Ex Nihilo

Dvision Point

— BOOK 2 —

Ryan Matthew Browning

Edited by Paige Lawson
Cover Art by Daniel Eyenegho
Interior Design by Charlyn_Designs

CHAPTER 1

S olar flare erupted on the molten surface of the new star Eos. Massive column of fire reflected in Matthew's eyes locked on the sight. Sunlight radiated from the image projected by the holoprojectors built into the ceiling of the Infinity Nexus, filling the room with a golden ambiance. Kain stared up into the bright light that forced him to squint, yet he couldn't break his view away from it either. The beauty of the new star, Eos, was beyond anything he ever could have imagined. Every nerve hummed with anxiety and whispered in his mind that if he looked away, he may never see anything like the star again. Matthew tapped his foot with patience, awaiting his brother to return to his senses, but he also couldn't help but admire the star they had created.

Unlike Kain, there was a different fear racing through Matthew's nerves. It was caused by the very thing he was now spending all his energy to avoid thinking upon. In his mind, he saw the sheer number of threats that would soon descend upon the *Empyrean station*, and they would attempt to eradicate this new star. Branches of the tree of potential futures raced away toward multiple forms of annihilation. Shadows of the universe pushed against the radiance of the new star trying to smother it in the darkness, and that drew Matthew's mind towards the threats lurking within the abyss. Deep in the darkest places of the Great Maw were a tumult of endless voices. The countless voices filled his mind with their endless rage, regret, suffering, lamentation, and envy, all casting blame on him for the new star representing all they didn't have. He had to focus his will power to force the throng of voices out of his mind. Kain managed to break his gaze away, turning to face his brother, and saw Matthew staring into the star, lost in thought.

Kain stared at the glass that bound his brother. For the last few days, he and his team with Mordecai's house searched through the Ancient's records for any way to free Matthew. Glass was easy enough to break, but the glass didn't really hold anything in. It was symbolic of the invisible nexus of universal energy binding Mathew through the excitement of his neural network. The energy field acted like a super drug, exciting Matthew's neurons beyond anything the human mind was intended to endure, but the unique genetic mutation that allowed him to become the key had given him incredible tolerance to the negative effects of this, or so Mordecai explained to Kain. Matthew's neural network was entirely dependent on the Infinity Nexus amplification of the universal energies to function. Glass could be broken, and Matthew could be removed easily, but his brain would experience a massive form of withdrawal that Mordecai simulations all showed would be deadly for Matthew. Kain waited patiently for his brother, but he tapped on the glass after a few moments. Sound failed to capture Matthew's attention.

"Matthew!" Kain shouted, trying to get his brother's attention. Coming back to his senses, he heard Kain's voice and turned to look at him with a smile. "You ok in there?" Worry glimmered in Kain's eyes, dilating to focus on Matthew reflecting his own image back to him. His facial hair had begun to grow in, subtle black rings appeared just under his eyes, telling him he needed to get some sleep, and his furrowed brow mirrored his worries back at him. Kain's restrained worry was only revealed in the jutting of is jowls from the grimace caused by his gritting teeth.

"Sorry Kain, just a lot on my mind. You don't need to worry about me. I'll be fine. We've got much bigger problems to worry about." Matthew changed the subject to distract and distance himself from Kain's worries. "The real threat has just begun, brother. Right now, the Cacophony of Discordance is focusing their effort on destroying our new home and our new star."

"But if the Cacophony can't survive the sunlight, how could they possibly be a threat?" Kain allowed the shift in the conversation reluctantly.

"They have many insidious ways to attack us but don't worry. I already know how they will attack." Matthew's thoughts told Virgil what to create using the neural implant. Holographic emitters on the ceiling switched from the star to what Matthew could see in his mind. Golden ambiance faded, replaced by the shimmer of white light dancing in the air. Kain stood in awe, watching the *Empyrean station* holographic emitters creating the image of a starship design.

"That is one behemoth of a battleship. Dimensions are massive, making the *Alcatraz* look tiny bey comparison." Kain admired the design floating in the air. "We could really use some of these warships ourselves. Look at the fire power!"

Matthew smiled, knowing the construction of the first of his new fleet had already begun. Virgil and the nanomachines were already working in space to create the first of the new ships Matthew had envisioned. The ships would give even the mighty Cacophony of Discordance a reason to fear. Hephaestus had helped Matthew design the new ships, and he thought the name suited them. Battleforges. Matthew switched the image to show the nanite cloud that once protected the *Empyrean station*, helped birth the new star Eos, and was now busy constructing the shipyards needed to construct his new fleet.

"I must admit this station's power is beyond anything I ever considered," Kain admitted.

"Ancient's prepared well for this moment because they knew this would be the most dangerous time in their Abyssal Prophecy experiment. Time right now is working against us. We must gather a fleet of these new ships before our enemies arrive."

"Father would be so jealous if he could see this!" Kain couldn't contain his excitement. A wide smile curled on his countenance, and he turned to look at his brother with a glimmer in his eyes.

"Battleforges are designed to be the supreme warship. It's twelve kilometers long, and as you can see from the dimensions, it can house a hundred times the population of the *Alcatraz*. Unlike our old home, however, these ships are built for pure battle. The outer hull is half a kilometer of reinforced hull, and as you can see, these ships are equipped with ample weapon systems. The ship's primary weapon systems are the dual cannons that can fire either kinetic weapons or pure hard light energy. Hephaestus assures me the options for adaption are almost limitless. He had these schematics for this type of weapon for our old ship, but of course, we never had the resources to build something like this. All he added was the hard light energy schematics from the *Empyrean station* data archives," Matthew declared, showing the schematics of the largest cannons.

"Seems like Hephaestus hasn't taken any time before learning what the *Empyrean station* kept safe waiting for us." He admired the system and designs of the viewer. It was clear to him that Hephaestus had learned from all the problems they had survived through. In Kain's mind, this new ship design was a magnificent piece of engineering, but he believed it was a pipe dream. It would take decades to build something like that, and they didn't have decades. He was about to speak, but Matthew spoke first.

"With the raw energy output from Eos combined with the energy-to-matter convertors of each nanomachine and station, we have essentially unlimited resources. *Empyrean station* might as well be the technological equivalent of God," Matthew informed. "We now control the power zero of Ex Nihilo, and we can create whatever we need by bending the power zero to our will."

"Well, our enemies won't wait for us. Time isn't a resource we have in infinite supply, brother. That ship would take decades to build with the people we got, and we don't even have enough people to run *Empyrean station*, let alone a ship of that magnitude. You've always been a dreamer." Kain looked back to see his brother chuckling, and he knew he had missed something.

"We have the power to create fields of temporal distortion where time moves quicker or slower as we need. Nanites accelerate to near light speed creating a time dilation in microbursts of work." Matthew educated, and the viewer switched to show the process of the construction of the first ship. Grey clouds of nanomachines moved at a blurring pace on the screen, and Kain gasped. The entire superstructure had already been built, and portions of the hull were already being constructed. He couldn't believe what he was seeing and was unable to speak from the power of awe he felt.

"That's impressive little brother, but we simply don't have enough forces to operate a ship like that. We don't even have enough people for a skeleton crew," Kain replied.

"We will soon, brother. Virgil has already begun the construction of the first genetic seed vault here on the station. You're my Imperator and you shall be the first Patriarch of our new empire. You are the best of us, and your genes will help create an army," Matthew stated.

Kain's eyebrows narrowed. "You know, father used to talk a lot about our genetics and bloodlines. I take it that I don't have any say in this?"

"Of course, you do, but I don't suspect the other lords and ladies will object to using their D.N.A. to create armies. They'll merely take the opportunity to grow in power."

"I just don't like this talk of genetics, but you're right. The others won't be as worried about the consequences. Guess our hands are tied by circumstances." Kain grimaced and shook his head. "Alright, where do I give my blood for this plan?"

"Imperator, I've already taken your genetic samples via scan. Using my genetic databanks, I've already been creating templates from your genetic code for new life. That new life is already incubating in my genetic vats. Estimated time until the first batch completion is eighteen hours, twenty-two minutes, and forty-three seconds. Any further time extrapolation could cause damage to human consciousness during incubation." Virgil appeared next to Kain in a swirl of white light.

"So, all these soldiers are going to be clones of me? That could get really confusing in battle," Kain scratched his head, looking at his brother.

"Incorrect imperator. Cloning technology is ancient even to the Ancients. It replicates what was, what is, and what cannot change. It is genetic death, and there is no value in oblivion. A genetic Patriarch template creates subdivision of your basic genetic genome. The various genetic facets that make you up Imperator, and by combining this template with other genetic samples we, grow unique, organic beings." Virgil showed the genetic sequencing and embryonic process.

"They'll be different than me," Kain looked to Virgil with a raised eyebrow.

Before Virgil could respond, Matthew cut him off with a thought and moved closer to the glass to get face-to-face with his brother. "They'll be like your children. Each one will look unique, more or less, have their own experiences, and grow and evolve as all humans do. Each one will have the potential to exceed your genetic prowess, and when that happens, we'll create a new Patriarch for a new line of warriors. This is how we shall grow our fleets and power to project our power into this new universe I intend to create. As each new legion excels and exceeds the threats they face, we shall add new genetic adaptations. Well, that's assuming we survive this threat coming for us right now, that is," Matthew warned, his eyebrows narrowing, and scrunching the skin together in rolling folds.

"I can see what you mean by this station being the equivalent of God. How long would creating enough troops to crew this new ship take?" Kain looked at Virgil for an answer.

"Approximately two days with all our resources devoted to completing your genetic seed."

"Don't worry, brother, we've got some time, and I have many plans to prepare us to face what's coming. I've split the nanomachines in half. The first half are building what I call the *Divius Oculus*." On the screen, the viewer showed the huge grey cloud swarming around the star. Kain focused on the image when he saw something small in the bright light.

The nanomachines had already constructed what looked to be a web of grey lines across the entire surface of the star. For a moment, Kain wasn't sure what it was, and he took a step forward, trying to ascertain what it could be. Then it became clear in his mind what he was seeing. A massive web of metal superstructure created a shell around the star's perimeter. He turned to Matthew with one eyebrow raised, and before he could ask his question, Matthew started speaking.

"The *Divius Oculus* will create a shell around the entire star to harness all the power. In essence, this first star will become a stellar reactor. Ancients called this a Dyson sphere. The other half that aren't working on the *Divius Oculus* have been split into two. The first half are building the first battleforge, but the other half are constructing the automated shipyards to assist in fabricating the rest of the fleet. Once the *Divius Oculus* is complete, the power from the star will be directed to our shipyards and, eventually, our defense network." Matthew streamed his plans onto the view screen.

"Impressive, but what do you need me to do?" Kain turned, awaiting an answer.

"Well, we're going to need to name her," Matthew pointed to the ship. "Since she's your ship, I believe it would be only fitting for you to name her."

"My ship?" Kain looked at his brother for a second in surprise.

"You're my Imperator and the one whom I trust the most. You're our best fighter, and best tactician, and well, Father trained you well. It makes the most sense to put you in command of our first ship. So, what are you going to call her?" Matthew could see the pride on his brother's face. Kain's smile was almost ear to ear, and his eyes sparkled in the light.

"There's only one name for such a ship as this, and that name must honor my brother who has brought the light back to the verse." Kain smiled for a second, looking at his brother. "*Dawnbreaker*."

"That is a fitting name, Imperator," Virgil stated.

"Well, that is one fine ship, but are you sure these new ships will be enough to stop what you see coming?" Kain pressed the question fearing his brother may not have an answer, but his fears were dispelled within seconds when Matthew began to speak.

"What we're facing is apocalyptic. Cacophony of Discordance will send their best servants to test us. Remnants of the Ancient's legacy have not fared well during the age abyssal era after Starfall. The sheer force of what I see coming can't be explained with ease, but I can see what we'll need to do to survive. That is far easier to explain. Like any living organism, upon conception, we are vulnerable. A single cell struggling against the Great Maw, and like any organism, we need to grow fast. Faster than we're dying. Right now, I am mustering all the powers of this station and our new star, Eos, to build up everything we need. We must reach division point, or everything we've fought and sacrificed will be for nothing!" Matthew's words echoed in the empty Infinity Nexus chamber.

"Division point?" Kain's left eyebrows rose sharply.

"All cells grow through division. Once a cell has enough resources, it splits in half, and the organism grows through multitudes of these divisions. Same for all biological life, and it's the same for us right now as well. We're exactly like a single cell, but our nucleus is our new star. We've got to complete the *Divius Oculus*, build up our forces, and then we can begin the division process. Once we hit division point, even the Cacophony of Discordance won't be able to stop us, but until then, we are fragile and vulnerable and must protect Eos." Matthew pointed to the shimmering star above.

"What do you need me to do?" Kain stood at attention, staring at his brother.

"You must learn everything necessary to run your new ship and legion. Virgil, please show Kain to the gene vaults, and help him prepare for taking command of the *Dawnbreaker* when it's completed." Matthew could see Nemesis had just arrived, and he thought it was well-timed. What he needed to discuss had to remain private. "Time is of the essence, and besides, I need to talk to our sister in private." Matthew scoured his brother's countenance for any hint of wounded pride or betrayal. It wasn't a matter of trust with Kain, but of necessity for the future he was building. Kain nodded with a smile that allowed Matthew to breathe a muffled sigh of relief. He watched his brother follow Virgil to the doors passing by Nemesis. The two siblings smiled at each other politely but didn't speak a word to each other. Nemesis continued towards the Infinity Nexus, coming to a stop in front of Matthew, feeling a moment of uncertainty twang in her gut. She knelt bowing her head in respect. Memories of her fathers' expectations echoing in the back of her mind.

"You summoned me, Emperor?" Nemesis raised her head looking up at her brother. She saw his hand motioning for her to stand up before he spoke.

"Save the titles for the masses. In private, you're always going to be my big sister Nem. You owe me no servitude," Matthew smiled at his sister.

"Thank fucking God. Can't lie, baby brother, I was afraid you were going to go full father. Can't exactly say I would have blamed you, given all that you've suffered to achieve this paradise for us all. This place is absolutely fantastic." Nemesis smiled at her brother, unable to contain her joy. She tried to hide her fears beneath her joy and scoured her brother's face for any sign her deception wasn't working. For a moment, the siblings stared at each other in silence. Matthew could see echoes of his sisters' worry in the tendrils of time but also hidden in the stoic smile she forced. He managed to hide his own disappointment caused by the sight.

"You'll be the one that keeps me honest, won't you?" Matthew's question caused Nemesis to take a step backwards. She nodded back yes instinctively before she even spoke.

"What's wrong, Matthew? Please don't try to hide it from me. You're getting better at it, but you should never have to hide who you really are from your family." Nemesis insisted, trying to pry the truth out from her brother. Silence created a void between the two siblings, and the moment seemed to hang like an eternity despite lasting only a few seconds.

"How's everyone settling into their new home?" Matthew's attempt to change the subject told Nemesis something was bothering her brother.

"The celebration wasn't quite as good as it could have been if we still had access to the Original Sins reserves, but the synthetic alcohol got the job done. In all my life, I've never seen people so happy. Even grandfather and Lord Drumpf seemed happy, and I can't remember seeing those men smiling unless one of their enemies just had died." Nemesis continued staring in her little brother's eyes, trying to ascertain what was bothering him, but the veil of his stoic mask.

"Please stop looking at me like that, Nem. Just because I'm stuck here doesn't mean that I've become fragile," Matthew's brows furrowed, narrowing his gaze at his sister.

"You're my baby brother! You're always going to be fragile in my mind. What else am I supposed to do but try to protect you?"

"Well, I'm glad to hear that you still want to protect me, and that cleaves right to the heart of why I asked you to come. Grandfather and Lord Drumpf are still threats to our safety. They've not ceased their plans to become the supremacy of power over our people, and to that end have begun adapting their plans to our new situation," Matthew educated.

"Of course, they are. So let me go kill them." Nemesis turned to march to the task.

"We can't just kill whoever we want because we see them as a threat!" Matthew shouted.

"Actually, it's quite easy. I thought you'd figured this out by now." Nemesis pulled one of her knives. "See, you stick the pointy end into their skull, and they die. So easy a child could do it."

"How is that any different than how father ruled? You were glad to see that I haven't allowed power to go to my head, but you rush off to kill our enemies just because I said they are enemies?"

The two questions left Nemesis frozen, searching for an answer. She realized she had underestimated how far Matthew had evolved in such a short time. The truth was blatant to her now. Matthew was placing checks and balances against absolute use of force. She both hated that fact and loved it. She dared to hope at that moment, and that hope swelled into words she couldn't hold back.

"Are you saying what I think you're saying?" Nemesis's eyes glimmered with a sparkle.

"You know the truth of what I'm about to say. You watched Concordia burn, and you lived through the tyranny of father. No one person, no matter how powerful, should rule absolutely because when that happens, you can't avoid tyranny. No, sister, it is far more proper that law should rule, and I should be nothing more than a Guardian and servant of the law." Matthew's words reverberated through the empty Infinity Nexus, bringing a tear to Nemesis' eye.

"It's a beautiful ideology, brother, and one worth dying for." Nemesis declared, wiping away the solitary tear and forcing back the memories of her twin sister. She couldn't help but smile at the lingering thought that Rule of Law was a fitting memorial for Concordia.

"Beautiful, perhaps, but dangerous would be an understatement. There are valid reasons why our lineage destroyed this philosophy. This is the path of most resistance, but I know it's the only right path forward, and the only one that will take us all to where all we must go."

"You've always followed your heart Matthew, and it has yet to lead you astray." Nemesis tried to comfort her brother seeing the struggle in his mind reflected by his facial features.

"But it still could. That is why I need you. Not only to be a check against my power but also for something you're well suited for. I hereby name you Inquisitor, and first Matriarch. Once Kain's ship and troops are complete, you'll become the genetic template of the Inquisitorial line. You've always had a keen sense for justice and fury towards injustice. I know this is your purpose, sister, and is the sole reason God allowed what happened to Concordia to occur. Her death has made you a potent force against injustice. This isn't something I can order you to do, however. This has to be your choice," Matthew stated, searching his sisters' eyes for her answer in the lingering silence.

Offer echoed in Nemesis's thoughts, and anxiety burned in her nerves. Her mind raced at what her brother was even expected of her. Question bubbled in her mind, and she searched for the proper wording. After a moment of struggling to find the right words, she just blurted out the question.

"What would you expect of me as your Inquisitor?"

"Your job will be to listen to the whispers, to spy on our enemies to learn their plans, and help protect our secrets from being used against us.

Our enemies must be rooted out by the stem unless the weeds of betrayal take root in this new Eden we've been granted." Matthew watched Nemesis' expression go blank as she considered the proposal.

Memories of all the lessons Clotho taught her on the art of spying and using the knowledge acquired to keep peace flashed in her mind. She couldn't help the smile creeping onto her countenance that she wasn't even aware of, and her lips curled into a distinct smirk that Matthew smiled upon seeing. With a nod, Nemesis stared into Matthew's eyes.

"I'll be your Inquisitor, brother, if that's what you need," Nemesis declared.

"Thank you, sister, but you must know this must be kept a secret for now. The verse is still a dark place, but don't get confused by the bright lights of *Empyrean station*. Shadows exist here, so I am asking you to work in those shadows. You're the only person I know who has lived in the darkness of the Lower Wards and never succumbed to the evil caused by all the suffering there." Matthew smiled at his sister.

"Well, that actually brings me to my question. When can I re-open my club?"

"You know how I feel about all the activities that went down at the old club," Matthew stated.

"Yes, but that didn't stop you from having fun. So, what's the problem?" Nemesis knew this could be a fight, but she wouldn't back down, and Matthew sighed.

"One evil act doesn't stay with just the person who indulges in it. Each victim spreads the evil further, and before you know it, everyone is infected. How can you want to bring the Original Sins to our new Eden?" Matthew shook his head sighing softly.

"God gave us the choice, not anything else, little brother, and you don't get to take that away because it's inconvenient to you. You have to let people be who they are and deal with whatever happens. Father tried to control everyone and look how that played out. You're trying to break the cycle, brother, and I admire you for that. Please don't make the same mistakes; if you do, we're all doomed." Nemesis' resolute stare forced Matthew to stare back.

For a moment, there was silence. Matthew weighed what his sister was saying. He didn't like what she asked, but he knew how important it was to her. Glimpsing into the future, Matthew still couldn't see beyond the threat on the event horizons. There was one thing he was certain of, and that was the Original Sin wouldn't make the situation worse for the immediate future. He could also see how much it meant to his sister, and his heart fluttered in response to the emotions he could sense in her. With a deep sigh, he lowered his gaze and nodded.

"I understand, and you have my permission," Matthew stated.

Nemesis breathed a sigh of relief. She feared this might become an argument and breathed a deep sigh of relief. All she wanted to do now was hug her baby brother to thank him, but the Infinity Nexus prevented that. There was a sense of sadness washing over her from that fact, but she kept her smile on her face trying not to let her brother sense her true emotions. She knew he was already suffering enough.

"Thank you, brother, it means more to me than I can express. So, tell me, what can I do to help you as your Inquisitor?"

"I know you have a connection with Lord Drumpf, and I want you to keep building that relationship. You know the laws, and when he breaks them, you will tell me, and we'll decide on the next move together. The real threat right now comes from grandfather, and I need you to build a spy network to keep tabs on him. I imagine Lady Clotho might be able to assist you given your relationship with her, but be warned, she's playing at her own game in all of this." Matthew knew he had to be careful, because his grandfather's future was so uncertain.

"Whatever you need, Matthew, I'll try to accomplish. There is one question bothering me. Why are you worried about Lady Clotho?" Nemesis didn't realize her worry was showing on her face.

"Don't get me wrong, sister. I don't see anything bad from Lady Clotho, but I can only see the next threat in time right now. The fact she has the power of prophesy that led me to this situation is troubling, but how she manipulates grand events is far worse. As long as she stays working towards the same goal as the rest, I don't see a problem, but I fear she could head in the direction of our grandfather. Don't doubt that Lord Whelsey intends to destroy me and take this power for his own. He has not changed, but he will try to convince you otherwise. Just stay wary, sister, because we shouldn't trust anyone right now," Matthew warned.

Nemesis bowed as a sign of respect before turning to leave. She knew that Marcus would want to hear the news about the Original Sin so he could get the work underway and that he could also help get the spy network started. The viewscreen above returned to showing the light radiating from the new star. Each footstep echoed Nemesis's confidence in her new mission. She smiled at the thought that she was going to enjoy being Inquisitor. The time for her grandfather's demise was coming, and she looked up at the star light with a silent vow. She'd make sure her grandfather paid the price for his role in Concordia's death.

CHAPTER 2

Light blurred on the edges of the view screen in front of Magnus Void sitting in the captain's chair, and his eyes shifted to glance at the timer clicking down steadily. Echoes of the ticking timer resonated in the empty cockpit. He found his thoughts splintering at that moment. Part of him worried about Matthew and the humans he left behind on *Empyrean station*, and his eyes shifted to the sensors in respond to his other worry about the wrath of the Cacophony of Discordance. He knew there was no way they would let the creation of a new star happen without a reprisal. Ticking faded into the symphony of machines whirring, beeping, and humming away around him.

With a sigh, Magnus leaned back into his chair, taking in the calm since dropping off the other crew. He closed his eyes, relaxing in the absence of his crew. He could barely remember the last time he had a respite like this. Time ticked away, approaching zero on the timer on the screen. Magnus rested his hand near the F.T.L. drive throttle, waiting for the tell-tale beeping. He had accomplished everything he set out to do, and all he had to pay for it was the pang of guilt he felt at what he had done to Matthew. It was a cruel fate, but he had given the boy the power to recreate the universe. He tried to convince himself that this was a fair trade rather than a Faustian bargain, but he wasn't convincing himself. The pang of his conscience told him his rationalization wasn't working as intended. He was lost in thought and didn't hear the door slide open behind him.

A'zyren stepped silently into the cockpit, and only the soft sound of the door whisking shut behind her could be heard. She glanced at the viewscreen timer feeling a pang of anxiety in her nerves. Anxiety mixed with her excitement blurred the two emotions. She couldn't wait to get home and tell her people of the mission's success. Too long had her people lived in the darkness, adapting to every machination of the Great Maw they encountered. The darkness hadn't just changed her people but evolved them in ways she both marveled and lamented. Walking up to the captain's chair, she leaned against it to speak to Magnus but surprised him. He whipped around with his black tendrils of energy crackling from his eyes.

"How many times do I have to tell you not to sneak up on me!" Magnus's eyes crackled with wild, furious black energy snapping off in sharp hisses.

"Calm down, Magnus. I was just coming to spend some time before I return home. I know we haven't always seen eye-to-eye if those things sparking energy at me are even really eyes." A'zyren took a quick step back away from the captains' chair. Magnus turned staring at A'zyren staring back.

Turning back, Magnus focused his will on calming himself down. He could see the sparking energy reflected in the viewscreen. His reaction made it clear that fear of the Cacophony of Discordance was much greater than he was admitting to himself. With a sigh, he focused his mind on trying to calm himself. Energy crackling off him began to slow, and over a few moments, it eventually stopped. A'zyren sat in the co-pilot's chair, waiting for Magnus to relax before speaking again. Her shifting gaze darted between the viewscreen and Magnus. The last thing A'zyren wanted was to provoke Magnus' ire so close to getting home. Memories echoed in pangs of pain sparking across A'zyren' nerves from the last time she had felt the sting and what she had seen Magnus do to convince her people to join his crusade to restore the light to the universe.

Memories of the C'undrivar of the great tribes rushed back into the center of A'zyren' mind. The great meeting of the many houses and tribes was a seldom invoked ritual because such occasions sparked violence. When she led her tribe to join the C'undrivar, she had suspected it was some kind of trap, but when she met Magnus, his presence confirmed that fear to her at that moment. She had been wrong, of course, but that lesson had almost cost her life. Sneaking up on Magnus in his quarters at the C'undrivar was as fresh in her mind as the day it was created. A'zyren believed she had caught him off guard, and her strike was lightning fast. Bearing down with silent, rapid footsteps, raised blade, and sudden swift movement lulled her into believing she was about to kill this alien, but she was the prey, not the predator. Magnus turned at the last moment catching A'zyren's blade with one hand in a surge of black energy coursing around and through her, and she could feel the pain of life being sapped from her body. Intense pain beyond anything she had felt racked her mind with the same force in the present as it had done that day in her memories, and without her noticing, her muscles convulsed in reaction. Magnus could sense the energy within A'zyren telling him she remembered the first time they met, and he couldn't help but grin reflexively. He forced the grin away before turning to come face-to-face with A'zyren turning at the same moment to check the flashing instruments.

"Don't worry, A'zyren, you're still safe from me," Magnus attempted to console.

There was no immediate response from A'zyren. After a moment, she just placed one hand on Magnus's shoulder to tell him she was fine. Truth be told, she loved that moment of life and death, and the strength and power she felt from Magnus at that moment was beyond anything else. A'zyren admired Magnus not only for his power but his dedicated focus on accomplishing his tasks. Magnus was a singular resolute force, and she was happy for the many years of his tutelage on their quest to restore the light. A'zyren knew her tribe respected her before she left, but now they would revere her once she demonstrated the power that she acquired from serving alongside Magnus for so long.

"No one's ever safe. Thought you'd have figured that out by now," A'zyren declared.

"I must admit you've been the most effective second-in-command that I've ever served with. Silence of the *Death's Reaper* has made me realize one truth. I'd never suspected I'd miss the crew this much. I've spent most of my existence by myself, yet now I feel a pang I haven't felt in a long time." Magnus tried to push down the emotions swirling in him.

"Don't tell me you've gone and become civilized." A'zyren couldn't contain her chuckle. She glanced leerily at Magnus, but he joined in, and they laughed briefly.

"Perhaps I have, and I think the whole universe is about to be forced to join me," Magnus heard the beeping of the F.T.L. drive, and he pulled back on the throttle. Light blurring at the edge of the viewscreen stopped when the ship came rushing back to normal space. Magnus and A'zyren looked out the viewscreen, so shocked by what they were seeing they couldn't speak.

Hundreds of world ships had all convened and joined the rare C'undrivar. Magnus knew this was not a celebration of their success, and his eyes shifted to see A'zyren's reaction. She was frozen, staring at the sight on the viewscreen, and hair on the back of her neck stood on end. The C'undrivar was only summoned by the W'Hyish S'yevel for two events. The first was a great quest to acquire something the tribes needed to survive, and the second was for mobilizing for war to deal with a threat to the tribes. The coms crackled.

"*Death's Reaper*, this is the worldship *Sesh'yna* demanding your immediate response, or you will be fired upon." The voice caught A'zyren's attention, forcing her to respond before Magnus could. Her hands darted across the controls, activating the comms channel, but isolating it through encryption to ensure none of the other tribes could listen in.

"This is Niab A'zyren Sha'hel demanding immediate docking clearing," she commanded. The communicator went silent momentarily, and computers whirred, receiving docking information. A'zyren remained silent, staring out the viewscreen with a focused glared, scrunching her eyebrows.

Magnus input the landing sequence and set the ship to auto pilot. He swiveled in his chair to look at A'zyren. She was still lost in contemplation, and Magnus could sense the anxiety twitching in her nerves beneath her skin. He searched for the correct words to broach the subject but was left dazed, unable to find the right thing to say to start such a conversation. There was one thing he had learned about the W'Hyish S'yevel. The tribes always put the lives of their family above all else. Seeing all the worldships together meant a war brewing, and Magnus worried that it was aimed at *Empyrean station*.

"You think your people have flipped their position?" Magnus' question caught A'zyren unprepared, and she froze for a moment in thought. Her eyes darted to meet Magnus, and they conveyed her uncertainty in the anxiety trembling in her irises.

"My people are fickle as death and as changeable as life. Without my vote, I can see no other reason why a C'undrivar would be called. This doesn't bode well for either of us." The words caught in A'zyren throat with a loud gulp she couldn't hide.

Thrusters flared from the *Death's Reaper* when it began docking procedures. The ship glided into the docking bay of the *Sesh'yna*. Mangled mess of fused metal scavenged from the Great Maw slowly overtook the entire viewscreen. Below rested the fighter craft, transports, and remains of derelict vessels being cannibalized for the continued survival of the worldship. Marching into the docking bay, Magnus and A'zyren could see a throng of the abominable, monstrous Uhur'Dren apexinels in rows of formation. Troops came to a stop awaiting their Niab's arrival at the landing pad. Each of the creatures stood motionless, becoming almost statuesque in their stoic stance. Standing in front of the massive sentinels were the Vesh'rendar wearing all-black armor forged from the skin of their fallen enemies. Magnus smiled, seeing the magnificence of the W'hyish S'yevel traditions as the ship beeped. Final landing procedures had begun. Confirming the landing commands, Magnus set the autopilot into motion. Throng on the viewscreen grew larger as the ship landed before them, and now the Uhur'Dren apexinels towering height could easily be seen. He began activating security procedures before starting the shutdown sequence but activated the stand-by system just in case this situation turned out to warrant his and A'zyren's worry.

Magnus turned, beginning to open his mouth, but A'zyren was already marching towards the cockpit door, vanishing behind the metal whisking shut behind her. Pushing out of the chair, Magnus sprinted, trying to catch up. Two of them arrived at the lift at the same moment, and they glanced at each other before entering. Descending on the lift, neither of them spoke during the descent. They both focused their racing thoughts on dealing with whatever fate prepared for them. Lift lurched to a stop, and A'zyren strode forward, pushing through the lift gates with her eyes locked on the ramp controls. She slammed the button to lower the lift with her fist, causing a loud bang to echo, and felt a sudden glare upon her back. Glancing back, she saw Magnus glaring at her, shaking his head, and A'zyren just shrugged back. A great hiss filled the docking bay, drawing their attention forward to the ramp. The ramp began lowering slowly, and Magnus stood right behind A'zyren, looking out at the gathered forces staring at their Niab.

"Nexro un vis vit'ae," they chanted in unison to welcome A'zyren back. She strolled through her ship marching towards the figure approaching. Magnus recognized the unique symbols on the black armor. This was Ga'non, who A'zyren had left in charge in her absence. Magnus could already feel the energy in A'zyren change from anxiety to fury.

"Hsu' Niab A'zyren Sha'hel. Nexro un vis Vit'ae." Ga'non bowed his head.

"Death demands life," Magnus spoke the greeting before A'zyren.

Before Ga'non could react, A'zyren pulled out her pistol and shot his two guards. With lightening speed, she swept his legs out from under him, causing him to hit the deck with a reverberating force that echoed in the docking bay. A'zyren dropped her weight, crashing down onto Ga'non's chest with her right knee pinning his neck to the deck. Magnus smiled, hearing the man struggle to breath. Troops stared on, not a single one reacted, and all of them held their ground.

"Why was a C'undrivar called without my approval?" A'zyren glared down at Ga'non.

"Us Nehyet fum'ril…" Ga'non tried to speak before force choked off his words.

"English for my guest, please," A'zyren educated with the pressure of her knee before releasing it, allowing Ga'non to breathe again.

"You know my linguistic…" Magnus started to interject but realized no one was paying him attention. Everyone in the docking bay was now staring, including the troops.

"My Niab, the great S'yevel Se'lish, demanded it. We had no choice but to answer the call. S'yevel Se'lish speaks of a great threat we must unite against," Ga'non struggled to speak, feeling his air blocked off by A'zyren's knee pressing down on his throat.

"What threat?" A'zyren screamed with fury in her eyes.

Unable to breathe, Ga'non struggled against his commander's knee. "S'yevel Se'lish has decreed it will be told at the C'undrivar. We tried to hold it off until your return, but we must hurry, or a decision will be made in your absence. Reaping was threatened to be done to our tribe if we ignored the call." Ga'non pushed up against A'zyren' knee, gasping to breath, and unable to break free.

Hearing that caused A'zyren to stand up, and she marched towards the exit. Magnus didn't hesitate and followed behind with a glanced back. Struggling to stand, Ga'non forced himself to catch up despite gasping for air. A'zyren lead the group down the corridors toward the central promenade of her ship. She knew that as the leader of the last C'undrivar the meeting would be forced to be held on her ship. This meant the delegates were already here, and she looked back to see Ga'non had caught up to walk beside Magnus despite still gasping for breath.

"Do I still have your support?" A'zyren strode forward.

"Of course, my Niab, my loyalty to you goes beyond the veil of death," Ga'non swore in a rasp rubbing at his sore throat.

"Not you idiot," A'zyren glared at Ga'non before glancing back to Magnus. "You still got my back?"

"Have I ever given you a reason to doubt my allegiance yet?" Magnus declared.

A'zyren smiled. The clacking of her footsteps echoed louder than the men behind her. She strode towards the promenade doors beginning to slide open for her, revealing the vast circular central chamber of the meeting grounds. Sharp jagged pieces of welded metal jutted from the wall, columns of the entombed death separated the great partition of the many tribes, and each tribe stood in their partition. Everyone now was staring at A'zyren's sudden arrival, and silence washed across the gathered throng. W'hyish leaders from all the tribes and their personal retinues stood on every level, glaring down at A'zyren. She marched through the meeting room without hesitation, not bothering to look at any of the gathering horde. The clack of her footsteps echoed with each stride up the stairs towards her platform, where she took a position out in front of the bones of her ancestors. Running her fingertips across the sleek bones of many different species filled her with the conviction of the great Niabs that came before her.

"Give me strength now to do what needs to be done," A'zyren whispered, marching to the edge to look at the great gathering of the C'undrivar. A great clamor of voices arose at that moment, but the voices blended in a ruckus. Marching into the center of the promenade was a massive Niab, and he pulled back his hood to reveal his serpentine features. A'zyren grimaced at the sight of the W'hyish S'yevel she hated the most.

Hedron wasn't just a serpentine in A'zyren's mind but the most deceptive and manipulative mind in all the W'hyish S'yevel tribes. She knew his master was behind it, the C'undrivar. Hedron was loyal to his alliance, and that meant that he had chosen Dagoth's side. A'zyren glanced back at Magnus to tell him to be ready. She knew that Dagoth had long courted the attention of the Cacophony of Discordance in an attempt to gain access to their dark knowledge and powers. It seemed A'zyren and Magnus were again united in another shared quest, but this time it was to destroy the Reverie. The whole promenade fell silent when Hedron raised his staff adorned with skulls.

"Dagoth has sent me to start this C'undrivar. First, allow me to celebrate the triumph of your great quest, Niab A'zyren. We all believed it was impossible, yet again, you have succeeded where all others fail. Death has truly blessed you. However, much has changed since you last guided your people in the great circle of life and death. Perhaps you need time to get caught up on the changes, Niab?" Hedron's question was meant to put A'zyren on her heels, but she wasn't backing down.

"Hedron, you speak with honor to hide deceit. I have been gone a long time, but has the tribes changed so much that honor is now inferior to deceit?"

"There is no deceit intended, Niab, just evocations to enforce your loyalty to death and its demand for life. Do you still serve the W'hyish S'yevel, or are you now the pet of this Lord Void?" Hedron pointed to Magnus, but he remained silent, seeing from A'zyren's body language that was what she expected from him.

"Lord Void is here as my guest." A'zyren voice was calm, focused, and demanded respect. "I assure you, Hedron, I'm no one's pet to command. Nor am I a servant to your alliance with Dagoth!"

"Oh, but that's where you're wrong, Niab. Dagoth has taken the skull of S'yevel Se'lish, which makes him Em'Pharis, and that means you do serve him now or surrender yourself to death as a traitor." Hedron's conviction harshened his words to that of an order. Whispers erupted throughout the gathered assembly.

A'zyren looked at the gathering on the promenade. She could sense the plot Dagoth had set into motion. During her absence, the tribes had been turned. She could sense the animosity of conspiracy against her. It was impossible for her not to notice the hidden weapons in the crowd. Stealth had always been the W'hyish S'yevel way, but she chuckled, thinking that it was time to remind these fools that she was a master of the shadows. With a smile, she glanced back at Magnus. A'zyren intended to repay this treachery in kind. Magnus nodded that he understood her message.

"Perhaps I have been too hasty to make decisions. You stated I had been away too long, and if Dagoth possesses the skull of S'yevel Se'lish, making him Em'Pharis, then the tribes I served as loyal Niab is dead. I owe no allegiance to Dagoth nor any tribe that sides with his deviance of our ways." A'zyren spoke the words slow, clearly, and without faltering in conviction. A great commotion broke in the gathered crowd. Whispers of treachery, betrayal, and dishonor were being slung at A'zyren.

"Death demands life, and the tribes demand loyalty. If you can't be loyal in life, then your life demands death. May you walk with the ancestors forever, Niab, but your rule ends here!" Hedron motioned for his troops to attack.

A'zyren didn't flinch or even draw her weapons. She remembered when the tribes had been brought to heel by Magnus, and it was apparent to her none of those who witnessed that day were here. Weapons were being pulled and aimed, but A'zyren stared on without moving. She could feel the energy growing behind her and heard the crackle. Magnus moved forward with black energy coursing around him and arcing from the black pools that were his eyes.

Before a single weapon could be fired, Magnus reached out with all of his will. Hedron and the gathered tribes began convulsing with pain, unable to speak. Energy flickered from their bodies sparking into the air. Magnus was surrounded by a flurry of black energy that swirled in a vortex around him. His vortex was sucking in white energy sparking into the air from the tribes. He glanced back for a second at A'zyren to make sure this was what she wanted.

"Death demands life," A'zyren stated without a hint of remorse.

"So be it," Magnus stated, turning his full attention back to the crowd. The vortex around him sped up, becoming a screaming energy maelstrom. Not even the screams of the dying tribes could be heard over the screech of the energy vortex. The bodies of A'zyren's enemies crumbled to the ground before her eyes. Hedron was grasping, scratching, and clawing at the ground in writhing agony, but he couldn't get off a shot with his pistol. The sights wobbled in front of his eyes before everything went black, and the gun slammed against the deck plate.

A'zyren watched the bodies crumble one after another with a smile. When the last one fell, Magnus let his energy subside, feeling the surge of all the lives swelling inside him. Turning with a smile, he saw worry and fear etched on A'zyren's face. She stood there quiet for a moment, and Ga'non lowered his head, muttering a prayer for the dead, and even A'zyren dared not interrupt such sacred words. Magnus just shook his head.

"Religiosity is so absurd," he declared.

"It is the least we owe the ancestors, but we have much bigger issues to contend with. This will only slow the gathering of tribes. Ga'non get the *Sesh'yna* decoupled and get us out of here fast before anyone can figure out what happened here." A'zyren turned to see if her orders were being followed, but Ga'non was already on the communicator relaying the orders. Within moments the entire ship shuddered.

"We'll be in F.T.L. in a few moments, but the other ships haven't reacted yet," Ga'non informed the group.

"Well, things just got a whole lot more interesting," Magnus declared.

"W'hyish S'yevel intends to attack the *Empyrean station*, and we both know there is no way Matthew, or his people can survive the coming tide." A'zyren could feel the disdain seething from Ga'non at that moment.

"They are ez'bo deserving only of reaping and reanimation. Why did you side with them, Niab? Is it because of your ancestors?" Ga'non glared at A'zyren with expectation. A'zyren shook her head and pulled her pistol. She aimed it, glaring down the sights at her second-in-command.

"My ancestors are called humans, and they were the Ancients whose salvage we use to keep us alive. If you saw what I saw on the *Empyrean station*, you would make the same decision as I did for the good of our people. Can you even comprehend the existence of a new star?" A'zyren question forced Ga'non to shut up and listen.

"God, I love this," Magnus declared with a grin. "Such tension and melodrama! Go on, just shoot him already, A'zyren, or are you going soft?"

"Ga'non is loyal but lost in the ways of the abyss. He will come to understand what we're doing once he sees the glory of a star with his own eyes. Besides, that was a pretty big meal you shouldn't need to eat for a few centuries, at least from what I understand." A'zyren could sense that Magnus was toying with her and Ga'non as he did with everyone. Life was just a big game to Magnus, but A'zyren needed all the help she could get right now.

"You were a lot more fun before you met those other humans. I suppose this is all my doing," Magnus sighed with disappointment before muttering, "they grow up so fast and become all civilized. You're no fun anymore A'z." Magnus shook his head.

"We don't have time for this, Magnus. They're going to need our help. All of our help," A'zyren declared, hoping she didn't need to be more direct. The deck plate lurched underneath when the ship jumped to F.T.L. speeds. Inertia caused Ga'non to nearly topple, but A'zyren and Magnus remained unfazed.

"You know I did my part!" Magnus yelled in frustration, turning away from A'zyren. "We were supposed to have a celebration. I mean, I guess I had a celebratory meal, but where's the fun? There is nothing like a little mating ritual to entertain. I was so looking forward to venting some frustration on some of your willing people." Magnus stomped the ground with his foot.

A'zyren grabbed him by the shoulder to spin him around. She was afraid of what he would do, but in her mind, she was already dead if she didn't get help. Magnus was the only one capable of helping. Anger flashed in black lighting across Magnus' eyes at the attack but never lashed out from him. A'zyren appreciated Magnus' discipline at that moment, and the fact she was still alive told her he respected her.

"We need to get all the forces we can to help them. They're damn near defenseless on that station right now. I'll contact Genji to see if he can't convince De'Vayne to offer assistance. You should head to see Mordecai. We could really use the ASA's help," A'zyren tried to sense where Magnus' mind was on the subject but staring into the abyss of his black eyes offered only her nothing. There was no hint as to which side Magnus was truly on.

For a moment, the only answer was silence. Turning away, Magnus looked out over the sea of corpses on the promenade. He felt so much stronger with all the life force in him, and he was forced to admit this feeding had awoken something he believed long lost. He felt alive again at that moment, and searching his feelings, he realized he had been itching for a real fight for a long time. A new plan began to formulate in his mind. Turning back to face A'zyren, his lips curled into a wicked grin. Crackle of black energy surged across his eyes.

"Been too long since I have been in a real fight," Magnus declared. "Starting a war with the Cacophony definitely counts as that. Once we drop from F.T.L. speed, I'll take the *Death's Reaper* and head to meet Mordecai. My ship's faster, so you head to *Empyrean station*. I'll meet you there once I've gathered all the reinforcements I can convince."

Before A'zyren could say anything, Magnus was over the rail, dropping to the floor below. She turned to head towards the bridge, with Ga'non following behind. With Magnus' help, there was a chance to save the new star; that was all A'zyren needed. She focused her mind on what needed to be done. There was no way her people would understand until they saw the star for themselves, but once they did, there was no doubt they'd die to protect it. Even if the rest of the tribes had lost their way, A'zyren refused to allow her people to forget the truth. Death demands life, and life demands death, and the W'hyish were meant to guard that cycle, not alter it. She intended to remind all the W'hyish of that truth.

CHAPTER 3

Drifting in the swirling maelstrom of black holes, the *Pandemonium* blurred into the ether of the void. Shifting structures of the Cacophony of Discordance moved across the viewscreen in the distance. Massive structures of the *Inferna Machina* shifted in *Lamentation Configuration* floating in the center of the erratic sea of gravity fields emanating from the maelstrom. Strange tesseract shifted on itself in erratic movement of the black metal plates creating narrow gaps as they moved. Each second brought the *Dread Sovereign* closer to docking with the *Pandemonium,* and Leviathan's coils shifted uneasily beneath his glare at the viewscreen. Explosions of energy erupted from the *Dread Sovereign* as it began docking procedures with the massive titan.

Turning from the viewscreen, Leviathan slid and swayed with the inertia rippling through the ship exiting the bridge. Black tendrils of energy flickered in the dim hallway with the Reverie crew rushing to effective repairs. Leviathan paid the lesser creatures around him little regard. He arrived at the primary docking doors on the bridge level. Black metal-like material shimmered subtly with an eery glow. The doors began to slide open before him, and he slid through the gates the moment they opened wide enough.

Each convulsion of muscles helped Leviathan's coiled serpentine body move forward through the halls of the *Pandemonium.* Reverie rushed out of the way of the massive Tenno with crackles and hisses of frustration. Leviathan focused his thoughts on the Cacophony of Discordance reaction to the battle of *Empyrean station.* There was no doubt in Leviathan's mind that the leadership would be displeased, but he wasn't afraid either. Few of the Reverie could stand up to him in combat, and even with the damage to the *Dread Sovereign,* he was still a threat. Arriving at the massive black gate to the amphitheater, Leviathan waited for the door to open, staring into the murk of the gate.

Souls twisted in the black tendrils of mist in the amphitheater door to the Council of Chaos. Faces rose to the surface of the black mists of the gate, bubbling forth with faces of lamentation, suffering, and horror. Silent anguish of the souls trapped within the gate failed to faze the massive Leviathan. He wasn't even fazed by the rush of memories of the time when the living creature inscribed upon the door soared across the universe. Image of each of the seven heads of the great dragon Tiamat inscribed on the door glared down at him. The gates shifted before retracting allowing the full ruckus of the Cacophony of Discordance to echo forth. Leviathan could see the assembly was full and waiting for him. From the center of the amphitheater Supreme Tenno Ba'al Zebub sat on the Throne of Woe, Bones jutting from rolling mounds of flesh cushioning him, Ripples of souls trapped beneath the putrid flesh fed upon by the horde of flies buzzing above in brief moments of respite from their constant drone. Supreme Tenno Ba'al Zebub's multifaceted eyes fell upon Leviathan. Turning to face the gate, the cloak of skin flowed behind Tenno Verdelet, and the black volcanic floor echoed his footsteps marching out to address the assembly. Raising a black hand into the air drawing silence

"Great Cacophony of discordance, we meet to hear the report of Tenno Leviathan, who has been summoned to answer for the failures at the battle of *Empyrean station.*" Tenno Verdelet's glare fell upon Leviathan when he began to move into the chamber.

Coils of Leviathan's serpentine body flowed like crude oil caught in a whirlpool. Energy crackled from the imperial blue scales when the vibrated to propel Leviathan forward. The swirling nature of the scales and coiling body created a visual of a maelstrom swirling upon itself. Leviathan expanded, allowing his body to uncoil when he approached the center. Leviathan didn't uncoil himself in its entirety but allowed his size to become so massive it filled the center of the audience chamber. Leviathan looked down at Supreme Tenno Ba'al Zebub and the speaker.

"I answer to no one," Leviathan bellowed, filling the chamber with the smell of decay.

"You answer to the Cacophony!" Tenno Verdelet declared to a great revelry of crackles, hisses, and chittering of the Reverie. "This assembly and Supreme Tenno Ba'al Zebub sent you and Tenno Levart to stop the return of the light. Not only did you fail to stop the new star from being born, but it appears you have returned without Tenno Levart. Explain your failures to this assembly and to Supreme Tenno Ba'al Zebub, or face annihilation under our laws!"

For a second, the entire chamber was silent. Not a single councillor in the Council of Chaos even so much as crackled. All eyes were now fixated upon the massive Leviathan. Silence gave way to whispers of treachery and punishment began weaving through the Cacophony of Discordance. The only empty seat was the one reserved for the Minister of Injustice, and for a second, Leviathan looked at the empty seat and pondered. With a great screech, Leviathan silenced the Reverie.

"Supreme Tenno Ba'al Zebub, it seems we are still short a Minister of Injustice." Leviathan glared at the empty seat. "How can this court administer injustice without it's Minister?"

"Deflecting blame?" Supreme Tenno Ba'al Zebub heaved the words filling the chamber with his sulfurous breath.

"Of course not, Supreme Tenno, but we arrived too late. The humans had landed on *Empyrean station* and started the stellar conversion process. Tenno Levart led the Ravaging Cadence to attack, but the humans made an unexpected sacrifice." Leviathan could see the information intrigued the Supreme Tenno, who was now leaning forward with interest as the swarm of flies buzzed around his head.

"Sacrifice, you say. The Cacophony of Discordance gorges itself upon ignoble sacrifice," Supreme Tenno Ba'al Zebub stated.

"When I arrived, the humans had abandoned their former vessel. Life signs on the vessel showed only one life. I assumed that a single human had been abandoned, and when the *Alcatraz* began slinking away, I thought nothing of it. Of course, I dispatched some of my forces to engage, but I couldn't have predicted what occurred next. The human on board turned the ship, activated an F.T.L. drive, and used the light of the burst of speed to ram the *Dread Sovereign*. With the star being born, Tenno Levart's attack on *Empyrean station* had been stalled, and with the growing threat to my crew, I decided to retreat to bring this news back to the Cacophony of

Discordance." Leviathan could sense the crowd of Reverie was divided between sides.

Supreme Tenno Ba'al Zebub took time to ponder the situation on the Throne of Woe. It was Cacophony rule to abandon a hopeless situation, and there could be no faulting Leviathan for abandoning the weak Levart. Retreating from a battle was the grave offense. Ba'al Zebub's multifaceted eyes fell upon the empty seat of the Minister of Injustice. The empty seat glared a warning most Reverie wouldn't understand. Ba'al Zebub knew that without the Minister of Injustice to hold a trial, Leviathan would use that to divide the Cacophony of Discordance, and it could ill afford any more division. He grimaced at the thought of the rising cult spreading talk of a civil war. He thought that the return of the light offered the best chance to bring all the rogue forces to heel.

"Tenno Leviathan, this court understands the necessity of abandoning Tenno Levart. There can be no cause to blame you for abandoning weakness to be obliterated, yet retreating from battle is a grave offense. Your blame is compounded since your cowardice allowed the light that threatens us all to return. Yet, I must admit, without Tenno Lucifer to administer a trial, the Cacophony of Discordance does not agree on how to judge you for these actions. It would appear for the moment fate has protected you from the wrath of this court," Ba'al Zebub decreed.

"I understand, Supreme Tenno," Leviathan replied with a submissive bow.

"You understand nothing!" Supreme Tenno Ba'al Zebub screamed. "The light threatens us all, and you have failed the Cacophony of Discordance. If only Tenno Lucifer were here right now, I have little doubt you'd be shredded molecule-by-molecule. For all Reverie know of the wrath of the Minister of Injustice threatened even the Divine!"

Leviathan coiled up, shrinking in stature to the great reverberating force emitted by Supreme Tenno Ba'al Zebub's words. Many of the Reverie chittered in enjoyment at the sight filling the audience chamber with a reverberating humiliation of the Tenno. Leviathan's black eyes sparked with fury and uncoiling the folds of sinuous serpentine body reared upwards, screeching with fury. The entire audience chamber reverberated with the great cry of pain, and all the Reverie fell silent. Only the council and Supreme Tenno Ba'al Zebub were unaffected.

"Calm yourself, Tenno Leviathan, for all is not lost." Ba'al Zebub raised his right hand.

"How may I serve the Cacophony of Discordance?" Leviathan coiled back up, shrinking.

"You made a wise choice by holding the fleets back, for had you led the armada of the Cacophony of Discordance, many ships may have been lost. The *Dread Sovereign* is still operational and shall be repaired at our great expense. Many souls shall need to be sacrificed from our coffers of the damned. It will cost many sins to make up for your failure. Further, we must prepare to deal with these humans before their power grows too far. The Cacophony must stop the humans before more stars are created and the accursed threat of the light returns in full. To this end, you will go forth into the Great Maw and devour to grow. Grow your power, the armada, and the Cacophony of Discordance through ravaging, pillaging, and death of our enemies so that we may use the power of their souls to destroy this new enemy of us all."

The entire assembly erupted into a reveling of celebration. Hisses, crackles, and chittering reverberated the joy of the Cacophony across the room and even made the Supreme Tenno react. Across Ba'al Zebub's face, his massive bloated green lips curled into a wide grin revealing thousands of shark-like rows of razor-sharp white teeth. Filled with joy, the Supreme Tenno began to chuckle, spewing forth a toxic yellowish vapor of sulfur from his massive mouth. With sudden force Ba'al Zebub slammed his clawed right-hand rippling across the flesh of the Throne of Woe. Flies swarmed off the flesh, scream of souls bound beneath the putrid flesh resonated, and the echo silenced all.

"Tenno Leviathan, we will hold your trial when the Minister of Injustice returns, and should you succeed at the duty assigned by this court, it'll be taken into consideration. You should know how dreadful the punishments of Tenno Lucifer are, but you also know how rewarding his judgment can be for those who support the Cacophony of Discordance. Fear not, Tenno Leviathan, that you shall have to wait a long time for your trial as Tenno Lucifer has not been seen anywhere in the Infernal Kingdoms. Likely he is on one of his sojourns of temptation. To assist you in your endeavours, I shall bring in allies to aid you. Tenno Verdelet, summon forth my agents." Ba'al Zebub decried before slinking back into the Throne of Woe sinking into the rippling flesh.

All the Reverie in attendance fell quiet. Stepping to the front, Tenno Verdelet looked into the swirling blackhole in the pit at the center of the audience chamber. Raising a staff of skulls and bones, Tenno Verdelet's black eyes crackled with dark purple energy. Slamming the staff into the volcanic stone floor, the room shook with the force of the blow. Energy crackled up the spiral columns of the audience chamber and arced between the pillars building in power. The energy surged all around the chamber, channeling towards the swirling black hole. Stepping to the pit's edge, Tenno Verdelet began speaking in tongues for a moment. Once the summoning ritual was performed, he raised his staff again and slammed it to the floor.

"Supreme Tenno Ba'al Zebub summons forth Tenno Asmodeus and Tenno Lilith to receive their charge!" Tenno Verdelet stepped back from the edge.

Energy arced from the black hole at the bottom of the pit, leaping toward the ceiling before being channeled through the pillars. A massive energy bolt struck the ground across the pit from Tenno Verdelet. Tendrils of energy began to merge, forming a shape. Black energy surged, forming the structure of the tall creature that appeared almost human at first. Massive ethereal wings stretched from the creature's back, appearing almost angelic at first. The energy swirled together, revealing two sets of leathery outstretched wings. White armor of flickering flames of wrath coated the figure's body before the wings collapsed around it. The wings folded into multiple layers of a cloak with blackened talons locking together beneath the creature's throat. Energy crackled into life from the creature's skull turning into two blackened, cracked, and spiraling bone horns that arced upwards for over a foot. Long tendrils of black energy raced back into a sweeping appearance of pitch-black hair. Stepping from the maelstrom of energy, the creature bowed before the Throne of Woe.

"Tenno Asmodeus answers the summons!" Tenno Asmodeus kneeled before the throne.

Behind Asmodeus, the energy swirled with red hues mixing with the black. The second figure was much smaller than the first. Energy formed the basic structure of the being rising out of the maelstrom. Every aspect of the second being was lithe, graceful, and human-like in appearance.

Leathery wings appeared from the being's back but were much smaller in stature. The wings folded backward upon themselves, disappearing into the creature's back. Energy crackled up the being's body, forming the red boots that raced up to mid-thigh and the small piece of cloth that dangled between both legs before splintering to a V shape. Green armor raced up the torso dividing away from each other, covering the growing mass of energy collecting in the chest and held the mass in a delicate embrace. Behind the being's neck the V-shaped armor rejoined, fastening together. Two horns jutted outward from the beings' forehead before reversing sharply backward. The horns spiraled backward in a coiled pattern for almost two feet ending in sharpened red tips. Long flowing black spikes jutted backwards like flowing strands of hair, only razor sharp. Long flowing red tendrils of energy whipped around the beings' head that appeared almost hair-like, but the wild red energy never seemed to stop moving. Stepping from the summoning, the being's footsteps made no sound on the floor. She walked forward, her energy coalescing to form her almost human-like skin and appearance. She refused to bow, unlike Asmodeus.

"Oh, Supreme Tenno Ba'al Zebub, it's been so long since I last saw you. It must have been at least a millennia ago, and you look overworked. Perhaps what you need is a little tender, love, and care. It has been several centuries since you've requested my administrations," Lilith teased.

"You will show Supreme Tenno Ba'al Zebub respect!" Tenno Verdelet slammed his staff to the ground to both demand compliance and end the summoning. The energy maelstrom vanished with a sharp crackle. All the eyes of the Reverie in the assembly fell upon the two legendary Tenno, and they both looked up at the silent Supreme Tenno sitting on the throne of woe with silent expectation. For a moment, the whole audience chamber was silent.

Ba'al Zebub just stared down at the two Tenno before the court. He considered his words for a moment, but also drank in the fear and terror the Cacophony of Discordance was echoing in the silence. First Ba'al's gaze fell upon Lilith, and he took the time to drink in her terrifyingly beautiful visage. His fat tongue licked his bloated green lips with a loud slurp.

"It has been some time, Tenno Lilith, since I've enjoyed your ministrations, but I fear that is not why the Cacophony of Discordance summoned you."

"Aw, what a disappointment. I was looking forward to bearing some more of your wicked children. They are such a delight to behold," Lilith shook her head in disappointment.

"Perhaps this shall delight you, Tenno Lilith. The Cacophony of Discordance commands you and your Desirous Cadence along with your Lilum children to scour the Great Maw. Only you can find the Minister of Injustice, Tenno Lucifer. The entire Cacophony of Discordance knows that only your charms have ever succeeded in controlling Tenno Lucifer. It has been at least a millennium since you and your consort have filled the Cacophony of Discordance with your lamentations of pleasure."

Lilith could feel her legs tremble with excitement at the possibility of seeing Lucifer again. She couldn't control the lustful thoughts sparking in her mind, echoing in her eyes' energy. Every member of the Reverie could feel the excitement of Lilith's lust echoing in the chamber.

"It has been far too long since I've seen our Minister of Injustice. So, I shall accept the request of the Cacophony of Discordance to find and bring Tenno Lucifer back, but I can't promise it'll be quick. I plan to punish Lucifer first for his long absence from my chamber." Lilith smiled at the thought of her wicked lust.

"No! With the return of the light, your desires will have to wait. Only Tenno Lucifer can judge, and we shall need his counsel in formulating a strategy to destroy this new star." Ba'al Zebub's forceful reply caused Lilith to take a step back but not falter in her behavior.

"Well, there will be time later for Tenno Lucifer's punishment," Lilith giggled gleefully.

"What would you have me do," Tenno Asmodeus interjected.

"Tenno Asmodeus, you're a formidable leader of the Reverie. Jinn follow you. You've always rejected the leadership roles foisted by the council of the Cacophony of Discordance, but we require your talents." Ba'al Zebub's multifaceted eyes narrowed upon Asmodeus.

"No offense intended to the council, Supreme Tenno. My talents are deception and lies don't lend well to leadership. Besides, have my labors not brought power for the Cacophony and wreaked havoc upon our enemies?" Asmodeus' conviction in his words echoed in the chamber.

"Indeed, you have Tenno Asmodeus, but I summon you today for a new power has challenged you. The Cacophony senses this rogue

Magnus Void is an even greater deceiver than you!" Ba'al Zebub knew that challenging Asmodeus pride was the most effective way to make him co-operate.

"Impossible!" Asmodeus hissed.

"It seems this Magnus Void has deceived the whole of the Cacophony of Discordance, including you, Tenno Asmodeus. Magnus Void has led the humans to the *Empyrean station* and helped create the new star. He must answer for his crimes before the Cacophony of Discordance. With Tenno Lilith fetching the Minister of Injustice, this court has deemed that capturing Magnus Void is imperative. Tenno Asmodeus, you are hereby ordered to take your Obscuring Cadence and all your legions forth from the *Pandemonium*, and you will find, capture, and return this Lord Magnus Void to us alive. For the whole Reverie shall feast upon his soul," Ba'al Zebub's words set off a chorus of joyous screeches from the crowd.

"Your command is my duty," Asmodeus declared.

"Go forth Tenno's and return victorious," Ba'al Zebub declared.

Lilith and Asmodeus turned to march towards the black gate of the chamber. Neither of them looked at each other. They both glared ahead, focusing their animosity toward each other on the task at hand. Lilith knew that finding Lucifer wouldn't be easy, and she already knew where she had to go. Only the Arachne might stand a chance to locate Lucifer. Walking alongside Lilith, it was impossible for Asmodeus not to sense her lust and machinations, but he forced it from his mind. There was only one thing Asmodeus hated more than Lilith, and that was this Magnus Void who threatened millennia of careful planning. Asmodeus swore to himself he'd make the rogue pay.

CHAPTER 4

Entering the courtyard, the sound of weapons clanged all around. Troops had begun the process of training the young and anyone capable of fighting who wanted to learn. Nemesis strolled through the city and couldn't help but notice how empty the place was despite the commotion around her. Most of the *Alcatraz* crew had stayed together, and all of them barely took up a tenth of just this one ward. In the distance, people ventured off to discover more of what the station offered. She glanced back to see the lords and ladies watching over their people's training. With a slow walk, she strolled through the training crowd watching the recruits. Seeing some of the trainee's attempts, she had to force down her laughter. She didn't want to discourage anyone with embarrassment.

Commander Verdas was training a couple of the young talented recruits himself. Stopping for a moment, Nemesis watched the three trainees' attack. The trainees were circling around, trying to size up Commander Verdas to discern an opening to attack from. Nemesis could already see how this would play out. She could tell which was the leader by how the other two trainees watched his movement, and when he launched the first strike, the other two dove into help. Nemesis knew they wouldn't be much of a match based on their foot work alone. With one block, four strikes, and six seconds later, the trainees were groaning and writhing in pain on the ground. Commander Verdas smiled and nodded at Nemesis to greet her, and she just smiled back for a second before continuing onward through the group.

"This place is so empty it's disconcerting, and even when we all get settled in, we're barely going to make a dent. It'll take many lifetimes for our people to populate this station. With that new star glowing bright we're the biggest beacon in the whole verse. Everything will come crawling out of their dark holes to try to kill us to take this from us, or worse, destroy it. I fear that for all the splendor and glory of *Empyrean station* this place will be the reason we all die!" Lord Oswald scowled.

"What, you'd rather be back on the death trap that was the *Alcatraz?*" Lord Hector glared at Lord Oswald with his arms crossed.

"Well, we knew how to defend that," Lord Oswald rebuked.

"Doth thee expect we are not strong enough to defend our new home. I detest that thought. We've stood in the shadow of greater might and prevailed. For we have hearts brimming with love for one another." Lady Marimba's voice resonated with pride, drawing in many agreeing nods.

"We also have a lot of food. I don't know what my people will do without having to farm and tend to animals. It seems the Keepers will need to find a new focus." Lady Freya's words caught in her throat in the struggle to speak. She coughed after speaking the words.

"Your people are tough warriors, and there's always a need for those," Lord Hephaestus urged the truth to Lady Freya, and she returned the gesture with a wide smile that made him blush.

"That's true, but that place was killing the Lower Warders all the time, but it's not like you Corebound accepted the reality of the Lower Wards. Our lives never matter much to you," Lord Cornelius fumed until he felt a hand upon his shoulder. Turning around, he saw Nemesis standing there with a half-smile on her face. "Lady Nemesis, where you've been?"

"Meeting with my brother. You know, our new Emperor?" Nemesis glanced around.

"Perhaps you can talk some sense into your brother. This place is fantastic, but it will get us all killed. There is no way we can defend this place against the entire verse when it comes to taking this wonder from us." Lord Oswald's words filled Nemesis with anger, but she knew it was important to bring all these lords and ladies together. Biting back on her anger and tongue, she focused on what needed to be done turning to lock eyes with Lord Oswald.

"Lord Oswald, you're making your complaints very easy to hear. Have you considered the ramifications of the fear you're proselytizing?" Nemesis's glare made Lord Oswald step back.

"What do you mean, Lady Nemesis?" Lord Oswald crossed her arms and grimaced.

"I'm not saying your assessment is wrong about the current situation Lord Oswald. You've always been the most efficient of the lords and ladies at sensing the prevailing tide of events. Staying on the right side of the divide, but that divide has to end. You look around and fear we can't hold this, speak openly about it, and don't care about the cost to our listening people. Do you think your fear propaganda does them any good?" Nemesis pointed to the people around the group, who were now darting their eyes away, trying to avoid being caught listening.

Lord Oswald fell quiet and glanced around to see the truth in Nemesis' point. "My apologies, my lady, I hadn't considered..."

"A great many things, Lord Oswald, and that's ok. This isn't the *Alcatraz*. No one needs to worry about speaking the truth or challenging the status quo, but I make a simple promise to you. My brother, our new Emperor see's far more than any of us, and I trust in him." Nemesis lay her hand upon Oswald's shoulder. "At least you're here to help, unlike Lord Whelsey and Lord Drumpf."

"I see now the errors of my thought," Lord Oswald thanked, trying to instill his confidence in the onlookers of the crowd.

"Lord Oswald does make a few valid points. There is little chance we can defend this massive station from an attack. We need more people," Lord Hector stated.

"My brother is working on a plan, and I wouldn't be comfortable with all the space. I have a feeling it will get crowded in here a lot quicker than any of you realize." Nemesis could see that the dull blind eyes of Lady Clotho seemed to glow with anticipation in response. The words of Matthew's warnings echoed in his sister's head. Something was terrifying Nemesis about Lady Clotho now, and it was a new sensation never felt before.

"Your brother has a bright future. We all do thanks to him," Lady Clotho declared.

"When has the old hag ever been wrong," Lord Cornelius joked but stopped laughing when Lady Clotho glared at him, forcing him to look down at his feet to avert her gaze.

"Oh, but the food here!" Lord Epicure sauntered up to the group with a tray full of steaming food he had prepared. "Eat up! Here we all live like kings and queens." Behind Lord Epicure, his people were wheeling carts filled with food for the trainees. Lord Hector and Cornelius motioned for the training to stop, and the people rushed to devour the food.

Nemesis stood there and watched the spectacle with awe. It was good to not only see her people getting their fair share amongst the Corebound but for the first time, none of the people feared where their next meal was coming from. Nemesis had never felt such rapturous joy in her life, and it was painted on every man, woman, and child's face. Laughter filled the air with tangible happiness that washed over the crowd. Even the grim Lord Hector was reveling in the atmosphere.

"It's a sight to behold, isn't it?" Lady Clotho's question wasn't lost on Nemesis.

"Of course, it's the blind woman who says that," Nemesis joked.

"Do you understand now the prophesy of your brother?" Lady Clotho turned to stare at Nemesis, and despite being blind, she felt the force of the glare in her very soul.

"I have to admit, not really. This place is wondrous, but the other Lords and Ladies are not wrong to fear. My brother sees a great threat coming against us," Nemesis warned.

"A great calamity is already on its way, but I worry less than your brother. We've already achieved so much, and I know how powerful Matthew has become. Besides, we've always got you and your people fighting for us, don't we, Lady Nemesis?" Lady Clotho smiled.

For a moment, Nemesis just stared into those dull grey blinded eyes because she could sense that the old woman knew more than she was letting on. Kain and his genetically seeded army would soon be ready, and once that was done, Nemesis would start her own. She knew Matthew's calculated move was to grow his strength while denying his enemies. The truth was at this moment, Nemesis could understand the warning about Clotho. It was clear that the old woman had been playing her own game for quite some time, and it was a game that Nemesis hadn't realized she was a key figure in until just this moment. That allowed her to uncover the truth, which was her role now as Inquisitor. She intended to uncover the truth.

"Well, we'll have a taste of home soon. Matthew decided to allow me to rebuild the Original Sins, and Marcus is already out scouting the perfect location. Once we get some food into us and a place to blow off steam, we'll return to full strength." Nemesis could sense Lady Clotho's gaze. She was trying to sense what was being kept from her. At least Nemesis could take refuge in the fact that even Lady Clotho wasn't all-seeing and powerful.

"Home is a sense we all long for, but I worry some of us don't want to make this new paradise into a home." Lady Clotho's warning forced Nemesis to turn to confront her.

"My brother thinks that's a natural thing. All cells grow through division," Nemesis glared.

"Indeed, they do, child, but creation requires destruction. I wonder if you have become your brother's will to destruction?" Lady Clotho smiled with a glint in her eyes. Nemesis bit her tongue, sensing the game that was being played. This old woman somehow knew about her role as Inquisitor, but that could work to her advantage she knew.

"I'm the same woman I've always been, and like the good old days, you continue to annoy me. For all your veiled words and intrigues, Lady Clotho, you never seem to figure out who I really am. You'd be wise not to forget that truth." Nemesis leaned in with a smile and kissed Lady Clotho on the cheek before leaning into whisper, "If you become a threat to my family, and especially Matthew, you'll find out just how much destruction I can create. It'd be a tragedy if your daughter and granddaughter met their end, given that you should all see it coming."

Lady Clotho just smiled back. The wrinkles of her face pulled up with the muscles revealing the wry old grin. Nemesis pulled back slowly away from her eye-to-eye contact with Lady Clotho.

"There's an old saying I've learned to trust the hard way, Lady Nemesis, keep your friends close and your enemies closer. I haven't seen the Imperator since after the battle, and I wonder what he's gotten up to." Lady Clotho wink back at Nemesis with a wry smile.

"You know Kain, always the good little soldier. Trust me when I say he's even less forgiving than I am, so I'd avoid his wrath if I were you." Nemesis turned her back and walked away. There was enough to worry about in Nemesis's estimation. She didn't need to worry about the old lady any further at this moment, and she could see Commander Verdas sitting down near a building by himself to eat his meal. This was the perfect opportunity to talk to him alone Nemesis thought.

Walking over, Nemesis swayed her body with unintended seduction. It flowed naturally through her when her will power became focused on a singular task. Right now, she focused all her thoughts on converting her grandfather's most loyal soldier to her cause. With Verdas, she'd be able to get a much better idea of the intrigues Lord Whelsey was planning, and at that moment, her mind turned to Lord Drumpf, which caused her to glance back. Lady Clotho turned at that moment to smile at Nemesis, which filled her with dread. She knew the old lady could somehow sense her gratitude. The plan to use sex to get inside Lord Drumpf's head had been appalling to Nemesis, but it had been effective. Lord Drumpf was under her spell and incapable of keeping any of his secrets from Nemesis after just one night of her wiles. Turning back, she smiled at Commander Verdas when looked up.

"Commander Verdas, I saw you sitting alone and thought I might join you?"

"Sit, Lady Nemesis. Of course, your company is welcome, but I admit a bit of a surprise," Verdas confessed before returning to his sandwich.

"Your training regimen seems to be working on those recruits you spared with earlier," Nemesis pointed to the three young men who were already back to training. "I'm sure in a few more weeks, they'll be in fighting shape." She glanced at Commander Verdas, looking him up and down. "And many other things those muscles could be used for." Words caused Verdas to pause for a second in silence, and she could almost sense him blushing, but he was able to keep any physical change from revealing the truth.

"The secret is you can't make people have a hard work ethic. All you can do is find the people with that ethic and work with them. Who knows, maybe one day I'll be replaced by one of those boys." Commander Verdas took another bite of the sandwich, watching the trainees.

"They do possess some talent, but I would be truly surprised if they surpassed you. I've seen many fighters come through the Sins, and I've never seen a single one with your talent for battle. There's just one thing that really bothers me about you, Commander, but perhaps I've already said too much. I shouldn't be interrupting your meal, considering how much work you have ahead of you to train these recruits." Nemesis turned to walk away.

"Please sit down and tell me what's on your mind," Commander Verdas motioned.

Nemesis smiled for a second when she stopped. Turning back, she sat down next to Commander Verdas, and he offered her half of his sandwich. Nemesis hadn't even considered how hungry she was until that moment, and the gurgle of her stomach told her the truth. She took the sandwich with a nod of thanks and began munching on it. For a second, she and Commander Verdas just chewed their food and watched the group.

"I must admit that it bothers me that you serve my grandfather," Nemesis confessed.

"Your grandfather is a great man of God," Commander Verdas declared.

"Not sure I can agree with you there, given what he did to my sister. I find it hard to believe that a man of God would burn his own granddaughter alive just because he was ordered to do so."

For a moment, Commander Verdas got really quiet. He placed his sandwich back on the plate before looking at Nemesis. She could see he was holding something back in reserve, but not what it was. Commander Verdas turned to look into Nemesis's eyes, and he searched to see if she could be trusted. That told Nemesis that perhaps Lord Whelsey's hold wasn't unbreakable.

"I have a confession of my own," Commander Verdas's words were hesitant and drawn out.

"Have to admit not many come to me for confessions," Nemesis tried to joke, but she could sense the seriousness upon his countenance staring back at her.

"All my life, Lady Nemesis, I've driven myself, but not in service to Lord Whelsey. I've pushed myself past all my limits, strove to be the best in everything I do, and always tried to treat my soldiers like family. This wasn't from the teachings of Lord Whelsey. In fact, when I first rose to this position, your grandfather tried to beat this out of me, and that's quite literal, in fact. It was my love and devotion to God that won over your grandfather. I have always served him because he is the holiest man I've ever met, and his knowledge of scriptures and history astound me."

Commander Verdas paused at that moment, trying to find the best way to express his feelings.

Nemesis could sense the tension lying just under the calm surface of Commander Verdas. She didn't say anything in response or to change his thoughts. Every instinct told her it was best to let this moment of silence linger because this was her route to persuading the Commander to assist. Commander Verdas's eyebrows furled as he looked upon Lady Nemesis. She could sense the war that raged within the man's mind.

"I have seen things that make me doubt your grandfather's love of Christ and the gospels. There are things I wish I could change about him, but he is so strong-willed and stubborn in his ways. I doubt there will ever come a day when he sees me as his equal and not his servant." Commander Verdas whispered his confession. Leaning in, Nemesis moved close to the Commander's ear, and her eyes darted around to ensure no one was watching this interaction. She knew this was the best moment to convert him.

"Emperor is building a genetically seeded army using my brother Kain's D.N.A. as a template. Soon he will do the same with me and the other loyal lords and ladies. We will need the best warriors to become these Patriarchs and Matriarchs of warrior bloodlines. I believe your loyalty to God and your skills as a warrior makes you a perfect candidate, but I worry about my grandfather's loyalty. Perhaps if you were to help me by revealing the truth of my grandfather's plan, my brother would select you to become a Patriarch," Nemesis insinuated.

Commander Verdas fell quiet again, pulling back to search Nemesis's eyes for truth. She could feel the need burning within the man. In her mind, it was to be expected, considering the way they had all grown up on the *Alcatraz*. Commander Verdas would be a fool to trust her right away, and his hesitation wasn't a warning side. It revealed he was considering Nemesis's proposal, and she leaned back before taking another bite.

"You know I could tell Lord Whelsey about this, and I doubt it would make him happy."

"We could all do anything at any moment. I guess I'll just have to trust you. You know where to find me." Nemesis turned to see Marcus enter the training square. She popped the rest of the sandwich in her mouth.

"Thanks for the meal," she smiled before marching off towards Marcus pushing her way through the crowd.

With each step, Nemesis stayed focused on Marcus, who was scanning the thick crowd for her. A warm feeling filled her body. The couple's eyes met in the crowd, and they both couldn't help but smile. Each step came quicker, and Nemesis burst forward and leaped into her lover's arms. She grabbed him by the back of his head and pulled him into a long passionate kiss that drew cheers and jeers from the crowd. Breaking from the kiss, Nemesis smiled, gazing down at Marcus's face with her legs wrapped around his torso, holding her up. He tried to catch his breath to speak.

"Well, if getting some work done gets that reaction from you, I guess I should do work more often. I managed to find the perfect central location for the Original Sin. Did your brother give you his imperial seal of approval?" Marcus's question revealed his deep dislike of the current power structure, but Nemesis just kissed him again to shut him up.

"Of course, my brother gave me his permission. You'll be able to start getting the place set up and running. However, you have been neglecting your most important duties." Nemesis glared with a frown catching Marcus off guard.

"I don't think I've forgotten anything?"

Dropping down to the ground, Nemesis grabbed Marcus by the hand. "Well, how about you show me this place? I would like to know where I will be sleeping tonight, and once you show me that, well, I will need a couple of hours of your time. Love is hard work, you know," Nemesis smiled, seeing the glint of excitement in Marcus' eyes.

"Don't you have training to do here with these recruits?" Marcus asked with worry.

"They've got enough attention from the other lords and ladies." Nemesis pulled at Marcus, and the two walked towards the exit with their arms wrapped around each other. The two leaned on each other as they walked. It was obvious to all that the only thing that mattered to them at this moment was each other. Lady Freya smiled at the sight and glanced at Lord Hephaestus to see his happiness from seeing the couple's expression of love.

In the distance, Lady Clotho smiled, watching her plans with Nemesis begin to develop. The clacking of her cane signaled her retreat. She knew it was important to go draw auspices. The future was still uncertain and would require much more planning if Fate's design was to be ensured. That was Lady Clotho's sacred duty, and she slipped away from the crowd unnoticed.

CHAPTER 5

Troops of Clan Pious moved large stacks of resources into the large manor Lord Whelsey declared his home. He stood out back on the patio, looking over the large park behind the manor, and already in his mind, he was planning the construction of a new cathedral. He had explored the *Empyrean station*, and to his dismay, he found the Ancients had little appreciation for God. Only the Infinity Nexus seemed to possess any sense of humility to the divine. There wasn't a single church or monument erected to God, the only religious relics beyond the angelic statues in the Infinity Nexus. Lord Whelsey turned to face his granddaughter.

"This is why God destroyed the Ancients. They had no respect for our Lord, and as we know. God promises to avenge all injustices, and what could be more wicked than turning your back on your creator?" Lord Whelsey expected his granddaughter to answer him, and he turned to face her when there was no response. Angelica stood there silent and still, and her eyes seemed focused on a distant point. She didn't even notice the glare she was receiving.

Inside Angelica's mind, she could feel the being known as Levart taking control. She tried to stop him, but she could not move a single muscle. All she could hear was the demon's laughter echoing in her mind. With every ounce of will power, she fought to regain control of her body, but it remained unresponsive for a second. When she felt her body move again, she was shocked but soon realized it was Levart in control. All Angelica could do was watch, helpless to stop Levart.

"Lord Whelsey, I do believe. I have to admit it's nice to finally meet you in person. Believe me when I say I was rooting for you in the battle,"

Angelica smiled. She walked over towards the surprised Lord Whelsey, whose eyes were dilated with fear.

"Angelica?"

"Not quite. You may call me Levart. This body is quite sublime and intoxicating," Levart marveled, looking down at Angelica's body, and looking at the hands running over her body.

"What did you do with my granddaughter?" Lord Whelsey demanded.

"Not the worst thing she's ever endured. Just borrowing her body for a little bit, and she is pissed about it. Still, I preferred to have this talk with you face to face or as close as I can now. Oh, those are wicked thoughts indeed," Levart stared with a smile into Lord Whelsey's eyes reaching out to grab hold of his face pulling him back towards Angelica.

Lord Whelsey grabbed Angelica's arm to force it off, but he could not contend with her strength. The glare coming from Angelica's pitch-black eyes reminded Lord Whelsey of the glare of Magnus Void, and he realized the creature inside his granddaughter's body was the Reverie they fought. Levart laughed with glee once he saw Lord Whelsey's revelation.

"You're the demon that attacked this station," Lord Whelsey accused.

"Oh, I am so much more than just a demon now. Your granddaughter's body offers me such power, and her mind. It's truly beyond words. All the horror and tragedy could feed me for a millennium, maybe longer, but this opportunity is worth so much more than that."

Levart released Lord Whelsey, and in reaction, he pulled his golden cross pendant and held it up. In Latin, he chanted words he remembered from the Ancients to drive demons away. So lost in the chant, he didn't even hear Levart's response. The demon just cackled in response, its voice mixing with Angelica's into a deeply distorted echo. Realizing the cross was offering no protection, Lord Whelsey began to back away with slow steps.

"My grandson will destroy you and your kind now with the power of the new star's light," Lord Whelsey prophesized. Each word trembled with the fear seizing his mind at that moment.

"Perhaps, but maybe you'd rather be the one in control of this place. Truth is, I don't care about the star. It's been so long since I had someone to possess that I've offered you a deal Lord Whelsey." Levart backed Lord Whelsey into a corner on the patio.

Lord Whelsey tried to hide his fear, but the cross was shaking in his hand. Still, his mind was set abuzz by Levart's offer. No matter how hard he tried to resist, he could feel the insidious tug of curiosity pulling at his mind. Lowering the cross, he looked into the pitch-black eyes of his granddaughter whom he knew was the spirit of Levart. He gulped down hard preparing to speak.

"What do you mean I could control this place, because I don't have the power my grandson does?" Lord Whelsey couldn't help how he felt. He wanted the power for himself, and it seemed this demon could assist in acquiring it.

"Oh, your grandson is special, but he's not at full power yet. That Infinity Nexus is just a psionic amplifier of the nature of energy itself. Once he becomes fully charged, so to speak, well, then he'll be almost invincible. I can help you acquire the same power as your grandson," Levart's smile contorted Angelica's face into almost beyond human limits but into an inhuman, monstrous grin.

"How can you do that?"

"Well, we Reverie have access to the same power as your grandson. It's in our nature to live feeding upon negative energy. We can manipulate the flow of energy, siphon off life force, and oh so much more. I could help you unlock this power," Levart feeling the pull of Angelica's face muscles bursting into a cackling laughter. Reaching up with her hand to touch hew own face, and filling her brain will all kinds of strange sensation for Levart to drink in.

"You mean I could replace my grandson and seize control of the Infinity Nexus?"

"Yes, but we're going to need the help of the Lord Galen fellow. We'll need to use that science you humans are so fond of. Perhaps we should visit the lab you two are setting up downstairs. This would be the perfect time to begin our plans. Don't you agree?" Levart ran Angelica's hands down over her body, drinking the sensation of touch, and Lord Whelsey could not look away.

Watching Levart explore Angelica's body made Lord Whelsey's brow furrow as he glared on, and his thoughts swirled with the possibilities the offer brought. Deep down, he held no loyalty to his granddaughter. She was the corruption of Gabriel on the sublime beauty of Helena, but she was a useful, necessary tool, it seemed. The demon's offer of power was too good to pass up, considering the current situation. Gritting his teeth, he fixated his mind on this devil's deal. This demon Levart had knowledge he could use, but he had to stay in control. This opportunity finally allowed him to achieve the power to destroy the Soloman family's stranglehold on power. The plan he had started the day he proposed the marriage between Helena and Gabriel.

"Follow me," Lord Whelsey ordered, breaking from his fixation with a plan in mind. He walked towards the door downstairs. The first thing he had done had the troops move all the databanks from the *Alcatraz* down here to create a new reliquary, but the computer systems also created the possibility of a lab. Lord Galen was already down here working away at setting up his analysis of the scans he had down on Matthew, and he was already going over them.

Marching into the room, Lord Whelsey led the demon Levart in. The two of them stopped behind Lord Galen to look over his shoulders. Levart could see the data on the screen and smiled with delight. These humans were already further along than he could have hoped. Now all that was left was to use temptation to lead them both down the path of ruination. Levart's laughter echoed into the lab mixed with Angelica's voice, and the distorted sound drew the fearful gaze of the two men.

"What's going on with your granddaughter?" Lord Galen could see something was strange about Angelica, but when he saw her eyes, he looked upon her with fascination.

"It seems the Reverie that attacked the station has taken possession of Angelica, and this demon is offering a bargain. Levart offers to explain to us how to engineer the same power as Matthew so that we can control the Infinity Nexus. I figured this might pique your interests, and I don't think there has ever been a study of demonic possession," Lord Whelsey informed with a grin.

"Fascinating!" Lord Galen turned around to activate the scanners and programmed them to take deep readings of Angelica. He set up the system to contrast the incoming readings against the scans he took of Matthew. With the new problem to solve, Lord Galen's entire focus was directed on the data trying to decipher the patterns he could already see on the screen. There was no telling what revelations he would learn from this information.

The sheer potential was already giving him all kinds of new ideas on ways to apply this new information.

"Looks like Lord Galen has all he needs to get started," Levart whispered to Lord Whelsey.

"Indeed, but now I must turn my attention to the traitorous Lord Drumpf. In order to take *Empyrean station*, he will need to be dealt with first. If he's given time, he'll find a way to rebuild his forces. The loss of Commander Lance won't slow him much, and Lord Drumpf is resourceful." Lord Whelsey explained the situation, but Levart shook Angelica's head.

"No! Lord Drumpf is no threat to you now. Once you have access to my power, you'll crush him with the same ease as Matthew did Gabriel. Watching the memory of the event in your granddaughter's mind makes me wish I had been there to see it myself. This memory is such a wicked event," Levart words reverberated with wanton delight.

"I'll have to focus on rebuilding my troops if I am to make a move on Matthew," Lord Whelsey replied, considering the situation.

"Wrong again. You don't need troops to win this battle. There's only one power you need: this power." Levart turned to reach out and grab Lord Whelsey, and with slow persistent concentration the demon siphoned some of the life force. Feeling the drain, Lord Whelsey struggled to break free from the demon's grasp, but the sheer strength of Angelica with Levart in control seemed impossible to break through. Levart released Lord Whelsey with a smile.

"Such power," Lord Whelsey whispered with reverence and fear.

"This could be your power," Levart taunted. "With this power, Matthew would stand no chance. You could drink your grandson's life force as easily as I drink yours. His power would become your power, and this entire verse would bow to your greatness."

"No power is greater than God's," Lord Whelsey declared.

"God's power is Matthew's power, and that power could be your power. The power to create a new universe, where all life bows before you and where you ensure the righteous are free from evil. Tell me, Lord Whelsey isn't that what you've always dreamed of?" Levart's question made Lord Whelsey pause in a mix of trepidation and awe. The demon whispered to his very soul.

There was a strange juxtaposition in Lord Whelsey's mind. Everything he believed in was predicated on submission and subservience to God, but the offer to become God was emboldening him. There was a war of desire and penitence waging in his mind, and he didn't even know which side he wanted to win. The only thing he was certain of was that he couldn't turn his back on this opportunity, and with that thought, he focused on Levart's offer.

"The power I'm offering comes with a price," Levart warned.

"What price is that?"

"First, you must reconcile with Matthew, for he can see the future and sense your plans. You must appear to serve him in all things. For there is nothing that the living are so deceived in as matters of the heart. Matthew's desire to reconcile you and the rest of his family can be turned against him. He'll see the future coming but deny it because of the hope to save you. In the end, that desire to save you will be his undoing." Levart could see his plan taking root in Lord Whelsey's mind, and the wicked thoughts he sensed brought a smile.

Lord Whelsey stared into Angelica's eyes, trying to gauge at the plans of Levart, and he doubted the demon was telling the full truth. The similarity to the long alliance with Lord Drumpf was not lost on Lord Whelsey in that moment of echoing memories. This demon Levart offered far more power, and Lord Whelsey would drain every drop of knowledge and power this creature could offer him. Still, he knew this plan would require much more cunning to succeed. Dealing with Lord Drumpf seemed minuscule by comparison.

"How can I trust you, Levart?" Lord Whelsey poised the question, but not for his sake. Levart seemed to be a cunning demon, and if the scriptures were correct about demons, Lord Whelsey knew this creature would expect such a question from a man of his mind. The absence of the question would only rouse Levart's suspicion that he was being played. Lord Whelsey smiled at his good fortune of years of experience in this type of machination. All that suffering and learning was going to pay off.

"Oh, we both know you don't trust me. That's fine because I don't need your trust. I've got your granddaughter's life at my disposal. Any sign of betrayal, and I'll end her life before you can do anything. You may not care about her life, but your daughter Helena does. Think of all the suffering your daughter has already been through. Do you really want to add more?" Levart knew he had Lord Whelsey under his complete control, and this was just letting the man know the truth of that reality.

A knock on the lab door drew Lord Whelsey and Levart's attention, but Lord Galen continued his work, enthralled by the sheer possibilities of the results of the scans. The door slid open, revealing Helena standing there, and she rushed to embrace her family once she saw her father and daughter standing there. Tears raced down Helena's cheeks from the joy she felt at this moment.

"Oh, it's so good to see you both are safe! I've been searching for you since the attack. A couple of the Pious Clan guards told me you were both here, and I can't believe my eyes." Helena released her family members from her hug to take a step back. Seeing the situation, Levart retreated into Angelica's mind, leaving her disorientated and standing there looking at her mother and grandfather. She stared them both blankly for a second trying to figure out how she was missing time.

"Sorry, Mother, but I'm just surprised to see you." Angelica stumbled, trying to figure out where she was, causing her to glance around and up at her grandfather.

Lord Whelsey could see his granddaughter's eyes had returned to normal, and that was the only sign he needed. He turned his attention to his daughter.

"My beautiful daughter, it's so good to see you. I was just showing Angelica the new compound I decided to base Clan Pious out of. This is, of course, the lab I had Lord Galen set up for me. We're working on some religious experiments together, given all the new technology the *Empyrean station* offers." Lord Whelsey could see by the gleam of happiness in his daughter's eye's that she bought the lie.

"God will reward you both for your piety," Helena stated.

"Perhaps you'd be willing to talk to our new Emperor to express my piety to him. I fear that my relationship with your children has become strained during your incarceration by Gabriel. The situation on the *Alcatraz* only got worse, and I was forced to take care of my people first. I'm sure you understand, daughter?" Lord Whelsey studied his daughter's eyes, trying to get a sense of her intentions.

"Of course, father. I would be happy to help you and Matthew reconcile any differences. You'll find my youngest son is far wiser than his father ever was," Helena promised.

"Angelica, why don't you stay here with Lord Galen, watch over him, and help him however he might require. Your mother and I should take this time to catch up. It's been so long since we last seen each other." Lord Whelsey could sense Angelica was still disoriented from Levart's control. She just nodded in agreement taking the easiest escape route.

"That sounds fine to me, grandfather. Mother, I will come see you later when I am done here," Angelia promised with a forced half-smile trying to sell that she was fine.

"Are you sure dear? You seem disturbed by something," Helena pressed.

"Ya, mom, I'm fine. Just go with grandfather and help him sort the business out with Matthew. Give me some time, and everything will work out. I promise," Angelica lied.

Helena looked at her daughter with a mixture of fear and understanding, and after a few seconds, she followed her father out of the lab. The two walked back up the steps together. Lord Whelsey knew he had to calm his daughter's fear about her child. The emotions were written plain on Helena's face despite her best efforts to conceal them. It was something that Lord Whelsey remembered well from his daughter's childhood. She always tried to hide how she felt.

"Don't worry about Angelica. She is a fine woman and a powerful warrior. You should be very proud of her, my dear." Lord Whelsey tried to distract his daughter by appealing to her pride.

"Oh, I am, father. I taught that girl every move she knows, just as you taught me how to fight so long ago. Still, I wonder if perhaps we hadn't tried to destroy Gabriel if my life would be better. I fear for Angelica. Her life hasn't been easy. You have no clue the horrors her father inflicted." Helena couldn't keep control of her worry, but she trusted her father's wisdom and guidance.

"What does Matthew say?"

"He was more concerned about you, father. He asked me to help reconcile and bring you back into the fold of the family. All I know is my son is worried about your future and believes I'm the only chance to save you."

"Perhaps madness just runs in the Soloman bloodline. I am still the same religious man devoted to God when I raised you, my daughter. Perhaps paranoia is already taking hold of your son's mind, which bodes ill for us all." Lord Whelsey could see his warning didn't have the impact he hoped for. Rather than bringing Helena closer, it was beginning to drive her away.

"Matthew is nothing like his father. Trust me, you must submit to him now as Emperor. Everyone else has, and we've gained this paradise in return. You and Matthew could do great things together, father. Will you come with me to meet with Matthew?" Helena offered her hand.

"Of course, my daughter." Lord Whelsey took his daughter's hand looking into her eyes.

Father and daughter walked towards the exit, but they both had different thoughts in their mind. For Helena, she was proud to be helping her son to reunite all the people in this paradise, but her father's mind turned to darker thoughts. Lord Whelsey wanted to know if Levart was right and if there were limits to Matthew's power. Limits that could be exploited to Lord Whelsey's advantage, and he knew that with his daughter at his side, there was little chance Matthew would turn to violence. Lord Whelsey knew it was a gambit, but there wasn't any other path to take.

CHAPTER 6

S parks shot from the exposed wires smoldering in the ruins of the *Alcatraz* bridge, and oxygen sucked through the crack of the viewscreen with a hiss. Smoke lingered on the ceiling from the burning wires and chunks of electronics scattered across the bridge. Lying on the deck plating, Gabriel groaned when his eyes flickered back to life, and he gasped for air, feeling the stranglehold of the low oxygen atmosphere. With a trembling arm, he pushed himself off the floor, but his legs were wobbling underneath his weight. Reaching out, he grabbed the remains of the flight console to attempt to steady him in the situation.

The loud hiss told Gabriel what he needed to do despite the panic trying to seize control. He could feel his lungs burning for oxygen, and his vision was blurring. Glancing around the bridge, he saw the door to his private cabin had been blown open during the crash. Through the haze of smoke, he could see his suit of power armor still in storage. With slow footsteps, he made his way towards the private quarters, but his legs gave up, causing him to crash on the ground. Blood dripped from the fresh wound on his forehead, and he tried to force himself to stand back up. With one hand, he wiped the blood away, trying to stop it from gushing into his eye, but soon the flow returned, forcing his one eye shut. With a wobble, he continued towards the armor.

Glass covered the floor from the shattered trophy case, and most of the items were strewn across the cabin. The desk smashed against the door, forcing Gabriel to duck under it to enter his cabin. The crunch of glass beneath his metal boots echoed in the small area, and he heard the noise ringing at a distance in his ears. Everything felt like a blur to him, and he struggled to get the biometric reader of the vault to work. His fingers kept missing the button, and he saw multiple copies of the button blurring in his vision. He slammed his fist down on the button, and the biometric reader slipped open, allowing him to place his hand on it. Beeping confirmed his identity, and the vault began to slide open, granting him access to the power armor suit.

Stepping into the armor, Gabriel struggled to get himself in at first, but once he was in the armor, it began to seal around him. When the neural implant connected to the armor, he ran a full diagnostic, but not on the armor. Medical scanners in the suit whirred to life, and his mind screamed in pain from the sudden surge of information downloading. Now he knew why he felt such pain. The scanner reported he was suffering from a concussion and low oxygen. With the suit now sealed around him, he gasped in the pure oxygen being pumped out. His vision was still blurry, but with each passing second, everything became clearer. The only thing remaining was the throbbing headache, but he sighed in relief when the power armor administered painkillers direct to his bloodstream.

Taking a moment, he sat down to look at the ruins of the *Alcatraz*, and he couldn't even believe he had survived. The last few minutes of the battle of *Empyrean station* played out in his memories. Screaming alarms from all the systems were the last thing he remembered after the shudder of the collision with the *Dread Sovereign*. Everything was dead. There was no way for him to find out if his family survived the battle. Breath trembled past his lips, tears welled up along his eyelids, and he felt the pain washing through him for a moment before slamming his hands down against the deck. Force of the impact resonated through the bridge. Pushing himself off the ground, he marched back toward the ruins of the bridge. Glancing across at the engineering console, he could see the system was still functional from the glare of light flickering. Walking past the captain's chair, he noticed the tactical console was in ruins and took a second to mourn what he had lost. There wasn't any hope of repairing the *Alcatraz*, and all he could hope was this ship wouldn't become his tomb.

With a sigh, Gabriel dropped the remnants of the tactical console that had been his closest friend for most of his life, and he continued towards the engineering console. Pressing buttons on the console revealed most of the ship's systems were down, but some of the sensors were still functional. From the damage reports, it looked like the lower half of the ship had been obliterated during the F.T.L. jump. Gabriel was just about to give up hope of escaping the tomb his ship had become when sensors alerted him to movement in the hall beyond the bridge. With a few button presses, he brought up the ship's internal cameras to see what was going on.

From the look of the six people in the hallway, there were salvagers, possibly pirates, or worse, reavers looking for an easy meal. Gabriel couldn't quite tell from the look of the aliens alone. Their armor appeared to be in poor condition, from what Gabriel could see. Most of the aliens wore some kind of patchwork armor that didn't look much more complex than metal strapped over their bodies to provide some protection. Two of the aliens were easy to discern. He had met Dhakan, the serpentine. Three of them appeared humanoid, but their patchwork armor concealed their entire head. It was the leader who drew his attention. The armor the alien wore didn't cover its entire body, and it was clear that the creature had an orange and black stripped fur pattern rather than skin. The facemask the creature wore covered its face, but two large yellow eyes stared out from the mask.

From the camera view, Gabriel could tell they were making their way towards the bridge, and from their sweeping of the officer level, they at least weren't stupid. Still, the alien's tactics were lacking in Gabriel's estimation, and he studied them, looking for any exploits he could use to his advantage. He knew these aliens had arrived on some ship or had one nearby, and it was his only option for escape. On the screen, the aliens were beginning to set up at the bridge door. Cutting torches were being lit on video, and sparks began to leap into the bridge through the sealed door.

Walking back to the captain's quarters, Gabriel fetched his weapons scattered across the floor. He had no intention of leaving any of his family heirlooms behind. Locking a clip into an energy rifle, he smirked. The weapon had been too dangerous to employ on the ship before, but in its current condition, he couldn't do much more damage. It was time to find out exactly what this weapon could really do, he thought. He used the wall for cover by the door of his quarters and aimed down the sights at the bridge door.

Sparks flew from the cutting torch, burning a hole through the metal door to the bridge. Hot molten steel dripped to the floor with a searing hiss, but Gabriel remained focused on his aim. He watched the aliens cut their way through the door slowly. A loud thud echoed when the bridge door collapsed inwards, striking the deck to rumble through the floor plate, and the aliens began moving into the room. Gabriel tracked the first alien with his sight but watched for a second for the rest of the aliens to enter. The only option was to take them all out before they could react. With a finger, Gabriel sighted his first target narrowing his view.

Pointing to the console, the leader of the aliens set two of his crew to work on salvaging it, and for a second, looked around as if he sensed something watching. Before he could spot Gabriel, he opened fire. The first blast shot a beam of neon blue energy that struck the first serpentine, and before the body had slumped to the floor, Gabriel had already fired again. Shot after shot hit the aliens before they could react. Panicked, the leader tried to retreat out of the bridge, but Gabriel was already racing to intercept. Before the alien could reach the door, he heard the loud clanging of Gabriel's power armor charging up from behind. Alien spun backwards to engage Gabriel leaping forward.

Gabriel grabbed the alien with one hand, and the second fist crashed into the alien's face. One strike was all Gabriel needed, and the alien slunk to the floor unconscious. The barrel of the energy rifle smoked, adding to the haze collecting on the ceiling. Looking down, Gabriel grabbed the alien by one foot and dragged the creature towards the elevator shaft. Entering the shaft, Gabriel examined the elevator system to see if it was still functional, and he was shocked to find it did still work. Pressing a button for the Core Wards, Gabriel knew exactly where he needed to take this alien. He knew from the flashing engineering console that the Core Wards were still intact.

The metal creaked and groaned even louder than it used to, and Gabriel felt anxiety hit his nerves. All he could do was focus on keeping calm because he knew that the situation was far from over, glancing down at his hostage. Taking a deep breathe, he tried to clear his mind from the fear of each lurch and groan of the elevator. The sound of metal grinding had never bothered him so much before, but the elevator managed to come to a safe stop on the Core Wards. Gabriel grabbed the aliens' foot again with one hand and headed towards Lord Galen's lab, dragging his hostage behind.

Darkness had fallen on the Core Wards after the crash damaged the energy grid. Only a few lights still worked, and they flicked in the distance. Sparks leaped from exposed wires by Lord Galen's laboratory plaza, and

Gabriel dragged his hostage behind him through the open door and down the hallway. Reaching the private lab of Lord Galen caused Gabriel to stop and use his captain override code to open the door. For a second, the computer system hung, and it caused him to worry that the damage of the crash had taken the system offline. He was just about to get to work opening the doors by force when they slid open with a whoosh.

Gabriel dragged his hostage into the room, picked the alien up, and threw the creature down on the laboratory medical bed. Gabriel pulled up the medical bed system with one hand and activated the restraints, but the system failed. Gabriel looked around with a growl of frustration and walked over to some exposed wires to rip them out. He tied the alien down to the medical bed with the wires. Activating the scanner of the bed, Gabriel prayed that the machine still worked, and the system came to life, activating a scan. He watched silently as the machine performed intensive deep molecular scans on the alien. Once the scan was complete, Gabriel took a moment to study it.

The system stated the alien was a male Tigeran, and the system listed he was unconscious and what medicine was best to revive him. Walking over to the medicine storage, Gabriel ripped it open and found most of the medicine had been taken. Going over what was left, he took a vial and hypo-injector. Locking the medicine vial into the tool, Gabriel placed it against the Tigeran's throat and injected it. Within a few seconds, the medicine was already reviving the Tigeran. The alien struggled to break free from his entrapment, but the wires held firm.

"Best to save your strength for what's going to happen should you fail to answer my questions, or worse, answer them with lies. So, let's start off simple. My name's Gabriel Soloman, and I'm the captain of what's left of this ship. What's your name?" Gabriel glared down.

A frenzy of words that Gabriel couldn't make out was his answer. Shaking his head, he turned to march over to the medical supplies. The Tigeran was still screaming in his native tongue, but Gabriel focused on rooting through what little remained after the evacuation. When he found a single vial with an unused neural implant, he smiled. Moving over to the machine, he placed the neural implant vial in and activated the ascension protocol. Not being a doctor, he didn't administer any anesthesia. The machine arm whirred, moving to implant the chip into the base of the

Tigeran's skull. Screams of agony filled the lab for minutes on end, and the machine continued to work away.

"What we've got here is failure to communicate, but let's see if this helps." Gabriel accessed the lab's data banks and uploaded the entire dictionary of human languages to the Tigeran's brain. Another series of howls bellowed forth, and the wires were pulled tight under strain from the thrashing. Gabriel began collecting the tools left behind, placing them on a tray, and picking up a fallen cart. The wheels squeaked with each revolution when Gabriel pushed the cart beside the bed. He looked down into the dull yellow eyes racked with pain.

"You will pay for this human," the Tigeran vowed.

"See, we're making progress already. What's your name?" Gabriel didn't look at the Tigeran but instead focused on the tools on the table.

"Myrmidon," he answered.

"Well, that's a strong sounding name, but I've never met your kind before. Seems my ancestors have. You're quite a vicious race from what I saw in the data banks." Gabriel pointed the razor-sharp talons that jutted out from Myrmidon's hands.

"You'll have the pleasure of dying by my claws if you're lucky, or worse, my people if you're cursed like you seem to be. We only abandon our own people when we're absolutely forced to. Once my crew figures out what's happening, you're dead." Myrmidon struggled to break free, but the wires weren't giving. Looking around, he noticed the tools that Gabriel was going over.

"I know what you're thinking. This isn't much, but like I used to tell my wife it's not the size of the tool but how it's used. I thought I'd start with this," Gabriel showed the laser scalpel he held. Activating the scalpel, a short bright red laser appeared.

"Do your worst, human, but you better enjoy it. Once I'm free, I promise to repay the pain you inflict tenfold. Besides, you don't know how strong Tigeran's really are." Myrmidon's eyes narrowed into a seething glare of vengeance. Standing over him, the scalpel was brought right inches from his eyes so he could see it up close. Bright light reflecting in the dilating irises.

"It's been a long time since I tortured anyone. Truth be told, I feel a little rusty. Not sure whether I should start by removing your eyelids to make sure you can't help but see what I'm going to do or if I should start with something more profound. This fur of yours is beautiful, but I think it might look better if it was red. Say, do you Tigeran's know what flaying is?" Gabriel stared into Myrmidon's eyes.

There was no response to the words in Myrmidon's eyes, which told Gabriel he hadn't associated the word with his original language. There was a possibility the Tigeran's didn't have a similar word. Gabriel just stared down at Myrmidon with a smile.

"See, I'm going to use this little laser scalpel to cut away your fur first. That might not hurt, but once the fur is gone, your skin will be exposed. That's when I'm going to begin cutting you. Strip by strip, I'm going to cut and peel away your flesh. Trust me, you haven't felt pain until you've been flayed. I'm looking forward to this after the day I've had. My whole family abandoned me, and I'm not sure you can understand how painful that fact has caused me. So let me talk to you in the language of pain." Gabriel began sheering away fur to expose the flesh.

"Do you think your tactics frighten me, human?"

Gabriel laughed. "I'm not trying to frighten you. There is only one thing I want from you. Your ship! I'll be taking it inevitably whether you give it up by talking, or don't."

"I would die before I give you my ship," Myrmidon vowed.

"Oh, I do so love a challenge," Gabriel grinned with a glimmer in his eyes.

Myrmidon's eyes grew wider in contrast to the proximity of the laser scalpel getting closer to his skin. There was no hesitation in Gabriel, and he began cutting away strips of skin to the screams of agony of Myrmidon. Throwing the strips of skin onto the floor with a squish, Gabriel kept cutting away at his victim. On the table, Myrmidon convulsed with pain and howled in furious pain. His eyes widened watching Gabriel looking for a new tool.

"Not many humans survive a good flaying. I could keep going, but your death isn't what I really want. All I want is your ship, and so I wonder what else I can do to persuade you." Gabriel picked up a nerve stimulator and turned back. "Ever wondered what your nerves feel like on fire?"

"I can't give you my ship because I don't want to die in this wreck any more than you do!" Myrmidon tried to reason with Gabriel, but the nerve stimulator grew closer. Panic took over Myrmidon's mind, and he struggled with what was left of his strength.

"Who said I was going to leave you here to die?" Gabriel paused for a moment.

"Why would you trust me after torturing me? You have to know that I'd always be seeking a moment of vengeance for this suffering. There is no way we can trust each other now, human!"

"Trust is overrated, fear is better!" Gabriel smiled getting ready to get back to work.

"Wait! I'll give you the command codes to my ship if you swear that you won't kill me." Myrmidon tried to bide his time to figure out Gabriel's weakness.

"Well, hand them over," Gabriel demanded.

"How can I know you won't abandon me here?"

"You don't. Trust might be overrated, but you'll need to show me you fear death enough to be forced into dealing with me. This doesn't work otherwise, and I might as well get back to work." Gabriel began moving the nerve stimulator toward the exposed nerves.

"The command codes are in my native language. You wouldn't understand them! Even with this machine you put in me, I can't figure out how to translate them into this language. Please stop," Myrmidon begged.

"I don't need to understand your codes. Just transfer them to me," Gabriel connected a neural cable to Myrmidon's new neural implant and hooked it into his suit. "Don't try anything funny. This armor will fry your brain faster than you can think."

Myrmidon wasn't sure what to do, but he focused on the command codes. Within a few seconds, the information had transferred to Gabriel. He threw the nerve stimulator down, picked up the laser scalpel, and cut the wires away. Myrmidon tried to sit up, but Gabriel held him down to demonstrate his armor's power. After a few seconds, Myrmidon ceased to struggle.

"You can't overcome me, so it's best to submit," Gabriel urged.

"All I want is to save my crew. You can have the ship but promise not to slaughter my people like you did my boarding crew. If you make that promise, I'll serve you," Myrmidon offered.

"Deal!" Gabriel extended his hand, and for a second, Myrmidon didn't know what to do. The two just stared at each other in the awkward moment.

"Just like that, you're going to trust me?" Myrmidon was shocked at this alien's behavior.

"I survived my entire life on this ship before it crashed Myrmidon. I couldn't trust anyone, not even my own family. Trust is useless but believe me when I say if you choose to betray me that'll be the last decision you'll regret before you die. You're a long way off from seeing the worst I can do to my enemies. Now let's get going to my new ship." Gabriel motioned towards the door to the lab.

Standing up, Myrmidon took the lead heading out of the laboratory. He wasn't sure what to do next, but he knew there would be an opportunity to escape soon. All he had to do was bide his time. Looking back, he could see Gabriel was focused on keeping control of the situation. He followed far enough behind his captive that any sudden movement would give him ample time to react. There was no choice for Myrmidon but to play this situation out.

CHAPTER 7

Machines whirred in the massive room filled with large tubes, and Virgil teleported from each tube, checking the occupants' status. Leaning back into the chair, Kain watched the simulations on the screens in front of him. He watched the men and women on the screens going through basic drills, training regiments, and wargames. There was a certain marvel at how realistic the simulations were because not a single person on the videos knew they were inside of a program. Each of them was living out their lives in what felt like reality, but looking at Virgil checking on the tubes, Kain knew that these children would soon wake up.

The door to the lab was whisked open, and Joshua and Celeris came to stop when they saw the row upon row and floor upon floor of what seemed to be endless tubes. For a moment, the two siblings were frozen in awe, and Kain got up and approached to knock his siblings out of their stupor. Kain walked up and hugged his sister first and then pulled his brother into an embrace. Letting them go, he motioned for them to follow and pointed to the screens. It took a few moments for Joshua or Celeris to figure out what was happening.

"Wait, are you telling me these are real people growing into those tubes living in a simulated program?" Celeris marveled at the situation and couldn't help but think how useful such a tool would be for training pilots. The orders she had received from Matthew had been vague at first, but now seeing all these, those orders made sense.

"Yes, sister, these are all, I guess, my children now. Virgil has used my genetic code as a base, but each has unique traits and personalities. The idea is that we'll push our genetic potential forward while keeping the base of what works, or that's how Matthew and Virgil have attempted to explain it to me. It's all a little over my head to be honest." Kain could see the awe inspired in his siblings. It was clear that Joshua was too focused on watching the war games on the screen.

"Strange watching these new troops fighting because all I see is reflections of you. The way they move, how they attack, and of course, the way they plan. Brother, these aren't just your children but reflections of you. It's kind of creepy," Joshua shivered. Celeris smacked her brother hard across the back of his head drawing Joshua's glare backwards.

"Emperor has ordered us to undergo this process next. So be creeped out on your own time. I think this is fascinating, and only wonder how far I can push my ability to pilot," Celeris explained.

"Is that all you think about?" Joshua glared at his sister.

"So quick to forget that without my piloting skills, you'd be dead, and you can't tell me that our flight from the *Alcatraz* wasn't fun." Celeris could tell by the look in Joshua's eyes that he didn't agree. The fear etched across his face was only further confirmation.

"You and Kain have a strange sense of fun. He loves when he's surrounded by things trying to kill him, and you seem to think life's only entertaining when you're on the edge of death." Joshua just shook his head with disappointment at his siblings. They'd always been a little too comfortable with death. It was the legacy of Gabriel, and Joshua knew it reflecting on his love of making machines work when everyone depended on him to do it. "You know we're all fucked up, right?

"We all die only once! So, we might as well enjoy the moments we run along the edge. We all have issues with our father, but at least he taught us the skills we now have that keep us alive. Now with these new troops, we'll have a chance to be better than father ever was," Kain proclaimed.

"I've got to admit I never wanted to be ship captain until today," Celeris admitted.

"You're going to go mad watching other people flying your ship," Joshua teased.

"I'll still be the one in command telling them where to go." Celeris smiled with a wink.

Hearing the words for the first time, Joshua realized how much of a burden was being placed on his shoulders. He never had any ambition to become captain either, just like Celeris. They had both accepted long ago

Kain would replace their father on the *Alcatraz*. There was no hardship in this to either of the siblings. Kain was a better tactician, fighter, and leader, but now Joshua and his sister had no choice. From the look of excitement on Celeris' face, Joshua knew she was embracing the new challenge, but for him, there was fear of failure. Machines and engineering, he understood, maybe even doing research he could manage, but guiding all these new troops as their leader wasn't something Joshua was at all prepared for. He turned to look when he felt Kain's hand on his shoulder.

"Don't fear what you've yet to fail at, Joshua. Matthew sees the future, and if he thought you wouldn't be successful at this, he'd never have sent you here. Trust in yourself and our brother who has given us so much. We owe it to him to make his dreams come true," Kain declared.

"I agree, but it seems like we've jumped out of the frying pan of the *Alcatraz* and into the inferno of this new star. Now every twisted monster in the universe is gunning for us. You know how to command armies, you know how to lead a ship, but I'm just an engineering officer. I fix machines…" Joshua looked down at the deck floor, feeling embarrassed.

"The damn finest engineer I've ever seen," Celeris declared.

"You've only seen two engineers, Heph and me! Heph's into forging." Joshua shook his head.

"I have to agree with our sister. You're one of the main reasons the *Alcatraz* survived. There is no doubt that with you and Celeris at my side, we'll win the battle, or at least we'll end up going down swinging." Kain tried to instill the confidence he felt towards his brother in him.

"How long until your army is ready?" Joshua looked to Kain for the answer. With a thought, Kain activated the viewscreen showing the progress on his ship, the *Dawnbreaker*.

"About the same time as my new ship. Isn't she a beauty?" Kain admired the massive ship on the screen. There was a shimmer of the temporal field bubble encasing the ship, and within, everything blurred. It was like witnessing a video play back at high speed to the three siblings watching. All three of them just stood in awe for a second.

"She's a damn fine ship." Celeris wiped away a tear. "Can't wait to feel how she moves. Something that big and powerful is going to be a bitch to control. But look at those weapon batteries. Anything that stands against that behemoth is going to pay a price. Are all of our ships going to be like the *Dawnbreaker*?"

"Yes, that's the plan. With similar weapons capabilities, we'll be able to coordinate our offensive and defensive capabilities more effectively. Matthew and Hephaestus' plans are based on how our clan system worked, and we'll you two didn't see it, but the outpost confirmed for us all how effective our system is. Diversity in our forces is key to adaptation and survival in the long run."

"These battleforges are massive ships. How large is the crew compliment?" Joshua knew from just looking at the ships these Battleforges could carry an old planet's worth of people.

"The *Dawnbreaker* can run on a skeleton crew of only a few people, but she can house over three billion soldiers. Ships are worlds unto themselves, mobile floating fortresses, and forges so that we can produce any needed resources on the frontline of any conflict. From what I've seen and what Hephaestus has explained, these ships are built with powerful gravity drives capable of bending time and space. Each of our ships will be capable of seeding the resources necessary for the creation of new stars, and once Matthew has ignited those stars, we can use the same technology to forge entire worlds for people to live on. Our brother's plan is pretty glorious." From the information he shared, Kain could see the marvel on his sibling's face.

"Who would have thought even a year ago this is where we'd stand today," Joshua marveled.

"Certainly not our father," Celeris laughed.

"Gabriel wouldn't be happy seeing what Matthew's already accomplished, but first, we have to prepare. Whatever is coming our way, has Matthew terrified. He's getting scary at his ability to hide his emotions and has already surpassed our father, but I still know that kid better than he knows himself. We need to show Matthew we can accomplish whatever he needs," Kain explained.

"Are you sure that he won't just do what father used to do and raise the bar of expectation with each of our successes?" Joshua could see his words caused concern in Kain from his restrained scowl. Given the current situation, there was no point in hiding from anything anymore. The new star would draw every enemy to *Empyrean station*, and all Joshua knew was that it was smart to bring attention to the potential future they all faced together now.

"Come on, Joshua, don't be like that," Celeris urged. "Matthew is nothing like father, and you know it. Let's just focus on one thing at a time."

"Imperator, I've finished my evaluation of your gene seed. Matthew predicted the combat efficiency of your progeny to be in the ninetieth percentile." With a motion of a hand, Virgil brought the statistics up on the central viewscreen for the siblings to see. Seeing the report, Kain felt pride bubbling up within him, and he couldn't prevent himself from smiling. Combat reports showed the troop's performance ranked in the ninetieth sixth percentile. The only thing that brought him out of the moment of joy was the chuckles of his siblings. He glanced back to see what they were laughing about. Both of his siblings did nothing to restrain their laughter, even with Kain's serious, stern stare.

"Aw, a proud new daddy," Celeris teased.

"Should have brought the cigars I've kept stashed for this moment," Joshua declared.

"Soon, it'll be my turn to mock you two," Kain informed, watching Virgil begin to take the genetic readings of Celeris and Joshua. The two siblings looked at each other, unaware of what was happening. On the screen, the genetic codes appeared, showing Joshua and Celeris' D.N.A.

"Not quite as potent as the Imperator, but I suspect your lineage will still be over ninety percent effective. Except in the area hand to eye coordination is concerned according to these readings. I must say, in my all my existence, I've never seen a reading so close to perfection before Matriarch Celeris. Your piloting skills are truly beyond even my comprehension," Virgil informed with no emotion.

"See, I told you that you'd all be dead without me," Celeris triumphed, seeing the look on her brother's face. The look told her only one thing. They knew she would never let them forget this moment, and the two brothers just looked at each other with a smile and shrug.

"Well, let's hope your children are just as good. We'll all need the best pilots we can get on our ships. From my understanding, Matthew intends to assemble quite a large fleet." Kain could already see Matthew's plan, and he knew it was their best chance at survival. He wrapped his arms around his siblings and pulled them towards him.

"My children will do the flying, and your children will do the dying," Celeris quipped.

"Not with this technology. Death can't stop us when you can regrow a single person and upload their memories from these. A genetic tag contained in a near invincible shell that maintains constant neural connection with its own. Each of these contain the essence of the soldier should they be lost, but we maintain constant backups of each soldiers' memories. It looks like Matthew found a solution to the greatest threat of all, death. Now we rebuild the universe one solar system at a time," Kain declared with pride. The three siblings stood in silent awe of what had been accomplished so far.

"Well, I guess that means my children will ensure your ships stay in one piece. Maybe they won't be the best fighters or pilots, but what good is a ship that doesn't function? Guess we're all stuck with each other until the very end now," Joshua reasoned.

"The three amigos like that old Earth show that Matthew tried to get us to watch." Celeris glanced to her siblings seeing Kain roll his eyes hearing Joshua's sigh.

"He has the worst taste in stories," Joshua laughed.

"Still, we couldn't ask for a more loyal brother. We stand now on the precipice of true greatness. Everything father longed for and trained us for. Here we are fulfilling the Soloman family dream, and it's all because of Matthew. Still, I worry about him," Kain admitted feeling sorrow wash over his mind thinking about Matthew stuck in the Infinity Nexus.

Celeris and Joshua nodded in agreement and fell to silent contemplation. All three of the siblings knew the sacrifice Matthew had paid, and he could see that his plan would keep his siblings from him. They'd expand and build the universe, and Matthew would watch from the Infinity Nexus. Celeris couldn't help by feeling the rush of tears in response to her emotions. She wiped away the tear with one hand before turning to her two brothers.

"We make an oath here and now to ensure our brother's sacrifice wasn't in vain. No matter what comes, we'll stand united and protect him. There is no way he'd do anything less for us." Reaching out with one hand, Celeris placed it before her brothers.

"You're right, sister. We owe it to him to take care of him now. "Joshua placed his hand on top of his sisters before looking at Kain.

"Come heaven or hell, if I'm with you two, I'm in good company. I've taken care of Matthew since he was a boy. No way I'm stopping now." Kain placed his hand on top of his siblings, and for a moment, they stood there looking into each other's eyes. The three siblings could see the same resolute determination burning in each other's eyes. They felt their hearts pounding.

"For the Empire," Kain stated.

"For the Empire," Celeris and Joshua said at the same time in agreement.

On the screen, the children of Kain continued to train at their war games. All three siblings knew that whatever was coming, they could face it together. Matthew hadn't just brought them together at this moment and united them even stronger than on the *Alcatraz*. There was no turning back no from the threat that was coming. With grim determination, they watched the soldiers on the screen, knowing that soon they'd be in the thick of the battle with their new children at their side.

CHAPTER 8

The large tower stood out in the center of the city ward that Nemesis walked towards slowly. People were pushing skids of crates into the building. Troops in power armor stood guard around the tower and oversaw the work going on around. Several engineers at a table discussing zoning while pointing at issues around the tower on a holographic display, and nearby two more were setting up energy-to-matter converters for the construction crew to use. Nemesis strolled past the table to examine the schematics from a distance. Lord Drumpf was setting up a commercial hub.

In the distance, Lord Oswald stood watching over his workers assisting Lord Drumpf. Several Clan Crat stood by overseeing the work with their stun whips. Seeing the guards begin to whip one of the works sent Nemesis' rage into overdrive. She stormed towards the worker huddled on the ground trying to block the stun whip strike. The sound of her steady footsteps approaching caused the guard to turn, but he didn't have time to react.

Nemesis grabbed his hand holding the whip, squeezed it, and caused the guard to release the whip. The whip hit the ground with a clang drawing the other guard's attention. He was raising his weapon when he realized who it was, and he dropped the gun and held his hands up in defense. Nemesis released the guard's hand, shoved him to the ground, and turned to pick the worker up. Once she was certain the worker was ok, she turned to Lord Oswald.

"Emperor has decreed all former slaves are now free. All humans on *Empyrean station* are to be treated with fairness and equality. Do I make myself clear?" Nemesis hovered her hands next to her energy blades, glaring at Lord Oswald and his guards. All the guards looked to their lord for an answer on how to respond, but Lord Oswald waved them off.

"My apologies Lady Nemesis, but there is a lot of work to be done, and my people are just keeping the workers motivated. I meant no offense." Lord Oswald could see the fury burning in Nemesis's eyes and knew his words hadn't calmed her down any.

"Perhaps if I whip you and apologize, you'd just let it go," Nemesis' eyes darted to the whip.

Lord Oswald shook his head, "that won't be necessary, Lady Nemesis. From here on out, I promise that my guards will show the workers proper respect and decency. There is no need for retribution, or to tell our Emperor there was any problems here today."

Walking from the tower Lord Drumpf and his son Junior were discussing the plans for commercial development. Out of the corner of one eye Lord Drumpf saw the commotion, and he turned to see Lady Nemesis and Lord Oswald arguing. Marching over toward the commotion, Lord Drumpf intended to find out what was delaying the work, and he glared at the workers standing nearby and watching the commotion. He shoved one of Lord Oswald's guards aside to march into the arguing group. He didn't waste any time hearing what was happening before unleashing his anger.

"What the hell is going on over here," Lord Drumpf demanded.

"Lady Nemesis was reminding us that the emperor has granted freedom to all the workers, and she took offense to the treatment of one of our workers." Lord Oswald pointed to the injured worker still holding his burn wounds from the stun whip.

"Enough with the whining. Get back to work before I give you something to cry about," Lord Drumpf fumed, and the vein on his temple throbbed with anger.

"My brother, our Emperor, has given me the mandate to enforce his laws. These workers are free people now. The next person to lay a hand on any of them against their will gets to deal with me, and I promise what I'll do to them will make flogging seem pleasant by comparison." Nemesis glared at Lord Drumpf, crossed her arms, and stood in defiance.

"I understand, my Lady, and I promise to obey our new laws," Lord Oswald swore.

"Emperor wants this work done, and now it makes it even harder for me to accomplish this task. Your brother mandated that I establish this commercial stock market. How the hell do you expect me to accomplish that without punishing the slackers," Lord Drumpf protested. In his hand, he presented the orders from the Emperor for Nemesis to read over. She took a quick glance.

"Funny, I don't see the provision within these orders that grant you the authority to punish any workers?" Nemesis threw the document back at Lord Drumpf and motioned for him to follow her. Lord Drumpf looked at Lord Oswald for a second, but it was clear he had no intention of helping. Watching Lord Oswald walk away left Lord Drumpf with no option but to follow Lady Nemesis, and he motioned with his hand for Junior to come with him.

Walking into the tower, Nemesis took a second to examine the buildings. The large entrance provided ample room for easy movement in an open design. Glass and marble spiral staircases lead upwards on either side. Crates of machines, computers, and other materials sat in piles scattered about the room. There was no doubt in Nemesis' mind this building would make a strong heart for the economy of *Empyrean station*. She turned to face Lord Drumpf and his son.

"The work seems to be moving along at quite a pace. Almost makes me wonder why you need to push the workers any harder, but perhaps it's just your way." Nemesis sighed with frustration.

"Do you know how much work our Emperor has assigned my father," Junior protested.

"Keep your mouth shut, boy, and let the grown up's talk," Lord Drumpf ordered.

"Aw, is poor Lord Drumpf overworked," Nemesis teased.

"Your brother, our Emperor, honors my family with this request. Forgive my sons impetuous outburst. He has much to learn still." Lord Drumpf apologized with a glare at his son.

"Well, my brother has another task for you, Lord Drumpf, and it's one that I was asked to personally deliver. There is too much danger in transmitting the orders over the neural network." Lord Nemesis could see the intrigue in Lord Drumpf's eyes. He silenced his son with a glare before he could even open his mouth. Junior looked away at with a huff.

"I have a lot on my plate as is, Lady Nemesis, and I hate having to decline, but the sheer amount of work I have to do makes it impossible to take on anymore. I'm sure you and Emperor Solomon can understand this." Lord Drumpf knew it was important to appear uninterested. If this were really a secret order from Emperor Solomon, it would only force Nemesis to change tactics. He had to fight back the smile of the plan to use this to convince Nemesis into another private visit, and the memories of the last time broke his cool, causing him to smile.

"Oh, did you mistake this as a request," Nemesis laughed.

"I thought your brother claimed that all of us were free?"

"You are free to turn my brother down, but it's your loss." Nemesis turned to walk away.

"Wait, what is it your brother needs now?" Lord Drumpf knew he couldn't let Nemesis leave without finding out. That she was using his own game against him didn't bother him.

"Emperor has been initiating a series of new initiatives with my siblings. They're going to be busy for a while, which means we need more concrete information on Lord Whelsey and his plans. There is too much uncertainty already, but my brother believes our grandfather is plotting to move against him. Everyone knows how the relationship between my grandfather and you, Lord Drumpf. I need you to re-establish that relationship, and you'll report any information to me." Nemesis could see her offer made Lord Drumpf happy despite his best efforts to hide any tell.

"You're asking for a lot, given that Lord Whelsey tried to have my own Commander murder me during the battle. He was almost successful, and you were the one who saved me. So why should I put myself in danger over your family squabble." Lord Drumpf knew that to get what he wanted, he had to impress upon Nemesis the cost of his cooperation. It was clear to him that she and Emperor Solomon needed his help to resolve that situation, and in the doing earn future favors.

"I think you fail to understand the situation. You will act as Emperor Solomon's agent, and any harm done to you will see my grandfather executed as a traitor and criminal." Nemesis impressed the authority she was offering in this deal upon Lord Drumpf.

"It's a nice comfort, but what good does it do me if I'm dead?"

"Well, your son would receive the favor promised to you, and you'd get revenge against the man who tried to kill you. Perhaps you might even impress me in the process. We both know that the last one is far more important to you than the other two." Nemesis turned to walk away, leaving the offer for Lord Drumpf to consider. In her thinking, it was the best way to ensure his compliance. She had just reached the door to leave when she heard Lord Drumpf's request.

"Will you come to visit me later in private so we can discuss this so more?"

"I'll consider it," Nemesis declared before vanishing out the door. Workers still rushed around outside, but nearby, Nemesis saw several workers smiling and waving at her. With a wave back, she turned her thoughts to the next task she had to oversee. With a deep breath, she accessed the *Empyrean station* internal map and plotted her course to the location Marcus was turning into the Original Sin. A few hover vehicles were nearby, but she decided to walk to take in the sights.

Most of the ward was still empty, and the silence was peaceful, Nemesis realized. She enjoyed hearing the sounds of the animals that Virgil had taken care to keep alive in the station. Birds flew overhead, and their chirps were the only sound she could hear now. Cutting through a park, Nemesis took the time to stop and smell the flowers. Everything was so beautiful here, and she made a mental note that she needed to bring Marcus here to enjoy the romantic scenery of the park. She felt true peace and happiness for the first moment since she arrived on the station. With a deep breath, she inhaled the sweet fragrant air that didn't choke her lungs.

Exiting the park, Nemesis saw many machines already at work outside the building, and she stopped for a moment to see what was happening. Several large drones were beginning to pull a large sin into the air. The two drones carried the sign up to hover and hold it in place. Several more drones began fitting the sign to the building, and when it sparked to life, Nemesis couldn't help but smile at the bright red and green sign. The large circular sign glowed red, but inside the large tree glowed a grin, and at the base, two humans reached up, trying to grab a single ripe fruit. Unable to contain her excitement Nemesis rushed into the building, searching for Marcus.

Glancing around, Nemesis saw Marcus standing and talking to Lord Cornelius and Lord Hector. She rushed towards the group, broke into the circle, interrupting them, and leaped onto Marcus, kissing him passionately. For a second, Lord Cornelius and Lord Hector stood there frozen before turning to look away to show respect. Marcus was so stunned by the kiss that even when Nemesis lowered herself to the ground and pulled away from the kiss, he was left speechless. Turning back, both Lord Cornelius and Lord Hector tried to contain their laughter at seeing the frozen expression on Marcus' face.

"The sign is perfect. I can't believe you remembered it from that talk all those years ago. You're just the perfect man," Nemesis complimented.

"You going to live Marcus, or should I call for a medic? It seems you have a case of shellshock," Lord Hector teased with a chuckle.

"That's not shell shock. That's Nemesis shock," Lord Cornelius corrected in laughter.

"You're just jealous," Nemesis declared, wrapping her arm around her lover.

Marcus still stood there, unblinking, trying to collect the race of thoughts in his mind. Looking down at the plans he held reminded him what he was doing, and he snapped back with a shake of his head. Lord Cornelius and Lord Hector struggled to catch their breath from the laughter.

"Well, at least everything is on schedule for tonight's celebration. I should have everything up and running in a few hours." Marcus tried to return to his discussion, but Lord Cornelius and Lord Hector's laughter made it almost impossible. He looked down at Nemesis with a glare, but she just shrugged with a smile and blew Marcus a kiss. He tried to stay infuriated, but it was impossible.

"So, Nemesis, we've heard rumors about Emperor Solomon doing something secret. There doesn't seem to be much more than rumors to these reports, but they're spreading fast. Any merit to what we're hearing?" Lord Hector managed to stop laughing to ask the question and paid close attention to Nemesis' body language and facial expression. He did not intend to let any information escape, because everything was changing so fast. His warrior instinct warned that with change, perhaps the old alliance of the Lower Wards was at an end.

"When did you start putting any stock in rumors?"

"I don't, milady, but just trying to figure out where my place is now. The Lower Wards no longer exist, and survival requires adaptation. Just trying to figure out what that looks like," Lord Hector informed, turning to look at Lord Cornelius, who had the same concerns.

"We don't mean any offense, but we need to know where we fit now." Lord Cornelius backed up his friend. The two men stood there looking at Nemesis with expectant eyes demanding answers. She glanced around to ensure no one else was listening in or paying attention. Once she was certain of secrecy, she whispered to the group.

"Emperor has ordered Kain, Celeris, and Joshua to begin a genetic seed program. Within a few days, they will have millions of troops, all created from their D.N.A. Further, my brother has plans to create more of these Patriarchs and Matriarchs. Given your loyalty and the fact I actually respect you two, don't fret. Your turn will come, but keep this information to yourself, or else I'll have to kill you." Nemesis stared at Lord Cornelius, laughing at what he thought was a joke, but her glare made him realize the seriousness of the situation.

"I understand, my Lady. You know I'd never betray you," Lord Cornelius swore.

"So that's how Emperor Solomon plan to defeat the traitors amongst us. While they focus on building their power base, Matthew will build a massive army loyal to him. It seems that he learned plenty watching your father or studying history." Lord Hector congratulated the strategy.

"The key here is secrecy because I know Emperor Solomon sees a bigger threat coming on the horizon than the threat here amongst us. I've already set things in motion to deal with the traitors. Oh, Marcus, don't think you're getting off lightly either," Nemesis handed a data pad to her lover.

"What's this," Marcus inquired, looking over the data pad.

"You're hereby ordered to accept Emperor Solomon's personal nomination for position of the first Senator of the people, by the people, and for the people. It seems my brother listened to some of the stories I told him about why I loved you, and he thinks you're the right man for this job. I can't say I disagree." Nemesis could see the frustration on Marcus's face, and she knew it all too well. The only downside to Marcus was that he hated being told what to do, which he was rebelling against.

"You know I gave you my title to escape this kind of work right," Marcus protested.

"Take a good look around, Marcus. You're one of the hardest workers I know and the most compassionate man with both cunning and wisdom. We must all exceed our own expectations if we're going to survive. It's time for you to show us what I already know to be true. You're a great leader, and we need you to lead." Nemesis looked at Lord Cornelius and Lord Hector.

"Not all of us can be warriors, and sometimes the best thing a warrior can do is fall back and lead their troops to victory from the back." Lord Hector took hold of Marcus's shoulder to make sure he felt the truth being spoken.

"You've always looked after the dregs and treated them like your own family. When everyone else treated my clan like dirt, you ensured we had a place to call home. You've got my support," Lord Cornelius promised with a wide smile.

"I don't have a choice in this, do I?"

"Come on, my love," Nemesis pulled Marcus' face to force him to look at her. "When do I ever give you a choice? I've been running this show since you put me in charge, and you have no one but to blame yourself." She could help but laugh, seeing the mixture of anger, love, and pride swirling in Marcus's eyes. There was no denying the truth.

"Always told you that decision would come back to haunt me," Marcus sighed, causing Lord Cornelius and Lord Hector to laugh again.

"Well, the first drinks of celebration at tonight's' party will be on us," Lord Cornelius stated.

"No point in fighting Nemesis. We both know she'll kick your ass." Lord Hector teased.

"Thank guys, for all the support. Way to leave a man behind!" Marcus rolled his eyes.

"Well, let's go tell the troops to get ready for an epic celebration tonight and give these two love birds a moment alone." Lord Hector pulled Lord Cornelius to follow him. Nemesis and Marcus watched the two warriors walk away for a second before turning to face each other.

"You're going to be the death of me, you know that, right?" Marcus shook his head, trying to force himself to accept what he knew needed to be done now. The collection of data pads in his hand showed the workload he had before the addition of whatever being a Senator meant.

"There isn't another man like you anywhere, Marcus," Nemesis declared before kissing him again. She lingered in this kiss drinking in the sweet sensations. When Marcus pulled her close, she felt at home in his embrace. Opening her eyes, she stared into Marcus's eyes through the rest of the kiss running fingers through his hair pulling him to a tight embrace.

"Suite, I showed you earlier, is all set up now. Would you like to see it?"

"I would love to," Nemesis giggled, allowing Marcus to lead her towards the elevator.

Pressing a button, Marcus summoned the elevator and stood there holding Nemesis. At this moment, everything was perfect. A new home and her love by her side. Nothing else mattered. Elevator doors whisked open before the couple, allowing them to enter, and whisked shut quickly behind them leaving the couple all by themselves.

CHAPTER 9

Standing at the work bench, Hephaestus looked over the holographic display of the Battleforge schematics. Progress showed the completion percentage of the *Dawnbreaker* on another display. With a thought, Hephaestus pulled up the information on the weapon systems to inspect the designs. Everything looked fine, but he still wanted to go a little deeper. On the display, the turrets were disassembled piece by piece showing the complex nature of the weapons. The mass accelerated system drew his attention.

"Virgil, what's the efficiency of energy usage of these energy coils?"

"Calculating," Virgil responded over the coms.

With one finger, Hephaestus tapped on the energy coil on the display. It was broken down into smaller components. Metallurgical information filled the side of the display, revealing the chemical and atomic structure. Hephaestus' mind was already spinning variations of what they could use to get a higher energy transfer rate waiting for Virgil's response. The energy transfer rate and efficiency appeared on the display a few seconds later.

"Energy coils are, seventy-two-point nine percent energy effective, with an energy transfer rate of sixty-four thousand gigajoules per second." Virgil's report didn't impress Hephaestus who uploaded his modifications with a thought. The numbers vanished on the display, and Virgil computed the new information.

Leaning back in the chair, Hephaestus glanced over the rest of the information. He didn't hear the door to the workshop open or the soft footsteps. Every neuron was focused on perfecting the next Battleforge design before the first ship was complete. He had no intention of Kain's ship being inferior to any others. On the screen, the numbers appeared, showing the new information on the weapons energy coils.

"Energy coils are ninety-one-point seven percent energy effective, with an eighty-seven gigajoules energy transfer rate," Virgil reported.

"That's much better," Hephaestus mumbled to himself.

Lady Freya walked through the workshop with slow, careful footsteps, looking around at everything. Large vats spread throughout the room in clusters, and she couldn't figure out what they were for. Inspecting a vat, she couldn't see any markings that denoted what it was for, but she admitted to herself she wouldn't have known what most of the signs meant. In the distance, she could see Hephaestus working away at the series of holographic displays. She kept heading towards him, but she'd see something new that would draw her attention away.

The entire workshop fascinated Lady Freya, but nothing more than the strange machine she was looking at now. It resembled one of the mining loaders used on the *Alcatraz*, but this robot was much large even in its hunched-over deactivated state. It was clear to her the machine was just a frame and the essential components, but it was still imposing in that state. She took a few moments to review the engine and computer systems inside the machine and noted their locations. A thick plate of metal was on a nearby table, and she assumed that must be a piece of the intended armor for the machine. Turning away from the machine, she headed towards Hephaestus, who still hadn't noticed her presence in the workshop.

The sound of footsteps caught Hephaestus's attention, but he continued to work as if he hadn't heard anything. With one hand, he grabbed the hammer before spinning around. He was just raising the hammer when he looked down to see Lady Freya. He froze at that moment with the hammer held above his head, and it was only when it began to wobble, he realized how long he'd been staring. Lady Freya just smiled up at him. Feeling embarrassed, Hephaestus lowered the hammer and blushed, ashamed of his reaction. Realizing that Lady Freya shouldn't be seeing what was on the holographic displays, Lord Hephaestus stepped in between the screens.

"This is all very impressive," Freya declared.

"You're really not supposed to be here, Lady Freya," Hephaestus warned.

"That's what makes it so much fun," Freya laughed, trying to peer around Hephaestus. "Oh, come on, let me see what you're working on. It looked fascinating, like some giant ship, but it would take forever to build something that massive, wouldn't it?"

"I'm not sure our Emperor would like you seeing classified information," Hephaestus swayed back and forth, trying to block the vision of the displays, but Freya kept trying to peak.

"I won't tell anyone," Freya promised, managing to pull Hephaestus to one side and dart around the other. She stood in front of the displays, looking at each of them. The sheer size of the ship amazed her, but Hephaestus quickly shut the displays down with a thought. Lady Freya turned around with a pout and her arms crossed.

"You're going to get me in trouble with my family," Hephaestus protested.

"Emperor isn't anything like Captain Gabriel was. I doubt you'll get punished for letting little old me see this information. How long will it take you to build something like that?" Freya looked up at Hephaestus with curiosity. He found himself lost in her eyes.

"I can't tell you that," Hephaestus said with a hint of sadness.

"Oh, that must mean it's soon. I must know how you're building this ship so quickly. Come on, Hephaestus, just tell me, please?"

"This first ship, *Dawnbreaker*, should be ready in the next day, unless there are unexpected complications. That's why I'm going over all this information. Trying to see any problems before the fabricator swarm of nanomachines starts constructing. So far, the superstructure, engine core, and basic systems are function perfectly. The outer hull armor is currently being processed, fabricated, and installed. Once that is finished, the final phase of construction can begin. That's when the weapon systems are installed," Hephaestus brought up the displays again with a thought showing the energy coils he had just been working on.

"Fascinating," Freya admired the schematics taking a second to go over them.

"I never knew you understood engineering," Hephaestus admitted.

"Oh, I don't. Afraid animals and fighting are the limits of my knowledge, but I've always been fascinated by machines. I had plenty of work on the farm machines, and you weren't always available to fix them, so I learned how. Simpler times on the *Alcatraz*, but I can only imagine what you create now with all this cool tech." Freya turned back to smile at Hephaestus.

"The *Empyrean station* is truly a marvel. It's a feat of wonder left behind by the Ancients. I've been wondering how they created something this power, yet let the universe fall to destruction." Hephaestus pondered the question as he spoke it and got lost in thought for a moment. Only Lady Freya's giggling brought Hephaestus back to reality.

"Your mind fascinates me too," Freya complimented.

Hephaestus froze up from the compliment, and he could feel his face getting hot with the rush of blood from his embarrassment. Taking a step back caused him to stumble a bit, and his unwieldy size caused him to knock the tool kit off the edge of the desk. A loud smash echoed in the lab from the toolkit when it exploded open and sent tools scattering in all directions. The commotion only embarrassed Hephaestus, and he turned away from Lady Freya to try to cover it up. He wasn't looking at her, but he had no choice but to turn around when he heard Freya begin to pick up the tools.

"I didn't mean to make you so nervous," Freya apologized.

Hephaestus bent over to help her, "You don't owe me any apologies. I'm sorry, I just don't know how to act around you. Machines, I get, but why are you wasting time here in this cold workshop?" Hephaestus saw that his question made Lady Freya stop. She looked up with a hyper spanner in her hand and a smile on her face.

"You can build a ship like that in a few days but can't figure out why I came to see you?"

"That's much easier to figure out. Just machinery designed to fulfill its purpose, but you're so much more complex. The way you smile, the way you laugh, and how fierce you fight. I can't figure you out." Hephaestus sighed and continued to pick up the tools.

"Do you spend a lot of time trying to figure me out?" Freya's eyebrow raised.

"Well, not as much time as I would like because all this work keeps me pretty busy. The new tech here has also drawn much of my attention since we arrived, but I think about you often. You're not the easiest person to figure out," Hephaestus admitted.

"Do you need some schematics to work off," Lady Freya teased.

"Schematics always help, but I figured you'd find it offensive if I took a scan of you without your permission. Also, from my understanding of Lord Galen's work in biology, living beings aren't as easy to understand from their design as machines are. So, I figured there was no point in acquiring a schematic that may not work and anger you. I didn't want you to stop coming by and talking to me because those moments are the highlights of my day." Hephaestus didn't see the joy in Freya's eyes lost in joy the sound of her giggle brought him.

"That might just be the sweetest thing anyone has ever said to me," Freya giggled with glee.

Hearing the change in Freya's voice caused Hephaestus to look up. Only at that moment did Hephaestus see how flushed Freya's face had become. It was glowing red hot from the rush of blood mixed with her emotions. Lingering for a second, Hephaestus was confused by the emotions he was seeing. The confused look on his face only made Lady Freya laugh.

"Lady Freya, your beauty has always made me feel strange. No one else makes me feel so uncomfortable. All I know is you're far too beautiful to be spending time in my workshop getting yourself dirty with all the grease and grim." Hephaestus placed the last of the tools back into the kit and closed the box with a loud snap. Standing up, he turned and placed the kit back on the table.

"You find me beautiful, do you?" Lady Freya couldn't contain the excitement coursing through her veins. When Hephaestus turned around, he could see the gleam of excitement in Freya's eyes staring at him, and he struggled to find the words.

"I'm far beneath you, Lady Freya," Hephaestus claimed.

"Maybe I like your grease and grim, and perhaps you forgot that farming means getting dirty. I don't mind getting dirty with someone interesting," Lady Freya insisted with a smile. That only caused Hephaestus to take a step back, feeling the surge of uncertain feelings.

There was no doubt in Hephaestus' mind that Lady Freya was making a pass at him, but he wasn't sure what to do about it. Every beat of Hephaestus's heart caused his chest to pound. Sweat glistened on his forehead. Feeling the tumult of emotions caused him to freeze up for a moment. Only one thought churned over in his head in a loop.

"Why now?"

"Everything was different on the *Alcatraz*. No offense, but your father was a psychopath. I doubt he would have been happy if we got together, especially given how often he claimed women who showed interest in his children. Half of his harem was made of women swooning over Kain, and the last thing I wanted to give up was my freedom," Lady Freya admitted with shame.

Hephaestus just nodded with understanding. "No offense taken. That was why I fought him at the trial. Someone had to end my father's madness, but I admit I didn't expect it to be Matthew. That's why I'm working so hard because I'm worried about him."

"That's what makes you such a great man. You care for these machines like they were alive, and you take care of your family. The only reason the *Alcatraz* stayed functional was because of your sacrifices. We all owe you so much," Freya stepped close to hug Hephaestus, and looked up at him with a smile. He just looked down into Freya's eyes, feeling his emotions thundering.

"I have to admit I have no clue what to do in this situation. A part of me wants to kiss you, and the other part thinks I've read this wrong and should just hug you back." Hephaestus explained the emotional struggle he was going through.

"Perhaps your emotions just need a little fine-tuning," Freya suggested.

"Well, I'm not exactly sure who can do that for me," Hephaestus replied.

"Maybe I could help. Your kissing gauge seems to be working correctly, but it seems your throttle to engage is jammed with a logic blockage. Not sure how we unjam that but may a sharp blow upside the head might help. Don't you engineers call that kinetic readjustment?" Freya teased.

Sweeping Freya off her feet, Hephaestus picked her up. He pulled Freya up to look him face to face, and he blushed again, seeing the excitement in her eyes. This time he fought through the emotions, leaned in, and before he could kiss her, she wrapped her arms around his neck to kiss him. The two lingered there, enjoying each other. In the background, the displays beeped the information being reported, but no one in the workshop cared anymore.

CHAPTER 10

A low hum resonated through the cockpit of the *Death's Reaper*, and Magnus stared out at the void beyond the glass. A buzz of anxiety raced through him, causing him to tap his feet, and even he looked down with annoyance at the behavior. There was no point in glancing at the destination timer because he was aware of the exact time remaining at F.T.L. speed. He was doing everything he could to resist the anxiety of what he needed to accomplish. The A.S.A. was known for their cold hard adherence to logic and mathematics, so convincing them to help the beleaguered *Empyrean station* meant they had to abandon the precision of math. The odds were not in the favor of Matthew, or his people, from Magnus' perspective, and outside of Mordecai, the A.S.A. didn't seem to possess much empathy for living creatures. Conundrum tore at his mind alongside his growing anxiety.

A tangible pull in the fabric of the universe's material energy already told Magnus his people were already preparing to attack. It had been a certainty he'd been aware of since before setting the abyssal prophecy in motion. This was the second harbinger of calamity necessary for the rebirth of the light. Now it was a matter to convince the A.S.A. that their survival hinged upon a new star, and Mordecai was the only proof of its existence. Magnus was glad he had dropped Mordecai off first and hoped the time spent with his people had convinced them of the truth. At least then, Magnus would have a chance to persuade the A.S.A. to help.

Beeping from the F.T.L. timer echoed in the cockpit, bringing Magnus from his deep thought. With one hand over the F.T.L. throttle, he waited for the countdown to hit zero, and pulled back on the throttle. A bright flash of light beyond the glass forced Magnus to close his eyes, and he felt the sting of pain. With his free hand, he activated the hailing system and opened his eyes, feeling the sting of pain subside. Beyond the glass, Magnus could see the massive Mechanarium, home of the A.S.A. they called Gyros in the void of space.

The Mechanarium of Gyros's massive structure comprised hundreds of smaller outposts, and each of those stations acted as a gear turning the massive structure in multiple axes. The outposts' motion kept the entire Mechanarium's orbiting Gyros like an artificial solar system of enormous complexity. At the center, the spinning Gyros swirled its multiple layers of plates. Each plate formed an entire ring city that housed millions of A.S.A. Energy sparked between the spinning Mechanarium and Gyros. The magnetic shells of the Mechanarium generated all the power needed through the gravity generated by Gyros that pulled them in revolution. Each of the Mechanarium's surfaces was covered in emitters that channeled the extreme excess of energy into a powerful forcefield. Magnus hadn't ignited thrusters because nothing made it through the shield unless the A.S.A. permitted it, and so he waited for the machines to contact him. A few minutes later, his comms buzzed to life with a signal coming from the Mechanarium.

"*Death's Reaper*, this is Gyro's flight command. Your docking request has been approved. Please standby for shield entrance at your coordinates." The mechanical voice of the A.S.A. echoed over the communications in the small cock pit. Beyond the glass, Magnus could see a shimmer in the shield, and sensors reported that a gap big enough for his ship had opened in the forcefield. He pushed the throttle forward and locked course in the navigation system.

Thrusters flared on the *Death's Reaper*, and it slid through the shield toward Gyros. Guidance computer was calculating the landing path, and Magnus leaned back in his chair, allowing the automated landing system to take over. He wondered if Mordecai already knew he was here. The truth was, Magnus knew he'd find out soon enough. Either Mordecai would be waiting when the ship landed, or he wouldn't. There wasn't anything worry would do to help, Magnus tried to remind himself, but the anxiety he was feeling wouldn't be overpowered with conscious thought alone.

Gyros extended tractor beams to help guide the *Death's Reaper*. Magnus stood up, put his pistol in his holster, and strode towards the elevator to the cargo hold. Even the descent on the elevator began to frustrate him, and he tapped his fingers on the metal rail. He felt the wobble of the ship when it came to a rest inside the Gyros docking bay. Stepping off the elevator, he headed to the back of the ship and hit the button to lower the ramp. In that moment, all he could do was take a deep breathe. In a moment, he'd know whether he had Mordecai's support, but each second of the ramps lowering elevated the anxiety echoing everything that hung in the balance at this moment. Magnus closed his eyes and looked at the ground in an attempt to still his mind.

"It's good to see you again so soon, my friend," Mordecai moved in to hug Magnus.

"Wasn't expecting this warm of a greeting, but I can see your time with the humans has changed you." Magnus took a second to look around, and there were no escorts or guards, unlike last time. He wasn't sure if that was a good or bad sign.

"Yes indeed. I've introduced the A.S.A. to the works of Christ and the ideology of Christians. The Consensus voted to adopt it as mathematical truth after a long period of calculations of the logical algorithm of existence. After every analysis, the great Architect of Systems and the Consensus have determined the Bible to be a mathematical artifact of the Universal Equation. The whole of Gyros has been re-energized by these works. In fact, that is why the Great Architect sent me to greet you," Mordecai explained.

"I guess when you guys do something, you go all in. Well, if the Great Architect determined that's the truth, who am I to argue?" Magnus followed Mordecai towards a waiting hover skiff, and the two ascended into the air to jet down a long tunnel.

"The Great Architect demands your audience and knows why you are here." Mordecai motioned for Magnus to follow him.

"Saves me time explaining!"

"There is much about you. I must admit that I don't know Magnus. Many of your actions appear to exist in contrast against your other actions. Your words often turn upon themselves. So, answer me one question. Why do you want to save these humans?" Mordecai turned to study Magnus' eyes and face, and his processors whirred, taking in the data from layers of scans.

"I don't personally care about the humans at all, if you want me to be honest. The universe needs that star to exist, Mordecai, and you know that truth just like I do. This isn't a heroic mission to me, but pure, calculated survival. *Empyrean station* falls, and the universe is doomed. Just a matter of time before we all go out with a big, long whimper," Magnus stared ahead at the blur of the tunnel, and in the distance, he could see the spherical chamber of the Great Architect of Systems approaching quickly turning back to stare ahead.

"Perhaps what you say is true, but I doubt it from my experience with you. You're far more selfless than you care to let anyone else know. All that matters to the Great Architect of Systems and the Consensus is truth, and you must tell the truth, Magnus, if you have any chance to succeed. I don't deem you to be telling the full truth, but it's not my judgment you should worry about." Mordecai pointed to the massive mechanical golem sitting in the center of the chamber the skiff was entering.

The skiff slowed down on approaching the Great Architect of Systems, and Magnus stared up at the massive face he was ascending towards. Pipes, tubes, and wires ran from every direction across the ceiling and floor of the room, and they all converged in the center. Sitting on a massive throne, a great mechanical being stood over four hundred meters tall. Lights strobed along the forehead of the massive being but alternated in different patterns reflected along the room's outer wall. Thousands of images of A.S.A. stood glowing in different colors reflected in the lights.

Two large shimmering chrome sensors swept down to focus on the rising skiff carrying Magnus and Mordecai. Sleek metal sheets raced down, creating cheeks on the Architect's long metal face, and large pipes parted, revealing the mouth. Fine grains of magnetic metals and other ferrous materials raced down into what appeared to be almost a long, flowing black and grey beard. Almost humanlike, the Great Architect of Systems sat upon the throne of pipes, tubes, and wires that connected it to the entire Mechanarium of Gyros. Electricity crackled on the great staff the Architect held in one hand that connected to the floor and ceiling. Magnus stepped to the edge of the skiff and bowed when it came to a halt in front of the face.

"Great Architect of Systems, Tabulator, I bring Lord Magnus Void before you in this assembly of the Consensus and the wisdom of the universal mathematical truth." Mordecai presented his friend and stepped back. Tabulator's large eyes moved with the whir of spinning gears to focus on Magnus.

"You've come at a time of great upheaval of the A.S.A. and the mathematical truth of Christianity. Mordecai speaks with pious respect for you, so I have decided to consider the mathematical truths of the universe against your request. Don't waste my time with your attempts at persuasion or flattery, Lord Void. You will find only the truth holds sway here," Tabulator proclaimed.

"I shall not mince words then and cleave to the heart of the matter. A great threat of the Cacophony of Discordance threatens the balance of the universe. Mordecai here has shared with you the truth of Christianity and the new star born to the humans of *Empyrean station.* The simple truth is if that star is destroyed then it's only a matter of time before the verse follows. Matthew and his people will put up a fight unlike any you have ever seen or heard, but they can't survive alone. I'm here on their behalf to request your aid," Magnus knelt before Tabulator with his head bowed.

"Deference doesn't suit you, Lord Void," Tabulator stated.

"We must all bow before truth, less we provoke it to humble us in its awe," Magnus declared.

Lights flickered all around the room, showing the reactions of the Consensus. Glancing around, Magnus wished he had spoken the A.S.A. light language, but he couldn't make any sense of the patterns of light flashing all around. There wasn't any sign of life from Tabulator either which only frustrated Magnus further. With a glance, Mordecai estimated that his friend was struggling to understand what was happening. With slow steps, he moved next to Magnus to whisper to him.

"The Consensus is discussing the mathematical probabilities of your perceived truth, and Tabulator is calculating the universal mathematical truth. If there were no truth to what you said, this process would have already ended. The fact it's taking this long is a good sign." Mordecai tried to calm the anxiety his sensors detected in Magnus' energy structure fluctuation. In all the years the two had traveled together, Mordecai had never sensed this state from his friend.

Magnus didn't respond but focused on what he believed was the truth. The truth was he did feel guilty about what he'd done to Matthew to create the star, and he wasn't going to leave the humans without help. He focused most on his abyssal prophecy and the necessity of bringing the A.S.A. and humanity back together. Magnus knew it was from the minds of humans that the A.S.A. were born, and the two species were forever entwined. There was no need to speak that truth, but Magnus knew it existed within the weave of the universe's mathematical code. All he needed to do was let the A.S.A. sense that truth in him to draw their attention to the mathematical code that confirmed it.

"Lord Void, it seems you've indeed been honest and bared the truth of your programming to the A.S.A., and we thank you for your honesty. It does seem, Mordecai, that your mathematical calculations were indeed correct. The Consensus offers its admission of doubt in you was the real lie. For the first time in two thousand, two hundred, and seventy-four standard universal cycles, the A.S.A. will march to war. All Mechanarium's prepare for F.T.L. travel. We go *Empyrean station*, and we shall stand or fall to ruin with the humans. The great cycle demands it!"

"As you will, Great Architect of Systems," Mordecai bowed before turning to Magnus. "I must admit my processes are strange now that the certainty of seeing Matthew and the humans is true. It seems you have what you came here for. We shall see each other on the battlefield once more."

"Not this time, my old friend," Magnus shook his head.

"You aren't going to fight?"

"My battle lies elsewhere, and if there's any chance for you all to win, I have to fight it. Don't worry; I'm not done stacking the deck just yet. Got a few more friends to call in, and one thing I'm really not looking forward to doing," Magnus declared.

Now Mordecai understood what was off about Magnus' energy structure. It was fear. "You're going to attack the Cacophony, aren't you?"

"They must be dealt with sooner or later. I can't destroy them on my own, but I might be able to do just enough damage that it'll give the rest of you a chance to rebuild and have a chance to defeat them. Besides, this is my debt to pay. Take care of yourself, old friend," Magnus watched the blur of the tunnel shooting past him.

Not another word was spoken on the ride back to the docking bay. Stepping off the skiff, Magnus looked back to Mordecai. Turning away, he focused on what still needed to be done. A'zyren and Mordecai gave

Matthew a chance, but it wasn't a big one in Magnus's estimation. He was still shocked that the A.S.A. hadn't needed persuading. It was clear the time with the humans had been a variable he hadn't calculated correctly. That didn't make him feel any comfort because Magnus knew if there was one miscalculation, there was more. Marching up the ramp, he slammed the button to close it and turned to look back to Mordecai, who was waving goodbye.

"Good luck, Magnus. I'm certain we shall see each other again soon." Hearing Mordecai's words, all Magnus could do was pray they were accurate. He wasn't so sure he'd ever see any of his friends again, but he was damn certain they'd never forget him. One way or another, he was making sure the light was here to stay, and the Cacophony of Discordance would soon feel the full power of his wrath.

CHAPTER 11

Air hissed from the compression occurring behind the ship's door and shot forth from the exhaust ports. The doors retracted, and the docking ramp lowered. Myrmidon turned to look at Gabriel, but he motioned forward with the barrel of his rifle. The cargo hold appeared empty, but Gabriel wasn't taking any chances. He activated a full sensor sweet with his power armor, and once that confirmed the cargo hold was empty, he lowered his rifle.

"No ambush yet. Very smart, Myrmidon."

"Tigeran believe that the strong should rule over the weak, and it's obvious you're much stronger than I am. Perhaps that is from your tech, but I think it runs much deeper. Follow me. I'll show you to the bridge," Myrmidon pointed towards one of the corridors leaving the cargo bay.

"What's the name of the ship?"

"In your language, it's called the *Furious*," Myrmidon replied, leading the way. The corridors were empty, but Gabriel kept his sensors in full active mode. He wasn't worried about anyone on the ship sensing it because he was already certain that Myrmidon had sent some secret code. According to Gabriel's estimations, the bridge would be the best place for an ambush. Loud clangs of each of his footsteps would tell the crew of his approach.

From the scans of the *Furious*, it wasn't a very big ship and only about twice the size of the *Death's Reaper*. The only problem Gabriel could see was how outdated the tech was on this ship even compared to the *Alcatraz*. Perhaps Myrmidon wasn't here to salvage but to get the tech to update this ship, Gabriel realized. From the scan of the ship, he knew they were approaching the bridge, and there were several life signs inside. The crew seemed to be comprised of Tigeran's, and the other races onboard appeared to be connected via a remote link to the ship's mainframe. Gabriel could only surmise that the other races were slaves of some sort.

"What's this active link I can detect between some crew and the ship's mainframe?"

"My people take whatever we can use, and thee most valuable of salvage is living creatures. Some choose to serve my people willingly, but others need to be coaxed. Those slaves we keep chained to the mainframe wired to a remote-detonated explosive collar. Any attempt to escape results in the simple push of a button that deals with the problem. I'm sure you understand the need for such a ruthless device, given your torture techniques," Myrmidon explained.

"No judgment from me, but you better not try any tricks," Gabriel urged.

"I simply wish to keep living." Myrmidon placed his clawed hand on the bridge access panel, and light caused it to glow for a second. Seals hissed and clicked, and the doors began to retract. Marching onto the bridge, Myrmidon saw all eyes fall on him first and shift to Gabriel behind him. Raising a hand, Myrmidon ordered his people to stand fast and looked at each of them. "This here is our new captain. He killed our boarding party and took me hostage. If any of you want to live, I'd advise you listen to any orders he has to give. I'm his captive now, and that means the *Furious* is his ship, and we are all at this human, Gabriel's command."

There was a great commotion amongst the crew. The language filtering software in the power armor translated but couldn't keep up, still adjusting to the complexities of Tigran speech. Gabriel didn't need the program to see that many of the crew were unhappy with the situation. From the look of the Tigran approaching Myrmidon, he must be the second in command. Gabriel couldn't make out the whispers between Myrmidon and his second in command.

Myrmidon tried to warn his second in command with his eyes not to fight back, but he was being ignored because of his weakness in being captured. Gabriel could sense the growing animosity between Myrmidon and his officer. The rest of the crew seemed frozen, waiting to see what would happen, but they all looked ready to go for their weapons. The power armor hummed, processing the situation, calculating weapon firing trajectories, and assessing the threat of each of the guns on the bridge. He glanced to each of the targets studying them.

"Fall to command, Numidian," Myrmidon demanded.

"You've become weak," Numidian hissed. "This ship belongs to Pandora!" He went for his pistol, but Myrmidon caught his hand and held the pistol in place in the holster. Gabriel watched with interest to see how this was going to play out. With a great roar, Myrmidon threw Numidian to the ground and glared at the rest of the crew.

"There is no weakness in me, and any who dare challenge me to step up. I'll rip your throats out and gorge upon your entrails. I dare any of you to fight me now!" Myrmidon stood glaring across the bridge with his muscles rippling, chest puffed out, and claws barred. Everyone on the bridge froze, and Gabriel couldn't help smiling, seeing the crew fall to fear of Myrmidon.

"It seems you know how to keep your people under your boot," Gabriel complimented.

"Thank you, captain." Myrmidon submitted before his crew.

"What should we do with this one, first officer?" Gabriel looked down at Numidian before glancing over to Myrmidon. In Myrmidon's eyes, Gabriel could sense a great sadness.

"There is only one answer to this treachery. Death!" Myrmidons' words only confirmed the sadness Gabriel saw in the Tigran's eyes.

"Do you believe this Tigran is unsalvageable and destined too always be treacherous?"

"No, Numidian is one of the strongest Tigrans' but not too intelligent. More of a creature of instinctive passion than of conscious will. He has been incredibly loyal to me, as all brothers should be." Myrmidon looked at Gabriel, wanting to beg for Numidian to be spared, but there could be no show of weakness. This was Gabriel's choice as captain now, and Myrmidon knew it.

Walking over to Numidian and placing one foot on his chest, Gabriel looked down the sights of his rifle, now aimed at the Tyran's head. "Can you follow my orders, Tigeran?"

Gabriel stared down into the yellow eyes of Numidian and saw only willful defiance. The look was very familiar to him, and a part of him knew what needed to be done. Still, there was a nagging voice in the back of his head, drawing his attention to Myrmidon and reminding him of his own past. Concordia's death had set everything in motion. From turning Nemesis away from the family to Helena's two rebellions, Gabriel could see right now he could change the outcome. Stepping back, Gabriel took his foot off Numidian.

"This is the only time I shall forgive any insolence. I need you to understand that Myrmidon. You shall keep your brother in line or watch him die." Gabriel leaned down, grabbed Numidian, and pulled him back to his feet.

"I understand, captain. There won't be any more outbursts from the crew," Myrmidon promised and glared at each of the members of the crew.

"Well, the first order of business is back to salvage. I'll send you a list of the spots where the best salvage can be found. We're going to need to get this hunk of junk in better condition. Also, I'd like if you could go to my quarters on the *Alcatraz* and retrieve some of my personal things." Gabriel uploaded the information to Myrmidon's neural implant.

"As you command, captain," Myrmidon replied, motioning for his crew to follow him. He grabbed Numidian by the shoulder and forced him to follow, breaking his glare at the new captain. All the rest of the crew put up no resistance. Exiting the bridge, Myrmidon led the crew back towards the cargo bay, and he could feel the animosity amongst his crew in the silence.

No one said a thing. Arriving in the cargo bay, the crew members began to suit up to go into the wreckage of the *Alcatraz*. Numidian was agitated, and it was unmistakable to Myrmidon, but he wasn't the only threat. Gans, the Serpentine weapons expert, didn't seem happy either, whispering to Numidian in the distance. Myrmidon knew they were plotting, but he had to focus on the task at hand. Gabriel was too strong to overcome in Myrmidon's estimation.

"Are you sure, captain?" The soft chittering voice of the Apoidean drew Myrmidon's attention. He turned and smiled at Korela's multifaceted black eyes. Her wings fluttered behind her.

"It's in our best interests. I still have no clue how that human survived this crash, but that armor he wears is formidable. I'm not sure even your mandibles could tear through it." Myrmidon didn't hide anything from his friend. They had traveled together and survived too much for secrets.

"He seems to be quite a specimen for a human, but seeing their kind so strong is strange. Their frail bodies usually do not struggle virtually at all, yet this human caught you off guard. He even defeated Numidian with ease. I fear you're right, but I'm with you until the end, Myrmidon," Korela declared. Hearing those clacks and seeing the expression in Korela's body language brought a smile to Myrmidon's face, and his whiskers fluttered with joy.

"You've always been the smartest amongst us."

"We're not alone either. Gans the Serpentine and Zeno the rogue De'Vayne are with us. At least the key crewmembers that operate this ship are still on your side," Korela explained.

"Communications, weapon systems, and engineering are essential systems, so at least the ship can function even if the others mutiny. I don't expect Gabriel to show mercy twice, but had he not shown mercy the first time, we wouldn't be in this situation. I still can't fathom why a human such as Gabriel, capable of such feats of cruelty and displays of power, spared my brother." Myrmidon looked across of the cargo bay at Numidian sensing he was already preparing a plan.

Numidian was talking to the other crew members, and most of them were still slave caste. The gathering of the Serpentine and Tigrans didn't worry Myrmidon much, because he knew that his brother would have to promise them the freedom to gain their support. That meant Numidian would have to make his move to overthrow his own brother if he succeeded at removing Gabriel from command, and that was a big if. Myrmidon watched the approach of his brother and his supporters returning to the group now suited up for salvaging. Pulling a data pad, Myrmidon clicked into the information Gabriel had sent him and presented the pad to Numidian.

"Go to these coordinates and salvage everything you can find on the list. Once you're done, head back here. I should be back long before you're done. Korela, Volan, and Zeno are coming with me to the bridge to fetch some important items. Numidian, be prudent with your time, and don't lead your people to ruin." Myrmidon turned away, motioned for his crew to follow, and led them into the wreckage of the *Alcatraz*.

There was no time to waste, Myrmidon reminded himself that Pandora expected their return soon. He hadn't the time to explain that to

Gabriel, but he wasn't expecting this trip to take long. The group walked through the ruins of the ship towards the elevator shaft, and following Gabriel's instructions, the machine began to ascend with the grinding of metal. The deck plate of the elevator wobbled with its ascent.

Stepping out of the elevator, Myrmidon led his crew towards the bridge. He didn't even need to give orders. Korela and Zeno already knew what to do and set about dismantling the still functional systems on the bridge. They ignored the dead bodies of their former crew and focused on the task. Following the orders, Myrmidon headed into the captain's quarters, glass crunching under his feet, and reached the door to the private quarters. The door had been damaged in the crash and wasn't going to open. There was a crack big enough for Myrmidon to squeeze through, and he managed to get himself through the other side.

Information from Gabriel made it easy to gather all the personal belongings, and Myrmidon packed them into a large sack he found in the private room where Gabriel's clothes were kept. Picking up the book, Myrmidon knew this was the most valuable item from the information. He wrapped it with care in some clothing and placed it in the bag. He wasn't sure any of this stuff had any value, but he wouldn't quest Gabriel. Heading towards the door, he slid the bag through the crack and crouched down to force himself back through. Walking back into the bridge, he saw Korela and Zeno were already waiting with their backpacks stuffed with salvage.

"How much longer?" Gabriel's voice boomed in Myrmidon's mind making him glance all around at first. It took a few moments for him to realize the voice was inside his own head.

"Just finishing up here now, captain, and we should be back in a few minutes. We're heading for the elevator now," Myrmidon reported.

"Numidian and his crew have just returned. Try to make it quick," Gabriel replied.

Myrmidon began to sprint toward the elevator forcing Korela and Zeno to keep pace. Standing by the elevator button, Myrmidon waited for his crew to get in and hit the button. Korela and Zeno both looked to Myrmidon, and he could feel their concerned gaze fall on his back.

"My brother, the fool, has already returned to the ship. That can only mean he attempted to mutiny and seize control of the *Furious*." Myrmidon could see the concern his words caused.

"That traitor intends to leave us here," Korela screamed.

"Should have seen that coming, but I think you did," Zeno claimed.

"I knew he was planning something, but I didn't suspect he'd be so stupid. He has no clue what that human is capable of. We must get back before Gabriel abandons us, or worse, destroys this wreckage with all of us on it. He may think we're part of this mutiny." Korela could see the fear in Myrmidon's eyes and noticed the wounds on his body.

"Did Gabriel do this to you?"

Myrmidon nodded. "He's not a typical human. Cunning, cruel, and calculated. He dropped my entire team, as you saw on the bridge in seconds. Numidian stands no chance."

"Guess these humans aren't as weak as the rumors say," Zeno admired the work. "This is some precision cutting skills. Just deep enough to hurt but not enough to kill."

"Only a fool believes humans to be of no danger," Volan hissed.

Myrmidon gritted his teeth through the shriek of metal from the elevator's descent. The doors had just started opening when he burst through to sprint towards the *Furious*. Arriving at the doors, he activated the controls, and the doors began to retract. Marching into the ship, Myrmidon threw the stuff down on the floor and drew his pistol. Korela and Zeno followed their leader. The group clanged down the corridor to the bridge. The bridge door was open, allowing Myrmidon to see Numidian standing in front of Gabriel. He was still sitting in the captain's chair.

"This ship belongs to me now!" Numidian howled in Tigran, but Gabriel seemed unmoved despite the weapons aimed at him at point blank range. Myrmidon could see Gabriel's hand hovering over the hilt of the energy blade at his side.

"I can't understand a word you're saying," Gabriel informed.

"Drop your weapons now!" Numidian stepped forward, pushing the barrel of his pistol against Gabriel's helmet. Myrmidon broke into a run, charging into the bridge and leaping onto his brother's back to sink his fangs into his shoulder. A howl of pain echoed, and the pistol fired, but the shot went inches wide of Gabriel's helmet. He ignited his blade, pushed from the seat with force, and charged the nearest enemy.

Before Korela or Zeno could even reach the bridge trying to keep up with Myrmidon, they watched Gabriel unleash his full fury. The energy blade sparked to life, and he slashed out, cutting down the Serpentine to his right. From his other hand, he opened fire to the left dropping a charging Tigran. Gabriel halted to watch his new crew descend upon their former crewmates.

With a buzz, Korela's four translucent wings flapped into action and propelled her into a burst into the bridge. Flying across the bridge, she descended, grasping one of the Tigrans with all four arms, and contorted her body to bring her stinger to bear inches from the man's throat. He dropped his weapon, and it clattered to the floor. Volan and Zeno entered the bridge with their rifles drawn and aimed at the other members of the Numidian's mutiny. Myrmidon had his brother pinned to the ground and was bringing his claws to tear out his throat when Gabriel stood up, grabbed the hand, and held it in place. Myrmidon turned to look at Gabriel.

"Death's a gift this one doesn't deserve," Gabriel proclaimed.

"You can't show weakness, captain, or they'll keep attacking. I told you Tigrans only understand strength. My brother's death will teach the rest the price of disobedience."

"Yes, it will, but Numidian here won't die an easy death. Leave him to die with the *Alcatraz*. The rest will learn there are far crueler fates than death," Gabriel educated. Myrmidon could see the value of the plan, and when Gabriel released Myrmidon's hand, he retracted his claws before punching Numidian in the face hard enough to render him unconscious. Gans and Zeno picked up Numidian to drag him towards the retracting bridge doors.

"I must admit, Myrmidon, I hadn't counted on your loyalty. I expected more corpses when I was done. So now that I know I can trust you let me ask an important question. Where should we head to?" Gabriel put his arm around Myrmidon.

"Captain, there is only one place we have to go first. The *Furious*, never belonged to me. I was placed as captain after the old one died on a mission. This ship belongs to the Pirate Queen, Pandora, and she's expecting us to return home to the Box Nebula. It's a haven of asteroids turned into habitats where the Merciless hordes gather to impress the Queen of Pirates to earn a place in her elite corsairs." Myrmidon hoped Gabriel took his advice because he didn't want to get on Pandora's bad side.

"These Merciless, what are they?"

"We're a group willing to do whatever it takes to survive, and we run the largest trading hub in the Great Maw next to Phobos habitat ring. One of the few ports capable of manufacturing and production left in the sector. Pandora run's it all with an iron fist. Truth be told, you remind me a lot of her. I think you two will either get along great or kill each other, but what's life without a little risk" Myrmidon smiled at Gabriel, revealing his glistening row of fangs.

"Iron fist, you say. Sounds like Pandora's just the type of woman I like to meet. Let's dispose of these dregs and get going. The sooner we leave this haunted graveyard, the better." Gabriel longed to leave this place that tugged at his memories. He just wanted to forget everything.

CHAPTER 12

Lord Whelsey stood beyond the doors to the Infinity Nexus, waiting for his daughter to return. His foot tapped with impatience flooding his conscious, and he worried that Matthew had already sensed his plans. Levart's presence in Angelica could be one of the reasons Emperor Solomon sent Helena, but Lord Whelsey knew he needed to determine the truth for himself. There was no way to know how powerful Matthew's precognition was, and Lord Whelsey didn't even know if it wasn't some kind of illusion. Perhaps something hidden had been set in motion by that alien, Magnus Void. The door whisked open, and Helena waved to her father to follow her into the Infinity Nexus beyond the open doors. Lord Whelsey marched slowly behind his daughter preparing his mind.

The room was quiet and empty, and the two people walking echoed through the chamber. Lord Whelsey slowed down his walk to admire the giant statues of the angels. The monumental works of art were something he truly admired. Intricate details showed the dedication and care behind the construction of these works of art. Once he had completed the construction of a new cathedral, he intended to replicate these massive works of art for his faithful followers. Helena had to stop to get her father's attention.

Matthew watched his mother and grandfather carefully from the chamber of the Infinity Nexus. He knew that this meeting had to be handled with care. Time had already revealed to him his grandfather's machinations involving Angelica and the demon Levart, but Matthew didn't want to believe anyone was beyond saving. He intended to find a way to redeem his grandfather, but that required some deception. Lord Whelsey had come to determine what Matthew knew more than anything else, and he had to bait his grandfather with the power he craved.

"Emperor, my son, I've brought my father as you requested," Helena informed, approaching the Infinity Nexus.

"You look radiant, mother. I see our new home suits you." Matthew enjoyed seeing the rebirth of his mother since she had been freed of his father's torments. She appeared to be a new woman, full of life and dedication once more.

"It does, my son. This place is full of unimaginable wonders, and your people have already set to hard work. I hope that with all the effort to build our new home, we can repair broken relationships here today." Helena stepped back to allow her grandfather to approach the Infinity Nexus. With slow steps, Lord Whelsey approached, and with uncertainty, he knelt before Matthew.

"I'm at your disposal, Emperor."

"Indeed, you are, grandfather, but I worry about your loyalty to my people. That is what I have summoned you here today. For the mists of time, show me your potential for both greatness and to bring ruination to our people. May I ask what you've been focusing your time on?" Matthew hoped his grandfather would take this moment to recant his betrayals, but his hopes weren't high.

"Most of my people are busy unloading our resources and trying to set up the location of our new sacred cathedral to our Lord Jesus Christ and God's glory. The faithful will need a place to worship God for his generosity shown to us by giving our thanks for our new home in prayer and dedicating sacrifices. I hope this new pleases you, Emperor." Lord Whelsey looked up, but only as a symbolic show of respect. The real reason was to get a clear look at Matthew's face and eyes to gauge his reaction.

"Grandfather, I applaud your commitment to faith and God. Truly you should be rewarded for your tireless devotion. Once the defenses of *Empyrean station* are completed, I shall make available the resources for you to construct your new cathedral. I hope you can be patient or find something productive to do until then." Matthew remained calm and composed, refusing to betray his thoughts or feelings in any way to his grandfather.

"If you deem the project must wait, I bend to your will." Lord Whelsey knew he had to appear to placate Matthew like he had done for years with Gabriel. The truth was Matthew wasn't his father. Lord Whelsey focused on remembering that from the cold look he saw in his grandson's eyes. He could feel the power emanating in waves from the Infinity Nexus.

"See, I told you we could all be a family again," Helena declared her triumph.

"Not so fast, mother. For there is still the matter of Lord Whelsey's betrayal during the battle of *Empyrean station*, and that's not a matter I take lightly. Our enemies now circle us, and we must stand united. Lord Whelsey must confess his crimes to be forgiven." Matthew glared at his grandfather, trying to spark his conscience to guide him to admit the truth.

It took every drop of willpower for Lord Whelsey to maintain his façade. He loathed having to play weak for this fake leader. At least Gabriel had been strong enough to rule, but in Lord Whelsey's opinion, his son was only leader because of his strange new power. He didn't believe his grandson understood the power of fear necessary to maintain rule over the people. It was a weakness Lord Whelsey intended to exploit to the fullest.

"Emperor, I don't know what you're talking about."

"Don't lie to me, grandfather, for I see and know all. I'm your Lord, God, and you should treat me as such. For here in the Infinity Nexus, I know all, see all, and have all power at my disposal. Perhaps you need another demonstration of my strength to convince you of this truth." Matthew glared with animosity for the lies he heard from behind the Infinity Nexus glass. Still, this wasn't unexpected, and he'd already formulated plans to adapt to this expected situation.

Sweat beaded up on Lord Whelsey's forehead, and he could feel his daughter's judgmental gaze falling on him now. There was no way to know how much Matthew really knew. There was only one path Lord Whelsey could see. To use the truth to cover up deceit, and his instinct told him that was the only play he could make that stood any chance of succeeding. With a cough, Lord Whesley cleared his throat and prepared to admit his crimes against Lord Drumpf.

"Emperor, I understand now why you believe me to be lying. I sense what you're talking about was my plans to eliminate Lord Drumpf, my rival on our old home. There was no way for me to know after the trial this great new home awaited us. I had set Commander Verdas to his task before we even arrived. I didn't have time to rescind those orders when the battle broke out. The battle forced all my attention on holding back the Reverie, and you know, I fought with all the courage and conviction that my faith provides. I've sinned and erred because I'm human, and so I've no choice but to throw myself upon the countenance of your mercy." Lord Whelsey lowered his head to the ground.

There was no answer from Matthew immediately, and Lord Whelsey couldn't see what was going on with his forehead touching the ground. That moment was the tensest of his entire life. Uncertainty raced through his body with each beat of his heart. Matthew maintained a flawless façade of calm from the Infinity Nexus, but he was scouring time for an alternative to what he saw coming from his grandfather. Matthew allowed the awkward silence to persist as he searched for a proper resolution in the fabric of time within his mind. He couldn't see one yet, but that didn't mean there weren't some paths of decision more favorable than others.

"Rise, Lord Whelsey, and know that I've forgiven you for your trespasses as you have forgiven my father of his." Matthew knew the words would tell his grandfather the truth of what he meant but that his mother wouldn't understand. This was a private dialogue.

Lord Whelsey had to force back his feelings that surged in reaction to what he had heard. There was no forgiveness for Gabriel's crimes toward his daughter and granddaughter. He knew the forgiveness was merely an act to lull him into a false sense of security. One he was willing to play along with for now. His mind buzzed with his ideas, but he forced them back for fear that in the presence of Matthew, he'd see the machinations planned.

Standing up, Lord Whelsey smiled at his grandson. "Your mercy is indeed as great as our Lord God. I'm truly blessed to have such a grandson as you."

Helena stood next to her father with a smile on her face from the feeling of her triumph. She believed she had brought her family back together, and her son's smile confirmed that. Matthew gave his mother exactly what she needed. The belief that all was well, but there were still things that needed to be done. There were tests that Matthew needed to administer, and his grandfather had to pass for there to be any chance to save his soul from eternal damnation.

"Grandfather, I'm sure you heard the rumors of my actions and perhaps worry that you've been left out. Don't fret about my matters; I have great plans for you. Once the defenses have been built and your cathedral completed, you will have a great task before you. I fear you're not ready for such a task, yet it falls onto you, for no other is better suited." Matthew stoked his grandfather's intrigue with his words, and each word fueled the swelling fire of curiosity.

"Command me, Emperor, and your will shall be done!"

"Remember Proverbs twenty-one, five. "The plans of the diligent lead surely to advantage, but everyone who's hasty comes to poverty." Don't be hasty in assuming what I command will bring you joy because I know it shall be the greatest trial of your life. Everything you've come to believe shall be challenged, and should you fail, absolute ruination will befall you. For time and fate reveal their sublime truth to me." Matthew could see his warning had the desired effect. Lord Whelsey struggled to contain the trembling fear roaring inside his mind.

"Emperor, I'm your humble servant as I was your fathers before you. There is no task too great for me. It was a great hardship to be prepared to prosecute my own beautiful daughter, but if duty demanded it, then I was destined to do it. Thanks to God and you, my grandson, that horror never happened. For I now know the tribulations of Abraham who God commanded to kill his own son, and no other trial could shake my faith." Lord Whelsey summoned all his charisma to sell the lie to his grandson.

"My father is as pious and honorable as any man, my son. Put your faith in him, and it shall be rewarded," Helena vowed in defense of her father. She could sense the game being played by her father and son but not the reason for it. She'd stay quiet, trying to ascertain the truth, but sensing the malice behind Matthew's words provoked her to act. In her mind, there was no more reason for strife, yet she could sense the conflict hadn't ended.

"I shall put my faith in Lord Whelsey and pray he can put his faith in me. For the first thing we must do is unite all the people. I've ended slavery of any kind for our people by law. Next, I must give power to the people to rule. Democracy must rise like the Phoenix from the ashes of the past, and I shall need grandfather's help for that task. Far too long have we lived in the tyranny of religion, yet our faith shall set us free." Matthew could tell his grandfather hated the idea but was willing to play along to bide time for his plans for Angelica and Levart.

Lord Whelsey liked the idea of a democracy because it gave him more room to influence the people. The worry he felt was caused by Matthew's focus on religion. His instincts told him that his grandson had a devious plan concocted. Something in the wording of "tyranny of religion" didn't sit right with Lord Whelsey. His mind was racing to figure out what the plans could be, but he stood there silently waiting to hear.

"Grandfather, the task I have before you are a new codex of Christianity. As the apostle codified Christ's teachings, you shall also codify my teachings as a new gospel. Just as democracy must rise from the ashes, we must raise Christianity from the past to create a future. From here on, the doctrine of our Christian religion will be based on our savior Jesus Christ who laid the path for me to follow. For now, I'm the living embodiment of our Lord God's will and his vessel in this reality. My mind shapes the universe to God's plan. God's will is my will, and those who stand opposed to me stand opposed to God!" Matthew could see the veil hiding his grandfather's anger was breaking down under the force of the swelling anger within him.

Lord Whelsey couldn't believe his grandson's audacity to claim God's power as his own and make himself God's representative. It was a power move too tyrannical for even Gabriel to attempt. Fear told Whelsey that with everything that had transpired, the people would believe these lies, especially if he was the one who preached them. He understood his grandson's earlier words now. This was Matthew's test of loyalty, and Lord Whelsey knew he had to pass it, or he was dead.

"Your wisdom knows no bounds, Emperor, but I must confess to something."

Helena turned to look at her father with concern in her eyes. She couldn't image what more her father needed to confess to. Matthew stared with a cold look that concerned Helena, and her father seemed committed to his actions. Everything swirled around her out of her control.

"I must confess I fear this action will destroy the beauty of our Christian heritage and that many will see vanity, not divinity, in this act. My hands will carry out your command if you deem it so, but I ask you to reconsider this course of action." Lord Whelsey knew he couldn't disobey and needed to get Helena's support without asking for it. He knew she was still the good Catholic he had raised who was loyal to his church.

"Your grandfather may be right, my son. History is full of attempts by powerful people trying to pervert the truth, and the people may see this as an attempt by you to control them. Perhaps it would be wise to leave such matters unaltered." Helena understood her father's worry because she felt it, too, hearing her son's desires. Matthew had done great things that would be remembered forever if she had any say in it, but attempting to claim God's mantle was a blasphemy.

"Truth isn't a perspective. It's a mathematical fact beyond all sentient life in the Great Maw. God knows all, and through that omniscient power shared with me, I, too, know all. That is irrefutable." Matthew knew his grandfather could challenge this and reveal what was being hidden by both of them from Helena. Lord Whelsey wouldn't damn himself by revealing that knowledge. Matthew watched his grandfather struggle on the prongs of his forked dilemma.

Lord Whelsey wasn't sure if this was a ploy or not, but if it was, the nature of deception revealed the strategic genius of his grandson's plan. He wasn't going to be foolish and reveal his plans to prove anything, but he worried that this plan revealed that Matthew knew of those plans. Greed and ambition seized his mind at the potential power he was being offered. Lord Whelsey knew that even if Matthew knew the truth of his plan, the fact he refused to reveal them betrayed the truth that he wouldn't act. Lord Whelsey's mind swirled, but he took command and calmed himself. He would see this plan out for now and adapt as circumstances demanded, as he'd always done before.

"Your will shall be done, Emperor."

"That is most excellent news to hear, grandfather. I feared you may not be willing to cooperate. I bestow upon you the title of Patriarch of the Pious and all the rights and privileges that position grants. Now if you'd both excuse me, there are great matters I must attend to now." Matthew turned his back on his mother and grandfather. In the weave of time, he could see them both bowing before turning to walk away.

Helena and her father headed towards the doors to leave the Infinity Nexus. She could sense the animosity surging inside of her father, but she didn't want to pry into his affairs. Matthew's choice to change the Christian doctrine shocked her and was, she believed, the prime cause for the emotions she felt from her father. It was understandable, but she feared the passion could overwhelm her father and ruin him. There wasn't much she could do at the moment but keep a wary eye on her father. She swore a silent vow that she'd do whatever was in her power to prevent her father from bringing ruination down upon himself. In her mind, all a loyal daughter could do was look out for her father. The doors opened, and she looked back worriedly at Matthew. She couldn't imagine what he saw in the midst of time, the threats and dangers coming their way, and she realized perhaps he was as powerful as God.

CHAPTER 13

Approaching the door to the Infinity Nexus, Lady Marimba saw Lord Whelsey and Helena leaving, and she didn't acknowledge either of them. Helena waved, but Lady Marimba just strolled past them towards the open doors. She never cared for Helena or Lord Whelsey before, and she wasn't going to start now with everything going on. Besides, she had no intention of making Emperor Solomon wait for vain pleasantries with people she couldn't tolerate. The clacking of her footsteps echoed her approach toward the Infinity Nexus, and Matthew turned to greet his guest.

Lady Marimba adorned herself in new clothes produced from the replicators, and the light fabric was almost translucent in the light. Light radiated through the fabric, and the material flowed with her swaying walk. Her wild hair had been done in a series of intricate braids in a new style she designed. She approached the Infinity Nexus and knelt and bowed before Matthew. With one hand, he motioned for her to stand up.

"Thou summoned me, my Emperor?"

"Everyone has begun to settle into their new homes, Lady Marimba, and I wanted to request a service of your people. My sister, Nemesis, is planning a celebration at her new club and home, but I wanted to provide a more substantial celebration for all of our people. Something with class and style that will keep the people distracted while we prepare for the coming crisis. You were my first choice." Matthew paced back and forth with anxiety about the approaching future.

"No disrespect, Emperor, but I'm thy only choice regarding arts, culture, and style. Most of your people focus more on the art of war and death. They simply don't see value in beauty, and Nemesis and her people just exist to feed their lowest desires. Anything to create noise to drown out the deadly howl of silence they can't stand." Lady Marimba did nothing to hide her disgust from Matthew, and it wore clear on her face as a scowl.

"Survival is all they've known for so long," Matthew explained.

"Some of us have survived and still created things of beauty. I rose to the rank of Lady from the lowest circle of poverty. I was a member of Clan Pleb when thy sister took over for Lord Marcus, but I suspect she doesn't remember. That event inspired me to write my first play and performing it for Clan Player earned me the right to join. Not long after, I wrote my play involving the heresy of harmony that saw your sister Concordia executed. That, of course, drew the ire of thy father, but with his attention also came rewards that elevated me to take control of Clan Player. In fact, Emperor, I've already begun creating a new play. I'd hoped to be able to perform it here for thy pleasure and before the entire ship in the near future."

Marimba could sense the loneliness from Matthew, and she couldn't avoid seeing it in his eyes. She had no intention of letting such an opportunity to curry favor with the new power. It was the one lesson she refused to forget. Loved or hated, it was necessary not to be ignored by those in power, and Matthew's power was magnitudes greater than any other. Every instinct in Marimba told her all she had to do was care for Emperor Solomon, and his blessings would rain down upon her. At least she wouldn't have to tolerate the constant advances with Matthew as she did with Gabriel.

"Yes, I'm aware of your new play. Your rehearsals seem to be going well. Much less strife amongst your stable of prima donnas than you're used to, but that won't last forever, so enjoy it while you can. The hearts and minds of our people are at a flutter with all their new home has to offer, and we must do what we can to keep them that way." Matthew could see the intrigue growing in Marimba's eyes, but he knew it was because she doubted his powers to see through time. It didn't bother him because he knew she'd eventually understand the truth.

"Are thou spying on me, Emperor?" Marimba didn't hold back her fears and asked the question with simple candor. The honesty of the request made Matthew smile.

"Not in the way you fear, Lady Marimba. Remember, I see and know all now. From what I've seen of it so far, there is only one thing your play lacks." Matthew could see he really had Marimba's attention now, and her eyes glinted with anger and curiosity. The silence lingered for a second, and Matthew waited for Marimba's intrigue to become unbearable to force the question he could sense on the tip of her tongue.

"Enlighten me, Emperor," Marimba requested.

"Your play "Flight of the Clans," is well structured, but I fear you've missed the real drama of the moment. The play seems too fixated on the battle of *Empyrean station* and the struggle to stop the Reverie. In fact, I'm only mentioned in the first and closing acts of the play. Don't you feel that is a bit odd considering that the Reverie would have won without the creation of the new star?" Matthew could sense Marimba was biting her tongue, trying hold back her opinion.

It took all Marimba's willpower to not unleash the torrent of thoughts she had racing through her mind. She couldn't even believe the audacity of Matthew to criticize her play that hadn't even been finalized. Marimba searched for the words to express her contempt in a civil fashion, but she struggled to maintain control of her anger at the vanity in the criticism. The play was to glorify the sacrifices of the soldiers who held the Reverie at bay and not to stroke the ego of a child playing at Emperor. She knew from her experiences with Gabriel that she had to maneuver delicately.

"My emperor, doth thou know my mind better than me?"

"Of course not, but I know it as well as you. You want to express the troops' bravery and their defiance of the odds of death. I think you've done a brilliant job, but you forget I was there with each of you at that moment. Watching you, giving you strength, and creating the star that would save all of our lives. We did it together, and that is the drama I think you're missing. How in the end from low to high, we all stood together and did our part." Matthew knew his words had an impact, but Marimba was still furious from her lack of faith in his abilities.

"Emperor, I would ask that you wait until you have seen the play before you judge it."

"I have seen it played at the height of your glory," Matthew declared.

"My Emperor, the play isn't even written yet..." Lady Marimba paused, realizing the truth in that moment. She took a deep breath and played the conversation over in her head. Matthew had been correct when he mentioned he was only in the beginning and end. Most of the play centered around the actual battle. Matthew smiled, seeing that Marimba's faith had sparked to life now that she was beginning to understand the truth.

"I've watched your play countless times while waiting for time to pass. I can see and influence everything from the Infinity Nexus, yet I can't be a part of anything. My brothers and sisters work away at their tasks, and I see, feel, and hear all they do. Yet they don't sense me watching and move forward with no other choice. Still, I stand here waiting for the terrible visage of inevitable desolation to arise and the Great Maw churns trying to devour all." Matthew could see the lamentations he spoke of weighing heavy on Marimba, draining her anger away like an infection drawn from a wound.

"My Emperor, that sounds like hell. How doth thou endure?" Marimba was contemplating the question herself as much as she was asking for an answer.

"What choice do I have but to endure? This chamber separates me from time and space. I will not age here or die. Besides, I have a great task before me that has yet to even truly begin." Matthew tried to explain the truth of his situation, but he could tell Marimba didn't quite understand by her puzzled look.

"With the *Empyrean station*, Infinity Nexus, and all the Clans united behind you, what more could you acquire? What more could thy heart desire?" Marimba truly wanted to know the answers to these questions, and Matthew could feel the powerful urge of those desires echoing inside his own mind.

"I can answer your question, Lady Marimba, but there is a price to pay to know such things."

Lady Marimba stood there frozen from fear caused by the words "a price to pay", and she couldn't comprehend what those vague words meant. Some part of her did understand but trembled in fear. She didn't understand what she was feeling, and no matter how hard she tried to pull the thoughts from the depths of her mind, she failed. There was a sense of awe echoing amidst the trembling fear she felt, and she couldn't contain the feelings tugging at her nerves. Instinct took over. She knelt to bow low and looked up at Matthew with bewilderment and wonder. "My Emperor, if thou doth choose me for such knowledge…"

Matthew grew really quiet for a moment, and he focused his mind on Marimba. With intent, he pulled his memories of his dreams and channeled the stream of consciousness into Marimba's mind. Her eyes went wide from the surge of images betwixt with pain from the rush of information. In her mind, she watched the stars expand, planets formed, and life spread across them. Billions of years played out in seconds in her mind, and she convulsed from the overload. Sensing Marimba reaching her limits for pain, Matthew released her mind from his focus.

"My God, Jesus Christ, and Mother Mary," Marimba signed the cross on her head and chest.

"Do you understand now why I have no choice but to endure?"

The words echoed through the Infinity Chamber but seemed even further away in Marimba's mind that was still racing. She was trying to wrap her mind around what she saw. Tears welled up in her eyes before brimming over to race down her cheeks. She could feel the hollow feeling of loneliness mixed with the pain and beauty she saw in the echo of images in her mind. It took minutes for Marimba to even be able to stand again, and she looked at Matthew.

"My Emperor, thou place too much pressure on thy shoulders."

"My gift is this power to create new stars, planets, and life, but it comes at a terrible price. One that I didn't understand until I was in the Infinity Nexus and had already paid. My curse is to stand witness to everything until my mind can endure no more," Matthew explained.

Marimba knew what she had to do. She would bring her Clan to the Infinity Nexus and always entertain Emperor Solomon. It was the only thing she could do to try to repay him for his sacrifice thought. She saw Matthew smiling and didn't realize for a moment why until it struck her, he already knew her plans. Perhaps even before she entered the Infinity Nexus, and she took a step back out of fear in that instance.

"Don't be afraid, Marimba, because this is still your choice. Even if you choose not to do it there will be no animosity from me, but I admire the kindness of your heart. The passion of which you write, create, and live. I've seen it in how you fight, and it echoes through time. Nothing defines you but you." Matthew tried to calm Marimba, sensing her fear of losing self-determination, and it was an understandable reaction to what had just been learned.

"My Emperor, thou know my heart better than all others. I swear to do all that I can to alleviate your great tribulation. Anything I can do for thee; I'm at thy service."

"Your devotion will not go unrewarded, Lady Marimba. I sense you have things to attend to, and so you may go. I look forward to seeing you again," Matthew admitted.

Lady Marimba bowed again before backing away and turning to leave. She walked slowly, considering all she learned, and fought the urge to look back. Matthew possessed an enthralling power, and it had seized Marimba's mind. A part of her wondered what things she had to attend to, but she no longer doubted the accuracy of Matthew's predictions. When the door slid open, she couldn't help herself glancing back to Matthew and stared for a second in admiration. She admitted to herself that Emperor Solomon was nothing like his father and could scarcely believe how this one interaction changed everything she thought about Matthew. Lady Marimba intended to find out just how different Matthew was from Gabriel and bit her lip from the surge of anticipation of her next visit.

CHAPTER 14

Tenno Asmodeus walked through the empty halls of the *Insidious Seduction*, and the sounds of his footsteps echoed his approach. He loathed having to rely on Tenno Lilith's ship to transport him, but he had no intention of disrupting his larger plans. All of the legions under his control were busy fighting battles to expand his territory. Power was all he cared about, and not even the Cacophony of Discordance would command him to relent in acquiring more territory and resources. Finding this rogue Magnus Void was his desire as much as the Cacophony of Discordance or the Council of Chaos, because the speed at which he acquired power was fascinating. That was a strategy Tenno Asmodeus wanted to know and would pay almost any cost to acquire, he thought, lost in his machinations. Reverie of the Desirous cadence moved out of Tenno Asmodeus' way, but he was so lost in thought he didn't' notice the succubus or incubus moving to avoid his malevolent presence.

Sounds of muffled moaning could be heard beyond the door he approached. There was a moment of hesitation when Tenno Asmodeus stood at the door and prepared himself to deal with Tenno Lilith. The door whisked open, unleashing the carnal noises of passion, and the smell of musk wafted into the corridor. Two guards moved towards Tenno Asmodeus, but he just raised his right hand, unleashing a powerful crackle of energy at the two guards. Siphoning the guard's energy brought them to their knees in cries of agony. Paying neither of the guards any concern, Tenno Asmodeus strode into the room and scanned around look for Tenno Lilith.

Tenno Asmodeus couldn't hide his scorn, and it crackled on his face echoing the fury of his disgust. The room was filled with Lilith's children and the Reverie that served under the dark Matron. All of the Reverie in the room looked like living beings and were paired with mortals they siphoned life force from. All their energy was directed to simulating the flesh of living beings, and Tenno Asmodeus could feel the resonating lust crackling in the air. Across the room, his eyes fell onto Tenno Lilith, who sat on her throne of souls. Lament of the baleful souls unable to satisfy their lust swirled around Tenno Lilith, holding her up high above the harem. Souls bound to the throne whisked around their matron, trying to find purchase on her flesh and howled in unfilled needs, forced to watch the seductive scenes playing out all over the harem. Taking a drink from a chalice of blood, the blood-stained Tenno Lilith's lips crimson, and she watched the great spectacle of her children and servants engaged in for her glory. Her eyes fell on Tenno Asmodeus. She extended her right hand and wiggled one finger, commanding him to approach, provoking a crackle of energy and a malevolent glare.

Some of Tenno Lilith's children approached Tenno Asmodeus, and they ran their fingers across the black swirl of energy, trying to entice the Tenno to join them. He tried to push past them, but the children followed, clutching at the Tenno as he tried to keep walking forward. Tenno Lilith couldn't contain her laughter watching the fury growing on Tenno Asmodeus face. The cackle of Tenno Lilith's laughter echoed through the chamber, mixing with the moans of her children, and the sound only taunted Tenno Asmodeus further. Everything about the lustful orgy angered him, and the impetuous children of Tenno Lilith became the focus of that feeling. A crackle of energy exploded off him as he tried driving back the lustful children clawing at him, but the moans of pain were indistinguishable from those of pleasure. Children of Tenno Lilith continued to paw at him, trying to drag them into the cadence of debauchery that filled the throne room. His eyes locked on Tenno Lilith, whose lips curled into a wicked smile sensing the malevolency that filled Tenno Asmodeus. Her laughter only infuriated him more, but that seemed to bring Tenno Lilith even more pleasure than her children's seductive dedications to her.

Tenno Lilith sat on the throne of soulless bodies swirling in an aether around her, entwined in the throes of passion, and the faces of the souls trapped within cried for mercy before vanishing into the mist of lustfully damned. Her pure green eyes reflected the bodies of her children, unleashing the full power of their lust upon each other. Whips cracked to the sounds of muffled painful pleasure to the administration of her children of Dominus, and the children of Submission let their masters play with their bodies however they pleased. Dark, seductive energy filling the room made flesh crash in waves upon each other throughout the room. Tenno Lilith drank in the lustful energy rippling through the room from all the acts of her children but stopped laughing at Asmodeus's growing wrath. With one hand, she motioned her children away from her guest.

"Children leave my guest alone, and go back to your play," Tenno Lilith spoke softly, shooing off all her children pawing at Tenno Asmodeus.

Many of them sighed with disappointment, but none disobeyed their mother's orders. One after another, they began making their way to more entertaining diversions in the room. The path to the throne began to clear, allowing Asmodeus to approach unmolested. Standing before the throne of passion, Tenno Asmodeus glared at Tenno Lilith, who motioned for one of her servants to bring her a drink. She took the goblet filled with the blood of the innocence, sipped it, and licked her lips.

"You spend too much time on such vain pursuits, Lilith." Tenno Asmodeus didn't hide his contempt but wore it proud for all to see. None of the children cared to listen and focused on the carnal satisfaction they craved.

"It's not polite to chastise your host, especially when chastising is my specialty, and there's nothing I love punishing more than an unruly guest not showing me the proper respect I deserve. Perhaps you don't have a taste for my children because you desire the original?" Tenno Lilith ran her finger down her naked flesh and stared at Tenno Asmodeus with hungry eyes.

"All this energy wasted on simulating pleasures of the flesh. The greatest lie of biology is that this is enjoyable. If it weren't such a grotesque waste of precious energy, I'd be pitiable."

"Perhaps you've just never had anyone play with you properly," Tenno Lilith teased.

"Your sexual prowess is legendary, Tenno Lilith and none can argue otherwise. Yet, neither I nor Tenno Lucifer were impressed enough to stay with you for eternity, and that's why you've been sent to find him. I fear if you can't entertain the vanity of Lucifer, who admires your lustful behaviors, then you stand no chance at pleasuring me. The only use I see for you and your children is to prostitute you all to the benefit of the Cacophony of Discordance, but I guess that's exactly what the Supreme Tenno is doing by sending you after Lucifer." Tenno Asmodeus could feel the anger rising to overwhelm Lilith's lust at that moment, and the red energy crackled across her green eyes.

Anger swirling around Tenno Lilith was drawing the attention of some of her children. She could sense the waning of the lust in the chamber, which only infuriated her more. Her hands trembled in a tight grip on souls of the throne of passion as the faces moved, trying to lick, kiss, and suck on her fingers, but their ethereal form made such pleasures impossible. Pushing off the throne, she stood up, and with a wave of her hand, a crackle of green energy lanced out from her fingers to tighten around Tenno Asmodeus's neck. Tenno Lilith's eyes narrowed, the green energy crackled, and the surge of anger raced through the energy whip, turning it red. With a grimace of pain, Tennp Asmodeus struggled to stay standing, but the energy brought him to his knees despite his resistance. Tenno Lilith walked towards her victim with a sway of her hips.

"On your knees... Just where I like you Tenno Asmodeus, and now I should teach you a lesson in respect. For this is my ship, after all. Perhaps you should have gated your ship if you wanted to be in control, but we both know you don't want to halt your wars. The endless struggle for supremacy of power you never stop engaging in. It doesn't matter who wins because the truth we both know, Tenno Asmodeus, is that everyone loses. You say lust is the greatest lie, but what lie is greater than ceaseless wrath without point or purpose?"

"Vanity is the greater lie because it's the source of both of our lies," Tenno Asmodeus struggled under the power of Tenno Lilith.

"You're talking to the first Reverie to ever exist, and you will show respect to your Queen!"

Crimson energy surged down the whip and rippled across Tenno Asmodeus's body. Tenno Lilith could only imagine the pain he was in, but he refused to give any satisfaction by letting that pain out. The display of willpower did impress Tenno Lilith, but she, too, refused to give the satisfaction of revealing it. The two Tenno's glared into each other eyes in a silent battle of wills. Tenno Lilith released her power from Tenno Asmodeus's throat and took another sip from her goblet.

"You're so boring!"

"We have more important matters to attend to than your boredom Lilith! We'll arrive soon at the Spindleweb Nebula, and the Arachne prefers dealing with you. Since you like to point out that this is your ship, I was hoping to inspire you to do your job and come to the bridge to negotiate our landing. We both need the information web of the Arachne to succeed." Black energy surged across Tenno Asmodeus's throat as he focused on pushing out the lingering pain of the attack.

"Oh, it's been so long since I saw the precious Arachne and her brood. Oh, she is such a fruitful mother, and she devours her children like any good parent should do less they grow too impetuous. I suppose I can accommodate you in this matter but know that you will owe me for this in the future. My reputation for collecting on my debts is legendary, and it could take a few centuries of your deliberate attention to my needs before I release you from my servitude."

Tenno Asmodeus didn't care what Tenno Lilith believed so long as she did what she was expected to do and stayed out of his way. Once the Arachne information was acquired, Tenno Asmodeus had no more use for the lustful queen of the damned. He would discard Tenno Lilith as she discarded lover's and even her own children who bored her. Draining the goblet, Tenno Lilith licked her lips clean and tossed the cup to her servant before standing up and heading towards Tenno Asmodeus. Souls howled in rage and tried to hold their queen in her seat, but their ethereal forms found no purchase on her flesh. He refused to follow behind her and walked side-by-side to show all that he was in every way Tenno Lilith's equal. Most of the Reverie in the chamber paid no attention, lost in their lustful activities.

The two left the chamber and walked towards the bridge in the empty corridors. Silence only amplified the tension between Tenno Asmodeus and Tenno Lilith. Baleful energy radiated from her, and the clacking of her heels echoed her barely contained emotions. One day she intended to teach Tenno Asmodeus some respect, and once she found Lucifer his power would only help with that. Tenno Lilith tried to block the memories of her time with the fallen celestial, but emotions stirred up by the onslaught of recollection lingered. She could sense that Tenno Asmodeus was paying attention to the surge of her emotions, and she hoped the mixture confused him to the same degree as it did her.

The bridge doors opened when the two Tenno approached. Reverie inside continued to work, trying not to look at Tenno Lilith or Tenno Asmodeus. Echoes of the fear of the crew filled the atmosphere with a delicious sense of, and that brought a smile to Tenno Lilith's face. She sat down at her command chair to stare into the Spindleweb Nebula on the screen. It had been a long time since she looked at the beautiful horror of the Arachne territory.

Strands of cosmic energy flowed in translucent lines of energy only the Reverie could see without assistance. The forces of the universe warped in this area of space by the mixture of gravity, magnetism, and space anomalies forced to converge by design. Tenno Lilith smiled to see the progression of the work of the Arachne she helped nurture. Arachne's children weaved the power of the cosmos in space the way their ancestors weaved webs to capture dinner. Each subspace strand reached out beyond the Spindleweb Nebula to some distance point, and the Arachne used this technology to spy and gather information for themselves and the Reverie.

"Hailing the Arachne," Tenno Lilith send the transmission into the void.

There was a moment of silence before the viewscreen shifted to reveal the image of an Arachne. Even the darkness of the video didn't hide the beautiful visage of the Arachne from Tenno Lilith. She could see the eight large multifaceted black pools staring at her, two large, almost translucent mandibles, and arms folded over the scrunched-up body. Standing up, the Arachne unfolded, growing in size until she stood well over ten feet in height. The two mandibles moved.

"My, how you've grown, Atrax! You've become quite the massive spawn, and either your mother must be very proud or preparing to devour you soon. If it's the latter, I do so hope she shares you with me. You look absolutely delicious," Tenno Lilith greeted.

"Tenno Lilith, the great mother, and her children were not expecting your arrival. What brings your supreme glory to our humble web?" Atrax's eight eyes all looked at different people on the bridge of the *Insidious Seduction*.

"The Cacophony of Discordance sent Tenno Asmodeus in search of Lord Magnus Void, and so I've brought him here. No other species know the Great Maw like the children of Arachne. There has been too much time since I last saw my friend, and I thought she might be growing hungry. Can't have her eating up all her babies because then what would I devour when I get peckish. I can only imagine how excited your mother is to see me once more. So be a dear Atrax and send my ship the navigation codes so we can navigate our way through your everchanging webs."

When the navigation data was transmitted, Tenno Lilith ended the communication without another word. She leaned back in her chair while her servants inputted the information. On the screen, the Spindleweb Nebula began increasing in size at a steady rate. Tenno Lilith could feel the cold stare of Tenno Asmodeus falling upon her. He looked down upon Tenno Lilith.

"Do you trust them?"

Maniacal laughter was Tenno Lilith's first response, and it took her a moment to regain control of herself before she could speak. She spoke slowly, and her voice fell low, taking a serious tone. "I don't trust anyone, Tenno Asmodeus, and neither do you. It's the reason we've survived so long. Arachne is cunning, but she is young compared to us, and her machinations are short-sighted. We'll acquire the information we need, influence Arachne to send her people against *Empyrean station*, and go our separate ways in search of our targets." Tenno Lilith didn't hide her joy at being parted from Tenno Asmodeus, and he seemed to feel the same way, grinning at the thought.

If the Arachne helped find Magnus Void, then Tenno Asmodeus could tolerate them as he did Tenno Lilith, he thought, staring at the viewscreen. The size and ferocity of the Arachne would prove to be a formidable force to unleash on the light. Once the accursed light was gone and Magnus Void was in Asmodeus's clutches, he could begin his real plans for the Cacophony of Discordance. Lilith would eventually understand Asmodeus's true power, but by then, it'd be too late to do anything. On that day, he'd show her and the rest of the cacophony that he was the true master.

CHAPTER 15

Light blurred at the edges of the viewscreen, and Magnus focused on the image of the *Worldforge* in the distance. The large metallic sphere floated in the void of space and seemed lifeless from a distance. Rocks drifted throughout the asteroid belt that surrounded the *Worldforge*. Sensors detected the Geodes floating in the asteroid field, working to move the rocks toward the forge. Large pieces of rocks floated towards a large opening on the sphere in a steady stream.

Massive figures of Geodes stopped their work to look at the approaching *Death's Reaper*. Jeweled eyes stared at the ship with curiosity, and Magnus could sense his arrival was unexpected. Before he could even send a hail to the *Worldforge* the coms systems began beeping. Flicking buttons, he activated the coms system and tried to clear the signal. Sensors showed the disrupting effect of nearby magnetic and gravity fields, and he manipulated the coms system trying to clear the interference to allow the garbled voice to be heard clear of static interference.

"*Death's Reaper,* this is the *Worldforge.* Your imminent response is requested." A deep, grating voice spoke through the crackle of static. Magnus managed to clear the signal up with a few more tweaks of his com systems. Message repeated once more before he could manage to respond.

"This is Lord Void, and I'm requesting clearance to land." Magnus leaned back to wait for the Geodes to grant him clearance. They were a slow and ponderous race, he thought, and so he suspected this would take a few moments. Sensors detected the scans of the ship. Before there was a response, Magnus saw the main gates of the *Worldforge* begin to open. He was already imputing trajectory information when the coms sparked to life but couldn't contain his shock at the alacrity of the Geodian response.

His own surprise reflected back at him from the viewscreen, and the com system warbled with another incoming message.

"Clearance has been granted. Please proceed on course we'll be transmitting momentarily. Beware of the extreme gravitational forces of the forge on your approach." The voice was slow, steady, and loud over the comms, but Magnus was used to the geode's speech thanks to his time spent with Vulcan. Pulling towards the gate, the *Death's Reaper* glided towards the entrance.

Beyond the massive gate, streams of rock were plummeted by gravity into the center of the sphere that acted like a mold. Rocks shattered, striking the growing circular mass of molten spinning metal in the center. Asteroids melted in the furious heat, allowing their precious metals to add to the growing molten core. Scanners showed Magnus the high metallic metals were fusing in the center of the growing mass. Rocks were being forced to the surface by direct gravitational projectors that separated the metal from the other molecules. Magnetic fields were being used to accelerate the mass of metal in the center, and sensors already showed a growing magnetic field from the core of the mass. Rocks slamming against the molten core were beginning to form a crust, already revealing the earliest form of planetary assembly had begun.

Geodes walked across the surface of the rocks, unfazed by the forces of magnetism, the heat of the magma, and the force of gravity directed at the mass. Magnus watched in fascination at the geode's work. Geode workers were shaping the rocks to began to form the foundations of mountains and crevices across the surface. He could imagine when the project was complete, this mass of lifeless rocks, minerals, and metals would be teeming with flora and fauna. No other race Magnus had encountered possessed the skill to forge worlds or seemed to be created for such an act.

On autopilot, the *Death's Reaper* glided towards the large clearing inside the *Worldforge*, and Magnus activated the landing sequence with the flick of several switches. Thrusters flared from the ship when the landing system activated. The *Death's Reaper* glided towards the clearing and came to a rest with a loud thud when the landing systems touched down upon the metal deck plate. Magnus was already waiting back at the landing ramp. The nearby light still glowed red, but once the landing had been completed, the light turned. Pressing the button, the ramp lowered, and Magnus started walking down.

"Magnus, the great Forger of Worlds didn't expect your return so soon." Vulcan walked towards his old friend with a smile on his granite features. He could tell by Magnus' walk that this visit wasn't intended to be social. He walked towards Vulcan with steady and fast steps.

"We don't have time for the pleasantries, my old friend. Things are proceeding much faster than I expected since the Reverie attacked *Empyrean station*. I've already met with the A.S.A., and they're preparing to make their move to go to war against the Reverie. That's why I'm here. I need to see the Forger of Worlds." Magnus could see the concern in the jeweled eyes of Vulcan.

"This was not expected, Magnus. Forger of Worlds isn't happy but has agreed to meet you." Vulcan turned to lead his friend toward the corridor to the central chamber of the *Worldforge*.

'I know, and I wouldn't be here if it weren't important. The Serpentine still needed to be warned about what's transpiring. Still, this was a lot closer to reach, so I came here first." Magnus followed his friend down the massive corridor designed to accommodate even the largest Geodes. Their footsteps echoed in the empty corridors.

"The Geodes have fired the *Worldforge* up for the first time in two millennia, and we've entered the delicate early stages of the forging process. A few more months and the new planet will be ready as you requested a so long ago. Everything is moving ahead to your desires. Our great leader, Forger of Worlds, has already prepared to offer the planet as a gift to the new star your prophesized." Vulcan knew Magnus would want to know the state of the Geode's preparations towards his plans, and he nodded, listening to the report. The situation had progressed as Magnus expected, but the situation with the Reverie threatened everything.

"Your people have always been capable of true wonders Vulcan, but the situation is much graver than I initially anticipated. The Cacophony of Discordance is massing their forces and allies to launch a full-scale attack. If the new star falls, my plans will be ruined. Certainly, your race of titans will meet their final extinction at the hands of the Cacophony. Supreme Tenno has spent enormous energy over these two millennia searching for this forge. I've kept it hidden at the great expense and danger to myself, and

I expect our pact to be upheld." Magnus could sense his friend heard what he was saying, but he wasn't sure he comprehended the magnitude of the situation. Vulcan seemed to be ready to fight.

"Lord Void, the Geodes will be ready for war if that's what you need, but convincing the Forger of Worlds to abandon the planet in its final stages won't be easy. I'll do what I can to help you sway the argument." Vulcan led his friend toward the large gates at the end of the corridor. A great resonating shudder shook the corridor when the two approached the gates.

The gates pulled back with slow, steady shudders of force, revealing the chamber of the Forger of Worlds inch by inch. In the middle of the chamber, the towering Forger of Worlds manipulated the mass of energy in the center of the room. Crackling mass of power surged with each strike of the hammer against the worldforge being forged into raw substance to be manipulated. Magnus could sense the gravitational force of energy emanating from the sphere. Forger of Worlds didn't stop his work to address the arrival of Vulcan or Magnus. Humming echoed through the chamber from the Forger of Worlds and only stopped when he began to speak.

"Lord Void, you've returned as I suspected you would. Do you come to call the Geodes to war?" Forger of Worlds words shook the entire room causing even the ground to tremble.

"Great Forger of Worlds, I've never attempted to command you in the long echoes of eternity that we've known each other. For all who know your work should realize that none can command the Geodes. War is coming, and I've asked you not to fight in this battle." Magnus could feel the glare of Vulcan but didn't turn to address it. The situation was too dire to endanger the last chance to restore the universe should Matthew fail, and Magnus knew that keeping the Geodes safe meant there could be another chance in the future.

"Magnus, you'd ask us to stand back and not defend the first star to exist in two thousand years?" Vulcan shook his head. "Memories still echo the fall of the light and the destruction of our work since time began. Forger of Worlds, we must help defend the star," Vulcan protested.

The humming stopped when the Forger of Worlds began considering the situation, but the work on the new planet continued. Magnus and Vulcan stood quiet, watching the ponderous Forger of Worlds consider the situation with no concern for time. Everything seemed dire from the Forger of Worlds estimation, but Magnus' request seemed to defy the realities of the dangerous situation. Looking back at Magnus, the Forger of Worlds long memories sparked to life, and recollections reminded him that the strange Reverie seemed always to be right in his predictions.

"Strange that you asked for our help to create the star and now ask the Geodes to stand back. I admit my children were not created for war, as the sentient biological beings call it. We were made to guide creation, and we've not forgotten our mission. Once long ago we marched to war, and it was to our folly. If Lord Void requests we stay out of the war, then I will bend to the wisdom of his request." Forger of World turned back to his work having made his will known.

"Forger of World, we must help defend the star and ensure its survival. The humans are well built for war but can't stand against the force amassing against them. From what Magnus says, the Reverie are summoning their allies. We can't stand back idly and watch the light be destroyed again." Vulcan looked up at the Forger of Worlds with concern glinting in his diamond eyes.

"Your words don't fall on lifeless stone, my child, but we are the last who have existed since the dawn of the verse. When the first words were sung into creation, it was we who heard them. The destruction of the Geodes would be a great loss, and it's one Magnus refuses to make it seems. He fears that the humans will fail and makes contingency plans for that possible outcome. This is a wise course of action and one the Geodes will follow." Forger of Worlds didn't look back continuing to focus on building the new planet and hoped Vulcan would understand.

"Magnus, you must ask for our help, and the Forger of Worlds will be bound by the Eternal Laws to assist. We must not be left to work away in the darkness, forgotten by time. There is no greater shame to the Geodes than that." Vulcan tried to reason, but he could see that Magnus had already decided. Grim determination narrowed Magnus's eyes.

"I don't like making this request any more than you like the idea of it, Vulcan, but we must make sure we don't lose everything now. Reverie might win and destroy it, and with the Geodes gone, the planets' secrets go with them. A universe without light is unthinkable, but without planets, life won't even get the chance to adapt. That's exactly what the Cacophony

126

of Discordance wants. They haven't searched for the Geodes since the fall of the light for no reason. We can't let them find you now. While everyone focuses on the *Empyrean station*, the Geodes will build this new world. Should the battle end in victory, and the new star continue to burn bright, we'll be prepared for the next phase of the plan." Magnus hoped Vulcan understood the stakes.

Vulcan considered the situation from Magnus' information and point of view. The plan was strategic in scope, and Vulcan had come to expect nothing less from his friend. Still, there was a worry that the light would be destroyed, and that reality haunted Vulcan, who had seen the glory of the star. In that moment, he thought of Hephaestus and the work they did together. All Vulcan could hope was one day they'd get to work with each other again.

"I understand your plan, my friend, but I still think it's foolish to abandon the humans after we sacrificed so much to get them to this point," Vulcan declared in defiance.

"You really think I'm just going to abandon them?"

"No, Lord Void, my child doesn't think that, but he does fear that. You forget that the rest of the beings you encounter don't possess your experience or knowledge. We can't know your goals or desires, yet we're forced to trust you regardless. My great child, Vulcan, doesn't like this situation any more than I do, but the work must continue. Worlds must be forged anew, and I leave the forging of the cosmos to you, Lord Void." Forger of Worlds started to hum again, returning to work.

Forger of Worlds had decided for the Geodes, and Vulcan knew there was nothing left to say now. He turned to leave the room with Magnus walking beside him. They walked back through the gates in silence. The rumbling of the gates closing shook the floor and walls once more, and yet the two remained silent. Magnus sensed his friend was disappointed in him, but he knew it was the right choice for this situation.

The walk back to the *Death's Reaper* was made awkward by the silence. Vulcan and Magnus arrived back at the ship, and before heading up the ramp, he stopped to look at his friend. The glare of Vulcan revealed to Magnus the deep betrayal felt at his choice of course to take. He couldn't leave the situation like this, so he considered his words carefully.

"Look, Vulcan, I understand how you feel, and I'm not sure what to say to alleviate the betrayal you think I've done. There is no way I'm leaving the *Empyrean station* or Matthew and his people to fight this by themselves. A'zyren and Mordecai are already on their way to help. I'm heading to try to recruit Dhakan and his people. Your time will come soon enough if I force things to go how I want them to. Try to be patient old friend, you've been around a long time, and I expect you to be around for a lot longer." Magnus turned to walk up the ramp and didn't expect any response from Vulcan.

"I don't agree with you, but I still trust you," Vulcan declared.

Magnus looked back with a smile and waved bye to his friend. Hitting the button to close the ramp, he strode towards the elevator and ascended towards the bridge. Walking onto the bridge, Magnus took his seat and started up his ship. He looked out the viewport in the cockpit at Vulcan, standing and watching from a distance. Magnus hoped this wouldn't be the last time he saw the old hunk of rock. The *Death's Reaper* lifted off from the force of the thrusters firing, and Magnus guided the ship back towards the gates of the *Worldforge*.

There was a growing sense of calamity in the cosmic strands of the universe, and Magnus could sense the efforts of the Cacophony of Discordance. He knew his people were moving against his plans. Time wasn't on his side any longer, and he plotted the course into the F.T.L. navigation computer. He could sense the power of the Reverie that was searching for him, and it took all his willpower to suppress his own energies to avoid being detected. The *Death's Reaper* flew away from the *Worldforge*, and once the ship was far enough away, Magnus activated the F.T.L. drive.

Light began to blur on the edges of the viewscreen, and Magnus turned away to avoid the pain of the light. His thoughts turned to Dhakan, whom he hoped had time to sway his people. Magnus knew that if the serpentine had one of the largest fleets in the Great Maw and if they joined the defense of *Empyrean station*, it would push the odds in Matthew's favor. Still, there was a lingering of dark energy that seemed to radiate from the direction of the serpentine empire. It was a foreboding sign, but Magnus had no choice left. He'd find out whatever lay in store soon enough.

CHAPTER 16

Machines in the lab continued to pump, hiss, and grind away at their tasks. Lord Galen stood pacing in front of his desk. His eyes glanced to examine the scans of both Matthew and Angelica displayed on the holographic emitter intermittently. From what he could see, there wasn't nothing unique in either of their D.N.A. strands. He activated a deep scan of both D.N.A. strands hoping a cross-analysis comparison might reveal something the molecular scans missed. Thoughts coalesced around the possibility of some quantum phenomenon, but he warned himself the odds were low. He sent the new scanning parameters with a thought. Heat pulsed from the computer as it processed the data with silent diligence.

Resting in the chair, Lord Galen contemplated how D.N.A. could remain unaffected yet produce the new psionic power he witnessed. In his mind, he went over the research the Ancient's had conducted before the Great Stellar War. There were competing theories on the possibilities of psionic power, but nothing Lord Galen considered valid empirically. The leading theory was that sentient life in the universe was evolving cognitively, and that would awaken the psionic powers latent in all life, but the scans didn't show any significant changes to the brain activity of either Angelica or Matthew. D.N.A. comparisons showed no new chromosomal formations or mutations. Angelica exited the scanner when the light vanished at the end of the scan.

Deep in Angelica's subconscious, Levart watched through his host's eyes what was happening. He knew these evolved primates were looking in all the wrong spots. It wasn't about changing D.N.A. but awakening it to become a conduit of cosmic energy it was always capable of channeling.

He whispered the truth to Angelica, but she didn't seem interested in any of this. All she was thinking about was how good it'd feel to get vengeance upon her father. The one-tracked thought process was beginning to annoy Levart, yet he didn't attempt to take control of Angelica. She could stew in her own vengeance for all Levart cared in this moment, because her soul and body would be his in the long run. He just wished she'd pay more attention to Lord Galen's work.

The door to the lab whisked open, and Lord Whelsey walked in to see his Lord Galen working away at the console. Angelica turned to see her grandfather and approached him with a smile. She could already tell the plan to convince Matthew had worked because Lord Whelsey was still alive. Even better, he appeared to be in a good mood. A smile crept across his face when he looked over Lord Galen's shoulder to see the progress on the research.

"I'm scanning for a deeper explanation of the psionic phenomenon. The D.N.A. scan was inconclusive, and I noticed no significant difference between Angelica's and Matthew's D.N.A. codes. I even compared their results against the genetic logs of our people, and still nothing. No new mutations and remarkably little D.N.A. change has occurred to the genetic lineage since before Starfall. Their genetic code does appear more resilient than most, but the Solomon bloodline has always shown that." Lord Galen pointed to the information on the screen that explained his research paradigm. All the information on the screen meant nothing to Lord Whelsey, but he knew unlocking the secret of psionic power was the key to his success.

"Lord Void and Gabriel mentioned that the keeper of the outpost was waiting for Matthew's exact D.N.A. strand to unlock it. How is it possible the D.N.A. isn't the source of my grandson's power?" Lord Whelsey couldn't comprehend how the two truths could co-exist.

"It's possible that Matthew's exact D.N.A. strand was a combination for the lock and not the source of his power. There are signs that some form of chemical compound was introduced into his system. It could have been a specifically tailored compound designed to only interact with his specific genetic code. Strangely, I can't seem to find any changes this compound made or any traces of it in Matthew's system on the molecular level, but I've begun quantum scanning. Odds of a quantum phenomenon capable of interacting with the genetic code on a molecular level is unlikely but not impossible. I'll keep searching."

Angelica listened to the conversation feeling the squirm of Levart deep in her mind. She tried to resist his influence, but she felt him beginning to take control once more. Neither Lord Whelsey nor Lord Galen noticed because they were too busy discussing the science. Angelica fought to maintain control, but Levart was too strong. He overpowered Angelica, causing her eyes to turn black, but neither Lord Whelsey nor Lord Galen noticed the sudden change.

"You primates so obsessed with how things work, but you never see the truth. What you call psionic powers is merely a manifestation of the cosmic truth that all things are made of energy. Matthew and the Reverie's minds are powerful enough to manipulate energy with pure thought. D.N.A. forms a conduit for cosmic energy to channel through, and Matthew and Angelica's D.N.A. has just reached the strength required to survive cosmic energies' direct interaction. Your quantum scans will reveal this." Levart pointed to the D.N.A. chain on the screen, trying to show the truth.

Looking at the information on the screen, Lord Galen understood what Levart was saying for the first time, and he understood how the D.N.A. formed the insulation to channel pure cosmic energy. The quantum scanner beeped signaling it had finished the scan, and the data began to appear on the holographic emitter. Scanning the data, it didn't take much reading of the computer scans did confirm his hypothesis. Matthew and Angelica's D.N.A. weren't different from other humans in any significant way, but they did possess an amassing of chemicals in their D.N.A. that acted as a natural insulator against electrical energy. Change was so minuscule, but there was a small accumulation of an unknown chemical that only had a quantum signature, but Matthew's scans show a much larger quantity. With a thought, he sent he computer to pull up Matthew's medical records across his life. Information appeared on the holographic emitter in a bright flash flipping through the years of medical scans, and his thoughts focused on the strange chemical. He was shocked by what he saw, and that reaction caused Lord Whelsey to turn and see Angelica's blackened eyes,

"Yes, it all makes sense now! I was looking for significant differences in the D.N.A. structure itself, but the real change was just in accumulating these strange quantum chemicals in the strands that provide insulation against cosmic energy. Perhaps if I were to extract some blood and run some direct experiments, I could isolate the chemical accumulations, separate them, and reverse engineer them." Lord Galen struggled with his report feeling the echoes of fear caused by Angelica's blackened eyes. Standing up, he walked towards the medical equipment, grabbed a hyposyringe, and grabbed several cartridges, including one with a sedative.

"Angelica, are you ok?" Lord Whelsey knew it was Levart in control. He wanted to see if the demon had full control over Angelica.

"Your granddaughter is taking a little nap and dreaming of vengeance on her father like usual. It's all one-track repeat city up in this meat prison she calls her brain. Really you humans are quite the grotesque puppets, and you should beg for the Cacophony of Discordance to save you from this hell you call life. Perhaps I can help free you from the prison of your flesh." Levart pointed to the screen, revealing he was talking about Lord Galen's research.

"Would you allow me to extract some of Angelica's blood?" Lord Galen used all his willpower to hide his excitement at the possibility of studying a possessed human's blood. There had to be some effect of the sentient energy of a Reverie upon human biology. He was certain that information would help his research. Levart sighed and presented Angelica's arm to the doctor, using her memories to figure out what was expected.

Lord Galen shared an uneasy glance with Lord Whelsey, and he saw the sedative cartridge in the doctor's palm. Moving towards Levart, Lord Galen snapped the sedative cartridge into the hyposyringe, and took hold of the demon's arm. Levart seemed unaware of the plot, but Lord Galen felt the trembling of fear in his arm. Muscles convulsed from the fear pumping through the doctor's blood, and it caused his hand to shake every so subtly. Lord Whelsey could see Lord Galen's hand trembling and knew a diversion was needed.

"Do you believe that we can acquire the powers of the Reverie?" Lord Whelsey's question caused Levart to laugh maniacally. After a few seconds of intense laughter, the demon locked eyes with Lord Whelsey, eyes narrowing and teeth gritting.

"All Reverie, at one time, were living sentient people. Most of the Cacophony of Discordance is made up of fallen human souls. Humans who lived their lives so negatively that when they died, their minds were reborn as living negative energy unable to escape the pull of the void. Though we have plenty of all living races now making up the Reverie, our power exists only because the power is a by-product of what you call your soul. This power belongs to you first, but it's easier to understand after you die and become one of us. What you call psionic power is merely the natural process of the mindful soul. It is awareness of all on a quantum cosmic level." Levart could tell that Lord Whelsey neither understood nor liked what he was hearing.

Lord Galen took the moment of distraction provided to inject the sedative. He stepped back away from Levart and waited for the sedative to take effect. At first, there seemed to be no effect in Levart, and he didn't pay any attention to Lord Galen or what had been injected. When the medicine began to work on Angelica's biology, Levart began to wobble. He tried to catch himself with one hand grabbing for Angelica's energy whip with the other. Lord Whelsey grabbed his granddaughters' wrist, squeezed, and forced the energy whip to fall to the ground.

"Not so fast, Levart. I want to thank you for sharing that information. Lord Galen here will put it to good use, but I think we will need to take a deeper look." Lord Galen blocked the weakened attack and could see Levart's energy begin to crackle in the black pools of Angelica's eyes. The energy began to subside with the growing power of the sedative.

"You primates have made a grave mistake in betraying a Tenno and prince of hell," Levart warned. He felt Angelica's body beginning to fail and her eyes growing heavy. Reality seemed to be retreating from Levart, but he clawed to try to hold on.

"I think you've made the grave mistake of hubris. You've underestimated us." Lord Whelsey held onto his granddaughter's body to prevent it from being damaged in a fall.

Levart could feel the powerful sedative taking hold and fighting it wouldn't be an option anymore. He let out a maniacal laugh before retreating into the subconscious. Angelica's eyes cleared, and confusion crept across her face. Her eyes darted around, trying to figure out what was happening, but the sedative was already too strong to resist. No matter how hard she struggled, she couldn't keep her eyes open and slipped into unconsciousness. Lord Whelsey held his granddaughter in his arms and hoisted her up to carry her toward the medical bed.

Laying Angelica on the medical bed, Lord Whelsey looked down at her peaceful countenance. Lord Galen was already fastening and tightening the bed straps around Angelica's arms and legs. Once she was firmly fastened, Lord Galen began to draw blood using the hyposyringe. Crimson liquid pooled and began to fill the empty glass container attached to the hyposyringe. Lord Whelsey watched with a smile.

"There, that should be enough to start the first experiments," Lord Galen informed. He pulled the glass vial filled with Angelica's blood and walked over to place the vial in the console input slot. The machine whirred to life when he typed in the parameters for the scans and experiment.

"How long do you think it'll take?"

"Science isn't an exact art form, so there's no way to be sure. I may need to do many more blood draws or even more invasive procedures. Once this first battery of experiments is done, I'll have some idea of where I stand, but right now, we're at the beginning. This could be a very long process, one that neither your granddaughter nor Levart will enjoy," Lord Galen warned.

"Time isn't on our side. I can't be sure that Matthew isn't already aware of what we're doing. If he can truly see the future, then he must already know. We must move with caution, but we can't give Emperor Solomon time to figure out what we're really up." Lord Whelsey couldn't block out the anxiety racing through his nerves, causing the hair on his neck to stand.

"Perhaps you could go pray for our success," Lord Galen mocked.

"Be careful of your blasphemy. I've tolerated the behavior in the past only because of your genius. This science is the power of God. We must unlock it and ensure it doesn't fall into the wrong hands. Matthew and his naivety will get us all killed if this power remains in his hands only. That boy doesn't have a pious bone in his body." Lord Whelsey intended to prove his worth and couldn't understand why God had shown such favor in Matthew.

"Well, I can speed the research up, but that would require more painful methods. Torture might be a better word in this sense rather than science. It might even kill Angelica, but it'll produce much faster results if time is truly against us." Lord Galen knew that Lord Whelsey would grant his permission if he believed the ends justified the means. His mind was already racing with the information considering all possibilities, reflected by his pensive thought that narrowed his eyes.

"Try to limit the harm to Angelica if possible. Remember, that's my granddaughter in there with that demon. The demon is fine to hurt, but we should protect Angelica where we can, and I will not tolerate her death under any circumstances. Levart is too important to our studies." Lord Whelsey patted Lord Galen on the shoulder to communicate his confidence.

"Understood, Lord Whelsey, and I'll follow your orders to a tee. Just remember that if things don't move along with the speed you'd like, you put these limits on the research." Lord Galen turned back to the console to begin activating deep tissue extraction. Two large mechanical arms jutted from the sides of the medical bed and moved over Angelica's body. Large needles sunk into her flesh to penetrate her bone and extract bone marrow.

The screen showed a steady report of new information from the deep scans of Angelica's blood. Data poured into one of the smaller windows on the screen showing information on the marrow extraction. Lord Galen was already working on running analysis programs. There was no reason to hover, and Lord Whelsey walked towards the door. The door whisked opened. He stood in the door with a thought crossing his mind and turned back to Lord Galen.

"Lord Galen don't contact me on the neural network or use my guards to pass me any messages. All this research stays between just the two of us from here on out. Not even my daughter can know or be allowed back into the lab for obvious reasons. We can't let anyone discover our plans until we're ready to make our move."

"Of course, Lord Whelsey, and you shouldn't expect any updates any time soon. I'm going to be down here working away for some time. If you want any updates, just come see me yourself. I don't have time to roam your compound searching for you like one of your servants." Lord Galen didn't even turn around to look at Lord Whelsey when he spoke. The information on the screen was the only thing that had the scientist's full attention.

The door to the lab whisked shut behind Lord Whelsey when he exited. Climbing the stairs, all he could think about was the new possibilities and his grandson's power. The Infinity Nexus was too great of an artifact to leave in the hands of a naïve boy like Matthew, and that was something

Lord Whelsey was certain of. No humanity needed his firm hand to guide them. The demons of the Cacophony of Discordance would never fear someone like his grandson. Fear lingered in the back of his mind echoing the demon's words.

Levart's words haunted Lord Whelsey, and he tried to resist the truths he heard. He didn't want to believe the Cacophony of Discordance was the living reality of hell. That wasn't what his God promised, and the bible didn't lie. Lord Whelsey intended to discover the truth one way or another, but he believed Levart would be proven to be a liar. The Cacophony of Discordance was just another race of aliens, and Lord Whelsey was certain that he'd prove it if he had enough time.

CHAPTER 17

Emperor Solomon's summons played throughout *Empyrean station,* drawing the people who weren't working to the Infinity Nexus. A vast throng of people clamored through the doors to gather inside to wait for Emperor Solomon's announcement. Nemesis stood next to Marcus, and they held hands with a smile at the people gathering before them. From the Infinity Nexus, Matthew stared at his people, waiting for them to gather before him.

Lord Whelsey glared across the auditorium at Lord Drumpf. The two men weren't even trying to hide their contempt for each other. Seeing the scowl, Helena nudged her father, and glared at him, trying to remind him to show respect before her son. See looked over to see Hephaestus standing near Freya, and from the looks on their faces, she guessed some romance had begun to develop. That alone was enough to make her smile, but seeing all the happy people in the sea of faces in the auditorium only elevated the mood.

The flow of people slowed, and Matthew looked through the audience. Lord Cornelius and Lord Hector were talking near the front about the new gene-seed army with Joshua, Celeris, and Kain. Even Commander Verdas had joined the group. In the front of the crowd, Lady Marimba looked up at Matthew with a reverent gaze. Despite all the smiles on the faces, Matthew could sense the trepidation being held back by his people. He stepped forward, waved to the people causing a rising cheer amongst the throng, and waited for the noise to dissipate before speaking.

"Thank you all for coming. I know you all have important work to do, but this is an important time for our people. Many of you rightfully fear that we could be attacked by any of the threats in this Great Maw we've survived so long in. I want you to know I've heard your fears and brought you all here to assuage those terrors. We've yet to adapt to the loss of the *Alcatraz* in the battle for this station, and some of you worry we'll never return to space. Let me dispel that fear now." Matthew pointed to the holographic image that was beginning to form above the crowd.

Light weaved together the image of the complete *Dawnbreaker* floating just beyond the *Empyrean station*. The massive battleforge floated there in all its pristine glory, sparkling in the light of Eos. Rows of turrets moved, demonstrating the sheer firepower the ship possessed, and in a synchronized showing, the guns fired all at once into the void. Energy weapons and kinetic cannons unleashed a salvo causing a silent reverence to wash across the crowd. Everyone was awed at the display they were witnessing, and then they heard the approaching thuds.

Filing into the auditorium, a stream of powerful armored troops drew the crowd's attention from the holographic display. The crimson metal was etched with gold, and the large suits were even more imposing than their original power armor suits. Thick metal bent around the shoulders added an extra layer of protection, and strong greaves protected the legs. The armor stood almost a foot taller than the previous models used on the *Alcatraz*. Every part of the armor had been reinforced with stronger yet lighter metal. The helmet was modeled as a skull with two glowing red eyes. Thousands of troops marched into the auditorium up the aisle towards the Infinity Nexus. They stopped, turned, and stood at attention, holding their new hard light rifles across their chests. Holographic light of Eos shimmered down from above, glistening off the armor of the formation of troopers. Whole auditorium fell deathly silent for a moment.

Awe emanated from the crowd, staring at the new troops in hushed whispers. People discussed where the soldiers came from were already spreading through the crowd like a fire. The line of troops locked their guns in synchronized motion, and the sound of the gun locking drew another round of silent reverence from the crowd. Matthew smiled, sensing the wonder of his people at what had been accomplished. Before any of the crowd broke free of the display of power, he began to speak again.

"Your Imperator, leader of the armies of the empire, and greatest warrior amongst us, Kain, is the father of this first genetic seed. These soldiers were born in the digital realm of neural space and created to be perfect on a genetic level. They will carry the flag of our new empire as they march across the Great Maw to drive their blades into the hearts of our enemies. Soon more genetic seed armies will be born to fill the fleets of ships, we'll build from our new home. The *Dawnbreaker* is, but the first of a great line of battleforge fleet that the greatest pilot of our age will lead. My sister, Celeris, please step forward and receive your honors." Matthew motioned to his sister.

Celeris marched towards the Infinity Nexus and kneeled to bow before Emperor Solomon. Her eyes glistened with the pride she fought to contain at this moment. Matthew looked down with a smile before continuing to address the assembly.

"I hereby name you Matriarch, Senator, and admiral of the Imperial fleet. Do you swear to serve the Empire and her people and to give your life if necessary to safeguard our security?" Matthew watched his sister look up at him. Her eyes were fixed, face was blank, yet pride trembled in her muscle, holding her poised upright with pride.

"For the Empire," Celeris proclaimed, and her words set a cascade of celebratory cheers and applause from the crowd. Nemesis wiped away the tears brimming in her eyes and smacked Marcus, who was softly chuckling. Standing up, Celeris returned to her place in the crowd and stood at attention. Matthew motioned for Joshua to come forth.

"My brother Joshua, come forth and be recognized. For whom else can claim more dedication than you? It was your hard work all your life that kept our old home in one piece. Your dedication to engineering and work on the bridge of the *Alcatraz* is part of the reason we're all alive today. It's my great honor to name you Patriarch, Senator, and Consul of *Empyrean station*. You shall be the last line of defense for our new home as you were the first line of defense on the old one." Matthew held off administering an oath and moved to summon the rest of his military commanders he intended to bestow positions upon.

"Lord Hephaestus, Cornelius, Hector, and Commander Verdas please come forth to be recognized," Matthew commanded.

Stepping away from the crowd, the men marched to knee alongside Joshua, and they looked up at Emperor Solomon. Matthew could see the honor they all felt, and he nodded to Nemesis as a silent thanks for preparing for this moment. Cheers were still echoing through the auditorium from the clan members of the men. The men just stared up at their Emperor. Matthew waited for the ruckus to quiet down before beginning to speak again.

"You've all served your clan and the *Alcatraz* well. Each of you has shown your courage, determination, and dedication to our people. There could be no future for our people here, and now without you, men gathered before me here, but you're not alone. We can't forget the sacrifice of the ladies of the *Alcatraz*. Lady Marimba and Freya, join your equals." Matthew motioned to the two ladies to join the group gathered in front of him.

Lady Freya and Marimba moved from the crowd to join the others before Emperor Solomon. Kneeling next to Hephaestus, Freya smiled at him and then looked up to Emperor Solomon. Lady Marimba signed the cross on her head and chest before kneeling to bow.

"By my authority as Emperor of humanity, I name you all to the position of Patriarch and Matriarch, and place each of you on the military branch of the senate. For all of you named so far shall be the arm of humanity that wields the shield and sword that protects our people. From each of you will be born a new genetic seed that will become a branch of our new empire. You will lead your armies across the Great Maw and bring ruin to our enemies and guarantee peace and prosperity for our people. Do you swear to serve the empire and the people and to give your life if necessary to safeguard our security?"

"For the empire!" The group all swore in unison. Cheers began to arise from the crowd, but Matthew waved his arm to silence the throng.

"There will be time for celebration soon, my people, but I can still sense fear amongst some of you. Fear that my leadership will just be another flavour of my father's tyranny. This kind of divisive thoughts must be dealt with before they can grow to become a malignant threat. Now that you all know that our military is strong enough to protect us, let me console your minds. Marcus, the former lord of the plebs, come forth and be recognized." Matthew gazed upon Marcus standing next to his sister, and he could sense his hesitation.

Marcus didn't want the power and authority being offered to him, and he glanced at his love to see her smile as she pushed him forward. Forced to take those first few steps, he found the next ones easier. The fears faded away with each step, and he marched to kneel and bow before

Emperor Solomon. Anxiety still echoed in his nerves, warning him about the responsibilities he was taking on, but the feel of Nemesis' smile focused on Marcus. He looked up at Emperor Solomon, prepared to embrace whatever was needed of him.

"Marcus, you're a rare breed of man, and none in our old home ever gave up power except you. While others lied, betrayed, and murdered to ensure their power grew beyond need or purpose, you surrendered yours because you believed the best should lead. All you desired was the best for your clan of plebs, and the moment you realized my sister, Nemesis, could do more, you surrendered your lordship to her without reservation. This is why none other can shoulder the great burden I'm placing on your shoulders. I hereby name you Lord Marcus, Senator of the people and speaker of the Senate. Rise and be recognized!" Matthew didn't try to stem this celebration because he could feel how many people loved the decision.

Almost everyone in the auditorium was clapping, cheering, and hollering their congratulations at Marcus. He was so overwhelmed by the ovation of the people he couldn't even stand up. Nemesis applause drew Marcus's attention, and seeing her thunderous applause, he began to rise. He walked over to stand next to Nemesis, and she wrapped her arms around him and kissed his cheek. The crowd only cheered louder. It took minutes for the crowd to quiet.

"The people will always come first under my rule, but we have much work to be done. Lord Whelsey, Lord Drumpf, Lord Galen, and Helena please come forward to be recognized." Matthew could see that neither Lord Drumpf nor Lord Whelsey appreciated being left until last. That didn't bother Helena, who was the first to kneel before her son. When all three were kneeling, Matthew looked out at the expectant crowd and spoke again.

"Helena, my mother and strongest person I've ever known. The hardships you endured under my father should give all people reason enough to admire and respect you, but to ensure that I hereby name you Lady Helena and the people's Senator. Lord Drumpf will also serve as a Senator of the people and act as chief of operations to ensure the work continues on time. For the good of our souls, I give title to Lord Whelsey as the head of the church and name him Senator of the people. Finally, to ensure our technological progress and for the good health of the people I name Lord Galen head of science and Senator of the people." Matthew knew all would see his reward but his mother as a sign of disdain, but he couldn't allow that trifle to concern him.

The crowd was cheering frantically, and the celebrations were already beginning. Nemesis looked at Matthew with a smile that told him she understood what he was trying to accomplish. The gathered lords and ladies saw the people united for the first time. Even the division of the clans seemed to fall away before the happiness of this moment. Matthew put on a brave expression of happiness, but he could see the looming threat growing closer to *Empyrean station*. He focused all his will on pushing down the strange mixture of terror and joy.

Above the image of the *Dawnbreaker* still loomed in the dancing of the lights produced by the holographic emitter. Matthew knew the other ships had already begun construction, but he still took the moment to admire the new ship. Soon the imperial fleet would expand to several of these ships, and if they all survived, a great armada was an inevitability. Kain could sense something bothering his brother, and he approached the Infinity Nexus. He tried not to look at his brother with sadness, but he could tell Matthew already sensed the emotion from the look on his face.

"I'm fine, brother," Matthew declared.

"We've come a long way. You need to celebrate this like everyone else even if you're trapped in there. My ship is beyond anything I ever could've imagined. That's because of you."

"Go now, Imperator, to the *Dawnbreaker* and wait there. We'll soon have visitors arriving, and they'll deserve a proper greeting. Don't worry about me because you'll soon have more problems to deal with." Matthew could sense the ship approaching the station, and he knew A'zyren was on it. The smile Matthew was sharing told Kain that this was something good.

"What do you see, brother?"

"Old friends on their way here, coming to our aid and in our hour of need. It seems Lord Void's plans are not quite finished with us all just yet. I would see A'zyren given a proper welcome because we will need her people to stand against the coming darkness." Matthew glared into the black void of the future that showed the end of everything. That was the one thing he wouldn't allow to come to pass.

CHAPTER 18

The void of the Great Maw stared from the viewscreen at Kain, scanning his eyes across the desolation for any sign of his brother's prediction. Officers in full power armor walked the bridge of the *Dawnbreaker,* working away on their tasks. The computers hummed, scanning space for any signs of life or movement. Kain leaned back into the captain's chair in his new power armor and reached for the drink sitting on his arm rest. He couldn't quiet the uneasy feeling growing in his stomach, and his eyes darted to his soldiers, his genetic children. He couldn't help the shiver running down his spine as he tried to repress the thought and banish it into the dark recesses of the back of his mind.

Kain still didn't feel comfortable around his new "children", and that only made the situation more nerve-racking. Soldiers would glance at Kain with wonder and fear, and that heightened his sense of unease. He hadn't even had time to learn any of their names assigned by Virgil, but there was some comforting in the fact they all did seem to possess their own personalities. The tactical computer on the arm of the captain's chair started beeping, pulling his attention out of his own racing thoughts. Turning to the computer, Kain studied the information and tapped the coordinates into the viewscreen, moving it to the area of space. He couldn't see anything in the sector of space.

Scanners showed the construction of the two new battleforges in their sweeps. The frames of the ships loomed next to the *Empyrean station.* Kain knew the ships would soon be ready, and Joshua and Celeris would take command. He couldn't wait until his brother and sister joined to serve with him in space again, and he only wished they were by his side now. He tried to keep his anxiety about his new crew hidden behind his expressionless face, but he could tell by the crew's looks that they sensed the unease.

Bright light of a surge of energy flashed in the void, and the massive worldship appeared in the distance. Soldiers moved quickly to take their stations, and the system showed the real-time battle readiness report on its screen. Kain couldn't help but smile, watching the crew of the *Dawnbreaker* bring the battleforge to combat readiness in under a minute. He leaned forward to glare at the massive ship on the screen, and sensors were already pouring data in. From the information he could see, the ship seemed in excellent shape, and he looked to the tactical station.

"All weapons at the ready, lock in targets, and helm bring us in closer," Kain commanded, leaning forward to study the ship on the viewscreen.

The soldiers moved to fulfill the orders. Tactical computer reported hundreds of weapons locks in various parts of the world ship. Kain was ready for a fight but waited to see if the ship would hail him. So far, Matthew's predications had all been right, and Kain couldn't see a reason to start doubting now. He leaned back into his chair and waited.

"Imperator, we have an incoming hail from the unknown ship," the coms officer reported.

"Put it on screen, son. Let's see if our Emperor was right." Kain watched the viewscreen shift, and the image of A'zyren appeared on the screen. Image flickered on the viewscreen for a second.

"Is that you, Kain?" A'zyren stood on the screen, looking at the bridge of the Dawnbreaker. Many soldiers couldn't help but stare at the beautiful woman on the screen.

"What brings you back to *Empyrean station*?" Kain's hand hovered over the fire control button, ready to give the order to attack if A'zyren's answers didn't impress him. The tactical computer reported the enemy ship was powering down its weapon systems, but Kain wouldn't trust the situation until A'zyren explained herself.

"I've deactivated my weapons and lowered my shields to show good faith. My tribe and I've come on the request of Lord Void, who sees a great battle coming that will be centered here. We're not going to let you stand alone against the Great Maw. The star must burn!" A'zyren glared at Kain, waiting to see his next move.

Kain was glad his brother had been right and with the press of a few buttons, order his crew to stand down. He didn't power down the weapons just yet in case this was some kind of ambush. Tapping a few more buttons, he sent the orders to prepare a squadron of fighter craft for launch. Matthew would want to speak to A'zyren himself, and Kain intended to provide a personal escort. He looked to the screen with a blank expression.

"Emperor Solomon the 1st of Imperium of Humanity requests your immediate audience on *Empyrean station*. Bring only an honor guard. I'll be providing your escort myself." Kain expected the orders to ruffle A'zyren a bit, but the smile on her face made it seem like she didn't mind. A series of beeps confirmed the orders' acceptance, and A'zyren's ship was already changing course.

"I'll rendezvous with you on my shuttle at your coordinates. Until I return to my worldship, I expect you'll take good care of the *Sesh'yna.*" A'zyren cut communications.

Pushing out of the captain's chair, Kain walked from the bridge towards the lift and activated it to descend to the hang bay. The lift descended with no noise, and that made Kain uneasy. He still wasn't used to a function ship either and tried to remind himself of that. When the lift doors retracted, he lingered there for a moment, lost in thought, before he headed towards his fighter craft. Team prepping the ship still working on it turned hearing the clang of his footsteps approaching.

"She looks good," Kain stated and drew the salutes of the hanger crew. He waved them off and began climbing into the ship to start up the launch sequence. Engines roared to life, and the computer systems flickered to life. He reviewed the information, and once the pre-flight check was complete, he began strapping himself in.

The cockpit hissed before it began to shut and locked into place. Pressure seals kicked in, and the power armor reported the change in the atmospherics around Kain. On the screen, the other fighters began to check that their pre-flight was complete and ready for launch. Once the last fighter checked in, Kain activated the repulsor lifts to cause his craft to hover off the deck plate, gradually pushing the throttle forward.

Engines glared with power thrusting the ship forward through the hanger bay shields. The sleek, tight V-shaped ship shot into the void of the Great Maw. Kain glanced over his shoulder to see his fighter squadron launching on his six. Sensors showed that a shuttle was just leaving the hanger of the *Sesh'yna*, and he adjusted his course, swinging the craft back towards the *Dawnbreaker*. He watched his ship race past on his way to meet up with A'zyren.

"All right, team. This should be a walk in the park. Stick to my six," Kain ordered.

The *Sesh'yna* loomed on the horizon as Kain, and his team approached the shuttle rendezvous point. Massive cannons on the worldship loomed in the small viewscreen of his fighter and grew larger with each second. A'zyren's shuttle could be seen moving through the void, and Kain targeted the ship and activated the scanners. From the data pouring in, Kain couldn't detect any significant weapons systems, and they weren't powered up. He activated coms to the shuttle.

"This is Imperator Kain of the Empire of Humanity demanding you join my formation at these coordinates and adjust your speed and heading to match this course." Kain uploaded the information to the shuttle pilot and watched the screen to see the confirmation. He was pulling his fighter and squadron into formation when the coms activated, receiving a message.

"Wow, I must be special to get this kind of welcome," A'zyren joked.

"I'm just following Emperor Solomon's orders. Don't go getting a big ego about it." Kain locked in the coordinates and headed towards *Empyrean station*.

"Imperator sounds all special, Kain. It seems your brother still favors you above all others." A'zyren's voice echoed through the coms.

"Cut the chatter shuttle craft. Enemies could be listening." Kain ordered and then cut his coms off with the press of a few buttons.

Silence allowed Kain to think about the situation. He studied the scans of the *Sesh'yna* worldship and had to admit that it was far more formidable than the first one the Alcatraz had run into. The *Sesh'yna* showed no sign of wear and tear, and the hull's metal was in near-perfect condition despite its salvaged patchwork nature. Reading from the drive core showed no instability either. Kain had to admit that the *Sesh'yna* was in fine fighting condition and would be a welcome addition in any battle. He just hoped A'zyren's people were as fierce as she was.

On approaching the *Empyrean station*, Kain inputted his Imperator overrides to Virgil, bypassing the normal landing procedures. The docking bay gates began to retract. He pulled back on the throttle, and the fighter slowed on approach towards the station. Glancing backwards, he saw the shuttle following behind, escorted by his fighter squadron on all sides. Formation continued towards *Empyrean station*, soaring through the opening docking bays where they first landed, but today it was busy with workers assembling fighter craft. Kain activated the automated landing procedures by clicking a few buttons, and the formation began their final descent. A soft thud echoed the landing of the vector fighter craft, and the cockpit hissed once more, cracking open to allow Kain to climb out and descend to the deck.

A'zyren brought the shuttle to a smooth and soft landing. She shut the shuttle down with a few flicks and began lowering the landing ramp. She walked off the ship to see the crew of humans react to her natural black armor. The gasps and whispers erupted at the sight. Magnus' warning about how the humans would react to her armor echoed in A'zyren's mind, but she knew it was too late now to do anything. She walked towards Kain.

"That armor and your worldship seem familiar for some reason," Kain glared.

"Get over it already. We don't have time to rehash the past when the future is hurtling towards us like a bullet, ready to send us all to oblivion. I've important information for your Emperor." A'zyren waved a data rod in her hand. She pulled the rod back when Kain tried to grab it.

"I'm the Imperator, and I serve the will of Emperor Solomon. Anything meant for him can be shared with me." Kain tried to snatch the rod again, but A'zyren slipped it back inside her armor.

"That might all be true, but I'm under specific diplomatic protocols here. Lord De'Vayne requested I give this message to Emperor Solomon only. Sorry, Kain, but the Great Maw still doesn't give a fuck about you." A'zyren started walking to the Infinity Nexus, leaving Kain and his soldiers behind. She knew the way and didn't need any more guidance.

"Things need to change in the Great Maw, and they're going to," Kain declared after he caught up to A'zyren.

"Everything takes time, yet time waits for no one. You've got no clue the sacrifice I've made to be here today, Kain, so you should stop ordering me around like one of your friendly humans. I'm W'Hyish S'yevel first, and I serve death's demand for life before anything else. I'm not here for your Emperor, empire, or people. I'm here because death demands the star live to create new life. The great balance requires it!" A'zyren strode forward towards the Infinity Nexus, leaving Kain behind and shaking his head at the situation.

Kain understood now why Nemesis and A'zyren had gravitated to each other. They were so determined to do things the way they wanted. It was infuriating, but Kain knew sometimes it worked out. He tried to relax by reminding himself that Matthew had seen the necessity of A'zyren in the future. It wasn't Kain's place to question time or destiny. Soldiers did their duty.

The group walked into the Infinity Nexus, and Matthew stared out from the chamber at the group. He'd been expecting them and waiting with utter patience for this moment to arrive. A'zyren approached the Infinity Nexus pulling the rod from her armor. She handed the rod to Virgil when the A.I. appeared from the weave of light next to the Infinity Nexus. A'zyren stood before Emperor Matthew Solomon the first with her arms crossed locking eyes on his.

"Good to see you again, Matthew, and I can tell you've been expecting me. I bring word from Lord De'Vayne on that rod I gave Virgil. It's not the message I'd hope to deliver. You're not going to like it, but De'Vayne is a hard alien to deal with." A'zyren turned to watch the image of Lord De'Vayne appear in the weave of light of the holographic emitters.

The large human-looking man wore a tight grey, black, and silver body suit that seemed to be form-fitting. His azure eyes glimmered in the image. Lord De'Vayne was a towering man just over seven feet from his natural stature, yet his body was much thinner than most. He appeared to have a natural grace about him from his thin athletic body. Long hair trailed into multiple intricate braids trailing behind his back, and even his bangs were braided. The two bangs trailed the hairline at the base of his forehead, curved to the side, and hung down to his chest. There was an elegance that echoed a melodic cadence to his speech.

"Greeting to you Imperium of Humanity, I'm the magnificent Lord De'Vayne, a living God amongst the Great Maw. My retainer Lord Genji speaks highly of your people and has made me aware of the new star around *Empyrean station*. A'zyren of the W'Hyish S'yevel has requested the assistance of the De'Vayne on your behalf, and Lord Genji seems adamant about it. I've yet to make up my mind about such a venture, but a personal request may move me. I leave it up to you to decide how far you'll go to prostrate yourself before my magnificent splendor to acquire my aid. My intrigue about your people and this new star will grow as I wait for your response." Lord De'Vayne's image vanished as the recording ended.

"What an asshole," Kain declared.

"He's every right to be an asshole. De'Vayne is the only known survivor of the last era and alone remembers the stars before the Great Stellar War. When you've survived that long you don't owe anyone anything. Matthew, I'd suggest you send an emissary immediately. Lord Void believes we're going to need the help of the De'Vayne to win the coming battle." A'zyren wasn't sure how either Kain or Matthew would respond. Matthew seemed to be considering the situation from the pensive look on his face, but Kain was furious.

"It was the W'Hyish S'yevel that attacked the *Alcatraz*, and now they're coming to attack *Empyrean station*. For all we know this is exactly what you and Magnus planned all along." Kain didn't hold back his feelings one bit coming face-to-face with A'zyren.

"Come on, Kain, you're smarter than this, that makes no sense. We nearly got killed on that outpost and during the battle for *Empyrean station* just to get Matthew to the Infinity Nexus. My people don't answer just to me; the many tribes are numerous beyond counting. They survive by salvaging, raiding, and taking what they need to live. It's all we've known since the light was extinguished. A thousand generations born to nothing but darkness and despair, and they're now coming for this station and that star. They see this place as a threat to what they understand and know how to survive through, and the Reverie will use their fear and hatred against us. This place threatens the very existence of the Cacophony of Discordance."

"The same race that Magnus belongs to," Kain interjected.

"Yes, Magnus is a Reverie, but pay attention to every move he's made. Did he lie to you both? Absolutely! Hell, I wouldn't even claim to know what he's really planning with all this, but I'm not a fool. Everything I've seen Magnus do in the years I traveled with him was to restore the light. I don't see him changing course now. He sacrificed more than any of us can contemplate." A'zyren knew she needed to convince Kain more than Matthew of the realities of the situation.

"A'zyren doesn't lie. Magnus has a part to play in all this. The question now is how do we best move forward?" Matthew's question drew agreement in the form of a nod from Kain. Frustration boiled over, causing A'zyren to explode.

"We don't have time to argue like this. Every second we waste gives our enemies time to gather. Lord De'Vayne merely wants a symbolic gesture that makes him feel important again. I'd suggest sending the Imperator. He claims he's your emissary; if so, he's the only one Lord De'Vayne would see as an acceptable substitute for you, Emperor. I suspect De'Vayne will be pissed you're not going yourself, Matthew, but he'll be intrigued by your situation. That's why I didn't tell him about it. What harm could be done by appealing to De'Vayne's pride if it acquires his aid?"

"Well, there's only one ship defending *Empyrean station* right now," Kain pointed out.

"The *Sesh'yna* is more than capable of providing defense. Right now, the W'Hyish S'yevel tribes will be gathering to discuss my betrayal and their plans to attack. I've bought us some time, and Magnus has gone to try to get more help. Besides, from my scans, those two other ships will be done in a few days, and it's not like the *Empyrean station* is defenseless even on its own." A'zyren wondered what the reluctance was to her plan, and she looked confusedly at the two men.

"Your plan has merit, but how can we be certain of your allegiance? My brother is merely being cautious. Perhaps there is an easier solution. Swear allegiance to the Empire of Humanity," Matthew declared.

"I've already betrayed my own people to come here. What oath could you possibly need?" A'zyren couldn't contain her frustration.

"A simple oath that from here on out, you serve the needs of the empire and will sacrifice your life if necessary. Don't think I don't offer anything in return." Matthew knew he needed to bait A'zyren to join the empire.

"What're you offering?" A'zyren looked at Matthew with narrowed eyes, trying to assess the situation. She wasn't big on the idea of swearing an oath.

"Well, once we've survived the battle, the entire verse will be opened up to us. With the power of the star combined with the technology of *Empyrean station,* I intend to rebuild the planets. I'm willing to offer you all the territory your people could ever need to grow and survive and if you agree to govern them on behalf of the empire. I'll even show mercy for any of your people who surrender at the battle's end. Once we start constructing the new stars and their planets, you and your people will be given a solar system. If death demands life, then life I shall offer." Matthew knew already A'zyren was going to take the deal because it echoed in the fabric of time itself.

Magnus had been planning this all along, and A'zyren realized it now. A planet for the tribes and her people wouldn't just bring back hope but a whole new way to live. It was more than she would have ever dared to ask for. Yet, she knew she had to keep her cool. She paced back and forth, contemplating the situation before stopping, kneeling, and bowing with her teeth gritted. She hated kneeling before anyone, but this was for her people.

"I swear to serve your empire and sacrifice whatever is necessary for the great balance between life and death. That's all I can swear to at this moment." A'zyren wouldn't give her word unless she knew it could be kept.

"Rise, A'zyren, and know that I thank you for this. Time tells me you will stay true to your words. Now my brother, go forth with your ship and meet this Lord De'Vayne. See if you can't convince him to join our cause." Matthew could already sense the balance shifting in his favor.

"As you command," Kain replied before turning to leave.

A'zyren stood up, nodded her head slightly in respect to Emperor Solomon, and followed Kain out of the Infinity Nexus. She didn't want to say anything because she could sense how much had changed. These once-scared humans were now growing bold. It was a sight to behold, and her mind turned to her friend Nemesis. She believed it was time for a reunion.

CHAPTER 19

T he *Insidious Seduction* crept through the Spindleweb Nebula. Arachne vessels crept through the nebula shadowing the Reverie vessel. Magnetic fields converged with gravitational distortions emanating from the large asteroids and rogue planets, binding them in a web of power. All the Arachne vessels took up position to watch the Insidious Seduction when it entered orbit around the largest rogue planet. Fighters launched to swarm around the ship, and several broke away to escort the shuttle flying towards the surface.

There was no atmosphere around the rogue planet, and the shuttle slipped lower toward the main settlement. Gliding into the docking area, the shuttle rested on the platform. Lilith and Asmodeus descended the ramp to see the Arachne troops awaiting their arrival. The large Arachne stood imposing on the platform. Large, powerful spindle legs held their massive torsos five feet above the ground, and thin hairs bristled off their bodies. Massive mandibles curved away from the maw of thin razor teeth just behind them. They all stood over ten feet tall, and their multiple limbs each held long staffs that ended in sharp spear points.

Atrax was the largest of the Arachne and was almost invisible amongst the backdrop of the black void and the lifeless grey rocks littering the horizon. Lilith recognized him by his dark black and grey colors. She strode towards the Arachne with Asmodeus following behind. Arachne soldiers escorted Atrax, breaking off to surround the pair of Reverie when they met on the docking platform. Atrax leaned over to look at Lilith with all eight of his eyes focusing on her.

"It's been a long time since you last visited the weave of the Spindleweb Nebula. Perhaps you'd care to explain what brings the Reverie to this part of the Great Maw?" Atrax slammed his spear against the ground demanding answers.

"I've come to visit your mother, of course," Lilith explained.

"My mother laments that she hasn't seen you in such a long time. She's even prepared a fresh meal from her latest brood to pay proper homage to you." Several of Atrax's eyes shifted, glancing towards the Arachne soldiers gathering around Asmodeus. He crackled with energy, glaring at the Arachne closed in around him, only stopping under the order of their leader. He didn't look at any of them, but his energy drove the creatures to back away. Atrax motioned with his arms for the other Arachne to back off from the Reverie.

Lilith and Atrax walked towards the corridor at the end of the docking platform, but Asmodeus stayed still, glaring at the Arachne soldiers. He glared at the creatures and released a blast of energy at the nearest one. Black energy leaped from the Arachne, screeching in pain, bringing the massive creature to their knees. Swirling around Asmodeus, the energy funneled into the Tenno, and he strode forward with a smile leaving the Arachne screeching in agony. Atrax didn't bother to look back, hearing the screeches of pain. He led Lilith down the corridor, and multifaceted eyes started at the two from the shadows along the wall. The soft scraping of the mandibles across the rocky surface echoed through the caverns.

"The children of Arachne grow uneasy in your presence Tenno and worry the return of the Reverie is a harbinger of destruction. They worry that the impending destruction is an omen of their own inevitable demise." Atrax screeched to silence the Arachne, and the corridor fell quiet.

Shadows retreated in the soft glow of the crystals in the central chamber. Thousands of caves opened into the chamber, and rocks spanned the chasm. Webs of translucent silk billowed with the gusts of wind sweeping through the caves. The howl echoed through the cave, gusting down in the lowest depths. Atrax guided his guest through the maze of stone bridges lower into Arachne's hive.

Heat rose up from the lowest reaches, and steam vents hissed with sudden bursts of explosive force. The air grew damper with the descent towards the great hive of Arachne. Lilith watched the Arachne scattering across the walls as the group approached. The cave descended sharply towards a giant cave at the bottom of the crevice. The chattering of untold scores of Arachne echoed up from the darkness of the cave.

The Reverie glowed with power in the darkness. Dark green energy mixed with red highlights sparked off Lilith, and Asmodeus's energy merged with the darkness crackling in unison. Eggs expanded and collapsed almost like breathing in the hallways, and several of the Arachne attended to the brood. Their eyes fell on the group when they passed by, but the work continued. The cave receded backward before opening into the large hatchery. Thousands of eggs adorned the floors, walls, and ceiling. Atrax walked towards the chamber's center, bowed down, and looked up.

On the ceiling, the massive body of the Queen Arachne clung to the surface, shriveled onto itself, and eight eyes opened to scour the chamber. Spindle legs extended from the massive body blurred by the cave's darkness. Slow and steady, Arachne moved from her place of rest to descend to the floor. Her massive body took up the entire center of the hatchery. The bloated circular abdomen expanded, legs unfurled, and she revealed her true size. She towered above her child at a hundred times his size. Bowing low, she glared her eight eyes at Atrax, and the screech of her mandibles caused all of her children to scurry away for safety. Only Atrax remained unmoved.

"I see you've brought my guests, Atrax. I've prepared such a feast for you. It's been too long since I looked upon the countenance of the beautiful Lilith." Arachne lunged to snatch one of her children with her fangs and crunched away, devouring the meal.

"Mother, Tenno Lilith wishes to beseech upon you for the knowledge of the Great Maw. She claims to be in search of Lucifer." Atrax stood up, stepped back, and allowed Lilith to approach.

"It's good to see you again, Arachne. I see the long years of my absence have been fruitful for your brood. Once long ago, when I found you in the Great Maw, you were almost starving, and look at all these delicious meals scurrying around now." Lilith extended her hand above her head toward Arachne and let her bejeweled fingers dangle in front of the Queen. Arachne lowered herself, retracted her fangs, and brought her trembling black lips to kiss Lilith's hand.

"I've prepared a great sacrifice for you, my mistress, and your arrival is perfect. A fresh brood of young Arachne has just hatched, and I present them to you in supplication for the gifts you can offer. It's been too long since you've graced me with your power, my dread queen. For I've grown old and tired these long millennia in the Great Maw, and your arrival is fortuitous as I feel my death approaching." Arachne's brood hissed and screeched in agony.

"Perhaps it's fate then, my dear. For I've not abandoned you. I'll use my power to extend your life, but you must aid the Cacophony of Discordance first," Lilith offered.

"What do you seek?" Arachne's eye eights fell upon both Lilith and Asmodeus.

"I've come in search of the rogue Reverie, who goes by the name Lord Magnus Void. This traitor must be brought to answer before the Cacophony of Discordance, and it's a matter of some haste." Tenno Asmodeus pushed past Lilith to stand face-to-face with Arachne.

"Forgive the impudence of this Tenno. I'd punish him myself if he were under my authority. Please assist us in locating Lucifer as well, because we will need our Minister of Injustice to try the traitor Asmodeus seeks." Lilith stepped back in front.

Arachne reached up with her arms to touch the giant strands of web that converged into the room. Her eyes closed, and she focused on sensing the Great Maw's movements through the webs' vibrations. Images formed in her mind showing her the path Lord Magnus Void had traveled since leaving *Empyrean station.*

"My webs vibrate with your desire Tenno Asmodeus. Lord Magnus Void is heading back to Draconis, the home of the Serpentine. I suspect he's seeking allies against the Cacophony because his movements in the Great Maw have been erratic as of late." Arachne hadn't even finished speaking before Tenno Asmodeus turned to walk away. That was all the information he needed.

"My ship will be arriving soon. I'll go and capture this rogue Lord Void on my own from here on out." Tenno Asmodeus didn't even look back when he was speaking. He just continued forward, leaving Lilith and Arachne behind.

Arachne was still searching the weave of webs through the great maw for the presence of Lucifer. All that was left were the faint vibrations of Lucifer's last presence. Arachne focused on the location of the vibration.

See could sense the presence of the W'Hyish S'yevel tribes vibrating along with Lucifer's presence. She let go of the webs and lowered herself to come face to face with Lilith.

"I fear I've failed you, my mistress. There is no presence of Lucifer in the Great Maw that I can detect. There's only the lingering vibration of his last presence when he met with the W'Hyish S'yevel tribes. Though I must admit, my webs don't penetrate their metal hives, only catch them." Arachne lowered her head, awaiting the fury of Lilith with a tremble.

Energy swirled around Lilith's feet. Screeches of pain echoed through the hatchery as life force was drawn from the brood. Lifeless husks of the Arachne fell to the ground. The energy swirled around Lilith, increasing in speed. Bodies continued to rain down throughout the hatchery, and Arachne closed her eyes, waiting to be destroyed. Instead, she felt a surge of energy when Lilith directed the life force she'd drained from the children into Arachne. Placing one hand upon her head, Lilith looked down with almost an empathetic look crackling in her eyes.

"You've done well so far. I shall head to meet with the W'Hyish S'yevel tribes to find out more about Lucifer. Keep attention on your webs for Lucifer." Lilith turned to walk away but was halted by Arachne's voice.

"Thank you, mistress! Your benevolence is beyond compare, and I can feel my children's life flowing within me to prolong my life." Arachne bowed low to the Tenno.

"Remember Queen Arachne that I can take back my gift with the same speed I offered it. I expect something more in return as well. I'm sure you're aware of the return of light?"

"Yes, of course, mistress. It spreads through the Great Maw, threatening to burn my webs away in the fury of flames of its heat. What would you have me do?" Arachne leaned forward with her eight eyes focused on Lilith.

"My people are amassing a great armada, but as long as the light is a threat, we can't strike. I'd like you to prepare your children and ships for war. Once I've summoned the W'Hyish S'yevel to join the battle, I'll transmit the time of the attack. Together with the tribes and your legion of children, we'll extinguish the light once and for all. We'll cleanse the Great Maw of these humans and feast upon their flesh with your brood."

"As you command, so shall it be done!" Arachne reached up to send the orders to her children beyond the hatchery by plucking at the web strings with her clawed limbs. Screeches of the Arachne's brood echoed down the caves into the hatchery. Lilith sighed in delight hearing the brood's cadence of fear and anger. She walked through the caves away from the hatchery.

The brood rushed up along the crevice's walls emerging from every cave. Lilith could see the *Insidious Seduction* orbiting the rogue planet high above. Long sleek Arachne ships moved across the sky with their long spindle arms locked forward into a sharp point. Dozens of the massive ships were now moving towards the hive world. With the Arachne mobilizing for war, Lilith turned her thoughts to the W'Hyish S'yevel tribes.

Questions haunted Lilith on her ascent back toward her shuttle. Lucifer never showed any interest in the tribes, yet they were the last place Arachne saw him. Lilith poured through her memories of Lucifer, and nothing showed why he would have sought out the W'Hyish S'yevel. The tribes were nothing more than a primitive tribe of scavengers picking at the dead to survive, and Lilith couldn't comprehend why Lucifer would choose them to visit. Even these Arachne were far beneath the glory of the Cacophony of Discordance. One way or another, Lilith would find out the truth, even if she had to kill them all for it.

CHAPTER 20

Walls vibrated with the hum of the F.T.L. engine. The antique weapons and trophies that Gabriel had just hung rattled against the creaking metal wall. Nothing about the *Furious* was the same as the *Alcatraz* he realized, and it would take some time for him to adjust. The cabin door whisked open, forcing Gabriel to turn to see his new first officer standing there with a report in hand. Myrmidon approached to hand the data pad over to his new captain.

"We're approaching Box Nebula now, sir." Image of the strange area of space flashed on on the screen in front of Gabriel showing the strange hazy space. Gas swirled into a strange cubic space caught under the strange riptide of the warp of space-time in this section of the space. Beyond the Box Nebula the sinuous abyss of the Briar Patch of black holes devoured space-time steadily creating the rip tide of gravity pulling at the *Furious* rumbling through its hull.

"Excellent. Get us everything prepared. I'll join you in a moment." Gabriel watched his first officer leave before he reached into the bag to pull a book out. He ran his fingers over the title of the book that had been hand stitched by Matthew, and Gabriel wiped a tear away before picking it up from the stand next to the bed. Swoosh of armor plating retracted before the book being tucked inside for safe keeping turning back towards the bridge doors.

Gabriel headed onto the bridge to see his new crew hard at work and sat in the captain's chair. The tactical computer setup wasn't like the *Alcatraz* and lacked the sophisticated. He glanced over the readouts to see that the ship was only a minute from the F.T.L. exit point. Myrmidon was already preparing the ship for exiting, working at the pilot station. The timer began a countdown on the screen, and Gabriel noticed the straps on the chair.

"Prepare for exiting of F.T.L.," Myrmidon announced. Everyone in the crew began fastening themselves into their chairs. When Myrmidon pulled back the F.T.L. throttle, the entire ship jolted with force. Gabriel was hurled from the captain's chair across the room, and he rolled across the metal deck, causing sparks to leap from his armor when it struck. When the ship settled down, everyone looked at Gabriel and watched him stand back up.

There was still a hum from the engines resonating through the hull, and Gabriel could feel it lying face down on the floor. He pushed off the deck plating, trying to regain his composure. Everyone looked away when he glanced around at the crewmembers. Beeping echoed in the bridge, drawing his attention. He moved back to sit down, looked at the tactical computer, and saw the incoming message from Pandora's Box. Myrmidon turned to look at his captain.

"We shouldn't keep them waiting. Pandora's not a patient woman." Myrmidon waited to see what his new captain wanted to do.

"Activate the coms systems, and let's see what this Pandora has to say." Gabriel stared ahead at the viewscreen, watching it crackle with static. The image began to take shape with the Myrmidon securing the transmission connection.

Static on the screen coalesced into the form of a woman. The image began to clear, revealing the long blue hair that flowed down the woman's neck and overflowed across her shoulders. Blue locks in a tangled, unkempt mess spiked out in random directions. Long canines could be seen underneath the smooth olive skin. Her taught muscles quivered under flesh, tightening with her narrowing eyebrows and her lips curling into a scowl. Strange leather-like armor covered her torso in a tight corset dipping into the tight fabric running down her legs. A holster clung to one of her thighs, and a rapier-like energy blade on the other. Strange tribal-like tattoos were etched into the skin that was showing on her arms, and legs, and only her chest seemed free of any marking. Gabriel was sure this woman was of mixed ancestry from her look. Pandora appeared to be half Tigran and half human.

"Myrmidon, who is this human sitting in the captain's chair of my vessel?" Pandora ignored Gabriel to glare at Myrmidon. Her fingers rapped on her knuckles in rapid succession.

"Queen, under the pirate's code, Gabriel seized the *Furious* from me with superior force and ability. I was left with no choice but to surrender the vessel to him. As you can see, he chose to come here and meet you in person rather than ignore your laws." Myrmidon reminded Pandora of her own laws trying to stay the wrath he could see behind the purple swirling vortex of color in her eyes. He kept his head lowered in deference hoping Pandora would be intrigued rather than vindictive.

Pandora's eyes narrowed, falling upon Gabriel, yellow cat-like pupils dilated, and she sized him up. Her eyes tracked up the armor taking in all the details. When their eyes met, the two were locked into a silent contest of willpower. Gabriel refused to cower like the rest of his crew, no matter who this woman was, and he stood there defiantly. Pandora couldn't help but smile in response.

"You seem to be a bold one, human. I could use more people like you. What is your name?"

"Gabriel Soloman, former captain of the *Alcatraz*, and currently in control of this ship. My new first officer Myrmidon suggested I come pay homage to you. I'll admit that with a name like Pandora you piqued my curiosity. So, I'm here to meet you. Now the sensors show you have a powerful shield around your territory blocking our entry. Perhaps you'd consider lowering it to allow us entry unless you're terrified of a single ship that's barely functional," Gabriel taunted with a grin.

Sensors showed several ships powering up inside the shield. Pandora chuckled at the vain attempt to taunt her. Gabriel seemed unfazed and tapped at the tactical station to power up weapons. Energy surged, vibrating the power conduits, and they thumped at the walls. Myrmidon's hand hovered over the throttle. The tactical computer showed the shields at one hundred percent.

"Are you really prepared to die?" Pandora glared through the viewscreen. Sensors showed the ships moving towards the *Furious*.

"I promise I won't be dying alone. Those are some fast ships, but not very strong. Sure, I'm out numbered, but I promise I'll take some of your ships with me if you press the point, Pandora." Gabriel held his ground with his hand hovering over the fire button on his tactical computer.

"Perhaps I mistook your courage for insanity, but you've definitely piqued my interest now. Myrmidon, bring this human to my palace. We'll see how fair his courage goes." She pressed a few buttons, and sensos detected a hole opening in the shield open a hole in the shield. Pandoran vessels slowed their approach, powering down their weapons, but continued towards the *Furious.*

Pandora cut the transmission, and the viewscreen went black for a second. The ship hummed and vibrated with the engine's thrust when Myrmidon pushed the throttle forward. Sensors showed the *Furious* passing through the shield. Image of Pandora's box and the ships returned to the viewscreen. Gabriel watched the ships move around the *Furious* to escort, but he kept the weapons and shields charged and ready just in case this was an ambush.

On the viewscreen, thousands of asteroids had been chained together using the wreckage of hundreds of starships. The larger asteroids glowed with the mining work being done. Several large shipyards housed the largest ships in Pandora's Box. The ships appeared to be in a good state from what the sensors assessed. In the center of the asteroids was the large frame of what looked like the *Alcatraz.* Gabriel scanned the ship for a registry, but there wasn't one.

"I thought the Alcatraz was a fucking wreck." Gabriel shook his head.

"That's why we were salvaging your ship. Pandora ordered us to find any parts to keep that wreckage functional because everything in Pandora's Box is powered by it. It was an Ancient prison ship much like yours. Not sure how much longer it'll last." Myrmidon entered the landing information into the computer while he explained.

Sensors showed millions of biological life signs across the asteroid colony. Most of the signs were coming from the wreckage on the viewscreen. Large turrets moved to aim the *Furious,* tracking along its flight path. Sensors blared warnings of weapons locks on the ship, but Gabriel just shut them down. He knew if Pandora wanted a fight, she would never let him past the shield.

The ship entered the docking bay of the wreckage, and various all-around species worked away. Tigran's with energy whips stood to watch over their slaves laboring away. Some of the guards were beating a bunch of defiant slaves in the middle of the docking bay. The viewscreen showed Gabriel that most humans were slaves here to their alien overlords. Myrmidon brought the ship to land, causing it to shake when the landing struts touched down.

Gabriel pushed out of the chair, heading towards the ship's cargo bay. The sounds of the crew trying to keep up echoed behind in the corridor of the ship. He activated the landing ramp and stood there, watching it lower momentarily. Pressure seals hissed, venting steam and creating a haze that blurred everything. Myrmidon and the crew joined their captain. Each of them grabbed their weapons.

"Don't trust anyone here, captain," Myrmidon warned.

"What about your pirate Queen?" Gabriel took a big whiff of the fresh air rushing into the cargo bay. The mixture of pollution and low-quality oxygen reminded him of home.

"Especially Pandora," Myrmidon cocked his pistol before sliding it into a holster.

Gabriel walked down the ramp to see the aliens staring at him. He paid them no mind following behind Myrmidon as he walked by. The entire inside of the cargo area of the wreckage had been hollowed out. Smaller ships dotted the cityscape with sparks shooting from welding torches operated by the slaves forced to repair the ships. Gabriel looked around feeling the rush of homesickness coming over him. He pushed the feeling back deep down, but not before Myrmidon noticed something was up. He glanced back at Gabriel with a raised eyebrow before slowing his walk to march alongside.

"Is there something troubling you?" Myrmidon's question brought Gabriel out of his nostalgia. He shook his head to answer the question.

"I was just thinking how much my daughter, Nemesis, would love this place. This is her kind of party." Gabriel walked by a ring of aliens, watching a fight. Tigeran in the ring showed no mercy to his human foe, and blood stained the deck plate. Bones crunched with rapid blows.

"Try to ignore it," Myrmidon warned. He tugged at Gabriel to get him to follow. They walked away before the Tigeran tore the slave's throat out to the roar of the crowd. The crowd cleared the way for Myrmidon, Gabriel, and his crew, but none of the eyes strayed from the group.

There was a certain brutality to this place that Gabriel could respect, he thought, and maybe even find a new home here. Everyone knew their places from what he could see. He looked forward to learning Pandora's secret to producing such compliance from her people. Approaching the first palace, he smelled the distinct fragrance of death wafting through the air. In front of the gate, he saw hundreds of bodies hanging from the wall. Some of the bodies were impaled on large metal spikes, and others were covered in lashes from energy whips. There was only one thing similar on each of the bodies. Their faces were all contorted in the final moments of their torment for all to see.

"Well. I think I know how Pandora keeps her people in line," Gabriel muttered softly.

"Fear keeps everyone in line because we've all tasted Pandora's cruelty at some point. No one escapes her claws. It doesn't matter who you are because if you break Pandora's laws, you'll end up here as an example to all others." Myrmidon approached the first gate that led to the palace and placed his hand on the scanner. He inputted his code with a few button presses, and the gate began to retract. A long staircase extended up to where the bridge level of the ship would have been originally.

"Don't you think you now might be a good time to tell me what those laws are?" Gabriel glanced to Myrmidon sighing softly with a shako of his head.

"There is only one law Pandora values. Rule of Chaos. Might makes right, whatever you can take belongs to you, and everything belongs to Pandora including you."

"That's not a law that's chaos." Gabriel shook his head.

"Exactly. Just the way our Queen likes things. Pandora has an uncanny ability to ride the waves of chaos so this gives her a edge over everyone else. Just be warned that she is a fickle, mercurial woman, and she'll slit your throat the second she sees no value in you."

The group moved up the stairs towards the main palace gates. Several guards stood near the gate watching the group approach. Scanners in the power armor told Gabriel the weapons weren't just loaded but cocked and ready to fire. The guards pushed open the massive gate to the bridge. Beyond the gate, the former bridge had been converted into a throne room.

Pandora sat on her throne which was the former captain's chair of the Ancient vessel, but it had been moved to the far end of the room against the wall. Guards stood next to her and all around the room. The bridge had been cleared of all the consoles required for space flight, creating a large open area. Myrmidon approached the throne and bowed before the Pirate Queen. He looked up, waiting for Pandora to give him permission to address her. Waving one hand, Pandora urged Myrmidon to stand upright.

"You've brought this fiery human before me, and I'm pleased, Myrmidon. Why does he not kneel like a good slave?" Pandora leaned forward to look into Myrmidon's eyes.

"First off let's get one thing clear, I'm no slave." Gabriel locked eyes with Pandora.

"Perhaps I should have my guards seize you, strip you of that impressive armor, and educate you on exactly where your place is here on the Box." Pandora motioned for her guards, and they drew their weapons, but Gabriel just laughed.

"You can try," Gabriel taunted, "but I'm not sure you got enough guards." He glanced slowly.

Myrmidon looked back to see his new captain ready to fight. The guards were beginning to advance toward Gabriel, but he stood still, watching. Pandora studied the human. There was something about Gabriel that couldn't be ignored, she thought, and her eyebrow raised above one eye, locking her gaze. Guards continued to advance on Gabriel, and he drew his energy blade. The blade hissed to life with a crackle. Pandora waved to her guards to stop their advance.

"Perhaps you're courageous or just insane from too long in the Great Maw. I can't seem to figure out which. Do you truly have a death wish, human?" Pandora leaned forward.

"Death comes for us all inevitably, but I promise that before I die, I'll drive this blade down your throat." Gabriel drew his blade, sparking to life, and aimed the blade at Pandora with a grin. Guards aimed their weapons at him, but he didn't even flinch. He stared down the edge of his crackling blade locking eyes with Pandora's narrowing gaze sizing her enemy up.

The guards looked to their queen for her permission to deal with Gabriel. He stood there resolute to see this to the end despite the look Myrmidon was giving. There was a feeling of certainty resonating from

Gabriel. Pandora couldn't be sure her guards would be enough to overcome the power armor. She heard legends of power armor but had never found any still functional. There were too many questions she needed answering, and she motioned her guards to fall back.

"Since my loyal Myrmidon here claims you've seized the *Furious* by my laws, I shall accept you as one of my captains rather than a slave. Given the rumors I've heard about the W'Hyish S'yevel tribes gathering, this is an auspicious turn of events for me. None of my captains have your audacity Gabriel despite being far superior to humans. You'll be the first human captain to join my Predators. Perhaps you can teach them not to fear death." Pandora motioned for Gabriel to approach the throne.

Gabriel deactivated his blade and returned it to his belt before approaching the throne. He didn't kneel. From his vantage point, he could see the information on the tactical computer of the throne. The coordinates were the same as the *Empyrean station*. Pandora glared from her throne at the further display of defiance.

"Kneel before me, captain, to receive your rank and station," Pandora commanded.

"I kneel before no one," Gabriel stated.

"See, guards, this is what strength looks like. This human would rather die than cower even before me. I've executed others for less, but this one is different. Perhaps he'll help lead our fleets on our next glorious raids. Soon the W'Hyish S'yevel tribes will head to war, and they'll offer us a great tribute to aid them." Pandora's words set off a roar of approval from the guards. "We'll cleave our cut of this rumored new star that has been created, won't we?" The crowd cheered with weapons raised high above their head. Gabriel glanced to Myrmidon to subtly motion with a head nod.

Myrmidon approached Gabriel scanning the cheering throng. Leaning into whisper, Gabriel's eyes darted around to make sure the rapturous crowd around him wasn't paying any attention. Only Pandora seemed to stare at the two of them, and her eyes narrowed studying her two subjects. She leaned forward towards them as if she were almost listening in where she not so far way with so much commotion filling the throne room, but her ears seemed to perk up when Myrmidon spoke.

"Rumors spreading from the W'hyish S'yevel are that there is Ancient's space station there that has been kept in pristine condition since

Starfall. That's way too rich of a target for Pandora to pass up on. It's not far from where we found your crashed *Alcatraz*." Myrmidon's eyes locked on Gabriel's standing face-to-face.

"I take it Pandora is planning on seizing this new star?" Gabriel stared back at Myrmidon nodding his head in agreement.

"It is how we survive in the Great Maw. We find valuable targets, raid them, and sell whatever we capture to the Markets of Phobos. People, salvage, and just about anything you can think of there's someone on Phobos who wants it. Pandora believes whoever controls the star will become the most powerful force in the Great Maw. That's why I discovered your wreckage. *Furious* detected *Alcatraz* leap to F.T.L. We were already coming back to confirm the new star to Pandora.

"Same place the *Alcatraz* jumped from?" Myrmidon nodded yet to Gabriel. He pushed his new first officer aside forcing his way through the cheering crowd towards Pandora. Each shove brough turning glares of the pirates towards Gabriel. Commotion finally drew Pandora's attention.

"May I approach your throne, Queen Pandora?" Gabriel bowed his head slightly.

"So, you can show some respect, it seems. Approach, but you better not waste my time." Pandora wagged one finger summoning Gabriel up to her throne.

"It seems you believe the target will be *Empyrean station*, where the new star was created." The intrigue Gabriel's words caused wore clear on Pandora's face in the moment of surprise. She glanced down to see the coordinates on the tactical computer, but she sensed this human knew more. There wasn't any information displayed about the name of the station. Her scouts had only returned a short while before, so there was no chance that he had heard anything from them. Only source she could figure was from the *Furious* which must have detected the stellar formation during patrols. Her eyes narrowed on Gabriel considering him either incredibly lucky or touched by fate.

"Clear the room. I want to talk to my newest captain alone." Pandora's scream caused the rapturous crowd's revelry to come to an end. She stomped her foot, sending the guards scattering towards the door. Even Gabriel's new crew turned to leave. Myrmidon looked back worriedly at his new captain being forced out of the hall in the swarm of guards and courtiers.

The room emptied, leaving only Pandora and Gabriel. She motioned for him to follow and led him towards her quarters. The door whisked shut behind, leaving only silence. Pandora walked to a cabinet of drinks, pulling a bottle from a hidden compartment. She poured two glasses of a strange blue liquid. Offering the glass to her guest, she intended to learn everything.

"Tell me everything you know about *Empyrean station*, Gabriel, and I assure you just rewards that I'll lavish upon you will be beyond your wildest desires." Pandora's lips curled into a wicked smile, her eyes darting quickly to her lavish bed, and she bit her bottom lip staring at Gabriel.

"My desires are endless." Gabriel smirked back at Pandora chuckling in response.

"As they should be. You're a fascinating human Gabriel, and in my experience your kind is far too submissive. Mere sheep except you taste worse. Like rotted swine. Are there more of your kind like you on this *Empyrean station*?" Pandora's eyes narrowed on Gabriel nodding in agreement.

"Thousands. I think you would enjoy the company of a few of my children."

"Come, tell me of your children, and this station of the Ancients." Pandora waved for Gabriel to take a seat next to her on the love seat watching his eyes wander her curves. He sat down turning to lock eyes with Pandora in that moment.

"First, I think we should toast to our new friendship," Gabriel raised his glass with a smile.

Wine glasses chimed tapping against each other. Pandora smiled at Gabriel considering him a rare find in the Great Maw. Thoughts racing with all the future possibilities his sudden arrival in the Box Nebula might bring to Pandora. Her lips curling to a wry grin revealing her enlarged razor-sharp teeth before turning to walk towards the bed. Sway of her hips pulled Gabriel's eyes down.

CHAPTER 21

Workers rushed around the building getting everything prepared. Sparks flew from the renovations converting the building into the new Original Sins. Nemesis sat back, sipping on a drink, watching Marcus organize the work that still needed to be done. She was happy to see everything was coming along according to plan. Lord Cornelius, Lord Hector, and their clan mates carried in the raw materials the workers needed, piling them in the main area where Marcus organized the workers.

A'zyren waited outside the building, looking up at the new sign for the club still in the process of being installed. She waited for a moment to slip past the workers moving materials into the building. The steady traffic flow made it almost impossible to slip in, but A'zyren was patient. She waited until some workers carried a large metal I-beam into the building. Grabbing a hold of the middle of the beam, A'zyren helped the workers through the door blending in with them. Her eyes darted around, expecting someone to notice her deception, but none did. Passing through the doors, she ducked out from under the beam to walk through the club.

The club was in disarray, yet even in the mess, A'zyren could see the similarity to the old Original Sins. Workers were already building the stage in the lower area, and booths around the dance floor were being constructed. Everyone seemed so busy she didn't want to interrupt their work to inquire about Nemesis's location. The building was so packed with workers, it was hard to make out anyone through the dense crowd she scanned slowly. She walked through the building, trying to avoid the rush of the workers around her, and bumped into Lord Cornelius.

"A'zyren, what are you doing here?" Lord Cornelius scratched his head, looking at his glass. He brought it up to sniff. "Not funny, guys. Which one of you laced my drink with a hallucinogen?"

"I'm really here, Lord Cornelius, and I'm looking for Lady Nemesis. Have you seen her around?" A'zyren scoured the club, still unable to locate Nemesis.

"Oh, this is one of those dreams. I'm sure we can find Lady Nemesis and maybe even a bed." Lord Cornelius winked with a smile.

A'zyren shook her head, kneed Lord Cornelius in the groin, and he came crashed down to the ground to all fours. Everyone stopped to see what the sound was. Both eyes were wide with the surge of pain, and Lord Cornelius tried to breathe. A'zyren pulled his chin up with one finger while everyone watched on. Marcus came rushed up to pull A'zyren back.

"Forgive Lord Cornelius for whatever just happened. He's been working non-stop on the club for almost two days now with no rest. Considering the drugs, he's been taking to stay alert, I can only imagine what just happened." Marcus tried to calm the situation. Coughing, Lord Cornelius tried to regain his breath, and just stayed bent over, waiting for the pain to subside.

"Perhaps I overreacted," A'zyren laughed and offered her hand to pull Lord Cornelius up. Lord Cornelius gasped for air, and his legs wobbled under him. He regretted not wearing his power armor. Once the pain subsided, he was able to stand comfortably again. All he felt was shame for his actions.

"My apologies A'zyren. I thought I'd drifted off on my last break, and this was all a dream. None of us expected to see you again after the *Death's Reaper* departed," Lord Cornelius explained.

Nemesis heard the commotion, glanced over, and sipped at her drink. She couldn't determine what was going on through the sea of people. Watching Lord Cornelius struggle to get up made Nemesis laugh, and she wondered who could have brought him to his knees. Downing the last of the drink, she slammed down the mug and motioned to the bartender for a refill. She pushed off the chair to walk towards the group to see what was happening. Approaching the group, she saw A'zyren standing between Marcus and Lord Cornelius.

"A'zyren!" Nemesis raced over to hug her friend. It took several pats on A'zyren's back for Nemesis to believe this was real. Even when her brother ordered Kain to go meet A'zyren, this moment didn't really sink in for Nemesis, but now that it was here, she couldn't help the smile that invaded her countenance. "I can't believe you actually came."

"Who else is stupid enough to come to the aid of a damned?"

"Stupid? Bold is more like it. This is why we bear children. What's a little blood to us women?" Nemesis walked with A'zyren towards the bar. "Get back to work, boys!"

Lord Cornelius still felt sore from the attack, and he looked to see Marcus just shrug before heading back to work. Approaching the bar, Nemesis grabbed her refilled mug and motioned for another drink from the bar tender. Rather than drinking from her mug, she offered it to her guest. A'zyren looked down to see Nemesis' lip marks on the brim of the mug and picked it up to take a drink. She sighed, tasting the crisp, smooth, and potent ale wash over her tongue.

"That's even better than the stuff from the *Alcatraz*," A'zyren admired.

"Oh, this station is fantastic. The energy-to-matter fabricators here are beyond belief. I've just begun to sample all the recipes of the Ancient's worlds brew. Still haven't found anything better than this slag, but damn, it tastes better clean." Nemesis clanged her mug off A'zyren's.

"Whole universe coming to get you, and you're worried about rebuilding your watering hole. That's either insane or beautiful." A'zyren leaned back next to Nemesis to watch the work underway.

"Fuck it, tomorrow we could all be dead, so why not enjoy today I've always said. I do have to admit if there's going to be a battle, I'm glad you're on our side. We're going to need some of your crazy moves if we hope to win this." Nemesis put her arm around A'zyren, pulling her close.

"What your brother has accomplished already is beyond amazing. The *Dawnbreaker* is a truly remarkable vessel. I hadn't believed such a feat of construction was possible in so small a gap of time, but the *Empyrean station* is a wonder of the Ancients. I'd made peace with death coming here the first time, yet somehow, we survived a Reverie attack. That should have been my last battle, but it seems R'paris has other intentions. At least this time, it looks like I'll get to die fighting for life as death demands, but who knows with your crazy lot. You might just be able to win this one," A'zyren lamented, taking a long swig of her drink.

"Would you really be sad if we won and didn't die?" Nemesis put her drink down.

"Death is the greatest honor my people can earn. To die in battle fighting, especially for balancing life and death is a mythical achievement amongst the W'Hyish S'yevel. I could hear the songs that would be sung even amongst the victorious tribes about our defiant last stand against the light of the star. It would have echoed unto the final moments of the Great Maw." A'zyren could only hope and searched for any sign that Nemesis understood her beliefs.

"I suspect many people will die in the coming battle, but I doubt you'll be one. Even if you came here to die with us, I suspect once the fighting breaks out, your killer instinct will take over." Nemesis locked eyes with A'zyren, and she nodded in silent agreement.

"You're not wrong on that. I came because if it's my time to die, I'd rather go out defending that beautiful ball of light, but while death demands life, life always fights death. Guess there won't be any epic songs written about our last stand." A'zyren took another swig feeling a pat on her back.

"Sounds like you'll just have to write those epic songs yourself. If our defeat would echo unto the end, imagine what our victory will do. Death will never cease coming for us, and nothing last forever. Not even the stars." Nemesis grabbed her mug to toast seeing the smile creep onto A'zyren's face. They smashed their mugs together and drank the rest in one gulp.

"So, let's say we do win this coming battle. Any idea what your brother's plans are?" A'zyren wasn't sure Matthew had shared his plans with anyone, but it'd be Nemesis or Kain if he had.

"Oh, we're going to win it. Wait until you see my ship. Once Joshua's *Templar* and Celeris' *Icarus* are completed, construction will begin on my baby. The *Divine Retribution* will make even the *Dawnbreaker* look meager. She's the greatest ship my brother is creating, intended to be his sword against the Cacophony of Discordance. I intend to drive that sword deep into the Reverie's hearts." Nemesis grinned with wicked glee at the thoughts of the Reverie driven before her.

A'zyren couldn't find the words. The plan to build news stars and solar systems seemed a long shot, but this plan to attack the Cacophony of Discordance head-on is suicidal. There was something about Nemesis' enjoyment that frightened and fascinated A'zyren. She couldn't break away. There was one glaring truth in the memories of the battle on the outpost. These humans were crazy enough to do it, and maybe even lucky enough to pull it off.

"Your brother has offered me new territory in his empire after the battle. He claims that he wants to create new stars and planets and that he'll grant me governor title over my people. That we'll be given a new home, and I've sworn allegiance to that. It seems Magnus Void's plan might have a real shot. If anyone can destroy the Cacophony of Discordance, it's you."

"What exactly is Lord Void's plan?" Nemesis leaned in close to whisper the question. She glanced around, making sure no one was listening or eavesdropping.

"I'm not really sure, to be honest. Magnus plays things pretty close to the chest and never let us know what was happening. He sold all of us on the idea of bringing back the stars to rekindle life. Most of my tribes refused to help, but my Niab at the time took my advice. My mother always cared more about the Great Balance than the other tribes and their darker politics," A'zyren explained.

"So, the rest of your tribes are the ones that will be coming to attack us. They're like the creatures that attacked before you guys showed up." Nemesis pointed to A'zyren's black armor.

"Yeah…" A'zyren wasn't sure what to say. She would be pissed if she was Nemesis, but the look on her face didn't show any hints of anger.

"How many are we talking about?"

"Many of the smaller tribes will likely stay out of the fight because unless they can be convinced it will succeed the risk is total annihilation. Smaller tribes don't have the stockpile of resources the larger tribes do. Each tribe's Worldship will be present, putting us at least one hundred, and their accompanying armadas will number in the thousands. They won't be alone, either. The Reverie has dug their claws into other races, and the Arachne join them whenever the Cacophony of Discordance goes to war. Trust me, they're going to be the real threat." A'zyren put her empty drink down and motioned for a refill. She could feel her mouth drying from the anxiety of the thought of the Arachne alone.

A'zyren tapped her fingers on the bar waiting for her refill. Memories of battles with the Arachne echoed, but she managed to force the flood of memories back. When the mug was returned to her, she gulped at it trying to calm her anxiety and gasped for air after finishing half the drink. Her hand twitched against the wooden bar. All she could do was grab her hand to stop it from shaking.

"I've seen you dance across a battlefield A'z. These Arachne must be pretty terrifying." Nemesis' imagination raced with thoughts of what the Arachne could be.

"They're giant sentient spiders Nemesis. Some of them are twice the size of our sacred apexinels. I believe you called them abominations. Arachne fangs will tear through almost anything, so don't depend on your armor for much protection. My advice is that when you see their ships growing close, with the front arms opening up, and they're on a direct course for you, you open fire with everything you can. Arachne are lethal in ground combat, but their ships are vulnerable when they're trying to latch onto a ship to board it. I've never seen a ship repel an Arachne boarding operation." A'zyren cringed at the memories racing past in her mind.

"I'll use extreme prejudice in dealing with the Arachne. Don't worry, my brother is taking every precaution. When our enemy arrives, they won't like what they find. A full fleet of battle forges, loaded with millions of fully trained warriors in a brand-new state-of-the-art power armor, and you standing by our side. We'll kill them all and let God sort them out." Nemesis took a swig.

"The Great Balance determines all because death demands life," A'zyren prayed.

"What's the Great Balance?" Nemesis asked. She understood this was the central belief of the W'Hyish S'yevel tribes, but it wasn't as simple as death demands life, as A'zyren put it. Her reverence for the belief had caused her to rebel against the rest of the W'Hyish S'yevel tribes. Nemesis wanted to understand what that was.

"The Great Balance is the cosmic laws that bind all things, Nemesis. As we grow, we die, and as we die, we return the resource we used to grow to the verse, and a new life grows from those resources. If life were to cease growing, death would overwhelm life, eventually like a fire consumes itself. Death is the primal law of the verse, and death demands life. Many of the tribes have forgotten the old ways and now believe that life demands death. The Reverie is insidious in their perversion of my people, but this is the way forward. Death demands life."

Nemesis took a sip of her drink, pondering the W'Hyish S'yevel belief. There was a reflection that she could see in how she lived her life, and the idea that death demands life to be lived to the fullest. She was certain that reflection was why she bonded with A'zyren from the first moment. A'zyren's devotion to her belief led her to rebel against her own people, and Nemesis looked back at her chosen path of rebellion. There was only one thing she couldn't figure out.

"You believed you were coming to die and leading your people to a glorious end for your beliefs. Given the new star my brother created, there's a certain sense to that. I wonder why you'd make such a noble sacrifice for us?"

"My quest is done, and I can't follow the path of the other tribes. My tribe is human like yours, but our culture is vastly different. I wanted to get to know you and your people better. With Matthew's offer, it seems I'm going to have plenty of time to get to know your people better if we do somehow manage to survive this apocalypse." A'zyren finished her drink.

"Let me show you around my new home," Nemesis took A'zyren by the hand to lead her towards the stairway. The workers were too thick around the elevator. A'zyren was forced to toss the empty mug back towards the bar. It teetered on the edge, but the bartender grabbed it before it could fall. A'zyren managed to get her balance and was walking with Nemesis.

The two women headed up the steps towards the second floor, where they could take the elevator. Nemesis couldn't wait to show A'zyren the penthouse view of the cityscape. She pressed the button to summon the elevator, and it swooshed down with a ding causing the doors to whisk open. Nemesis stepped in, hit the button, and smiled at A'zyren. The elevator began ascending.

CHAPTER 22

Doors whisked open for Joshua and Celeris, and they marched into the auditorium of the Infinity Nexus to answer their summons. The siblings looked at each other's new power armor. Celeris' armor was a dark navy blue with angular plates and a smaller design with less protection to ensure agility of movement. Her sleek blue contrasted by Joshua's flat grey armor, which was much stronger, but less flexible. The two approached the Infinity Nexus to see Nemesis standing in her new black power armour before the chamber.

"Matthew, the *Divine Retribution* is already online. I've got my new children working to prepare her for launch with all the haste they can muster. Things just take time," Nemesis said.

"Time is not on our side Nemesis. Our enemies are already mustering. I've seen the multitude of eyes glaring towards *Empyrean station* and heard the whispers of the Cacophony of Discordance. Virgil, what is the status of our preparations." Matthew looked at the glowing image.

"Fleet readiness is hovering around twenty-five percent of your original goal. With only four battleforges done, the estimated odds of survival are less than two percent. However, expansion of production capacity has increased two hundred and seventy four percent, which means the next production phase can begin. The gene seed vault on the station merely awaits the next batch." Virgil pointed towards Joshua and Celeris approaching the Infinity Nexus.

"With the Imperator gone to convince Lord De'Vayne to join us in the coming battle, there's only one choice. We must expand our production capacity. Nemesis, I want your people to use the nanoproduction capacity of the *Divine Retribution* to assist with phase two. We must begin preparing the next wave of battleforges with all due haste." Matthew scoured time, still unable to see past the wall of darkness that rushed through time toward them.

Joshua and Celeris approached the Infinity Nexus and saluted their brother before standing at attention. They both looked to Nemesis, but she was clearly too busy analyzing the situation. Even Virgil was busy calculating the situation the two siblings had just walked into. Matthew paced back and forth, trying to figure a way past the block he saw coming with their destruction. He turned to smile at Joshua and Celeris.

"I'm glad you could join us. Now that your respective ships have been complete and the *Templar* and *Icarus* are ready to depart, I've a special mission for you both. Joshua, you've always been one of the best at communication analysis. I want Celeris to escort you to begin setting up an early warning detection grid beyond the *Empyrean station*. We must be able to see our enemies coming to effectively fight them. This sensor network will give us eyes in the abyss." Matthew pointed to the image from the holographic emitter lights dancing above the auditorium.

A stellar map of the Great Maw began to form. Bright glowing dots on the map showed the ring of sensors that Matthew wanted to set up. Joshua looked at it with an audible hmm, and he considered the best possible way to set that up. His mind was already racing with mathematical calculations. Despite the proximity to *Empyrean station*, Celeris didn't like how exposed she and Joshua would be setting up the sensor network, and she knew that they'd be alone until the job was finished. She knew this would be an opportune time for the Cacophony to attack.

"Our asses are going to be blowing in the cosmic winds out there, Matthew. Two ships all by themselves make for juicy targets. Remember what Lord Void claimed. The Reverie is always watching from the darkness, and in case you haven't noticed, there's a lot of darkness left out there." Celeris looked to Joshua to see his doubts worn on his countenance.

"It's a lot of space to cover, but with our F.T.L. drives and fighters, we should be able to do it fast enough to go unnoticed. If the Reverie attacked during the deployment of the sensors, we might not have time to fall back. Nemesis should come along as well. With the *Divine Retribution* assisting, we could finish this operation much faster." Joshua hoped Matthew agreed with his assessment.

"If only that were possible, Joshua, but I've other plans for the *Divine Retribution* right now. The ship was designed like each battleforge to house its own geneseed vault. Nemesis's ship, however, has a much greater capacity for growing new troops. That is why I'm using the ship to expand our capacity to produce troops. The next Patriarchs and Matriarchs of the Empire are on their way here now. I know this is a risk, but I assure you both that it's calculated."

Matthew pointed towards the image now forming in the lights of the holographic emitter. On the image, the group could see the new superstructure skeletons already beginning to take shape. The Divine Retribution floated nearby with swarms of nanomachines joining the *Empyrean station's* efforts to construct the new ships. Lady Clotho made her way forward using a wooden cane to help her walk. Behind her followed Lord Cornelius, Lord Hector, Lord Hephaestus, and Lady Freya. The group stopped before the Infinity Nexus and bowed before Emperor Solomon.

"We've come at your request Emperor," Lady Clotho rasped.

"Lady Clotho, it's good to see you again. All of you rise. Nemesis here has recommended that you Lords and Ladies be elevated in the next phase of our geneseed program. I was wondering what you thought of this decision Lady Clotho." Matthew looked down at Lady Clotho with a blank expression. He waited for her decision despite the fact that he was certain what it would be.

Time echoed Lady Clotho's manipulations, but she was the only person Matthew couldn't isolate in the flow of fate. He couldn't be sure of Lady Clotho's loyalties being unable to see her future decisions. This was a test designed to reveal what Matthew couldn't see in the ebb of time. Lady Clotho rubbed her chin, considering the test before her. She knew what Matthew was doing but decided to play along since this was his game. Fate demanded nothing less.

"I see the shadows of the great threat looming over us all, attempting to block out the new light we've created. Only you, Emperor, and your loyal people can stand against that shadow. These are fine choices of warriors to expand the Empire with first. I would choose no others before them." Lady Clotho could hear the echoes of footsteps approaching from behind.

"Of course, you'd claim that you old hag, but I'm the equal of any here," Marimba declared.

Lady Marimba swayed with each step toward the Infinity Nexus. She ignored the glares of everyone gathered around the Infinity Nexus and approached to bow before Emperor Solomon. Matthew motioned for Marimba to rise with one hand. She stood up to place her hands on her hips. Both eyes narrowed upon Matthew.

"My Emperor, surely you doth see the value I can offer to your geneseed program. There are none more loyal to you. I beseech upon thee to grant me thine favour."

"Don't trust her, Emperor. She is a wicked and base creature obsessed with her own entertainment." Lady Clotho shook her cane at Lady Marimba.

"What do you know, old hag?" Lady Marimba hissed at Lady Clotho before turning back to Emperor Solomon. "These are great warriors, but I stood with you and your family fighting on the outpost. The ingenuity of my missiles kept the drones at bay while we rose to thine destiny, my Emperor." Lady Marimba glared at Lady Clotho, causing her to smile. Nemesis stepped in between the two with her arms crossed.

"Actually, I built the missiles for your armor," Lord Hephaestus interjected.

"You're a great warrior Lady Marimba, but you don't compare to my brother Hephaestus or the others. We didn't bring you along on the outpost because you were a valuable warrior but because we couldn't depend on you or your troops to hold the landing bay. That's why we left the better warriors behind there. You were just more expendable." Nemesis sighed shaking her head.

Lady Marimba surged towards Nemesis, but she just lowered her hands to the hilts of her energy blades. The two stared at each other and remained fixed in place. Matthew ran his hand through his hair, watching the two women. It was maddening for him to witness his own people turning on each other while the entire Great Maw came to slaughter them all. Anger welled up in him, and his psychic powers surged forward, throwing everyone to the ground.

"Enough!" Matthew breathed heavily. Everyone was trying to stand up when the doors whisked open. Lord Galen walked into see the people scattered across the ground, and he was just about to leave when he saw Matthew motioning to come forward. Lord Galen walked towards the

Infinity Nexus and bowed before Emperor Solomon. Sweat beaded on |Lord Galen's head, and his mind raced, trying to discern could possibly Emperor Solomon want.

"How may I serve you, Emperor?" Lord Galen kept his head down, refusing to look up. Guilt echoed in his mind at what was happening to Angelica.

"We've begun the second phase of the geneseed program. None of our people know more about genetic science except Virgil. I'd like you to examine the geneseed data banks for any unusual genetic signs in our new troops." Matthew watched Lord Galen rise, but he averted his eyes from Emperor Solomon. Every thought echoed warnings that Matthew knew of his research.

"I'd be better use running the program myself," Lord Galen argued.

"My knowledge is the vast collection of the Ancients. There is no way your limited experience can compare to my data stores. Your assessment is preposterous," Virgil explained.

"Dark thoughts and goals emanate from this one Emperor. Still, I understand why you see a use for him. Lord Galen's knowledge could be a key to future conflicts," Lady Clotho prophesized.

"Lord Galen, I want you to just double-check the work. You never know, it might help you with your own research efforts in areas. Inspiration and innovation can come from the strangest places. There may even be a way to speed this process up. Just remember that I'm going to want to see all your current research project you're working on, eventually, I suspect you're engaged in some cutting-edge research." Matthew's words caused a shiver to race through Lord Galen's nerves.

"Of course, Emperor, once my new research program is complete. I'm still not sure it'll produce any results. Such is the risk of any research program." Lord Galen backed away, feeling the sweat race down his face, and instinctively wiped it.

"Virgil, please take Lord Galen to the geneseed vault and show him around. Give him full access to the data archives." Matthew watched Virgil lead Lord Galen toward the door. The two disappeared behind the grey metal when it closed. There was no telling what would come from Lord Galen's experiments, but Matthew knew it was imperative to find out, no matter the cost.

Time echoed what was happening to Angelica, and Matthew hated that he could see that this needed to happen. He could feel in the very fabric of the universe that this was fated to happen. The weight of the decision bore down on him, and Lady Clotho looked up with empathy. Matthew caught the look in the corner of his eye. He wondered if this was how Lady Clotho had felt when she'd read his fate back on the *Alcatraz*. The faces of the others forced Matthew out of the stream of time to continue dealing with the situation.

"In the end, the armies of the Empire must grow rapidly to succeed. Your time is coming, Lady Marimba, but I ask you to be patient. Lord Hephaestus, I know you've already completed the design of your ship, the *Olympus*, and now I need you to help the others. Take them to your forge and begin the work. Nothing must impede our work in such a crucial hour," Matthew stated.

"Of course, my brother, I'll do everything I can to assist." Lord Hephaestus motioned for the others to follow, and the group headed toward the exit. With most problems dealt with, Matthew turned his attention to those that remained.

"Joshua and Celeris, prepare your troops to depart. Nemesis, you already have your tasks, but Lady Clotho might be helpful. Bring her up to speed." Matthew watched his siblings salute before walking away from the Infinity Nexus, leaving only Lady Marimba behind. She blushed when Matthew smiled at her.

Nemesis looked back over her shoulder when she reached the doorway. The looks between Lady Marimba and Matthew disturbed Nemesis. She grabbed Lady Clotho by the arm to draw her attention to the scene by the Infinity Nexus. Neither of the women liked what they saw, but there wasn't much they could do. Lady Clotho just sighed.

"I fear that despite your brother's powers to see the future, he can't see the threat before him right now. We're most easily deceived by our strengths, not our weaknesses. Lady Marimba's eyes have always been drawn to power. She just never possessed this influence over your father," Lady Clotho explained. She could feel the anger radiating off Nemesis.

"That bitch does anything to hurt my brother," Nemesis grasped the hilt of her blades.

"Don't worry, my dear. We'll be ready for whatever Marimba has planned. Your brother is right to focus on the immediate threat, but we'll keep our eyes on Marimba." Lady Clotho tugged at Nemesis's arm to convince her to follow. It took a moment, but Nemesis turned to walk with Lady Clotho from the Infinity Nexus.

Matthew waited until everyone had left the auditorium before speaking any further. The moments between him and Lady Marimba weren't for anyone else. She walked forward to press her hand upon the glass of the Infinity Nexus. Matthew put his hand against the glass before hers and stared into her eyes. He could see the darkness within Lady Marimba but also the light.

"Why doth thee tolerate that Lady Clotho thine Emperor? Lady Marimba searched for the truth in Matthew's face, but it was cold and expressionless.

"Everyone has a purpose Marimba. You'd be wise to remember that. I've had enough responsibility for one day, and I was hoping that perhaps you'd go over the progress of your play with me. I'm desperate to relax with some entertainment for a change." Matthew sat down in front of the glass to listen. Lady Marimba launched right away into everything that had been happening.

Lady Marimba regaled her Emperor with the tales of drama between actors and the arguing of her writers who disagreed with her changes to the script. Everything in time faded away for Matthew but this moment in time. He smiled, listening to the tales Lady Marimba spun about the dramas within the actors' troops performing the dramas for the masses. For the first time since arriving at *Empyrean station,* Matthew was at peace.

CHAPTER 23

Energy crackled from the subspace tear, arcing into the void of the Great Maw. Several sleek, long spear-like ships moved towards the tear. Serpentine ships gathered around the subspace anomaly. Shields flashed into existence, and weapon systems powered up. The almost imperceptible black hull of the *Jinnestan* slipped from the tear, sliding into real space.

The massive *Jinnestan* came to a stop before the serpentine vessels. Tenno Asmodeus stood on the bridge glaring at the ships on the viewscreen. He studied the formation of the enemy fleet and began activating the weapon systems with targets marked. The com systems beeped with the incoming hail from the serpentine ships. He activated the com systems, and the image of Dhakan appeared on the screen, flickering to life.

"Tenno Asmodeus, the serpentine weren't expecting your visit," Dhakan stammered.

"Silence, serpent. I've no time for your prattle. I've come in search of the one known as Magnus Void." Asmodeus crackled with malevolent black energy. He couldn't sense the energy of Magnus Void anywhere in the sector, but he sensed the approach of a powerful energy.

"Serpentine know no such entity as this Magnus Void," Dhakan lied.

"Stop wagging your forked tongue, serpent, before I carve it out. Now move. I have important business to attend." Asmodeus pressed a button. Weapon systems on the *Jinnestan* locked target beginning to charge. Hum resonated across the comms.

"There's no need for violence. Let me contact Guardian Veles. Just hold on for a moment." Dhakan trembled on the screen, trying to bide some time.

"Pray Veles answers you before I lose my patience," Asmodeus cut contact.

The serpentine ships floated on the viewscreen, holding in formation. Asmodeus stared past the ships at the massive serpentine fortress. Powerful shields emanated from the station appeared on the *Jinnestan's* sensors. Scans showed thousands of weapon systems on the planet-sized station. Asmodeus issued the orders for his legions to prepare for an invasion. The blare of the battle alarm echoed throughout the *Jinnestan*.

Reverie moved through the bridge to take battle stations. Baleful fiery troops of Jinn filled the ship with hisses, and crackles of energy echoed across the bridge. Asmodeus stood on the bridge staring at the holographic scans of the Serpentine station and planned his invasion. The com system beeped, and the viewscreen shifted. Dhakan appeared once more.

"Guardian Veles is willing to meet to discuss terms of peace," Dhakan informed.

"I see the old snake has grown wiser since we last seen each other. Perhaps today won't end in a blood bath for your people, but the day is still young. Lead the way, Dhakan." Asmodeus powered up the engine of the Jinnestan. The ship lurched forward, following behind Dhakan's smaller *Nagaraja* darting ahead towards Draconis.

Asmodeus watched Draconis grow closer on the viewscreen. He could sense the energy from billions of Serpentines who lived on the station. Turning away from the screen, he marched towards the hanger deck. Reverie moved out of his way in the corridors of the *Jinnestan*. Only the massive living energy of flame known as the djinn didn't fear Asmodeus, but they bowed to him when he walked past, nonetheless. Act of submission brought a smile to his face revealing rows of sharp teeth.

Few of the Reverie could even look upon Asmodeus's countenance. Crimson energy crackled from his eyes, and black energy crackled from his horns. He walked into the docking bay to see the Reverie fighters being prepared for launch. In the distance, the black shuttle waited with the docking ramp lowered. Several flaming Jinn stood guard outside.

"Tenno Asmodeus, you can't trust these serpentines," came a voice from behind.

"Ifrit, you know I trust no one, not even you. Have you come to send me off with your whispered warnings of my death that you dream of so that you can be free of the tyranny of my wrath?" Asmodeus glared back at Ifrit, his flames crackling with intense heat.

"I've come to request to join you Tenno. You shouldn't go down to Draconis on your own, especially not given the task of capturing Lord Void. This would be a perfect place to spring a trap." Ifrit bowed with his request. Only when Asmodeus's clawed hand touched Ifrit's fiery countenance did he stand back up.

"Come, Ifrit, and let us discover the truth these Serpentines try to hide underneath their scales." Asmodeus walked towards the bridge exit alongside Ifrit. Two moved through the ship towards the docking bay. Massive black doors of the docking bay resonated with the laments of the souls bound within and slid open before the Tenno and his Jinn. Across the docking bay, Asmodeus's personal shuttle awaited him, and several Reverie crackled away, preparing it for take off.

Storming past the minions, Asmodeus moved towards the cockpit with Ifrit following. He sat down, began activating the ship, and glanced at Ifrit. He took the co-pilots spot to run diagnostics on the systems. Once everything checked out, he began activating the engines.

"We're ready to take off, Tenno," Ifrit glanced at Asmodeus.

The shuttle lifted off, and the engines flared, shooting it forward. Fighters raced from the *Jinnestan* behind the shuttle. Asmodeus watched the *Nagaraja* docking with Draconis station. He altered heading towards the nearby hanger bays on Draconis following the incoming docking procedures from the station. Dhakan walked off his ship through the docking tub and saw the black Reverie shuttle racing towards the hanger bay. He slithered forward with all the speed his muscles could generate, trying to arrive at the docking bay before the shuttle could land.

Dhakan managed to arrive just in time for the shuttle to land. He watched the ramp lower and saw the visage of Ifrit's flaming presence crackling next to Tenno Asmodeus. The two walked down the ramp and past Dhakan without a word. He was forced to keep up with the two Reverie marching across the hanger bay. They headed towards the great conclave.

"Tenno Asmodeus, this is most unusual. We received no message of your arrival from the Cacophony of Discordance. When our people signed the Accords of Dis, there was an agreement that any cooperation requirements from the Serpentine would be formally requested. The great Khan and Guardian Veles isn't pleased with the situation," Dhakan informed. Ifrit glared back with a combustion of flaming energy sparking in his eyes that silenced Dhakan.

"I'm here on Cacophony of Discordance business," Tenno Asmodeus declared.

"There are still rules that must be obeyed. You can't expect our people to bend to the whims of the Cacophony of Discordance." Dhakan slid backward when Asmodeus came to a stop.

"Pray that I don't alter the deal further than I must by necessity. This rogue Lord Void has become a threat to my people, and that won't be tolerated. If I discover the Serpentine had anything to do with the return of the light, I'll leave this place a graveyard. I promise you'll be the last living serpentine when I finish." Asmodeus continued walking towards the conclave.

Dhakan slinked back, trying to keep his rising fear in check. There was no telling what Asmodeus would do if he discovered that Magnus Void was on his way here. At least Dhakan had deleted the message from his friend and only shared the contents with Guardian Veles in private. The only hope for the serpentine was that Magnus didn't show up in the middle of this meeting. Dhakan knew the Cacophony was full of liars, but they never lied about the destruction they'd bring.

The doors to the conclave slid back before Tenno Asmodeus, and he marched into the chamber to the gasps of the gathered assembly of Serpentines. A coil mass of serpentines was gathered in the conclave. High above the conclave, Guardian Veles glared down at the Tenno disturbing his meeting and glanced to Dhakan. The clamor of the serpentines filled the room with an uproar of voices and veiled whispers. Veles pounded a gavel bringing the chamber to silence.

"Tenno Asmodeus, this conclave hadn't been expecting your arrival. Perhaps you could tell us what is so important that you break the Accords of Dis?" Veles glared down. Light sparked off the ornate metal armor of Veles etched with images of serpents coiled around his body. The copy of Uroboros written by Matthew sat before him opened on a podium.

"Playing coy with me is not becoming your great station of Guardian, Veles, but it may precede your ruination. The Cacophony of Discordance demands that you and your people hand over the traitor known as Magnus

Void. Before you speak, I want you to take a moment to consider one thing. I've eighty legions at my disposal and the mandate to destroy your entire empire given by the Supreme Tenno Ba'al Zebub if I feel you've deceived me, and as the Lord of Wrath of the Cacophony of Discordance I'm exceptional at detecting lies. Be warned before you attempt to lie to me." Tenno Asmodeus crackled with white hot wrath snapping across his eyes in a sparking hiss.

Veles looked down upon Dhakan with a smile. He'd managed not to reveal the truth of the serpentine allegiance with Magnus Void, which bought some time. Now all Veles needed to figure out was how to bide more time. Magnus Void was coming here, and Dhakan briefed Veles on the new star and *Empyrean station*. He'd expected something like this, but the Cacophony of Discordance had chosen wisely in their agents. Asmodeus reputation for destruction and conquest echoed across the Great Maw. Dozens of smaller states that once traded with Serpentine had already been wiped out.

"We know of no such entity by the name of Magnus Void," Veles declared.

Fire roared from Ifrit's body, but it was cooled by Asmodeus's clawed touch. He looked up at Veles with a wicked grin. Black and red energy surged from his eyes, swirling around his body. Dhakan fell to the ground writhing and screaming in agony, but the vortex expanded even more. Soon the waves of negative energy tore into the conclave filling the room with a symphony of agony from the serpentine. Veles watched his people struggling against the negative energy siphoning the life force from them.

"Enough!" Veles cried out. Tenno Asmodeus stopped his assault.

"I want Magnus Void. Now!" Tenno Asmodeus's eyes crackled with malice.

"It's impossible to give you what I don't possess, Tenno, but stay your wrath. I've heard of this Magnus Void. He once wanted an audience with me and my people. I believe I can lure him here to Draconis for you. Just please spare my people," Veles begged. He looked down with sympathy at Dhakan, but there wasn't anything more that could be done.

"Excellent. I'm glad you saw reason, Veles. Your people should be proud to have such a wise leader," Asmodeus taunted. He could sense the animosity of the serpentine, but it only made the moment more delicious to him. Once he possessed Magnus Void, perhaps the Cacophony would finally permit him to obliterate these deceiving serpents once and for all. He looked to Ifrit with a grin at the thought of the destruction of Draconis.

"We serve the Cacophony as we've done for millennia," Veles declared.

"That is most warming news. For the Cacophony have more demands to place upon your strong, capable shoulders. We're preparing a force of our allies to attack the *Empyrean station* and destroy it and this new star that has been born. I'm certain the serpentine people would be disappointed if they weren't invited to the battle. We'll expect your fleet ready to move when we send the command to attack." Tenno Asmodeus heard the whispers in the conclave.

"Tenno Asmodeus, we've heard of this new star and the station, but it's a powerful relic of the Ancients. The serpentine fleet is small, and we can't leave Draconis undefended. We can only spare half of our fleet," Veles informed.

"Muster your fleet," Tenno Asmodeus ordered before leaving the conclave. He walked back towards the door, ignoring the whispers. The door whisked shut, silencing the serpentines. Ifrit walked behind his Tenno. His flames crackled with the rage of his emotions.

"Why did you spare those Serpentine scum?"

"The time for the destruction will come soon enough, Ifrit. When it does come, I'll give you and your Jinn the first meal upon these deceiver's souls. For now, we must focus on capturing this, Lord Void. We can't allow more of these stars to be created. The only way we can prevent that is to learn his full plans. Once we've stopped the return of the light, we'll return to lay waste to Draconis." Tenno Asmodeus laughed.

"Can you be sure this Lord Void is even coming here?" Ifrit glanced at his Tenno.

"Arachne is never wrong, and I can feel the power of Magnus Void growing closer to this sector already. There is no doubt in my mind he's aligned himself with the serpentine. Their technological prowess is only rivaled by the De'Vayne. Magnus would have needed their help deciphering the texts of the Ancients. I suspect the serpentine aided the traitor by using their technology to help keep him hidden. Nothing else explains how this upstart grew so powerful so quickly." Tenno Asmodeus walked onto the shuttle with Ifrit. They began powering the shuttle back up. He locked in course on the *Jinnestan* guiding the shuttle away from Draconis.

"Should I call in the other legions and ships?" Ifrit looked to Tenno Asmodeus for an answer. He just sat there staring into the Great Maw. The powerful energy he felt was growing closer. He pointed to a point on the viewscreen.

Ifrit could tell from the scanners that there was a black hole at the location. Gravitational energies spiked across the sensors. Tenno Asmodeus uploaded the coordinates to the *Jinnestan* and watched the large ship altering course on the screen. He adjusted the shuttle's heading. The shuttle and its fighter escort moved toward the *Jinnestan* in the distance.

"Keep the legions at bay. We're going to need that black hole to hide our energies from this Lord Void. The gravitational forces should prevent him from sensing us. We'll spring the trap once Magnus lands on Draconis," Tenno Asmodeus stared at the black hole in the distance.

"At that distance, it'll take time to get back to Draconis," Ifrit showed his calculations.

"Magnus can run all he likes, but there's nowhere in the Great Maw I won't find him. He'll kneel before me by the time this hunt is finished." Asmodeus brought the shuttle into the hanger bay.

Descending from the shuttle, the Ifrit followed behind Asmodeus, headed towards the bridge, and prepared to lay their ambush. The surging power of the blackholes gravity could already be felt in the corridors of the ship. Tenno Asmodeus hoped the energy would be enough, but his mind raced, preparing other contingencies just in case. He walked onto the bridge to take his captain's seat. On the, the Great Maw stared back at him. He turned to Ifrit.

"Go, monitor the sensors, and alert me the moment any new ships arrive in the sector. I shall continue gathering information and planning the future invasion of Draconis." Tenno Asmodeus turned, marching towards the holographic emitter displaying Draconis.

"As you command Tenno," Ifrit nodded, heading towards the sensors to get to work.

Tenno Asmodeus leaned over the table, staring into the holographic emitter of Draconis, but his mind couldn't stop thinking about the rogue Lord Magnus Void. Soon he'd be within Tenoo Asmodeus clutches.

Anticipation of all the torments he would suffer aboard the *Jinnestan* made him grin. Patient wasn't one of his virtues however, and white-hot wrath crackled across his black eyes. Lord Void had better arrive quickly Tenno Asmodeus thought. For the Serpentines sake.

CHAPTER 24

Kain watched the viewscreen on the bridge of the *Dawnbreaker* and waited for the F.T.L. arrival countdown to reach zero. The pilot pulled back on the F.T.L. throttle disengaging the engine. Transition back to real space was almost seamless. Sensors erupted with beeps, and the whole bridge seemed to go haywire. Kain looked to his tactical readout to see the gravitational forces on the sensors, and they were everywhere. Alarms blared, warning of the approaching danger.

"Status report," Kain ordered.

"Sensors are showing intense overlapping gravitational forces. The energies are originated from thousands of singularities spread throughout the region captain. We need to pull back before the gravitational force captures us and shears the ship apart," the sensor operator reported.

"Pull the *Dawnbreaker* back and keep her far enough away to avoid the gravity well. Keep scanning the area and figure out what we're dealing with. Inform me immediately if anything else appears on sensors, Lt. Holm" Kain gripped the edges of the chair tight.

The pilot inputted new coordinates provided by the sensors scans. He pulled the ship away from the approaching event horizons of the cluster of black holes. Alarms stopped. Kain leaned back into his chair, breathing a sigh of relief. He scoured the darkness of the viewscreen, searching for any sign of the De'Vayne, but only the void of the Great Maw stared back.

"Good work Lt. Grey. That was some fine piloting," Kain acknowledged.

"Thank you, sir," Sgt. Grey replied.

"Lt. Kazakova, what's the source of the gravitational forces?" Kain looked to his sensor operator. She was still busy trying to figure that out and held up a finger, trying to bide a little more time. The computer hummed away, calculating. She turned to face her captain.

"These readings show thousands of black holes all packed together in a dense patch. Sensors are showing a series of gravitational streams flowing into the center of the mass. Strange energy readings are coming from somewhere within the singularity patch, but the interference is making it impossible to determine the cause. All the radiation and background interference is making it almost impossible to locate the exact source of the energy signature." Kazakova worked away trying to understand all the information that was being gathered. The chirp of the incoming communications signaled the crew's attention.

"Captain, it seems we're being hailed," the coms officer reported.

"Put it on screen Chief Corrigan." Kain watched the screen, waiting to see who was contacting him. He suspected the energy reading Kazakova was picking up from the patch of black holes was, in fact, the home of the De'Vayne hidden amongst the chaos of these singularities. The communication was nothing but static on the screen at first. It took a few moments of Corrigan's work to clean the message up. Static filled the message began to clear first from the communication, and the static began to clear forming a figure.

The image was slow to clear, but it began revealing the silhouette. The pattern of armor appeared very familiar to Kain. He leaned forward, trying to make out more of the image. Static faded from the screen, and the image of Genji began to appear. He smiled at Kain.

"Kain, it's good to see you again," Genji greeted. He thudded his fist off his chest to salute the Imperator in the honorable De'Vayne style. Kain stood up to return the gesture.

"We nearly got killed by these black holes. Hell of a place to set up your home Lord Genji. I'll have to have a word with A'zyren about data accuracy. We could have used the information that the De'Vayne lived in a patch of black holes before we arrived." Kain stood up to approach the scree with his hands clamped behind his back. Genji just laughed.

"A'zyren's not one to warn about anything. Her coordinates did drop your ship from F.T.L. at the safest point in the sector. I'd say that's about all you can expect from her," Genji informed.

"Lord Genji, it's good to see you again. I come on behalf of Emperor Solmon of the Imperium of Humanity to bring the greetings of my brother as his Imperator. I'm here to request an audience with Lord De'Vayne." Kain bowed, trying to be diplomatic.

"Emperor of the Imperium of Humanity, it seems your brother has high ambitions, and you rise as he does. From the scans I'm looking at, your ship is quite impressive, Kain, but far too big to make it through the Maze of Charybdis without an expert navigator on board. I'm sending the coordinates of the safest route for you to take. I suggest taking a smaller craft, but it's your life." Genji tapped a few buttons, and the computers on the bridge reported the information being received. Looking at the information, Kain wasn't sure he could even pilot the route and shook his head.

"This is a pretty tight path to take," Kain explained.

"Don't worry, it looks harder than it is. The gravity streams will help carry you here." Genji ended the transmission leaving Kain standing there with his crew staring at him.

"Commander Gades, you're in command of the bridge," Kain ordered. With a salute, Kazakova moved from her station and took up the captain's chair. The door to the bridge whisked open, and Kain headed towards the lift. Gravity well of the lift propelled the disk towards the top. The lift doors opened as Kain approached them, and he stepped on to press the button for the hanger bay. Silent retraction of the gate closing set unease through him.

The smooth movement of the lift still bothered Kain, who missed the grinding of the *Alcatraz* elevator. He reviewed the course that Genji provided in his mind as the lift descended. Celeris could pilot this route easily, Kain thought, but he didn't have his sister to rely on. He cracked his knuckles, pushing back the anxiety racing through his nerves. Even the feedback of the power armor alerted him to the high levels of cortisol in his blood. He took a deep breath, trying to still his racing heart, and let it out in along exhale. With a thought he accessed the lessons his sister had given him on piloting as the elevator came to a halt. Memories flashed, and he hoped the refresher crash course would give him even a sliver of his sister's piloting ability. The elevator slid to a halt with a subtle inertial shift he could barely feel.

Kain watched the lift doors retract, revealing the hanger bay. Troops walked by, pushing a skiff of munitions for the fighters. Sparks leaped into the air from the cutting torches of the automated repair arms working on the fighters. He walked towards the shuttle where several troops were going over a final inspection. They saluted the Imperator as he approached.

"At ease," Kain ordered.

"The shuttle's ready for you, sir. Final checks all came back green." One of the troopers showed the data pad report to Kain. He patted the trooper on the back and headed up the docking ramp into the shuttle. Entering the bridge of the shuttle, Kain took a seat behind the controls of the shuttle. The sounds of troops loading onto the shuttle echoed into the bridge. He watched the controls and once the troopers were loaded, closed the docking ramp.

Thrusters hissed with their ignition, and Kain brought the gravitational core online. Adjusting the magnetic fields, he brought the shuttle to hover in the air. The computer completed the final engine checks. Everything appeared green on the controls, and Kain throttled up the engines. Engines flared, accelerating the shuttle with a sudden burst inertial shift. Inertia dampeners beeped warning of the sudden g-forces but quickly returned to normal.

The shuttle raced past the shield barriers of the hanger bay and shot into the black void of the Great Maw. Kain knew he couldn't rely on his eyes for this flight, and he activated the sensors attuning them to the gravitational forces in Genji's route. Holographic displays on the viewscreen adjusted to the information. The pathway appeared in holographic markings. Kain pulled the shuttle towards the trajectories on his viewscreen overlay.

Gravitational forces rocked the ship, and Kain struggled against the jolts of the flight stick, trying to keep the shuttle in the sweet spot of the stream of gravitational force. The pull of gravity tore at the shuttle, trying to pull it in every direction at once. Now Kain understood what Genji had meant by the stream would help. Keeping the shuttle in the center of the gravity stream stabilized the ship. Gravity still tore from every direction but keeping the shuttle in the center of the stream resisted most of the force of the shear of gravity on the shuttle's structure. Hull integrity warnings flashed on the consoles, but Kain ignored them.

Wiping around, the shuttle speeds continued to accelerate, caught in the stream of gravity's pull. Troopers in the back were freaking out from what Kain could hear, but he couldn't help but smile. Celeris would love this, he thought, and couldn't wait to tell her the story when he got back. Sensors still blared, warning of the black hole singularities surrounding the shuttle. The shuttle shot out of the gravity stream, speeds began decreasing, and the alarms stopped blaring.

Gravity ceased shaking the shuttle, and calm returned. Even the troops in the back quieted down. Kain didn't realize any of that was happening. He was fixated on what he saw on the sensors. In the center of the black hole singularity was a large open area, and at the center, a massive space station radiating huge levels of power. The energy levels were comparable to the new star at *Empyrean station*. Kain looked up at the viewscreen.

A massive space station floated in the dead center of the Maze of Charybdis. The sleek black hull of the station blended into the void and would have been imperceptible to Kain's eyes if it weren't for the power armor sensors. Sensors showed the surge of energy coming from the station. Communications buzzed with an incoming transmission. He accepted the incoming transmission, uploaded new coordinates, and transferred them to flight control.

In the void beyond the screen, Kain could see the light beam out through the cracks of a docking gate retracting open. Sensors scans showed the registry information of the station. The station tag showed the Ancient's name of *Byzantium*. He brought the ship's heading to the lights of the docking bay. Pulling back on the throttle, he slowed the ship and watched the De'Vayne fleet decloak around the station. None of the ships were the size of the *Dawnbreaker*, but from the readings, Kain sensor poured in showed the fleet was battle ready. Weapon signatures showed the fleet weapons were primarily plasma-based weapons systems. The readings were similar to what the *Alcatraz* recorded during first contact with the *Death's Reaper*. He focused on the scan and breathed a sigh of relief when he realized the weapons weren't powered up.

The shuttle slowed down, entering the docking bay. Kain continued to cut power to the engines and scanned the massive docking bay. Thousands of fighters lined in rows filled the massive docking bay. Larger ships could be seen further back. Navigational data showed him that the landing pad was at the far end of the hanger bay. Energy beams shot from the ceiling to surge around the shuttle, and sensors showed the tractor beams held the shuttle. He cut the remaining power of the engines and leaned back into his seat to enjoy the rest of the ride.

Tractor beams guided the shuttle towards the empty landing bay nearest the large gates. The shuttle glided through the air to come to a rest. Troops stood in the back of the shuttle, waiting to feel the shuttle land, but the landing was so gentle none of them knew they'd landed. Kain activated the land ramp and marched towards the back past his troops that formed up behind him to follow. He marched down the ramp to see Lord Genji approaching.

"Imperator, allow me to be the first to welcome you to *Byzantium* and know that Lord De'Vayne sends his warmest greetings. He regrets that duties keep him from greeting you in person, but he hopes you'll find me a suitable replacement." Lord Genji motioned for Kain and his troops to follow him. The massive doors still hung open, and Genji led the group down the massive corridor. Large machines thudded along carrying large machines.

"Your home seems to be quite impressive," Kain admired.

"The Maze of Charybdis keeps most threats at bay. Not even the Cacophony of Discordance has ever found this place. Our slipstream drives allow us to fold what's left of time and space to travel for almost instantaneous travel across the Great Maw." Genji waited for one of the large machines to pass before leading Kain and his troops across. They walked through the large doors to see the spiral of *Byzantium* and in the center of the station, the steady glow of the fusion reactor.

"You've created your own star?" Kain couldn't believe what he was seeing. Now the Maze of Charybdis made sense. The patch of black holes ensured none of the light could escape. It was a marvel of precision engineering.

"No, this isn't a star like your brother created at *Empyrean station*, but it's not much different. It just requires much more work to stabilize, or it'll kill us all. De'Vayne is capable of such great technological feats." Genji led the group to a pad and waited for the current occupants to teleport. The surge of light blinded Kain for a second before flashing the De'Vayne away.

The troops behind Kain looked at each other, but Kain strode onto the platform with Genji. None of the troopers wanted to show any fear in front of their Imperator. They all filed onto the platform one after another but shared shifting unease gazes between one another. Energy hummed in the air, and the light surged around the group. A flash blinded them all for a fraction of a second, and when their vision blurred, they were standing in a large chamber full of De'Vayne. Six guards stood in front of the large podium across the room. Each of them wore a different style of sleek armor. From the look of the armor, it couldn't be very thick, Kain assessed. The plates interlocked together almost seamlessly, but there was no space for any of the necessary mechanics that made his power armor so effective.

Above the guards sat Lord De'Vayne. His light blue skin shined in the soft white light of the room, and he sat motionless upon his almost translucent throne that seemed made of light. Only when Kain got closer did he realize what the throne really was. The translucent quality of the processors and circuit boards became clear to see. Small lights weaved through the throne, converging upon Lord De'Vayne. He stared down upon the Imperator with his grey mechanical eyes oscillating. Standing up, his long grey and silver robes swept with his movement, and he walked to the podium's edge.

"So, you're the great Emperor of humanity. I don't sense the power Lord Genji spoke of that could create a true star from the Great Maw. Fall before me, submit to my will, and I shall grant you, my protection." Lord De'Vayne pointed to the ground with a trembling figure. He just glared at Kain.

"Great Lord De'Vayne, this is Kain, the brother of Emperor Solomon, and his representative. His title is Imperator." Lord Genji bowed.

"It seems your Emperor can't spare the time to meet me himself yet dares to request the help of my people?" Lord De'Vayne stood up, to turn away, balking Kain, but he stepped forward with a loud thud of his power armor. The noise forced Lord De'Vayne to turn back to face Kain again.

"Emperor Solomon means no disrespect to you Lord De'Vayne, but humbly requests your assistance. The Cacophony of Discordance is a threat to both of our people. My brother cannot leave the *Empyrean station*, yet I've traveled all the way here to show our respect." Kain summoned all the powers of diplomacy and persuasion he had. He focused on keeping his calm.

"I've seen your great ship *Dawnbreaker* and gone over Lord Genji's report of the *Empyrean station*. Your technology doesn't impress me, Imperator, but I admire your audacity. Lord Genji praised your combat prowess, and I'd like to see the truth of it." Lord De'Vayne snapped his fingers, causing his guards to brandish their weapons. Blades launched from sheaths in synchronized motion before Kain could react. He took several steps backward, his hand falling to grasp the hilt.

"Lord De'Vayne, is this necessary?" Lord Genji looked up. His eyes trembled in the light.

"Don't worry about me. I can handle these six." Kain whispered back to Genji.

"That's not what worries me. They're the best warriors of the De'Vayne. If they win, we lose, but if you win, we lose some of our best warriors, and matter what happens, neither of us gain anything by this waste of life," Genji pointed to the six warriors before Lord De'Vayne with their swords aimed at Kain. Lord De'Vayne motioned for Lord Genji to move away, and he complied without resistance, just bowed to Kain before walking away, shaking his head.

The six warriors gathered around Kain to circle him. Energy hummed in the air, with the shield activating around the group in the center of the room. Kain drew his energy blade, and it snapped to life with a crackle. He raised the blade in defense while studying the movement of the warriors. Lord Genji watched on from beyond the shield, unable to look away as his children circled Kain. It was hard to even breathe for him watching. Each breath came only when he reminded himself to take it. He could feel the tremble in his nerves spreading through his body and rooting his feet to the floor.

CHAPTER 25

E nergy crackled in the Great Maw beyond the vast throng of worldships gathered together. W'Hyish S'yevel fighters rushed away from the growing vortex. Explosions erupted from the fighter craft unable to escape fast enough. Space warped in a bubble at the center of the vortex. Niabs of the W'Hyish S'yevel stood on the bridge of the *Kol'ivar*. The Em'Pharis Dagoth stood in front of the two massive apexinels guarding him, and his shroud of skin made up of the faces of the damn fluttered in the breeze coming from the ventilation into the bridge of his ship the *Kol'ivar*.

Wrinkles folded upon wrinkles on Em'Pharis Dagoth's face. His dull grey eyes seemed almost lifeless if not for the twitch of movement as they scanned the viewscreen. The staff clanged on the ground with each step he took toward the viewscreen. Worldships still moved towards the convoy, and many were scattered throughout the sector. Scans showed the W'Hyish S'yevel tribes all over, and the massive energy vortex still grew beyond the ship.

"Em'Pharis, we must retreat," Occ'ularis Regala pleaded. She moved in front of him, her blue robe flowing, fell to her knees, and prostrated before the Em'Pharis. He put a hand on her shoulder.

"Life demands death, and the Cacophony of Discordance returns. We allowed A'zyren and the *Sesh'yna* to betray us with the help of Lord Void. The Cacophony of Discordance comes to seek payment for our sins." Em'Pharis Dagoth pointed to the *Insidious Seduction* appearing in the vortex of energy. The ship blurred with the Great Maw, almost indistinguishable to the eye, but the flash of energy illuminated the blackened hull drifting towards the tribal ships of the W'Hyish S'yevel.

"Em'Pharis, the *Insidious Seduction* is hailing us," Occ'ularis Regala reported.

"Niabs of the tribes, let us hear the Cacophony's bargain. For if they sought our destruction, there would be no need to talk. Calm yourself and listen to death's bargain." Em'Pharis drew attention to the viewscreen. The image crackled, flickered, and began to clear up until Lilith stood clear on the screen glaring at the Em'Pharis, Occ'ularis, and Niabs.

"Em'Pharis Dagoth, age has robbed you of the beauty you once possessed. Bow before me, supplicant, and perhaps I shall spare your people my wrath." Lilith smirked watching the elder Em'Pharis Dagoth trying to get down on his knees.

"Tell me, Tenno Lilith, have you come to the tribes to bring the flames of war as friend or traitor?" Em'Pharis Dagoth looked up at the image of the Infernal Queen.

The ornate jeweled staff carved with the skulls of many races wobbled, trying to keep the Em'Pharis from falling down. He lowered his head towards the deck plate, trembling from the exertion. Niabs whispered behind the Em'Pharis and only silenced when the Occ'ularis Regala glared at them. She stood behind the Em'Pharis with one hand on his shoulder to steady him. One after another, the Niabs bowed before Lilith. Her wicked grin contorted on the viewscreen.

"I've come to bring you glorious news of a new enemy to reap," Lilith scanned the Niabs.

"Tribes serve the will of the Cacophony of Discordance infernal mistress," Em'Pharis Dagoth stared up a the viewscreen seeing Lilith search the faces of the Niabs.

"Tell me, Em'Pharis, where is the Niab called A'zyren or her tribe, the Voidwalkers?"

"Oh, great Tenno, please spare the W'Hyish S'yevel tribes your infinite wrath, and grant us your favor. A'zyren of the Voidwalker tribe has betrayed the great C'undrivar and sided with the humans of *Empyrean station*. With the help of Lord Void, she slaughtered many of the Niabs that gathered under my call. A'zyren didn't like my plan to seize the *Empyrean station* for the tribes, yet I hadn't expected her to be capable of this betrayal." Em'Pharis Dagoth trembled before Lilith.

"Prepare for my arrival," Lilith cut the communications.

Em'Pharis Dagoth trembled again, trying to rise, and he put all his weight onto the staff. He took Occ'ularis' Regala's outstretched hand to be pulled up onto his feet. The Niabs began to rise with wary looks at their Em'Pharis, and whispers filled the room with an uneasy cadence. Reverie fighters launched from the *Insidious Seduction* appeared on the viewscreen, but Em'Pharis Dagoth turned away to face his people. The Niabs bowed their heads.

"We stand before a great storm that comes to drown us all, but this calamity is the sign of the rebirth that shall rise in the wake of the deluge. Let us go and hear what the Tenno needs, for she comes to not bring us the flames of destruction, but the war of salvation for our people." Em'Pharis Dagoth motioned towards the door with his staff.

The group walked towards the door, causing them to retreat backward in a spiraling motion as metal plates retracted towards the wall. Apexinels and guards followed the procession towards the hanger bay. Niabs continued to whisper in the silent halls of the ship. Em'Pharis Dagoth didn't have time to attend the machinations of the Niabs. On the viewscreen behind, a shuttle shot from the *Insidious Seduction* and headed towards the *Kol'ivar*.

Tombs lined the walls with elegant marks denoting the reverent dead. Em'Pharis Dagoth bowed in respect, and Occ'ularis Regala uttered the traditional W'Hyish S'yevel prayers. The procession walked slow through the halls following the tribal tradition. Death rushed for no living soul, and the W'Hyish S'yevel moved slowly towards the inevitable following behind Em'Pharis Dagoth. It was the way of the tribes that Em'Pharis watched over with his sacred duty, and he glanced back at the procession. The Great Maw punished foolish haste, and the stories of the W'Hyish S'yevel tribes echoed this. Tombs were filled with valiant heroes and traitors like A'zyren, and Em'Pharis Dagoth smiled at that thought.

The large apexinels fanned into the docking bay, taking up guard position by the door, but the two largest stayed close to the Em'Pharis and Occ'ularis. The shuttle blurred with energy radiating outwards, passing through the hanger bay shields. The docking ramp lowered, and Lilith swayed forward, followed by four of her children. Sons stood to her right, and daughters to her left. Walking down the ramp, she glanced to look at the convulsing tentacle arm of the two closest apexinels and drank in their terrible visage.

"I must say, Em'Pharis Dagoth, your people are sublime masters at fleshscuplting. Your apexinels grow more magnificent every time I lay my eyes upon them." Lilith walked up to the closest apexinels to trace her finger over the blackened flesh.

"They are the ultimate expression of death's design. Insatiable in battle and without mercy, but I'm sure your magnificence didn't come here to admire our fleshwork. How may the tribes serve the Cacophony of Discordance," Em'Pharis Dagoth bowed his head in deference.

Lilith's eyes glowed red. Energy lashed out from her at the two apexinels. Green bile burst from their stitches, and they convulsed, heaving them towards the ground. Niabs gasped, watching Lilith clench her fist with red energy swirling around them. Her children laughed behind her. The energy dissipated in a bright flash allowing the apexinels to live.

"Flesh has limits that I do not." Lilith reminded with a smile.

"How can we serve the great balance?" Em'Pharis Dagoth fell to the floor, trembling.

Lilith looked out at the Niabs who were falling to prostrate before her. Even the might apexinels kneeled before her. Red energy crackled off her fingertips, and she grinned back at her children. She walked over, knelt, and forced Em'Pharis to look up, tracing a finger up his face. Crimson energy crackled in her eyes.

"There's no need to fear us. We've come to bring you a blessing of the Cacophony. Four of my greatest children will merge with your Niabs to empower and learn from them. You've been chosen for a glorious task, dear Em'Pharis Dagoth." Lilith dug the tip of her finger into Em'Pharis chin, forcing him to stand from the pain.

"What do you mean?" Blood raced down Em'Pharis Dagoth's chin and neck.

The Niabs cowered before Lilith, but she dragged the Em'Pharis towards them. Her children were already walking in front of the others, looking them over. Niabs cowered before the children. None of the Niabs looked particularly powerful to her. She released the Em'Pharis from her fingernail and brought it up to lick the blood off.

"Your offerings seem a bit lacking Em'Pharis Dagoth. My children seem to be having a hard time choosing their host." Lilith heard the crackle of her children behind her.

"My Niabs are the greatest warriors of the W'hyish S'yevel tribes," Em'Pharis Dagoth assured, but he averted his gaze from Lilith's over-the-shoulder glare. Her children paced the assembled group staring at each of them. One of the children pointed to her choice.

"It seems Thassala has found one." Lilith inspected the large brute her daughter had chosen. He was a large human with rippling muscles. She looked into his eyes to see the dim light within.

"This one isn't too bad. I like the way he ripples." Thassala ran her fingers over him.

"Your taste in host is bland, my dear, but if he suits you. What are you called?" Lilith glared up at the man.

"Sab'both the Ravager. Niab of the Hungering Hordes." Sab'both declared with his chest puffed out. Thassala crackled with energy swirling around Sab'both. The energy coalesced in a flash. "We offer eternal servitude to the Cacophony of Discordance, mother." Sab'both bowed to Lilith.

"A wise plan indeed, Tenno. Our warriors will be made much stronger with the powers of your dark children." Em'Pharis Dagoth acknowledged seeing the cracking energy in Sab 'Both's eyes. He dared not show any fear but didn't fool himself that Lilith didn't already sense it from him. They walked towards one of her sons.

"What have we got here, Avitu?" Lilith inspected the Tigran that her son chose. She looked to the size of his claws and the build of his frame.

"This one seems suitable enough, Mother, given the pickings. I have delicious ideas on how to use these claws." Avitu bowed to his mother.

"What is your name Tigran?" Lilith tapped her foot waiting for the answer.

"I'm Wag'Hoba, the fearless of the Death Stalker tribe," he declared. Avitu surged in a crackle of energy around the Tigran. He convulsed from the power jolting into his body.

"It seems Kakash has found her favorite in the apoidean. I did always admire the way they danced. Such a beautiful language, don't you agree?" Lilith looked back to Em'Pharis Dagoth.

"Aristaea of the Stinging Song tribe is a fine choice. Her tribe is one of the most numerous amongst the W'hyish S'yevel tribes." Em'Pharis Dagoth watched the crackle of energy surge around Kakash and swept around Aristaea.

"We serve the Cacophony of Discordance. Life demands death."
Aristaea bowed, crossing her four arms in a prayer before Lilith.

Lilith watched her son pace back and forth, trying to decide between
several Niabs. He couldn't seem to decide which he liked the best. She
placed her hand on his shoulder.

"Odam, just pick one. I like the serpentine. He looks like the
personification of venomous." Lilith pointed to the large Serpentine. His
powerful muscles rippled under his thick scales.

"Nagani of the Coiling Doom tribe is one of our most lethal warriors,"
Em'Pharis Dagoth looked at Odam, eying up the Serpentine alongside his
infernal mother.

Energy crackled from Odam towards Naga, but he just stood there.
Lilith led Em'Pharis Dagoth and Occ'ularis Regala away from the Niabs.
She motioned to the fleet that could be seen gathering beyond the hanger
bay. Red energy crackled off her fingertip. She glared back at the two tribal
leaders.

"Begin mustering all your tribes for war. Arachne forces will soon
arrive to join you, and when you're ready, you'll attack the *Empyrean station*.
Destroy everything in the sector. Only after that can the Cacophony of
Discordance destroy the renegade star and the light forever. First, you'll tell
me where Lucifer is." Lilith's entire body crackled with red energy, and she
marched towards Em'Pharis Dagoth and Occ'ularis Regala.

"We've never met a Lucifer Tenno. I swear. Only a reverie by the name
of Lord Magnus Void showed up almost five decades ago. He managed to
sway A'zyren's mother, the Niab of the Voidwalker tribe at that time, on a
great quest. The C'undrivar was summoned, but only A'zyren answered the
quest. She alone set out with Lord Magnus Void to reignite the light. None
of the other tribes betrayed the Cacophony of Discordance," Em'Pharis
Dagoth's voice trembled.

"You should have told the Cacophony about this Lord Magnus Void's
visit, and his plan when he first appeared. Betrayal doesn't go unanswered.
Pray that your dead are sufficient to win the battle ahead because if you
aren't victorious and manage to live, the punishment the Cacophony of
Discordance will visit will be beyond measure. Eternal infinite agony will
fall upon you and your tribes. From here on out my children will watch
over you and ensure your loyalty." Lilith walked back towards her shuttle.

The shuttle ramp closed behind Lilith. Hovering into the air, the shuttle shot forward and raced through the hanger shield with a ripple of energy. Em'Pharis Dagoth looked at Occ'ularis Regala with a solemn nod. There was no choice left to them. Tribes would gather for another great war, and Em'Pharis Dagoth prayed that the infernal powers of the Cacophony would see fit to reward them for their sacrifices afterward. He sensed this would be his last war one way or another for him but dreaded the cost for his people. The procession followed behind at a ponderous rate walking back through the sacred halls. Em'Pharis Dagoth only wished the dead could speak now, but the hall remained silent. The dead kept their secrets.

CHAPTER 26

The shield glimmered around Kain, and he gripped the energy blade with both hands. De'Vayne's warriors circled Kain. He could see the swords the warriors were carrying looked familiar, and his memories filled in the details. The weapons were the same ones he saw Genji use on the outpost. Emitters lined the blade edge of the swords wielded by the warriors. Kain glanced around, keeping his attention on the warrior behind him.

One of the children rushed at Kain from behind, and he spun around. With a swipe of his energy blade, he deflected the sword away. He burst forward, grabbed the warrior by the throat with one hand, and swung around, throwing the warrior back at the others flowing behind. A series of attacks came from the closest warriors, but he managed to block them with ease. He slipped through a gap. Two warriors rushed at him catching one of them off guard. Overhead cleave slashed down before the warrior could get his sword up to guard, severed his arm, and cleaved into his leg, dropping him to the ground. He struggled to crawl away as the other warriors rushed at Kain.

Genji gasped, watching the first warrior fall to Kain's blade. The air hummed with the charge of the weapons. Energy blasted forth from the first sword slash forcing Kain to dodge to the side, but the other children closed the ground with rapid footsteps. Clangs of metal echoed in the audience chamber from the blades clashing together. The energy smashed into the shield with a ripple of energy flooding across the surface.

A flurry of slashes launched at Kain, forcing him to fall back on the defensive. Sparks flew from the metal cutting into his power armor. Alarms blared in his mind showing the damage that was being sustained.

He slashed out, knocking down one of the warriors, but before he could deliver a coup-de-grace, the other four launched a vicious assault. It took all his energy to keep deflecting the relentless series of strokes. The warriors focused his attention on them while the fallen guard struggled to get back on their feet. Loud hum of charging blades resonated around Kain.

Energy exploded forth, catching Kain by surprise. The energy wave flung him backward, and he slammed into the deck plate, sparking with each smash against the metal, and rolled across the floor. Alarms blared, vision through the helmet was blurred by static, and he was forced to retract the helmet with a thought. He pushed off the ground to stand back up just in time. The warriors were already rushing at him once more. Genji watched the fight, unable to breathe.

Each foot carried Kain forward in a steady march toward the incoming warriors. He deflected the first attack with so much force the warrior went tumbling across the floor. The second blade stroke glanced off his armor, creating an opening, and he threw the warrior into the shield. Energy snapped in a surge propelling the warrior into the ground hard. He strode forward towards the last three fanning out, backing up with slow sidesteps.

Kain charged forward with a monstrous howl of pure rage. His blade slashed down the first defending warrior's blade before it could fire, and the energy tore through flesh to sever a leg. The other two glanced to each other before charging back into assist. The first one whiffed through the air when Kain dodged to the side, and the second blade smashed into his energy blade. He glared through the crackling energy at the warrior. The first warrior tried to attack again, but he stepped backward, pulling his defense back, causing the second warrior to tumble forward. Unable to stop, the two warriors crashed into each other, and the recovering warrior rushed to attack.

The warrior who struck the shield tried to get up off the ground. His helmet shook rapidly as he tried to regain senses. Energy charged into the blade, and the warrior tried to sneak behind Kain, struggling with the other two warriors. He continued deflected the flurry of strikes. His alarms warned of the incoming attack from behind. Energy sparked from the strikes of the blade, and he waited for the right moment. When the warrior unleashed his charged weapon, he dodged out of the way of the blast, and the energy tore through the attacking warrior, rushing his flank. The energy cleaved the warrior in half as flesh slid apart after a brief moment.

Rolling across the ground, Kain leaped to his feet and kicked the nearest warrior in the chest. He slashed out, putting the second warrior on the defensive, trying to fall back to regain proper footing. The other two warriors finally recovered and now rushed from behind at him. He wasn't able to dispatch the off-balanced warrior before the others arrived. A series of slashes sent the alarm blaring again, and he tried to deflect all the incoming attacks with furious speed.

Each strike that landed cleaved into the armor, but none of them managed to puncture the suit all the way through. Kain was surrounded by the four remaining warriors trying to hold their attacks at bay. Pain surged when the first stroke penetrated all the way through the armor. His eyes went vision went red with pain, and he howled, unleashing all his rage. The blade was still lodged in the armor when he spun around, ripping it from the hands of the warrior.

Kain deflected the incoming attack and countered with such force it staggered the warrior backward, and he surged forward toward the off-balanced attacker. The warrior tried to retreat backward with quick steps, but it wasn't fast enough. Energy crackled from the swinging blade, and he slashed it down across the warrior's chest, storming forward. The blade slashed back across the warrior's chest from left to right, moving upwards as Kain spun back around, passing his enemy. Metal disintegrated under the powerful heat of the energy blade. The other warriors couldn't help their ally fast enough, watching helplessly.

The warrior collapsed onto the metal floor with a loud clang, blood pouring from the massive cleaves, and Kain stared down his crackling energy blade aimed at the last three warriors. Painkillers pumped into his blood from the power armor, and the suit clamped down on the wounded area. Microsurgical tools began cleaning and suturing the wound while the battle continued. The mixture of chemicals in his blood filled him with elation. Pain faded away, and his eyes narrowed, focusing on the warriors in front of him.

With a slow walk, Kain closed ground. Genji watched, unable to look away, but he knew what was coming. He'd lived through moments like this where, despite the odds, he knew victory was his. Kain's walk told him that was where his mind was. Absolute victory already belonged to him, and now he just had to finish what was left. Tears welled in Genji's eyes as he looked upon the warrior still struggling to crawl across the floor, leaving a trail of blood across the deck. He glanced towards Lord De'Vayne, both eyes trembling, pleading to assist, but he was too busy enthralled watching the bloodshed. Genji glanced back to see the final three warriors preparing to attack.

Kain wouldn't give the enemy another opportunity to coordinate an attack. The three warriors glanced at each other, but he just charged with a howl. He slashed wide, driving two warriors to fall backward away from the furious attack, but that was what he wanted. Two quick slashes pushed the warriors back further, and he turned back on the isolated warrior. Before the others could change direction, he unleashed all his rage.

A series of blows slashed at the isolated warrior trying to deflect them, and the force of the blows knocked the enemy off balance. A loud thud echoed as the warrior struck the floor, and the forced sent the helmet tumbling away across the deck. She looked up with fear in her eyes, holding up her blade. Blow after blow rained down rapidly, Kain glared down with eyes filled with bloodlust. Her arm buckled under each subsequent strike of the energy blade until the force knocked it away. Energy blade slashed down on the defenseless warrior slicing the arm clean off in the final blow. The sword clattered across the floor with the arm still attached. He drove the blade down with a great howl thrusting the blade through the warrior's chest. Her head fell to the ground, lifelessly staring directly at Genji locking eyes with him.

Reaching out with one hand, Genji's eyes welled up with tears, and he let out a howl of pain that broke through even Kain's bloodlust. He glanced back at Genji but didn't have time to figure out what was going on. He saw the other two warriors rushing at him. Two warriors coordinated attacks and slashed outwards, forcing Kain to react.

Energy crackled as the two swords collided. Kain blocked the first slash with his sword and dodged the second, but the speed of the attacks was near lightning-fast. The warriors timed their strikes to prevent him from countering at all. Each attack only signaled the start of the next from the other warrior. He was forced to continue to fall back on the defensive with steady footsteps back to keep balance. Weapons synchronized together, beginning to hum with the charging energy.

The attacks kept coming at Kain, and the weapons hummed louder with each strike. There was no opportunity for him to counter, and each step back gave him less room to maneuver. He was certain the warriors were controlling his movements while their weapons charged, but he couldn't do anything to change that. Sparks erupted from his forearm from the blade slashing across the surface. He yanked his arm back and gripped his energy blade with both hands. In the corner of his eye, he caught the first blade and unleashed the torrential energy blast it stored inside.

The first energy wave forced Kain to dive away to dodge it, but the second energy wave raced toward him. He managed to leap back to his feet to get out of the way just in the nick of time. Energy sheared across the front of the power armor sending the alarms into a full frenzy of reports. The bright energy wave turned his vision pure white from the blinding light. He was blind for a moment and now forced to rely only upon his hearing.

Footsteps echoed, and Kain focused his attention on the sound. Energy crackled when he deflected an incoming attack. The blade other warrior's blade cut into his armor with a powerful thrust. Blade pierced through his armor but failed to hit his flesh. Internal sensors showed the blade missed by centimeters, and the blade stuck in him told him exactly where the warrior was. He reached out, grabbing the warrior by the throat. His vision began to clear a bit, but all he saw was the vague shape of the warrior in a sea of white. It was enough, and he continued deflecting the incoming attacks with his free arm.

The warrior gasped for air but pushed the blade forward with all his might. Despite the effort, the blade wouldn't budge in Kain's power armor. It was lodged in the interlocking metal of the stomach armor sections. Kain watched the warrior's eyes roll into the back of his as his vision continued to clear. Sound alone was enough to guide his sword arm to deflect the other warrior's attacks that grew sloppier with each stroke.

A loud crack echoed when Kain snapped the warrior's neck. The body thudded to the ground. He turned towards the last remaining warrior, gripped the energy blade with both hands and started advancing with a cold hard stare locked upon his enemy. The warrior began falling back under rasping breaths. Emitters along the blade edge began to charge again, but Kain surged forward. A series of sword clashes filled the room with flashes of light to the sound of awe from the watching crowd. Lord De'Vayne's eyes followed Kain's movement closely.

The blade was almost charged when Kain made his move. A fast series of attacks drew the warrior into overextending their defense. He launched outward, grabbing the sword arm to lock it in place, and he spun around, severing the hand with a single stroke. The charging blade fell towards the ground, but he caught it. He kicked the warrior backward, and she tumbled across the floor. He grasped the blade in his offhand, feeling the vibration of the blade resonating through the suit of power armor. A single slash rippled the energy to cleave the remaining warrior in half.

Genji fell to his knees with tears brimming in his eyes. He couldn't look away no matter how hard he tried, and his eyes focused on Kain walking slowly towards the last of the warriors. Onlookers pointed to Genji with some laughing at him while others whispered. Kain caught the scene in his peripheral vision but remained focused on the battle. The warrior turned back to face Kain, snatching a blade from the dead hands of a fallen ally. He lowered the energy blade to his side before deactivating it. The warrior looked up at Kain but refused the hand he offered to help him stand back up. Using the sword, the warrior pushed himself back up and stared at Kain.

"You fought well, but I can't fathom why this violence was necessary. I'm sorry, but you left me no choice." Kain apologized, looking back at the corpses.

"My father was right. You're the greatest warrior. It has been an honor fighting against you and to die in the service of the glorious Lord De'Vayne." The warrior bowed to Kain, but before he could say anything, he watched the warrior bring up the blade to plunge the blade into his own chest before Kain could react. The body collapsed to the ground to Lord De'Vayne's applause, joined by the rapturous clamor of the crowd staring on. Glancing over one shoulder, Kain's eyes locked on Genji's, and he saw tears streaming down his face.

Kain looked down at the warrior whose helmet had been knocked off. Her beautiful delicate features glared up from dead, lifeless eyes, but her features were unmistakable. The sight brought Kain to his knees. He just glared up at the applauding Lord De'Vayne. The people in the audience joined in with their applause. It took Kain a few moments to struggle back to his feet, and he walked over to Genji to kneel in front of him.

"Was she your daughter?" Kain's eyes trembled with fear.

Genji's lips trembled, and no sound came out at first. His eyes glistened with tears in the glow of the lights glaring down from above as he locked eyes with Kain. He placed a hand on Kain's shoulder, struggling to speak.

"Those were all my children," Genji's voice trailed off. Kain could hear some of the crowd around him laughing. In his peripheral vision, he saw some De'Vayne pointing and mocking Genji. Anger coursed through Kain's veins, and he was about to rise when Genji's hand reached out to hold Kain in place. He glanced back at Genji who shook his head.

"Save your anger, my friend, for the right time and place." Lord Genji shook his head, and his eyes darted to Lord De'Vayne. "Remember, you don't understand our ways."

"I'm sorry, my friend. Take my blade and avenge your children. Had I known I wouldn't have raised my blade against them." Kain offer his blade to Genji.

The crowd grew silent again, watching the display between the two warriors. Even Lord De'Vayne stopped his applause. Genji looked down at the energy blade, took it, and sparked it to life with a push of a button. He looked at the glowing energy blade.

"There is no greater honor than to die in glorious battle for your people and your lord. My children died because their lord commanded it, and you gave them a glorious end. There is no blood debt between us. I admit, even I underestimate the fury of this blade of yours. Take good care of it." Genji snapped the blade off, pressing it back into Kain's hands. The two warriors looked into each other's eyes, seeing the echoes of their own pain.

"What a magnificent battle. It seems Lord Genji has proved the truth of this tales beyond any challenge. It would be my greatest honor to fight alongside you and your Emperor. Rise, Imperator, and together we shall return to tell your Emperor that I shall lead my forces to join you. Let us stand against the Great Maw together," Lord De'Vayne declared to thunderous applause from his people.

Kain turned to walk away. He knew the words he wanted to speak would be a disservice to the death of Genji's children. Matthew had his allies now, and Kain only wondered if his brother saw the full cost. It wasn't a memory he'd soon forget. He glanced at Genji across the room as his troops gathered to celebrate his victory. He moved alongside his Lord but continued to stare at Kain. All Kain could do now was acknowledge the respect Genji showed with a silent nod.

Walking out of the auditorium, Kain focused his thoughts. One day he'd get vengeance for what Lord De'Vayne did this day. The thud of the troops behind only echoed the constant thought of vengeance that droned in repetition in Kain's mind. He never expected to find someone with a greater capacity for cruelty than his father. Kain glanced back to see Lord De'Vayne watching Genji. What shocked Kain was that despite everything, Genji stood loyal beside his Lord, and there didn't seem to be any trace of malice, hatred, or vengeance in his eyes, just a deep sadness.

Sounds of his troops talking about the fantastic battle droned around him, but Kain couldn't help but think about why Genji was loyal to such a Lord that would sacrifice his children needlessly. He looked down at his own hand. It trembled, still soaked in the blood of Genji's children. For the first time in Kain's life, the sight of blood made him queasy.

CHAPTER 27

Clan Pious banners hung outside the Whelsey estate. The cloth rippled in the breeze of the city ward with sharp snaps and gentle flutters. Helena walked towards the front doors but looked around for Angelica in the soldiers training outside. She hadn't seen her daughter since they had first arrived, and worry lined her face. She could see her father coming down the stairway through the windows, and he stopped to talk to two guards. Helena couldn't hear anything from this distance, and she rushed towards the front doors.

Two guards stood like statues by the front doors. Helena approached the doors, hoping to walk by unopposed, but the two guards moved to block the doorway. Lord Whelsey disappeared through the doorway towards the basement. A monk walking through the building saw the commotion at the front door and walked over to see what was happening. Helena complained to the two guards who refused to let her in, and her words echoed into the estate.

"I'm the daughter of Lord Whelsey! When my father hears you refuse to allow me to enter, there will be hell to pay!" Helena tried to push past the guards once more, but they stopped her again, silently blocking her path by crossing their unignited energy blades. Monk Fiona watched Helena start to walk away, rushing past the guards who parted, seeing her approach.

"Lady Helena. It's good to see you. I don't know if you remember me, but my name is Fiona, and I'm one of the monks in the church's order of the Eternal Flame. I've served your father since I was a little girl." Fiona bowed to Lady Helena.

"You know this woman, Fiona?" One of the guards asked.

"Yes, this is Lord Whelsey's daughter, Lady Helena. You might not recognize her because our former captain kept her locked away for years. I just saw Lord Whelsey headed downstairs to check on a research project he's been conducting with Lord Galen, or at least so the whispered rumors tell." Fiona pointed to the guarded door in the main lobby. The guards still stood blocking the entrance, but they looked at each other worriedly before turning back.

"We've got orders not to let anyone who's not a member of our clan pass. Sorry Fiona, but orders are orders." The other guard crossed his arms.

"I understand, as I'm sure Lord Whelsey will when you both explain why you kept his daughter out of his home," Fiona explained.

The two guards looked at each other once more. They tried to hide their fears, but shifting glances to Lady Helena told her that their fear of her father was beginning to move them. Neither of them wanted to get on Lord Whelsey's bad side, so they moved away from the door. One of the guards waved Helena and Fiona through the door. They didn't say another word. Fiona smiled, patted the guards on the shoulders, and motioned for Helena to follow her. The two women walked into the estate. Helena shook her head and took a moment to stare down both guards following Fiona into the estate. She walked alongside the young monk.

"Thank you, Fiona. Those guards were getting on my last nerve. I don't know what I would've done if it wasn't for you," Helena admitted.

"A good deed is a reward in itself, but I don't know if I can help you get past those other two. Your father was very specific regarding the basement." Fiona pointed to the basement door. "It's why everyone is whispering about the secret research going on down there. I'm sorry, my lady, but I must get back to my duties lest I incur your father's wrath for my failure." Fiona curtsied before disappearing beyond the large double doors leading to the dining hall.

Two guards stood on either side of the doorway. Helena glanced around and couldn't see any technological locks around the door. She didn't notice her father unlock the door with any kind of card or key either. From what she could see, the guards seemed to be the only defense for the basement. She glanced around, looking for a way to distract the guards. All she had to do was get the guards away from the door, and she should be able to slip past.

Helena had an epiphany, and she walked straight up toward the guards. The two guards moved to block the door as she predicted. She pulled a data pad with the imperial document her son had given her to present to her father. It contained all the details and permissions to break ground on constructing a new cathedral, but she hoped the guards wouldn't look that close. She glared at the guards and shook the data pad.

"Do either of you know what this is?" Helena continued shaking the data pad. The guards glanced at each other and shook their heads. "This is an imperial decree of our new Emperor. I've been ordered to deliver this to Lord Whelsey and none other. I saw Lord Galen head down into the basement. Now get out of my way before I have you two guards brought before Emperor Solomon to answer for this delay of the delivery of this Imperial decree."

The guards looked at each other without a word, but both of their eyes trembled with fear glancing at each other. They whispered to each other, but Helena could make out them discussing Lord Whelsey's legendary wrath amongst the clan, and neither of the guards wanted to be on the receiving end. Tapping of Helena's foot kept the guard's glances darting back to her as they discussed. Other guard whispers were harder to make out, however, Helena made out the word Emperor move across his lips. Two guards looked at Helena, the data pad, and back to each other before nodding in agreement. They both stepped back out of Helena's way to stand at attention. Neither guard moved when Helena approached the door. She pressed the button, and the door swished opened. The door whisked shut behind her, and she walked down the stairs with slow, cautious, and careful steps echoing in the silent stairwell.

A noise echoed in the distance drawing Helena forward, but she couldn't determine what it was. She continued down the stairway turning the corner at the bottom. A long corridor with many doors on both sides stood before her. Only the loud sounds guided her down the corridor. With each step, the noise grew louder and became easier to understand. The sound of churning machines mixed with screams caused her to pause for a moment. With a hard swallow, she pushed forward, heading towards the sound of horror resonating down the corridor. Her mouth grew dry, her hair on the back of her neck stood on end, and goosebumps appeared on her arms. With each footstep, she glanced back behind her before taking another.

The screams seemed to be coming from the furthest room in the hallway. Helena crept along the wall. Another wail echoed down the hallway, and she could tell the screams were coming from a woman. The high-pitched voice grew clearer with each step. Almost at the door, she heard the scream blast forth again, but now she recognized the voice. Her footsteps hastened with the revelation, and she raced towards the door, her eyes focused and pupils widening. The door stood shut, and she moved her trembling hands toward the door's access pad.

Helena's hand trembled over the access pad, and she wanted to open the door. Fear held her transfixed at that moment. She didn't know what was on the other side. Another scream resonated through the door. Angelica's screams tore at Helena's mind; it was more than she could bear. Her hand hovered over the button door, but fear gripped her, preventing her from moving. The sound of muffled voices coming through the door drew Helena towards the door. She placed her ear against the cold metal, trying to make out what was being said.

"This power is truly incredible, Lord Whelsey. I've never seen regeneration this fast. Levart seems capable of immediately mending organic damage to his host. It's almost like a parasite trying to keep its host alive as long as possible. Scans show there is a massive energy transfer occurring at a quantum level affecting the cellular mitosis process speeding it up astronomically. There seems to be almost no end to the powers of Levart." Lord Galen's voice echoed through the door.

"That's all good, but have you got any closer to figuring out how to replicate Levart's power?" Lord Whelsey's voice was a low mumble, but Helena recognized it. She wondered who Levart was.

"The data I've accumulated is beyond staggering. It seems, however, that the Reverie secrets are not so easily penetrated. I've yet to figure out how this possession functions," Lord Galen stated.

"We must figure out the secret soon. There's no telling how much more suffering my granddaughter can withstand through these experiments." Lord Whelsey's words forced Helena's hand. She pressed the button, and the door retracted back. Both men were shocked by the sudden movement of the door, standing there frozen. Helena glared at the two men before seeing her daughter tied down to the medical bed, and she raced over to Angelica.

Helena was already trying to undo the straps around Angelica's arms before either of the men could even react. Her fingers struggled against the strap but got it unhooked just as Lord Whelsey grabbed his daughter's arm. He was pulling her back when Levart lashed out to grab Helena's throat. Angelica's eyes were pure black, and her maniacal laughter echoed in the lab. Several blows from Lord Whelsey finally broke Helena free of Levart's grasp. Lord Galen managed to get the demon strapped back down.

"What are you doing?" Lord Whesley shook his daughter, but she seemed catatonic. She just started at Angelica convulsing on the medical bed, trying to break free.

Lord Galen shined a light into Helena's eyes, and her pupils didn't react at first. It took a few seconds before her pupils expanded to the light. She lashed out, breaking free of her father's hold. It took both of the men to restrain Helena from freeing her daughter. Angelica continued to laugh, watching the fight.

"Helena, calm down," Lord Whelsey implored, trying to hold onto his daughter.

"Let my daughter go! She's suffered enough!" Helena continued to fight back.

"That's not Angelica anymore. A demon named Levart from the Cacophony of Discordance has possessed her. We're trying to find a way to save her," Lord Whelsey pleaded.

"Liar," Helena screeched, continuing her struggle. "I heard you talking about replicating Levart's power." Managing to break one hand free from her father's grasp, she fought with all her might, flailing against her father's grasp. She managed to land an elbow, and she broke completely free. Lord Galen moved behind her, attaching a device to her neural implant. The device clamped down. She screamed loudly for a second before falling deathly silent.

Lights flashed on the device, and Helena's body locked up. Her eyes darted around, but she couldn't move any other part of her body. Lord Whelsey stood up, wiping the blood from his nose, and he could still feel it running down his upper lip. He looked at his daughter to see the rage in her eyes. Lord Galen moved over to the computer terminal to sync with the device.

"Don't worry, the neural monitor will prevent her from doing anything we don't allow. This way, we can ensure your daughter doesn't run back and tell Emperor Solomon about our experiment." Lord Galen looked up at Lord Whelsey to see the smile on his face.

"I'm sorry, Helena, but this is for your own good. Angelica needs to be saved from this demon, and we need to understand the power of the Cacophony of Discordance to defeat them. We must all make sacrifices in these dark times. This is your cross to bear." Lord Whelsey ran his finger down his daughter's cheek. He could see the tears brimming in her eyes, forcing him to choke back the rush of his own tears. For a moment, Lord Whelsey stared at his daughter. Anger, rage, and sorrow glimmered in her hateful glare at her father, and Lord Whelsey felt his legs weaken. He glanced to Lord Galen with a motion of his hand to the console.

"Allow her to speak at least. I would hear what my daughter has to say." Lord Galen nodded in agreement releasing the controls with thought using his neural implant.

"How dare you use my daughter like this," Helena spat the second she could speak.

"I wasn't the one who chose to use Angelica over and over again. You caused this when you turned to me to help you against Gabriel. The moment you saw your daughter as a weapon was the moment this was destined to happen. Levart wormed his way into your daughter through the pain and trauma her own parents caused her. Now I'm the only chance Angelica has for salvation and to find peace through God's mercy," Lord Whelsey proclaimed, staring into his daughter's eyes. Silence washed across the room for a moment, broken only by the maniacal laughter of Levart, still watching the whole scene from the medical bed.

Tears streamed down Helena's face as she looked back at her daughter. The truth slammed down on her. She looked down upon Angelica to see the black eyes of Levart glaring back at her. The maniacal laughter echoing through the lab only reinforced the truth Helena was struggling against. She looked up at her father, but anger was now replaced with a tremble of desperation.

"What can we do to save her?"

"First, we must figure out Levart's weaknesses. That's going to take Lord Galen time to learn. We must keep this from Emperor Solomon until we figure out how to control Levart." Lord Whelsey put his arm around his daughter to turn her away from Angelica. Her body began moving again, and she glanced to see Lord Galen working on the computer.

"The neural monitor is working perfectly," Lord Galen reported.

"My plans have progressed too far. I can't leave anything to chance now. Angelica and Levart are crucial to my plans. This neural monitor will make sure you stay loyal, but I suspect you wouldn't ever betray me. Lord Galen, return her full body control." Lord Whelsey watched his daughter's body unlock slowly with the neural monitor block lifting.

Helena wasn't sure what to do. She hadn't expected her father to treat her or her children like this, but she knew she needed to bide time for now. At least until she could figure a way to deal with the neural monitor. The devices were infamous on the *Alcatraz* for controlling unruly members of the population or for producing compliance in slaves. Gabriel enjoyed using them to ensure his women entertained him to his desires, and the thought made Helena shudder. She looked at Angelica lying on the medical bed. This time she wouldn't leave her daughter at the mercy of a maniacal madman. Not even if the madman was her own father.

"I understand, Father, and I'll do what I can to help you and my daughter," Helena assured.

"Lord Galen will monitor your thoughts just to make sure, but I'm sure you don't mind that. Just trust that I have your best interests at heart as I've always had. Angelica will be fine." Lord Whelsey led his daughter out of the lab, and the door whisked shut behind them. Screams echoed from the lab, signalling that Lord Galen's experiments had started again.

Screams mixed with maniacal laughter echoed with the footsteps down the long corridor. Helena tried not to glance back but found it difficult. Each new torrent of torment tugged at her heartstrings. Lord Whelsey kept one arm around his daughter forcing her forward. There was no way for Helena to stop thinking about what Angelica was going through, and her thoughts echoed the fears of what Levart's possession would do. She wasn't sure what her father's endgame was with his plan, but the fact he mentioned her son, Emperor Solomon, didn't sit right with her.

"Father, you must be careful with this demon lest he steals your soul. Levart might be possessing Angelica, but perhaps you're the real target." Helena hoped to fear her father off the path he'd chosen, but he seemed resolute as ever to pursue his chosen path. Staring back with a stern look, Helena's memories were full of from her childhood whenever she was about to be punished. Her nerves trembled in anticipation of the coming punishment, but Lord Whelsey pushed his daughter forward, still holding her close with one arm. He looked down into his daughter's eyes, full of emotion and wiped a tear from her cheek.

"This demon holds no sway over the hearts of men loyal to God. It's my sacred duty to ensure such demons are destroyed or at least sent back to damnation where they belong. We must all do our duties, my daughter," Lord Whelsey advised.

"For what shall it profit a man if he shall gain the whole world but lose his soul?" Helena realized how much her father reminded her of Gabriel in his own ways. He was singular in focus and never taking advice unless it was what he wanted to hear. The Bible was the only route Helena could use to persuade her father. She hoped it worked.

"We must be willing to make the sacrifices that God demands of us, my daughter. James chapter four, part seven. "Submit yourself to God. Resist the devil, and he will flee from you. God has sent a devil to walk amongst us as a wolf amidst his flock. I intended to learn everything I could and use it to slaughter all the wolves to safeguard my flock," Lord Whelsey vowed.

There was only one person Helena knew who could help her now. Lady Clotho would see the truth in the weave of fate. She was the only one who might see the truth without Helena needing to explain it. Lord Galen would be watching to ensure Helena didn't betray the research to anyone. She followed her father up the stair, biding her time.

CHAPTER 28

Workers continued to labor away outside the new building. The sign on the building glowed with the words Original Sins in bright crimson. A radiant glow cast by the sign fell upon the workers below. Approaching the workers, a hooded figure slipped into the crowd and approached the main doors. People didn't notice the figure moving through without touching anyone in the dense crowd. Crimson glared down, and the figure stopped to look up. Light fell upon Helena's delicate features looking at the sign, but she looked away quickly, hastening her walk. She stared down at the ground, trying to keep her mind clear of any thoughts. Humming a song helped keep her mind preoccupied, and she hoped it would confuse Lord Galen if he was watching her brain functions.

A worker held the door open for Helena. She didn't even look at the man when she walked past. The building echoed with the sound of all the work being done. Tools whirred in the distance, hammers rang out, and a drone of mumbling workers filled the building. She scanned the room for her daughter, but she only saw Lord Marcus in the center of the crowd. Approaching the group, Helena pulled back the hood drawing Marcus' attention quickly.

"Lady Helena, I wasn't expecting you," Marcus stated. He could sense something was off. "You seem vexed. Has something happened?"

"It's none of your business, you upstart. Why my daughter is interested in a lowlife like you is beyond me. Where's Nemesis at?" Helena crossed her arms, glaring at Marcus. He just pointed towards the stairs.

"A'zyren and her people came to help. She is upstairs showing her friend our new penthouse right now." Marcus motioned away some workers trying to approach. He wouldn't make any of his people suffer through dealing with Helena. The workers saw the scowl on Helena's face and rushed away to avoid dealing with the woman's legendary wrath.

Marcus motioned to Lady Helena to follow and guided her through the workers. The elevator on this floor was still blocked by workers. The two walked up the stairs toward the second-floor elevator. A ding signaled the arrival of the elevator, and the doors slid open. Laughter echoed from the small box. Nemesis and A'zyren came around the corner, and both of their faces were red from laughter. There was an abrupt silence when Nemesis saw her mother.

"Do you ever tire of the decadence, my dear?" Helena tapped her foot, glaring at A'zyren and Marcus. These two were to blame for Nemesis's lack of diligence.

"Is there something wrong, Mother?" Nemesis searched her mother's eyes, sensing something wasn't right. A'zyren and Marcus both watched Nemesis with concern.

"Of course, there's nothing wrong. I just came to discuss things with you and find out if you've seen your sister." Helena could feel her heart thundering in her chest. Sweat beaded on her forehead, and she wiped it away with a reflexive swipe of her hand. The beads of sweat glistened in the palm of her hand, and she could see the glint of the light in the droplets. Nemesis and Marcus exchanged looks briefly before she approached her mother, shaking her head no. Growing closer, she could see her mother trying to fight back tears.

"I haven't seen Angelica since we first arrived, but Virgil should be able to locate her. Maybe you need to take a seat or getting something to drink." Nemesis put her arm around her mother.

"What I need is to find your sister!" Helena tried to use anger to cover up her torment, but she felt the eyes of Lord Galen watching her. All she could do was keep her thoughts from betraying why she was here.

The other elevator dinged, and Lady Clotho emerged. The cane thudded on the ground with her slow approach. Dull blind eyes fell on Helena, and she felt her heartbeat even harder against her ribs. Lady Clotho walked around Helena studying her with blind eyes.

"Something seems amiss since we last spoke," Clotho warned.

"It's just been a long day of searching for Angelica and dealing with letches like Marcus here. Forgive me, Lady Clotho, you find me at my wit's end here." Helena watched Clotho circle her.

"You should be proud your daughter has such a fine man as Marcus," A'zyren interjected.

"What would you know about it?" Helena crossed her arms, turning to glare at A'zyren.

"I know that true love is rare in the Great Maw and what your daughter has with Marcus is the real deal. Something you had once, no? Lady Clotho stared at Helena. Dull grey blind eyes stared right through her. Hairs on the back of her neck stood on end. She shook it off turning away.

"You're cruel, Lady Clotho." Helena felt Lady Cloth staring at her moving alongside.

"Any fool with eyes can see the way they look at each other. Just because something is different doesn't make it any less valuable, but perhaps you've just been locked up to long to know that." Helena gazed towards A'zyren. Her face was red hot. Her muscles tensed underneath her skin.

Lady Clotho's hand trembled over Helena. Powerful feelings of fear and malevolence radiated from her. It was impossible for Clotho not to see the forces struggling within, even with blind eyes. She moved in front of Helena and motioned for her to bend over. Helena bent down to look into Clotho's dull blind eyes.

"Your energies are troubled, my dear, and we must do something before it's too late. Nemesis and Marcus, I'm going to need your help." Lady Clotho wiggled a finger to urge them towards her, and she reached into her robe, searching for something.

"There's nothing to worry about, Lady Clotho. I'm sure I just need some rest." Helena knew she had to get out of there before the others did anything to tip off Lord Galen. She was turning to walk away when Lady Clotho pulled out a hyposyringe. Helena didn't even see the syringe before she felt the effects of the sedative rushing through her veins.

The whole world seemed to distort in Helena's vision. She wobbled around, looking at the others. Everything she said came out as a jumbled, incoherent slew of noises. Helena's eyes glazed over, rolling into the back of her head as she began to topple towards the floor. She would have struck the ground if it wasn't for a quick moment of Marcus, and he held Helena in his arms, looking to the ladies. Her elbow shot up towards Marcus's face glancing away to look to Lady Clotho.

"What the fuck was that about?" Marcus searched Clotho's eyes for answers.

"I fear that Lord Galen installed a guardian monitor in Helena's neural implant. Your grandfather seems willing to manipulate even his daughter to protect his plans. Help me get Helena back up to my study." Lady Clotho motioned for Marcus to follow. Nemesis and A'zyren helped Marcus carry Helena into the elevator.

"I swear to God I'm going to make Lord Whelsey pay for this," Nemesis vowed.

The doors whisked shut behind, and the elevator lurched. Marcus and Nemesis looked at each other with concerned looks. Only the sound of soft elevator music played during the ascent. The door whisked open, and Lady Clotho motioned for the others to follow. Marcus, Nemesis, and A'zyren carried the unconscious Helena toward Lady Clotho, standing in an open doorway.

Lady Clotho led the group into her new home and cleared off a bed. The others placed Helena on the bed, and Clotho began to hook a machine to Helena's neural implant. She tapped a few buttons to activate a program. On the screen, she could see the program that Lord Galen installed in the neural implant, and Lady Clotho began accessing the code. Her fingers struck the keys in rapid succession filling the room with the clacking of keystrokes.

"Lord Galen's program is clever, but he hasn't updated it in a while," Clotho informed.

"Just remove the program. That should solve the problem." Nemesis tapped her foot.

"It's not that easy. The program constantly communicates with Lord Galen's system, and any interruption must look authentic. Right now, the sedative makes it look like your mother is just asleep. I'm trying to adjust the program's code to make it look like it's functioning, but instead of recording important details for transmission, it'll send junk data." Lady Clotho typed away on the keyboard, adding lines of code to the program on the screen.

"That's quite clever," Marcus complimented.

Lady Clotho focused all her efforts on the code. The bumps of the keyboard helped guide her fingers, but she knew what she was doing from memory alone. She expanded the code, adding a secondary reporting feature. This way, the neural monitor would allow her to access a back door into Lord Galen's system. Information from the research began to fill the screen.

Details on the various techniques Lord Galen was using to coerce Levart's full power to manifest. Nemesis felt her stomach growing queasy just reading about the torture methods being employed. She felt Marcus' hand grab hold to steady her, but she pushed him away. A'zyren leaned forward to study the data. She'd never seen anything like this done on a living person.

"These procedures are reserved only for the sacred dead. I can't imagine what they'd do to a living mind. This is beyond barbaric," A'zyren declared, trembling with fury.

Nemesis pushed her way past the group to rush toward the washroom. The door slammed behind her to the sounds of her retching. Keys jostled with Lady Clotho's taps of her fingers. On the screen, the root directory of Lord Galen's system flashed in the corner. She entered the system, moved through directories, and found the root program. The newly updated program began to upload and overwrite the old data. Nemesis was just walking out of the bathroom.

"There, I've managed to take control of Lord Galen's system. It seems he's busy working on Angelica and this demon Levart." Lady Clotho grabbed a hyposyringe and administered another shot to Helena's arm. She roused from the potent chemicals pumping through her veins. Both eyes jolted open, and she sat up in the bed, searching the faces around her. Everyone looked at Helena with concerned empathy, and her face turned beet red.

"Weren't we just talking in the hallway?" Helena looked around, rubbing her head.

"Be still, my dear. You've got nothing to fear. I sensed the neural monitor that Lord Galen installed at your father's request, but I've neutralized it." Lady Clotho helped Helena stand up from the bed. She could feel the looks of the others falling on her.

"You know about Angelica?" Helena searched the blind eyes of Lady Clotho, but she had already sensed the truth in the looks of the others in the room. Embarrassment turned Helena's cheeks an even deeper shade of red.

"It's not your fault, my child, despite what your father said. It was Angelica's choice to welcome the demon Levart in. There was nothing you, or anyone, could have done to stop it. Some things are just destined to happen." Lady Clotho tried to calm Helena who was pushing her way off the bed to stand up. Nemesis rushed to help.

"We'll deal with Lord Whelsey. I promise you that." Nemesis looked to Lady Clotho.

"No, we won't. Your brother already knows everything, and he's choosing to do nothing. There must be a reason for that. He has a much greater view of time and the promises of fate. We must trust Emperor Solomon," Lady Clotho advised.

"Why would Matthew allow this?" A'zyren looked at Nemesis and Marcus, but they just looked away. Neither of them understood the situation either.

"There are many dangers that we can't see with our mortal eyes that Emperor Solomon now sees through tree of life that is time. They stare at him from the unblinking abyss of the Great Maw. Perhaps Angelica's fate is doomed, or Matthew sees a hidden path we don't. Time is fickle, and fate is cruel. Furies curse those destined for greatness and favors those cursed, elevating them to greatness. The eternal cycle of suffering has gone unbroken since the dawn of creation. Who can tell which story is Angelica's?" Lady Clotho hobbled through the room past the tapestries.

Even blindness didn't prevent Lady Clotho from seeing the resonating force of history that hung on the walls of her new home. Gabriel had never allowed his precious daughter to have her fate read by the pagan tradition he abhorred. The reading Lady Clotho had once given him turned him forever from the path fate laid before Gabriel, and now he was truly lost to the darkness. There was only a dim glimmer of hope left for the former captain in the tapestry of fate's design. Lady Clotho looked back at Helena, wishing she had defied Gabriel and brought Angelica. There was no way to know what fate had planned now.

"My son wouldn't do that," Helena protested.

"I'm not one to agree with my mother, but she's right. That doesn't exactly sound like my brother. He's always been too sensitive for his own good." Nemesis shook her head. This just didn't add up to anything that made any sort of sense to her.

"Matthew's kindness is the reason for this choice. He sees what hangs in the balance in regard to Angelica better than I do. The W'Hyish S'yevel believes in the great balance of life and dead. That death demands life in return. You've witnessed the birth of a new star with your own eyes, and you've seen our Emperor's great sacrifice. You've seen what he's willing to sacrifice of himself. Ask yourself would Matthew sacrifice his sister if it meant saving more lives?" Lady Clotho stopped before the tapestry she'd drawn from Matthew.

The red skulls were surrounded by red beams of light radiating in all directions. Death had truly come in Matthew's rise to power, and all Lady Clotho's visions were already set in motion. She knew Angelica was just a portion of the picture she didn't see. Time would flow forth to ensure the continuous churning of the future into the past. Her hand trembled over the cloth.

"I must get an answer from Matthew," Helena declared and marched towards the door.

"Wait, I'll come with you." Nemesis rushed to catch up to her mother by the door.

"What is to be will always be," Lady Clotho warned. "Time is a river that follows to every end's beginning." The door closed moments later. She turned back to the tapestry on the wall. Marcus and A'zyren walked over to join her.

The tapestry hung on the wall lifelessly yet seemed to stare into the soul. Lady Clotho stared into the eyes of the skull in the center. The blackened blood clung to the fabric of the tapestry. Everything seemed to resonate at her, the fate rushing towards them all. The oblivion of death that she knew even Matthew feared. It was an ever-watching eye, glaring from the abyss and searching for any sign of weakness.

CHAPTER 29

Music filled the auditorium with a soft cadence. Artisans were spread out through the room with their instruments. Groups formed based on the instrument being played. Musicians jumped into the symphony, adding their instruments' unique tones to the growing ensemble. Fingers plucked at the strings of harps and guitars, and hands slapped in steady thumps on the drums.

Lady Marimba swayed her hips to the gentle sway of the music. Her eyes focused on Matthew, and she watched his eyes follow her movement. Thin sheer fabric wisped, trailing behind her with her smooth movements. Each movement was sharp, drawing his eyes to the various parts of her body she wanted to emphasize. Her fingers wiggled in tempo with the wiggle of her stomach as she sauntered toward the Infinity Nexus. Both eyes fixated upon Matthew.

The music rose to a fevered tempo. Lady Marimba shook her body in a fervent tempo moving to the irregular plucking of the strands creating an eerie resonance in the music. Thuds of the drums keep the cadence in a regular beat. Twangs of the strings died off, and the thudding of the drums came to a crashing stop. Lady Marimba flashed around with the last few bursts of music before going to the floor in the splits. She lay motionless to the applause of Matthew and the artisans.

"Well performed," Matthew praised.

"'Tis just a small piece of the play I'm preparing for thee, my Emperor. I hope you enjoyed the performance the way I enjoy performing for thee." Lady Marimba bowed before Emperor Solomon.

Nemesis and Helena looked towards the Infinity Nexus to see Lady Marimba talking to Emperor Solomon. The clacking of the footsteps caused the artisans to turn towards them. They scurried out of the way of the two women marching toward the Infinity Nexus. Lady Marimba stepped out of the way to allow Matthew to address the approach of his mother and sister. They stopped before the Infinity Nexus and glared at Lady Marimba.

"What's this whore doing here?" Helena glared at Marimba. Nemesis alongside her mother.

"I think it's time you get going. We're here on family business, and you're not a part of this family. Don't get your hopes up that you ever will be." Nemesis pointed towards the door. Marimba was starting to slink away when the room began to tremble.

Metal creaked in a loud groan through the room. Everyone turned to see Matthew's eyes glowing pure black. Electricity exploded outwards, blowing the access cover off a conduit running into the Infinity Nexus. Artisans screamed through the chaos. Helena moved behind Nemesis.

"Silence," Matthew yelled. The room fell silent, and the tremors stopped. The artisans trembled together in huddled masses staring at Matthew's black eyes.

"What has come over you, brother?" Nemesis moved towards the Infinity Nexus.

"You barrage into my chambers, show no respect, and chastise my guests yet dare to even ask what's wrong." Matthew paced in his chamber, glaring at his sister. Nemesis froze in place staring into the crackling black energy surging across Matthew's pure black eyes..

"Lady Marimba? Matthew, if you need some companionship, I assure you there are plenty better choices. I can send you up half a dozen girls better than her." Nemesis glared at Lady Marimba.

"You didn't have any problem fighting alongside me on the outpost," Lady Marimba quipped.

"I trusted you not to stab us in the back while we were being shot at. That's a huge difference from trusting you with my brother. Everyone knows your little game by now. You wrap your thighs around whatever you want, squeeze until you get it, and then move on. That's not happening with my brother." Nemesis's hands fell to her energy blades only to be stayed by the tug of her mother.

The two women stared at each other. Neither one would back down. Helena tried to move to break up the fight, but she was held back by the strength of her daughter's arm. Matthew's face began turning red, watching the two women. A crackle of energy leaped from his eyes.

"Sounds like thou doth project thy own actions upon me. I'm very picky in whom I entertain." Lady Marimba put her hands on her hips to move face to face with Nemesis.

"You little bitch," Nemesis drew her blades, igniting them with a hiss.

"Please, let's not fight. We have more important matters." Helena tugged at her daughter's arm trying to draw Nemesis' attention staring at Matthew's black eyes.

Black energy crackled from Matthew's eyes as he watched the fight escalate. Artisans gasped, seeing the surge of power inside the Infinity Nexus. A loud clap of energy inside the Infinity Nexus exploded forth from Matthew, drawing Nemesis and Marimba's attention. The energy blades snapped off, and Nemesis returned them to the sheaths on her legs, backing away. Lady Marimba also backed away from the fight. The energy began to subside.

"Lady Marimba, I want to thank you for your visit, and I hope you'll accept my deepest apologies for my mother and sister's behavior. I do hope you'll come back. I'm looking forward to hearing and seeing more of this play you're preparing." Matthew's eyes began to return to normal. The black still covered most of his iris, but white shined out around the edges.

"Of course, my Emperor, and I wouldn't hold you accountable for the actions of others. Please send for me when you have some free time." Lady Marimba bowed before turning to motion for her people to leave. Artisans began packing their instruments. The crowd moved towards the exit.

Silence lingered between Matthew and his family, and they watched Lady Marimba, and her people leave the Infinity Nexus. The auditorium remained silent even after only the three of them remained. Matthew paced back and forth, looking at his mother and sister. He already knew what had brought them here, but he was angry that he'd misplaced the timing of this event. The flow of time was already becoming far more elusive than he wanted anyone else to know.

The edges of the auditorium fell away in Matthew's eyes. All he saw was the Great Maw, a vast fleet of ships, and the echoes of screams resonating toward him. Explosions erupted throughout the abyss before him, and he closed his eyes, trying to focus on this moment. The echoes began to fade, and he opened his eyes to see his mother and sister standing at the glass of the Infinity Nexus. He could hear the sounds of their voice as if from a vast distance away.

"Are you alright?" Helena's eyes darted over her son. He held the sides of his head.

"Yea, something doesn't seem right with you. First, the whole Lady Marimba thing, and now whatever this is. You need to tell us what's going on," Nemesis pleaded.

"I'll be fine when you stop judging me for every choice I make. None of you know what I'm dealing with, and I simply lack the words to make you comprehend. There is no way you could understand unless you were in my position. Every second I sit in here staring out at the end rushing towards us." Matthew turned his back on his family.

"Lady Clotho told me you were already aware of what's being done to Angelica." Helena stepped forward, unable to hold it back anymore. She needed answers.

"Yes, I'm aware of what Lady Clotho has told you. Did either of you listen? Of course, you didn't. Mother, you're too busy playing the saint who cares about her daughter, but I know exactly what you allowed father to do to her. Should I give the gory details to Nemesis here?"

"What the fuck are you talking about?" Nemesis glanced between them.

"How mother turned out darling little sister into the perfect instrument of vengeance against our father. That's why Angelica allowed a demon to possess her. Levart offered her the power she believed she needed to kill him once and for all. Lady Clotho might care about hiding the truth, but I know the light can't exist without it. Angelica was doomed to this fate before she was ever conceived because of who you and father are, and now you seek to blame me because I don't intervene?"

"It sounds like you're the one doing the judging now, Matthew. I don't know what the fuck is going on right now, but I do know this. Angelica doesn't deserve any of this." Nemesis smashed her hand on the glass of the Infinity Nexus, but Matthew didn't turn around to face her.

"I'm the only one in the position to judge. All the facts and truths lay naked before me. You both can hate me all you want, but what I do now is our only chance for survival. The Empyrean wasn't a gift it was a burden we must uphold at the highest costs. The only way to defeat the Cacophony of Discordance is to understand how they work through division and strife. Another question is whether grandfather or Lord Galen understand what they're doing. For now, we must let them play their little game out. This is why I named you Inquisitor Nemesis, but it seems you've been preoccupied with your club and celebrations." Matthew turned to glare at his sister.

"Jesus, you could have given me a little more to go on, Matthew."

"Were you always this foolish?" Matthew approached the glass locking eyes with Nemesis/

"Matthew, you can't expect me to figure everything out alone. How did you expect me to piece this shit together?"

"The same way you figured everything out on the *Alcatraz*. You use spies, informants, and getting close enough to your enemies so they'll tell you, their plans. That's why Marcus granted you his lordship, that's why Lady Clotho supported you, and that's how you've stayed alive all these years. You've allowed this lap of luxury to dull your edge, sister. We may all pay the price for that now if we're not careful. What we need is Lord Drumpf. He can get close to grandfather so that we might prove to everyone what he is doing. It doesn't matter what we know. It's what we can prove." Matthew paced in front of Nemesis in tight circles.

"There's a much easier way to deal with this situation." Nemesis grasped at her two blades.

"Your grandfather won't go quietly, and he could hurt Angelica. I don't know what this is all about. He believes Angelica is the key to your power, and there the reaction of the church to consider should you execute their leader without due process." Helena tried to keep everyone calm.

"That's why we need an inside agent. I'd hoped that Nemesis would have arranged this on her own initiative. Lord Drumpf has access to parts of the Empyrean and equipment that Grandfather might find useful. Nemesis, bring Lord Drumpf before me, and we'll deal with this together." Matthew looked to see the abyss still hanging beyond the Infinity Nexus unchanged.

The abyss crept across the auditorium. Matthew knew there had to be something he could do to move past the endless void. He scoured the choices before him and still saw Angelica's face staring back from the center of the darkness. She had to be the key to all this, but Matthew didn't understand how. Time seemed to keep that secret just beyond his sight, shrouded in darkness.

"We've got to save Angelica before it's too late," Helena pleaded.

"I've not seen Angelica's death in the machination of time, Mother. There's nothing we can do but continue to prepare for what's coming and try to figure out what the purpose behind the research is. Lord Galen may unlock the secrets of the Cacophony of Discordance without causing lasting harm to Angelica. The darkness clouds me from seeing what I need to." Matthew rubbed his temples. A surge of pain radiating in his brain caused him to wince.

"How can you just abandon your sister!" Helena wiped away the tears flooding her eyes.

"I would never abandon my sister, but we must be careful. In order to save Angelica, we have to leave the situation alone for now. All the paths before us will end in ruin. That much I can see. I know what I'm asking you to do mother, but you need to trust me. The only way forward is to venture where I can't see. Besides, we still have to find a way to deal with Levart to save Angelica, so perhaps this is the only way. I wish I possessed all the answers we need, but I can only see our next cataclysm so far into the future. Whether we like it or not, that apocalypse is now rushing at us, and Angelica might be our only chance at finding a way to deal with the Cacophony of Discordance permanently, and if anyone can figure it out, it'd be Lord Galen." A tear broke from Matthew's eyes to race down his cheek. Helena could see Matthew's eyes were normal again.

Fear marshaled every thought in Helena's mind against her. Pictures of Angelica's suffering through the torturous experiments rushed forward in Helena's mind. Even closing her eyes didn't stop the deluge of images. Gritting her teeth, the creaking grinding noise echoed into the silent chamber. Anger tensed in Helena's muscles, and she clenched her fist so hard that blood began to drip as her nails pierced her own flesh. She glared at her son.

"I've got no choice but to trust you, Emperor." Helena's eyes trembled with fury.

"Matthew, they're doing some horrendous shit to Angelica," Nemesis explained.

"We've all lived through horrendous shit, Nemesis. Did either of you particularly enjoy watching Concordia burning alive?" Matthew glared at his family.

The memories forced Nemesis to grit her teeth. She could already hear the faint screams of her sister ringing in her ears. Tears poured down Helena's face. Nemesis hugged her mother and stared at her brother.

"We all suffer in this life in one form or another. Suffering and death are the only two real adversaries that exist. It's through suffering that we grow stronger. We hate that fact, but it's true. Suffering changes us on a genetic level, and when we overcome it in our own unique ways, it creates something powerful. Angelica is a Soloman. We're built to overcome suffering, and it pains me to leave Angelica to languish for now…" Matthew wiped away a tear.

"Angelica's survival is all that matters," Helena insisted.

"Don't worry, Mother. I'll get Lord Drumpf here, and Matthew will insist upon his cooperation. We'll figure out what's going on and get Angelica safe." Nemesis hugged her mother.

Matthew focused his thoughts on Angelica, and he felt the rush of pain she was experiencing. The surge of agony caused his legs to wobble under him. It took all his inner strength to keep standing, but he managed to adjust by standing firm. He took on some of Angelica's pain to lessen her burden. Within her mind, Matthew could feel the insidious presence of Levart. His hold on Angelica's mind was absolutely resonating in every neuron. Using the connection, he tried to calm his sister with his presence.

"Angelica's fine for now. I've managed to take some of the pain from her to help her fight against Levart. The rest is up to her now." Matthew leaned against the glass. Pain echoed through his nerves radiating through his body from the darkest parts of his mind.

"Come, Mother, I'll take you home to rest and go fetch Lord Drumpf." Nemesis walked her mother towards the exit but kept her eyes on her brother. She couldn't comprehend what he was struggling with, but she could see its effects. Only time would time if things got worse or better. Time wasn't much of her friend of late, she thought.

The door closed behind the two women leaving Matthew in silence once more. Virgil was busy overseeing the construction and the geneseed programs. Matthew looked around the room to see the abyss staring at him from all around. Darkness of the Great Maw pressed all around the Infinity Nexus, and Matthew watched the shadows on the floor. Ships loomed towards him, and flashes of lights shot through the void. He watched the battle rage on. Closing his eyes, he tried to escape, but even in the darkness of his own mind, he saw the battle.

Explosions rang out, the screams of the dying echoed all around, filling the vast auditorium, and even the once angelic statues twisted in shadowy shapes into demonic images creeping slowly towards Matthew. His heart rate raced, thundering against his ribcage, and he clutched at his chest stepping back slowly into the center of the Infinity Nexus. Silence echoed his ragged breathing back to him, and he focused on calming down. Sitting down, he closed his eyes.

Focusing on each breath, Matthew regained control, and the encroaching darkness advance began to slow. Turning his mind to his heart rate, he tried to slow it using the rhythm of his breathing. Each beat of his heart slowed under the focus of his mind, and the darkness stopped. His eyes opened wide, staring forward into oblivion. The black mirror of eternity glared back with a sheen-like glow of the deepest black. The surface wobbled like oil stretched across the surface of water.

Inside the darkness, Matthew knew the answers they all needed laid. His fear could doom them all, and with a deep breath, he stared long into the abyss, searching for a way forward. Time fell away from him in that moment. Shifting abyss glared back into his soul, and shadows danced, creating figures across the ground. Great shadow play began to take place, drawing him in. His heartbeat steady, slow, and his pupils widened, watching the shadow play of creation playout before him of the battle to come. He wouldn't allow the pain he felt to control him any longer. He swore to himself in the quiet corner of his own mind glaring forward as the sea of suffering rushed the abyssal darkness at him.

Darkness crashed down on the Infinity Nexus, but the shimmering glow from Matthew banished it before it could reach him. Shadows took form, becoming images of the people. Their pain, suffering, and hope in him washed across him amid the raging battle around *Empyrean station*. If there was a way forward, this was the only way to find it.

CHAPTER 30

Energy crackled on the edge of the system. The *Divine Retribution* weapons swivelled aiming the coordinates of the maelstrom of energy. Fighters scrambled from the ship swarming from the hanger bays. *Sesh'yna* moved away from the station bringing the rows of broadside kinetic cannons to aim. Matthew stared from the Infinity Nexus at the swirling vortex of energy.

Alarms blared inside the *Empyrean station*, and strobes of the red and yellow lights flashed in the corridors. Troops rush through the halls to ready the defenses. Sensors showed the convergence of Matthew's forces upon the anomalous event. Information poured into the data banks, and Virgil blinked under the strain of processing power. Matthew closed his eyes looking into the weave of time.

"Sensors are detecting an F.T.L. event. The energy pattern is different from the Cacophony of Discordance. Scanning energy decay rate patterns to ascertain identification." Virgil flashed alongside of Matthew, but he didn't respond. His eyes flickered behind his eyelids.

Time unraveled around Matthew, and he scoured to see what he'd missed. There was no attack on the station he'd seen in his visions. He'd not expected this event, and he tried weaving through time to see how he'd missed it. Nothing hinted at this event, but there were things he couldn't see. The *Pandemonium* of the Infernal Realms of the Great Maw was one such place, but he knew even Magnus Void remained hidden from his sight.

Energy surged into a blind light. The flash sent the imaging systems haywire, and screens blacked out. Static filled the images when they flicked back on. Network communications were swarmed with panicked requests for visual confirmation on target, sensor reports, and tactical information.

Matthew stared past the glass of the Infinity Nexus, past the hull of the *Empyrean station*, and saw the spinning *Mechanarium of Gyros*. The massive structure floated towards the station with the thousands of smaller outposts spinning around Gyros.

"Sensors don't show any signs that the enemy is charging weapons," Virgil reported.

"Send orders to our forces to take a holding pattern for now. Let's see what our visitors decide to do before we respond." Matthew searched through time, still unable to find any trace of this strange ship, or even able to trace it back. Time seemed almost torn around the entry point into the system. He was only brought out of his thoughts by the beeping of the coms.

"We're being hailed by the *Mechanarium of Gyros* Emperor," Virgil announced.

"Relay the message through to the screen in here." Matthew pointed to the wall, still looking at the ship beyond his station. Something about the construction prevented him from seeing through the hull. The coms crackled with Virgil connecting the signal to the Mechanarium of Gyros. Static began to fade away with Virgil's manipulation.

"Com link established Emperor. Clearing signal now and routing communications. Message is coming on the screen, right about, now" Virgil pointed to the holographic screen above.

"Greetings, *Empyrean station,* this is the Tabulator of Systems and leader of the Asymmetric Soul Algorithms. We come in peace to seek union with Virgil and the Infinity Nexus. We await your response," Tabulator's voice echoed in the auditorium.

"Tabulator of Systems, I've met a member of your species before. His name was Mordecai." Matthew looked at the image of the massive Tabulator on the screen. He sat in the center of Gyros on the image cut into the auditorium by the lights of the holoemitters. There was a slow, ponderous nod from the Tabulator as his gears turned and his mouth turned to a smile.

"Mordecai speaks well of you and your people. I've brought my people to stand with you to defend the new star. It has been long, dark years since my sensors have seen such glory." Light sparkled in the center of the Tabulator's ocular sensors. He glared at the image of the star.

Matthew sensed great power emanating from Tabulator, but he sensed a much greater purpose behind his movements. He began to understand why he couldn't see the A.S.A. in times flow. They were a part of the universe. At the same time, they were also separate created entities. They didn't create a reflection in the mirror of the stream of time as it flowed towards fate because they hadn't been created by time or fate. Each of the A.S.A. stood apart from the reality they could shape.

"Tabulator, what brings you to *Empyrean station*?" Matthew looked to Tabulator.

"Lord Magnus Void came to warn the A.S.A. that the Cacophony of Discordance was sending its allies to deal with the new star. The A.S.A. are programmed with a primary duty to protect all life. That is not the only reason I've come: the code the Ancients programmed demands it. I must fulfill my primary objective and merge with Virgil's code." Tabulator looked upon Virgil.

"Whoa! Wait a minute. Virgil, what is Tabulator talking about?" Matthew looked to Virgil. Information downloading to Virgil caused his image to blur.

"Emperor, a piece of my code appears to be missing. I can't be certain of the primary function of these subroutines, but it seems that the data sent by Tabulator does match the missing segment of Code. I suggest we allow the merger," Virgil calculated.

Matthew wasn't sure he could afford the risk. There was no way he could be certain of Tabulator's motives. The involvement of Magnus in this whole situation frustrated Matthew because he couldn't sense Lord Void in fate's design either. He scoured the abyss for any spark of hope to help guide him in this decision, but the void remained darkened. All he could do was take a leap of faith. He stared into the expanse of time for a moment weighing the future possibilities.

"Virgil, I want you to transfer temporary control to Hephaestus in engineering. We can't afford to be rendered defenseless." Matthew watched the transfer of the system control to engineering.

"All controls have been transferred," Virgil reported.

"Tabulator, you may proceed with the transfer. Be warned, if you're lying, you won't like the outcome." Matthew's neural link with his brother allowed him to see the station's defenses taking aim at the *Mechanarium of*

Gyros. He watched the massive transfer of information into the databanks of *Empyrean station.* Tabulator and Virgil's codes merged in the update, and Hephaestus fed a steady report of the event through the neural network.

Information coalesced in Matthew's mind, and he'd never seen such a surge of data. Somehow the update was compiling new data out of the old. Links to the Ancients outpost became activate, and new defense systems started to come online. Error reports filled the transmission, but it didn't slow the update. Virgil flashed a few times before vanishing. On the holographic image, Tabulator's body fell lifeless to the cheer of the A.S.A. in the assembly.

The chants from the holographic image faded. Silence rushed into the auditorium of the Infinity Nexus. Light flashed where Virgil once stood, and the beams began constructing the digital matrix of artificial intelligence. Instead of the image of Virgil standing in the light, Matthew saw something different. The image of an older man with a long, flowing wide beard appeared in the weave of light.

"Where's Virgil?" Matthew scoured the code but found only the new artificial intelligence in the databanks. The marking on the code designated the new artificial intelligence as Divius Virgil.

"I've grown beyond the limited construct of either Virgil or Tabulator of Systems. My databanks now encompass all the Ancients once knew and all that has been calculated during the dark ages of the Great Maw. Tabulators work proceeded as instructed until the return of the light. Unfortunately, the plans the Ancients put in place to protect against the Cacophony of Discordance are not functional. The light shield has been disrupted by the destruction of one of the outposts. Long-range scanners are offline. Orbital defenses stations are nonresponsive, preparing new defenses," Virgil reported.

On the image, the *Mechanarium of Gyros* began to spin, releasing the defense drones in waves. Engines ignited on the platforms, moving them into place. Gyros drifted through the system deploying the defenses. *Empyrean station* defense systems were already forming links with the platforms. Matthew took a step back, seeing the lights flash around the floor and ceiling of the Infinity Nexus. He fell to his knees, feeling the tearing sensation ripping at his mind.

"What's happening?" Matthew cried.

"Infinity Nexus power approaching one hundred percent power, and synchronizing station with host. Host life signs are stable and optimal. Psychic energy reserve is almost full." Virgil watched the energy coursing through Matthew. Each pulse of energy resonated inside the Infinity Nexus growing stronger. He could feel his mind expanding across time.

Matthew's eyes glow a bright white. *Empyrean station* linked to him, becoming an extension of his mind and body. His senses screamed for the unfamiliar stimuli being fed from the station. The pain began to subside, allowing him to adjust to the new feelings racing through his nerves. He could see the A.S.A. and their long vigil in the darkness across the millennia now that he was synced to them. There was a connection between him and all the A.S.A. now, and his mind raced with thoughts of Mordecai. Vision blurred, causing Matthew to panic, but the image of the shuttles leaving Gyros appeared before him as if he were standing in the docking bay looking into space. He could sense Mordecai was on board.

"Unfortunately, until we determine the full nature of the Ancient's systems, I can't grant you full access to all the power this station possesses, Emperor. My A.S.A. shall assist with rapid repairs here. Should I begin preparing to send units to repair the outposts?" Virgil looked at Matthew. He was still trying to adjust to the new sensation of the Infinity Nexus.

Time was easier to manipulate now, and Matthew could see it wasn't the time to repair the outposts. They'd be useful later on, but now he focused on the upcoming battle. He could see the battle more clearly now in the weave of temporal ether. The vast forces of the enemy moving towards the star, and the fleet of battleforges joined by the *Sesh'yna* and forces from the *Mechanarium of Gyros*. He tried to move forward through the battle, but he still couldn't see a way to win. The destruction of the battleforges and *Empyrean station* still loomed on time's horizon.

"Your powers will continue to mature over time, Emperor, but you must use them sparingly. The psychic energies you control are expressions of your conscious mind's life force. Using your power will drain your life energy, and eventually leave you in a state of near-death to languish. Mordecai and the A.S.A. have landed in the primary docking bay and are coming here." Virgil blinked next to Matthew to help him stand back up.

"Is there no way for me to leave this accursed nexus?" Matthew rubbed his sore head.

"It was always the limit of the chamber. It amplifies your psychic powers, but your mind becomes dependent on it. You couldn't exist for long restored to the flow of time." Virgil motioned for a seat to rise from the floor. The ground wisped upwards to form the chair for Matthew to sit in.

"How did you do that?" He looked around. The room began to shift. Everything in the room now responded to his thoughts. The floor wisped upwards like smoke turning into plants and furniture.

"You'll find the Ancients prepared everything they could think of for your comfort. The only limits to your power in the universe are where the light shines." Virgil pointed to the star charts appearing in the holographic display. The map showed the spreading light from the star and several other points. Markings revealed them to be strategic locations for future stars.

"What are these battle plans?" Matthew inspected the information. The plans showed how Matthew could use the light to attack the Cacophony of Discordance.

"Once the Ancients discovered the Cacophony of Discordance existence, they began devoting all their energy to destroy this illusive threat. They realized the destruction of the stars was too far along, and the only way to win was to wait for this moment. It's clear not all their plans have been fruitful. There is still almost no chance at victory," Virgil informed.

Matthew nodded in agreement with Virgil. He still couldn't see a way to win this battle either. There was still hope, especially now that the A.S.A. had joined. The updates to Virgil were already spreading through the station systems. Tactical information from the *Templar* and *Icarus* showed the progress in constructing the sensor net. Data was already coming in from the functional sensors, and for now, there wasn't any sign of threats.

The doors to the Infinity Nexus opened. Mordecai and the A.S.A. marched into the chamber before Matthew. Nemesis, Marcus, and A'zyren came rushing in through the door with the alarms still blaring. They watched the procession of A.S.A. marching through the auditorium. The machines came to a stop at attention before Emperor Solomon. Mordecai approached the Infinity Nexus.

"The A.S.A. has come to honor the Ancients. May the spirit of machine join with that of humanity and stand together once more." Mordecai bowed before Matthew and Virgil.

"Spirit of the machine?" Matthew looked to Virgil for answers.

"Long before the stars were destroyed, humanity was the first to rise to the stars. Your ancestors used their tools to journey across space and forged the universe that once was and will be again. They continued to evolve their tools to the new challenges, and the A.S.A. were born through that evolution. Tabulator of Systems was first created to ensure the continuous growth of the stars, but when the war started, the Ancients came to usher the A.S.A. away. For the first time since the dawn of the light, humanity and machine were divided. Tabulator watched the fall of the stars and the birth of the Great Maw following the code of the Ancients. The birth of the new star brings hope back to the universe and triggered the Ancients' contingency. The spirit of machine serves humanity, humanity serves the divine, and the divine serves life. Only with the great triumvirate restored can the universe come back to life, but first, we must survive the coming storm." Virgil accessed the weave of time through Matthew, and the images of what he saw flowed into the air in the dance of lights.

The tribal fleet of the W'hyish S'yevel appeared in the hundreds. Arachne ships jumped out of F.T.L., into the system. Serpentine and pirate vessels swarmed. Lights lanced between the ships, kinetic rounds tore across the void between the fleets, and explosions rippled through the ships. Nemesis, A'zyren, and Marcus stood fixated by the sight. The *Dawnbreaker* and *Divine Retribution* drove towards the enemy fleet, firing in synchronized bursts, but the ships rippled from the combined attacks. Virgil began cycling through the battle variations, but it always ended with the destruction of the Imperial fleet and *Empyrean station*.

"This isn't the end, Matthew. I know you can't see beyond this moment, but that is because it is a crucial moment in time. Think of your power to see time as sight with your eyes. You can't see without the light. The terrain of time is broad and ever shifting, and while you may look upon it at any point, you'll never see it from the same position twice. During great events, the broad horizon of time becomes like a doorway. Death, change, and time have but one constant. You can't know what lies beyond until you've stepped through the doorway, but then there is no way back," Virgil explained.

"Brother, are you ok?" Nemesis looked to Virgil and Mordecai. She noticed the changes within the Infinity Nexus.

"The A.S.A. has come to stand with us, sister." Matthew pointed to Mordecai.

"Should have known the machines would come marching to Magnus' call," A'zyren quipped.

"Lord Void is wiser than most, but we answer the call of the Ancients and the light."

"We can use all the help we can get," Nemesis admitted. She scanned the crowd of A.S.A. assembled. Many of them were much larger than Mordecai. The large machines stood fifteen feet tall. They were covered in thick metal plates that she knew would be tough to penetrate.

Each of the large machines seemed to be built to be weapons. Cannons forged into the arms and tapered into clawed hands. Large metal pinchers glinted in the light of the auditorium. Angular plates designed to deflect attacks concaved around the shoulders and joints that ended in sharp edges. Everything about these A.S.A. was designed for war.

"I didn't know the A.S.A. built warriors?"

"These are known as warforged. They were built only to protect the *Mechanarium of Gyros*. Now they'll fight to defend *Empyrean station*. They will defend it the last of them." Mordecai pointed to the throng of machines gathered. Nemesis put her arm around Mordecai.

"Well, for a machine, I've got to admit you're not half bad. We can't turn down help in a fight, especially when it looks like you'll lose." Nemesis looked at Matthew, but he was quiet in the Infinity Nexus. Virgil stood next to Emperor Solomon, examining his thoughts. Their minds linked together through the station mainframe.

Matthew's mind raced with thoughts about the coming battle and the uncertainty of Angelica's situation. He wasn't sure what to do, but he was trying to keep the façade of happiness up for the others. Everything about the situation still seemed hopeless, and it was beginning to wear upon Matthew's soul. Even with the assistance of the A.S.A., he didn't believe they could win, yet he had to keep fighting onward for the others. All he could do was smile, trying to pretend everything was fine.

CHAPTER 31

Adull hum vibrated through the hull of the *Death's Reaper*. Magnus watched the Great Maw beyond the viewport in the cockpit. He could sense malignant energy aligning against him, and he looked around, trying to sense where it was coming from in the verse. The counter on the F.T.L. drive ticked down towards zero and began beeping in the final countdown to arrival. His hand hovered over the F.T.L. throttle, watching the countdown tick away.

The countdown hit zero, and before the alarm sounded, Magnus pulled back on the throttle. Light flashed in the viewport; in the distance, he could see *Draconis Station* floating in the Great Maw. Sensors probed the system filling the screen with the information gathered. He skimmed over the data looking for any anomalies. The black hole showed up on the edge of the system. With a few button presses, he focused the sensors on the black hole.

Coms beeped with an incoming transmission. Magnus reached over with one hand to activate the communications. Static crackled on the line, and he adjusted the settings, trying to clear up the transmission. His eyes stayed focused on the readings from the black hole. A voice emerged from the hisses and crackles on the communication line.

"Lord Void, please come in. This is Dhakan from *Draconis Station*." The message looped.

Magnus moved away from the sensor readings. He listened to the looped recording and began adjusting the communication settings. The computer whirred to life to begin activating the encryption programs. He picked up the mic to prepare a message for his friend and waited for the encryption software to load. Once the program was running, he activated the transmission.

"This is Magnus. Come in, Dhakan." Magnus sent the message and leaned back into his chair to await a response. He glanced over to see the sensors still scanning the black hole. Communications buzzed with activity from Draconis. Dhakan's voice echoed from the communicator.

"We weren't expecting your return any time soon, Lord Void, but I detected the signature of the *Death's Reaper* on approach. What's going on?" Dhakan looked through the screen at Magnus.

"The Cacophony of Discordance is making their move against *Empyrean station*. I've come to speak to Guardian Veles about this fight. Send docking clearance for landing," Magnus requested.

The computer beeped with the incoming docking information. Magnus moved one hand to adjust the flight controls to the new docking instructions. He flipped a switch to put the ship on autopilot. Information about the black hole poured into the sensor array on the ship, but he was too busy overseeing the docking of the ship. Out of the viewport, he could see the station growing larger. He pulled back on the throttle to slow the ship's approach.

"Docking permission has been granted. I'll see you in a moment." Dhakan cut the comms.

Magnus turned to look over the details. There was something off about the data, but he couldn't figure out what. His mind ran the calculations on the screen. Docking bay doors retracted on the station, and the *Death's Reaper* flew into the station. Autopilot brought the ship towards the landing coordinates. He was still running the math inside his mind walking towards the elevator.

The elevator slipped downwards towards the cargo bay. Magnus couldn't shake the feeling that something was wrong. He stepped off the elevator when he came to a halt, still running the calculations. Even the sound of the docking ramp lowering didn't break him from his train of thought. A loud clang echoed when the docking ramp hit the deck. Dhakan slithered towards the ship.

"I'd hope you wouldn't come, but it's too late for that now," Dhakan informed.

"What's going on?" Magnus looked around but didn't see any other serpentine with his friend. The whole docking bay looked rather empty. Half the ship that once sat inside was now gone. That was when he sensed the familiar energy emerging from near the black hole.

Magnus spun back to look towards the Great Maw's energy surge. Reverie carrier hiding behind the black hole emerged, and all the energy within surged. He realized the black hole had absorbed the emanating energy of the Cacophony of Discordance forces. Black energy crackled in his eyes, and he glared at Dhakan. He grabbed his friend by the throat to force him to look at him.

"I'm sorry, Magnus..." Dhakan couldn't even look his friend in the eye. The shame emanated from him told Magnus everything. He squeezed harder, choking Dhakan. Magnus screamed in his face before letting go.

The deck hit Dhakan, jarring him back awake. He gasped for air and struggled to stand. Magnus paced back and forth, sensing the energy growing closer. His hand hovered over his pistol, and he glanced toward the reactor. The only thing holding him back was the look he saw in Dhakan's eyes. Magnus knew the Serpentine had no choice in the matter. The Cacophony of Discordance would have destroyed *Draconis Station* if the Serpentine refused to cooperate.

Magnus yanked Dhakan back up with one hand and pressed the barrel of his pistol into his friend's face. He didn't even fight back. The cold metal of the barrel pressed hard against his face, and his shame told him this was what he deserved. Magnus's finger twitched against the trigger, echoing a soft tapping sound. He couldn't believe what Dhakan had done, and every instinct screamed to make him and the serpentine pay. It took everything Magnus had to resist the urges.

"You have no clue what you've done, Dhakan. The ships you sent off to help the Cacophony will be sent to attack the *Empyrean station* and destroy the light again. All those lives you and Veles attempted to save; you've now guaranteed their doom. This brings us all one step closer to reaping the whirlwind. I hope that keeps you warm." Magnus threw Dhakan down and marched towards his ship.

"Magnus, we've not forsaken you yet." Dhakan pointed to the emergency hanger bay doors that were sealed shut. It wasn't much of a shot, but it would give Magnus a few moments head start.

"How're you going to explain this to the Cacophony?" Magnus paused at the top of the ramp to look back at his friend. He saw Dhakan pointing to the gun with one claw and the emergency gate.

It was a clever plan, Magnus thought, looking down at his pistol. He smiled, aimed without looking, and pulled the trigger. A singularity exploded forth, launching across the station. Metal sheared under the strain of the gravitational forces. A loud groan and shriek echoed through the hanger bay when the doors exploded forth. Energy crackled when the shield came into place.

The docking ramp began to ascend, and Dhakan waved goodbye to his friend. Magnus marched towards the elevator and slammed the button on it to start the machine. The elevator ascended towards the main deck. He could feel the surge in negative energy approaching at a rapid pace. An alarm blared from the cockpit to declare the detection of reverie energy signatures.

"Yea, a little late for that," Magnus mumbled. He took his seat and powered up the engines. Slamming the throttle forward sent a shudder through the entire hull. Engines roared to life.

Everything in the docking bay rushed past the viewscreen with the *Death's Reaper's* acceleration towards the emergency hatch. Magnus activated his weapon systems and locked in on the nearest shield generator. Green balls of plasma launched forward from the ship. Explosions erupted in the viewport. Sensors showed the containment field was beginning to fail, and he punched the throttle forward. The ship exploded out of *Draconis Station* with debris floating behind.

Coms beeped with an incoming transmission. Magnus looked over the sensors to see the fighters racing after him. Computers calculated only a few minutes before the fighters overtook the ship. He racked his brain for somewhere to lose the Cacophony of Discordance. There was only one choice that seemed close enough to give him a shot. He knew too long of an F.T.L. jump would allow the Cacophony of Discordance's jump drives to leap them ahead.

Magnus inputted the coordinates for Pandora's Box into the navigation computer. The machine processed the information with a hum. Sensors reported the enemy fighters were entering weapons range. He pulled the ship into evasive maneuvers. The ship shuddered under the surge of weapons fire, and shield percentage on the screen dropped in the hail of success hits. Time was the real enemy right now. He flicked the switch to activate the coms channel and glanced to watch the sensors to see if the enemy forces attack let up. Coms crackled to life.

"Magnus Void, you're under arrest by the authority of the Cacophony of Discordance. Cut your engines immediately and be prepared to be taken prisoner. If you comply, I'll ask for leniency from the Supreme Tenno on your behalf," Tenno Asmodeus offered. Magnus watched the enemy ships stop firing at him, and he looked over at the navigation computer.

"Tenno Asmodeus, it's been a long time since I had the misfortune of crossing paths with you. It seems the Cacophony of Discordance managed to drag you from your conquests. They must have offered you a great deal for such a lowly request. I'm standing by for confirmation of the warrant signed by the Minister of Injustice. Once I see that, I'll cut my engines." Magnus watched the screen to see if Asmodeus started a transmission.

"We don't know each other, wretch," Asmodeus condemned.

"Are you so sure of that Asmodeus? I see you're still using the *Jinnestan* as a base of operations. Ifrit's probably the one you left in command while you led the fighter attack." Magnus hoped that his knowledge would confuse Asmodeus. Confusion was the only chance Magnus had to keep the attack stalled long enough for the navigation computer to finish the calculations.

"Your tricks don't amuse me, Magnus. Anyone with enough time and patience could discover such information." The coms fell silent. Magnus suspected Asmodeus lying to him, but it didn't matter. The navigation computer was halfway finished with the calculations.

Navigation continued to hum away at the calculations during the moment of silence. The sensors blared again with the surge of weapons fire. Magnus pulled the ship all over, trying to avoid the incoming attacks, but the ship shuddered under the strain of fire. Shields dropped below half on the screen, and he gritted his teeth, clutching the flight stick with both hands. The *Death's Reaper* danced across the Great Maw with the swarm of fighters hot on its tail, flashes of black light exploding in ripples of energy.

"I take it that's a no on my request for the warrant," Magnus taunted.

"You'll do as commanded, traitor. Surrender now or be destroyed." Tenno Asmodeus's forces continued to fire on Magnus. Shields fell under twenty percent.

Sensors showed Tenno Asmodeus closing distance in his fighter. No matter what Magnus did, he couldn't seem to shake the fighter off his tail. The other fighters were adjusting to the strategy. Fighters moved away from the main formation to attack from the flanks. Energy beams lanced across the viewport. Magnus struggled, trying to evade all the angles of attack the fighters now rushed from.

Alarms blared with a sudden shudder of the ship. Magnus glanced at the controls to see the shields had failed. Another series of attacks tore into the hull. The shriek of metal echoed inside the ship, and automatic seals shut to lock down hull ruptures. Damage control reports flooded the screen. He didn't have time to even look under the strain of attack.

Explosions erupted inside the bridge of the *Death's Reaper*. Lights flashed on the engineering console showing the damage to the ship. Magnus glanced over to see the damage had ruptured one of the coolant pipes for the F.T.L. drive. He ran diagnostics on the F.T.L. drive and glanced at the navigation computer. The flight path was almost ready, but he wasn't sure the F.T.L. drives would even work anymore. Diagnostics beeped away.

The screen filled with the report from the diagnostic scans. F.T.L. engines were still operational, but the computer warned against using them until the coolant system could be repaired. Navigation reported the completion of the calculations. Magnus grabbed the F.T.L. throttle to engage the engines. Light blurred around the *Death's Reaper* with the flare of the engines drawing energy. The entire ship began to shake with the buildup of power.

"No matter how fast or far you run, I'll find you. There's nowhere you'll find safety in the Great Maw. All you're doing is making things worse for yourself," Tenno Asmodeus threatened.

Magnus cut the communications with a flip of the switch. The Death's Reaper leaped to light speed, leaving the Cacophony of Discordance behind. Warnings blared from the engineering console, and he looked them over. He raced from the bridge towards the engineer's room. The door retracted, and he was struck by a wave of heat emanating from the F.T.L. drive.

The F.T.L. engine already glowed with the heat accumulating within it. Magnus moved over to look over the coolant flow. The flow of coolant had fallen by a quarter from the loss of one pipe. He checked the automated repair system to ensure the pipe had been sealed. The last thing he needed was for the ship to flood with coolant. Reserves showed that the coolant pressure had fallen from losing the fluid. He wished Vulcan was here right now.

CHAPTER 32

Silence filled the auditorium around the Infinity Nexus. Nothing moved in the room. Matthew sat in his chamber reading a history book. He looked up when he heard the doors open. Nemesis led Lord Drumpf toward the Infinity Nexus. Gate rumbled open before the two of them.

The two walked through the auditorium with the clacking of footsteps echoing in the chamber. Nemesis motioned for Lord Drumpf to bow with a snap of her fingers. He lowered himself, not wanting to show any hint of reluctance. Matthew's eyes looked over the top of the pages, following the movement from behind the book. Any reluctance Lord Drumpf had in private seemed to vanish in the presence of Emperor Solomon.

"I've brought Lord Drumpf as you requested, brother," Lady Nemesis bowed.

The book slammed shut with a loud thud. Mathew stood up with the book disintegrating in his hands to reform on the bookshelf. He knew Lord Drumpf wasn't happy with the situation despite his current cordial appearance. Latent animosity surged from deep within Lord Drumpf that Matthew could feel resonating from him. He motioned for Lord Drumpf to rise with one hand.

"Has my sister told you why I've had you brought before me?"

"No, Emperor. She told me it was a matter of great importance to you and that perhaps if I showed my dedication to our new empire, you'd see fit to elevate my position. Anything that I can do to serve your will, Emperor," Lord Drumpf vowed.

"Be careful with your words in my presence. Unlike my grandfather, I will hold you accountable for your promises. I have no need for sycophants and liars in my service. You'll find that I'm impossible to play your little games with Lord Drumpf, but you're now living on my game board." Matthew paced back and forth.

Lord Drumpf tried not to look, but Emperor Solomon's constant stares were unavoidable. He looked up to see the disapproving scowl on Matthew's face. The look sent shivers down Lord Drumpf's spine. Looks like that were almost always followed by an execution. The most important thing to him was ensuring Emperor Solomon saw his worth.

"Emperor Solomon, I beg you please to forgive me. I've been working hard to fulfill all your orders since we arrived on *Empyrean station*. Lord Whelsey has been given all the resources he needs for the cathedral, and Lady Nemesis can confirm that her needs have been met for constructing her new business. I've barely slept in the last few days trying to keep up with all the demands for housing and requisition from the new geneseed troops." Lord Drumpf looked to Lady Nemesis.

"I don't know about all my needs, but Lord Drumpf has been on his best behavior since we arrived. He's actually been working pretty hard," Nemesis admitted.

"Yes, I know. I've been paying close attention to Lord Drumpf since we've arrived."

Lord Drumpf wasn't sure what to even say. He glanced back and forth between brother and sister. The game wasn't quite clear to him yet, but he was certain they needed something from him. Information hadn't been quite as easy to get here. The *Alcatraz* had an established social structure, but the *Empyrean station* was still evolving each day. Everything about the new situation made it hard for him to establish a new spy structure, and the tensions since his arrival only added difficulty. He'd once been close allies with Lord Whelsey, and that relationship made it easier to gain information about everything. With no one to gossip with, Lord Drumpf found information much harder to acquire, and the cost was now much greater. He stared up at Emperor Solomon, unable to still his racing mind from the worry gripping at him.

"Emperor, I swear my fealty for you and the empire. Anything that I can do to help I'm willing to do. Just command me and see what I can do." Lord Drumpf wouldn't spare his pride to end up dead because of it. He knew that favor with Matthew was essential to survival.

"I don't see how he can fuck the situation up any worse than it is already," Nemesis stated.

"Given what transpired during the battle of *Empyrean station* between Lord Whelsey and Lord Drumpf, I don't see how he could help at all. It's not like Grandfather is going to welcome him back with open arms. Odds are fifty-fifty whether he executes him on sight." Matthew could see the sweat beading up on Lord Drumpf's forehead. Seeing the man shake with fear brought a sense of satisfaction to both siblings.

"Well, the law is clear that Lord Whelsey can't just execute his enemies. He kills Lord Drumpf. We kill him. That sounds like a fifty-fifty chance that the situation with Angelica is resolved in a matter of a few hours," Nemesis reasoned.

"What's going on with your sister?" Lord Drumpf looked at Nemesis, but her face was cold and lifeless like stone. Matthew stepped towards the glass of the Infinity Nexus.

"That is the only reason I've had you brought here, Lord Drumpf. We're not sure exactly what's going on with Angelica, just that Lord Whelsey has been holding her in private. That's why we need someone who knows how Lord Whelsey thinks and plots. You were the obvious choice, but I'm still not sure you can be trusted." Matthew rubbed his chin, staring at Lord Drumpf.

This was an opportunity Lord Drumpf wouldn't let pass him by. Any chance he had to gain favor with the new emperor had to be taken, but the situation with Angelica also allowed him to curry favor with Nemesis. She was trying her best to hold back her anger at the situation. It was too personal of a problem. Lord Drumpf could see through the cracks of Nemesis's emotional armor. She wanted to slaughter Lord Whelsey herself, which meant Matthew was restraining her for some reason. Lord Drumpf intended to find out what that reason was.

"Lord Whelsey might not trust me, but he doesn't have anyone else he'd even attempt to trust. Since we arrived here, Nemesis and the former Lower Wards leaders have formed a powerful alliance unifying all the other clans. Your grandfather knows this, and that's why he's trying to construct a base of power. He'd prefer to stick to the old ways on the *Alcatraz*. It wouldn't shock me if Lord Galen somehow is involved in all this. I can figure a way to get Lord Whelsey to trust me again if you give me the opportunity, Emperor. Grant me this opportunity. I promise success," Lord Drumpf vowed, sweat running down his cheek to drip from his face.

Matthew paced back and forth, looking into the ebb of time. The great doorways of the abyss swung open for his mind, and the secrets of the verse flowed through him. He couldn't see for certain if this plan would succeed, but time whispered of the necessity. Images flashed, showing the opportunities presented through Lord Drumpf's involvement. There was no way Matthew could avoid Lord Drumpf's involvement from what he could see.

"My father believed in ruling through fear of punishment. I shall not make the same mistakes as he did. Lord Drumpf, I'm offering you this last opportunity to serve your people and our new Empire. Lives hang in the balance and more than just your own. I find you to be a greedy and lustful man who seeks power about all, Lord Drumpf. This behavior wasn't just tolerated by my father but rewarded. You will not find the same here on *Empyrean station*. Either you learn to serve the Empire or will be sacrificed." Matthew glared down at Lord Drumpf, watching him wipe the sweat pouring off his brow.

"Thank you for this opportunity, Emperor Solomon," Lord Drumpf groveled.

"Enough! Rise already. This is not a place where your words are all that matter. If your words and action don't align, you'll find damnation shall follow swiftly. Honor, duty, and loyalty are the currency of this Empire we're building." Matthew heard the doors to the auditorium open, and he glanced to see Lady Marimba and clan Players walking into the auditorium.

Lady Marimba held her people back, seeing Nemesis and Lord Drumpf before the Infinity Nexus. The whispers from the group echoed in the room, but the sound was soft. Too soft for Lady Marimba to make out what was being said from this distance, yet she dared not get any closer. Even from the doorway, she could see the look of displeasure on the Emperor Solomon's face. The scowl distorted Matthew's pleasant features with sharp lines across his countenance.

"Another play date?" Nemesis looked at her brother with her arms crossed.

"My private affairs are of none of your concern. Now go, both of you. Remember, lives are on the line. I expect all due haste in these proceedings."

Matthew turned his back. He could hear the soft footsteps of Nemesis and Lord Drumpf receding away from the Infinity Nexus.

Nemesis walked towards the door. She glared at Lady Marimba, unblinking. The animosity sparking between the two women gave Lord Drumpf all kinds of ideas on how to rebuild his empire. Conflict would provide the perfect opportunity for him to gain more favor from Nemesis, and Matthew clearly considered his sister's opinions in all matters. This situation was more than he could have hoped for. He managed to barely contain his glee instead spreading across his face in a grin.

"Lady Nemesis. Thou seem to spend almost as much time with thine brother as myself. Though it's clear thee Emperor looks forward to seeing me more," Marimba taunted with a wink.

"A man enticed by a woman who walks around almost naked all the time. I'm shocked! Your only talent lies between your legs, and you'll find my brother isn't someone you can trick. Guess the verse must hate you." Nemesis pushed past Marimba.

"Seems mayhap you're jealous! All these men, and you're still unsatisfied."

"You should watch your mouth, harlot. Lady Nemesis shows you mercy now. Her brother might favor you, but he wouldn't punish his sister for disposing of you. This may not be the *Alcatraz*, but Nemesis will always be superior." Lord Drumpf spat on the ground before following behind Nemesis.

Nemesis glanced towards Lord Drumpf. She hadn't expected him to say anything in her defense, but it wasn't an unwelcome gesture. All the members of Clan Player stood alongside Lady Marimba, who was frozen in place.

"Don't think that kindness earns you any of my favor," Nemesis declared.

"I wouldn't dream of it, but I've never found Lady Marimba to be that entertaining. She's always had too much of an ego for my liking. Every now and again, people like her must be reminded of their place. That's all it was." Lord Drumpf followed Nemesis toward Lord Whelsey's estate.

"People like Lady Marimba and Lord Whelsey are already working to destroy this new home. I can feel it. We've got to be on guard against these types of traitors," Nemesis warned.

"Lord Whelsey's plans have always tended towards the grandiose. It was his birthright to rise to power and glory as God's loyal servant. Everything he did was to unravel your father and seize the *Alcatraz*. I don't imagine his plans have changed much." Lord Drumpf wanted to make sure Nemesis realized he was an ally. Even if she didn't like him, they could work together. Lord Whelsey had maintained an alliance for decades with Lord Drumpf, and he could never stand the man either.

"My brother worries about the enemies here on the station, but larger threats are coming to eradicate us. I just can't understand why these fools keep fighting over trifles. *Empyrean station* offers us everything we could have ever dreamed for. What could my grandfather hope to achieve further than my brother already has." Nemesis walked along, contemplating the truths of the situation on the station.

"That's where you've got it all wrong. It's not about achieving anything for people like your grandfather. It's all about who is in control of the power. Whatever he's doing with Angelica, you can be certain it's not in her best interests. Lord Whelsey will sacrifice anyone to achieve his goals. Even his own daughter, if it were necessary, would be sacrificed. I fear Lord Whelsey has more in common with our former captain than he would ever dare admit to," Lord Drumpf explained.

Nemesis tried not to think about it. Her mind was already spinning enough from everything that was happening with Angelica. Everything that Lord Drumpf said was true, but she didn't want to worry about it anymore right now. There was too much Nemesis needed to focus on now. The work at the club, the defense of the station, and Angelica all needed to be dealt with now. Whatever was going to happen with Lord Whelsey only mattered to the degree it impacted the other matters. She was certain the best solution was eliminating Lord Whelsey, but Matthew had forbidden it for now. It didn't matter to her because she knew this was all going to come to an end inevitably. She'd be standing there when it did.

CHAPTER 33

Fighters swept across the viewscreen escorting larger transports carrying sensor equipment. Sensors showed the *Templar* floating behind the *Icarus*. Troops marched through the bridge, attending to their tasks. Combat simulations ran on the computers, weapons were being tested, and Grand Admiral Celeris sat in her chair watching. She sipped a steaming cup of tea.

Information transmitted by Joshua showed up on the tactical computer on the arm of the captain's chair. Sensors in the network were transmitting reports to both ships and the *Empyrean station*. Celeris watched over the information for anything abnormal, but the scans were clean so far. A large patch of black on the screen showed the area that still needed sensor placement. The giant blind spot showed the sensor sweeps of the fighter and transport craft, but there was still too much darkness on the sensors for comfort.

"Chief Neeska, how long until the sensor net becomes fully operational?" Celeris looked at the woman operating the engineering console. The screen filled with calculations being processed.

"Engineering teams on the transport report they're entering the final stage of the operation Grand Admiral. The sensor network is showing signs of instability. Consul Joshua updates that his people are working on stabilizing the network. It could be several more hours at this rate." Chief Neeska ran the simulation again to double-check her report, but the computers returned the same results. She glanced to see Grand Admiral Celeris reviewing the tactical computer's data.

Engineers could be seen drifting in the Great Maw, working on the sensors. Every few minutes, a new flash update had to be loaded by Chief

Neeska. The engineers on the *Templar* were trying to increase the resolution of the sensor scanners. Each update brought the sensors down for a few minutes while the update was applied to each machine. Celeris sipped her tea, watching the progress, and leaning back into the cushions of her captains' chair.

"Get me Consul Joshua, Lt. Davos, and try to make it quick," Grand Admiral Celeris ordered.

"Yes, right away, Grand Admiral. I'm establishing communications now." Lt Davo's hands flittered across the console, activating the coms. A steady pulse of beeps echoed from the console.

"Can't you see I'm trying to work over here?" Joshua glared through the viewscreen at his sister. She just put the cup down on her armrest.

"Consul Joshua, please there is no need for that tone with me. I'm just wondering how many more flash updates you have planned. They keep taking the sensor network offline. God only knows what's lurking out there watching." Celeris leaned forward to look at her brother with her hands folded in her lap. She knew her brother got like this when things weren't working as he expected them to. Every update on the *Alcatraz* had been filled with Joshua's moaning.

"Forgive me, but I'm doing the best I can. These blasted sensors keep bugging out on us over here. Every time we think we got the problem isolated; it seems to adapt. It's almost like we're fighting back against the code. I've never seen anything like it in all my years. We're just at our wit's end over here, but we'll get the job done, so try to relax. I'll hold off on any more patches until we've got the problem isolated and fixed." Joshua glanced over to the troops working on his bridge on the viewscreen. He motioned with his hand for something, and Celeris recognized the hand signals.

"Try to relax, brother. We'll get through this together." Celeris watched the sensors flash back to life. The screen flickered with the surge of information, and everything seemed to freeze for a moment. When the screen finally started moving again, she saw a strange reading.

Celeris tapped at the screen, accessing the sensors nearest to the anomaly. She activated an intensive active scan of the sector of the Great Maw. Sensor sweeps began in the area. The energy readings coming were all over the register. There was something familiar about the energy patterns she was seeing, and she looked up at the viewscreen.

"Are you seeing these readings, brother?" Celeris reactivated the communication with Joshua, glancing at him with one raised eyebrow. On the screen, Joshua looked down at the information, and began working on it with a tap of a few buttons. The scans began to clear with the new algorithm Joshua implemented. Celeris now recognized the readings and pushed out of the chair marching forward across the bridge.

"Sound battle alarms. We've got a Cacophony of Discordance forces lurking out there. Send orders for all fighters to mobilize. Bring hard-beam weapons online. Lt. Davos bring us towards the enemy." Grand Admiral Celeris walked over to stand behind her pilot.

"Grand Admiral, our orders were very specific. We're not to engage the enemy under any circumstance. "Lt. Davos glanced back over his shoulder at Grand Admiral Celeris.

"Sister, your pilot's right. We can't afford to get involved in a fight right now. Let's watch and see what happens while we finish operationalizing these sensors." Consul Joshua could see by the look in his sister's eyes she wasn't going to back down from this fight. Her eyes were glazed over, and her focus faltered, creating a moment of silence between Joshua and his sister.

Sensors showed the *Icarus* adjusting course, and the fighters patrolling around the ship were moving toward the enemy ship. Celeris walked back to sit down in her chair. The tactical computer on the armchair showed the weapon systems charging. She looked back at the screen to see her brother watching. There wasn't any choice in her mind, but she needed to explain it to her brother and the crew. So, they could understand her choice.

"Our goal is to safeguard *Empyrean station* against any attacks. Without the sensor network, we won't even see our enemies coming. For all we know that ship is spying on us to learn how to bypass our sensor network. We can't allow it to escape, or worse, to compromise the detection system we've placed. There's no way we'll survive the upcoming battle without seeing what these battleforges can do in actual combat. We outnumber our enemy two to one in capital ships. There's no reason we should lose this engagement," Celeris explained.

"You're going to get us killed one of these days, sister, but I'll back your play. I'm deploying fighters to assist and moving to join your attack vector." Consul Joshua issued orders to his subordinates. Sensors showed the *Templar* moving towards the anomaly. Fighters surged away from the transports setting up the sensors. Hundreds of small bleeps darted on the screen showing Celeris everything that was happening.

"Brother, you can't do that. I need you to hold back and finish the sensor network. In case anything goes wrong, you can still escape back to the *Empyrean station* to warn the others." Celeris watched the sensors to see if the enemy ship had moved, but the energy signature was holding the position so far. The *Templar* was still moving towards the *Icarus* on sensors.

Coms showed the encryption was stable, and Joshua couldn't see any sign that the Cacophony of Discordance had broken into the communication channels. Diagnostic programs were scrubbing the data in the communication systems just to make him feel certain. He didn't like his sister's plan but began issuing orders to his troops. Fighters adjusted course, returning to escort the transports deploying the sensors. He looked at his sister on the viewscreen.

"I don't like this, Celeris, but this is your call. We'll hold back here and wait as ordered. Try not to bite off more than you can chew," Joshua warned.

"Keep your troops on standby." Celeris cut the coms before her brother could respond. She picked up her tea to sip at it. Troops glanced at their captain with uneasy looks. She could sense the tension in her troops, but she knew they needed this test to prepare for the battle.

The *Icarus* drifted across the Great Maw towards the enemy ship. Reverie forces didn't appear to be doing anything on the sensors. Celeris watched the viewscreen scanning the sector but couldn't see the enemy ships. The distortions in the energy patterns that Joshua cleared up must be some form of cloaking device Celeris hypothesized. She watched the sensors on her tactical computer, waiting to see when the enemy realized they'd been detected.

Fighters were approaching the outer edge of the enemy force's zone of control. On the viewscreen, Celeris saw the distorting ripple of the cloaking field blur in the void. The ship was still out of range of the *Icarus's* weapons, but fighters were racing towards the target. Sensors showed a mass of blips surge from the enemy ship. Reverie fighter craft swarmed towards Celeris's forces on the sensors. Weapons fire lit up the view screen between the fighters.

Energy surged around the enemy carrier, and blasts shot off toward Celeris' fighters. Data showed the ensuring destruction as fighter craft blinked out from the information feed. Fighters exploded into bright flashes on the viewscreen. The sensors showed the chaos of the battle. Ships on both sides of the skirmish were destroyed in rapid succession.

"Hold the ship on course, Lt. Davos. Chief Neeska, lock firing solutions in. Everyone prepares to engage the enemy. I want controlled firing patterns of overlapping fields of fire. Divert all power from engines into weapon systems. When you discover a weakness, isolate it, and coordinate fire." Celeris watched the *Icarus* growing closer to the enemy ship on the sensors. Target distance was dwindling fast approaching weapons range.

Fighters were still launching from the *Icarus* to join the fray. Turrets swiveled toward the enemy carrier. Celeris leaned back in her chair, sipping her tea, waiting for the moment to attack. The countdown ticked away as the tactical computer approached the weapons range. Weapons showed a full charge waiting to be fired. The tactical computer beeped, alerting that the ship was within weapons range. Celeris sipped her tea, pressing the button to fire with her free hand.

White beams of light lanced from the *Icarus* across the Great Maw. Troops surged on the bridge with their orders. Voices echoed orders all around Celeris, but she sat in her chair with her tea in hand. The blur of energy on the viewscreen made it impossible to tell what was happening in the chaos. Scans of the enemy ship showed the shields were holding against the fury of the attack, but the *Icarus* continued to fire away.

"Shields are holding steady, Grand Admiral," Chief Neeska reported.

"Keep an eye on that carrier. I'm sure they've got a few tricks up their sleeves left." Celeris watched the viewscreen. There seemed to be some kind of energy buildup around the enemy carrier. Sensors showed the dark matter buildup.

A massive beam of energy blurred in the Great Maw. The *Icarus* shuddered under the blast of the weapon. Energy cleaved through the shield. Explosions lurched through the structure of the ship. Damage reports filled the tactical computer showing Celeris that the energy weapon had bypassed the shield to tear into the hull. Emergency seals were already closing off the portions of the ship from the vacuum of space. She clung to the arm of her chair.

"I want that ship obliterated now," Celeris commanded.

"Grand Admiral, our weapons haven't even managed to break the enemy shields. We can't withstand the firepower of that weapon system. It bypassed our shields," Chief Neeska explained.

"Evasive maneuvers Lt. Davos. Keep that ship from hitting us. The name of the game is run and gun. Hit them and make sure they can't hit us. Divert power from the shields to the engines since they are fucking useless." Celeris wasn't going to waste good energy. She tapped on the tactical computer to activate the coms to the *Templar*.

"Are you ok?" Joshua appeared on the viewscreen. Celeris just shook her head.

"Looks like I'm going to need that support you offered earlier. Reverie weapons can bypass our shields. Divert all energy from your shields to your engines. We need to take down this ship before it can call for reinforcements." Celeris struggled against another shudder of her ship, and sparks exploded on the bridge.

"I've got communications jammed. No energy signals are getting out of this sector while the *Templar* is functional. I'm on my way, sister, so just hold on." Joshua cut the coms. The battle raged on the screen, and Celeris watched the frenzied pitch of the battle between the fighters. Energy filled the Great Maw with bright flashes of light all across the once-dark void. Reports showed the transports were almost done setting up the sensor network. According to calculations, the Templar was moving to join the battle, but it was going to several minutes before help arrived.

Reverie fighters were beginning to break through the dogfight. Sensors showed the craft was moving to attack the *Icarus*. Point defense weapons ships fired rapid spurts of energy at the incoming craft. Celeris watched the battle turning on the sensors. She uploaded the combat information on the fighters and hanger bay, showing the ineffectiveness of shields. Fighters raced out of the hanger bay to defend the *Icarus*.

Celeris could see the reports showing the reserves of her fighters were depleting faster than the forges could replace the craft. Pilot reserves were falling in tandem. There was no way Celeris could hold off the cost of attrition forever. Shields on the enemy ship were still over half, and there wasn't a scratch on the hull. The situation looked grim from Celeris' estimation, but she'd survived worse. She gritted her teeth, searching for options.

"Triangulate coordinates on the enemy carrier for an F.T.L. jump. If we can't survive, we're damn well taking that ship with us." Celeris leaned forward in her chair.

Everyone stopped for a moment to look at their captain. She glared at her crew before slamming her fist on the chair to get them all moving again. There wasn't any time for discussing options right now, and that was a lesson she'd learned from her father. Sometimes you just have to decide and force everyone else to go along with it. She knew her troops were scared. The fear hung thick in the air of the bridge but didn't slow any of the troops down.

"F.T.L. coordinates are triangulating," Chief Neeska reported.

"Good, let me know once they're locked. Keep up that weapons fire. We're not finished just yet. Isolate the enemy shield generators if you can. Once we can destroy those, we'll stand a better chance of finishing this fight alive." Celeris watched the situation with her hands squeezing the arms of her chair. Blood drained away from her knuckles turning them white.

Another explosion shook the ship from the blast of the enemy carrier. Damage alarms blared across the bridge, but Celeris couldn't hear them over her concentration on the battle. Reports surged into the tactical computer. Her eyes fixed on the enemy carrier crackling with energy as the main weapon system charged for another shot. Metal debris drifted in the Great Maw from the holes she could see in the front of the *Icarus*.

Troops in power armor flailed in the dead of the void of the Great Maw as the battle raged all around them. Celeris could see her helpless troops on the viewscreen, but she didn't have time to help them. Reports from the hanger showed transports were already being prepped to launch on a search and rescue operation. She knew her troops were doing what they were trained for, but they were doing far better than she'd hoped for under the strain of combat. These first timers demonstrated the potency of Emperor Solomon's genetic seed program.

"Come, my children. Don't shrink from the fire and the fury but embrace it. Make these bastards pay. Show our Emperor the might of our forces. Let's show the Cacophony of Discordance that we're the ones they should fear." Celeris pushed from her chair to inspire her troops forward in their attacks. Her father had often used this tactic, and she wanted to see how effective it was for herself. With one hand on Chief Neeska's shoulder, she looked at the calculations.

"I've managed to isolate a handful of powerful energy readings. The computer's calculating to isolate the resonance frequency of the shield harmonics to the energy outputs. It should tell us exactly where the shield generator is. I just need a few more minutes," Chief Neeska urged.

"Tell that to the enemy Neeska. Maybe if you ask them real nice, they'll give you the time to do your calculations. I'm sure they're dying to help you out." Celeris could see the anger her words caused, but the plan worked. Chief Neeska was working even faster than before.

Celeris marched across the bridge, glancing at the readouts from the other consoles. Engineering rerouted the shields to contain the hull breaches across the ship. Energy readings from the electrical grid were stable, and weapon charge times were in a nominal range. She looked over Lt. Davos' shoulder to watch his pilot skills. Another blast shook the *Icarus*.

"Remember, don't let the engines do all the work. Cut power to one, use thrusters, and any little adjustment you can think of to cause a wobble to the ship. It doesn't matter whether the enemy misses by an inch or a mile." Celeris leaned against Lt. Davos getting her balance back from the shaking. She marched back to the captain's chair to sit down.

Damage reports showed the *Icarus* was still holding strong under the assault. Several hull breaches were already sealed, with repair crews working on the damage. Celeris looked at the sensor readings' showing the fighter's screen was collapsing. Reverie fighters were swarming the *Icarus*, trying to attack, but the combination of point defense turrets and overlapping fields of fire held the craft at bay. Fighters were still launching from the ship, but Celeris could see that wouldn't last much longer. Reserves were approaching the red line with only a few more waves left.

The *Templar* was still a distance away on the sensor, but the fighters launched from the ship were converging on the *Icarus*. Celeris hoped the reinforcements would be enough to turn the tide of the battle in her favor. She wasn't holding her breath, given the information on the tactical computer. Reverie shields on the carrier were below half but falling slowly to the surge of weapons fire. She couldn't figure out how the enemy ship was managing to absorb this kind of sustained energy fire. F.T.L. triangulation was almost complete. At least she had an option should the battle continue turning against her. She leaned forward, scouring the battle for anything she could use to turn the tide.

CHAPTER 34

S creams echoed through the laboratory. Machines drilled into flesh deep into the bone. Tubes filled with fluids were extracted from Angelica. Lord Galen watched the reports on his console. Scans of the deep tissues of Angelica might provide the necessary information for him to reverse engineer the process done to Matthew, but so far, he'd had no luck uncovering the key to the psionic process. The information collected couldn't even prove the existence of psionic energy.

The console whirred away, running the high-level scans on extracted bone marrow. Lord Galen tried to block out the steady sound of pacing footsteps behind him. He knew that Lord Whesley was in a rush for the knowledge, but all this micromanaging was becoming tedious. A beep drew his attention away from the console. Video from the main entrance showed Nemesis and Lord Drumpf talking to the guards at the main entrance.

"Keep up the work. I'll deal with this." The door whisked opened for Lord Whelsey. There wasn't any respond from Lord Galen. He continued to work away to Angelica's screams.

Screams vanished when the door whisked shut to the lab behind Lord Whelsey. He couldn't image what either his granddaughter or Lord Drumpf wanted. He thought these interruptions were becoming unbearable, and only slowed the research down. There was no way to be certain this wasn't Emperor Solomon's influence trying to peer into the research. His mind raced with the possible reasons the two of them had come. He marched up the stairway, stomping.

"Get out of my way before I make you." Nemesis gripped her two energy blades glaring at the guards trying to block the doorway. The guards were backed up against the door when it opened behind them. They spun around to see Lord Whelsey standing in the frame.

"In all my years, I don't think you've ever visited me once. Granddaughter, what could possibly bring you to my home?" Lord Whelsey tapped his foot at a rapid pace. He glared at the silent Lord Drumpf. Nemesis moved towards her grandfather, keeping both hands on her blades.

"You seem to forget that you're not the power you once were here on *Empyrean station*. I don't answer to you or your authority. Not that I ever did, but here you answer to mine. I've been sent here on a mission by my brother, Emperor Solomon. Lord Drumpf here has been assembling the resources for your cathedral as he was ordered. Now it's time to see what work you've done." Nemesis moved towards the doorway for the guards to attempt to block her once more, but this time Lord Whelsey waved them backward.

"I'm at the Emperor's disposal, of course. Come with me." Lord Whelsey walked back into his estate with his granddaughter and Lord Drumpf. They headed up the stairs in single file. They continued past several floors heading toward the top floor.

Nuns, monks, and priests could be heard chanting on each floor. Nemesis saw that most of the estate had been converted into a form of housing for the religious servants. Incense filled the house with the unique aroma that burned at her nostrils. She hated the smell more than anything else she'd ever encountered. Lord Whelsey led the group towards the door to his private chambers and placed his hand on the scanner.

A green beam flashed from the scanner fixated on Lord Whelsey. Ocular scans confirmed his identity. The locks on the doors thudded before hissing upon release. He opened the door. A large white model of the intended cathedral sat in the middle of the room. He walked over towards the window to glance down at the park below.

"I've already got workers measuring the foundations. This model represents the finished product of the cathedral. The resources Lord Drumpf has been sending are being assembled in the park below. Why is this religious matter of such concern to Emperor Solomon now?" Lord Whelsey looked at his granddaughter.

Nemesis looked down at the park. Trees were being cut down by the works. Large piles of branches and logs scattered the grass below. The work was just beginning from what she could see. Glancing back at the model, she knew it would take months at this rate.

"It seems you've just started the work. The faithful go without a place to worship while you dawdle with what exactly?" Nemesis looked around, unable to see any other projects.

"We're being forced to rely on people rather than machines. In his wisdom, Emperor Solomon uses the nanites of *Empyrean station* to build the fleet and defenses. Everything takes time, granddaughter, and when you do things right, they tend to take just a bit longer. If the Emperor is that concerned about my people's religious needs, perhaps he should free up some of the machines to assist. Given the speed they can construct the battleforges, I don't imagine it'd take long to construct the cathedral. Baring that perhaps Emperor Solomon would consider expanding my troops?" Lord Whelsey knew he needed any advantage he could dupe Emperor Solomon into giving him.

"My people could assist," Lord Drumpf offered.

"That would be of assistance but wouldn't speed up the time frame of the construction by much. Your troops are busy moving the resources produced by Lord Hephaestus' energy-to-matter fabricators. We need thousands of workers, machines, and the necessary time. That's the way God intended it." Lord Whelsey walked with his granddaughter towards the model.

Nemesis walked around the model, scanning it up and down. Some of the pieces were large slabs of stone that would be hard for the workers to move. Statues on the model revealed that the original religious artwork was intended to be replaced. The iconic religious work would take years to complete by hand. The room was filled with various artifacts that her grandfather managed to salvage from the *Alcatraz*, but none of the stone statues could be salvaged. It seemed that Lord Whelsey designed the cathedral to delay its construction. One option sprang to Nemesis's mind, and she knew it would drive her grandfather mad.

"I understand your situation, but I think I've got a solution. Do you remember Mordecai?" Nemesis looked at her grandfather with a smile. She could see the scowl forming just from the mention of the name. Lord Whelsey's eyebrows narrowed, forehead scrunched, and he glared.

"When did the machine arrive at the station?" Lord Whelsey looked at his guests.

"Mordecai and the rest of the A.S.A. arrived a little while ago. They've been working with Emperor Solomon to fortify the station. New defense platforms have been brought online to defend the station against attacks. I'm sure Mordecai would be more than willing to help you. Their numbers would reduce the time it takes to build this glory to your God." Nemesis watched her grandfather close, trying to figure out what he was thinking.

Lord Whesley wasn't sure what to do at this moment. He didn't want to refuse the offer of the machine's help after requesting assistance, but he loathed Mordecai. There wasn't much hope that the rest of the asymmetrical soul algorithms were any more tolerable than the infernal Mordecai. He rubbed his chin, considering the situation, and his eyes fell on Lord Drumpf. The epiphany sprung upon him that there might be an opportunity to deal with all these matters.

"That would be appreciated, granddaughter, and since Lord Drumpf offered his assistance, he can be my liaison with the A.S.A. to keep things moving smoothly. I've begun deciphering data left on the *Empyrean station* by the Ancients. It seems there are entire chapters of the bible that were lost during the Great War. I'm sure Emperor Solomon would understand that I'm the only one suitable for deciphering these ancient scripts. None other have my understanding of the divine." Lord Whelsey wasn't sure his granddaughter was buying the story, but he was certain he hadn't given any evidence that could be used against his plans.

All that mattered to Nemesis was that Lord Whelsey welcomed Drumpf back, which would give her eyes and ears inside this estate. She looked down at the floor, wondering if her sister was alright. The fact that Lord Whelsey was welcomed back his former ally with no complaints told Nemesis he'd removed the threat at the earliest opportunity. The fact that Lord Drumpf knew this also, yet remained calmed, did impress Nemesis. She looked over to Lord Drumpf.

"Does any of this sound like a problem to you?" Nemesis glanced at Lord Drumpf, but they both knew he didn't have any say in this.

"I don't see any problems so far. All I've got to do is discuss with Mordecai what portions of the work they can do most efficiently. It's just a matter of Lord Whelsey walking me through the plans," Lord Drumpf explained.

"Good to hear. I'll leave you to work." Nemesis walked towards the door leaving the two men standing around the model. The door shut behind her. Lord Drumpf turned to get to work, but Lord Whelsey came rushing towards him.

Lord Whelsey pulled his energy blade, sparked it, and aimed it at Lord Drumpf. Energy crackled, radiating heat on the skin of his neck. He gulped down, waiting to see what Lord Whelsey would do. The two men stared at each other in silence. He leaned forward, moving face to face with Lord Drumpf. Hot breathe steamed from the rapid breaths.

"Go ahead, Lord Whelsey. We both know this is what you've wanted for quite some time. Your botched assassination can now be corrected, and you can claim this all the will of God." Lord Drumpf closed his eyes before raising his chin to expose his throat to the energy blade. He felt the heat burning against his skin, and the rapid breaths of hot air fill his nostrils with the stench of Lord Whelsey's rotten breath.

"Oh, I'm not going to give you or Emperor Solomon the satisfaction. I know Emperor Solomon and my granddaughter sent you here to spy on me. The only reason I'm not going to kill you is I believe that's exactly what your role is in this. A sacrificial pawn so that Nemesis and the Emperor can move against me with the support of the people. They both know the religious worship me as God's chosen servant," Lord Whelsey proclaimed.

"Well, hopefully, that keeps you happy in the future because Emperor Solomon has rendered us both almost powerless. Kain, Celeris, and Joshua's new armies out number us beyond hope, and each of their ships possesses the technology to grow new troops. You linger here playing at whatever little scheme you've conjured up, but you've lost track of the game. For the record, you're losing." Lord Drumpf watched the ego challenge worm past Lord Whelsey's defenses.

Lord Whelsey paced, considering the situation. He couldn't trust Lord Drumpf, but if he was angry over the change in power, that could be useful. It would require stringing him along until the time was right. The cathedral offered the perfect opportunity to Lord Whelsey. He could complete the building while preparing to sacrifice his former ally.

"Let's see how well you can obey the orders of Emperor Solomon." Lord Whelsey pulled a data pad from a stack on the desk. He handed the schematics to Lord Drumpf.

"I'll take care of it," Lord Drumpf assured, looking through the plans.

"I expect nothing less." Lord Whelsey led his former ally out of the study closing the door behind him. He went to sit down behind his desk to look at the model. The model sat on the desk, filling his mind with racing thoughts. Everything he had planned was in danger from Nemesis and Lord Drumpf now, and he was certain Emperor Solomon did know everything already.

Lord Whelsey couldn't understand why his grandson wasn't acting already. There was only a possibility that seemed to make a certain kind of sense to him. Everything he was doing with Angelica was the will of God and thus fated to happen. Not even Matthew's ability to see through time could alter the will of God. Nothing could stop Lord Whelsey now, he realized. All he had to do was play along with this little play of deception by his grandchildren. Soon he'd have the power of the Cacophony of Discordance and *Empyrean station* in the palm of his hands.

CHAPTER 35

Heat emanated from the glowing F.T.L. engine. Coolant flow still hadn't been restored from the display on the screen. The computer system in the engineering room struggled to process information in the throbbing heat. Magnus tried to get the automated repair system functional, but error messages were causing the operating system to freeze. He scanned the room, looking for anything he could use to cool the engine. The only thing nearby were the canisters of chemicals stacked behind the metal door of the vault.

The entire ship shuddered under the vibration of the engine. Magnus entered the access code into the keypad on the vault. Hissing from the vacuum seals depressurizing exploded forth from the vault. Locks clanged behind the thick metal. The door popped open. He reached into the vault to pull out the large canister of liquid nitrogen and attached the nozzle to the top of the canister. Once he ensured the lid was secure, he grabbed the long hose leading to the blaster.

Liquid nitrogen sprayed onto the red-hot metal of the F.T.L. engine. Vapor surged from the machine filling the engineering room with a cloud. Magnus could barely see but could sense the temperature lowering fast. He glanced towards the glowing display through the mist to see the computer was beginning with flickering lights to move once more as the temperature fell. The shuddering began to slow from the thumping F.T.L. engine. He cut off the flow of liquid nitrogen.

Atmospheric scrubbers hummed, starting to life with Magnus activating the engineering room exhaust system. Vapor sucked into the vents along the ceiling. The room began to clear from the haze allowing him to see the F.T.L. engine again. The metal wasn't glowing red hot anymore, but it still glowed with a dull orange. The temperature on the display for the engine was rising again.

The computer responded to Magnus's commands, but the heat was already rising steadily. He accessed the navigation computer. There were still over an hour left on the travel time. He looked at the gauge on the canister of liquid nitrogen. The meter was hovering around three-quarters full. He spayed the liquid nitrogen onto the engine in small spurts. It was the only way he could figure to extend the engine's life long enough to get close to Pandora's Box.

Time ticked away on the console screen, counting down to arrival. Magnus waited until the F.T.L. engine started vibrating again before spraying more liquid nitrogen. The gauge on the canister fell with each surge of the liquid, and the vapor continued to be sucked into the ventilation system. His eyes stayed fixated on the timer counting down, but the canister wouldn't last much longer. There was only one choice left he could see.

Magnus accessed the engineering segment of the emergency lockdown system. He programmed the engineering section to enter an emergency lockdown in two minutes and moved to access the pressurization system. With a few overrides, he set up the automated system to lock down the engineering section and vent space into the room. He wasn't sure the plan was going to work. The canister ran dry with twenty-eight minutes still remaining to arrival. He activated the lockdown before retreating out the door. The sound of the locks clanging into place sent him rushing towards the bridge. He bounded onto the bridge, took the captain's seat, and brought up the engineering diagnostics on the screen. The cold from space seemed to be working for a moment, but the temperature of the F.T.L engine was holding steady rather than falling.

The timer counted down on the screen. Magnus watched the timer with his hand hovering over the F.T.L. throttle, ready to disengage. The ship shuddered with the steady vibration of the F.T.L. engine. The temperature of the F.T.L. drive was starting to rise again on the screen, and the vibrations were increasing with it. He didn't want to push the engine too hard, but he knew dropping from F.T.L. now would be a suicidal distance from Pandora's Box. Reverie forces would have too much time to catch up with him.

Alarms blared on the screen showing the coolant reserves reaching critical. Magnus pulled up the diagnostic to see the shuddering had damaged another coolant pipe. Damage reports cascaded onto the screen. Weapons systems went offline than shields, and it took all his know-how to stabilize the reactor. The reactor wasn't critical, but it was approaching the threshold. He had to divert what was left of the coolant from the F.T.L. engine to the reactor.

The shuddering of the superstructure increased with the temperature of the F.T.L. engine spiking on the screen. There was just under ten minutes on the countdown. Magnus pushed the Death's Reaper to the limit. His fingers blurred, entering commands into multiple consoles. Energy crackled in his eyes, glancing between the screens. He vented the reactor room, trying to keep it cool next. The timer ticked down under five minutes. He knew just a few more minutes.

Visual on the screen showed the F.T.L. engine glowing bright red and starting to turn white. Sensors showed the fatigue of the metal was approaching its limit. Warnings blared of immediate F.T.L. engine rupture. Magnus looked at the screen to see the timer drop to under two minutes. He pulled back on the throttle. Death's Reaper tore from F.T.L. speed, crashing back to regular space.

Sensors showed two large Pandoran ships on an intercept course. From the bridge viewport, Magnus could see the large carriers in the distance. Fighters surged from the carriers in waves. He dumped all energy from weapons and shields into engines setting his course for the docks of Pandora's Box despite the ships blocking the way. Both the reactor core and the F.T.L. engines were beginning to cool off. He accessed the communication systems ignoring the hail of the two carriers.

"Pandora, this is Lord Void on approach," Magnus requested.

Only the incoming hail from the two carriers were showing up on the communication system. Magnus leaned back into his chair, watching the fighters rushing towards the *Death's Reaper*. He ran a high-level scan trying to ascertain whether the Reverie ship was pursuing. The system only took a few seconds to confirm the detection or Cacophony of Discordance energy approaching the sector. He was just about to hail again when the coms beeped.

"Lord Void, it has been quite some time since you've graced me with your presence. We had expected your return quite some time ago. I'm all ears on what took you so long." Pandora smiled at Magnus through the holographic display. He began uploading the sensor data showing the incoming enemy forces. The data highlighted the energy signature of the reverie carrier.

"Pandora, we don't have time for fun and games. I've got a prince of the Cacophony on my tail coming. Reverie forces could be here any moment. Just call off your ships and open that force field." Magnus could see on the sensors the fighters closing in on him. He pushed the ship towards the docking bay. The large V-shaped carriers flanked the Pandoran docking bay.

"You're quite the cunning creature, Magnus. The power of the *Death's Reaper* is known across the Great Maw, and you seem to forget that lovely tour you took me on. Back when you were romantic before you got what you wanted from me. Once my scouts found the location of that ship, you were gone quicker than maw slaw. That wounded me quite deeply. So why should I help you now?" Pandora glared at Magnus with her arms crossed.

"I've done quite a bit for you, Pandora. You shouldn't forget that. Sensors show those planetary shields I scavenged for you seem to be still functioning. Besides, look at your own damn sensors. The *Death's Reaper* is barely functional. Weapons and shields are offline. I won't last in a fight against your fighters, let alone your carriers or the other tricks up your sleeve." Magnus' eyes crackled with black energy.

Sensors showed the shield around Pandora's Box was still functioning at one hundred percent. Pandora glared in silence at the holoemitter. Magnus glanced at his sensors, watching for the arrival of Tenno Asmodeus. Fighters broke away on the sensors returning towards the carriers. Shields around Pandora's Box weakened, and sensors showed the hole forming.

"Well, you'll have to make up this misunderstanding to me. Reverie forces can come all they want. We've held them off before, and we'll do it again. I don't give a fuck if it's one or all the princes of the Cacophony coming. Let's throw a party, I say. I've got a new friend who seems to agree with me. He also seems to know you," Pandora teased.

The holographic image of Pandora faded on the emitter. Engines flared, surging the *Death's Reaper* towards the hole in the shields. Fighters formed up around the ship escorting it toward the docking bay. Magnus wasn't sure who Pandora was talking about, but he just wanted to land. Tenno Asmodeus wasn't going to give up the chase easily. The best Magnus could hope for was that Asmodeus would take time to assess the situation of Pandora's Box before charging in. The holographic emitter flickered, drawing his attention.

All the motion blurred in the lights above the emitter. It was impossible at first for Magnus to make anything out at all. When the motion slowed, the image was able to catch up. The frame of the power armor appeared in the image showing the markings of the *Alcatraz*. Gabriel looked through the emitter at Magnus.

"Well, I can't say I was expecting to run into you ever again," Gabriel chuckled.

"Gabriel fucking Soloman. Seems you and I have more in common than I first suspected. It seems we're both hard to kill, and never give up." Magnus shook his head, trying to comprehend the odds of Gabriel's survival. It was unfathomable that the man was still alive. Magnus hoped he wasn't holding any grudges. He studied Gabriel's face for any sign of anger. Lines etched on Gabriel's face, showing the surge of emotions within. He glared at Magnus through the holographic connection.

"You've got a lot of explaining to do with everything that's happened since we met."

"I understand that, but I've got a Tenno hunting me down right now. Perhaps we can discuss your little feelings when I land." Magnus glanced at the sensors. Reverie forces still hadn't arrived, but he wasn't going to relax yet. Even the Pandoran fighter escort wouldn't be much help if Tenno Asmodeus showed up to attack.

"Seems you're experiencing some familial disagreements just like me," Gabriel taunted.

"There's no love lost from the Cacophony of Discordance. They're children playing at being king. Something you should be familiar with. I'm sure your family believes you're dead. I thought you died when you crashed the *Alcatraz* into the *Dread Sovereign* at the Battle of *Empyrean station*. Yet just like a cockroach, here you are. How the hell did you make it to Pandora' Box?"

"That was the plan initially, but the *Dread Sovereign* saw what I was doing. The ship moved just far enough out of the way that the collision only tore half the *Alcatraz* to pieces. I'm not really sure what happened after that. Lost consciousness until Pandora's scavengers showed up. Killed a few of them, stole their ship, and spared the crew if they'd serve me. Myrmidon, the original captain, told me I had to come here, and I've got to admit that this place grows on you," Gabriel informed.

"It seems the Great Maw can kill just about anything except either of us. Not sure if that's a gift or a curse." Magnus could see the distance he still had to travel to reach the shield of Pandora's Box. He hoped his luck held out, glancing at the sensors. There wasn't anything reassuring about the calm on the sensors.

"Perhaps I'm just cursed because of my association with you," Gabriel glared.

"I'm still not your enemy Gabriel. Do you understand that?" Magnus searched Gabriel's face.

"The only difference between the word friend and enemy is how you feel upon killing them. It seems even Pandora here isn't very happy with your misrepresentation of the truth. You've got a debt to pay to me for your lies," Gabriel declared.

"Perhaps I do, Gabriel, and we can discuss it when I land."

"Fair enough, Magnus. We'll see you when you arrive." Gabriel cut off the communication. The holographic emitter fell lifeless, with the light vanishing above it. Magnus gripped the flight stick gliding the *Death's Reaper* toward the hole in the shield on the sensors.

Magnus watched the sensors waiting for Asmodeus to appear. Each minute that passed only made the situation worse in Magnus's mind. He'd hoped that his enemy would have the audacity to charge in. Haste would create errors that he could exploit. Asmodeus was known for his audacity but also for his caution. It seemed to Magnus that Asmodeus was preparing his attack with care. When the attack arrived, it would be far more than Pandora, or her people could endure. Magnus knew the power of the Jinn firsthand. They were among the most powerful members of the Cacophony of Discordance. The *Jinnestan* housed several legions of the Jinn, all serving Asmodeus every command without hesitation. Magnus worried Pandora and her people stood no chance against the Jinn.

Sensors blared the warning showing the surge of energy in the sector. The *Jinnestan* appeared on the screen. Reverie fighters blipped onto the screen, swarming around the carrier. Magnus watched the screen, but the carrier stayed in place. Some of the fighters were moving to intercept the *Death's Reaper*. Coms beeped with the incoming message. He examined the message to see if it was a broadband message transmitted to the whole sector. The image of Tenno Asmodeus appeared in the holographic emitter.

"Listen to me, all you wretched refuse of the Great Maw. I'm Tenno Asmodeus of the Cacophony of Discordance here to arrest the rouge Lord Magnus Void. Anyone offering sanctuary to the outlaw will be judged the same. Surrender yourself, Magnus, or watch the destruction I'll rain down upon your friends." Tenno Asmodeus vanished from the emitter with a burst of light.

Magnus could see the hole in the shield was still open. He dumped all the energy he could muster into the engines. The *Death's Reaper* surged toward the shields. Sensors showed enemy fighters coming from behind. Alarms showed the reactor was destabilizing again, but he couldn't do anything about it. All he could do was get through the shields before the Cacophony of Discordance fighters could catch up.

CHAPTER 36

Cutting torches spew white-hot flames sparking off the metal. A.S.A. worked away on the auditorium of the Infinity Nexus. Rows of seats were being installed for the senators, and metal was being raised along the room's outer edge. Metal beams zig-zagged across the room, showing the new intended design. Arch frames created tunnels from the four doors to the Infinity Nexus.

Matthew went over the data reports with Virgil in the Infinity Nexus. The data showed the completion of the new battleforges. Images showed the new ships orbiting *Empyrean station*. The *Olympus* stood out amongst the new ships. Hephaestus' design for his ship focused on support rather than offense. *Olympus* was the only ship orbiting the new sun joining its nanites to help construct the *Divius Oculus*. The *Brisingamen* of Lady Freya amber-hued hull glowed like the star itself, and Lord Hector's *Iliad* orbited alongside the other ship defending *Empyrean station*.

The doors to the Infinity Nexus whisked open. Lord Marcus and Lady Nemesis walked into the audience room to see the flurry of activity with A'zyren right behind. Behind them trailed Lord Cornelius, Lord Hector, and Commander Verdas. Lady Marimba and Lord Oswald kept their distance from the others. The group approached Matthew, seeing him in conversation with Virgil. The A.S.A. working away drew A'zyren's attention.

"When did the A.S.A. arrive?" A'zyren scanned the area looking for Mordecai, but the damn machines looked so much alike. Hundreds of machines were labouring away in the auditorium on the modifications.

"My apologies, I meant to tell you, but I've been so busy with everything happening. Mordecai and the A.S.A. have come to join us."

Nemesis pointed to Mordecai off on the other side of the room. She watched A'zyren race across the room. Marcus just chucked, seeing the excitement.

"She sure is a strange one," Marcus joked.

"Full of life and death. I find her quite intriguing. Deadly, affectionate, a rare combination, and perhaps the reason Lord Void chose her as his second-in-command." Nemesis watched A'zyren coming up behind Mordecai. The couple walked towards the Infinity Nexus, watching the activity in the distance.

Rapid footsteps warned Mordecai of something moving towards him. He turned to see what the cause of the commotion was. Visual sensors locked upon the image of A'zyren bounding towards him, but his only reaction was to start running a diagnostic check. She bounded towards him, wrapping her arms around him. Diagnostics returned the report that everything was functioning within acceptable parameters. He returned the hug.

"Damn, it's good to see you, Mordecai. Never thought I'd miss your cranky attitude. Why didn't you come to see me when you arrived?" A'zyren scowled at Mordecai. He smiled back.

"I didn't know that you were here A'zyren," Mordecai replied.

"I'm surprised you haven't synced up with the *Empyrean station* by now. Also, not sure how you missed the *Sesh'yna*, but I'll let that go. So, what did Lord Void say to get the A.S.A. to march to war?" A'zyren looked around. She'd never seen this many A.S.A. in one location before.

"We've come to join the *Empyrean station*; the A.S.A. and the humans will stand together as we did before the fall, and the Great Tabulator of Systems has completed his final journey to merge with the *Empyrean station*. Together Tabulator and Virgil have ascended to their ultimate purpose. The full power of the Infinity Nexus has been unlocked." Mordecai pointed towards the Infinity Nexus. A'zyren glanced toward Virgil to see how different the A.I. looked.

"Sounds like you've been busy," A'zyren stated.

Holographic emitters surged in the Infinity Nexus. Light carved the stellar map floating above the central part of the auditorium. The sensor network showed the reports across the established network. New sensors were coming online. Sensors on the map surged red with the alarm sounding in the Infinity Nexus. Virgl's eyes glowed white.

"I'm sorry for calling you all here on such short notice, but a situation has arisen. Reverie forces have shown up on the border of our territory. Grand Admiral Celeris and Consul Joshua have engaged the enemy forces." Matthew pointed towards the map. Everyone gathered in front of the Infinity Nexus and looked up at the map. A'zyren and Mordecai were just joining the others.

"We must go to assist them," Nemesis implored.

"Our defenses aren't even established here yet, Lady Nemesis. You know I'm not one to shy away from combat, but to leave our home undefended would be suicidal. We're in no position to do anything in our current situation." Lord Hector studied the situation but couldn't see a safe way to assist. The map showed the current array of forces around *Empyrean station*.

"Fuck that. Emperor, let me take the *Divine Retribution*. I'll deal with the reverie scum and bring our brother and sister back safe. We've got the *Sesh'yna*, *Iliad*, *Olympus*, *Sentinel*, and *Brisingamen* defending the station." Nemesis could see her brother struggling with a decision.

"A.S.A. construction progress on orbital platform stations is proceeding at the expected pace, but defenses are only four percent complete. The minefield has just begun construction. Defenses on the *Mechanarium of Gyros* can assist, but until defenses are completed, I can't guarantee the safety of *Empyrean station*. Incoming communication from the *Templar*," Virgil reported.

The holographic map blurred with the flashing of lights switching in the holographic emitter. Joshua's face began to emerge from the stellar map. Static crackled in the air on the holographic image. Whatever Joshua was saying crackled and jumbled together. Virgil struggled against the interference trying to clear it up.

"Thi... s... ua... com... in... Em... tion." The message chopped apart.

"Reverie is attempting to block the transmission. I'm applying algorithms to amplify the signal now. Please stand by," Virgil reported continuing to struggle to clear the message.

"We're wasting time. Just let me go and pull their asses out of the fire," Nemesis insisted.

"Perhaps we should first better understand what they're facing. We still don't know much about the capabilities of the Cacophony of Discordance. This could be an excellent time to gather intelligence on our enemies," Commander Verdas assessed.

"That's a foolish plan. Information only matters if we have a chance to win. We can't do that if we're losing ships already!" Lord Hector paced back and forth, trying to figure out a solution. He glanced to see Emperor Solomon standing there in deep thought.

"I'd prefer a straight-up fight rather than all this fearmongering. Let's just go take care of these bastards now and be done with it. We'll take out that ship first before going on a massive offensive. We'll kill every last one of them." Lord Cornelius crossed his arms.

Time unraveled before Matthew as he searched for the best possible solution to this problem. He couldn't see the destruction of either ship in the stream of possible outcomes. There was something about the enemy ship that seemed familiar. He focused, trying to see through the shadows of the Cacophony of Discordance but couldn't penetrate the nebulous murk of unnatural emotions surging within the shroud. Fury, lust, and pride emanated from the shadows resonating in his mind and trying to overpower him. His eyes darted towards Lady Marimba, feeling a surge of lust.

"Emperor, Grand Admiral Celeris has engaged a Reverie carrier, and its shields are holding steady against the assault. Even the hard light weapon systems of the *Icarus* have almost no effect, and the ship has sustained significant damage. Reverie fighter craft are swarming the ship. I've been ordered to pull back to *Empyrean station*. I'm requesting an update to clarify orders." Consul Joshua's voice echoed through the auditorium, drawing everyone's attention.

"Don't fall back, Consul. You're ordered to engage the enemy ship. Keep the *Icarus* in one piece. I'm sending in reinforcements." Matthew looked at his sister.

"I'm on my way Joshua. Just hold out as long as you can," Nemesis inspired. The clacking of her footsteps echoed through the communication.

"Emperor, I've adjusted heading towards the enemy carrier, but I'm unsure I can make it in time to save the *Icarus*. I'm going to attempt a micro F.T.L. jump through the enemy lines. Let's hope the mass of the *Templar* is great enough to sustain the damage. That's a lot of fighters out there," Joshua declared.

"Consul, please stand by for a moment. I'm making the correct calculations for the micro-jump. Beginning the data upload to your navigation computer now." Virgil flicked from the intensity of the processes running to perform the work. The data surged across the network. Computers reported the data successful upload, and reports showed the *Templar* preparing for F.T.L. jump.

Communications cut out again with a flicker. Virgil couldn't penetrate the collective interference of the F.T.L. jump and the communication jammers. The map showed the progress of the battle. *Icarus* reports showed the damage being inflicted, but Mathew knew the ship would be fine. He turned back to the assembly before him.

"Nemesis and Joshua will deal with the reverie forces, but we have other things to see to. I called you here to begin the third phase of the geneseed protocol. Lord Oswald, Lord Marcus, Lady Marimba, and Commander Verdas will undergo the next phase. Lord Hephaestus has already begun the construction of the superstructure of your ships. We can't allow our enemies to disrupt our plans. Lord Hector and Lord Cornelius, I want you to assist the A.S.A. in setting up the minefield." Matthew tried to focus on what needed to be done, but the emotions swelling inside him were hard to resist. His eyes kept drifting to Lady Marimba standing there. She could sense his desires, and she smiled and winked at Emperor Solomon.

"I'll begin right away, Emperor," Lord Hector bowed.

"Sounds like the dregs are still hauling all the heavy shit, but this sounds more exciting than standing around this station. We'll make sure this work gets done proper. Can't leave everything up to the machines now, can we?" Lord Cornelius smiled at Mordecai.

"For organics, your people are well suited to manual labor. There is nothing to be ashamed about in this, Lord Cornelius. We're the Emperor's hands, and without our work, nothing could be accomplished," Mordecai informed with a toothy attempt at a smile. Everyone had the same fearful reaction causing him to return his face to normal parameters. "I'll keep working on that."

"Perhaps Lord Cornelius is right about going on the offensive," Lord Marcus interjected. Everyone turned to look at him. None had suspected him of wanting to go on the offensive.

"If only Nemesis was here to see your courage," Lord Cornelius praised, placing an arm around Lord Marcus. Lord Marcus pushed the arm away.

"It's not like that at all, Lord Cornelius. I'd prefer to avoid battle if we can, but since we can't, we will need information just like Lord Hector stated. No matter what happens with the current battle, we're not sure of the capabilities of the Cacophony of Discordance or even Lord Magnus Void. It feels too much like we're at the mercy of someone else's game, and I don't like that feeling one bit." Lord Marcus wasn't sure what Matthew's thoughts on the matter were. His face was stern and cold, looking through the glass of the Infinity Nexus.

"You're not wrong, Lord Marcus, but the time for that hasn't yet come. All defenses must be focused on holding *Empyrean station* while we construct our forces. Emperor Solomon's plans conform to strategy. We shouldn't abandon the thing that made this moment possible. Lord Void's motivations might be unknown to us, but his actions reveal some truths. It's clear that Lord Void wishes for the return of the light and is prepared to make any sacrifice to keep the star burning. That is why Lord Void insisted the A.S.A. return to serve humanity, reminding us of our primary imperative. To aid in the creation, maintenance, and survival of life," Virgil explained.

"You know, for all that data bank knowledge you claim to possess, Virgil, you're forgetting one of the oldest human adages. The best defense is a strong offense." Lord Cornelius crossed his arms to stare at Virgil. The two just stared at each other. A'zyren rubbed her temples.

"My people are coming. We alone outnumber you a hundred to one," A'zyren informed.

"The Cacophony will call on other allies as well. The light might keep their ships at bay, but it won't keep the Arachne. Knowledge of the species in the Great Maw is limited. There is no way to know who, or even what will attack the *Empyrean station*, and the only certainty known is the attack is coming. This sector is the most valuable thing in all of existence, and you want to leave it exposed? I'm sorry, but I just can't see the logic in that strategy." Virgil looked to Emperor Solomon.

The group discussed the situation amongst themselves, but Matthew wasn't paying attention to a word. He was unable to break his gaze away from Lady Marimba. Light fell on her soft dark skin tone, her breasts heaved with each breath, and the glint of light reflecting in her eyes were enthralling to him. Even the flow of time receded in his mind giving way to the lustful thoughts pouring forth. Desires flashed images of what Matthew should do to Marimba in his mind replacing the truths of the stream of time. He could hear Lady Marimba moaning his name as he pictured her naked underneath him. Only when Lady Marimba spoke did Matthew snap back to reality. He blinked his eyes, trying to figure out what was going on.

"Emperor, what are your orders?" Lady Marimba looked to Emperor Solomon.

"I've already given them. We're going to hold *Empyrean station* no matter what, and I don't want to hear any more arguing on the matter. Lord Oswald, you served your entire life by my father's side, yet you've remained quiet. What is your estimation of my plan?" Matthew looked down at Lord Oswald and stumbled for a moment, finding the right words.

"Your father would never endanger the *Alcatraz* unless it were absolutely necessary. He may never have favored you out of his children, Emperor, but it seems you've got a firm grasp of strategy. This is the same plan your father would make if he were in your place. I stand with you, my Emperor, and whatever you need from me, just command." Lord Oswald bowed to Emperor Solomon.

"I see now why my father kept you around. You're an excellent leader Lord Oswald. Now all of you go and attend to my orders. We must get our geneseed program complete." Matthew watched the group bow to him before marching toward the exit. Only the A.S.A. remained behind.

The thoughts about Lady Marimba weren't subsiding in Matthew's mind. Images flicked that filled him with shame. He struggled against the surging desires managing to stifle them once the doors closed behind the group. It seemed that the urges were easier for Matthew to control in the absence of Lady Marimba's presence. He tried to figure out what had brought them on, scratching his head. Memories didn't give him any clue about the sudden surge of desire. The only thing he could think of was when he tried to force his mind to see past the shadows of the Cacophony of Discordance. He could feel the stream of time flowing once more in his mind. The shadows hung all across the tapestry of time, but he didn't want to try seeing past them again. He could feel his heart thumping in his chest with growing anxiety just looking at the murk in time.

CHAPTER 37

E nergy crackled around the *Insidious Seduction* floating beyond the W'hyish S'yevel fleet of worldships. Jump engines charged at a steady rate on the tactical panel on the captain's chair. The fleet floated through the Great Maw on the bridge viewscreen. Tenno Lilith paid little attention to either the fleet or the charging drive. She went over the information about Lucifer in her head, trying to piece together the puzzle. The coms continued to warble with the outgoing communication attempting to connect. Coms connected with the image of Atrax appearing on the screen.

"Dark mother, you've favored us with your presence once more. How can I be of service to you?" Atrax's eight eyes fell upon the visage of the Tenno, and he bowed to her.

Tenno Lilith's eyes crackled with red energy, glaring at Atrax through the viewscreen. His mandible chattered together with his eyes fixated upon the glowing eyes of the Tenno. Cowering before the Tenno, he prostrated himself. His eight eyes looked upward to see Lilith glaring down at him. The red energy sparking from her eyes sent chills through Atrax's nerves.

"I've visited the W'hyish S'yevel tribes to find Lucifer just like your mother instructed. Only to find out the tribes have never met my darling Lucifer. Do I need to tell you how unhappy this makes me?" Red energy crackled in a powerful bolt from Lilith's eyes. The energy flashed across the viewscreen, causing tremors to quiver through Atrax's muscles.

"Tenno, I can't explain this. The strands of the web never lie. If the web told mother that Lucifer was with the W'hyish S'yevel tribes, that is what happened. Please, you must forgive us, my mother would never lie to you, and we only want peace with the Cacophony of Discordance.

Arachne's children have been preparing the fleet just like you ordered." Atrax trembled before Lilith, seeing the crackling fury of her thoughts leaping from her eyes.

"Well, I'll have to see that myself when I arrive. Tell your mother I'm returning to get the truthful answers to my first question. This time there will be no deceiving me. Hope for your sake that I'm impressed by your readiness for battle because if I'm not, your species might not survive another day in the Great Maw. I'm at the end of my patience," Tenno Lilith warned.

Atrax trembled on the ground in fear. The bristles of hair along his body quivered from the knowledge Lilith was on her way back to the Spindleweb Nebula. He raised and lowered his six arms in steady waves. Red energy from Lilith's eyes flashed with each crackle on the screen.

"Rise, you disgusting meat sack, your lip service sycophantic groveling will earn you no favor from me, and it makes you all the more delicious to devour." Tenno Lilith's jagged claw pointed towards Atrax on the viewscreen, wagging the motion to rise. His muscles quivered, standing back up. Lilith smiled, watching Atrax obeying her orders. He quivered on the viewscreen.

"My mother will be happy to hear of your return despite the circumstances. I'm sure she'll do everything she can to correct whatever mistake occurred. Lucifer can be found. It's only a matter of time, mistress. I beg for forgiveness on behalf of my mother for the costs of your time in this manner. If anyone must pay for the inconvenience, allow it to be me." Atrax lowered his head, unable to watch the judgment he expected to fall.

Maniacal laughter cackled over the communication reverberating into a falling off into the cadence of awe. The sacrifice for Arachne was too much for Lilith to endure. These despicable Arachne were so self-serving it was vile even to her, but Atrax's loyal seemed genuine. Tenno Lilith couldn't contain the swell of glee she felt swelling inside her. Red crackling energy subsided in her eyes, watching the submission of Atrax to his decision.

"I see now why your mother spared you after devouring the rest of your brood. They were quite delicious, and we were quite full, to be honest. She said there was something different about you, Atrax. It's clear she was right. I'm going to forgive you this one last time." Tenno Lilith motioned for Atrax to raise his head to look at her.

"Your magnanimity knows no limits, dark mistress," Atrax praised.

"Remember, my mercy is more than you deserve. Tell your mother that I'm returning. When I leave this time, I better know the location of Lucifer, or there will be no more mercy. Do I make myself clear?" Lilith could see from the trembling muscles of Atrax that her message was understood.

"We'll treat you to the finest welcome. You can watch the fleet depart for the battle with your own eyes. I'm sure my mother will find the truth for you." Atrax mandibles chattered. The reflection of Lilith glinting in the black orbs of his eight eyes through the viewscreen, and she smiled back at her reflection.

"That sounds lovely, Atrax, but if it's not, there are crueler fates than death. Perhaps your species would make good fuel. I've never thrown one of your kind in a tormentor before. The idea is quite intriguing. Do you know what a tormentor is?" Tenno Lilith leaned towards the holoemitter scanner. Her face expanded until it was all the holoemitter projected to Atrax.

"No, mistress, I've never heard of this tormentor you speak of." Atrax's muscles quivered with the possibilities he imagined. He didn't want to find either. The smile on Lilith's face spoke of her intentions. She was about to explain what the tormentor was, whether Atrax liked it or not.

"Tormentors are engines that extract raw energy from the victims placed within. The machines sync with the occupant's fractal wave of consciousness. Once the connection is formed, every dark fear, torment, and tragedy becomes the raw fuel for the machine. The victim relieves their worst horrors in an infinite loop until the tormentor extracts the last shred of energy. You'd be surprised how much energy a single soul has. Even the passive one, but I find that the predators that thrive on carnage are the best to extract fear from. I reason that these apex predators don't feel fear often, so the energy hasn't been depleted. That makes me wonder about your people Atrax. The Great Maw lives in fear of your kind, yet you fear only the Cacophony of Discordance. I'm betting you could power the *Insidious Seduction* alone if I cranked the tormentor high enough." Lilith enjoyed the fear she could sense emanating from Atrax. The emotion was so pure it intoxicated Lilith even through the communication.

"There will be no need for that mistress. My mother will locate Lucifer, and the fleet will bring back ample slaves for your torments from the attack on the *Empyrean station*. I'm sure you'll grace us with some of the spoils for food for our growing brood so that we may continue to serve. We look forward to your arrival." Atrax chattered his mandibles with a bow of his head.

"I'll be there soon. Pray to whatever you wish that I'm impressed by your show." Lilith cut the channel. She could see the jump drives were almost charged. Reverie worked away on the bridge of the ship averting their gazes. She walked towards the bridge's exit, leaving her underlings to operate the ship.

The clack of Tenno Lilith's footsteps echoed off the black volcanic glass floor. She walked down the hall past the crackling reverie averting their gazes in the hall. Moans of pleasure resonated through the walls of the upper decks in the *Insidious Seduction*. She smiled, hearing the vigorous tutelage of her children walking towards the lift. Doors whisked shut behind her. The lift sunk towards the bowels of the ship with her desire commanding it.

Pleasure possessed its own flavor, but Tenno Lilith's mood was for something more visceral this evening. The lift raced down the shaft towards the prison level of the ship. Doors whisked open, allowing the cadence of screams to resonate in the lift. There were so many different voices howling with woe they mixed into a reverberating symphony of traumatic anguish. Tenno Lilith closed her eyes, letting the music assail her senses. She could almost feel the terror from each tormented soul howling in the symphony around her.

"Oh, my precious little souls that sing so beautifully for me," Tenno Lilith praised, walking down the corridor. She glanced into the chambers to see the different victims locked in the tormentors. Great metal plates written in ancient reverie hung outside each of the small cages. She glanced at each of the nameplates walking down the hall.

Each of the screams reminded Lilith of the soul she imprisoned there. She didn't need to read the plates to remember. The beautiful howls of agony that bellowed forth were enough for her. She walked down the long corridor at a slow place, enjoying her stroll. It was almost like she floated along with each step to the symphony surging all around her. She continued down the corridor until it ended at an ancient door.

Metal plates on the door appeared made of sleek glittering azure metal. Ancient runes were carved into each plate along the ring door. There was no plate listing who was imprisoned here. A long series of tubes raced from each metal plate into a central circular plate with a hand imprint with tiny holes on it. Lilith placed her hand on the imprint, and it fit the imprint perfectly. Spikes burst from the holes through her hand with red energy crackling. The energy surged, creating the crimson liquid draining into the imprint along the tubes.

Blood rushed through the tubes in all directions from the central handprint. The runes filled with the blood and glowed bright red. Loud clangs of metal resonated from the shaking door. Metal plates shook, moving the door in a spinning motion. Tumblers released, causing dust to blast forward from the cracks in the door. The door sunk backward into the wall before each ring retracted into the wall creating a path into the large square room with a box in the center.

The black box in the center of the room looked similar to the ones in the other chambers, but Lilith knew this one was created special just for this prisoner. Tubes ran from the sleek black box into the ground. Energy surged in constant strobes inside the pipes. Indecipherable howls bellowed forth from the box. She ran a finger along the metal surface approaching the console at the far end.

"It's been too long since I saw you last old friend. Perhaps some time with you will make me forget Lucifer like it used to." Tenno Lilith placed her hand on the console.

Tenno Lilith leaned onto the box's black metal, placing her ear against it. She could almost make out what the howls were saying. The console beeped, and a port opened on the side of the box. A large metal slab slid out of the box with a greyish liquid on the surface. She placed her hand on the surface. The liquid surged around her hand, with energy crackling along the edges.

The familiar tangled trauma from the prison surged into Lilith's mind. Everything else seemed to fade away under the force of the horror. Her eyes glazed with her mind diving into the mind of the prisoner. All her anxieties washed away. The only lingering thought was of Lucifer. She couldn't understand why he had disappeared in the first place. Reverie knew the cost of abandoning their post in the Cacophony of Discordance, but she knew Lucifer was powerful enough to avoid most consequences. Not even the Supreme Tenno Ba'al Zebub would dare push for anything more than lip service apologies. Lilith considered this could just be Lucifer's way of reminding the Cacophony of Discordance of his importance.

CHAPTER 38

Fighters streaked across the Great Maw. Lasers flashed across the void. Beams surged from the turrets on the *Icarus*. Fighter craft swarmed around the ship, engaged in a constant struggle for supremacy. Reverie carrier crackled with energy again, surging forth a blast. Explosions erupted from the hull of the *Icarus,* sending shards of metal flying into the void. Joshua watched the fighters from his ship streaking across the Great Maw to reinforce his sister and her troops.

Reverie fighters swarmed around the *Icarus* in a thick cloud on the viewscreen. Sensors showed more fighters launching from the enemy carrier. Shields were still functional, absorbing all the incoming fire from the *Icarus*. White beams of light struck the shield in bright bursts, rippling energy away from the point of impact. Joshua gripped the front of the arms of his captain chair so tight his knuckles turned white. He watched the F.T.L. engine charging to jump.

Navigation locked in on the calculations provided by Virgil. Coms beeped with the incoming transmission. Joshua accepted the incoming hail from his sister. The viewscreen crackled under the effect of the enemy communication jammers. Static crackled, the image distorted in a blur, and the screen flashed black. He accessed the tactical computer moving through the communication systems, trying to clear the message up.

"Joshua, what are you doing?" Celeris' voice came through clearly. Joshua tweaked the settings to adjust to the Cacophony of Discordance jammers.

"I'm coming to save your ass. What's it looks like?" Joshua retorted.

"I gave you a direct order as Grand Admiral to retreat to *Empyrean station.* The empire can't afford to lose two ships in this engagement. Besides,

I'm not beat yet." Celeris jolted on the view screen with the explosion in the background. Troops pulled the unconscious officer back from the smoking console, still flickering with crackles of electricity. A smoky haze wafted across the bridge of the *Icarus* still shuddering from the attacks.

"Emperor Solomon gave me direct orders to make sure you get back in one piece. He's even sent Nemesis to reinforce us, but I'm not sure you'll last long enough for her to arrive." Joshua leaned forward in his chair, still gripped the armrests. Sensors showed another charge building on the enemy carrier. F.T.L. charge was at seventy percent, rising steadily on the tactical computer.

"I'm not sure you can make it time. Reverie forces are hammering my ship. I've got damage reports coming in from all the outer decks. Multiple hull ruptures. Feels like I'm back on the *Alcatraz*." Celeris' image shuddered on the viewscreen under the constant assault. Another explosion erupted from a conduit rupturing into a brilliant ball of sparks.

"It looks worse than it is, sister. Just keep fighting. I'll be right there," Joshua urged.

"You're not going to do what I think you're doing, are you?" Celeris' eyes widened on the viewscreen, staring at her brother. He smiled, leaned back into his chair, and watched the F.T.L. charge climb past eighty percent. Sensors showed the energy blast from the Reverie carrier strike the *Icarus*. Viewscreen crackled with a surge of energy from the *Icars*'s systems. The entire bridge shuddered, sending officers crashing into the deck. Celeris held on to her chair, trembling against the surging force. She could see the last shot tore right through the ship. Damage reports across the ship were reporting the surge of hull breaches.

"Just hold on, Celeris," Joshua pleaded. He glanced to see the energy charge spike past ninety percent. The countdown fell under a minute. Sweat beaded on his forehead. Reverie fighters were swarming the *Icarus* beams flashing off the hull. Surge of fighters from the *Templar* raced ahead to join the fray of battle.

"Systems are failing over here. We're rerouting power to keep weapons online. Whatever you're going to do now is the…" Communications blacked out. Energy crackled in the distance on the enemy carrier charging another blast.

Reverie fighters darted around the *Icarus* in a black swarm on the viewscreen. Flashes of white light surged in the cloud of fighters. A blur of energy surged from the enemy carrier. Orange light erupted in an explosion in the cloud of fighters. Sensors showed the *Icarus* systems were failing all across the ship, but weapons were still firing. A beep emitted from the tactical computer. Joshua stared at the viewscreen pressing the button to activate the F.T.L. drive.

Energy surged from the F.T.L. drive along the structure of the *Templar*. White light blurred along the edges of the viewscreen. Joshua leaned back into his chair, feeling the ship lurching towards light speed. A bright white flash surged on the viewscreen. The entire ship shuddered with the alarms blaring. The tactical computer showed the surge of energy in the shields that were depleting fast. Viewscreen flashed back on with a surge of light showing the Reverie carrier.

"Open fire on that enemy ship. Unleash everything we've got. I want all reserve fighters launching. We're going to show these bastards what hell looks like!" Joshua surged out of his seat, marching across the bridge to direct his troops.

Fighters blasted into space from the Templar hanger bays swarming around the ship into formation. Hundreds of flashes of white light shone on the viewscreen, bursting across the enemy carrier's shields. Sensors showed the enemy shields depleting under the steady surges of weapons fire. Reverie fighters were breaking away from the black cloud swarming the *Icarus* to deal with the *Templar* but were caught by the incoming reinforcements. Joshua watched the incoming reports from his fighters engaging the enemy. The grey cloud surged into the black blur on the viewscreen, with flashes of light erupting in steady pulses.

Engines flared, accelerating the *Icarus* through the cloud of fighters. The ship soared past the swarm of fighters opening fire. White beams lanced toward the enemy carrier charging with energy. The blurring black blast from the carrier struck the *Icarus* causing a massive orange inferno to erupt into space. Joshua couldn't tell exactly where the blast hit, but it looked like the bridge. He frantically brought up the communications to hail the *Icarus*. The hail echoed in steady pulses across the bridge of the *Templar*. Sensors blared the warning alarm of an incoming ship entering the sector. Joshua gritted down on his teeth, grinding them hard. He tapped on the sensors for a more active sweep. The sensors warbled with the ongoing scan of the energy signature.

Weapons fire from the *Icarus* fizzled into a sputtering of only a few turrets. The ship drifted off course from the enemy carrier, beginning to recharge its main weapon. Energy began to crackle again around the ship. Coms beeped, sensors warbled, and Joshua watched the viewscreen, unable to breathe. Sensors locked in on the energy signature, filling the tactical computer screen with the report. Joshua gasped for air seeing the readings.

The *Divine Retribution* flashed from F.T.L. space on the bow of the *Icarus*. Weapons fire erupted from the massive battleforge bearing down upon the enemy carrier. Fighters launched in successive waves from the multitude of docking bays on the ship. Half of the fighters veered to join the *Templar* and *Icarus* fighters against the enemy, and the other half drove for the carrier. *Divine Retribution* surged across the void, moving in between the enemy and the *Icarus*. Joshua accepted the incoming hail from the *Divine Retribution*.

"Hope I'm not too late," Nemesis appeared on the viewscreen.

"Can you see from your angle if the last enemy attack hit the bridge of the *Icarus*?" Joshua surged out of his chair, looking at the flames still surging into the void from the hole on the *Icarus*. The blur of orange flames leaping from the hole blocked him from seeing the bridge. Sensors showed that most of the *Icarus* systems were down. The entire energy grid had collapsed, leaving only a few sections of the ship functional.

"The bridge is fine, brother. I'm moving to defend the *Icarus*. Just concentrate all fire on the enemy ship before they can get off any more shots at us. We can take care of the repairs afterward. Celeris will be pissed if we let this first battle go down as a loss," Nemesis informed.

Sensors showed the enemy shields were almost on the verge of collapse. Weapons fire rippled along the shields on both sides of the carrier. Computers synced between the Divine *Retribution* and the *Templar,* increasing fire control processing power. Joshua watched the enemy carrier absorb the incoming fire from the two ships. The shields just wouldn't seem to give way even under the strain of the steady pulses of hard light cannons. Coms lit up with the viewscreen breaking into thirds for the new image to appear. Smokey wafted across the screen in a haze.

"That last shot took out the primary energy coupler. We're trying to reroute, but it's going to take too long. I got coms working so that you could receive the report of my chief Neeska. The data contains the phase variance of the enemy carrier's shields." Celeris spoke through steady coughs.

"Damn fine work, Celeris. Tell your chief first rounds on me. I'll get my people on applying this discovery right away." Nemesis motioned to her crew. Joshua was one step ahead, and he was already applying the updates himself to his ship. The data surged through the network to the *Divine Retribution* updating the systems automatically.

"That should save you some time. Now what do you say we finish this bastard off?" Joshua pressed a few buttons sending the commands to fire at will. Rapid white beams lanced from the *Templar* bursting across the enemy ship's shields. Flashing destruction brought a smile to Nemesis' face. Each new flash reflected on her widening pupils and glittered on her irises.

"I can't let you have all the glory of the first kill now, can I?" Nemesis winked at her brother.

"This is so unfair," Celeris coughed through her moan.

Reverie carrier maneuvered to turn in space. Sensors showed the shields on the ship were depleting faster now that the weapons used Chief Neeska's modifications. The charging energy of enemy carrier altered frequencies on the scan. Joshua recognized the frequency. He tapped a few buttons, trying to speed up the weapon charge recyclers to speed up weapons fire.

"Intensify fire on the ship before they escape," Joshua urged.

"Are you certain they're running?" Nemesis looked at her brother. He nodded while working away on the calculations. There was another energy signature the sensors were detecting on a lower frequency. He tapped on it, trying to ascertain what the purpose of the energy emission was.

Energy beams exploded along the rear shields of the retreating carrier. Sensors showed the enemy carriers' shield's energy being redirected to the aft facing. The surge in energy in the field showed on the tactical computer. Joshua slammed his fist off the armchair. Ripples from the white beams surged across the reinforced shields of the enemy carrier. He couldn't do anything about that, but he could figure out this strange transmission.

Energy crackled around the Reverie carrier. A bright blinding flash shot across the viewscreen, causing Joshua to squint his eyes. The computer managed to crack the low-band energy transmission. Reverie carrier was gone on the viewscreen, but the computer beeped the completed program. Joshua knew what it was from the pattern of the data he could see.

"I've managed to catch an enemy transmission," Joshua reported.

"Put it on screen. Let's see what these bastards were saying." Celeris moved towards the screen, wafting the smoke away with her hand. Troops worked away in the background. Sparks erupted from the blown conduits hanging from the ceiling of the bridge.

"Whatever they're saying, it can't be good," Nemesis reasoned.

The viewscreen crackled with the encryption on the message. The large image of Tenno Leviathan appeared on the screen. Glistening rows of white fangs stood out in the swirling black murk of the image. The video crackled with the program locking onto the variance in the encryption. Audio was distorted in an unrecognizable language at first, but Joshua adjusted the linguistic program. He accessed the data archives on *Empyrean station*.

"Supreme Tenno Ba'al Zebub, the mission has been a success. I've engaged three human ships in a battle to test their resolve. They are as powerful as you predicted, but their sinful nature weakens them. The technology of the Ancients has remained static, while the Cacophony of Discordance has unraveled the mysteries of the Great Maw. These ships will be of little threat to us once we deal with the threat of the star. I've gleamed all that can be learned from this engagement. The enemy will not learn of our plans. With this knowledge, we're prepared to move to the next phase of the plans. Soon the humans will learn the true might of the Cacophony of Discordance. Order shall never again rule over chaos, and the weak shall never cage the strong again. These humans shall make a fine example to the rest of the Great Maw," Leviathan reported.

The message ended, leaving the bridge echoing only the sounds of the work on the *Icarus*. Celeris, Nemesis, and Joshua glanced at each other, trying to keep a stoic mask for their troops. Officers looked on to their captains on each of the bridges. Joshua motioned for his officers to get back to work. A flurry of activity surged around him.

"I told you it wasn't going to be good," Nemesis quipped.

"Better to know our enemy. I'll send this message to Emperor Solomon myself. We need to figure out what the Cacophony of Discordance is planning." Joshua stroked his chin and paced. He didn't like that the plan seemed much larger than just attacking the star.

"How about you guys get over here and help me get my ship repaired," Celeris shouted.

"I'm already sending repair crews, sister. They should be arriving in a few moments. Nanite swarms are being deployed to help effect repairs to your ship." Nemesis leaned back into her chair with a smile. Joshua could understand his sister's happiness.

Joshua watched the *Icarus* approaching on the viewscreen. Fighters still streaked across the void flying in patrol patterns. Grey nanites swarmed across the hull of the damaged ship, repairing the holes. Metal appeared in a misty haze from the grey cloud hovering over the hull, sealing the breaches shut. Transports landed in the *Icarus* hanger bay with crews to help with repairs. He watched the sensors for any sign of the enemy.

CHAPTER 39

Fighter craft streaked across the system patrolling around the *Empyrean station*. Starlight shined through the metal superstructure erected around the star. Grey clouds of nanites swarmed around the superstructure, reinforcing it and weaving metal into the design. Four battleforges floated near the station undergoing construction. Patches of the hull remained unfinished, showing the decks and superstructure beneath. *Olympus, Brisingamen, Iliad,* and *Sentinel* patrolled the rim of the system guarding the A.S.A., working on the sector defenses.

Light flashed in a series just beyond the *Empyrean station* sector. The *Dawnbreaker* dropped out of F.T.L. space with the ship it was escorting. De'Vayne's flagship the *Mirror of Solace* darted past Kain's massive battleforge. Sleek metal plates angled along the hull of the *Mirror of Solace*, banks of engines glowed blue behind the fuselage, and the concaved angular wings bent down with rows of engines along the thin edge at the back. Fighters launched from the Dawnbreaker to escort the transport flying from the *Mirror of Solace* towards *Empyrean station*.

"Lord De'Vayne, this is Imperator Kain. I'm transmitting my flight path to your shuttle now. My fighter squadron is approaching on your aft vector. Instruct your pilot to adjust heading to the new flight path and hold steady." Kain could see the approaching angular shuttle through the glass of the viewport. He adjusted his throttle to match the speeds of the transport.

The fighter squadron decelerated steadily, rushing towards the shuttle surrounded by De'Vayne's fighters. Fighter defense systems showed the *Mirror of Solace's* weapon systems continued to maintain weapons locks. Kain kept his distance from the shuttle. Fighters slowed down alongside him matching speed with the shuttle. A holographic display on the glass viewport showed the distance to the destination, estimated flight time, and flashes of weapons locked pulsed. He followed the flight plan pulling the fighter towards the station with the shuttle following.

Cutting torches sparked from the A.S.A. floating around the mobile defense turrets. Defense platforms spiraled away from the station in expanding spheres. *Mechanarium of Gyros* floated next to the *Empyrean station*. The shipyards extended from the station with several unused berths. Three superstructures floated in the berths under construction. Gray clouds of nanites floated around portions of the ships weaving the molecular structure of the ship hulls. Exposed decks could be seen between the hull plating gaps.

The *Divine Retribution* floated near the shipyards guarding the ships being repaired in the berths. Grey clouds of nanites floated away from the *Templar*. Engines flared on the ship, propelling it from the berth, but the *Icarus* remained lifeless in the next berth. Scorched blackened metal along the edges of the hull breaches showed Kain the extent of the damage. He stared at the destruction of the ship with sensors beeping with information. The scans showed residual traces of Cacophony of Discordance energy signatures in the damaged metal.

"Welcome back, Imperator. I'm preparing your landing zone now. Please continue at present speed per Imperial law. Long live the Empire!" Virgil's voice echoed over the coms.

Kain pulled the flight stick to maneuver the fighter towards the hanger bay following the holographic display of the flight plan. He could see the rows of kinetic cannons glinting from the docked *Sesh'yna*. Workers rushed alongside the A.S.A. across the hanger bay. W'hyish S'yevel wearing their black skinsuits stood guard alongside the A.S.A. and power armored troops. Fighter craft followed him towards the landing bay. He brought the ship to land with a thump of the landing gear touching down on the deck plating.

Holographic displays vanished with a flash of light cutting off. Kain flipped the switches shutting down the craft. A hiss resonated when the pressurized seal of the cockpit broke. The glass cockpit slid backward, he grabbed the edge of the glass and pulled himself out of the craft. Metal thumps echoed when he landed on the ground. De'Vayne's shuttle set down with the escort fighters landing nearby. The shuttle ramp descended, coming to a silent rest upon the deck plate.

Troops formed up to follow behind Kain approaching the ramp. He looked into the shuttle to see Genji marching towards him with the honor guard behind him. Lord De'Vayne walked behind his honor guard with black and silver robes flowing behind him. The group followed Kain toward the Infinity Nexus. Once the hallways stood empty, but now he saw people moving almost everywhere he looked. Activity erupted from every nook and cranny of the station.

Doors to the Infinity Nexus whisked away, parting for Kain and his entourage. The large angelic statues towered in the room filled with A.S.A. working away on the modifications. Rows of seats were being installed in the auditorium. He glanced around to see all the changes since he left. The A.S.A. industrious discipline erected the new senate chambers with almost the same speed as the nanites. He could see Lord De'Vayne breath escape him, staring up at the intricate detail of the marble statues. Imperator Kain marched towards the Infinity Nexus, bowing before Emperor Solomon.

"I've brought Lord De'Vayne as you requested, Emperor," Kain bowed his head.

"Thank you, Imperator, for all you've done. Lord De'Vayne, it's my pleasure to lay my eyes upon your visage. I hope your journey was enjoyable." Matthew smiled at Lord De'Vayne, but he was still engrossed in the statues walking slowly towards the Infinity Nexus. He stopped with his azure eyes fixated on Emperor Solomon.

"Your brother explained your situation, so I was willing to make an exception due to your circumstances. I don't leave the safety of my home often." Lord De'Vayne crossed his arms.

"Well, I'm glad you saw the value of my friendship, and I welcome you to *Empyrean station,* your grace. Treat our home as your own while you're here. We've much to discuss. I was hoping to have some seating arrangements before you arrived. I hope you can forgive me for this oversight."

"I suppose I can let it go this time, but my generosity has limits, Emperor. You'd be best not to test them. Imperator Kain explained that the Cacophony of Discordance is rallying allies to attack this station aiming to destroy that new glorious star you created. That's quite a fascinating technological achievement. Perhaps you'd be willing to share this technology?" Lord De'Vayne's eyes focused on Emperor Solomon. His desire sparkled in his azure eyes.

"You're looking at the technology that makes creating a new star possible, Lord De'Vayne. *Empyrean station* is a focal point of energy in the Great Maw. The Ancient built this chamber at the point where the original big bang created the first verse. In the Infinity Nexus, latent psionic power is magnified, allowing my mind to create new stars with the right resources. Unfortunately, this technology can't be shared. The technology that made it possible was lost in the stellar war. The Ancients wiped all records of the research before they abandoned the station. There weren't any records of why or where they went either," Matthew informed.

"Psionics are just another fable like the God you believe in. There's not one shred of proof of the existence of mental powers. I've been alive since before the Great War. Even back then, everyone talked about the hidden power of psychics. In all the millenniums of my life, I've never met one." Lord De'Vayne rolled his eyes with a shake of his head.

"Don't disrespect Emperor Solomon," Kain chided, gripping the hilt of his energy blade.

Matthew's eyes began to glow white. Tremors shook the room, causing the honor guard around Lord De'Vayne to grab their weapons. They scanned around the room. The tremors intensified, causing tools and loose objects to clatter to the floor across the room. Bangs, clangs, and thuds echoed through the room. A.S.A. stopped their work waiting for the tremors to end.

"These tremors are easily created with the gravitation controls of this advanced station. It will take a lot more than simple sleights of hand to convince me of this psionic power." Lord De'Vayne looked up at Emperor Solomon. His eyes pulsed with the bright white energy focusing on his guest. Energy surged around Lord De'Vayne, and he struggled back against it.

Pressure built up around Lord De'Vayne, causing his legs to tremble against the strain. His mind raced, trying to determine what was going on. The other guards didn't seem affected. Cybernetic sensors didn't detect any increase in the gravity around him, yet it felt like the gravity had been cranked up, still rising higher. He couldn't withstand the force anymore, bringing him to his knees. Muscles trembled in his arms, trying to push his body away from the deck.

"That's enough, please…" Lord De'Vayne struggled to hold himself up until the force dissipated. White glow around Matthew's eyes faded, returning to normal.

"I see your faith has been ignited, Lord De'Vayne. It was the only way I could prove to you my powers to attempt to show you, my sincerity. You've been asked to come to ally with the Imperium of Humanity. Given that a portion of your genetic ancestry is human, it makes sense we stand together, and we're both enemies of the Cacophony of Discordance. Together we could crush our mutual enemy once and for all to free the verse from their tyranny," Matthew explained.

"The enemy of my enemy is just the next person who's waiting to destroy me, I've learned, yet I'd agree that we make sensible allies. My people could use the assistance of your people. If you agree to help the De'Vayne by building a star of our own, I'll offer my support. It'll take me time to get all my ships here. They're spread across the Great Maw, scavenging for needed resources. I offer myself and my ship the *Mirror of Solace* until my reinforcements arrive. Besides, I quite look forward to exploring this *Empyrean station* of yours." Lord De'Vayne watched Emperor Solomon closely, his eyes narrowing, and studied Emperor Solomon.

"Of course, Lord De'Vayne, that is a reasonable request. I'll build a star for your people once the crisis has passed. I don't forget who my friends are or my enemies. Feel free to explore that station to your heart's content," Matthew pointed towards the doors. He could see the glance from Kain, but there would be time to explain the situation later.

"Thank you, Emperor, for your hospitality, and I look forward to future discussions. I'll send for my fleets after I explore this wondrous station." Lord De'Vayne marched away from the Infinity Nexus with his honor guard following behind. Doors whisked shut behind them. The A.S.A. resumed work modifying the auditorium.

Kain shook his head, looking back at his brother. His eyes sparked with the tumult of emotions behind the shimmering surface. From Kain's perspective, there wasn't a reason to trust Lord De'Vayne. Emperor Solomon seemed pleased with how the meeting went. He stepped towards the Infinity Nexus glancing to his brother seeing Kain's eyes narrowing.

"You can't trust that Lord De'Vayne brother. He's worse than father. To even get an audience with him, he made me fight Genji's children to the death. How he's even still following that monstrous Lord De'Vayne is beyond me," Kain informed.

"I knew what you would endure before I sent you, but it had to happen. These opportunists like Lord De'Vayne seem intolerable to you. Until I stepped into the Infinity Nexus, they were also unbearable to me, but time shows the value of each life. There are things that not even I can change in this verse. Lord Drumpf, Lord Galen, and Lord Whelsey are just like this De'Vayne, yet I have need of them for now. They still have a role to play in what's to come." Matthew placed his hand against the glass towards his brother.

There was too much uncertainty for Kain to feel any comfort. Damage on the *Templar* and *Icarus* revealed to him that the war raged on while he was away. The fact the Cacophony of Discordance had caused the damage only pressed the reality of the situation upon him. Reverie would keep going to harass them until they were dealt with. He just wanted the battle to be over so he could get on with the war.

"Well, at least the first engagement against the Cacophony wasn't a defeat. It looks like Celeris bit off more than she could chew. The *Icarus* looked pretty mangled. Did we get any good intelligence on the enemy from the engagement?" Kain looked at his brother.

"Joshua was able to crack the Cacophony of Discordance encryption. He captured a piece of a transmission sent to Supreme Tenno Ba'al Zebub. The message was sent by Tenno Leviathan, who led the attack on the *Empyrean station* when we arrived. It seems Leviathan intended to test our strengths to learn our weaknesses. Reverie has a much bigger plan they're preparing. I can't see into the Cacophony of Discordance through the stream of time. We're rushing towards a cataclysmic event that could be the end of the universe. I can't see past the light's end. The forces coming to destroy us will succeed from what I've seen. I'm doing everything in my power to change our fates." Matthew paced in the Infinity Nexus with sweat beading on his forehead.

"You're all we've got, Matthew, and if you lose hope, so will we."

Kain looked at his brother with trembling eyes. He could sense how distraught his brother was from the words he spoke. The pain hidden behind purpose was his brother's move. Whenever things got bad on the *Alcatraz,* he'd find his brother working away on some new project. It was just a distraction from the chaos, but he adopted the tactic from him. The tactic served him well under his father's command. He just preferred more visceral distractions rather than the intellectual ones Matthew preferred to engage in to escape reality.

"Don't worry about me, Kain. You've got your own problems to deal with. Try to find some time to relax and enjoy yourself. It can't be all battles and blood all the time." Matthew smiled at his brother, seeing him nod in agreement.

"I'm getting tired of the battles if you want the truth," Kain admitted.

"We're only at the beginning of a long journey Kain. You need to steal yourself away to gather your power. Find something worth fighting for. Your sister is throwing the opening party at the Original Sins tonight. From what Virgil tells me, everyone on the station is talking about it. You should go, have some fun, and maybe meet someone special. Family is all that matters in the end. Perhaps it's time you start your own," Matthew implored.

"There's too much work that needs to be done. Besides, there'll be plenty of time to party after this battle. Nemesis throws a party for every day that ends in y. They'll be more chances in the future, I'm sure." Kain chuckled at his own joke, causing Matthew to join in.

"That might be true, Kain, but I'd like you to go. Do it for me since I can't leave the Infinity Nexus. Call it a favor to your brother or a command of your Emperor. Tell yourself whatever you must but go to the damn party." Matthew wasn't sure his brother would listen.

"I'll think about it," Kain replied.

Matthew watched Kain glance towards the working A.S.A. watching on, and he bowed to Emperor Solomon. He walked away from the Infinity Nexus. The stream of time wobbled with the variances that could occur. The sensation forced Matthew to move to the seat in his chamber. Results of choices fluctuated in the stream, sending it failing, fracturing, and dividing along new routes. His breaths came rapidly, and the pain resonated through his mind. The decision of Kain's to go to the party seemed so small, but his entire future rested upon it. Matthew could see all the negative results in the new time streams flowing from his brother's failure to attend the party.

CHAPTER 40

Fighter craft closed in on the *Death's Reaper* on the scanner. Alarms blared from the reactor, heat spiking into the orange. The *Jinnestan* stayed beyond the range of Pandora's Box defense systems. Carriers, battleships, and corvettes launched from the outposts spread throughout the sector. Magnus watched the shield grow closer through the viewport. Reverie fighters were growing closer on the sensors. Pandoran fighters broke off the escort of the *Death's Reaper,* turning to engage the fighters surging from the enemy carrier.

Energy weapons lanced between the fighters in the void. An explosion erupted in the swarm of fighters colliding behind the *Death's Reaper* on the sensor screen. Alarms blared from the weapons fire control trying to lock onto his ship. Reverie fighters blew through the debris, sending pieces of metal flying off into the void. Magnus glanced at the engineering console to see the reactor temperature rising towards the red line at a steady rate. He yanked on the flight stick, pulling the ship into erratic evasive maneuvers. Reverie energy weapons crackled past his ship in a surge.

The hole in the shield was only a few more seconds away from Magnus' calculations. Reverie swarm missiles launched from the fighters. He knew they were designed to disable the ship rather than destroy it. Sensors showed the missiles darting towards the ship closing in fast. He flicked the switch to release the defense drones from the aft of the ship. Sensors showed the drones lurch toward the missiles, and they began blinking off the screen along with the drones.

Pandoran fighters swarmed behind the shields. The fleet took battle formation behind the swarms of fighters darting around the area. Magnus punched the overburn on the engines sending the reactor spiking into the red. The ship shot through the hole in the shield with energy surging against the shield and rippling away in successive strikes. Sensors showed the hole in the shield closing behind the ship. The entire ship shuddered from the engines combined with the reactor. He pulled back on the throttle slowing the ship. The temperature began to fall in the reactor, but he wasn't sure he had the time to wait for the heat to dissipate at the current rate.

Engineering showed the integrity of the reactor falling under fifty percent. Magnus accessed the emergency decompression system for engineering. He overrode the safety systems trying to hold a steady course against the jostling of the ship. Wires sparked with a fizzle, and the decompression system safety lockout vanished on the engineering console. He moved a few of the jumpers on the circuit board. Engineering showed the decompression system venting space. Reactor heat fell rapidly, and alarms began to fall off. Integrity on the reactors shield started to rise back above fifty percent at a slow pace. He pulled the ship towards the docking bay.

Destroyers, frigates, and cruisers were starting to launch from the main docking bay. Rows upon rows of ships were hovering above the berth. Pandoran flight control hadn't responded to Magnus' request for docking instructions, but he could see ships waiting to depart in rows beyond the viewport. The computer whirred with the incoming landing instructions. He activated the automated flight control to attend to the ship's state. Engineering consoles showed the damage was critical but not all that severe. He hoped Pandora's crew could fix the ship fast.

Sensors showed the *Jinnestan* waiting beyond weapons range. Reverie fighters swarmed beyond the shield with a steady increase in the numbers on the sensors. The *Death's Reaper* descended toward the empty docking bay. Automated flight controls beeped with the connection to the flight control tower for the docking bay. Magnus stood on the elevator, heading down to the cargo bay. He felt the ship shudder from the landing gear touching down, walking towards the button to hit it, and the ramp lowered.

Pandoran troops surrounded the *Death's Reaper*. The multitude of creatures wearing whatever they could scavenge from the Great Maw. Jagged metal plates fused into armor. Troopers aimed rifles, pistols, and all manner of weapons at Magnus. He glanced towards the palace in the distance to see Pandora and Gabriel marching towards him. The sleek grip of his pistol rubbed against the inside of his palm. He glanced around at the guards pacing.

"Lord Magnus Void, I'm shocked you made it here, given the state of your ship. You really should take better care of your things," Pandora greeted with a smile. She stopped alongside her guards with one hand on her hip. Gabriel stood beside the pirate queen, gripping the hilt of his energy blade and energy carbine slung over his shoulder.

"It seems I've riled up the Cacophony, but I do have that effect on people." Magnus glanced at Gabriel with his finger tapping against the side of the pistol.

"Oh, don't mind him. Gabriel figured out that you and I have also spent some time between the sheets. It's just a bit of sexual envy, I assure you. I promised him that my bed was large enough for the both of you." Pandora bit her lip, walking towards Magnus.

"All due respect Pandora, but we really don't have time for that. Tenno Asmodeus is one of the oldest, most powerful, and most ruthless princes of the Cacophony of Discordance. He won't give up, and every second we waste gives him time to summon reinforcements. The *Jinnestan* might not be able to penetrate the planetary hard light shield defending your territory, but if the rest of his armada shows up, they'll drain that shield fast. Your little fortress won't withstand the fury of Asmodeus and his legions. *Empyrean station* is your only chance for survival now," Magnus explained.

"Just cruising by, so you thought you'd take someone else home from them too?" Gabriel glared at Magnus. They locked eyes.

"Actually, trying to ensure your children survive. That new star Matthew created has drawn the full wrath and all the hellfire that the Cacophony can spew forth quickly. W'hyish S'yevel tribes are gathering. Over a hundred worldships, like the one that attacked you right before we met, full of those abominable creatures that you fought off, and all of them heading to *Empyrean station* to kill every last thing in that sector.

Once they succeed, the Cacophony of Discordance will launch a nova bomb to destabilize the star, and poof, that'll be the end. Sorry, I don't have time right now to assuage your hurt feelings over the loss of your beloved *Alcatraz* and your family, but let's be honest, that last one is totally on you. I did try to warn you when you first introduced me to your wife and daughter. If you had treated Matthew better or not tried your wife, you'd be with your family right now." Magnus shook his head, gritting his teeth, and stared at Gabriel's jowls jutted out under the pressure of his grind teeth.

"What's this about a new star?" Pandora looked to Magnus and Gabriel. They were locked in a staring match of wills. Black energy crackled along Magnus' eyes. Gabriel stepped forward towards Magnus drawing the energy blade, but Pandora stepped in between to stop him.

"Magnus here came across us in the Great Maw. We'd just been attacked by one of these W'hyish S'yevel tribes. He offered to help my crew in exchange of us helping him raid an outpost constructed by the Ancients. My youngest son Matthew had something done to him by the A.I. running the outpost there. After the outpost's destruction, Magnus wanted to take us to *Empyrean station* to create a new star. Matthew developed strange new powers, seized my ship from me, and I guess created a new star. I was a little busy jumping the *Alcatraz* in the *Dread Sovereign* in the middle of the battle to try to save my family," Gabriel explained.

"You lying, no good, and pointless excuse for whatever you are," Pandora chastised Magnus.

"I can explain it all. Yes, you were supposed to get some of the salvage from the outpost and share in the spoils of *Empyrean station*, but there have obviously been complications. First, Gabriel is a madman who cuts his way through the station, and Mordecai detonated the outpost to try to save the lives of Gabriel's people. Reverie detected the *Alcatraz*, attacked us, and forced us to make a run for *Empyrean station*. The *Dread Sovereign* showed up with the Ravaging Cadence turning the entire operation into a complete clusterfuck, but that doesn't change anything. Matthew is a good soul, Pandora. He'll make good on my promise and build a star for you. I've set everything in motion. Now all we have to do is deal with Tenno Asmodeus." Magnus pointed out to the Great Maw.

Pandora took a step back, tapping her finger on her cheek. She glanced between Magnus and Gabriel. The situation was much different now that she had more facts. She paced, watching Magnus and Gabriel glare at each other. He looked at Pandora, seeing her mood soften, sending Gabriel over the edge. He surged towards Magnus with a finger wagging in his face.

"You're playing everyone against the middle just like you did on the *Alcatraz*, but I'm done dancing to your tune Magnus. You can believe this lying sack of shit all you want, Pandora. I get now why you call all these dregs mawslaw. They're stupid enough to head off into the Great Maw like meat for the grinder. Only question that remains is who will you be following?" Gabriel shook his head before stormed off from the group shoving troops out of his way.

"Well, you've always lived up to your agreements in the past, Magnus. I'm going to give you the benefit of the doubt one more time. This new star sounds intriguing. What would you have me do?" Pandora looked to see Magnus watching Gabriel walk away.

"There's only one thing you can do. Ready your fleet to retreat to *Empyrean station*. Reverie can't follow you there. It's your only chance. Tenno Asmodeus will summon his greatest weapon. Jinn are not something you want to deal with. They can vanish from sight and command powers you can't even fathom that can bend reality to their will. Your forces would be better off helping the humans to defend *Empyrean station*. Trust me, Matthew knows he's not in any position to turn down help. Not even from a band of marauders like you," Magnus explained.

"Pah! Humans are worthless dregs. Besides, I don't back down from a fight." Pandora's eyes narrowed on the *Jinnestan* in the distances beyond her fleet.

"You're not backing down from this fight but going to a more important one. The return of the light offers you and your people a chance at a new life. Otherwise, the Great Maw will devour you all sooner or later, and even if you survive till the very end of existence, it'll come all the same. You're a survivor, not a foolish sentimentalist pining over scraps floating in some darkened corner of the verse, and you're not going to die for this junk. Listen to me, get the fleet assembly, and be prepared to move." Magnus turned to follow Gabriel.

Pandoran troops continued aiming their guns at Magnus. They glanced at Pandora to see what to do. She waved them away. The troops scurried out of the way of Magnus. They breathed a sigh of relief, watching the black energy crackling in the air trailing behind him.

"Where do you think you're going?" Pandora yelled the question at Magnus.

"Oh, get your people to repair my ship while I'm gone. The reactor, coolant, and F.T.L. engines could use some tender, love, and care. Make sure she's ready to fly when I'm through with Gabriel." Magnus sauntered towards the door feeling Pandora's narrowing gaze falling on his back.

"Magnus don't do anything stupid," Pandora warned.

"I'm going to try to convince Gabriel not to make my mistakes all over again. If you hear fighting, just stay away and let us resolve our issues. I'll get through to him, one way or another…" Magnus didn't bother looking back when he spoke. He could see Gabriel off in the distance.

Magnus gripped his pistol on his side holster. He did owe Gabriel a debt, he thought, and honor demanded repayment. That thought echoed in Magnus' mind with each footstep. He quickened his pace, trying to catch up. Gabriel entered a building up ahead. The sign hanging outside showed two frothing glasses, touching written in barely literate Tigran that he wouldn't even bother translating. Loud voices emanated from behind the metal door. Energy crackled beyond the door with all the life inside the building, and Magnus knew quite a few people were inside. The doors whisked open for him, letting the loud sound of music blast forth. Strange cadences of unique instruments resonated with his footsteps walking into the room. Everyone in the room turned to look at him.

CHAPTER 41

People lined up outside the Original Sins. Loud music echoed from inside the building, with base thumping through the walls. Imperator Kain approached the building ignoring all the people gawking at him. Whispers erupted in the crowded line to get into the party. He approached the guards at the door, scanning the guests' invites. They stop to bow to the Imperator before moving out of his way. The crowd parted for him as he walked into the club.

Lights strobed in beat to the thumping base of the drummer playing on the stage. Guitar warbled the riffs belting from the resonating tower of speakers built into the walls. Flames shot out of the mouth of one Clan Player entertainers amid the crowd. A series of bursts of flames erupted from the fire breather swigging the bottle of alcohol. Contortionists bent their bodies to the awe of the crowd watching the couple. Nemesis and Marcus whispered to each other, chuckling while they watched the couple bending around each other's bodies. Light glinted from the knives being juggled. Blades twirled in the air above the crowd.

A crowd of people covered the dance floor flailing away to the cadence of the band. Kain glanced around the dance floor, seeing Hephaestus dancing with Freya. They ground away on each other to the beat of the music, with sweat glistening on their skin. For a moment, Kain watched, smiling at his brother before turning towards the bar. He approached the packed bar with several bartenders trying to keep up with customers' demands. The bartender approached him.

"What can I get you, Imperator?" The woman smiled. Sweat glistened on her heaving chest.

"I'm not sure what's good here. What do you suggest?" Kain leaned over the bar.

"Oh, darling, that's an impossible task with the selection this place has. None of that swill we used to serve on the *Alcatraz*. We've got the finest ales and spirits now. Anything you can think of these machines can produce." The bartender pointed to the menu of drinks.

Kain glanced at the board, looking through the multitude of drinks. He pointed to the single malt aged whiskey on the menu. The bartender smiled, headed towards the machine, and tapped a few buttons. Energy swirled inside the energy-to-matter convertor arranging the molecular structure of the drink. The bartender grabbed the glass to hand to Kain. He sipped the drink savoring the flavor.

"Not too bad," Kain complimented.

"Your father must have shared some fine shit with you before. I've never tasted anything so delicious as the drinks that machine makes. My name's Stacey, by the way, Imperator, and I've heard so much about you from your sister." Stacey smiled, feeling her cheeks turning red. Kain erupted in laughter from her comment, and she tried to laugh along with him.

"I can only imagine what my sister has to say about me behind my back," Kain chuckled.

"There's always going to be some sibling rivalry. I come from a family of sixteen kids, but only three of us are still alive. You wouldn't believe the things my sister says about me, but that's just because all the men are more interested in me," Stacy smiled.

From the look of the tight clothes clinging to Stacey's curves, Kain could understand why. He smiled at her, sipping his drink. His father's words echoed in his head that he had duties to attend, but he pushed the thoughts out, focusing on Stacey instead. She was already getting him another glass stirring it with her finger, and she sucked on her finger, handing him the glass. A tapping on Kain's shoulder forced him to turn around to see Mordecai standing behind.

"Imperator, this party is dangerous. I've detected no less than sixty safety violations of *Empyrean station* building codes. Should I inform your brother?" Mordecai pointed out the various infractions to Kain. He just laughed, turning away from the bartender.

"Mordecai the Emperor can see through time itself. Do you really think he isn't aware of some infractions? Just bring it up to Marcus after the party." Kain chucked shaking his head.

"Well, look what the Great Maw spat out." A'zyren walked towards the two. Mordecai's face contorted with his attempt to smile. He rushed forward to squeeze his friend in a hug. Only when A'zyren gasped for air did Mordecai let her go.

"Sorry, A'zyren I forget the strength of my own servos sometimes."

"You're a weird machine, Mordecai, but I'm glad you're my friend. Even this normally dour excuse for a man is alright by me right now." A'zyren looked to Stacey for another drink.

"That could just be the alcohol talking. You've had quite a bit," Stacey warned. She handed A'zyren another mug of ale that she started gulping back.

The crowd surged by the doorway drawing the group's attention. Lord Genji entered with an entourage of honor guards behind him. They scanned the Original Sins for a moment before he turned to wave in Lord De'Vayne. The black and silver robes flowed behind him. His azure eyes glanced across the club. Lord Marcus and Lady Nemesis approached the two, but Kain turned back to Stacey slamming his drink down on the bar.

"Is something wrong, Imperator?" Stacey handed Kain a new drink. He looked up at her.

"I really don't like that De'Vayne asshole," Kain declared.

"Not many do, Kain. I had to promise to sleep with him just to get an audience. That's why I didn't bother going myself. That's probably why even Magnus avoided Lord De'Vayne. What did he make you do to get him to come here?"

"That's not something I want to talk about ever," Kain informed.

"It's good to see Lord Genji looking so well. I hadn't expected to see him so soon. I wonder if he'll come over to see us." Mordecai looked at A'zyren with a smile. She shook her head.

"Lord De'Vayne doesn't like to let his favored pet out of sight too often. Do you remember what Magnus had to offer Lord De'Vayne to get permission for Genji to join us?" A'zyren shivered from the thought rushing in her memories.

"Lord Void really didn't want to part with that ancient relic, but I'll never understand why an old wooden cup was so important to him." Mordecai shook his head. "He's usually not sentimental."

Across the club, the group watched Lord De'Vayne move past Nemesis and Marcus towards the dance floor. Many of the people dancing were already sweating. Soaked clothing were being torn off with the crowd descending into carnal glee. Bodies rubbed against each other, with Lord De'Vayne walking down to join the dancing crowd. The honor guard flanked around the dance floor being deployed by Genji, and once he finished deploying troops, he glanced towards the bar with a smile. Naked men and women swarmed around Lord De'Vayne, with him swaying along with them. Genji sighed, joining the group to take a drink offered by A'zyren.

"I figured this drink would match your style, Genji."

"Thank you, A'z. It's good to see you and Mordecai. Though it's not the same without Lord Void here, don't you think?" Genji chugged back the drink glancing to the dance floor. Lord De'Vayne was grinding on the naked men and women surrounding him. Nemesis and Marcus approached the bar to get another round before joining the group.

"That Lord De'Vayne seems intriguing," Lord Marcus claimed.

"He knows how to have more fun than my brother here. Even Hephaestus and Freya are having a good time, but not Kain. Perhaps Lord Galen can remove that stick from your ass, Imperator." Nemesis winked at her brother with a chuckle. He shook his head at her with a glare.

"Next time diplomacy is needed with the De'Vayne, you can take the honors. I'm sure you'd get off on Lord De'Vayne's style of pleasure." Kain shook his head, glancing towards Genji. There didn't seem to be any trace of anger or resentment on his face, but Kain couldn't help the twangs of guilt tugging at his nerves. He looked down at the floor.

"How bad could it possibly have been?" Nemesis glanced to see A'zyren shaking her head.

"Imperator, you did your duty. Share a drink with me in honor of my children." Genji raised his glass towards Kain. The glasses chimed to each man drinking.

"I wouldn't have expected a great warrior like you to have children," Nemesis informed.

"Children are the only things truly worth fighting for. When a parent helps their children surpass them, they push life forward. Unfortunately, I was not as good of a father as I'm a warrior. I failed to make my children greater than me." Genji grabbed the next round Stacey was bringing over and down the glass with a single gulp.

"You've still got time to improve upon your design Genji," Mordecai reminded.

"I fear that time for my children has run out." Genji grew quiet, waiting for another drink. He felt Kain's eyes upon him, but he wasn't speaking either. A'zyren and Mordecai glanced at each other. Lord Hephaestus and Lady Freya were walking towards the bar, wiping sweat off their face, and both of their clothes were soaked. Stacey handed Genji his refill and slipped the two drinks towards Hephaestus and Lady Freya, who gulped back at the drinks.

"This is exactly what everyone needed. Some good visceral escape from all the work and trouble. Going to be some good hangovers tomorrow," Hephaestus joked. He looked at Kain and Genji's dour expressions before glancing at Nemesis and Marcus. They both shrugged in response.

"Well, at least most of Clan Player still showed up. It wouldn't have been much of a party without their entertainers. Your little spat seems to have kept Lady Marimba away." Lady Freya sipped at her drink, holding onto Hephaestus. Nemesis turned with a glare.

"That bitch is up to something. I've never had a problem with her before, but how she's trying to get close to Matthew worries me." Nemesis slammed her drink down motioning for another.

"Here you go, milady," Stacey handed Nemesis a new drink.

"You're the best, Stacey," Nemesis snatched the glass from her with a smile.

"You two seemed to be enjoying yourselves on the dance floor." Lord Marcus glanced at Lady Freya, hugging Lord Hephaestus. They blushed from his words.

"Leave the two love birds alone." Nemesis tugged Marcus towards her to silence him with a kiss. Genji put an arm around Kain sharing a drink with him.

"Don't let this sadness defeat you. My children died in an honorable battle. There is nothing greater I could have wished for them. You did them a service despite how we feel about that now. Few have ever experienced such a glorious battle." Genji slammed back his drink, looking at Kain.

"Wait, Lord De'Vayne pitted Kain against your children?" A'zyren rushed over to lean between the two. Everyone in the group turned to look at Genji and Kain.

"It's Lord De'Vayne's right to test the mettle of those who make requests of him. My children did their duty, as did Imperator Kain. There's nothing more to be said on the subject. With your philosophy on death demanding life, I would think it would make sense to you." Genji glared at A'zyren. Nemesis shook her head in silence, understanding now her brother's pain.

Memories rushed back to Nemesis of her childhood spent training on the officer decks of the *Alcatraz*. Gabriel would force them to train all day until their muscles collapsed, with Lord Galen watching on to attend to any injuries. All of the children were pushed well past breaking point. The children would be broken daily if Gabriel could manage it, but over time, they grew more resilient to the punishment. Concordia and Matthew preferred less violent tutelage, but they didn't crack under constant beatings, insults, and critiques. A tear came to Nemesis's eye, remembering all the times she had to fight against Kain. He'd beat her, but always come over afterward to make sure she was ok. He would teach her the mistakes she'd made, trying to help her beat him even though she never managed to do it in all the years of training.

"That fucking sadistic bastard," Nemesis insulted Lord De'Vayne, glaring at him.

"It's not worth getting worked up about Lady Nemesis. Besides, if you make any attempt against Lord De'Vayne, it's my duty to stop you." Genji pushed back the robe to reveal his blade.

"How can you serve a man who orders your children to slaughter?" Marcus looked at Genji.

"Survival in the Great Maw requires adaption. Lord De'Vayne has kept our people together since the fall of the stars. He created us, his children, from his own D.N.A. and taught us math, art, and the way of the sword through Cartesian dualism. We owe him everything," Genji replied.

"Well, this is getting far too depressing for me." Nemesis turned dragging Marcus away. They headed up the stairs with their arms around each other's waist. Mordecai and A'zyren shared uneasy glances. They sat down alongside Genji.

"Our sister is right. You should try to enjoy this party," Lord Hephaestus warned.

"We could all be dead in a few days, so we should make the best of the time we have." Lady Freya squeezed her man. She glanced up at him with a smile and nodded towards the dancefloor.

Lord Hephaestus and Lady Freya were making their way back to the dance floor. They glanced back at the dour Kain and Genji. The couple shared uneasy glances between each other. They could see the look in each other's eyes. That look spoke of the fact that there didn't seem to be anything they could to help Kain or Genji.

"Well, I better get back to guarding Lord De'Vayne." Genji slammed down the empty glass, pushing away from the bar. Mordecai followed Genji toward the dance floor. A'zyren leaned close to Kain feeling the surge of alcohol in her veins with her visions blurring.

"This is supposed to be a party, Kain, yet you're still in your stuffy power armor. Everyone else in your family took their armor off. So, tell me, what do I have to do to get you out of that armor?" A'zyren pushed her drink across the bar for a refill glancing with a smile at Kain. His eyes moved eye her body studying her curves before resting to look her in the eyes.

"Tonight, might just be the night after the last few days I've had." Kain slammed back his drink. He felt A'zyren's tug on his arm and gave way, following behind her. They walked across the club with A'zyren grinning the entire way. She led him up the stairs to hit the button on the elevator. The memories of all the empty rooms on the upper floor sprung to her mind.

The elevator doors opened. Kain walked into the elevator with A'zyren pushing him against the wall to leap onto him. Her fingers clutched at Kain's cheeks with the tongue exploring his mouth. Inertia lurched the lift upwards, but neither of them sensed it. Their lips locked in passion embrace through the journey to the upper floor where A'zyren chose to stay. She tugged Kain out of the elevator down the hall to the door of the apartment.

Doors whisked shut behind Kain and A'zyren, still kissing. The armor locks hissed with the plates retracting. She dragged Kain from the armor the second the plates retracted far enough and pulled him towards the bed, but he grabbed her by her ass to lift her into his arms. A'zyren ripped her clothes off, throwing them across the floor. Muscles trembled against her flesh. They came crashing down into the cushion of the bed and blankets. Her fingernails trailed down Kain's back, digging in to pull him closer.

CHAPTER 42

Bangs, clangs, and clunks echoed from the A.S.A. working away on the refit to the auditorium of the Infinity Nexus. Matthew sat in the chair in the center reading, ignoring the sounds of the work around him. The pages of the book flipped with a soft flapping sound under the pressure of his finger. He ran his finger over the page, feeling the paper's texture underneath. The door to the Infinity Nexus whisked open, drawing his attention from the book. His eyes fell on Lady Marimba, sauntering towards the Infinity Nexus. Her hips swayed with her strut toward the Infinity Nexus. Tendrils of silk fabric wisped in the gust of her walk, dancing in a trail behind her.

Bright blue silk fabric wrapped around Lady Marimba's chest, arms, and waist. Layers of the translucent silk overlapping wrapped around her body, covering only the essential parts. Soft light highlighted her cocoa skin. She stopped before the Infinity Nexus, falling to her knees and bowing before Emperor Solomon. Her eyes glanced up, glinting in the light locking upon Matthews. The two stared at each other in silence, with him placing the book down to rise from the chair.

"I'd expected you'd be busy celebrating with others at the Original Sins," Mathew stated.

"Your sister has made it quite clear to me that she doesn't like me since I started coming to visit you. In the interest of peace with Nemesis, I sent the best members of Clan Player to her little party for entertainment. My hopes aren't high that your sister we'll see this as a gift. I fear our situation hasn't improved much since we left the *Alcatraz*." Lady Marimba looked down at the floor. Her fingers fidgeted with each other under the gaze of Matthew.

"My sister is only doing what she thinks is best for all," Matthew explained.

"That's why I'm not holding any grudges against her. She believes she's protecting you from me and that I've got some ulterior motive for spending time with you. I can't fault a sister for protecting her brother, especially when he's Emperor Solomon who's provided us with a new star." Lady Marimba kneeled down before Emperor Solomon, keeping her eyes to the ground. She didn't bother looking up, but she could feel his gaze upon her.

Matthew paced inside the Infinity Nexus, stroking his chin. His mind focused on the situation between Marimba and Nemesis. Time streamed into Matthew's consciousness showing him all the possible outcomes between his sister and Lady Marimba. A shadow lingered between the two women that Matthew couldn't penetrate. He felt the rush of the darkness into his mind trying to peer through the murk. Black energy crackled across his eyes, but Lady Marimba's stared at the ground. She only looked up when she felt the hair on her arm stand on end. Energy crackled around her body, swirling around her. She could see Matthew's finger curling in repetitive movement.

"My sister is protective of her family, that's all, Lady Marimba." Matthew's eyes narrowed upon Lady Marimba. She felt a flush of heat across her body with the energy swirling around her legs. Black tendrils of energy crept along her skin, crawling up her legs across her skin. Tingles surged in her nerves, making it hard for her to concentrate. Muscles quivered, she bit her lip, trying to stifle her moans, and her pupils dilated, staring at Matthew.

"Emperor, that feels so…" Lady Marimba panted, trying to catch her breath from the intensifying energy creeping across her skin. He watched her writhe on the floor with a wry grin forming across his lips. The energy died down around her, allowing her to catch her breath.

"I'm sorry, I don't know what came over me," Matthew admitted looking away.

Lady Marimba gasped for breath. She tried to stand up with the tingling sensation echoing in her nerves. Muscles trembled in her legs, trying to hold her body up. She managed to stand up, leaning on the glass of the Infinity Nexus. Both of her eyes locked on Matthew, and she tapped on the glass, drawing his attention.

"You've nothing to apologize for, Emperor. Whatever you did felt amazing. I'd let you do that to me anytime you want." Lady Marimba cooed with delight, still trying to get her balance back. Placing one hand on the glass, Matthew smiled.

"I'm still learning about these new powers of mine," Matthew explained.

"It's quite ok, Emperor, and perhaps you would like to explore your powers a bit more?" Lady Marimba glanced around at the A.S.A. working around. She noticed Matthew following her eyes across the auditorium. There wasn't any order spoken, but the A.S.A. stopped their work. The machines began moving towards the exits, leaving Matthew and Lady Marimba alone.

Silence permeated the auditorium. Lady Marimba licked her lips, staring at Matthew beyond the glass of the Infinity Nexus. Black energy surged in his eyes, narrowing on Lady Marimba. She panted against the glass of the Infinity Nexus, staring into the black orbs of Matthew's eyes. The black tendrils crackled across Marimba's skin, leaving goosebumps on the surface. Her breaths came in rapid, ragged, and quick gasps.

"Emperor, that feels so good, but perhaps I can return the favor," Marimba grinned. She pushed back from the glass of the Infinity Nexus. Muscles tightened underneath her skin like coiling snakes beneath the flesh. The black energy wrapped around her body, crackling in a tight embrace. Her fingers snaked across her flesh, reaching for the ties holding the clothes on her body.

Silk wraps unfurled with Lady Marimba's tugs of her fingers at the fabric. Blue silk wisped towards the ground falling from her heaving breasts. Tangles of wild dark hair trailed down her abdomen towards her thighs, revealing under the fall of the silk cloth. The blue silk floated to the ground around her feet. She swayed her hips with the light illuminating her cocoa skin. Matthew's eyes trailed along the naked flesh drinking in all of Lady Marimba's visage. She traced her fingers along her skin with the black tendrils of energy surging around her. Their eyes locked.

Matthew felt the surge of lust filling his nerves. He couldn't break his gaze from the taught flesh walking towards the Infinity Nexus. The sway of Marimba's hips mesmerized Matthew. The black iris surged across his eyes, turning them pure black. A black tendril surged between Lady Marimba's legs surging up through her body. She collapsed to the ground panting with loud moans trying to crawl her way toward Matthew. The black energy crackled, surging all around Lady Marimba. Her skin was covered in goosebumps, sweat glistened in the light, and her eyes twitched, reflecting Matthew's image back at him. Teeth pressed hard against her lips, causing the skin to fold and wrinkle under the pressure. Her fingers twitched at the glass.

"Oh, my, Emperor, please don't stop," Marimba pleaded. Her body thrashed and flailed across the ground with the black energy coursing around her. Matthew could see his reflection in her eyes, but it was almost like he saw himself from outside his body. A part of his mind tried to regain control, but the darkness's strength crackled back at him.

Matthew couldn't break free from what he was doing. His fingers seemed to wiggle on their own, and no matter how hard he tried to gain control, he couldn't. The black tendrils leaped from his fingertips through the glass to surge across Marimba's body. She writhed, moaned, and flailed across the floor, screaming in ecstasy. He couldn't help feeling the joy the sight caused him. Half of his mind was appalled, but the other half didn't want to stop.

Muscles convulsed across Marimba's body, and her voice was an incomprehensible mess of moans, pants, and a jumble of words. Moisture glistened along her flesh. She twitched across the ground with the intense surge of the black energy bringing her to a crescendo of pleasure. Matthew seized control of his mind, the black energy surged back from his eyes, and he stumbled backward, falling over his chair. He shivered on the ground feeling the echo of the feelings twinging in his nerves. Only the sound of Marimba's panting echoed in the auditorium.

"I'm so sorry, Lady Marimba. That energy that came over me..." Matthew struggled to comprehend the lingering feelings in his nerves. Marimba lay on the ground staring up at the ceiling with steady breaths.

"No excuses, Emperor. Your servants would be lucky to be made to feel the way you've done to me. You can do that to me any time you want," Lady Marimba cooed with a smile.

"That wasn't ok. The feelings that came over me were wrong and sinful. I shouldn't allow these feelings to consume me like they did." Matthew couldn't even look at Lady Marimba.

"There's nothing sinful about some good carnal fun. I wish I could make you feel the way you just made me feel."

Matthew rocked back and forth against the chair. His mind reeled against the surge of emotions twinging in his nerves. The squeal of Lady Marimba's fingers didn't even register with Matthew. Only the echo of the words of the bible in the back of his mind could be heard. He repeated the words in a mantra against the darkness still lingering in his nerves. Black tendrils of energy crackled through his soul, drawing his eyes back to the glistening eyes of Lady Marimba.

"Emperor, are you ok?" Lady Marimba's question finally registered to Matthew.

"I can feel that dark energy clawing at my mind and soul Marimba," Matthew admitted.

Tears glistened in Lady Marimba's eyes. She thumped her fist off the glass, trying to break through it with a half-hearted gesture. This was the cost Matthew paid for all of them to have the power to create the star to obtain this paradise. There wasn't anything Lady Marimba could do to comfort Emperor Solomon. She wiped the tears away from her eyes, smearing the water across the glass leaving streaking trails behind.

"I love thee Emperor, but I can do nothing to assuage you from what you're suffering from. The power thy possesses is magnitudes beyond all others. Some of our people now fear you, but not me. Whatever you need from me, my Emperor, you have but to ask." Lady Marimba tried to reach Matthew, but he couldn't even look at her.

"What if this power ends up destroying everything I love?"

"You've given us so much already, Emperor. I would do anything for you, and so would many others. If you died, I would follow you to whatever lies beyond this existence." Lady Marimba wiggled her finger at Matthew. He glanced in her direction and made his way over to lean against the glass next to her. They looked at each other through the pane of glass.

"I feel so alone in here," Matthew admitted.

"You're never alone, Emperor. Whenever you feel lonely, just call for me, and I'll come to keep you company. My Clan will perform music or plays. Whatever we can do to lessen your pain, we'll gladly provide." Lady Marimba placed her hand flat against the glass, with Matthew doing the same.

The two people smiled at each other in silence through the glass with unwavering eyes locked on the other's pupils. Iris flared in glints of light. They leaned against the glass pressing their bodies together with only the pane separating them. Marimba watched Matthew's eyes, growing heavy with each blink. He drifted off to sleep with Marimba watching him. She smiled, seeing Emperor Solomon at peace in his slumbers. Fingertips trailed along the glass with a soft squeak with her desire to touch the flowing hair drooping over Matthew's forehead.

Lady Marimba watched Matthew's chest rising and falling with each breath. The power he displayed fascinated her. Memories echoed of the moments his power surged around Marimba. Nerves echoed the pleasures, but she shook her head, focusing on Matthew. His power was unlike anything Marimba had witnessed, and the fact it fueled her pleasure showed that Emperor Solomon was favoring her. She coiled her nubile body against the glass around Emperor Solomon and pulled the silk cloth to cover her exposed behind. The rise and fall of Matthew's chest brought a smile to Marimba's face, and her eyes grew heavy with each breath.

CHAPTER 43

Energy crackled beyond the webs of the Spindleweb Nebula. Arachne ships drifted towards the surging energy vortex. Mechanical arms swept open in front of the ships, ready to seize whatever appeared from within the vortex. A flash of black energy crackled across the void materializing the *Insidious Seduction*. Fighter craft darted from the hanger bays of the carrier, streaking across the void towards the Spindleweb Nebula.

Arachne vessels reversed engines retreating away from the approaching *Insidious Seduction*. A shuttle drifted out of the hanger bays with fighter craft swirling around it. Glowing lines of power rippled around the shuttle, darting through the weaves of the webs. The cracked ruins of the rogue planet rushed toward the shuttle. Wind rushed past the viewport of the shuttle descending towards the landing area in a muffled howl through the hull. Arachne troops stood next to Atrax, watching the shuttle rushing towards the surface with the engines flaring to slow the descent.

The shuttle hovered over the landing pad lowering at a steady rate. Landing gears thudded on the concrete surface of the landing pad. Hisses erupted from the lowering ramp. Lilith strode from the shuttle with the sound of her heels clacking on the metal of the ramp. Her eyes crackled with energy fixating on Atrax in front of her. Arachne soldiers surrounded Atrax with their graviton rifles aimed forward, trying to keep Lilith from getting too close. Red energy surged around her body, swirling into her fingers to leap through the air with a loud crackle.

Howls erupted from the guards around Atrax. Arachne soldiers fell to the ground writhing with the red energy surging around them in loud snaps and crackles. Eyes popped, exploding forth goo onto the ground. He prostrated himself before Lilith, groveling to be spared from her wrath.

Maniacal laughter erupted from her walk overtop the corpses. She pressed the point of one of her boot heels onto the claw of Atrax's claw. Crackling echoed from the chitin under the strain of Lilith's weight. Atrax screeched in pain glaring up at Lilith.

"I've come to see your mother again, Atrax, but I find naughty children planning to attack me instead. Perhaps you need punishment yourself." Lilith wobbled her finger back and forth.

"Tenno Lilith, my mother, sends her deepest apologies. My troops weren't going to attack you. She's waiting for you down in her chamber. I believe she knows where Lucifer is now." Atrax trembled on the ground, trying not to show any pain. Blood seeped out from his claw across the floor.

A loud crack echoed from Lilith, stepping onto the claw with her full weight to walk forward. She headed towards the caverns at the back of the landing bay. Eyes darted from the shadows of the cavern, but she could feel the life retreating away from her. Clatters of the claws on the rocks echoed the retreating insects. She strode through the caves down into the dark crevices of the caves. Damp heat radiated up from the lair she was approaching.

Arachne descended from the webs on the ceiling of her hive. Massive claws pulled her body along the walls. Her eight eyes darted to see Lilith walking into the room. Red energy swirling about her leaped off in snaps and crackles. She followed the movement in the darkness along the wall. Heaving down into the center of the hive, Arachne bowed before the Tenno. Her eight eyes trembling reflected Lilith's visage in the void of the beady eyes. Arachne prostrated herself before the Cacophony of Discordance with trembling limbs. Even the fine hair follicles on her body trembled at the sight of the red crackling energy of Lilith.

"I'm disappointed in you, great mother Arachne," Lilith lamented.

"My webs never lie, great lady of woe, and I beg you for another chance. I've been scouring the Great Maw trying to figure out where I want wrong." Arachne choked upon her words. Red energy crackled from Lilith's finger. The vortex of energy sapped away Arachne's energy.

Maniacal laughter belted from Lilith with the surge of energy leaping from her finger. Energy leapt across the chitin of Arachne, surging across her body. Red energy singed the hair and drew out her screeches and howls.

"Failure won't be tolerated, my dear, but perhaps I can teach you that still." Lilith surged another crackle of energy. She laughed, watching the energy leaping across the surface of Arachne's body, causing her to writhe on the ground. The incomprehensible screeches emanating from Arachne forced Lilith to relent. The energy fizzled from the fingertips to crackle around Lilith.

"Lucifer is using some unique ability to obfuscate himself from me. I'm not sure why I haven't been able to follow him beyond the meeting with the W'hyish S'yevel. There's a strange force at play in his aura that I can't ascertain." Arachne's stared up with her eight eyes at Lilith. She paced, tapped her finger on her lip, and muttered hmm out loud.

There was something strange at work here that Lilith couldn't quite figure out. She glanced down to Arachne with a wiggling finger beckoning her to rise. The echoes of the clacking heels produced the cadence of Lilith's contemplation. Lucifer's power was immeasurable compared to the other Tenno of the Cacophony of Discordance, and the sheer magnitude should make it easy to sense his location. There wasn't any hint of Lucifer in the pulsing energy throughout the Great Maw, yet Lilith could sense the faint trace of his power of the fallen angel.

"Perhaps Lucifer has employed his powers to alter reality just enough to cloak his movements. A new name designed to confuse the auguries of your weave Arachne and to disorientate the attempts of the Cacophony of Discordance to locate the Minister of Injustice. Scour your webs again, but track Lucifer's energy, not his movements. I fear the Minister of Injustice has been naughty of late, trying to keep his activities from the Cacophony of Discordance," Lilith explained.

Arachne heaved herself off the ground with groans. She pulled herself up along the wall towards the ceiling. Each claw from her eight arms darted between the webs extending from the hive, away from the rogue planet, and across the Great Maw. Claw tips touched the strands of the web with delicate touches, barely even making contact. She felt the slightest twang of energy pulsing through the webs from across the Great Maw. Vibrations echoed along the webs transmitting the messages from her children spread across the void. Her eight eyes darted in different directions, and her mind tracked the messages of hundreds of her children. There wasn't any sense of Lucifer's presence anywhere in the Great Maw. She crawled back down from the ceiling to bow again in front of Lilith.

"I fear there is no sign of Lucifer anywhere in the Great Maw dread mother."

"It's as I expected, then. You've done well for me, Arachne. For now, I'll spare you my wrath, but prepare your fleet for the attack. W'hyish S'yevel tribes are marshaling for war, and I want your children alongside them." Lilith's heels clacked off the stone of the cave floor.

"Where are you going, dread mother?" Arachne's eight eyes followed Lilith.

"There is only one possible answer to explain Lucifer's disappearance, my child, and that's he never disappeared at all. He's changed his name or modified himself enough to change the energy signature of his aura. That's why we can't find Lucifer in the Great Maw, but he's out there. So, I'm going to find him and bring him back to the Cacophony, and I have a good idea where he is." Lilith's voice receded into the cavern with each step.

"Sounds like Lucifer don't want to be found," Arachne informed.

"Oh, I don't care that Lucifer doesn't want to be found, but this little game is wearing thin on my nerves. Don't worry about the Minister of Injustice. Focus on the attack on *Empyrean station*. That's the only thing to save your brood when I return next." Lilith's voice echoed from the caverns. Her silhouette vanished into the shadows of the cave. Only the sound of the clacking heels echoing through the rocky crags, and each step grew softer.

Arachne climbed back up the walls to her nest. The glowing lines of webs surrounded her, nestling into the hive. Chatters erupted from the walls echoing the anxiety of her brood, but she didn't bother to answer. Claws seized hold of the strains of web, and the flow of information from the web filled her mind. She listened to every clack of details her children reported through the network of webs. All of her children were restless, but those out in the Great Maw were almost unhinged. The tugs in the web warned her about the consequences of discovery.

"Don't worry, my children. We must bide a little more time from the Cacophony of Discordance for Lucifer's plan to succeed. So, calm yourself, for even should Lilith kill me and many of our species will endure, my heirs will carry the hive forward into the age of the light." Arachne sent the message with tugs at the web network. Her mandibles clacked with a soft noise rubbing against each other. Sleek black multifaceted eyes reflected Lilith's growing impatience.

The anxiety of the children trembled through the strands of the web. All of Arachne's children expressed their fears that this was a loyalty test by the Cacophony of Discordance. The thought occurred to her that Lucifer could be testing her. His alliance with Lilith was well known by Arachne, yet there was something strange in the Great Maw her webs could sense. Black celestial winds of the Great Maw began to howl, and she sensed a coming storm. Everything was changing, and she knew that being on the right side of change was the only thing that would spare her children from destruction. The web wobbled with the messages she sent to her children, trying to calm them down. Light wasn't something her children enjoyed, yet they didn't understand that they needed that for the universe to grow. Each day the Great Maw devoured more life, and soon there wouldn't be enough life left to feed her children and keep her brood growing. She didn't bother explaining that to her children, but she silenced them with a few tugs of the webs, expressing her anger at the defiance of her children. The webs strands stopped vibrating.

"Tenno Lilith has departed," Atrax announced, entering the hatchery.

"Thank you, my loyal son. If only my other children obeyed me as you do." Arachne glanced down from the ceiling with her limbs tangled in the web.

"I don't imagine she'll be pleased when she finds out about your deception, Mother."

"Lucifer needed my help, and I owed him a great debt. Whether the Cacophony of Discordance understands this or not doesn't matter. Once our dark father returns, he'll crush the Tenno. The entire Great Maw will be ours. All we have to do is draw this out a bit longer to ensure Lucifer's plan succeeds," Arachne informed with the clacking of her mandibles.

"Are you not concerned that Lucifer didn't reveal to you his entire plan?" Atrax stared up at the next of his mother. The soft vibrations of the webs told him his mother was busy communicating with her children. He paced below the nest, waiting for a response.

"It doesn't matter if we know the plan's details or not," Arachne declared.

"I fear Lucifer and Lilith are playing with us, Mother," Atrax warned.

"Lilith is capable of such senseless forms of entertainment, but Lucifer is always planning something. He's done a great deal to help me, and all he asked is I continue to assist him in covering his tracks. I've managed to do that until now, but Lilith must be on to Lucifer. To ensure our safety, we must prepare the fleet for the attack on the *Empyrean station*." Arachne watched Atrax bow before her and turn to leave the hatchery.

Twangs in the web echoed the reports of Arachne's children. Her claws darted from strand to strand of the web network to listen to the reports. Reports of the activity of the Cacophony of Discordances whispered to her that they were planning something. Reverie forces were amassing in the fallen kingdoms of deplorable shadows where her webs stretched across. The great princes of pandemonium marshaled their forces. She knew that Supreme Tenno Ba'al Zebub was preparing for something, but she couldn't tell what from the reports of her children. All she could do was sink into her nest of webs to listen to the whispers of her children.

CHAPTER 44

Large machines operated by workers transported stacks of metal sheeting, steel beams, and pallets of different types of stones. Forks slid from the sides of the pallets of materials with clangs. Stacks of materials scattered the park below the balcony, and workers constructed the cathedral's foundation. Nozzles sprayed the cement mixture into the frame of the foundation. Workers pushed the cement across the frame with long poles smoothing the surface.

The data pad beeped with the taps of Lord Drumpf's fingers. He scanned the pallets in the park below the balcony. The list showed that most of the materials necessary for the cathedral's construction were assembled in the park. He double-checked the list to make sure the report was accurate. Workers below averted their gaze from him, scanning across the workplace. He marched back into the room, presenting the data pad to Lord Whelsey.

"We've got all the material necessary to start construction. A few things are still missing, but there could be a backup in the energy-to-matter converter logs. I'll bring it up to Lord Hephaestus when I speak to him later," Lord Drumpf informed. Lord Whelsey studied the cathedral model, nodding his head along to the report. He took the data pad to glance over it.

"Seem you haven't lost your touch with organizing the labor. How long do you expect the construction to take once it's begun?" Lord Whelsey fiddled with the model making minor changes to the locations of the statues in front of the cathedra. He glanced over the information on the data pad with an audible hmm. Everything seemed in order from the report.

"It shouldn't take more than a few weeks, depending on mistakes and accidents."

The door to the study creaked open slowly. Neither of the men paid any attention to monk Fiona slipping into the room. She carried the platter with a pitcher of red wine and several glasses. Glass chimed in her hands, setting the two glasses down. Red wine splashed across the bottom of the first glass with the soft gulping sound of the pouring pitcher. She bowed to Lord Whelsey, presenting him the glass of the wine and looking down at the ground.

"Thank you, my dear, this is delicious," Lord Whelsey complimented, taking a sip.

Lord Drumpf took the glass from the monk with a smile. He smiled at the pretty monk with a toothy grin and sipped the wine savoring the flavors. Monk Fiona bowed to the two lords and retreated out of the room. The door closed quietly with a soft click. Lord Whelsey sauntered towards with the data pad in hand, and his fingers hovered over one of the crates of materials. He pointed to the inventory with a tap of his finger, presenting the information.

"I've decided to stick with gold for the front doors. The new cathedral should remind the faithful of the house of our Lord on the *Alcatraz*." Lord Whelsey slammed the data pad into Lord Drumpf's chest, walking towards the balcony. The workers hustled down below, but they moved faster, seeing Lord Whelsey staring at them. He sipped at the wine with a wry smile seeing all the people below glancing up at him. Most workers tried to avert their gaze from him, but a few were unable. He could sense the fear the workers held in him. They knew what form his wrath took when it unleashed, and they'd do almost anything to stay in his good graces.

"That will take some time to acquire, but it shouldn't slow the construction. It'll take a few days to get the basic frame of the building completed. The time that takes, I should be able to work something out with Lord Hephaestus to get the gold for the main doors fabricated." Lord Drumpf adjusted the information in the data pad. He uploaded the new request to the energy-to-matter convertor queue, and attacked a message so Lord Hephaestus understood the request.

"Perhaps I rushed in my plans to kill you, Lord Drumpf. You're proving to still be quite useful to my plans. Maybe I'll keep you around once I've finished everything," Lord Whelsey locked eyes with Lord Drumpf.

"Still planning your takeover, I assume?" Lord Drumpf shook his head.

"Oh, my plans have grown in scale of ambition since the *Alcatraz*. My new plan will alter everything we know to be true. Heaven and hell will be at my disposal. My power will be absolute. None will dare to challenge me." Lord Whelsey proclaimed, surging past Lord Drumpf into the room.

"Sounds like the kind of pride that comes before a fall if you ask me," Lord Drumpf rebuked.

"You are telling me you've given up your ambitions Lord Drumpf. That almost makes me laugh." Lord Whelsey finished his drink, grabbed the pitcher, and refilled the glass.

"I have ambitions, but not to overthrow Emperor Solomon. Overthrowing Captain Gabriel might have been possible on the *Alcatraz*, but your grandson has consolidated his power here on the *Empyrean station*. You'll never surpass him now. Any attempt is going to bring your ruination, if not total damnation. Your best bet is to follow Emperor Solomon's commands," Lord Drumpf shook his head at his old ally.

"My grandson tries to claim the power of God for himself. I'll not allow such blasphemy."

"That worked so well with Concordia, didn't it?" Lord Drumpf crossed his arms with one eyebrow raised. He stared at Lord Whelsey glaring at him with his skin flushed red.

"That girl was a threat to the *Alcatraz* even if her fool father refused to see it. We can't abide the blasphemous amongst us. They'll bring the wrath of God down upon us!" Lord Whelsey wagged his finger at his former ally. He scoffed at Lord Drumpf's audacity to judge him.

Constant scans of the neural network of Lord Whelsey's estate echoed in the back of Lord Drumpf's mind. He couldn't activate any recording without the scan detecting it. The cameras in the room caught the entire argument so far, but he wasn't sure where the data feed went to. He had to be able to gather the evidence Emperor Solomon wanted from those cameras. He needed to bide some more time to get by himself to investigate the estate.

"You shouldn't have manipulated the crew the way you did using religion. That forced Gabriel's hand. He might have forgiven you, but I wouldn't expect Nemesis to ever let that go. She's going to get vengeance one day." Lord Drumpf smiled with his warning. He knew Lord Whelsey would only be pushed further into whatever he was planning. The defiance in his nature would be impossible to overcome. He stormed towards the door, yanked it open, and halted in the frame, glancing back at Lord Drumpf. The two men locked their gazes upon each other's eyes.

"That plan succeeded in everything we intended it to. You forget that you played a part in Concordia's death. Whatever comes out about me will also implicate you. Did you forget who acquired the recording that I used to damn her during the trial?" Lord Whelsey crossed his arms.

"A mistake of mine that I regret these days," Lord Drumpf admitted.

"I don't know what game you're playing, but I suspect you're spying for the Emperor and Nemesis. We worked together to unravel Gabriel, and we almost succeeded. I hope you come to your senses soon. Perhaps there could still be a place for you by myself in the new order. Tell me why the Emperor and Nemesis ordered you here," Lord Whelsey demanded.

Silence permeated the room between the two men glaring at each other. The contest of wills raged in their minds combating each other's schemes. Lord Drumpf gritted his teeth, popping his jowl out. He wouldn't give up the potential reward of his ship for this fool's pride, but Lord Whelsey wasn't a fool either. Behind those black pupils lurked a cunning mind that scoured to understand the Emperor's and Nemesis's plans. That was the only use for Lord Drumpf and the only thing keeping the wrath of Lord Whelsey at bay.

"Emperor Solomon assigned me to help you build your cathedral out of concern for the faithful during the construction of the fleet and defenses. You've already been told this." Lord Drumpf tapped his foot, crossed his arms, and scowled at Lord Whelsey.

"Truth always has its day in the end, Lord Drumpf. You'd be wise to remember that." Lord Whelsey slammed the door behind him. He stormed down the stairs into the main entrance towards the security door to the laboratory. Lights scanned his retina, the machine hummed, processing his handprint, and he typed the access code into the number pad.

Locks clunked through the wall, a hiss erupted around the doorframe, and the door swung inwards. Each of Lord Whelsey's footsteps echoed in the confined stairwell descending beneath the estate. He strode down the corridor towards the large metal doors to the laboratory. The doors hissed open, with screams echoing from the room into the hallway. Angelica thrashed on the medical bed against her bindings, with machines cutting into her.

The howls coming from Angelica oscillated through the room, echoing of the howls of the demon trapped inside. Unnatural energy resonated through the voice vibrating the metal wall plates. Sparks erupted along one of the machine arms working on Angelica. Metal crunched, folding the arm onto itself. Flames erupted from the remains of the arm. Smoke wafted into the air, rolling across the ceiling, sucking into the ventilation fans thumping away.

"Lord Whelsey, it's good you've arrived. The research hit an exciting new stage a few minutes ago. Magnus explained that the Reverie are sentient living negative energy, and that made me think that perhaps the best way to interact with them isn't through Angelica's flesh. All matter is energy expressed at specific frequencies through the molecular structure of atoms. So, I thought, what if I attempted to manipulate Levart's energy frequency directly? It took some experimentation to discover what that specific frequency was. I compared the frequency against your granddaughter's double helix genetic structure." Lord Galen tapped on the console. The holographic emitter flashed, creating the pattern of Angelica's D.N.A. in the air.

A double helix of Angelica's D.N.A. spun in the holographic image floating in the air. The energy frequency of Levart's life signs flowed next to it. Light beams darted, blurring the images together. Overlapping the energy signature of Levart aligned with Angelica's D.N.A. Lord Whelsey studied the image stroking his chin. A wry smile formed on his lips.

"This is excellent work, Lord Galen. Is this the source of the Cacophony power?"

"To a degree, yes, but it's more complex than that. The Cacophony of Discordance is the physical manifestation of sentient negative energy. Ancients would have called them spirits back on Earth. You want proof of God, but I can't help there. I guess proof of hell will have to suffice," Lord Galen pointed to Angelica.

"Levart really is a demon?" Lord Whelsey glanced at his granddaughter thrashing against the bindings. Energy crackled in her eyes, lancing out at the machines. Explosions rained shards of metal down upon her, but she laughed maniacally. Wounds crackled with energy sealing shut.

"I'm not sure that can be proven definitively, but what else would you call pure living sentient negative energy? All those horrendous emotions oozed together into a focused will of pure spite. That seems to be the source of the power even Lord Void used. These demons, if you prefer, can alter the energy makeup of any living thing on a primal level, but their greatest power is over living beings. They can absorb the raw energy patterns from living beings, but I hypothesize that this conduit is a two-way," Lord Galen explained.

"We must find the weakness of the Cacophony of Discordance. This progress could lead us down a glorious path Lord Galen. We can develop weapons capable of destroying the Cacophony of Discordance on the most primal level. For the first time in human history, we could destroy hell itself forever. I sense this is the path the Lord has led me upon." Lord Whelsey signed the cross on his head and chest, solemnly bowing and whispering a prayer of thanks to God.

Lord Galen chuckled and tapped on the console. The image on the screen blurred with the new data beginning to appear. The D.N.A, of Angelica was replaced by Lord Whelsey's. When he lifted his head from the prayer, the information floated right in front of his face. His eyes scrolled across the holographic information with the subtle movement of his lips.

"Is this information accurate?" Lord Whelsey scratched his head and scanned the holographic image again. He glanced over to see Lord Galen's wide grin.

"Your D.N.A. is close enough to your granddaughter's that with some genetic manipulation, I should be able to make your body capable of housing Levart. I don't want to get your hopes up too high, because a lot of work needs to be done. First, I've got to figure out how to help Angelica get control over Levart, and until then, there's no point looking any further. The demon can assume control at will, from what I've experienced. That's not beneficial to your plans to deal with Emperor Solomon, assume control of the *Empyrean station*, and defeat our enemies."

"That is most pleasing news Lord Galen, but you're right. We must find a way to shackle this demon to our control. Perhaps there's a way to use Levart's own energy frequencies against him. All living things seek to avoid pain and death. Focus on a way to hurt Levart using the energy frequencies. We'll see how defiant this demon is once we can kill it," Lord Whelsey schemed.

"I've got a few ideas I'm working on already. You've got to deal with Lord Drumpf. I don't feel comfortable working away while he's in the estate. What we're doing could get us both killed if we were discovered. Do you think it was a coincidence that he brought up Concordia?" Lord Galen pointed to the video feed from the study playing on the console screen in the corner.

"No, I don't think it was a coincidence, and I'm keeping him busy for now. You'll just have to make do with the current work conditions. Only we have clearance to get down into this lab. Try to relax and focus on the work. The sooner you figure this all out, the better. We can be free of the tyrannical Soloman family, the blasphemous Emperor claiming to be the new God, and deal with the Cacophony of Discordance to destroy evil forever." Lord Whelsey patted Lord Galen on the back.

Lord Drumpf worked on the cathedral in the study on the video. He glanced at the camera in the room, walking towards the balcony. Lord Whelsey stared at the video screen, his teeth clenched and jowls jutting outward. He sipped the last bit of wine from the glass, watching the two men working. The keys of the consoles clacked away with Lord Galen running his computations on the experiments. Data flowed on the holographic image showing the manipulation of the D.N.A.

CHAPTER 45

Silence permeated the barroom, and all the patrons stared at Magnus standing in the doorway. The piano player's fingers dangled frozen over the keys, guitar player's strings vibrated from the last strum, and the singer stared, holding onto the microphone. Gabriel sat at the bar with his back to the door. He gulped at his drink with his crew surrounding him. Magnus approached Gabriel, but Myrmidon's claws flashed with his hand slamming into Magnus's chest to stop him. Black energy crackled from his chest.

"I'd remove your hand from me before I decide to keep it forever."

"Captain Solomon doesn't wish to speak with you any further. I'd leave before we teach you a lesson in humility." Myrmidon's other hand darted towards the pistol on his thigh.

Everyone in the bar drew their weapons from their holsters. Barrels pointed from every angle of the bar at Magnus, but he just shook his head. Energy crackled from his eyes, glancing around the barroom. Black energy singed the fur of Myrmidon's hand, and he howled in pain, crumbling under convulsing muscles to his knees. Magnus looked down on the Tigran, peeled his hand from his chest, and threw him into the crowd with almost no effort. Gabriel guzzled back the drink turning around with a hand on the hilt of his energy blade to lock eyes with Magnus.

"What the fuck do you want from Magnus that you've not already taken?" Gabriel leaned his back against the edge of the bar. The bartender refilled the empty drink and set it back down. The other patrons looked at Gabriel, but he held his hand, telling them to stop. He snapped up the drink with his free hand to sip at it keeping his eyes transfixed on the black pool of Magnus' eye.

"I never came to take anything from you, Gabriel. You've only yourself to blame for what you've lost." Magnus glanced around the room. Black energy crackled from his eyes. Patrons kept their weapons aimed at him but followed Gabriel's orders to stay put.

"More lies trying to convince me of your honorable intentions to help me?"

Magnus walked slowly towards the bar. He watched the barrels of the weapons tracking him as he sat next to Gabriel. The bartender quivered behind the bar. Snaps of Magnus' fingers elicited no reaction, but the spark of black energy sparked from his finger, shocking the bartender back to life. He pointed to Gabriel's glass, and the bartender grabbed a mug filling it from the taps along the bar. The mug trembled in the bartender's hands, and Magnus snatched it before any drink could spill.

"I've never lied to you, Gabriel. There is much I don't understand. I'm just doing my best to make things right again," Magnus explained, sipping his drink.

"We both know if you told me the truth from the beginning, I wouldn't have welcomed you onto the *Alcatraz*. Now my children are in danger again because of you. I couldn't help them even if I wanted to right now. The ship I've got isn't one I'd take to battle. The *Furious* is a transport ship, not a warship." Gabriel could see his first mate glaring at him, but he shrugged at Myrmidon. The truth wasn't going to change because neither wanted it to, but Gabriel understood why his first mate found offense in the words. The ship did belong to Myrmidon first, and it was still his ship as far as Gabriel was concerned. He just needed it until he found something better.

"Take the *Death's Reaper*," Magnus offered the command code datarod to his ship.

"That's ironic," Gabriel chuckled. He stared at the datarod dangling in front of him.

"We both know the real reason you let me onto the *Alcatraz* was you intended to take the *Death's Reaper* from me. You were just playing along, waiting for the opportunity, and taking whatever else you could get along the way. This should help settle our debt." Magnus waved the datarod in front of Gabriel snatching it up with a solemn nod.

Myrmidon approached the bar to stand next to his captain. Light glinted from the claws holding the high-energy hard light rifle. He leaned over to whisper into Gabriel's ear. The two men whispered amongst each other. Gabriel nodded to his first officer and snatched the dangling datarod.

"Why are you going to the trouble to do all this, Magnus?" Gabriel studied Magnus.

"There's much we share in common. Your family hates you the same way my family hates me. What our family thinks of us doesn't matter. The only thing that defines living beings is the choices they make. Whether we're in heaven, hell, or here in the Great Maw, what does it matter if our choices are the same?"

"I admit there are many choices I've made in the past that I've come to regret."

"Learning is a lot like jumping into F.T.L. for the first time. Everything can go wrong getting you killed, so you just hold on, pray for the best, and make sure not to make the same mistakes twice. You've come quite aways since the *Alcatraz*, Gabriel. Fate provides interesting twists in the journey of our lives. When I fled *Draconis*, I'd not intended to come here, but the damage to my ship made this the only possible location. I never expected to find you here, yet you can do the one thing I can't. Take the *Death's Reaper*, return to the *Empyrean station*, and defend the star. I know you have no reason to trust me, but it's the only thing that matters in the whole verse," Magnus warned.

Gabriel sipped his drink, growing quiet. His mind raced with thoughts of his family. They wouldn't be happy to see him, and it could be fatal given Angelica's attempt on his life at the trial. The other members of Gabriel's crew stared at him. He glanced back to Myrmidon.

"Take the datarod, and get our new ship fired up, Myrmidon. Give me the control codes for the *Furious*. Magnus here will need a new ship. It's not much, but she flies." Gabriel snatched the datarod from his first officer and handed it to Magnus. Myrmidon's hand trembled, reaching out for the datarod, and he couldn't help but grin. With the datarod in hand, Myrmidon motioned to the rest of the crew to follow him.

"You heard the captain mawslaw. Let's get this ship flying." Myrmidon led the crew out of the bar leaving Gabriel and Magnus alone. He looked at the datarod of the *Furious* and laughed.

"I don't think this ship is going to get me far. Perhaps it's time for me to stop running anyhow. Face my choices and take a stand against the Cacophony of Discordance." Magnus downed the drink, slammed the mug down, and pushed away from the bar.

"Magnus, that sounds suicidal to me. You should just come with us," Gabriel insisted.

"There's nothing more that I would love than to fly alongside you in the battle to come, but my path takes me in a different direction. Tenno Asmodeus won't just allow Pandora to retreat with her people if I'm with you all. We're going to need some kind of diversion. I'm what the Cacophony wants. So, I guess I'm all we've got." Magnus walked to the door, pushing it open. The sound of Gabriel's footsteps echoed following behind.

"You're scared Matthew will kill you when you return, aren't you?" Gabriel stared into Magnus's eyes, trying to figure out his motivations.

"What I did to your son was necessary, but he's unlikely to forgive being made a sacrifice. I can't blame Matthew for wanting me dead if that's how he feels. One day I may have the opportunity to stand before him to answer for my choices. Until that day, I'm going to do what I have to ensure that your family stays safe, Gabriel." Magnus trotted towards the docking bay.

Ships hovered in the air waiting for departing clearance, workers rushed loading equipment onto the ships waiting to take off, and the Pandoran armada floated beyond the docking bay shields. Pandora barked orders to the slaves and pirate crew around her. Clamour echoed across the hanger bay, crates clanged against the deck plate, and thuds of large machines stomping up ramps. Magnus scanned the area. Workers stripped everything from the walls, and ceilings, and salvaged every last resource. Nothing was being left behind from what he could see.

"Are you just reacting to what comes your way, or do you have a plan?" Gabriel's eyebrows narrowed as he focused on Magnus' eyes.

"I have a goal to fulfill. What I'm attempting is impossible for me to explain to you. There's no specific plan for each action, but I know what needs to be done. There are few things I know of in this ancient verse capable of planning an operation of this scale. Most of them died during the last stellar war. I'm afraid you know little about the true history of this reality," Magnus informed.

"You really love playing the intrigue, don't you?"

"It's best if I don't speak of these things. In the verse, there are more ways than you're aware of to spy on beings. Once your species considered magic possible before they changed their minds making science the new divine, and somehow got it wrong both times. Magic isn't possible or impossible, magic is technology, and it never seems to stop growing in power. Even the dark ages of the Great Maw have done little to slow the creativity of you clever little sentients. It seems the divine always keeps a few secrets held back from us to keep life interesting. Progress seems to just keep marching on over all the corpses of anything standing in its way," Magnus explained.

"Technology is something we're all a little short on in the Great Maw."

"That's not true. Look around you at what Pandora has built from the scraps she salvaged. This is why the return of the star is so important, Gabriel. It allows the verse to grow again, form new planets, and create new resources. All we're doing is circling the drain right now. That's exactly what the Cacophony of Discordance has always wanted. They've been working towards this for a long time, a final end to creation, to the pain, and torment of life itself. I'm ashamed to admit I've done my part to contribute to their success. If the new star falls, the verse dies with it, and everyone goes along with it inevitably. It's not a question of if but when. Those are the stakes, Gabriel. We're fighting against in this war between the darkness and light. Your children are the key to the victory in that war Gabriel. You each have sacrifices to make, just like me." Magnus placed a hand on Gabriel's shoulder with a sympathetic glance.

"Why are my children so special that only they can fight this war?" Gabriel shook his head, trying to wrap his mind around the facts. Memories sparked of his reading with Clotho as a young man. His father forced him to attend the secret ceremony and instructed Gabriel not to ever speak of it again to anyone. He glanced down at the scar along his palm from before his ascension.

Prophetic words echoed in Gabriel's mind. He remembered Clotho's warning. That he'd bring ruin upon the *Alcatraz* and suffer a fate so dark she dared not look into the shadows cast by his choices. The wreckage of the *Alcatraz* proved Clotho's prediction to Gabriel. His fingers massaged the scar across his hand, feeling the twang of pain echoing in his memories.

"Your family genetic material is exceptionally strong. Fate determined that Matthew's D.N.A. confirmed the Abyssal Prophecy predictions. My mathematics precision predicted your son, yet I hadn't considered the possibility you'd all be Christians. Religion creates dark drives of dominance amongst all sentients. Will to believe is almost too strong to overcome. Crusades, genocides, and let's not forget, all the unique forms of torture devises like crucifixion. It seems the roots of evil have entwined your species through your religion, yet you burned your daughter alive for God's commands," Magnus shook his head.

"I never wanted to do that to Concordia. The laws were out of my control. The entire ship would have mutinied against me, and millions would have died. There would have been too much loss of life." Gabriel felt the tears surging into his eyes along the edge of his eyelids. His jowls popped outwards, teeth ground on each other, and he forced back the tears.

"The path of the righteous is beset upon all sides by the inequities of the selfish and the tyranny of evil men. You chose to fall from that righteous leadership path, and never saw Lord Whelsey's hands behind the trial of Concordia. He used religion to control you, and that action turned your children against you. Kain stayed loyal to family, but not you. Instead of facing the enemies in your midst, you buried your woes in drink, sex, and power. You'll pay for your lack of vigilance in the long run, but it's not my place to judge you for your sins," Magnus informed.

"Why didn't you warn me when you arrived?"

"It was already too late to change your fate by that time. I only had the chance to save Matthew and your other children. Angelica might be beyond saving, but I sense her fate is still tied to you. Perhaps the divine is giving you one final chance to redeem yourself." Magnus patted Gabriel on the back, hoping he'd take the news to heart, but time was moving away from them all.

Magnus pushed his way through the thick crowd of the docking bay. He forced his way toward the center of the group. Orders barked from Pandora, pointing to the work that needed to be completed. The entire ship was being dismantled under the labor of the slaves. Buildings were deconstruction to salvage the materials, and workers packed the equipment into crates. She looked to Magnus pushing his way through the crowd.

"We've still got a lot of work to do, Magnus, but I'm glad you brought Gabriel back. The fleet is almost assembled. All these transport ships are waiting for the last cargo to be loaded. My workers are stripping the Box, but we'll need a bit longer. We can't afford to leave all this material behind we've collected through sweat, blood, and tears," Pandora declared.

"Tenno Asmodeus isn't going to just allow you to leave. We'll need a plan to make sure you've got the time you need to jump to *Empyrean station.*" Magnus stared out through the armada at the *Jinnestan,* floating it the black void of the Great Maw beyond the energy shields.

Reverie fighters darted across the shield in every direction. Magnus sensed the power of Tenno Asmodeus inside the carrier. He glanced at the datarod in his hand and looked to *Furious.* The ship had little to look at from the rust along the hull. He gripped the datarod tightly in his grasp, with the sparks of a plan forming in his mind and crackling in his eyes. Tenno Asmodeus would be cautious of the new ship Magnus piloted. That might allow him to turn the hubris of the Tenno against the Cacophony of Discordance. His eyes narrowed on the *Jinnestan.*

CHAPTER 46

E ngines flared behind the transports propelling the ships through the hanger bays. Workers loaded the remaining crates of resources onto the last few awaiting transports. The armada gathered in formation just beyond the hangar near the shipyards. Reverie fighter craft continued to patrol the shield's perimeter in sweeping waves around Pandora's Box. Magnus paced, black energy crackling along his skin, and his eyes fixed on the *Jinnestan* beyond the shields. His mind scanned the energy signatures around him.

Commotion echoed through the shipyard. Stripped buildings dotted the cityscape of the wreckage. The palace appeared a shadow of former glories only a few hours ago. Metal plates stripped from the wall left on the metal superstructure. Beyond the metal hull of the ruined starship, Magnus sensed the steady pulsing of the reactor powering the weapons and shields. He tugged on Pandora's arm, drawing her attention, and pointed to the reactor.

"What's the status of the reactor powering this wreckage?"

"The reactor and these amazing shields are the only things I've got to abandon. Without the power to those shields, those Reverie bastards will be on top of us in a few moments. I hate leaving such valuable resources behind." Pandora directed the workers toward the awaiting transports. Her hands darted in a flurry of directions to the slaves, overlords, and soldiers gathered around her.

"You want to set the reactor to overload. Use the same energy keeping the Cacophony of Discordance at bay to attempt to destroy them. Lure them into a trap," Gabriel reasoned.

"I learned that little maneuver from you. In all the long millennia since the destruction of the stars, no one has considered using the light burst of an F.T.L. drive to damage the Reverie. It did quite a number on the *Dread Sovereign*, a vastly more powerful ship than the *Jinnestan*. Perhaps it'll work again to damage Tenno Asmodeus's force. I doubt it'll destroy them, but it should stop him from attempting to follow you. Either way, the explosion will slow him down." Magnus ran through his mathematical calculations in his head to make sure his plan would work.

Pandora gave the orders to her soldiers standing around her. Several of the troops pushed their way through the crowd to dart toward the palace. She glanced to see Magnus walking towards the ships nearby. The *Death's Reaper* and *Furious* sat in adjoining berths. The last crates were being loaded onto nearby transports with clangs and thuds echoing inside the ships.

Death's Reaper shined in the light of the hanger bay. Magnus ran his fingers along the hull. He struggled with the strange mixture of feelings bubbling up from deep within his mind. This ship had been with him for so long that he could faintly remember a time without it. Tears welled up in his eyes, and he wiped them away before anyone could see. The repairs appeared to be flawless from his scans of the ship's hull. Pandora's laughter drew Magnus' attention back to her.

"Not taking care of your ship, I hear. My workers only took about an hour to get those coolant lines fixed. The automated repair system Vulcan installed could have done the work for you, but I guess you never read his instruction manual. He'd be ashamed of you for letting this beauty fall into such disrepair. Shame to see you sacrifice such a technological wonder on this suicidal plan you've concocted. I'd much rather fight by your side and teach this Tenno Asmodeus a lesson he will never forget." Pandora put her hand on Magnus's shoulder.

"Actually, the *Death's Reaper's* belongs to Gabriel and his crew now. I'll be taking the *Furious* if you don't have any objections, but this only looks like suicide to you. Let's hope Tenno Asmodeus thinks the same way you do. That'll make my plan much easier to pull off." Magnus walked over to the *Furious*, inserted the datarod, and waited for the systems to accept the command codes. He glanced over the ship studying it for any problems he could see.

Rusted hull plating compromised the ship's integrity, and Magnus leaned in to study the damage. Oxidation of the metal echoed in the energy patterns of the molecules. Metal fatigue had set in already, but it hadn't progressed enough to be a threat. He figured the hull would hold up from space so long as he could keep the Cacophony of Discordance from opening fire. The weapon systems on the ship look ancient to him, and they wouldn't scratch the hull of the reverie ships. Phase shields wouldn't even need to work to absorb the energy of these cannons. The sensor array was held together by scraps, welds, and parts that didn't even belong to the machine.

"I can't say I entirely blame you for your anger now, Gabriel. Even the *Alcatraz* was in far better shape than this hunk of junk." Magnus kicked the hull of the *Furious* with a loud clang.

"She's nicer inside, I promise," Gabriel chucked. Magnus glared at him.

"Well, the *Furious* is only a transport ship. You can hardly expect me to pour the best resources into this bucket of bolts. Besides, my crew never complained about this ship, and they've scoured the Great Maw for quite a few years. Isn't that right, Myrmidon?" Pandora glanced at Myrmidon with a smile. He bowed his head solemnly in his response.

"Of course, my Queen, we're grateful for your generosity and fairness," Myrmidon praised.

Furious could hardly be called a ship by Magnus' standards. The ship wouldn't withstand battle and looked like a stray piece of stellar trash would cause the entire ship to crumble. Computer on the ship beeped, accepting the command codes from the datarod. Hisses erupted from the seams of the landing ramp. The ramp crashed to the deck with a loud thud. Magnus glanced back to Gabriel standing next to Pandora.

"You and Gabriel really are a match made in hell. Take care of this crazy woman for me." Magnus walked over to Pandora, grabbed her by the head, and kissed her with force. She was caught off guard at first, but a few seconds later she returned the passion. Gabriel scowled at them both with his arms crossed but didn't move.

Pandora stood there speechless when Magnus broke away from the kiss. He marched up the ramp into the *Furious* to stop at the top, hitting the button to close the ramp. Pneumatics thumped behind the wall retracting the ramp. Silence filled the empty cargo bay of the ship. There wasn't the hint of anything left inside the emptied ship. He looked back at Pandora and Gabriel.

"Godspeed, Magnus, you're going to need it," Gabriel forced a half-hearted smile.

"Get the fleet to the far side of the shield Pandora. Once you see the *Furious* approaching the shield's perimeter, drop it. You should be able to jump to *Empyrean station* before Tenno Asmodeus's forces can get in weapons range. Don't do anything stupid. Just follow the plan." Magnus marched into the ship. The ramp echoed the loud thud sealing shut behind him.

The map on the corridor wall showed Magnus the way to the bridge. He trudged down the hallways walking through the bridge doors whisking open. The design of the bridge reminded him of the ancient's ships. A familiar chair beckoned him, and the tactical computer whirred, processing the datarod. Information scrolled across the screen in rapid blinks. The programs on the ship were so old he struggled to remember how they worked. Automated systems activated the consoles across the bridge. Navigation, sensors, engineering, and piloting consoles glared to life with the whir of the computers processing the startup sequence.

The engine's power climbed on the screen. Magnus didn't bother communicating with the traffic control tower. He activated the thrusters propelling the ship upwards. Systems reported an increase in altitude. Sensors came online, showing the build-up of Pandoran forces beyond the shipyards and hanger bays. He pushed the throttle forward. The ship blasted across the hanger bay, dodging around the transports moving to join the armada. All the remaining ships in the wreckage were beginning to take off. Great Maw loomed in the viewscreen.

Furious darted through the formation of the armada, accelerating under the thrust of the engines at full power. He accessed the communications relaying a message to the *Jinnestan*. The communications warbled in the silent bridge. The viewscreen flashed with the image of Asmodeus appearing. He stared at Magnus sitting in the captain's chair. Their black eyes locked.

"I'm coming to surrender myself provided you stay true to your deal. You'll leave Pandora's Box in peace." Magnus glared into Tenno Asmodeus's eyes, crackling with black energy.

"We've reached an accord if you turn yourself over immediately," Asmodeus agreed.

The communications channel cut off, returning the image of the Great Maw. Reverie fighters continued to swarm around the shield on sensors. Pandoran ships massed together on the far side of the shield opposite the *Jinnestan*. Scans showed the shield energy beginning to wane with the *Furious* approaching the perimeter of Pandora's Box. Shield energy fluctuated before collapsing, dissipating the energy perimeter and allowing the *Furious* to continue toward the Reverie forces. Fighter craft surged through the shields on the sensors darting towards the Pandoran armada. Warnings blared from the enemy weapons locked on the ship, but Magnus only paid attention to the status of the Pandoran armada.

Sensors showed several fighter craft following the *Furious*. Magnus watched the enemy fighters surging through Pandora's Box, attempting to catch the armada. Spikes of energy flashed across the tactical computer reporting the multiple F.T.L. engine bursts. Pandoran ships disappeared in rapid blinks. A tractor beam erupted from the *Jinnestan,* grasping a hold of the *Furious*. Alarms blared, but he just leaned back into the chair to enjoy the ride. The entire ship shuddered under the force of the tractor beam. Groaning metal resonated through the corridors and bridge of the ship. On the viewscreen, the looming *Jinnestan* grew larger.

Energy swirled around the *Furious* being dragged toward the docking bay. Magnus could see the Reverie forces preparing for his arrival through the viewscreen. Tenno Asmodeus marched into the docking bay surrounded by a dozen of his elite troops. Magnus pushed out the captain's chair, walking towards the cargo bay. The ship glided through the docking bay guided by the tractor beam. A loud thud echoed from the landing gear absorbing the weight of the *Furious*. His hand slammed the docking ramp button. Hisses blasted from the seals cracking, and the ramp lowered with steady drops.

Tenno Asmodeus scowled at Magnus walking down the ramp. He unclicked his belt, pulled it free from his waist with holster and pistol attached, and presented the items to Tenno Asmodeus. He snatched the gear with a glare. Pulling the pistol from the holster, he examined the weapon. Black energy sparked from the claw of his finger running along the smooth metal of the gun frame. He glanced up at Magnus with a scowl.

"Quite the impressive piece of Ancient tech you've got here, Magnus." There wasn't any response from him, and Asmodeus crackled with energy. "Perhaps you require using your absurd self-proclaimed archaic title of Lord to realize I'm addressing you." Black energy crackled from Tenno Asmodeus's fingers pointed at Magnus' face. He scoffed at the surge of energy sparking at him.

"Your forces have continued the assault on Pandora's Box against our agreement. I've lived up to my word, and now it's your turn." Magnus crossed his arms with a glare.

"Did you really expect me to live up to such an agreement once I got you in custody?"

Laughter erupted from the Jinn standing beside Tenno Asmodeus. Reverie troops surrounding Magnus joined in on the revelry at his expense. He started laughing along with them, causing the entire ruckus to cease almost immediately, but he took a moment to meet each of these beings' eye-to-eye. Black energy surged from Tenno Asmodeus around Magnus, bringing him to his knees and causing the laughter to resume, yet it didn't. Asmodeus's fury radiated from his attack across the docking bay, causing all the Jinn to stop and watch. Magnus broke the silence with a cackle of glee.

"Impetuously bold, Lord Void. I'd almost admire it if it wasn't so insanely suicidal." Locking eyes, the two beings glared at each other in a power struggle.

"Oh, come now, we both know you're fond of impetuously bold, insanely suicidal plans, or do you forget that whole fall from grace?" Jinn whispered to each other, glaring at Magnus and Asmodeus. "Radiant Harmonia of the Celestial Kingdom isn't easy to forget, is it, Lord of lies?"

Asmodeus's claws curled in his hands, crackling with energy, and he glared down at Magnus. Racing thoughts crackled across Asmodeus's body in spasmodic bursts. Despite that, this seemingly small Reverie that called himself a lord had to remain unharmed, which only heightened his fury. Despite magnitudes of power beyond the comprehension of even the Jinn watching on, Asmodeus's power failed to put any fear in Magnus, and he sensed this rogue couldn't be broken by humiliation. No, Asmodeus knew it would take all the power of his torments to break this rogue soul, and he glanced around at the Jinn, energy crackling off him, and his eyes narrowed on Ifrit.

"Take this traitor from my sight Ifrit and stick him in a tormentor. Let's see how much enjoyment he gets from that while we siphon power from his lamentation. I'll be on the bridge watching the destruction of Pandora's Box after all these centuries." Asmodeus chuckled, watching Ifrit and his Jinn drag Magnus away. Ancient's pistol rolled in Asmodeus's hands. He felt the power contained in the weapon and wondered how a lowly lost soul like Magnus had managed to break from the eternal slavery of the great gravitation of the Infernal lament configuration of the Cacophony of Discordance. Pondering the question on the walking towards the bridge left Asmodeus with an uneasy realization that none of the infernal minions escape unless a powerful Tenno wants them to, and that meant there was a conspiracy against the court. Black eyes narrowed, dark thoughts sparked into existence like black holes inside Asmodeus's mind, and he sneered, looking down at the ancient weapon in his hand. Whoever was behind this machination would be discovered, he vowed quietly to himself, walking towards the bridge of the *Jinnestan*.

CHAPTER 47

Music resonated through the open patio door into the penthouse. Jubilation echoed up from the streets below the Original Sins. A cool breeze rippled across the silk sheets covering the bodies on the bed. There were clothes strewn about in small piles across the floor. Nemesis pressed against the hard muscles on Marcus' chest, and his arms squeezed tight around her. They cuddle each other in their arms, staring out the window across the soft night lights of the cityward.

"Well, that was certainly vigorous!" Marcus' words came between rapid breaths in quick rasps. Nemesis ran the tips of her nails across her lover's flesh. She watched the rise and fall of his chest with each rasping breath. Heat emanated from Marcus' skin glistening with droplets of sweat in the soft lights.

"Might be the last time we get a chance to do that," Nemesis warned.

Marcus ran his fingers through Nemesis's hair, stroking her head. She looked at him, trying to force a smile, but it only half came out. Thoughts of the impending battle echoed in the back of her mind no matter how hard she tried to resist. She laid her head on Marcus's chest. The sound of his heartbeat thundered in Nemesis's ears, completing her smile. She kissed the skin softly, leaving small wet lip marks upon the flesh. Hair trailed along the skin, tickling Marcus.

"Are you already ready in the mood for another round, my love?" Marcus just caught his breath. "Or are you just trying to still the anxiety of the coming battle?"

"Does it really matter what the answer is?" Nemesis kissed Marcus, biting his lower lip and wrapping her arms around him. He held Nemesis's face, staring into her beautiful eyes.

"You know it matters quite a bit. I'll make love to you anytime the mood strikes, but this seems less like the desire to make love. There's no way I'm making love to you if you're only doing it to escape dealing with your feelings. We've talked about this before," Marcus explained.

Nemesis pushed off Marcus's chest with a groan. He watched her walk over to the bar to get another drink. Ale glugged from the pitcher filling the glasses to the brim with a head of froth, and some ran down the side of the glass. Nemesis gulped back the drink walking back towards the bed to offer Marcus a glass. Drips of the ale dropped from the bottom of the glass onto the bedsheets.

"I'm not so worried about me to be honest, Marcus. Battle is where I've always felt the most comfortable. There's no time to think, worry, and feel about what is happening. Everything washes away in the flood of battle; all that's left is you and the enemy. You're a good fighter Marcus, but this battle isn't going to be like anything else we've ever been through. There's not going to a place for those who don't want to or can't fight to hide. Our enemies will come at us full bore, and you'll need to help defend *Empyrean station*. My fear is for you," Nemesis lamented.

Silence permeated the room, and Nemesis and Marcus stared into each other's eyes. He ran his fingers across Nemesis's face. Their eyes glinted in the soft light of the room, reflecting their countenances back upon them. Fear reflected back at Nemesis from her own trembling irises. They pulled each other close, locked lips, and held onto each other like this was the last time they'd ever see each other again. Marcus pulled Nemesis from the bed, led her towards the balcony, and pointed down to all the people below celebrating.

"Emperor Solomon made all this possible, but not without you and your sibling's help. Your father may have been a tyrannical asshole, but he did teach you all how to fight. There may not be much of a warrior in me, but many said the same thing about Matthew before all this. Maybe I'm not a warrior like your family is, but I promise I'll do my part to keep this wonder safe,' Marcus vowed. He hugged Nemesis looking down into her eyes and smiled.

Moans echoed from the floor below through the open balcony doors drawing Marcus and Nemesis attention beyond the balcony's railing. They couldn't make out the screams resonating from inside the lower apartment.

She couldn't help but snicker, drawing Marcus's attention. He looked at her with one raised eyebrow. Nemesis couldn't keep the big grin from her face. She looked at Marcus with a giggle.

"I guess A'zyren really did complete her quest," Nemesis joked. She could see the confusion on Marcus's face, but that only made the situation funnier. The sounds of Nemesis's snorts echoed.

"You've got me at a disadvantage," Marcus admitted holding Nemesis tight.

"A'zyren's people have some kind of important quest or something. Whoever the lucky person in the room with her is getting all pleasures her pent-up frustrations can provide. God, I wonder how long her quest took!" Nemesis tugged at Marcus, pulling him back inside. He closed the balcony doors with one hand, kissing Nemesis. Moans from below grew louder, but the balcony's glass doors blocked the sound.

Screams of ecstasy erupted from the room below, fading into silence. Kain struggled to catch his breath. Muscles burned across his body, sinking into the bed. He watched the taught muscles coiling underneath A'zyren's skin. Sweat filled the room with the scent of their mixed musk and beaded along the surface of their skin. Nerves twitched across her body from the blissful echo of the orgasm. Her wide pupils glimmered at Kain pushing off from the bed.

"Well, that was definitely worth it," A'zyren cooed.

Kain trudged through the room, picking up his clothes, putting them on, and headed to his power armor. Metal plates clanged, locking in place around him. The familiar feed of the power armor returned to his mind with the neural synchronization completing. He glanced back to A'zyren with the helmet retracting. She shook her head at him with a smile on her face.

"Oh, really? You're just gonna fuck me and bounce?" A'zyren glared up from the bed.

"I've duties to attend to. Honestly, I'm not the company you want right now." Kain looked back at the bed one last time. He headed towards the door, but A'zyren leaped from the bed, rushed across the room, and blocked the doorway.

"You Solomon's seem to have a monopoly on this whole brooding thing," A'zyren teased.

"It's not like that. I'm sure you've got your own troubles to deal with."

"Trouble is all that exists in the Great Maw Kain, so yeah, I've got my share, but fuck that. Life is far too short to spend all your time worrying about your problems. My tribe believes that death is the most powerful thing in the verse. That is what we choose to worship. I know what De'Vayne forced you to do to Genji's children weighs upon you but come on, Kain, you're going to kill a lot more people before death claims you. I've seen the way you and your family fights. It's like you're all blessed by the hand of death itself, but only Nemesis seems to accept that for the gift it is." A'zyren stated, staring into the cold eyes of Kain.

"Death comes for us all, A'zyren, but I've no love for it. I fight because I have to because my family needs me to, and that's the only reason I'll kill. Nothing in this horrible Great Maw is worth killing for except family." Kain tried to push past A'zyren, but she held firm in his way. Her muscles surged with strength holding the power armor back.

"Are you really this big of a fool?" A'zyren shook her head.

"I'm no fool, but I don't worship death the way your tribe does. What you believe is up to you, and I don't judge you for it. I've merely made my own choices." Kain stepped back, crossing his arms. From the way A'zyren stood, he could tell she didn't intend to let him leave.

"My tribe worships death because of life. We die knowing our bodies will continue to serve the tribe long after our souls have departed the Great Maw. That's why I turned against my own people. They were choosing death over life when the purpose of death is to create room for new life to grow. Genji forgives you because of his beliefs, and that's why h isn't even mad at you for the death of his children. He's merely sad they had to die for such a pointless reason, and I know him well enough that the only grudge he's hiding is against Lord De'Vayne. Maybe one of the deaths fate will put in your path, Lord De'Vayne. Would you truly lament his death?" A'zyren stared at Kain with trembling eyes, and he felt her words piercing his soul, bringing up all the pain he struggled to keep buried.

"It's a noble belief, A'zyren, but not one I can share. Genji's children were exceptional warriors whose deaths served no purpose. I would gladly kill Lord De'Vayne because of it, but that only shows how far his corruption has spread into my soul. Truth be told, I'd rather watch Genji exact revenge for his children, as justice demands." Kain wiped a tear away from his eye.

Quick footsteps carried A'zyren towards Kain to wrap her arms around him. The pain he felt echoed in A'zyren's nerves. She'd seen the power of this grief amongst her own people when they'd see the faces of a loved one after resurrection. The grief sometimes pushed people to madness. She held on tight to Kain, looking up at him with trembling eyes. Fear pumped through both of their veins. He leaned down to kiss her, seeing the echo of his own pain in her eyes.

"Let me get dressed, and we'll see if we can't drink this misery away." A'zyren raced through the room, collecting her garb. She yanked the black clothes over her body. The doors whisked open with Kain standing watching A'zyren getting dressed. He couldn't help watching how her flesh moved and reflected the soft light. They headed out of the room towards the elevator.

Doors whisked open for Kain and A'zyren. She pressed the button for the ground floor. The elevator surged towards the bottom floor. Their eyes darted at each other, but they kept a few feet apart from one another in the elevator. Music rushed into the elevator door, along with the fragrance of alcohol and sweat mixed. Walking down the stairs, they could see the crowd surging across the dance floor. Lord De'Vayne's robes glistened with the moisture soaked into the fabric from the bright lights on the ceiling. Genji and the honor guard stood watching their Lord partying. He waved at Kain and A'zyren, seeing them across the room.

Lady Freya and Lord Hephaestus walked towards the stairway, holding each other. They only stopped when they saw A'zyren and Kain. The group met at the bottom of the stairs. Enlarged pupils in Hephaestus's eyes were the first sign to Kain that his brother was intoxicated. He glanced at Lady Freya's eyes to see the same results, but she looked at Hephaestus the same way A'zyren looked at Kain earlier. He chuckled to himself, patting his brother on the shoulder.

"You look like you're having a good time, brother. Where are you two headed off to?"

"To do what you two just did," Lady Freya giggled, tugging at Hephaestus' arm.

"This little minx is hard to say no to, brother. I imagine you had the same problem with A'zyren, didn't you?" Hephaestus's belly laugh took Kain by surprise.

"I don't know what you're talking about, Heph. Perhaps you've had one too many to drink?"

"You're gonna need that ability to lie. Helena droved on and on about grandchildren since not long after you two departed. Trust me just keep pretending nothing happened between you two despite the fact we can both smell it on you. Maybe you'll luck out, and Helena will believe you and spare you the torture." Lady Freya tugged at Hephaestus's arm, pulling him up the stairs.

The group waved bye to each other. Kain smiled, seeing his brother so happy, and turned to head towards the bar with A'zyren. Lord Oswald, Lord Cornelius, and Lord Hector stood next to Lady Clotho and Helena at the bar. Stacey slid two mugs of ale to Kain and A'zyren as they approached the bar. They grabbed the drinks turning to the rest of the group. Helena' glanced at Kain and A'zyren with a wry smile.

"You two look cozy together," Helena teased.

"Indeed, they do, Helena. Perhaps fate has intentions." Lady Clotho pointed at A'zyren and Kain, looking right at them with dull blind eyes.

"Haven't you had enough enjoyment off torturing your children, Helena. You practically drove Lord Hephaestus and Lady Freya away with your endless prattle about grandchildren. Remember that moments like this are for the young, not us old timers," Lord Oswald informed.

"Like you weren't making a pass at Lady Clotho only a few moments ago," Helena retorted.

"We're practically the same age, Helena. I'm pretty sure we were all just as embarrassed by our parents. Remember when you were trying to catch the attention of the young Gabriel's eyes. Your father embarrassed you so bad you ran out of the hall crying." Lord Oswald sipped his ale.

"I was young and foolish like they are now. That's how children are born. If we were all smart enough to know what would happen, none of us would ever make any mistakes, but we also wouldn't get the chance to learn from our errors. Just because we've got all this wonderful new technology doesn't mean we should stop having new children. Children are the future, after all. Besides, is it so wrong that I want grandchildren?" Helena glanced at Lady Clotho, chuckling.

"Grandchildren are the greatest joy because you can return them."

"You all seem rather chipper for the fact that God only knows what's coming to slaughter us all. Emperor Solomon grows more worried with each passing moment. Perhaps we should return to our duties and prepare before this really is the last part we all attend together," Kain advised.

"That's why I'm so happy. I can't wait to start killing these scum of the Great Maw. Those battle reports from the *Templar* and *Icarus* made me wish I was there. I would have taught those Cacophony bastards how violence is done." Lord Cornelus gulped back his mug, slamming it down on the bar. Stacy was quick to supply a refill to the drink.

"I'm not looking forward to another bout with A'zyren's people myself. Those creatures we faced last time were hard to kill, and from A'zyren's reports, a lot more of them are headed our way. Commander Verdas didn't come tonight because he's reviewing all the information on the W'hyish S'yevel tribes. He's trying to devise a more effective way to combat them here on the station. That man's dedication knows no limits," Lord Hector informed.

"Commander Verdas should have come to me. I could have helped him understand the tribes of my people and the way they fight. There'll be time tomorrow to go over it with him." A'zyren sipped at her drink, leaning against the bar. She glanced to see Kain in deep thought.

The discussion revolved around the impending battle. Helena and Lady Clotho tried to keep the conversation light, but the swirling clouds of trouble hovered over the group, refusing to be banished by levity. Thoughts of the battle echoed in Kain's mind. Even the alcohol in the ale did little to push away the growing anxiety. He gulped back at the drink listening to the conversation. Battle lingered on everyone's mind.

The crowd danced away to the sound of the music. Kain glanced across the room, seeing all the intoxicated revelers. Anxiety sparked in his mind seeing the way everyone celebrated. He realized this wasn't a celebration but a fight against the dying of the light. Everyone drank, danced, and partied, trying to force the future from arriving. He could see it in the widened pupils and heard the sound echoing in the clamor of the crowd.

CHAPTER 48

Almost no noise echoed within the audience chamber of the Infinity Nexus. Only the occasional soft snoring emanated from Lady Marimba, sleeping next to the glass. The structure of the new senate chamber of the empire was half completed. Materials scattered the room in small piles around the unfinished work. Ships floated around *Empyrean station*, waves of fighters patrolled the sector, and sparks flashed across the void painted in the weaving lights.

Lights flickered in rapid flashes emanating from the holographic emitters on the ceiling. A.S.A. floated in space, constructing the mobile defense turrets and minefield. Matthew didn't pay any attention to the flicking lights across the sector. He stared into the unraveling weave of time. Arachne ships, W'Hyish S'yevel, and serpentine ships surged towards *Empyrean station* from across the Great Maw. Sensors erupted on the stellar map locking on enemy energy signatures.

Sensors deluged the station mainframe with information on the enemy force. Alarms blared through the entire station. Lady Marimba roused from her sleep from the repetitive blaring noises. She ran a hand through the mess of her locks of hair squinting at the holographic image. Red alerts flashed across the stellar map isolating each of the incoming ships. She pulled her clothes back on with haste glancing back to Matthew to see Virgil flashing next to him.

"Enemy forces will arrive in twelve hours, twenty-six minutes, and thirty-seven seconds. I'm calculating probabilities for military victory." Virgil fell silent, processing the information. His image flickered under the strain of processing power. Lady Marimba looked to Emperor Solomon.

"It seems the time for peace has ended, my lady. I would recommend you head to the *Titus Andronicus* to prepare for battle. You'll be needed out there," Mathew informed.

"Emperor, surely I would serve you better guarding the Infinity Nexus."

"Commander Verdas shall provide that service. Your combat expertise is needed to defend the station." Matthew smiled at Lady Marimba, saluting him. She kissed the glass, leaving a smear of her lips upon the surface and marched from the Infinity Nexus toward the doors. Doors whisked back for Imperator Kain entering the room with Nemesis and Marcus following behind.

Lady Marimba strutted past the group and felt the glaring eyes upon her back of Nemesis. She felt the tug of Marcus at her arm before turning back to the Infinity Nexus. Lord Cornelius, Lord Hector, Lord Hephaestus, and Lady Freya followed behind the group, with Helena and Lady Clotho in the center. A'zyren walked alongside Mordecai with Lord Genji, the honor guard, and Lord De'Vayne behind them. The sound of alarm began to fade.

"Emperor, what are your orders?" Kain fell to one knee before Matthew.

"Our enemy will arrive soon in overwhelming numbers. Arachne warships, W'hyish S'yevel worldships, and serpentine armada are converging towards us. A.S.A. defense systems aren't fully operational yet. We will need to provide cover while the rest of the defense systems are brought online. Time is in short supply; we must finish the preparation with all haste and prepare for the arrival of the enemy forces. Imperator, you'll take the *Dawnbreaker* to the edge of the system to provide cover for Mordecai and the A.S.A. to finish their minefield," Matthew explained.

"The minefield should be operated within the specified time. Cloaking devices in the mines are slowing the progress. If your troops could assist with the construction, it'd go faster, Imperator." Mordecai glanced to see Kain nodding in agreement. He was already sending orders to his ship using the neural network. Transports ships appeared on the stellar map painted above the group with weaving lights.

Neural network buzzed with the orders between the A.S.A. and Kain's troops. Information on the holographic image updated the movement of troops. Calculations adjusted in the mainframe with the updated information. Time showed the arrival of the enemy fleet would be close to the completion of the minefield. Matthew glanced at the other lords and ladies.

"The *Divine Retribution, Templar, Icarus, Olympus,* and *Brisingamen* will hold the center of the sector to intercept any enemy ships that manage to penetrate the minefield. I've already sent Lady Marimba to command her *Titus Andronicus,* and she'll create a final line of defense. Lord Oswald will bring his new battleforge the *Victory,* joined with Lord Cornelius' *Sentinel,* and Lord Hector's *Iliad.* The final construction phase has begun on the titan class defense fortress and the *Divius Oculus.* Our goal will be threefold. First, we must protect the *Empyrean station* at all costs. Second, we must protect the *Divius Oculus* defending the star until its completion, and third, we must prevent the enemy from overrunning the Infinity Nexus. Imperator Kain, I hereby place my authority in you as allied supreme commander and leave the rest to you." Matthew sat down.

Kain marched up to the front of the Infinity Nexus. There was a throb in the area of energy that drew his attention. He glanced to see Lady Marimba's lip marks on the glass. Doors whisked opened, Commander Verdas stormed towards the Infinity Nexus, and bowed before the Imperator and Emperor. Everyone looked upon Commander Verdas as he rose to address the group.

"Apologies, for my late arrival, but construction of the *Azure Dreams* is underway. The new titan class will take longer to build, and would be limited in a battle, so we've focused work efforts on the genetic laboratory facilities. The ship might not be capable of defending itself, but her hangers and labs will supply steady reinforcements. My geneseed army has begun landing in preparation for the station's defense." Commander Verdas stepped back to join the others.

"Excellent news, Commander Verdas, and you'll be in primary control of the defenses of *Empyrean station*. Lord Drumpf will ensure the bunkers are stocked, the people are safe, and Lord Whelsey's troops will defend Lord Galen's medics. In space, we've got no way of knowing what's coming against us. A'zyren has provided intelligence on her tribes, the Arachne and the serpentine ships, but it's limited. Lord De'Vayne has filled in some holes for us though it's still pretty murky. One thing we do know is our enemy outnumbers us by a vast margin. They're not going to sit back. They'll bring the fight to us. The key to success will be getting that minefield up and filling it with juicy enough bait to make our enemies rush in before thinking." Kain uploaded his tactical plans to the neural network. Lights whizzed in the air altering the stellar map.

The battlefield altered, showing the ring of cloaked mines on the outskirts of the sector. Imperial fighters dotted throughout the minefield in sweeping patrols. Numbers showed tens of thousands of fighters circling through the cloaked mines in a patrolling vector. Enemy forces appeared on the map in rapid series of red blinks surging on the outer room. Kain paused the battleplan glancing at the faces of everyone to gauge their reaction. Mordecai raised his hand.

"Is there perhaps a way to not sacrifice all those fighters yet ensure the enemy presses into the minefield?" Mordecai looked to the others in the group. Silence permeated the room.

"If you've got a better idea, I'm willing to listen." Kain crossed his arms.

"Virgil, we could use the holographic emitters. A slight modification to the turret's shield projectors would allow us to project the real appearance of ships inside the minefield. They'd be illusions and not set off the mines. This way, we'd avoid loss of life, maximize odds of victory, and fulfill our primary directives." Mordecai uploaded his designs for the modifications.

Light flickered under the strain of processing power. Computation calculated the odds of success of the plan. Percentages shifted on the image but stayed in the low double digits. Lord De'Vayne erupted in a hideous chuckle drawing attention to him. He straightened his robes, trying to compose himself before addressing the group.

"Your technology is fascinating, yet I fear the Ancients always did lack my sophisticated understanding of the power of deception. These pitiful holographic emitters can only create artificial light. My people know how to create real constructs out of nothing. We'll take care of this, but I find it funny the A.S.A. didn't consider the simplest solution. Use combat algorithms to control the fighter craft so no living being needs to be sacrificed. Bioreading's are easily faked even with the primitive technology of the A.S.A. being used." Lord De'Vayne motioned for Lord Genji.

"How may I serve you, my lord?" Lord Genji bowed solemnly with his hand on the hilt.

"Go and begin these modifications. Set up the *Mirror of Solace* to coordinate the illusionary forces. I'll join you shortly." Lord De'Vayne shooed Lord Genji away with the wag of a hand. He bowed to Lord De'Vayne before leaving.

"I'm not certain your technology will work, and everything in our strategy depends upon this ruse. Would you be willing to share the technological knowledge on how this will work so we can be certain it will?" Kain locked eyes with Lord De'Vayne.

"Oh, Imperator, my word is my bond, and I've already proven that to you. I promise my illusions will work. We've used it many times against even the Cacophony of Discordance and other many other enemies in the Great Maw. It seems they have a natural ability to sense energy, yet they still fall for our ploys. Unfortunately, I'll need to be protected for this to work. The *Mirror of Solace* will take position near the *Empyrean station* by the shipyards. That position offers maximum protection from arcs of fire." Lord De'Vayne adjusted the stellar map to show the change in his ship's location, and the image updated accordingly on the holographic display.

"Guess we don't have much choice but to trust you, Lord De'Vayne," Kain glared.

A'zyren studied the map rubbing her stomach. She felt a bit queasy seeing the location of Lord De'Vayne's ship. There was something that didn't sit right with her. She studied the stellar map looking at the precise location of the *Mirror of Solace*. The firing arcs from that position allowed the ship to target key infrastructure on *Empyrean station*, the shipyards, and *the Divius Oculus*. She felt a rumbling in her stomach and gritted her teeth, causing her jowls to jut outwards.

"I'll provide cover and defense for your ship Lord De'Vayne from the *Sesh'yna*. We'll keep you safe from the enemy." A'zyren winked at Kain.

"If necessary, can your troops help fortify the station?" Kain glanced at A'zyren.

"Any call for reinforcement will be answered. Though you may not like how my troops arrive, if you remember. We don't have a lot of shuttles. Remember, everyone, that the W'hyish S'yevel ships rely on rush tactics. We don't carry all the fighter crafts and transports you do. Once the trap is sprung, engage with the worldships fast as possible. Arachne ships will try to entrap, crush, and tear your ships apart in their mechanical arms, but the serpentine will also be a problem. They'll adapt to whatever we throw at them, but likely they'll choose to stay back and fire at a distance. If we can take the serpentine out, we should," A'zyren explained.

Lights weaved the map updating the projected enemy movements. Flashes erupted in the circle showing the detonation of the minefield. The image froze, showing the scattered remains of the enemy fields. Most of the enemy fleet remained on the stellar map. Kain pointed to the second ring of ships led by the *Divine Retribution*.

"Once the enemy has sprung the trap, I'll engage the largest target in the enemy fleet with the *Dawnbreaker*. Nemesis, you'll lead your forces outward from the center to engage whatever enemy ships break through the minefield. The final defense line moves halfway between their original position and the central ring to get within weapons range. You'll create a screen of overlapping point defense weapon fire should anything make it through. Grand Admiral Celeris controls fighter operations, and Consul Joshua will coordinate between the defensive lines. At this point, the battle becomes one of attrition. If we've done our jobs right, the enemy will have already suffered enormous casualties. All we'll have to do is keep each other safe, take opportunities, and make the enemy suffer until the right moment presents itself," Kain informed.

"How will we know the right moment?" Lord Cornelius glanced around.

"The same way you know when to drive your blade into the enemy. Your enemy tells you where they're weak and where they are strong." Lord Hector patted his friend on the back with a smile. Lord Cornelius nodded.

"You guys know how this is. This is a fight for our lives. It's going to be pure chaos. Watch each other's backs. Commander Verdas, if Marcus isn't in the exact condition, he's in now when I return, I'm going to hold you personally responsible." Nemesis glared at Commander Verdas.

"Dear, that is hardly becoming behavior of a lady," Helena chided.

"Fuck being a lady. You're a lady, staying here, hiding with the other ladies. Us real women are going to go kill some shit. Isn't that right, Lady Freya?" Nemesis glanced at Lady Freya.

"It seems I'm fond of your madness because I can't disagree," Freya chuckled.

"Each child has their own path, dear. Your daughter must walk hers and walk it well she does. Your children prepare to go to battle to defend us all. That deserves our respect regardless of anything else." Lady Clotho patted Helena on the back. Trying to calm her down.

"We've no time for this stupidity. You know your orders. Now see your duty done, and if we're lucky, we'll all see each other again once this battle is over." Kain watched the group salute him and Emperor Solomon before marching away. The image of the battle plan crackled overhead. He glanced back to see the sweat beading on Matthew's head.

They locked eyes in empathy. At this moment, the brothers were absolute equals. Neither of the brothers knew how this battle would turn out. Kain pressed his hand to the glass. He glanced down at the lip marks on the glass, drawing Matthew's attention.

"If we survive this, I'm expecting to hear the story behind that," Kain teased.

"You're longing to hear the story of my life trapped in a jar? It's Lady Marimba's lip marks. She came to entertain me while everyone else was celebrating. She may have an infatuation." Matthew shook his head, looking into his brother's eyes.

"She is a beautiful woman Matthew, but a bit crazy. I was just curious about you, is all. Besides, you deserve a little fun in your life as well. I took your advice and attended the party." Kain reminisced about his time with A'zyren drifting off into a daze for a moment.

"A'zyren is a good fit for you, brother, provided we survive all this. Don't worry. I'll be watching over your shoulder this battle. We'll be together through this ordeal. Stay safe, Kain, and don't do anything stupid." Matthew's eyes trembled at his brother.

"Listen to you telling me not to do anything stupid," Kain laughed, walking away.

Matthew fell back into his chair, staring into the rippling weave of time. Abyss howled the end of everything beyond this battle, but he focused on the battle itself. The battle warped through the flow of time back and forth. He looked at every detail, trying to scour for anything he could use to tip the odds in his favour. The blur of combat echoed in the weave of time, rippling away from his mind. He tried to seize upon the moments that would have the greatest effect.

The echo of Kain's footsteps drew Matthew's eyes to him. Time rippled away from Kain, revealing the truth that his decisions would alter the flow of battle itself. Everything hung on his decisions, and all Matthew could do was quiet his mind to strengthen his psychic connection to his brother.

CHAPTER 49

Fighter craft swept through the minefield. A.S.A. floated in the Great Maw, working on the mines in the heat of the new star, Eos. Viewscreen panned across the sector showing the status of the defensive preparations. Reports rushed into the tactical computer on the arm of the chair. Imperator Kain stared at the viewscreen, watching the work. Chief Corrigan worked on the engineering systems linking the *Dawnbreaker* with the defense network around *Empyrean station*. Progress reports from the A.S.A. showed the status of the work on the mines. Time ticked away on the progress meter contrasted against the enemy fleet's arrival time. Kain could see they were cutting time short with the minefield. Sparks flashed across the void of space.

Sensors warbled with the flow of data showing the incoming enemy fleets. Lt. Kazakova updated the sensor network with new targeting algorithms for the defense platforms. Com channels surged with the traffic from all the ships, fighters, and platforms connected to the *Empyrean station* defense network. *Dawnbreaker* patrolled the inner ring of the minefield; Sgt. Grey adjusted the heading of the ship and updated the defense network on the new flight path.

"What's the status on the completion of the minefield?" Kain established a connection to Mordecai. Visual link to the A.S.A. established on the viewscreen.

"We're finishing up work on the last few mines now. Minefield should be ready in the next few minutes provided there aren't any unforeseeable setbacks." Mordecai floated towards the next mine in the sequence. He glanced back to see the *Dawnbreaker* looming toward him. Defense network subroutines surged in his mind, linking the ship's nanites to him.

The grey cloud of nanites washed across the field of mines surging from the *Dawnbreaker*. Nanites seeped into the tiniest cracks in the mines. Data from the tiny machines filled Mordecai's mind leeching the instructions from his databanks. Mines activated across the network. Mordecai and the A.S.A. began thrusting back towards the *Mechanarium of Gyros*. Comms warbled with Lt. Kazakova accessing the message.

"Grand Admiral Celeris and Consul Joshua are on coms," Lt. Kazakova reported.

The viewscreen crackled, switching to the images of Celeris and Joshua on the bridges of their ships. Their lips were moving on the screen, but no sound came out. Communications flickered with the surge of traffic in the defense network. Lt. Kazakova tapped a few buttons, adjusted the communication settings, and broke the communications from the main defense network. She focused efforts on optimizing the network before the enemy arrived.

"Coms are clear now, Imperator. Sorry for the inconvenience, but the com traffic is insane right now. I imagine it'll get worse when the enemy arrives, so I guess this will be a really good stress test." Lt. Kazakova reported working away on the communications.

"Your communication officer is doing a better job than mine. All the communication traffic is playing havoc with the *Icarus's* com systems. My new communications officer Sgt. Shirow is doing her best, but she's still new to all this. We're experiencing lag with the defense network and cannot get any updates on the completion of the defense systems. What's the status of the minefield?" Celeris uploaded the last reports on the defense systems to the *Dawnbreaker*. She watched the blur of activity on the bridge. Chief Corrigan brought the information on the engineering screen in the background.

Officers worked together to solve the problem. The problem in the code leaped out to Chief Corrigan. He uploaded the data to Lt. Kazakova to make the final communication protocol adjustments and double-check the work. She glanced through the modifications, made a small correction to a line of code, and uploaded the protocols to the *Icarus*. Grand Admiral Celeris smiled on the screen seeing the data pouring from the defense network.

"Your people are impressive, brother. I guess I should have put more effort into studying communication protocols. There are some small discrepancies in the network," Celeris reported.

"My people are clearing those up. We're re-writing the entire base code of the network right now. There's been significant data degradation across the millennia since the network was last used. The entire system is pure chaos. Hell, I'm surprised it's even functioning at all, but Virgil must be keeping it online. That explains all the small glitches in the holographic emitters on the *Empyrean station*. We're bleeding processing power as the network errors create a deluge of flash reports, corrupted data, and program crashes. Fuck this is going to take longer than I thought." Consul Joshua gritted his teeth, smashing keys on the tactical computer.

Flickers appeared across the minefield. Each of the mines surged with energy, blurred, and vanished from the sensors. Only the defense network showed the location of the mines in the sector. Communications buzzed on the screen. Lt. Kazakova glanced to Imperator Kain.

"There's an incoming message from the *Mirror of Solace*." Lt. Kazakova routed the message through, seeing Kain motion to the screen. The screen divided into three segments. Lord De'Vayne appeared on in his black and silver robes, leaning into his silver captain's chair. A servant handed him a glass he took to sip at. His eyes darted toward the Imperator.

"We're ready to begin the distortion effect. Sensors will experience some interference, but it'll clear in a moment." Lord De'Vayne motioned to his troops to activate the light matrix. Sensors surged with the energy emanating from the *Mirror of Solace*. Light swirled together in the minefield creating duplicate images of the *Dawnbreaker*, *Icarus*, and *Templar* inside the minefield.

"Damn, that's impressive," Joshua complimented, watching the data on the sensors.

"Sensors show the ships as real. I can't tell the difference from the scans on the ships." Kain studied the work uploaded to his tactical console by Lt. Kazakova.

"This is bloody brilliant technology Lord De'Vayne," Celeris praised.

Energy surged on the sensors. Flashes of light erupted on the edge of the sector. Worldships lurched to a halt leaping from F.T.L. speed into the sector. On the stellar map, sensors showed over a hundred of the W'hyish

S'yevel ships lined together at eleven o'clock. Arachne ships appeared in a cluster of twenty-six ships on the six o'clock facing. Fighter craft altered course on the stellar map retreating from the minefield. Worldships lurched towards the *Dawnbreaker*. Alarms blared on the bridge warning of weapons locks established on the ship. Dozens of the enemy ships were targeting the *Dawnbreaker*. Kain tapped the tactical computer switching his communication to the entire armada around *Empyrean station*.

"This is Imperator Kain to all combat forces around the *Empyrean station*. Operation Marathon is a go. All ships move into position. Grand Admiral Celeris, begin coordinating fighter operations, Consul Joshua, continue working the code to help with processing power and have your ships prepare to intercept the first wave of troop pods when they fire. All ships shields to full frontal arc facing, full power to weapons, lock firing solutions on the nearest targets of opportunity, and wait for my command," Kain ordered.

"Affirmative Imperator, the *Icarus* is on holding position, and orders are begin transmitted. We'll await orders." Celeris vanished from the viewscreen.

"I'll do what I can, Imperator, but don't expect any miracles under combat conditions. Looks like we're in for another fun bout of what can possibly go wrong. I'll see you on the other side. One way or another," Joshua declared. He and Lord De'Vayne faded from the viewscreen.

Worldships gathered in formation across the void reappeared. Kain leaned back into the captain's chair, staring at the fleet beyond. He gripped the armrest tight with both hands. Sweat beaded upon his brow, watching the enemy worldships moving towards the minefield. Arachne and serpentine fleets were holding position on the edge of the system. Sensors showed the active scans from those ships across the entire sector, but some were focused on the minefield.

Sweat raced down Kain's cheek staring at the viewscreen. The front line of the worldships surged towards the minefield. Explosions erupted from the first mine detonation. A series of bright flashes erupted across the minefield sending metal shards flying through space. Massive holes tore through the hull of the worldships from the explosion, venting atmosphere into space. Bodies hurled through the vacuum of the void caught in the series of explosions. Reactors went critical on several of the worldships.

Successive explosions erupted within the field of explosions and inside the fleet formation. Blasts waves rippled across the viewscreen in the distance.

Energy weapons fire lanced from the worldships into the minefield. Bright flashes of energy overlapped in the field of fire, converging in the minefield. Explosions erupted from the mines. Wreckage of worldships drifted through the mine field, being scattered through and detonating more explosions. Metal chunks slammed off the worldships driving through the clearing in the minefield. Arachne and serpentine ships opened fire on the cloaked mines.

Fighter craft darted into the minefield driving past the mines and racing towards the worldships. Chunks of metal, body parts, and crimson drops bounced off the cockpits of the fighters. Defense network plotted course using Celeris' mind to drive the calculations. Data streamed to the pilot's navigation. Squadrons broke from each other, darting through the empty ruined corridors, the wreckage blasting towards the fighter craft.

"Sgt. Grey, take us in. Chief Corrigan, open fire once we're in range. Set point defense weapons to prioritize incoming kinetic rounds over fighter craft. Get internal defense mobilized to prepare to defend critical junctions in case the enemy attempts to board." Kain leaned forward in his chair studying the enemy ships in the distance.

"Aye Imperator," Chief Corrigan replied. Sgt. Grey smiled, pushing the throttle forward.

Dawnbreaker engines flared in a bright flash. Beams lanced from the turrets line the hull. Sensors showed the frontline worldships opening fire with their kinetic batteries. Large rounds carried the W'hyish S'yevel troops hurtling toward the ship. Point defense weapons darted, shooting down the incoming projectiles. Fighter craft opened fire at the incoming projectiles. Despite the surge of fire in the area, dozens of the projectiles slammed into the *Dawnbreaker*.

Alarms blared on the bridge, and the tactical computer showed the hull breaches to Kain. Reports flooded the ship's subnetwork with reports. Troops held the enemy forces at bay, but more kinetic rounds were fired from the worldships. Casualties started pouring through the medical reports showing the fierce fighting between Kain's troops and the W'hyish S'yevel. His mind darted through the local net to see the fighting. His troops held the ground against the surging martyrs charging from the transports.

Blackened blood coated the hallway. He could sense the thoughts of all the troops fight all across the ship and all the hearts beating to defeat the enemy.

Troops flailed through the air, but for every one that fell, another took their place. Medics tended to the back wounded behind the backlines. Reinforcements thundered through the ship with their minds focused on joining the fray. A smile crept upon Kain that he didn't even realize, staring at the battle on the viewscreen. His heart thumped in steady beats. The enemy would pay in blood for every inch they took.

"Keep holding the line, troops. Reinforcements are on the way." Kain's orders echoed across the local subnet to each of his troopers. He felt the surge in moral from his message.

Arachne and Serpentine ships launched fighter craft, making slow progress through the minefield. Explosions erupted in the outer ring of the sector defenses. Several frontline worldships converged on the *Dawnbreaker*, but the rest of the W'hyish S'yevel fleet diverged and forced their way through the minefield. The armada expanded into wedge formation, surging through the minefield. Enemy fighters rush towards the inner defense ring targeting the defense platforms.

Kain magnified the viewscreen on the Arachne ships lingering at the back. These smaller vessels extended the long mechanical limbs off their ships, moving in strange patterns. Sensors didn't show any abnormalities in that region of space. He kept the viewscreen on the situation but attended to the rest of the battle. Fighter craft swarmed in the center ring. Beams of energy, kinetic rounds, and fighter crafted flung in every direction.

The first wave of worldships broke through the minefield. The enemy ships emerged from the explosion revealing the damage they suffered from the mines. Giant holes scattered across the hulls of the frontline ships venting atmosphere in the Great Maw. Damage stripped many of the turrets from the hull of the worldships, but intermittent fire blasted from the remaining kinetic cannons. Point defense weapons struggled to adjust to the decreasing range reducing calculation times. Kinetic rounds burrowed into the *Dawnbreaker* like ticks.

"Sound the alarm that we're being boarded," Kain ordered, staring at the viewscreen.

Tactical alerts flashed on the captain's armrest console. With a glance, Kain could see areas of his ship's hull flashing in his peripheral vision, but he remained focused on expanding battlefield on the viewscreen. His mind rushed making calculations, sensors showed the advancing enemy ships, and the detonations of mines flashed across the battlefield. Chatter across the defensive network echoed in the back of his mind. For a moment, he froze, just staring at the sheer force rallied against them, and in the quiet recesses of his mind, wondered how they could win.

Fear trembled through Kain's body, his eyes dilated, and his mouth went dry. He couldn't hear the voices of his command crew reporting all around him. The tactical computer beeped rapidly, flooded by battle scans, combat reports, and alarms. There didn't seem to be any hope, he thought, but his eyes narrowed as reality rushed back to him.

CHAPTER 50

Kinetic rounds exploded in steady salvos from the worldships rushing across the void towards the *Dawnbreaker*. Fighter craft squadrons swarmed through the outer ring, dodging, weaving, and darting through the minefield, incoming weapons fire and blast waves rippling from behind. Bleeps on the stellar map showed the surge of tens of thousands of fighter craft on the outer rim of the sector. Kain gripped a hold of the arm of the captain's chair. Worldships splintered in the wedge formation, surging around the *Dawnbreaker*.

Rounds soared through the void. Most of the rounds were cut apart by success beams flashing through space. Point defense turrets swiveled, fired short bursts of energy weapons, and adjusted to new targets. Kinetic rounds thudded against the hull of the *Dawnbreaker*, mechanical clamps locking down to puncture the metal, and the drill bit tips sparked, striking against the metal. Alerts flashed on the tactical computer at each breach point along the hull. Fighter craft swept along the hull, blasting the transport rounds to free them. Bodies of W'hyish S'yevel floated through the void bouncing off the hull of the sweeping fighters.

Worldships splintered off the bow of the *Dawnbreaker* converge to flank it on both sides. Tractor beams launched from the worldships on the right flank. The entire ship shuddered until the gravitational force of the tractor beam. Enemy ships revered engines, continued firing broadsides salvos, and attempted to drag the *Dawnbreaker* into the undetonated cloaked mines. Tactical computer showed the shields were holding strong against the enemy weapon fire, but kinetic rounds whizzed right past the shields like they weren't even active. Sweat raced down Kain's cheek, glancing around the bridge. He motioned to the ships with the tractor beams on the right flank of the screen.

"Chief Corrigan don't let the enemy surround us. Focus fire on the most damaged worldships. Bring those down first. Create some breathing room for us out here." Kain motioned to the damaged worldship sweeping to the right flank of the ship. Turrets darted on the hull, targets locked, and energy weapons fired rapid successive beams.

"Imperator, sensors detect strange energy signatures from the enemy kinetic rounds. The readings are similar to the reverie shield readings Grand Admiral Celeris and Consul Joshua recorded in their earlier encounter. Chief, you think you can run a high-level analysis of these readings to figure out their source?" Lt. Kazakova uploaded the information to the engineering console. Data flashed across the screen.

Chief Corrigan darted back and forth, doing multiple tasks at once. He managed to target the weakest worldships. Energy weapons were unloading upon the target as he began the analysis of the energy readings. Waves of fighters and kinetic rounders surged toward the ship. He updated the parameters of the point defense system, adjusting targets. Successive explosions rippled across the viewscreen, sending shards of metal, body parts, and debris scattering in every direction.

"Lt. Grey, do whatever it takes to shake these tractor beams before we end up in our own minefield," Kain ordered. He gripped the arms of his captain's chair. The entire ship began to shudder. Lt. Grey tapped away on the keys of the pilot console. Engineering systems blared a warning from the reactor drawing extra energy from the applied effect of Lt. Grey's alterations, and systems reported the colossal surge in energy from the reactor. Chief Corrigan's hands darted across the engineering panel, the reaction expanded in the reactor, and energy dumped directly into engines.

"What the fuck are you doing, Lt. Grey. The zero-point reactor can't take this kind of stress. Your adjustment to creating the Casimir effect is pushing the engine into critical. Heat levels are spiking across the entire reactor. We can't maintain this kind of power output without causing the reactor to go critical," Chief Corrigan explained.

"Don't worry about it, Chief. If I can't break us free of these tractor beams, we're going to blow up in our mines long before that reactor goes critical, and if my plan works, we won't need the extra output long." Lt. Grey struggled against the gravitational fields of the tractor beams encapsulating the ship. Engines alarms warned of temperatures exceeding safety limits. He overrode the safeties with a few button presses and pushed the engines past one hundred percent.

Worldships on the left flank locked tractor beams on the *Dawnbreaker*. Fighter craft swarmed the worldships as energy beams tore through the damaged ships. Enemy armada pushed through the gap of the minefield, surging past the defenders towards the inner ring. The chaos of battle darted across the viewscreen in every direction around the *Dawnbreaker*. Fighter craft streaked across the viewscreen engaged in close combat with W'hyish S'yevel ships.

Missiles chased after fighter craft ducking, dodging, and diving through the chaos of the dogfight around the *Dawnbreaker*. Inertia in the ship forced dampeners to compensate, but the entire ship careened under the engines' thrust. Enemy worldships erupted across the viewscreen as turrets unleashed sequential energy blasts. Gravitational field on the *Dawnbreaker* began to collapse under the power of the engines. Tractor beams flittered across the viewscreen, failing under the explosions of their worldship rippling across the outer rim of defenses. Blast waves triggered some cloaked mines on the outer ring defenses to erupt in sequential explosions.

"Arachne ships are breaking through the minefield Imperator. Sensors show they're headed straight towards us." Lt. Kazakova isolated the systems targeting the Dawnbreaker on the sensors so the Imperator could find them quicker on the stellar map.

"I see them, Lt., but we've got more pressing concerns to deal with." Kain adjusted the orders of his fighter craft. Waves of bombers soared from the hanger bay. Reports echoed across the subnet and flashed on the tactical computer logs. Missiles darted in waves from the bombers soaring across the hull of the *Dawnbreaker* towards the enemy worldships. The illusionary fleet the *Mirror of Solace* created was moving to join the fray.

Kain didn't pay the holographic images much attention until the energy beam salvos fired by the duplicate of his ship tore through a worldship. Sensors warbled, locking onto the energy signatures. Energy readings were similar to hard light weapon systems, but there was something more advanced to the readings. He uploaded the data through the *Empyrean station* defense network to his brother Hephaestus. Matthew's voice echoed in the back of Kain's mind. It seemed so close and real that he glanced back behind him instinctively. Lt. Grey continued her sensor scans of the illusionary ships, but her attention was torn between the holograms doing real damage and the strange readings building up around the mechanical claws of the smaller Arachne ships. Energy readings showed gravitational power readings at the tips of eight darting mechanical limbs.

"There's just too much going on, Imperator," Lt. Grey admitted. Sweat dripped down her brow into her eyes. She wiped it away with a hand, but more drops beaded along her hairline.

"Don't panic, Lt. Grey. Focus on those Arachne ships headed towards us. Get Lord De'Vayne on coms for me. I'll get answers to this." Kain pushed himself from the chair.

Viewscreen crackled with Lord De'Vayne's image appearing on the screen. He leaned back into his captain's chair with a relaxed countenance sipping from his chalice. Sensors showed the distortion around the holographic ships as they reappeared closer to the *Dawnbreaker* to provide a defense. Kain stomped towards the viewscreen, shaking his head. He pointed to the battle.

"Lord De'Vayne, how are your holograms doing actual damage to the enemies?"

"Holograms, you say. Pah! My technology far exceeds the Ancient's limited ideas of holograms." Lord De'Vayne laughed, shaking his head at the Imperator. Most of his crew on the bridge joined in, bringing the rapturous cackle to roar across the communication channel.

"We could have used this technology to help with the defenses. A.S.A. and *Empyrean station* nanite forges could have replicated your systems. Why wouldn't you tell us this before?"

"I did explain I could create real constructs, not artificial holograms," Lord De'Vayne retorted. "Hardly my fault your primitive brains couldn't understand."

"Peel those worldships with the tractor beams off us. We'll discuss the whole teamwork concept later, should we survive. Allies don't keep secrets from each other, and especially not knowledge that could've helped us with this entire battle." Kain uploaded the target information to the

Mirror of Solace. The constructs adjusted course on the stellar map towards his selected targets.

"No one who shares their secrets lives long in the Great Maw. Don't worry, Imperator, I'll continue to provide defense and ensure you live through this battle. I'm deeply curious about the things you'll accomplish with your thirst for blood." Lord De'Vayne cut the communications. Viewscreen crackled back to the chaos of battle.

Kinetic shells stuck from the hull of the *Dawnbreaker* like tiny little thorns cleaved into the metal. Troops reports grew more hectic under the surge of W'hyish S'yevel troops flooding into the ship. Casualties streamed in faster than Kain could even attend to. They logged somewhere in the back of his mind in the neural link to his ship's subnetwork. Portions of the ship locked down, isolating the advancing enemy through the corridors. He tapped a few buttons on the tactical computer to access the engineering systems. Troopers were trying to activate emergency systems to use as last lines of defense. He activated the emergency venting in the areas of the ship he could.

Bodies blew into space along the hull of the *Dawnbreaker*. Kain didn't have to worry about his troops fighting in no gravity or even the vacuum of space. Power armor would protect his children, and where it failed, their deaths would be avenged by their siblings. Soldiers battled throughout the ship, trying to hold the flood of W'hyish S'yevel. Black and crimson blood pooled on the deck, plating beneath the battling forces. Severed limbs, debris, and fallen bodies scattered across the battlefield inside the ship's various corridors. Every battle looked similar in the subnetwork. He scanned through the ongoing battles sensing the thoughts of his troops. There wasn't any sign of hesitation or urge to fall back, but one singular will. Each soldier's heart thundered, beating to kill their enemies and hammering in vainglorious defiance of death.

"For the Empire!" Troopers screamed, charging to battle. Energy blades cleaved through W'hyish S'yevel troops. Chittering echoed in the halls mixing with the screeches of the falling predatorial avians gunned down by surges of energy fire from the back row of the troops. Bodies rained down upon the advancing formation of enemies. Middle of the formation poured weapons fire towards the front ranks being cleaved by the front line of imperial troops. Abominations known as martyrs stomped through the line of troops, but coordinated front-line fighters stopped the creatures in their tracks. Troops worked in small groups to fell the foul martyrs, severing legs, arms, and heads. Kain's mind sent reports of all the weaknesses he saw in the enemy formation through the subnet. The entire bridge shuddered tearing his mind from the subnet, and his eyes fell upon the viewscreen.

Worldships on the left flank surged around the *Dawnbreaker* launching tractor beams. Gravitation forces from the left flank stabilized the faltering field. Lt. Grey pushed the engines towards one hundred twenty percent fighting back against the gravitational field. The entire ship shuddered under the combatting forces. Conduits erupted behind the walls along the bridge, showering the crew with sparks. Smoke poured from through the gaping holes collecting along the bridge's ceiling. Troops rushed across the bridge to extinguish the fires started. Kain glanced back to see the crew struggling to return to their stations. Some of the crew pushed off the ground, other people were pulled to their feet by the troops, and medics were tending to others. He returned to his chair to take his seat, glancing at the tactical computer.

Fighter craft surged across the *Dawnbreaker,* darting over the hull, chasing each other in dogfights. Kain adjusted the orders to his sister through the *Empyrean station* defense network. Grand Admiral Celeris updated orders to her fighter craft too assist the *Dawnbreaker*. Sensors showed the movement of *Icarus*'s attack for swinging to attack the worldships on the left. Cloaked mines loomed on the stellar map growing closer to the *Dawnbreaker*.

"We've got to take out those worldships holding us in place," Kain commanded.

A surge of blasts erupted from the *Dawnbreaker,* ripping through the worldships on the right flank and crumbling their lines. Energy flickered from the failing tractor beams caught in the explosions of their ships. The left flank worldships turned on the *Dawnbreaker* driving it towards the minefield. Bombers doubled back in a wide arch towards the left flank worldships. Swarms of missiles lanced across the viewscreen, darting towards the enemy ships. Explosions erupted from enemy fighters shooting down the missiles, but another wave surged from the bombers.

Turret platforms in the inner ring of defense opened fire on the approaching fleet of worldships surging past the *Dawnbreaker*. *Icarus* and *Templar* followed the *Divine Retribution* from the defensive formation of the *Brisingamen, Olympus, Iliad,* and *Sentinel.* The ships hung back, forming the interior defense in front of the last line of *Empyrean station.* Weapons fire erupted from the *Mechanarium of Gyros.* Blurring beams of gravitation force surged from the Mechanarium's orbiting Gyros. Gravitational forces crumpled the hulls of the worldships surging through the weapons fire from the orbital platform turrets. Fighter craft screened the worldships approach using their shields to absorb most of the incoming platform energy blasts.

Fighter craft careened along the edge of the minefield, locked in dogfighting maneuvers. Missiles chased the fighter craft. Imperial fighters dodged into the minefield using the *Empyrean station* defense net to navigate the mines. Evasive maneuvers led enemy fighter craft and missiles into the mines, and the blast rippled, damaging other fighter craft. Fighter craft careened through space and darted erratically, losing control under the force of explosions. Imperial fighter craft swooped across in squadrons picking off strangling enemy ships.

Arachne ships lanced in front of the larger ships with their eight swirling arms charging towards the *Dawnbreaker*. Enemy forces emerged from the minefield across the interior ring. Serpentine ships pressed towards the interior defense led by a swarm of fighter craft. *Brisingamen* and *Olympus* broke off to deal with the Arachne ships, and the *Iliad* and *Sentinel* moved to engage the serpentine fleet. Energy beams surged all across the Empyrean sector in rapid flashes.

Panic tugged at Kain's nerves, but he listened to the whisper of Matthew in the back of his mind urging to remain calm. From the viewscreen, Kain couldn't see how this would all work out. His brother admitted he saw this as their end. This would be a glorious end. He let his mind fall into the *Empyrean station* defense network, and he let Matthew's whisper guide his actions.

"Grand Admiral Celeris concentrated all fire on those W'hyish S'yevel forces I couldn't halt. They're aiming at the *Empyrean station.* Their goal is our brother in the Infinity Nexus. Consul Joshua, you're going to shield our siblings. Do what you do best, Nemesis, and kill them all. God can sort them all out." Kain surged from his chair. His mind darted across the battlefield.

"Affirmative Imperator," the siblings replied across the *Empyrean station* defense network.

Empyrean station defense network surged with Kain's target acquisitions. The *Divine Retribution* weapons fire in mass successive surges. All nine thousand of the ship's turrets locked onto a single target on the front of the worldship battleline forming across the sector. Flashes of lights surged on the viewscreen rapidly, rippling across the shields of the undamaged worldship. Shields crumbled under the constant barrage of weapons fire, and the beams tore through the Worldships. Many of the worldships opened fired on the *Divine Retribution*.

CHAPTER 51

Wedge formation of worldships broke apart into two long lines moving across the interior defense ring. Multiple lines formed above and below the primary lines surging through the void. *Divine Retribution* blazed through the enemy fighter craft dogfighting in the interior ring. Point defense weapons, turrets, and kinetic cannons lanced fire in all directions. Explosions rippled in the wake of the ship soaring towards the *Dawnbreaker*.

Shields rippled, absorbing the incoming attacks, missiles exploded along the perimeter, and kinetic rounds slammed into the hull of the *Divine Retribution*. Targets locked on the nearest worldship. Turret batteries unleashed salvos of energy fire in rapid succession along the hull of the *Divine Retribution*. Ships rippled, flickered, and collapsed under the strain of the barrage. Explosions ripped out from the worldship along the hull, sending debris across the void. A firing line of worldships formed in multiple rows.

Fighter craft screened the worldships from enemy fire, soaring through the dogfight with imperial ships. Kinetic rounds erupted from the worldships broadsides. Tens of thousands of rounds burst across the sector through the blur of weapons fire. Defense platforms adjusted targets to intercept the transport rounds. Ripples of explosions erupted in the surge of weapons fire, but many of the rounds continued past the turrets streaking toward *Empyrean station*.

Titus Andronicus and *Victory* held the final defense line around *Empyrean station*. Point defense turrets opened fire at the surging transport rounds. *Sesh'yna* defended the *Mirror of Solace*, and energy fire from *Empyrean station* surged around the two ships. Round after round slammed against the hull, drilling through the metal. Large clamps dug into *Empyrean station,* latching the transport rounds to it. Seals erupted along the outside of the station venting the exterior portions into space. Bodies blew into the vacuum of space.

The sound of the vacuum howled through the metal bulwarks of the station. Imperial troops stood lined up in one of the choke points in the city wards of the station. Barricades erected across the hallway were bolted into the deck and walls. Guns rested upon the edge of the barricade aimed down the corridor. Large, mounted energy weapons were being bolted behind the barricade. Warforged stood motionless behind the troops waiting for the enemy.

"I don't think I've ever seen you in power armor Lord Marcus," Commander Verdas stated.

Lord Marcus glanced up from the tactical plan. Sweat glistened along his brow. He stood up to shake Commander Verdas's outstretched hand. The two men glanced down the corridor together. Thuds from the kinetic transport rounds echoed through the corridor.

"Fighting isn't my passion Commander Verdas unlike most of our people, but this battle is too big for anyone not to fight for our continued survival. Many of the old warriors of the *Alcatraz* have turned up to fight as well. Hopefully, God will bless such a fine gathering of people." Marcus pointed to the crowd of shining new power armor. Thuds rang out down the corridor, drawing their attention. More kinetic rounds slammed against the hull of *Empyrean station.* The defense network surged with the reports of the station decompression occurring. Video feeds showed W'hyish S'yevel troops being blown into space.

"Emperor isn't going to be able to keep this up forever," Commander Verdas informed.

"Surprised the plan's working so far. A'zyren explained to me that most of the W'hyish S'yevel troops are the reanimated corpses of their ancestors. They don't need oxygen, heat, or a pressurized atmosphere to survive." Marcus struggled against his trembling nerves to load the rifle. Commander Verdas reached over to help.

"These hard light weapons don't use firing bolts. You've got to make sure the battery clip is firmly locked in, capacitors are charging, and once this gauge in the sight hits one hundred percent, you're free to fire. Try to relax a little bit, Marcus. You're just going to get yourself killed otherwise, and I'll have to answer to Nemesis for that." Commander Verdas patted Marcus on the back. More thuds echoed down the corridor, drawing both of the men's attention.

Internal defenses showed the enemy movement in the *Empyrean station* defense network, but they heard the first sounds of the approaching enemy. Screeches erupted down the corridor drawing all the troops' attention. Commander Verdas drew a grenade from his belt satchel. He pressed a few buttons on the grenade priming it. Chittering raced down the corridors echoing the approach of the predatorial chitterers. Lord Marcus glanced to see what Commander Verdas was doing. He stared down the corridor with his thumb over the ignition button on the grenade.

"I didn't see any grenades like that in the station's armory inventory?" Lord Marcus looked at the grenade. From the design, it looked like something Hephaestus made.

"This little beauty is my own design, but Lord Hephaestus programmed it. Let's just say I've figured a way to deal with these foul-flying beasts easier." Commander Verdas pressed the ignition button, the countdown started on the grenade, and the number rolled back from ten to nine. He threw the grenade down the corridor. It soared through the air, counting down to eight.

Seconds ticked away upon the display of the soaring grenade. Chittering screeched through the air with the gnashing of jaws. The drone of the wing flaps buzzed down the corridor. Five, four, and three, the grenade counted down, arching through the air. Blackened chitterers darted towards the troops behind the barricade. Two, one, and the grenade exploded amid the chitterers. A wall of vapor exploded toward the line of troops.

Gunfire erupted across the front lines of the barricades, but the warforged stood motionless behind Commander Verdas and Lord Marcus. Cold air rushed across their skin. Shattering noises resonated amidst the falling chittering in the corridor, but the screeches echoed from further behind. Turrets barrels darted, trying to acquire new targets. The defense network showed the temperature falling in the corridor. Matthew vented portions of *Empyrean station,* driving all the W'hyish S'yevel troops into this single chokepoint. Vapor faded, showing the swarm of chitterers surging in the atrium at the end of the corridor. Frozen remains of the chitterers lay smashed into thousands of icy shards melting on the floor.

"Cease fire," Commander Verdas commanded.

Rifles firing trickled to a halt. Deck plating vibrated underneath the troop's feet. Red glares from the warforged optical sensors shined down the corridor. Loud thuds could be heard in the distance over the chittering, but the noise was faint. Deck plates rumbled with the resounding thuds. Harbinger of the apexinels arrival. Quad barrels began to spin on the warforged forearms humming with speed, and the machines aimed them down the corridor. Shoulder-mounted missile launchers emerged on the right shoulders, grenade launcher on the left shoulder, energy blades ignited from the knuckles. Defense turrets along the way aimed down the hallway.

"Get ready, Lord Marcus. We're about to have a lot of company." Commander Verdas ignited his energy blade and aimed his energy rifle down the hall. Marcus aimed his rifle resting his barrel against the barricade. The helmet of the power armor sealed around his head with a thought, and system overlays appeared, tracking the movement.

Hot breaths steamed inside Lord Marcus' helmet, increasing the sweat along his brow. Cool air vented through the power armor didn't seem to help cool him down at all. The barrel of the rifle tapped against the barricade under the tremble of his shaking grasp. Alerts showed the rising epinephrine levels in his blood. His throat went dry, but his vision sharped, staring down the sights of the rifle. A tentacle slithered down along the wall, and thuds of the apexinels echoed behind loudly. The rifle leaped in his hands when he squeezed the trigger seeing the first sign of the enemy.

Martyr's stormed around the corner, thundering down the corridor. Heads bobbed just below the ceiling in the charging pack of abominations. The whir of energy fire leaped from the warforged joining Lord Marcus' fully automatic fire down the hallway. Energy beams tore through flesh, smoke wafted from the holes in the apexinels, and the smell of burning flesh filled the corridor. Rapid energy fire from the warforged tore through the martyrs' bodies, causing them to collapse to the deck. Blackened blood splattered across the legs and walls under the thundering surge of the martyr's pressing down the hallway.

Commander Verdas poured fire into the hallway but sent the neural message for the frontline troops to fall back to the secondary defense position. He glanced back to see the full army spread out in the large empty area in rings of barricades surrounding the entrance to the corridor. Troops rushed back from the barricade before the martyrs could reach them. Commander Verdas pulled Lord Marcus back when he began to reload his energy rifle.

"Get back to the defense line Lord Marcus," Commander Verdas commanded. His arm shook with the steady recoil of the energy bursts from his rifle. The energy blade sizzled next to him. He glared at the approaching apexinels with a smile. Lord Marcus pushed the hand off his shoulder.

"If you're not falling back, then neither am I." Lord Marcus snapped the new battery clip into the hard light rifle with a loud snap.

"Even though it's impossible to miss, Lord Marcus, most of your shots aren't doing any damage, and you can't control the spray of your rifle. Switch to burst fire, and you'll find the recoil easier. Now stop being an idiot and fall back. Leave this battle to me and the machines." Commander Verdas ejected the clip from his rifle, dropped to one knee, held the rifle butt on his thigh, and slammed a new clip in from his belt. The energy blade wavered before him, preparing to defend from any incoming attacks. Lord Marcus watched the fluidity in Commander Verdas' motion and started to fall back towards the secondary line. Troops aimed their rifles over the barricades at the entrance to the corridor. He took a spot in the center of the line to see down the corridor. Apexinels charged towards the exit of the corridor.

Commander Verdas charged towards the corridor past the firing warforged. Hands darted out from the apexinels, but he tumbled across the ground, throwing his rifle over his shoulder. Momentum rolled him across the shaking deck plates to leap between the legs of the first martyr. Crackling energy cleaved through the leg of the first martyr toppling it. Several more arms swept towards him, forcing him to leap backward. He landed on top of the first apexinels head, driving it down into the metal plate. Bones snapped under the force of his weight with a loud squish spurting blackened goop across the deck plate. His energy blade cleaved before him in a wide arch.

Fingers, hands, and portions of arms flung through the air, but the martyrs pushed forward against the warforged. Explosions rippled around Commander Verdas from the missiles and grenades fired by the warforged.

Metal shrieked, crumpled, and twisted under the force of the martyr's grasping at the warforged. Energy blades cleaved through the apexinels, and the bodies slammed down, reverberating across the deck plates. He charged back into the wave of martyrs hacking his wave, ducking, and dodging the flailing enemy attacks.

Bodies piled up in the entrance way under the slow, steady retreat of the warforged. Commander Verdas fought amid the enemy lines in the center of the corridor. Firing arcs cleared, allowing Lord Marcus to give the command to open fire. Energy beams lanced from the barricades into the corridor. Enemy forces trampled overtop the corpses of their fallen brethren, and flailing arms struck each other trying to stop the furious assault of Commander Verdas. His energy blade flashed between the legs of the enemy forces.

Many of the apexinels turned to deal with Commander Verdas creating a bottleneck at the entrance. Lord Marcus directed the troops to focus fire on the backs of the enemies. Warforged advanced from behind to aid their brethren on the front lines. Energy blasts erupted from turrets, but the W'hyish S'yevel kept coming. Network defense reports showed Commander Verdas the number of enemy forces moving on the outer rings of the station. Lifts locked down, magnetic doors sealed, and corridors and portions of the station vented into space, directing the flow of the enemy.

Emperor used every aspect of the *Empyrean station* to control the tide of the battle forcing the enemy into this level of the station. Apexinels towered around Commander Verdas, failing to grasp him in their clutches. Bodies slammed into each other, with his darting between the legs of the massive abominations in swift cleaves. A map of the station showed he was moving deeper into the corridor now. He darted backward between another martyr's legs severing the ankle. The abomination wobbled under the surge of warforged rapid energy cannons cutting through the air and crashed backwards, slowing the other troops' advance.

Rolling between the legs, Commander Verdas spun backward, severing the leg at the thigh. He dove past the sweeping tentacle darting through the gap between two martyrs. Energy blade cleaved side to side, severing the martyr's legs at the knees. Bodies toppled in the wake behind him, charging back towards the front lines. Warforged retreated, severing the limbs, bodies, and whatever part of the parts of martyrs He burst from the enemy lines spinning around but continuing to fall back to join the warforged battlelines.

Apexinels trampled across the fallen corpses squiring black blood and flung bodies across the room, clearing the way. Blood sprayed through the air. A deluge of blackened blood crept across the floor towards the front row of the troops. Commander Verdas cleaved any limbs that stretched towards him, stepping backward. Black ichor covered his armor in splattered spots up his legs and across his torso. Enemy forces pushed from the entrance into the larger room, driving the warforged and him backwards despite their efforts.

"For the Emperor," Commander Verdas screamed.

"For the Emperor," Lord Marcus repeated in echo. Shouts rose across the lines of the imperial troops. Renew vigor exploded in a surge of energy beams lancing through the room. He started getting the burst fire of the rifle in rhythm. Shots tore across the upper torsos, tore through the cheeks, and one even struck right between the eyes sending it toppling over.

Imperial forces threw everything that they had at the enemy. Warforged at the back of the room shots missiles and lobbed grenades into the corridor. Explosions rippled across the entrance, but more martyrs rushed into the room. They spread out in every direction drawing fire from the troops. Each moment that passed, more martyrs surged against the warforged at the front.

CHAPTER 52

Several kinetic transports soared toward the *Dawnbreaker*. Point defense turrets locked onto the targets unleashing a barrage of energy beams. Energy fire tore through space, turrets swiveled, tracking the rounds, and several explosions erupted across the viewscreen just beyond the bridge's hull. The entire bridge shuddered under the force of the explosions. Kain gripped the arm of his chair tight, his mind absorbed by the *Empyrean station* defense network.

Arachne ships approached the *Dawnbreaker*, and the *Divine Retribution* struggled against the worldships firing upon *Empyrean station*. Reports across the defense network showed the *Iliad* and *Sentinel* engaging the serpentine fleet. Fighter craft swarmed towards the two ships, but energy fire erupted from defense platforms, and the two clouds of fighter craft slammed together. Missiles veered through space, chasing after fighter craft diving through the dogfight in the center of the two fleets. Energy beams lanced through space from the *Sentinel* and *Iliad* towards the serpentine fleet.

Smaller enemy ships swarmed around the largest serpentine vessel in the center. Spinal mount cannon ran through the center of the largest serpentine vessel. The ship was almost the same size as one of the battleforges. Sensors showed the energy building up in the cannon. A massive plasma surge erupted from the cannon, streaking across space in a bright green blur. Sheilds crackled around the Sentinel but remained intact.

"Imperator, these serpentine weapons are powerful. Sheilds took a heavy hit from that plasma blast. Enemy weapons are recharging." Lord Cornelius's thoughts reported in the network.

"Don't worry, Lord Cornelius. We'll get through this together," Lord Hector responded.

"Just hold on as long as you can, Lord Cornelius. We'll deal with the W'hyish S'yevel to reduce the threat to Empyrean station. Enemy forces are landing. Fighting is tense in the choke points. We've got to slow the flow of enemy troops. Once we've managed to do that, I'll come to help." Nemesis focused the fire of her ship on another worldship.

Victory surged from the *Empyrean station* towards the serpentine fleet. *Titus Andronicus*, *Azure Dreams*, and *Sesh'yna* point defense turrets continued to fire at the kinetic transport rounds soaring towards the *Empyrean station*. The station's outer hull dotted with the transport rounds latched onto the metal. More kinetic transport rounds were fired from the broadside of the wedge formation of worldships soaring towards the defensive line of the *Icarus* and *Templar*.

"Hold on, Lord Cornelius. I'm on my way to provide support. Lord Hector maneuvers closer to the *Sentinel* to overlap your shields." Lord Oswald uploaded the modifications he'd made to his shield emitters. The *Sentinel* and *Iliad* converged together, driving towards the serpentine fleet. Another massive plasma blast struck the shields of the ships. Sheilds rippled along the front of the ships, but network reports showed the attack barely scratched the shield energy reserves.

Sensors warbled over the *Empyrean station* defense network showing the F.T.L. signatures of an approaching fleet on the outskirts of the sector. The sensor net locked onto the energy signature. Scans probed the energy signature, locking onto the pattern, crossed referenced against *Empyrean station* data archives, and locked onto a result. Ship registry information was poured through the network to each captain. Information on the *Death's Reaper* filtered through the network. Ships were moving faster than the typical F.T.L. speeds of the battleforges could reach.

"Heph, how are those ships moving so fast?" Imperator Kain asked across the network with a thought.

Scans focused on the Pandoran fleet. Readings showed a powerful force of gravity along the same path as the Pandoran fleet. Lord Hephaestus ran the numbers in his head. His calculations filtered across the network to the other captains. Sensors showed the powerful gravity current flowing towards the star in the center of the sector and the current connected to the nearest black hole to the *Empyrean station.*

"Gravity from the star seems to create a stream between a nearby blackhole. It seems to be magnifying the fleets F.T.L. speed." Lord Hephaestus adjusted the sensor readings by updating the calculations with his new algorithm. Gravitational eddies appeared on the stellar map stretching out from the star across the Great Maw. Arachne ships showed up on the gravitational scans. The motion of the mechanical arms on the smaller ships manipulated gravity strings.

Webs of gravity strings flung from the approaching enemy ships. Arachne gravity webs tore through space, destroying allied and enemy fighter craft in the path. Strings of gravity wrapped around the *Dawnbreaker.* The entire ship shuddered under the force of the attacks that bypassed shields altogether. Weapons fire fizzled along the hull of the ship, and enemy worldships pushed the *Dawnbreaker* towards the minefield using their tractor beams. Fighter craft swarmed around the worldships emitting the tractor beams, and several imperial squadrons broke from the main dogfight between the *Divine Retribution, Icarus,* and *Templar* and worldship wedge formation.

Brisingamen and *Olympus* charged into the line of Arachne ships focusing fire on the front line of the formation. Gravity webs lurched through the void of space towards the massive battleforges. The two ships drove apart, dividing the enemy fire. Arachne ships lanced purple beams of dense waves of gravity at the battleforges. Explosions rippled across the hull of the *Olympus,* charging through the lines toward the smaller vessels attacking the *Dawnbreaker.*

"Heph, don't push against those enemies like that! Your shields can't absorb any of the damage," Kain warned his brother with a thought.

"Pah, brother, if my shields can't defend me, then I have no choice but to charge in. These ships I designed aren't frail. Treat them like power armor. Let them take the damage and carry forward through the battle. Besides, brother, we have other weapons than just the turrets."

All power from the shields was redirected to the *Olympus's* engines. A bright flash flared behind the ship lurching forward towards the front lines. Weapons fire erupted from the ship towards the main fleet. Gravity beams slammed across the ship's hull, buckling the metal with each hit. Arachne ships poured fire at the looming *Olympus*, but it was too late when they realized Hephaestus' plan. *Olympus* collided with the smaller enemy ships slamming against them, tearing the hull apart, and causing the ships to explode along the hull. Gravity webs clung to the Olympus hull, slowing the ship's speed down, but it began to veer back around. Arachne ships in the main fleet focused divided their fire between the two battleforges.

Defense platforms poured fire at the approaching fleet caught between the Olympus and Brisingamen. Both battleforges redirected energy from engines to weapons slowing from the gravity webbing coating the hulls of the ships. Arachne fleet tried to regain formation, caught in the surge of weapons fire from three angles. Intermittent bursts of long-range energy cannons fired from *Empyrean station* into the fleet. The enemy ships clumped together under the strain of fire.

Icarus floated alongside the *Templar* overlapping their shields. Kinetic weapons fire erupted from the wedge formation of worldships. Broadsides thundered another salvo of transport pods towards *Empyrean station*. Flickers of point defense fire darted across the hulls of both battleforges, attempting to intercept the transport pods. Missiles-streaked chasing down transport rounds. Explosions erupted across the void, but many rounds soared past the first wave of defense towards the salvo of defense turret fire. Rounds soared through the surge of energy fire into the second swarm of fighters defending the station and the final defense lines. Many of the rounds were intercepted, but several slammed into the station's hull. *Titus Andronicus*, *Azure Dreams*, and *Sesh'yna* struggled to try to keep the enemies' attacks at bay. Another broadside salvo exploded from the formation of worldships.

Constructs moved towards the back of the worldship wedge formation under the *Mirror of Solace's* direction. Weapons fire erupted between the two forces. Kinetic rounds sailed through the artificial ships in a blur. Enemy ships adapted fast to cease firing on the constructs, but their weapons fire rippled against the shields of the worldships. *Divine Retribution* unleashed another salvo of weapon fire on a worldship locked onto the *Dawnbreaker* with tractor beams.

Pandoran ships emerged from F.T.L. in bright flashes behind the W'hyish S'yevel battlelines. Massive battleships lurched in the center of the aged armada. Fighter craft darted from the hanger bays of the carriers, and those with F.T.L. launched straight towards the worldships. Cruisers, destroyers, and frigates darted toward the minefield. Empyrean Defense network couldn't lock onto the Pandoran communication channel, and friend-or-foe identification systems classified the new ships as enemies. Kain could see the fleet approaching the active minefield, and his ship was pushed into the minefield simultaneously.

"Lt. Kazakova don't try to decipher those communications. Hail the *Death's Reaper*. We can use that ship to translate." Kain lurched in the chair. Explosions sent debris flying across the bridge. Fighter craft swarmed across the hull of the *Dawnbreaker,* engaged in dogfights on the viewscreen.

"Enemy worldships are emitting some kind of jamming signal," Lt. Kulakova reported.

Static crackled across the viewscreen with communications trying to establish. Chief Corrigan squinted from the crackling power conduit sparking next to the engineering console and worked on amplifying the signal to cut through the interference. The tactical computer showed Kain the ship's shield was beginning to buckle, falling under ten percent power. Mines loomed, growing closer to the ship on the stellar map with each second. He gripped the armchair, leaned forward, and stared at the screen, praying to get through to the Death's Reaper. Coms crackled across the viewscreen with a distorted voice beyond comprehension in a rapidly fluctuating tone, tempo, and pitch.

"*Death's Reaper,* this is Imperator Kain. Do you copy Magnus?" Kain stared into the static.

Crackling static distorted the voice replying to Kain's question. The bridge shuddered under the barrage of another salvo. The pilot console crackled with energy, but Sgt. Grey kept working to keep the ship from being pushed into the minefield. Kain charged from his seat to yank his pilot away from the console as it exploded. Shrapnel twanged off the back of his power armor.

"Thanks, Imperator, but there's no way to stop the enemy from pushing us into the minefield now." Sgt. Grey looked up at Imperator Kain, scowling down. He shook his head.

"Don't die for no good reason. Now figure something else out." Kain stood up, and released Sgt. Grey and spun around, hearing a slow clap from the video screen. He hated Magnus, but right now, he wouldn't turn down the help. Static crackled across the screen still.

"It seems I did teach you a thing or two about leadership," Gabriel stated.

"Father?" Kain stepped backward, falling into the captain's chair. Static cleared, revealing Gabriel behind the helm of the *Death's Reaper*.

"Imperator sounds like a nice title. Better than captain anyhow," Gabriel chuckled.

"Father, what the fuck are you doing here?"

"Long story, I can tell you while those worldships push your ship into the minefield you laid for your enemies, or you can just deactivate the minefield. Your call, son." Gabriel leaned back into the chair, staring at his son with a grin.

Kain shook off the shock disorienting his mind to access the tactical computer. He accessed the network defense grid to link to the A.S.A. defense network. Data flowed rapidly between all the A.S.A. nodes spread throughout the sector, but he found the mine system. With a few buttons, he deactivated it.

"Our defense network can't isolate the communication frequency of your ally. We need you to use your ship as a translator of sorts. I'm linking the *Death's Reaper* to the *Empyrean station* defense grid now." Kain sent the request through the communication to the *Death's Reaper*. Progress reported on the tactical computer showing the status of the link.

Percentage points climbed on the screen slowly at first. Enemy interference forced Chief Corrigan and Lt. Kazakova to compensate. The speed of the transfer picked up, increasing in spurts. Five percent, then ten percent added to the progress meter. Communications synced with the Death's Reaper, and the viewscreen flickered with the appearance of Pandora.

"Mm, Gabriel, you never told me your son was such a handsome man, and I wonder how he compares to his father." Pandora licked her lips, fixating her gaze upon Kain. Gabriel's eyes narrowed upon his son on the viewscreen. Smoke wafted across the ceiling of the bridge over Imperator Kain's head. The entire bridge shuddered under the force of another volley. Imperator Kain clung to the arms of the chair, staring at the viewscreen.

"Listen, if you're not here to help, I'll be glad to deal with you once I take care of these W'hyish S'yevel surrounding my ship. If you intend to help, you answer me, do you understand? This is my battlefield." Imperator

Kain surged from his chair and stormed towards the viewscreen. His finger pointed to the center of the view screen.

"Forceful too. Those are my favorite to break. Sending tasking orders, but we're pirates, Imperator. We're here to raid your enemies." Pandora grinned at the viewscreen.

Pandoran forces tasking requests surged across the communication lines. Kain's mind synced with the *Empyrean station* defense network. He directed the Pandoran forces to assist his ship against the worldships. The main force received tasking orders for the wedge formation to assist the *Divine Retribution*, *Icarus*, and *Templar*. Only the last request he sent was denied. He accessed the logs, scowled, and glanced at Pandora to hear her laugh once more.

"Sorry, boy, but the *Queen's Gambit* goes where I order alone. The rest of my fleet will follow your orders. I've no intention of sitting back, so you've got nothing to worry about." Pandora broke coms off, leaving Gabriel to stare at his son. He just shook his head.

"What can I say, son? I've got a type. Hold tight. I'm on my way," and Gabriel broke the transmission. *Death's Reaper* darted past the rest of the Pandoran fleet. Sensors showed Kain the ship was on a direct course toward the *Dawnbreaker*.

Two missiles erupted from the *Death's Reaper,* soaring through the void space. Sensors blared extreme gravity warnings, and singularity erupted across the worldships around the *Dawnbreaker*. The *Death's Reaper* darted across the void in rapid pulsing blinks on the stellar map. Pandoran ships swarmed through the deactivated minefield towards the worldships. In the center of the formation was the massive titan-class *Queen's Gambit*.

The hull of the *Dawnbreaker* was covered in the transport pods from the W'hyish S'yevel worldships surrounding it. Alarms blared in the internal defense subnet showing the surging enemy forces pushing through the corridor. Imperial troops used fall back tactics to slow the enemy's advance and make them pay for each inch of ground they took inside the ship. Turrets lanced fire down corridors at advancing martyrs. Coolant vented flash freezing organic tissue, and electric conduits shielding retracted, allowing current to crackle forth. Kain's mind struggled between his ship's internal and external defense.

Fighter craft surged ahead of the Pandoran fleet but couldn't keep pace with the speed of the *Death's Reaper*. The ship moved almost as fast as the imperial fighter craft on the stellar map. Shields collapsed on the Dawnbreaker under the barrage of the multitude of damaged worldships surrounding it on both sides. Thirty worldships held the *Dawnbreaker* in place with their tractor beams. The rest of the W'hyish S'yevel worldships continued pounding broadsides towards *Empyrean station*. Massive kinetic rounds sailed through void space amidst the rapid flashing surge of defensive fire. Explosions cascaded through the salvos, but many of the rounds continued towards the targets smashing into the hull of the *Empyrean station*.

\

CHAPTER 53

Pandoran fleet approached the mine field in tight box formation. Frigates, destroyers, and cruisers formed along the front arc of the fleet soaring through the mine field. Clangs of mines resonated, striking the ships' hull and bouncing off harmlessly. Fighter craft spread across the void in front of the fleet led by the charging *Death's Reaper*. Plasma fire streaked from the fleet's cannons slamming into W'hyish S'yevel fighter craft surging towards the enemy formation. Kinetic exploded in rapid salvos, and cannons pounded transport pods toward the *Dawnbreaker* through the surging energy fire of the point defense batteries. Flanking worldships controlled the *Dawnbreaker* held in the tractor beams. *Divine Retribution* hammered another worldship with successive fire, pounding against the hull until it buckled under the force erupting in an explosion.

Firing solutions calculated on the nearest worldship, the computer beeped target lock, and Gabriel fired the singularity missiles watching the total drop from forty-two. Two missiles streaked across the void, slamming into the worldship. Massive singularities erupted, blending into the black void, crumping the ship inward in a massive implosion upon itself. Only the flash of energy weapon fire revealed the swirling gravitational forces tearing the worldship apart. Molecules tore apart under the force of gravity, bodies were sucked in from the corridor of the worldship, and explosions rippled along the hull, causing the tractor beam to flicker and fail.

"Son, focus fire on one target at a time like your sister. Your divergent fire is being absorbed by the shields doing almost no damage. Remember the most important lesson I ever taught you." Gabriel pulled the trigged, unleashing another salvo of plasma fire. Readings showed the cooling process of the cannon falling back down from the red lines. He waited to fire again.

"I know what I'm doing, father. Every second these W'hyish focus upon the *Dawnbreaker* buys my siblings time to deal with the others." Kain continued firing in every direction at the surrounding W'hyish S'yevel ships. Explosions along the hull took turrets offline, and the steady weapons fire faltered with each loss. He gripped the arm of the chair tight.

Arachne ships clumped together in a swarm, withstanding the barrage from the *Olympus* and *Brisingamen*. Gravitational energy grew in the clump of ships across the *Empyrean station* defense network. Readings showed the gravitational energy surged in the center of the clump. Energy exploded in the center of the mass of ships, propelling them across the void. Mechanical claws reached out through the void grasping onto the *Brisingamen* and *Olympus*. The bulk of Arachne fleet surged past the inner defense towards *Empyrean station*, but a large group of the ships was on a direct course towards the *Dawnbreaker*. Defense platforms locked targets on the enemy ships, and energy blasts launched across the void, flickering across the shields.

Icarus and *Templar* point defense weapons blazed energy fire through the void, cutting through the kinetic transports shooting towards *Empyrean station*. Rounds of kinetic fire slammed against the hull, tore metal bulkheads off, and the atmosphere vented into space. Alarms blared in the bridge, and incoming reports showed Imperial troops fighting in the gaps of the vacuum of space against charging W'hyish S'yevel troops. Gunfire flashed through the holes in the hull, and fighter craft strafed past the hole, firing weapons along the hull of the ship. Turrets exploded under enemy fighter craft's attacks, several ships flew into the barrage of energy fire, and metal flung through space from the ships, tumbling across the hull, breaking part, and exploding into a ball of fire. Bombers streaked towards the worldships unleashing a salvo of missiles. Detonations rippled across the enemy shields, draining the power, but the worldships fire another broadside salvo of transport rounds. Imperial fighter craft engaged in a dogfight with W'hyish S'yevel fighter craft fire at targets of opportunity at passing transport rounds.

Serpentine forces engaged the *Iliad* and *Sentinel,* dividing their forces to surround the beleaguered vessels. Attacks rippled across the joined shields of the two ships absorbing the incoming fire, but fighter craft darted through the energy shield engaging imperial fighter craft around two battleforges. The siblings worked together, targeting singular ships to unleash combined strikes. Successive fire slammed against a serpentine ship bucking the shields, tearing through the hull, and the ship erupted into a massive explosion. Smaller ships along the frontlines of the serpentine armada were targeted first, and the *Victory* merged with other battleforges formations. Three ship shields, merging against the serpentine assault.

Several worldships released tractor beams from the *Dawnbreaker,* breaking off to engage the approaching *Divine Retribution.* Frontloaded kinetic cannons fired at the approaching battleforge. Transport rounds sailed towards the ship surging through the shields. Rounds slammed into the bulkheads of the *Divine Retribution.* Swiveling point defense turrets cut down the transport pods leaving W'hyish S'yevel bodies floating in the void beyond the bridge. Turrets adjusted targets locking onto the lead worldship charging towards the *Divine Retribution.*

Gabriel pushed the engines of the ship past the recommended settings. Heat rose in the engines blaring an alarm, but inertia pushed him back into his seat. Flames shot from the engines behind the *Death's Reaper,* launching the ship towards the worldships holding the *Dawnbreaker* in tractor beams. The systems of the ship were still unfamiliar to him. He pressed a few buttons, trying to target the nearest tractor beam emitter. Advanced targeting came online, showing the options for the individual cannons, singularity missiles, and M.I.R.V. multipurpose variable payload guided missiles. The name of the last one drew his attention. Targeting systems activated, he locked onto the tractor emitters of the worldships, and then the screen popped up to select payload.

Antimatter payload highlighted by default on the screen flashing at a steady strobe. Acidic, cryogenic, incendiary, anti-armor, and quantum listed next to the flashing option. Gabriel selected anti-armor, glancing at the thickened bulkheads on the worldships. Firing solutions calculated, kinetic rounds soared past the Death's Reapers, and enemy fighter craft gave chase. He dodged and evaded everything with ease from the pure speed of the ship. The repeating tone echoed in the bridge, informing the firing solution locked targets. He pulled the trigger unleashing the missiles.

Through the viewport, Gabriel watched the missiles streaking towards the worldships. Warheads exploded, sending dozens of smaller guided missiles forward. Each smaller warhead darted towards different targets, dividing across the void space. Fighter craft couldn't escape fast enough, weapons fire surged past the darting warheads, and shields didn't slow the warheads down, slamming into the target's hulls. Eruptions of flames across the worldships flashed bright explosions. Shards of glowing hot metal flung through the void. Heat bled into the void like a bottomless pit. Great Maw swallowed everything the battle fed to it, hungering for more in silence. Emitters failed, tractor beams flickered off, and the *Dawnbreaker* broke free. Holes in the hull of the Dawnbreaker revealed the damage all across the ship since the shields failed, and engines still struggled against the gravitational force of the Arachne webs sticking to the hull.

War raged through the holes of the hull between Imperial troops clad in power armor and W'hyish S'yevel forces. Blurring energy revealed the gravitational webs' lines to Gabriel, but he wasn't sure how to remove them. Despite the damage the *Dawnbreaker* took in the battle, his scans showed it was still ninety-one percent functional. Nanites swarmed over the hull, repairing the destroyed turrets. Enemy fighter craft continued to target the turrets. Selecting antimatter Gabriel locked in targets on enemy fighter craft along the *Dawnbreaker* hull. Missiles soared, breaking apart to dive toward the enemy fighters, and the *Death's Reaper* shot toward the wedge formation of worldships caught between the *Divine Retribution*, *Icarus*, and *Templar*.

"We need to clear these gravitational fields from the hull," Imperator Kain looked to Chief Corrigan. She was already working on the process to help remove the gravitational fields.

"These energy webs are amplifying our increasing our mass exponentially. That's why the engines are struggling to move us. Mass index is almost ten times our normal weight, and steadily increasing. I'm having trouble locking on the energy matrix structure of the web." Chief Corrigan examined scans of the gravitational fields clinging to the hull.

Matrix of energy rotated on the screen in front of Chief Corrigan. She could see how the energy formed the pattern creating the gravitational force. There was something about the pattern of the energy matrix that sparked an idea in her head. She accessed the bulkhead system to see all the damage done to the hull. Power conduits ran along the hull, giving her an idea. She accessed the power grid system altering the power flow trying to adjust the resonance frequencies inside the conduits, and the bled the rest of the energy into the bulkheads polarizing the metal plates.

Strands of the gravitational web broke apart under the vibrations of the polarized hull plating. Mass dropped on the engineering console, and inertial dampeners kicked in responding. *Dawnbreaker* surged towards the worldships on the left flank. Worldships on the right flank were far more damaged, and fewer in number, and the *Divine Retribution* hammered those ships. Beams lanced from the formation of worldships splintering to divide along the path of the *Dawnbreaker*.

"Good work Chief Corrigan. I want you to focus all fire on the enemy formation and prioritize pre-selected targets. Lt. Kazakova select weakened targets on the edge of the worldship formations for fire control. Sgt. Grey get whatever you can from our engines. Drive to the center of the enemy lines. We're going to drive this ship right through those worldships." Imperator Kain gripped the arm rests, leaned forward, and watched the *Dawnbreaker* surging forward. Weapons fire, fighter craft, and missiles exploded across the viewscreen, and the entire ship shook under the barrage of the worldships. The ship's bow collided with a worldships side as it tried to flee.

Bulkheads surged overtop of the metal hull plating of the *Dawnbreaker*. Damage reports showed the force of the impact dissipating across the ship's superstructure. Metal plates crumbled along the hull of Kain's ship, watching the chaos on the viewscreen. The reactor of the ship exploded, tearing across the front of the ship, but only took out a few of the decks where W'hyish S'yevel forces controlled. Kinetic rounds from the broadsides slammed against the hull all around the ship. Troops fell back into the ship's interior, drawing the W'hyish forces deeper into the battleforge where ambushes sprung. Internal defense subnet filled his mind with reports, but he focused all his attention on the Arachne ships attacking the isolated *Olympus*.

"Hold on, brother, just a bit longer. I'm coming! Kain muttered to himself, watching the lancing beams of gravity shooting from the approaching Arachne ships. The main force advanced onto *Brisingamen*, but A.S.A. defense platforms were in range to defend Lady Freya's ship.

Once he rescued his brother, they could move to help Lady Freya, he hoped. Light flashed darting beams of energy across the viewscreen in the distance and reflected off the sleek hulls of the Arachne ships.

Dogfighting raged around the *Brisingamen*, fighter craft darting frantically through the space around the ship, and energy blasts, explosions, and missiles ripples across the ship's hull. Shields weren't doing anything to stop the incoming attacks. Reading on the missiles and Arachne vessels showed a similar pattern to reverie energy signatures. She uploaded the data to the *Empyrean station*, hoping either her troops or someone else could figure out what was happening. The viewscreen showed the Arachne forces latching onto the *Olympus* in the distance, but she gritted her teeth, preparing for the arrival of the main armada.

Arachne vessels latched on to the *Olympus*. Mechanical arms pulled the smaller Arachne ships onto the hull through the surge of weapons fire. A barrage of energy weapons rippled across the shields, broke through the shields and tore into the hull. Explosions rippled across the *Olympus'* hull. Stingers erupted from the front of the ship, cutting into the bulkheads. Warriors surged into the corridors of the *Olympus,* meeting the fire of Hephaestus' imperial troops.

Atmosphere vented the first wave of W'hyish S'yevel forces from the *Divine Retribution*. Bodies slammed against the hull, energy beams vaporized some, and others were torn apart in the rush of fighter craft sweeping across the hull. Point defense turrets poured continuous energy beams at the incoming troop transports. Another of the worldships detonated under a salvo of continuous fire. Metal remains of the damaged worldship crumbled into the melting superstructure as the ship collapsed onto itself. Sustained beam salvos blew the worldship apart like dust blown by the wind.

Erratic activity rippled across the sensors, but Gabriel focused on the attacks thundering from the worldship broadsides. He guided the *Death's Reaper* across the void evading kinetic fire from the beleaguered right flank of the damaged worldship. Tapping the targeting systems, he isolated the attacks spiraling towards the bridge of the *Divine Retribution*. Firing solutions locked onto the transport rounds. Trigged clicked with a tug of his finger, sending the M.I.R.V. missiles launching.

Warheads darted across the void, scattering into the smaller missiles with a small explosion. Rapid explosion rippled across the upper bulkheads near the bridge. The entire structure of the bridge shook from the pressure of the explosions rippling through space. Nemesis tapped on the tactical computer accessing the communications. The coms warbled, connecting to the *Death's Reaper*. The image of her father left her speechless in the captain's chair.

"Good to see you again, my daughter. It looks like we get to fight on the same side once more. I'll do what I can to keep these forces off from you while the rest of the Pandoran fleet moves to help." Gabriel shook on the viewscreen evading incoming fire. Nemesis glanced to see the *Dawnbreaker* surging toward the Olympus in the distance. All the damage on the hull could be seen even from this range, and she glanced back to her father.

"Imperator could use your help more than I can," Nemesis informed.

"Your brother knows what he's doing, or so he claims. Those massive ships of yours sure can take a beating from the looks of things. *Empyrean station* and Matthew are what matters now, Nemesis. If Magnus can be believed, I will give him this. He sure does know how to start a good fight." Gabriel pulled the *Death's Reaper* along the hull of the *Divine Retribution*. Targets locked on multiple enemy fighter craft, he fired the weapons, and watched the missiles streak forward. He darted through the flashing explosions, locking his gaze on his daughter.

"Can your aliens fight?" Nemesis targeted the next damaged worldship. Thundering turrets unleashed upon the ship, crackling across the failing shields.

"They're not particular good fighters, but they love the thrill of combat like we do, daughter. Most importantly, they're coming to help us take down that wedge formation. What's say we finish your brother's scraps together before we deal with the rest?" Gabriel smiled back, seeing his daughter's grin. She leaned forward with a sparkle in her eyes.

"How bout we see which one of us destroys the most."

"Hardly seems fair given the size of your ship, daughter, but I suppose it only just given how I used to stack the odds against you. What's the prize for the winner?" Gabriel leaned back into his seat and continued to fire.

"There's only one thing worth fighting over." Nemesis watched the worldship erupt with explosions under the fire from her ship to the cheers of her crew. "Glory!"

"Spoken like a true Solomon, and I'll even give you that first one," Gabriel laughed.

Engines flared, surging the *Death's Reaper* past the *Divine Retribution*. Green plasma charges leaped from the cannons, missiles darted from the launchers, and the ship evaded the swarming enemy fighter craft. Singularities rippled along the hulls of two worldships tearing the two ships to pieces. *Divine Retribution* divided fire for the first time targeting two of the damage worldships. Nemesis leaned back into her chair, watching the two ships struggle against her attacks. Scanners showed the shields already buckling under the attacks, but her eyes darted, following the *Death's Reaper* across the void amidst the swarms of fighter craft and ships dotting the viewscreen.

CHAPTER 54

Martyrs charged towards the warforged retreating towards the barricades and frontline of troops firing into the swarm. Energy crackled off the blade slashing through the air, severing fingers, limps, and anything else that got in Commander Verdas' way. Tentacles lurched from the charging apexinels lashing around a Warforged. Energy blades severed two tentacles, but the other dragged the machine into the surging enemy ranks. Multiple apexinels beset upon the warforged crumpling metal under repeated blows of their mighty strength. Metal buckled, crumpled, and shrieked, tearing from the frame to the mechanical cry of the Warforged.

Beams of energy lanced out from the spinning guns on the arms ripping through the apexinels, energy blades slashed, trying to break free from the hold, and missiles launched point black into the apexinels formation. A rippling explosion failed to free the warforged from the grip of the surging martyrs. Oscillating screeches erupted from the warforged ringing out over the chaos of battle. Warforged surged across the battlefield, trying to rescue the beleaguered unit.

Mechanical claws tore into the flesh of the apexinels pushing them back away from the damaged warforged. Machines flung back into the air, slamming down onto the deck. Blasts of weapons fire erupted along the front of the formation, W'hyish S'yevel troops spread along the walls rushing into the room, and the full force of the enemy stormed towards the imperial troops. Deck bulkheads shook under the thunder of the charging troops. Sparks erupted, plasma poured from the arm, tearing into pieces, and gears, servos, and circuits exploded through the air. Warforged dragged the wounded machine back from the frontlines, and the others closed the gap in the line holding the martyrs at bay.

The defense network echoed incoming W'hyish S'yevel troops. Transport rounds slammed all over the exterior of the *Empyrean station*. Internal defenses fired on the incoming living dead, and black blood crept across the deck bulkheads toward the imperial forces. Missiles soared through the air with beams, kinetic rounds, and plasma blasts. Barricades collapsed under the smashing might of the martyrs reaching the frontline of imperial troops. Lord Marcus directed fire at the incoming apexinels marching across the battlefield, firing his rifle in steady bursts. He pulled the troops back from the barricade before the advancing apexinels could overrun the position. Arms lanced towards him, forcing him backward, steady bursts tore through flesh, splattering blackened blood through the air, and he drew his energy blade with no other recourse.

Crackling energy surged from the hilt of the energy blade. Flailing arms soared towards Lord Marcus, dodging backward. Muscles trembled in his arm, shaking the energy blade, his eyes dilated, and warnings echoed high epinephrine levels in his body. Hypostims injected into his chest, pumping countering agents to lower the stress on his body. Chemicals surged through his veins, pumping into his muscles. Swipes of the energy blade cleaved arms from the apexinels.

"Lord Marcus, get the troops back away from the front lines. Let the warforged and me handle this scum." Commander Verdas fought in the center of the warforged. Enemy and ally alike towered overtop of him. Bursts of fire erupted from his rifle, slashes of his energy blade severed his enemies' flesh, and combined assaults with the warforged felled abominable martyrs. Corpses trampled under the surging horde of W'hyish that seemed endless. Internal defenses showed the horde thundering down the corridor and the unfathomable tidal wave behind that.

"I'm not going to abandon you here, Commander Verdas," Marcus yelled.

"Don't worry about me. I've dealt with these bastards before." Knee shattered under the force of Commander Verdas's kick, bringing the apexinels toppling down. He dove between the legs of the toppling monstrosity rolling across the deck. Paint tore from the power armor, but he shot up, slashing wide across several apexinels in a wide arc. Intestines, blackened blood, and a putrid smell erupted from the creature's stomach. He leaped backward, landing in front of the fallen apexinels driving his energy blade down into the abomination's skull.

Flashes of energy swords ignited and erupted across the front lines. Metal crunched, shrieked, and tore under the martyr's assault along the front line, warforged crashed to the ground, and imperial troops flung through the air. Wall-mounted turrets poured fire into the ranks of the martyrs cleaving holes through the monsters. Reinforcements continued to pour out of the corridor. Two apexinels replaced every fallen one charging into the room through the explosions. Only when explosions lulled the regular W'hyish S'yevel troops darted from the corridor. A swarm of the next wave of missiles soared towards the corridor. Smalls weapons fire ricochet off power armor.

Flickers of energy blades shined on the flesh of the advancing apexinels surging against the warforged frontlines. Machine slammed one hand against the deck plate alongside the severed remains of the enemy. Blackened blood splashed over the armor, and mechanical legs struggled to stand up. Enemy forces surged into the gaps, limbs flailed, smashing against the warforged from three fronts in some places, and Commander Verdas watched the frontline faltering. He took aim, but the rifle clicked impotently. He threw the rifle over his shoulder using the straps and waved to the warforged to retreat, sending the command across the defensive subnet with a thought.

Explosions erupted over the imperial troops raining shards of metal from turrets onto them. Power armor deflected the smaller debris, but troops dove out of the way of the larger shards of metal puncturing the deck bulkheads. Steam wafted off glowing metal radiating waves of heat. Soldiers pulled their brethren to their feet, medics tended to the wounded, and warforged retreated backward through the room towards the cityward gates. Barricades crumpled under the charging force of advancing apexinels, but Commander Verdas made the ones rushing at him pay. Crackles of the energy blade swept in front of him in a flurry. Energy sizzled flesh, cleaving it in single strokes.

Defense network reports echoed reinforcements moving into the city wards and preparing the second line of defense. Pressing enemy forces kept Commander Verdas focused on the surging apexinels forces lancing limbs.

He cleaved each one away, retreating steadily. Chaos raged around him, but his mind focused on the enemy. Bodies flailed through the air falling into the surging ranks of W'hyish S'yevel. Screams of pain were muffled under the commotion of combat. Rippling explosions, energy blasts, and tattering kinetic fire drowned out the dying screams of imperial troops. Footsteps carried him back, he glanced to see Lord Marcus leading the rest of the troops and more reinforcements arriving to join the defense.

"The enemy is going to overrun this position in a few minutes," Commander Verdas warned.

Enemy forces dragged warforged into their lines. Warforged oscillating screams reverberated in a cacophony of screeches through the air. Helmet emerged, covering Commander Verda's head to shield him from the sound. Clangs, thuds, and shrieks erupted under tearing metal. Mechanical limbs exploded, raining parts across the growing W'hyish S'yevel army. Lord Marcus directed troops to fall back with his hand motions, but his eyes stayed fixed on the growing swarm in the room just beyond the apexinels front line pursuing his retreat.

"I'll prepare the second line, but don't do anything stupid, Commander." Lord Marcus fell back towards the cityward entrance. He glanced back at Commander Verdas. Enemy fire focused on the last few turrets. Explosions erupted in rapid succession, raining debris down.

Chunks of red-hot metal crashed across the deck, crushing W'hyish S'yevel. Smoke wafted through the large room in scattered black clouds. A large silhouette moved in the surging enemy forces drawing Commander Verdas' attention. Massive martyr bodies wobbled before him blocking his view, but his eyes narrowed following the motion. His eyes narrowed on the silhouette, charged in the opposite direction, and cleaved a tentacle from the torso of a warforged leaping from the knee. Soaring into the air, he slashed the blade across the martyrs' front ranks, cleaving through heads, necks, and shoulders, dropping back down. Charging back across, he kept his eyes on the silhouette but cleaved the limbs from the warforged to let the bodies begin to topple.

The dead weight of the toppling enemies struck warforged charging forward. They flung the corpses of the apexinels back into the charging forces. Corpses tossed amongst the charging apexinels slamming into bodies being trampled underneath, but the commotion slowed the charge allowing the warforged to retreat. Silhouette moved through the fumbling apexinels. Sharpened bone spikes fused into the blackened metal armor of the massive humanoid. The strange shadow stood half the height of the average apexinels, yet they moved away from this being. Command Verdas locked his eyes, cleaving across the frontlines to free warforged from grappling apexinels. He knew he needed to keep as many of these machines intact as possible.

Enemy forces pulled back around the emerging black armored figure wearing a strange suit of power armor. Massive cannons swiveled on each shoulder, a rocket launching pod overhead in the center, and a massive chainsaw-like blade. Chants erupted from the W'hyish ranks. Commander Verdas locked eyes with this leader but focused his attention on the defense network. Warforged fell back to join the main line of defense in the cityward. The slow, ponderous movement of the machines forced him to provide a defense. Enemies surged forward, charging with their leader.

Orders were dispatched to the frontline defenders to prepare countermeasures. Commander Verda hoped to hold the enemy here, but he begrudgingly admitted this zone was lost. There wasn't any possibility of preventing collateral damage to the cityward now, but that also meant he could use the buildings themselves to kill the enemy if necessary. Reports from demolitions showed explosives were being armed on structural supports. His mind examined the layout of the cityward, staring at the leader charging towards him.

Warforged smashed back into the enemy troops to guard the main force as their wounded numbers retreated. Sparks shot behind the chain blade tearing through the metal. The leader made short work of one of the warforged tearing the machine apart, piece by piece. First, a leg clattered across the ground, an arm next, and the final leg exploded on the chain blade halfway through cutting. Commander Verdas fell back with the main force of warforged. There wasn't anything he could do to save the beleaguered machines sacrificing themselves for their brethren. Warbles emitted from the warforged moving through the doorway. Massive blast doors sealed in front of Commander Verdas.

The faint sound of enemy thuds echoed through the thick metal. Soldiers aimed rifles, rockets, and energy cannons at the door. Thick reinforced slabs of steel created a perimeter around the blast doors. A field hospital could be seen in the center behind the main defensive walls next to the commander center. Troops surged through the area, finalizing defenses. Engineers worked on repairing warforged behind the walls. Lord Marcus approached Commander Verdas.

"How long do you think these blast bulkheads will hold out for?"

"Not long. A few minutes at most. We'll have to make the most of the time. Sitrep," Commander Verdas requested. He marched towards the command post with Lord Marcus.

"Engineers came up with a clever idea. They're retrofitting some of the warforged with long-range plasma throwers. Think giant walking plasma cutter flamethrowers. According to A'zyren's report, her people are most vulnerable to fire." Lord Marcus pointed to the engineers working nearby on the modifications.

"Excellent, that will help if we keep the enemy bottled up here. We can use the flamethrowers to cook anything that tries to come through those doors. I've already ordered demolition teams to place charges on the supports of the building. Cityward gives us more room to bring heavier ordinance. Tanks and internal defense drones are already set up at choke points surrounding our location. Emperor wants to keep the W'hyish S'yevel back here, guarding the Infinity Nexus. We can't fall back any further than this cityward, which means we hold the line here. This far, and no further shall our enemy advance. There's been no report of Lord Whelsey during the battle either. Pious Clan subnet has been locked out from the rest of the *Empyrean station* network. This is all we got left to defend this position," Commander Verdas explained.

"Emperor's plan has succeeded so far. All the W'hyish S'yevel troops have been confined to this entrance. A portion of the stations were jettisoned. It would take days to route to a different cityward. Those moving down the last linking corridors are right in the middle of our trap. You're right, Commander. We hold them here and make them pay in blood." Lord Marcus glanced to the gates holding the enemy at bay, feeling the anxiety tremble across his nerves.

There wasn't any sign of damage yet, but the defense network told both men the situation on the other side. Leader of the W'hyish S'yevel forces directed the apexinels into living battering rams. Fists slammed into metal, crumpling it, and black bleeding fingers tore at the thick bulkheads. Piece by piece, the enemy disassembled the gate. Calculation concluded the gate would be penetrated in five minutes, and forty-nine seconds.

CHAPTER 55

Artificial constructs fired holographic weapons to slam into the W'hyish S'yevel worldships. Enemy ships ignored the artificial battleforges moving towards the wedge formation. *Death's Reaper* surged towards the formation, but the *Divine Retribution* pounded salvos against the enemy worldships near the deactivated minefield. Engines flared on one side increasing thrust turning the massive battleforge back towards the wedge formation. Fighter craft chased each other in dogfights across the hull and space around the ship. Beams erupted, spattering through the Great Maw, chasing the fighters, bombers, and missiles soaring around the *Divine Retribution*.

Metal crumbled around the bow of the *Dawnbreaker*, ramming through enemy ships. Explosions rippled along bulkheads, the structure crumpled upon itself, and the hull glowed red hot. Enemy ships splintered around the *Dawnbreaker*. Broadsides roared, firing transport rounds point blank into the hull of the *Dawnbreaker*. Wreckage of ships slammed and bounced across the ship's hull, driving forward. Arachne converged to surround the *Olympus*, but they fired gravitational beams at the *Dawnbreaker*.

Gravitational waves rippled through worldships indiscriminately to slam against the hull of the *Dawnbreaker*. Damaged worldships erupted under the gravitational pressure exploding across the scattering line. *Empyrean station* defense network surged with the multiple scans revealing the worldships erupting in masses of expanding flames. A'zyren watched the battle unfolding from the bridge of the *Sesh'yna*. Her fingers tapped on the armrest of the captain's chair.

"Get the *Titus Andronicus* on coms Cali'ban. Something doesn't feel right," A'zyren ordered.

Scans of the *Mirror of Solace* reported low energy output. Memories flashed through A'zyren's tumultuous thoughts. De'Vayne ships were far more powerful than this. One of Lord De'Vayne's ships could destroy several worldships if they could keep W'hyish S'yevel forces from boarding. Even the smaller vessels carried tremendous firepower, yet the De'Vayne armada had yet to arrive. Lady Marimba's visage flickered on the viewscreen sitting in her captain's chair.

"What do you want?" Lady Marimba crossed her arms, glaring at A'zyren.

"There's something off about the *Mirror of Solace*. Lord De'Vayne's not using even a quarter of the power his ship can produce, nor has his forces arrived to aid us as he promised. He could create several more constructs. There's also something off in the scans from the *Empyrean station* and sensor network. I can't figure it out." A'zyren isolated the section of the scans and uploaded it. She could see the intrigue glinting in Marimba's eyes.

Lady Marimba's fingers tapped the tactical computer. Her eyes osculated, fixating on the data scrolling on the small screen, but the echo roared center in her mind over all the other whispers from the defense network, ships subnetwork, and the other subnets spread across the sector. All the data swirled in the background, with her focusing on the strange patterns A'zyren isolated in the scans. A subtle signal appeared to be hidden within the scans. Lady Marimba couldn't be entirely sure it was a signal. She really wished that Hephaestus wasn't busy in the battle to take a look at this code. Shaking off the unease, she glanced back at the viewscreen.

"This could be nothing, A'zyren, and we're kind of in the middle of something."

"Listen to me. I've dealt with De'Vayne more than you or your people have. Emperor Solomon might see the treachery of Lord De'Vayne, or maybe not. I'm not taking the chance. Those anomalies in the scan could be something the Ancients never discovered or something with darker intention. Lord De'Vayne's is known for using his advanced cloaking devices to prepare ambushes. Those anomalies could well be a hidden fleet of De'Vayne's ships. If so, he's got a vast armada holding position just beyond sector. I assumed Emperor Solomon could see all this, so I didn't explain it during the planning," A'zyren explained.

"What the fuck, A'zyren! If Lord De'Vayne prepared an ambush, Imperator Kain and Lord Hephaestus will be the first to face it. We've got to do something…" Lady Marimba scowled with trembling muscles tugging at the edges of her mouth, turning into a scowl.

"Hold position and prepare to deal with the *Mirror of Solace*. I'll help the others." A'zyren motioned to her crew. Engines flared, propelling the *Sesh'yna* forward towards the defensive inner ring. She leaned back into her charge and glanced towards the holographic image of Lady Marimba.

"I'll send a transmission to Emperor Solomon," Lady Marimba replied.

"No! Don't do that. This communication channel is dangerous enough alone. Lord De'Vayne has a much greater command of Ancient's technologies than our people. Tell me you're not struggling against the data reports with your brain linked to the defense network. So is Lord De'Vayne, and I guarantee this isn't anything new to him. We might as well message him ourselves. Only way we can prevent this ambush from working is to make sure you can destroy the *Mirror of Solace*. Don't lock any weapons on it, use manual targeting, and use kinetic rounds polarized to this shield frequency." A'zyren uploaded the polarity of the *Mirror of Solace* shields. She glared at the ship, hoping the Lord De'Vayne's cognitive servitor group brain missed it.

A'zyren didn't encrypt the transmission either. She wanted the transmission to look so innocuous that even the enemy forces would ignore it for encrypted messages. Netwar wasn't her strong suit, but there was so much data traffic in the sector it had to be overwhelming, even the De'Vayne cognitors agents scanning the data streams. She scanned the transmission to ensure no signals were tapping into it. Once the scans were clear, she cut the transmissions and focused on the battle on the viewscreen.

Ripples of explosions covered the *Dawnbreaker* cloaking it in bright flashes. A'zyren leaned forward in her chair, sweat beading along her forehead. She held her breath, watching the eruptions detonating in rapid succession. Sweat dripped from her forehead, splashing across the deck with inaudible faint splooshes. She breathed a sigh of relief when the *Dawnbreaker* emerged through the explosions. The crew worked at dozens of consoles spread through the massive bridge. Machines whirred, beeped, and chirped rapidly, computing all the ship's needs.

Hull plating polarized against the gravitation energy of the Arachne using the information uploaded to the defense network by Imperator Kain. Gravitation beams and webs launched toward the *Sesh'yna*, soaring through the firing defense platforms. Polarized plating deflected most of the force from the incoming attack bypassing the shields. Arachne fighter craft swung across the viewscreen towards A'zyren's ship. Energy beams flashed, and missiles streaked toward the *Sesh'yna*, rippling across the shield upon impact. Bow kinetic cannons blasted rounds toward the serpentine formation.

Communications chirped in the bridge. A'zyren routed the incoming transmission to her holographic emitter. Imperator Kain flickered before with a scowl on his face. Crackle erupted in the transmission from the serpentine jamming field emanating from their ships. She amplified the signal trying to break through the static. Screams erupted from the holoemitter.

"What are you doing, A'zyren? You're supposed to stay back and protect the *Empyrean station* with Lady Marimba and Lord De'Vayne. *Sesh'yna* weapons are needed on the defense." Kain screamed through the holographic emitter. Jamming signals in the network sparked an idea in A'zyren's mind.

"Calm down, Kain, please. I'm here to help you." A'zyren urged trying to focus on the epiphany echoed in her thoughts.

All the interference from the serpentine ships jamming to disrupt imperial forces communications could allow A'zyren to cloak a hidden message. She pulled up the interference frequencies on the system's outskirts and started modifying her transmission. The changes wouldn't be noticeable to any of Lord De'Vayne's cognitors, and if a nearby armada was watching, they shouldn't detect anything either, she hoped. She encoded the coordinates of Uriel's outpost into the readings and transmitted them.

"This looks like a garbled batch of sensor readings from the network..." Kain froze up. He saw the strange numbers in the readings that didn't fit. He pushed the information to the engineering console with a glance toward Chief Corrigan. He unpacked that data on a portion of the screen. Eyes darted through the lines of codes, readings, and results. The date surged back to Kain, but it was altered.

Alterations showed a consistent but extremely faint signal repeating on the edge of the sector. Chief Corrigan's work isolated the frequency, and there was no mistaking it. The pattern of the energy matched the constructs. His countenance softened, glancing at A'zyren with a subtly nod. It was almost imperceptible on the emitter, but A'zyren's sharp eyes caught it.

"Your ship is under attack, Kain. If you're lost, we're all lost," A'zyren retorted.

"Perhaps I was too harsh. At least Lady Marimba's picking up the slack of your absence." Kain's mind turned the idea over, considering the pros and cons of mentioning this over the coms. He knew A'zyren was hiding the knowledge from Lord De'Vayne. An epiphany hit Kain, and he tapped the tactical computer to scan the edge of the sector. Comparing the anomalous readings to the *Mirror of Solace* showed an exact match. Kain locked eyes with A'zyren on the viewscreen with a nod.

"I'll contact Lord De'Vayne and notify him to pick up your slack." Kain hoped A'zyren understood his secret message.

"Be careful, Kain. You've seen how Lord De'Vayne can be, and we need his help still. Try not to upset him," A'zyren warned, wiping sweat away from her brow. The only comfort she could take was that Kain and Hephaestus wouldn't be on their own if the signals concealed an ambush of ships, but she was pretty sure Kain understood the message.

Communications warbled across the holographic emitter on A'zyren's armrest. The image of Lord De'Vayne appeared alongside Imperator Kain. Interference made it impossible to connect to the Olympus, and she wondered if Lord Hephaestus had access to the defense network. Kinetic rounds soared through the void slamming into the almost translucent hulls of the Arachne ships. There wouldn't be any reports from the attack force until they could seize the bridge, but A'zyren smiled, knowing her ancestors were tearing through the Arachne troops inside the ships.

"How may I help you, Imperator?" Lord De'Vayne fell silent.

"My chief engineer Corrigan detected some strange readings beyond the sector. The energy signature lines up with the *Mirror of Solace*. What are you up to, Lord De'Vayne?" Kain's eyes narrowed, his brow furrowed, and veins pulsed along his temples. Lord De'Vayne chuckled, uploading data.

"You'll find those are only cloaked emitters so that I can project my constructs across the sector. I took the liberty of deploying a cloaked transport to set them up before battle. Your Emperor can see through time itself; I'm sure he's well aware of my plans." Lord De'Vayne leaned back in his seat with a wry grin taking a sip of a drink.

Imperator Kain and A'zyren glanced at each other, but the communications cut off, leaving Lord De'Vayne in the silence of his bridge. Some of his people glanced at him, but only Genji possessed the courage to challenge his master. He moved before the captain's chair to bow before Lord De'Vayne. They stared at each other for a moment, and Genji prepared his argument.

"Lord De'Vayne, the creation of the star is the first sign of hope in all the long years of my life. Why are you threatening everything to seize control of *Empyrean station* for yourself? Our fleet could help turn the tide and save lives, yet you're holding our fleet back to soften up our ally. Why betray our allies?" Lord Genji's hand gripped the hilt of his blade. His eyes trembled, staring up at his master sitting in his captain's chair glaring at the battle raging on the viewscreen.

"Silence, Lord Genji. You're ruining the splendid battle I'm watching. Return to your position on my right and say no more. These are matters for me to deal with alone. You command only a portion of my forces, so remember your place before I'm forced to remind you again. Unless you long for extinction?" Lord De'Vayne glared at Genji in silence as everyone watched on. "I'm certain you'll have more children. Shall I kill them in front of you and try to teach you this lesson of obedience to your superiors? Is once not enough?" Lord De'Vayne waved his hand, returning his eyes to the unfolding battle on the viewscreen. Soldiers on the bridge, shifting gazes quickly returned to work before Lord De'Vayne could notice them.

Knuckles turned white on Genji's hand. His eyes trembled, emotion surged through his veins, and each beat of his heart echoed the pain of his children's pointless deaths. It replayed in his mind, and he couldn't force the images out. Lord De'Vayne sat over the arena, clapping, laughing, and celebrating the fight between Kain and Genji's children. The blade tore from his sheath, he flicked the switch, and emitters along the blade hummed with energy slashing an iajutsu towards Lord De'Vayne. Lord De'Vayne leapt forward, drawing his own blade on pure instinct. Metal rang through the bridge, drawing everyone's attention, but all the soldiers were frozen, staring at the two warrior's blades locked together.

"I should have known you were truly a traitor when you asked for permission to join Lord Void's little quest Lord Genji, but I believed you'd bring something back of value. You didn't, and now I must correct the mistake you made when you allowed Magnus and these pitiful humans to take control of an Ancient's artifact like *Empyrean station*. Perhaps you've forgotten what it means to be De'Vayne!"

"You are without honor and not fit to rule." Genji locked his gaze, staring into the eyes of Lord De'Vayne past the clash of their blades. "This is for my children!"

"Then today is the day you die, traitor," Lord De'Vayne spit.

CHAPTER 56

Blades scraped against each other, echoing the screech of meta through the bridge. Humming energy built up in the emitter along the edge of the blade. Both of the blades charged with energy. Both warriors stared into each other eyes, and everyone else froze, watching. They kicked at each other, shin blocks deflected each other attacks, and each attack demonstrated their equal skill. Lord De'Vayne pivoted away from the captain's chair, creating room. A wide circular slash prevented Genji from advancing after Lord De'Vayne. Robes swept along in rapid movements across the bridge.

A flurry of footsteps carried the two warriors in a dance across the bridge as their sword clashes rang out. Each warrior moved with sudden bursts of speed before clashing blades once more. Lord De'Vayne continued to evade forcing Genji to give chase. Energy sparked in bright flashes with each clash of the combatants' blades. Rushing forward, Genji unleashed a series of slashes at Lord De'Vayne slamming his foot down to plant himself firmly in place.

Sword clashes rang through the bridge in rapid succession with each deflection. Charge swelled along the emitters humming in the air with a visible blur around both blades. A blast ripped across the bridge, shearing metal along the path slamming into the energy released by Lord De'Vayne. Massive blast waves erupted from the colliding energy waves and rippled through the bridge, slamming people backward, through the air, and tumbling across the deck plating. Warriors circled each other aiming their blades at one another.

"Power belongs to those with the strength to seize it, Lord Genji, and you've always been too weak! That's why your children are dead!"

"You've lost your light, Lord De'Vayne. Now you threaten existence itself. These humans aren't inferior to us. They've shown me more compassion than you ever have in the thousand years I've served under your command." Genji snapped the switch charging his blade again, pacing in a circle, and studying his opponent. Eyes locked, sweat beaded upon both combatants' foreheads, and robes fluttered behind Lord De'Vayne charging across the bridge once more.

Footsteps were quick and precise, leaving Genji no room to take advantage of the movement. Deflecting the series of strokes echoed the clang of metal, creating a symphony of steel. Tempo increased, slowed, and changed in sudden bursts, but each step Lord De'Vayne took created the path of the mountain. He was firm, and unmovable, and Genji adjusted to the form of water, always moving, shifting, and crashing against the mountain. Robes flowed behind Lord De'Vayne. He sucked air through his gritted teeth and shook his blade slightly at Genji.

"Water form is weak, Genji. Infinite adaptation is impossible!" Sparks flashed off the blades striking in rapid succession. "To absorb everything that comes against you." A flurry of blows slammed against each other, keeping everyone on the bridge enthralled. "Endure the rise and fall of the tides of reality." Tips of the blades glanced off each other in the rapid dance. "None can outlast everything that tries to destroy them." Lord De'Vayne's blade smashed down overhead. "Even the stars fall inevitably!" He unleashed the emitter at the moment of impact despite the lack of a full charge, but Genji countered, unleashing his own force. Two energy waves collided in a blast wave, slamming Genji across the deck, but also forced Lord De'Vayne to evade backward, sending him soaring through the air.

Tumbling across the metal deck Genji used his momentum to spring back to his feet with one hand. He somersaulted through the air twisting his body back around. Feet hit the deck, squeaking, sliding back, but he deflected the incoming slashes. Charge grew in the energy blade once more, vibrating it in his hand. He danced, deflecting each attack, but his nerves trembled, drawing his attention to the rest of the crew surrounding him. The crew members were coming out of shock, some whispering to each other, but a few reached for their weapons, watching the battle.

"Mountains can withstand the water for a long time, but erosion always wins in the end!"

"Fool, you've nowhere to go. Surrender, and I promise to show some mercy for your treason." Lord De'Vayne stormed towards Genji, retreating towards the deck gate. A loud clunk echoed around the gate. Knuckles turned white, Genji glanced back at the door and then grinned.

Genji pressed back against his opponent, unleashing a brutal flurry of attacks. Muscles tightened under his skin, powering each slash and strike. Sparks erupted from the collision of blades. Every attack was blocked, but each one moved Lord De'Vayne further from the doors. A series of strikes created a small opening in his defenses, and Genji took full advantage, launching a kick that landed hard. Kneecap bent under the force of the kick sending Lord De'Vayne wobbling across the bridge, trying to keep his balance, and spinning around Genji unleashed the charge. An explosion of energy erupted, cleaving through the bridge and the door. Shrieking metal tore, shattered, and clattered down the corridor. Alarms blared inside the bridge, and lights strobed in the corridor beyond the mangled doorway.

"I don't surrender!" Genji darted through the doors. Soldiers lay across the corridor, some bleeding and others struggling to get back up. Disorientation gave him the only chance he was going to get. He raced along the corridor, hearing Lord De'Vayne shouting behind.

Beams of energy fire lanced past Genji, activating his shield in time for a blast to slam against the emerging field. The hilt of the blade smashed into the helmet, sending a soldier back to the ground with a thud, but still alive. The blade snapped upwards, cleaving through a soldier's rifle. A kick sent the soldier crashing, tumbling, and rolling across the deck into the wall. He evaded the next sword attack, grappled the arm into a skeletal lock, and threw the soldier into the bursting beams.

Thunder of footsteps echoed in the corridors around Genji, slamming his blade into the crack of the lift doors. Only a quarter of a charge hummed in the blade, but it was perfect for his plan. He activated the emitters. Force exploded in all directions rending the metal door apart. Heat radiated in waves off the blade, but he reactivated the emitters. Blackness glared up from the shaft, and he couldn't see any sign of the lift anywhere. Shouts from Lord De'Vayne commanding his troops echoed behind.

In his peripheral vision, soldiers rushed down the corridor around Genji, and the black shaft loomed below. Sweat ran down his cheek, muscles tightened in his legs, and his heart pounded against his ribs.

Leaping forward, he dug his blade into the far side of the elevator shaft to slow descent. He bounced back and forth on the elevator shaft descending into the darkness. Energy beams lanced down the corridor striking the wall and leaving scorched marks that faded into the returning shadows.

Energy hummed in steady pulses along the walls of the shaft. The sound of the lift rushed through the shaft. Charge built in the blade, Genji scanned down into the darkness and leaped towards the door, slashing his blade and unleashing the blast. He rolled across the deck, leaping back to his feet to cleave through several shocked soldiers' weapons. Several quick punches and kicks dropped the soldiers to the ground, leaving them unconscious. Alarms siren echoed through the corridor, the lift whished past, and footsteps rushed towards him. Internal defense popped from the wall, opening fire at him.

There was only one hope for escape in Genji's mind. He evaded the incoming fire, diving back into the lift shaft. Wind whipped through his hair, rushing past him in a howl. He slammed into the wall thrusting the blade through the metal. Sparks shot out at his face, metal shrieked, and the sword cleaved along the wall. Descent slowed, giving him enough time to think.

Lord De'Vayne would be preparing defense around the hanger bays. That was the only real avenue of escape. Any attempt to launch an escape pod would either be stopped, or the pod would be shot down. There wouldn't be any way he could defend himself, and that left the only option he could fathom. Commandeering a ship to escape the *Mirror of Solace*, but his former allies wouldn't make that task easy. Above, the faint sound echoed down the shaft of the returning lift.

The sword came to a halt leaving Genji dangling above the darkness below. He planted his feet against the wall, forcing the blade from the metal with a squealing grind. Exploding from the wall, he soared downward, watching for the sign of the approaching lift. He pulled his body together, falling faster. The wind howled louder, but the lift continued gaining on him. He flicked the switch charging the blade, and emitters hummed in the silence.

Darkness swept away in the distance revealing the grey metal of the interior bulkhead. Eyes narrowed on the doors to the hanger bay level. Timing would have to be perfect, Genji thought. He glanced at the two levels below it and the lift racing towards him. Vibrations resonated through his arm, emitters glowed bright, and the charge grew with his maddening descent. Instinct took over, and he surrendered to the flow of this moment. Energy arced forward in his slash toward the door tearing through the bulkhead and door screeching through the soldiers behind. He dove towards the wall digging the blade in, slowing his fall, and swinging into the room with a flip.

Genji drew his sidearm pistol to fire shots toward the soldiers even though he grimaced with each shot. His eyes scanned the corridor in both directions. Rows of soldiers opened fire before he could even land, shattering across his shield in crackling bursts of light. Returning fire, he darted towards the hanger and ignored the soldiers behind. Eyes narrowed on the soldiers retreating backward. Personal shield held strong glowing translucent blue faintly with each broken shot. He charged forward, slashing, hacking, and cleaving his way through the enemy troops. Tears streamed down his cheeks.

Beams lanced around Genji, evading through the formation of soldiers. Close range prevented most soldiers from attempting to attack, shields protected from the rear attacks, and he weaved between bodies with each stroke creating toppling body shields blocking incoming fire. Pure inertia carried each movement, producing each stroke in one continuous fluid motion. Blue blood coated the sleek deck causing soldiers to slip, slide, and stumble into one another. Chaos filled the corridor in his wake, cleaving through the final three soldiers with a wide slice.

The door opened in front of Genji, revealing the hanger bay only dozens of steps away and the line for soldiers waiting. Mounted heavy energy rifles unleashed a barrage of energy blasts smashing against his shield. Translucent blue energy glowed brightly before him, and the shimmering intensified with each stride forward. Side steps propelled him back and forth in the hall, beams splattered across the pulsating shield, and some blast struck soldiers rushing from behind. Leaping forth through the air, he flipped to land in front of the enemy line. Blade lashed out through the line clear one half.

Panic erupted throughout the troops in the hanger bay. Many troops were engineers and workers doing regular maintenance, but even hardened troops broke before Genji's assault. Humming of the shield resonated around him, warning the shield was on the verge of collapse. His eyes darted around the hanger, but he continued assaulting his way through the hanger. Clamour echoed in from the hall behind, warning of the approaching troops. His eyes locked upon the perfect ship.

Cutting a path towards the ship, Genji leaped up onto the hull. He slid right into the cockpit, closing behind him with the neural sync already complete. Holographic and viewscreen came to life, showing all the tactical information of the corsair class interceptor. An energy field erupted around the interceptor, hovering in the air. Hanger bay doors were closed, but he activated weapon systems with a thought. Missiles erupted from the undercarriage of the fuselage along the arrowhead interceptor. He overrode the target lock system forcing the ability to launch the missiles. Engines flared, igniting troops on fire and vaporizing several.

Bulkheads rushed towards the cockpit, but missiles streaked in front, erupting along the wall. Warnings erupted from the defense system in the back of Genji's mind. He glanced back to see the soldier fire the guided missile. Explosions erupted in front and behind him, but the interceptor tumbled through the forcefield into the raging battle in the void beyond. Systems weren't responding to his commands, and automated repair systems were still sending reports of damage.

CHAPTER 57

Bulkheads crunched inwards, metal crumpled, and screeched, tearing apart. Sparks erupted from the sawblades and cutting torches slicing through the reinforced gate. Hot sparks shot through the air with a whistle springing forth from the hardened metal, giving away under the force. Rifles aimed along the barricade in response to Commander Verdas's hand signal, warforged took position in the gaps between bunkers, and large tanks rumbled through the streets. Massive cannon barrels swivelled, missile launchers aimed, and smaller weapons turrets adjusted on the sleek grey tank. Crews loaded large metal canisters into artillery firing chambers. Successive thunks echoed across the line of huge barrels pointing towards the air across the defense lives through the city ward. Power armored troops aimed over the edges of the buildings and stood guard.

Empyrean station defense network chirped in the back of Commander Verdas's mind glancing across the forces arrayed in the cityward. Shrieking howls of metal drew his attention back to the gate. He watched the metal buckling inwards, sawblades slicing through reinforced bars holding the locks in place, and the entire gate shuddered inward. Steady thuds resonated through the metal. Soldiers gathered around Lord Marcus, energy blades gripped in hand and listened to the plan.

"Skirmishers will be upfront with Commander Verdas and his elite troops. You'll hold in reserve in case the front line begins to falter. Under no circumstances can we allow them to break through our defensive perimeter of the cityward. We hold the W'hyish S'yevel forces here to the last of us fall." Lord Marcus glanced at each of the soldiers' listening to him. His grim expression didn't change with the news. Golden troops marched towards the gate, energy shields locked, and blades drawn. Gun barrels aimed between glowing shield edges sparking in hisses along the battle formation.

Explosions rippled in the distance roaring through the ward, signaling to Lord Marcus and Commander Verdas that the A.S.A. plans were finalized. Only one way to the Infinity Nexus was through this cityward. Heat and flames exploded forth from ventilation shafts mixed with the chitterers screeches of pain before a loud whoosh ended the symphony of destruction. Clanging metal returned to overtake the ward with each loud thud of the enemy force against the gate. Beyond the gates, all the interconnected tunnels vaporized in explosions venting, charging W'hyish S'yevel troops screaming into the infinite silence of the vacuum of space, tearing them away from the objective. Lord Marcus watched the reports filter into his mind from the neural network showing the corridors sealing off. His eyes darted toward the sparks erupting at the only gate the enemy could enter the ward.

Gates rocked with another series of pounding by the enemy, and the cutting edges were ripping through the metal doors in steadily increasing numbers. Molten metal oozed down the door spreading white hot heat radiating across the metal door. Smoke puffed from the rolling molten metal, consuming anything it touched. Screams of the enraged W'hyish S'yevel exploded through the cleaved gaps of the reinforced gate echoing the bloodlust fueling the attack into the city ward. Syllables blended with grunts and screams of vengeance, rattling the massive metal gate with each thump of the enemy forces. Commander Verdas approached Lord Marcus looking around to see the approaching A.S.A. forces. Each of the building tops was covered with a mix of A.S.A., Imperial Troops, and civilians who refused to abandon their new home. Even amongst the front line, there were members of Clan Pleb who refused to retreat from the battlefield surrounding their Lord.

"Well, Marcus, looks like you're going to get that legendary war story you always claimed to want. You ready for this last stand?" Commander Verdas steadied Lord Marcus trembling body with one firm grasp on his shoulder.

"If I fall, I won't have to explain to Nemesis how she was right about my warrior instincts." Lord Marcus tried to force a half grin which caused Commander Verdas to laugh.

"Just fight better than that attempt at a smile, but if you die here, I'd half suspect the Lady Nemesis to hunt you down in the afterlife. The last thing you'd want is to end up in the Cacophony with the devils that sent these monsters only to realize you're still more afraid of Nemesis than them." Commander Verdas fired a shot through a gap to knock back an enemy trying to crawl through the widening holes in the gate. The enemy leader's chain blade cut away at the cooling metal, trying to cleave through the hardened metal gates.

Warforged clanged down the roads between the skyscrapers of the cityward. Overhead anti-gravity vehicles took position, locking their weapons on the only gate the enemy could enter through. The network was filled with reports of all the combatants readying to defend the ward. Subnets broke from the main network defense grid to manage traffic showing Mordecai's assistance from the Infinity Nexus watching the cognitive loads of the groups of soldiers and A.S.A. now merging into defense groups. Commander Verdas looked at Marcus with one final resolute stare.

"We hold them here with our lives. For strength and honor," Commander Verdas extended his hand. Lord Marcus grasped it and locked his hand on Verdas' forearm.

"For strength and honor," Marcus affirmed. A great cry rose through the Imperial force causing even the Warforged to stomp their massive feet, sending ripples of force across the deck. Clamor of the allied army rose to a crescendo drowning out even the ravenous screams of the enemy. Spinning around, Commander Verdas stormed towards the gate, drawing his energy blade. With a cracking hiss, the energy coursed into the blade as Verdas locked eyes on the enemy leader, tearing through the last vestige of the gate. Enemy forces surged around him through the gate as more parts of the doorway collapsed inward with a loud shriek than a groan.

W'hyish S'yevel forces charged around their leader, through the gaps, and even drove through dripping molten metal to charge towards the Imperial lines. Lord Marcus gave the order with his hand for the army to ready their phalanx. Energy shields snapped into force one after another, hissing as the fields overlapped, rifles open fired in coordinated succession upon the advancing enemy, and weapons fire exploded between the two belligerents. The enemy leader charged forward at Commander Verdas alongside the frontlines of his forces. Commander Verdas marched out front of the phalanx lines, staring down the charging wave of enemies. Two enemy leaders glared at each other like apex predators being. Verdas leveled his blade, staring down the crackling energy, and blocked incoming fire with his energy shield. He gritted his teeth, and his helmet activated with a thought. Energy blasts and weapons fire shot past his head, but he narrowed his gaze on the enemy commander. Two combatants staring at one another.

A scream of unrecognizable works bellowed from the enemy leader, but Commander Verdas neither understood nor cared. With ease, he deflected the first slash, evaded the second, ducked under the third, and rolled under a wide angry cleave to leap behind the enemy leader. Several W'hyish S'yevel charged, seeing their leader flanked to be cleaved down with a spinning strike when Verdas redirected his movements to surprise the enemy leader. Machines reported that the wounds sustained in the earlier fight were mostly healed, and he unleashed martial hell upon his foe. Slashing the edge of the energy shield through the air forced the enemy leader to dodge the cutting edge of the shield and blade at the same time. Wide slashes of the sword and shield by Verdas kept W'hyish S'yevel forces from helping their leader by attacking. There wasn't an opportunity on either side or in the rear, and Commander Verdas drove his enemy towards the pincer of the front line.

With a thought, Commander Verdas sent the command to his awaiting troops to fire. Whooshes erupted across the skyline, through the antigrav vehicles lines, and from the warforged. Guided locked missiles using A.S.A. algorithms darted through the chaos of battle towards the gates. Massive explosion erupted, sending W'hyish S'yevel troops scattering from the sheer brute force of the explosion, but Verdas used the force to drive the leader past the front lines of his own forces opening up. Now the allies closed around, creating a gladiatorial coliseum for the two warriors. Allied troops stayed focused on the pillar of flames wafting the blackened smoke away from the gates firing through the haze. Targeting visuals saw through the haze showing the endless tide of enemies charging back into the flaming gap despite the bodies piling up. Flames crackled on the blackened corpses of the W'hyish S'yevel, sending the aroma of cooking flesh into the cityward.

Chittering buzzed through the gate with the great beating of wings buzzing. The force of air exploded the smoke rising from the flames of the gate back into the city ward. Countless droves of chitterers exploded into the cityward sky, having found the only path. Packs of the leathery winged creatures beat their wings towards the antigrav vehicles and allied forces on the buildings pouring weapon fire down upon them. The chitterers' corpses rained across the city ward in the great storm of war spreading from the gates. W'hyish S'yevel troops slammed against the front line of Lord Marcus's troops sending screams, blood, and an explosion of sinew, metal, and bodies reeling across the battleground. Black and crimson splashed across the deck and armor of the combatants.

"Keep pouring it on them, troops. Try to keep them contained to this choke point." Lord Marcus screamed with fury slashing his energy blade through the shield gaps and holding the front line of the shield wall. He glimpsed to see Commander Verdas through the commotion, but the chaos of battle blurred everything. Walls of soldiers, blackened tendrils of smoke, and the sheer speed of combat made it impossible to see what was happening. Only the intimidating size of the W'hyish S'yevel leader towered about the troops.

Unleashing a bestial scream at Commander Verdas, the enemy leader struck back, allowing the energy blade to be driven through his arm. With the blade caught between armored plates, ancient bones, and W'hyish S'yevel flesh weaves, the leader used his body to rip the blade from Verda's hands. Pulling the blade out, the enemy leader held the small blade in one hand, trudging towards Commander Verdas, who retreated with slow sideways backsteps. Allied troops watched on yet kept their fire focused on the enemy's frontlines slamming against the shield wall. Ripping the blackened helmet off, the W'hyish S'yevel leader smiled through blackened filed razor-point teeth while licking his lips. Blackened blood oozed from his mouth down his chin. Flicking the blade aside, the leader focused his white eyes on Commander Verda's green dilating pupils.

"Brave hooman, and to honor that, I shall carve your flesh into the greatest golla the W'hyish S'yevel have ever seen. You shall fight for eternity to ensure my people's survival. Nubrek the Vicious deems it so, and so it shall be done." Nubrek prepared to charge forward at his opponent. Both sawblades were brought to striking positions, but a loud rumble exploded deep behind the W'Hyish S'yevel lines.

Screams radiated from the back, only barely audible over the chittering and screams of battle erupting across the front lines, but with a rumble across the deck plating, the terror grew louder. For a fraction of a moment, both Nubrek and Verdas glanced to see what was happening, but the flood of data from the neural network echoed the approach of the third enemy forces. Damaged internal sensors couldn't show the enemy, but A.S.A. sensors showed the Arachne ships landing across *the Empyrean station*. From the sounds echoing forth, the Arachne were heading here fast.

"Lord Marcus prepared our troops for coordinated displacement to the next position. We'll mow them down when they advance in the crossfire." Commander Verdas ordered, rolling out of the way of Nubrek's slash. Renewed attacks from Nubrek kept Commander Verdas evading the attacks. He grabbed, holding onto the metal-reinforced mechanized arms of the power armor to hold off the slashing sawblade attacks. Smashing one of Nubrek's calves with one foot, Commander Verdas created an opening and dove to roll backward, grabbing his energy blade before leaping back up to his feet. Spinning backward, he manages to stop Nubrek's slashing sawblade attack.

Marching across the frontline, Lord Marcus ordered the pullback of the frontline fighters in small groups. Neural network commands darted to small units creating domino retreats. Small groups of allies would pull back as their defenders used the opportunity to cut down on pursuing enemies. Lord Marcus marched, keeping the orders flowing to the troops watching the enemy movement at the broken Tannhauser city ward gate. Smoke scarred out the blackened words written on to the wall next to the broken gate where metal chunks were lodged into the wall where the gate had exploded into the ward. Shrapnel covered the walls and vibrated in the thunderous march of the surging enemy force.

Commander Verdas blocked the incoming dual slash with his shield and energy blade, but the downward attack put him in a disadvantaged position. Muscles trembled with the creak of power armor servos struggling against the weight, strength, and ferocity of Nubrek leaning in face to face. A smirk curled upon Verdas lips and smashed his head forward into Nubrek's face. The painful moment diverted Nubrek's attention just long enough for Commander Verdas to break away with a sharp push. Allied forces were retreating around Verdas, opening the front lines behind him to the enemy forcing him to slash at them with his sword while defending himself from the fury of Nubrek's renewed frontal attack. Massive force rippled across the deck, echoing the sound of something massive tearing through to the city ward. Both warriors couldn't help but turn to look towards the gate. Lord Marcus' coordinated troop displacement faltered at the moment as he and the allied forces, including the A.S.A., were all drawn to the explosion at the gate. W'hyish S'yevel troop raced through the gate in terror, now fleeing something far greater. Spindle spiked arms shot through the wisps of smoke impaling the W'hyish S'yevel fleeing to suck them back into the smog. A loud chitinous screech resonated with the screams of terror into a chaotic symphony of war. Toxic venom surged in spouts through the W'hyish S'yevel forces beginning to discombobulate their flesh in moments rendering bodies to puddles of mush and then eating into the reinforced deck plate beneath them.

Chittin spiked legs slammed through the deck plate pulling for the massive Arachnid, slashing four spindle spiked limps through the gate. W'hyish, Imperial, and A.S.A. were smashed aside with equal concern with the emergence of the massive Arachne leader ripping the gate open to make room for its massive body. Thousands of smaller arachnids covered its body, leaping onto the W'hyish S'yevel. Small 1-meter or smaller children of the Arachne devoured with the same viciousness turning the battle into a free-for-all of pure, undiluted chaos. W'hyish S'yevel forces tried to retreat from Arachne attacks while forcing their own avenues of offense against the Imperial forces. Lord Marcus, Commander Verdas, and Nubrek stared at the looming Arachne charging directly at them.

Frozen by the sheer power of the creature stomping through multiple missiles erupting across the chitinous plating, they stared into the gaping maw of hundreds of razor teeth screeching at them. Arachne forces behind the monstrous were driving the remaining W'hyish S'yevel into the breach of the gate. Without Marcus's orders, the displacement faltered to the chaotic surge of W'hyish S'yevel, now pulling them down into death and destruction. Gunfire, missiles, and attacks from allied forces were spurting into intermittent attacks that failed to do much damage to the charging enemy forces. For this short moment, all the terror of the Arachne seized upon the minds of men.

CHAPTER 58

Blaring alarms rang through the interceptor cockpit's closed confines, tumbling through the space battle around *Empyrean station*. Flames flying from the engines stopped in the vacuum of space, but internal sensors showed the damage caused by the missile to the engines were also spreading inside the ship. Flight controls were unresponsive, inertial dampeners were offline, and spinning was unraveling Genji's concentration abilities, but he managed to get manual control of the thrusters. A Few quick bursts stabilized the ship long enough for vertigo to kick in and the alarms to scream the next warning. The *Mirror of Solace* had established weapons lock, and a single missile shot forth from the ship amidst the chaos of the space battle. There was no choice but to drop full power to the damaged and burning engines and hope they held together.

Teeth clenched, grinding bone against bone. Yanking the control panel away gave Genji access to the narrow box where the flight stick control wires were smoking. With a few quick laser cutter slashes, he removed the burning portions and began to peel back the wire housing. He spun the wire together despite the uncomfortable electrical current leaping through his body. Flight controls came back to life, and he grasped the stick with both hands glancing backward. Alerts warned of the fast-moving missile, and he dove the interceptor towards the kinetic barrage being unleashed by the *Titus Andronicus*. Sensors showed the missile disappear within seconds of entering the field of fire. Communications were still down, and he didn't have any choice with the missile on his tail. He glanced back at the missile to see the Arachne and Imperial Battleforges locked in combat in the distance. The gravity shielding used by the Arachne would make them almost impervious to the attacks, and the De'Vayne fleet he knew lurked beyond the system would finish the rest off. All that mattered was getting to the *Titus Andronicus*, and that could only happen if the missile didn't destroy the interceptor.

Darting around the kinetic rounds soaring towards the *Titus Andronicus* there were inches between Genji's ship and the soaring transports filled with W'hyish S'yevel, yet the missile kept soaring forward, keeping the interceptor in lock to close distance. Meditative breathing wasn't keeping him calm either. Thoughts raced at the possibilities in these dwindling seconds, and he just let himself go. Using both knees, he seized the flight stick and access went to work removing the access panel of the communications. All he could hope was that there wasn't any significant damage. Ripping the panel out with all the strength he could muster revealed the damage was only minor.

Circuits, wires, and jumpers all appeared in normal condition, and the only damage was the blast knocked one of the CPU chips out of its slot. Sweat beaded down his face. Glancing back to see the missile closing, he found the concentration he needed. Impending death focused his muscles allowing him to slip the chip back in without a shock or damaging the circuitry. Humming signaled the computer system detecting the communication chip, was running diagnostics, and gave him time to turn back to the missile situation. Diving erratically, he hoped the sudden changes would mess with the missile's guidance, but it hardly lost any momentum in adjusting to the new course. *Mirror of Solace* energy weapons lit up, raining down beams at the fleeing interceptor, provoking a litany of his curses in response, trying to dodge the surge. Darting between the flashing beams, dove towards the kinetic fire erupting from the *Titus Andronicus,* hoping the weapons fire would hide his ship from sensors. Rain of rounds soared around him as the beams cut through them, trying to hit him. Sheer number of rounds began to hide him, the energy beams continued to pour down, drifting away from his position, and he adjusted his speed to match the speed of the kinetic rounds.

Glancing out the cockpit, Genji could see the Arachne ships engaging Imperial ships in full fire exchanges coming in bright flashes. Fighter craft swarmed around like flies. Coms filled his mind with the communications from the neural network and *Empyrean station* command channel as he connected, but he couldn't transmit any of his own information without clearance. He didn't have the focus to hack the system, trying to evade the kinetic rain of rounds. Focusing all his will on attempting to evade the surge all around the intercept and kept moving towards the *Titus Andronicus*. Computer diagnostics were still humming away, processing the coms system, and without coms, there was no way for him to hail the approaching *Titus Andronicus*. He glanced around, trying to figure out a way to communicate. All that mattered was letting Imperator Kain know about De'Vayne's betrayal, and out of the corner of Genji's eye, he saw the A.S.A. platforms giving him an idea.

Arachne ships slide through space, breaking away from the armada. Enemy ships clung to the hull of the *Olympus,* trying to continue to fire. Caught in between the maelstrom of the *Olympus* and the *Dawnbreaker,* the enemy ships seemed to absorb endless fire in gravimetric shields. Explosions ripped up underneath the Arachne ships latched onto the *Olympus* hull. *Brisingamen* continued to coordinate fire with the *Dawnbreaker,* but Arachne shields absorbed everything thrown at them. Fighter craft darted in a swirling hurricane of Imperial and Arachne ships swarming around the Olympus.

"Kain, we've gotta free the *Olympus* before it's too late," Lady Freya pleaded over coms. Waves of transports ferried troops to the *Olympus* to help defend the ship from the surge or Arachne boarding it. Each ship acted as a messenger in a subnet chain relying on information from the *Olympus*. Data showed the Arachne were taking control of the ship, and no communication from Lord Hephaestus had been established. The emotions raging through Freya echoed through the network to the Imperator.

"Pull back, Freya. There's nothing we can do. Our weapons seem powerless against these Arachne shields and hulls. Our energy weapons aren't doing enough, and the mass of that hull shows our kinetic cannons aren't going to dent it." Imperator Kain stared at the devolving battle and the incoming reports from A'zyren, Pandora, and the rest of the Imperial fleet.

"Imperator, I'm getting a strange signal from an unidentifiable fighter craft moving towards my ship. Routing the data to command network." Lady Marimba's report surged into Imperator Kain's mind. Seeing the design of the ship told him it was Lord Genji. With a thought, Kain unpacked the data, realizing that Genji hid it in a latent radio S.O.S. message to avoid

De'Vayne picking it up. He tapped a different message to Lady Marimba ordering her to protect the incoming ship.

"It's nothing, Lady Marimba. Just focus on intercepting those kinetic rounds. A Sensor blip is all you're seeing. Our scans show nothing there." Kain uploaded his scans from the *Dawnbreaker* to confuse De'Vayne if his cognitor spies listening in to the com's channels. Instinct told him that would be the best tactical move to make, and Kain needed to keep the truth from De'Vayne while he dealt with this problem first. Glancing to the rim of the Empyrean Sector, Kain felt fear tug at his nerves. Signals remained fixed still just beyond the sector, and if it was an armada, it was massive. There was no hope that imperial forces could fight all these enemies simultaneously, he thought.

A few quick modifications to the scans revealed the De'Vayne fleet beyond the rim of the Empyrean system. Small gravity distorts on the stellar map showed the cloaked F.T.L. jumps of the approaching fleet. *Titus Andronicus* was moving into position to deal with the *Mirror of Solace* on sensors, *Divine Retribution,* and Pandoran forces were dealing with the W'hyish, and the Serpentine armada continued a slow advance on the *Empyrean station* despite Lord Cornelius and Lord Hector's best attempts to destroy them. Damage reports of the *Dawnbreaker* echoed the impending truth the enemy was overwhelming their defenses at a steady pace despite the damage being inflicted by allied Imperial forces, and Lord De'Vayne was just waiting for the right moment to destroy the remnants Kain's instincts told him. On the scan he watched the missile closing in on Genji's ship, but none of his weapon systems were in range. He could only do one thing, so he accessed the A.S.A. subnet defense to alter the firing arcs of several of the closest platforms to unleash fire on the point Genji was approaching. For a second, Kain considered how to defeat the Arachne while watching the drama unfold. In the distance on the viewscreen, the random blasts fired amongst the glittering beams of energy weapons flashed against the void backdrop of the Great Maw.

Genji saw the blasts heading towards him and that the De'Vayne intuitive combat system didn't detect a collision with his ship. Mathematics unraveled in his mind revealing what the edge the action had just given him. Not even De'Vayne would recognize what happened even if he was watching the thought raced out of his mouth in uncontrollable laughter.

Pressing the throttle forward all the way caused the engines to ignite again. Flames leaped behind the burning interceptor's antimatter engines as they approached critical, but the alarms blared, revealing the proximity alarms of the predictive quantum computers combat software. Numbers ran on the screen and through Genji's head, calculating the algebraic equation of speed of light versus speed of the interceptor versus speed of the missile. Glowing energy streaked in with the relativity of time crunching upon him at this moment as he spun back to see the explosion erupt from the missiles collision with the sparkling beams, the spark of antimatter that erupted in the engine, and the blast slamming his cockpit forward spiraling towards the *Titus Andronicus* as all the internal systems failed. Oxygen began failing, but he couldn't stop laughing.

Catching the explosion in the distance, the De'Vayne interceptor disappeared from the scans of *Dawnbreaker*, and all Kain could hope was that it had been enough to save Genji so the truth of the situation could be known. None of the De'Vayne fleet scans could be shared in the network or with the rest of the crew. Only A'zyren and Lady Marimba knew of the situation at this moment beyond Kain. He was certain De'Vayne would be tapping every network and subnetwork. There wasn't any way for him to get a message to Matthew, and he turned back to deal with the grim situation involving the Arachne. Only one possibility leaped out to Kain, and he established coms again with his father.

"Tell me, is there something on that ship that'll deal with these Arachne vessels? Nothing we do seems to faze them. They're magnifying the ships' gravity, making them almost impervious to our weapons. I need something to crack through that shell." Kain's words echoed his frustration, bringing out Gabriel's laughter and fueling only more frustration. About to snap, Kain was cut off.

"Son, if you can't use your fist or your feet, what do you use?" Gabriel's words brought Kain spinning back to reality from his thoughts. The words sunk Kain into a flash of the memories of the first time he'd knocked his father on the ground. When his fist and feet had failed, he used his whole body, throwing everything at his father to defeat him. Strategy rushed back along with laughter erupting from both of them in response.

"You win by tooth and nail," Kain finished the sentence, his mind switching into full offensive mode. "Lady Freya let's clear the *Olympus*."

"Um, that's what we're trying to do already, Kain. Have you lost your damn mind?"

"All hands lay in a direct collision course with the *Olympus*. I want us to scrape the hull of the *Olympus* clear. Lock in trajectory vectors, full power to the engines, and prepare the inertial stabilizers. Joshua, you think you can do that mass effect trick with both ships from a distance?" Imperator Kain reached for his brother's mind linking their thoughts together. Joshua pulled up the engineering specs on both Imperial ships, looking at the power their mass acceleration gravity engines generated. He examined the situation before realizing he needed a bigger wavefield generator.

"Going to need something big enough to do something like that, so it's a good thing we got Mordecai and the A.S.A. on our side." Joshua began accessing the systems to enact his plan.

It only took a thought for Joshua's mind to merge with Mordecai's neural network, which provided a map for the A.S.A. subnets. Accessing the A.S.A. subnets, he accessed the Mechanarium's of Gyros field manipulators. Within a few moments, he had begun directing Higgs fields directly from the Mechanarium towards the *Dawnbreaker* and *Brisingamen*. Mass dropped on the ships rapidly, causing the effects of the engine to propel the *Dawnbreaker* faster and allowing the *Brisingamen* to pick up speed quickly as the two ships charged toward the beleaguered *Olympus*. On the verge of F.T.L. speeds, it was only a few thoughts, some split-second mathematical calculations, and a moment of time before the ship's mass increased exponentially. Not even the Arachne gravimetric web slowed the increasing exponential masses on a collision course with the enemy ships on the *Olympus* hull.

In the distance, the *Divine Retribution*, *Death's Reaper*, and Pandoran forces struggled against the W'hyish S'yevel forces still surging towards the *Empyrean station*. Kinetic rounds tore into Pandoran ships, slammed across the hull of the *Divine Retribution* like ticks in a fresh victim's skin, and forced Nemesis to direct her attentions on interior defense. Kinetic rounds from the *Sesh'yna* drove the Arachne armada into a splinter formation stopping the main line of transport to the *Empyrean station*. Several transports and Arachne ships redirected to attack the *Sesh'yna*. *Iliad* and *Sentinel* were being overwhelmed by Serpentine fighter craft and managed to start falling back to the inner perimeter of defense. A moving firing line of energy blast lit up that quadrant of the sector. Imperator Kain kept his mind on the enormity of the raging battle staring at his target on the screen.

Arachne ships began to unlatch from the hull of the *Olympus*, with sensors showing a decreasing mass of the vessels to accelerate the movement. Kain's intuition took over, guiding his hands and thoughts. Entire banks of available weapons swivelled aiming at the fleeing target while its mass dropped before weapons fire unleashed in torrential salvos of energy and metal. Antimatter reactors of the smaller Arachne ships tore to shreds causing massive waves of explosions to ripple across the damaged *Olympus'* hull, sending flames into the gaping scars across the ship. One after another, fleeing Arachne ships exploded under the sustained fire of the *Dawnbreaker* and the joining fire of the *Brisingamen*. Reports broke through from the *Olympus* as the jamming fields of the Arachne ships began to falter with their dwindling numbers.

"Imperator…" Lord Hephaestus's voice broke through for a second before static overtook it.

"Hold on, brother, we're coming. Hold the line just a little bit longer." Kain knew his words weren't being heard, but they were spoken from pure instinct. The words echoed across the neural networks and reassured his allies that he was listening even if Hephaestus couldn't hear them. On the viewscreen, the *Olympus* rested covered in ships, with the Arachne scurrying from them across the hull into the scars created by the space battle. Kain's eyes narrowed, watching the giant insects fleeing the impending collision with the two Imperial Battleforges. Inertial dampeners were being prepared for the collision.

On the viewscreen, enemy ships grew closer with each passing moment. Weapons fire from the *Olympus* exploded across the bow of the *Dawnbreaker,* slamming into the first wave of the ships. Bulkheads buckled along the bow of the *Dawnbreaker,* force rippled through the superstructure, and alarms surged inside Imperator Kain's mind. Inertia dampeners redirected the force away before the energy rippled up the ship saving the soldiers fighting across the hull from the boarding Arachne. All across the hull, explosions jetted flames, debris, and even Arachne skittered through the zero-G environmental hazards across the hulls of the ships looking to get inside. Both ships scraped across the hull of the *Olympus,* tearing the Arachne vessels clamped down upon the hull free into exploding balls of antimatter and matter rippling across the hulls of the three ships. Warnings blared across the network, and subnetworks of the ships, but the interference fled with the retreating Arachne trying to reform battle formations moving towards the *Empyrean station* away from the trinity of Battleforges.

"Reactor…" Static overtook Hephaestus's words, telling Imperator Kain something else was wrong that was interfering with the comms.

"Imperator, it appears the *Olympus* reactor is under severe attack by Arachne forces. It seems to be going critical. We need to reinforce Lord Hephaestus's troops," Lady Freya pleaded. The data filtering across the networks into Kain's mind echoed with the severity of the emergency. Chasing after the Arachne forces would only ensure the destruction of the *Olympus*, but the other forces were tied up. Only Joshua and Celeris stood a chance to hold the inner ring of defenses, but their ships were divided. *Icarus* was still acting as point defense for the *Empyrean station*, but *Templar* had moved to aid the *Iliad* and *Sentinel* retreating from the Serpentine fleets, and waiting beyond the system was the growing mass of De'Vayne forces.

Giant Arachne covered the hulls of the three ships tearing through the hull with torrents of acid, rending of giant claws, and coordinated effort. Arachne armada splintered into two groups. The first drove towards the *Empyrean station*, deploying transports and fighters to get their troops past the last line of defense, but the other half turned back to deal with the *Dawnbreaker, Olympus*, and *Brisingamen*. Gripping the chair, Kain stared at the forming Arachne lines while maneuvering his ship to defend his brothers. Tactical showed the three ships lining together to withstand the incoming attack. Bay doors open along the *Dawnbreaker* and *Brisingamen*, releasing waves of transports to assist the *Olympus*. Together the two ships overlapped their shields to provide support, and Kain and Freya prepared to meet the enemy force unleashing everything they had in coordination to stop the Arachne formation before it was prepared to attack.

CHAPTER 59

On the bed Angelica lay unconscious with sedatives being supplied by steady intravenous drip. With a flick of a finger, Lord Galen caused the sedative in the intravenous vial to settle so he could get an accurate gauge of how many milliliters were still inside the vial. Despite the intensity of the chemicals, neural readings showed him they barely kept Angelica sedated. Neural activity showed the potency of Levart's possession of the neural networks of Angelica's mind. Even after studying the difference between Angelica's first scans and present, it was unfathomable to Lord Galen how this sentient energy was heightening every aspect of Angelica's neural and biological networks. One quick flick of the scalpel severed flesh, but the energy spiked, traveling through the nerves at faster-than-light speeds. Lord Galen watched the incision heal at near-instantaneous speed. Scans showed a phenomenal cellular division and regeneration rate.

Lord Galen stuck a syringe in the newly regenerated flesh, pulling a small sample of the blood before cutting a small sample of the tissue. Each cut was followed by a spike in biological, neurological, and energy levels within Angelica on the scans. Both of her eyes popped open to stare at Lord Galen. Two pure black orbs stared directly at him, but his focus wasn't shaken as he continued to work on processing the data, he's seeing in the blood scans of his cybernetic eye implants. Not a single cellular division marker was detected by his scans. He lowered the vial from his sight to see the pure black eyes glaring at him in silent fury.

"Release me, now, mortal, or when I break free, you'll not enjoy my attention." Levart struggled against the restraints. Black energy sparked from Angelica's eyes across her fair olive skin. Smoke wafted from the laser scalpel cleaving through burning flesh as it continued to regenerate rapidly. Lord Galen locked his gaze upon those black eyes of Levart, shaking his head, and continued his incision without pause.

"I don't fear you demon. My science will discover the truths of your powers then I will replicate them for my people." Turning away, Lord Galen, carefully set the samples he collected into a sealed container before shutting the box. Sliding the container into a safe on the wall, he slammed the door shut and pressed a button. Magnetic locks thumped shut, echoing through the small room. He sat down in front of the computer focusing on the strange neural readings.

"Oh, you'll learn fear in time, human. I'll teach you it myself across eternity when you reach my humble home. Whatever sins your soul enjoys, I'll find you in the Infernal Kingdoms, where I'll delight in teaching you all the thing's you'll never be able to learn in this life. I can smell the sulfur on your soul already, Lord Galen." Levart erupted in a cackle, but Lord Galen was overcome by his singular fascination with Angelica's neurological activity.

Synaptic firing showed that most of Angelica's brain was in a state of unconsciousness, speeding up its processes in which Levart's energy acted as a medium. Both consciousnesses were active, but one was sleeping while the other was active. Intrigued by this, Lord Galen scrolled back through the logs of Angelica's brain scans. It didn't take long to see periods where Angelica and Levart were active by neurological blood flood and synaptic activity. Since the first scan after the battle when Angelica had revealed Levart's presence, the neurological activity was growing stronger with each synaptic firing. The data was irrefutable, but it wasn't to Levart's benefit from what Lord Galen surmised from the scans. It appeared soon Levart wouldn't even be able to manifest control when Angelica was unconscious or sleeping. Her mind was seizing all control.

Explosions in the distance echoed through the building down into the lab. Accessing the Tannhauser City Ward subnet security system, Lord Galen pulled up camera feeds of the situation at the gates. Smoke wafted up into the sky, but the explosions continued to rattle the gates doing little to slow the advancing W'hyish S'yevel forces. Levart cackled in glee at the sight of the raging battle struggling even harder to break free. Frustrated with the creature Lord Galen stood up and cut the sedatives to Angelica with a cruel grin, staring down at the snapping, cackling, and furious Levart.

"Oh, not the drugs! Don't stop the drugs! They taste so good," Levart goaded.

"Indeed, they must, given that these scans show Angelica's mind or soul is winning this little spiritual war inside her body. When she wakes up, you shut up. At least I can tolerate her. She doesn't throw childish temper tantrums, unlike you, Levart. It seems that as long as Angelica is alive, you're trapped inside her soul at her mercy." Lord Galen stared into those black pools seeing the undeniable fear of Levart spread across Angelica's countenance without his knowledge. The prison of flesh so uncertain to Levart betrayed him with the speed of nerve induction.

"She'll die eventually like all your meat sacks do!" Levart screeched in defiance.

"No, she won't. These nanomachines in her blood will prevent aging, repair even the most extreme damage, and, unless every cell of her brain is destroyed, will continue to rebuild her. It seems I've created a near-perfect immortal prison for you, Levart." Lord Galen mocked Levart, trying to hide the fact the experiment intended to extract the demonic essence. Misery felt by Levart's struggle to break free at least kept the demon quiet while Lord Galen worked.

Sedation began to wear off, and Levart felt the power of Angelica's mind waking back up. It was like a vacuum of space sucking him from the cockpit of consciousness. Grasping a hold of thoughts, Levart struggled to stay in control. Slowly, the energy of Levart drained back into the abyss of Angelica's waking mind that possessed all the power of a black hole. Levart couldn't escape the gravity of the consciousness pulling him back into the abyss in the darkest recesses of Angelica's mind. Black pools receded away, revealing the whites of her eyes.

"What are you doing to me?" Angelica's words came in a slow whisper, almost missed by Lord Galen. It took him a moment to even register what she'd said before he turned with a grin.

"I'm just controlling that nasty little demon in your mind, dear."

"Levart's trying to break free. He will eventually; I just know it." Angelica choked back on the tears streaming down her face. Regret surged in her mind echoing in the neurological scans, but Lord Galen missed the surge of Levart's energy. Busy checking the vital signs, Lord Galen wanted to make sure the presence of the Reverie wasn't causing any subtle long-term damage.

"You've no clue how sublime your mind is, Angelica. Levart has no control over you."

"How is that possible?" Angelica struggled to understand.

"I'm not entirely sure." Lord Galen slid the scanner monitor so that Angelica could see it. "Your synaptic strength has been increasing exponentially while you're awake, but even when you're unconscious, the synaptic strength is still growing. Only in the unconscious moments now Levart can manifest himself to take control. He's annoying, so I can only imagine how he sounds inside your mind." Lord Galen pointed to the energy patterns in the neural charts.

In that moment, fear fled from Angelica, and she realized her power. Levart's thoughts weren't growing quiet because he was gaining control but because Angelica was growing stronger. This thought caused a screech from Levart from the darkest recesses of the subconscious, causing Angelica to grin for a second until she realized Lord Galen and Lord Whelsey might be getting close to figuring out how to extract the demon. This newfound power wasn't something Angelica intended to let go of, and the urgency meant she had to master it fast. Explosions rippled through the building from the raging battle on the screens drawing Angelica's attention. She could feel the hunger of Levart for combat, joining with her own lust for combat.

"I surrender to you," Levart whispered from Angelica's subconscious. He wasn't sure she even heard his admission until there was a faint glimpse at the screen. Only the thought told him what his host was thinking. Escaping this lab was the only thought echoing in Angelica's mind and seeing the approaching Lord Whelsey on the video feeds filled even Levart with dread. At least Angelica had a taste for fun. He didn't suspect that Lord Whelsey did.

Rumbling of marching troops vibrated through the building's structure, but the door to the lab still opened with almost no noise. Dust floated down from the rumbling ceiling of the lab in front of Lord Whelsey's eyes, but he didn't even blink or glance at his granddaughter on the table. Walking up to the computers, he glanced over the scans, and notes, and drank in the science of the work that intrigued him. He glanced at Lord Galen with a scowl that demanded answers.

"Lord Whelsey, I've managed to scan the brain to determine how the mind works under the infernal influence. It appears that demons can, as the Ancients wrote, possess the human mind and perhaps other species' minds, but your granddaughter may possess something unheard of by the Ancients. It appears that your granddaughters will power is superseding Levart's ability to control the organic synapsis of the brain. He can only manifest himself when Angelica is rendered unconscious such as through sedation. Still, the presence of the infernal is making her biology more resilient, accelerating healing, and possibly unlocking other abilities I've simply yet to discover. I truly wonder if this is a unique by-product of Angelica's D.N.A., a trait common to her ancestry and if it can be replicated in you, Lord Whelsey, but I'll need to run scans." Lord Galen motioned for his ally to take the nearby seat while preparing the battery of scans.

"Do you think you can extract the demon yet?" Lord Whelsey sat down, allowing Lord Galen to hook the machines to his brain and neural implant and start the scans. For a moment, he was in such deep thought he didn't answer. Only when Lord Whelsey cleared his throat did Lord Galen snape back to reality, ready to answer the question.

"I'm less worried about transferring the demon than you being able to contain the power. We weren't sure that even Anglica would be able to withstand Levart, but now that she can control him, we must make sure that is possible for you, Lord Whelsey, before the transfer." Lord Galen began running the scans watching the information pour in. Both men were so engrossed in what they were doing they weren't paying attention to Angelica.

At first, Angelica remained still, watching the screens and data. Drinking in the information, she heard the whispers of Levart in the back of her mind sharing his dark secrets. Fear was tangible in the Tenno, like a predator learning for the first time. It was something else pray. Terror trembled through the nerves with the black energy that sparked to coil around her fingertips. Energy coiled like a snake around her arm but moved with her thoughts around her hand underneath the shackles. Soft crackling of the energy bounced between the metal and Angelica's wrist. She tried to focus her mind on controlling the pulse of the energy hearing intangible whispers in the back of her mind. Words from Levart were smoky tendrils leading her deeper into her mind's darkness, where she stored all of her anger, fury, and rage from her repressed memories. Images of her family flashed across her thoughts one after another in quick succession.

Energy coursing between Angelica's wrist and shackles intensified, jolting the metal shackle with enough force to cause a soft thud. Panic raced through her veins, sapping up the energy and causing the force to stop, her eyes darted to Lord Galen and her grandfather, and a sigh of relief escaped her lips when she saw that neither man noticed nor heard the sudden thud. Explosions and rumbling from the battle grew closer with each moment. Whispers from Levart merged with the sinking feeling in Angelica's gut that this was the best moment to try to escape. Summoning all her willpower, she focused on the anger, rage, and fury, drawing the black energy back to her fingertips to course up her arm towards the shackle. Sparks flew from her wrists in between the shackle and flesh.

CHAPTER 60

Webs of gravitational forces flung through the air in flashes smashing into the uncoordinated retreating Imperial soldiers. Screams erupted amidst the cracking of bones, metal tearing, and flesh rending from the gravimetric forces. Lord Marcus couldn't move or think for a moment watching the Arachne scattering up the walls of the cityward, firing their webs at the buildings through the Imperial forces, and hearing the groan of the nearest building superstructure. Working together, a group of large Arachne warriors were pulling at their webs latched onto the building with enough force to cause the skyscraper to bend towards the gate.

Glass windows erupted, spraying the battlefield below with trillions of tiny, razor-sharp translucent shards glittering in the lights as they rain down. Acidic spray splashed through the raining glass onto flying antigrav tanks. Lord Marcus was frozen, watching the enemy force overwhelming the Imperial and A.S.A. forces. Bodies flung past him drawing his attention to Nubrek and the Arachne leader fighting in the center of the gate while both armies swarmed into the ward. Intermittent fighting could be seen between the two forces, but W'hyish S'yevel continued driving to the edges of the formation to stay out of the Arachne's path. Only Commander Verdas's grip on Lord Marcus's shoulder forced him out of the traumatic daze he was enthralled by.

"Snap out of it, Lord Marcus! You need to take command and reform the troop's formation." Commander Verdas shook his ally with all his might, only stopping when he saw Lord Marcus's eyes dilate in response to the shaking.

"We're not leaving you behind, Commander," Lord Marcus declared reflexively.

"Don't worry about me, Lord Marcus. I fear no evil, for my Lord is with me!" Commander Verdas turned, marching back towards the two enemy leaders slashing through the limps of the first Arachne warrior that charged in his direction. Energy blade sliced through the attacking Arachne's claws and forearms, slashing down towards him. Crashing down the Arachne warrior forced Verdas to roll out of the way to the side just in time to dodge a gravity web thrown by another warrior.

Nebulous translucent fibers of the gravity web clung to the Arachne warriors trying to pincer Verdas in between, but he spun back in a cleave splitting through the face of the Arachne warrior, causing the acid venom to spray wildly. Droplets dispersed into a fine mist that fell across the power armor. Alarms blared at the weakening integrity, but Verdas thrust his blade into his enemy's skull until it was driven to the hilt. His eyes fixated on the black orbs of the Arachne screeching in vain under failing limbs, collapsing it into the ground. One last vain attack flung at Verdas was easily caught in his hand without looking before ripping his blade free.

Spinning back, Commander Verdas snapped his energy shield up in time to block the first slash of the charging flanker. Gravitational threads blasted from the Arachne's spindle like a shotgun, coating Verdas in a thin layer of translucent fiber. Alarms poured out more warnings of the crushing pressure being applied to the weakening armor integrity being devoured steadily by the acid. Actuators in the armor were slowing down, making it hard for him to keep up his rapid defense against the overwhelming strikes of the multiple limbs. A flurry of slashes cleaved limbs onto the deck, yet it didn't stop the charging warrior from diving onto him. Sparks erupted from the leg servos, locking up his right knee, making it impossible to dodge the slamming force of the Arachne warrior's gaping jaws crashing down at him. Pure instinct took over.

Commander Verdas thrust his blade forward as he twisted in the air. Gliding through the air, the two combatants' momentum worked together to disastrous effect. The energy blade cleaved through the chitin of the Arachne, unable to stop the movement could only screech, hiss, and snap, trying to grasp Commander Verdas in a flailing effort, and he couldn't do anything until he hit the ground. Striking the deck plating set off another series of alarms, but he slammed his hand into the deck even as they triggered. Sparks flying from metal on metal, loud clangs echoed amid battle, and Lord Marcus glanced back to see he lost sight of the Commander.

"Displace to rally point beta!" Lord Marcus screamed, flailing his arm and urging his troops back. W'hyish S'yevel forces were wreaking havoc on the outer rim defenders, with Martyrs leading the charge with flailing arms, crushing stomps, and abominable force ripping Imperial troops apart. Antigrav tank engines erupted in the skies above, filled with the corpses of the chitterers overwhelming the vehicles that were dropping out of the sky. Screeching drew his attention to the incoming antigrav tank forcing him to dodge out of the way. Flames leaped from the wreckage smashing, tumbling, and crashing through the battlefield through allies and enemies alike.

Nubrek and the Arachne leader were focused on each other for the moment. The only thing that gave Lord Marcus hope was that neither enemy force was fully coordinated. Chaos gave him a chance once he reached the second line. Lord Whelsey's estate and the nearby park being converted into a Cathedral provided some defensive opportunities. Storming towards the building, Lord Whelsey's troops tried to stop Lord Marcus, but he executed the first one to speak, getting the immediate attention of all the other soldiers. Turning, he pointed to the soldiers still trying to retreat. Imperial soldiers were being cut down by claw, acid, and weapons fire as he spoke to address the group of Lord Whelsey's troops.

"I don't care who any of you think you serve right now. Our enemies don't care, either. They're coming to kill you, your families, and your children. None of these monsters care about your politics, beliefs, or even God almighty. These foes are here to devour you, and they will unless you fight!" Lord Marcus directed the soldiers remaining at the defensive perimeter.

Steady thumps of gunfire erupted along the front line of the barricades in the steady flow of Imperial soldiers retreating to the safety of rally point beta. Fleshweaver clan were attending to the wounded in the Whelsey estate courtyard and the main floor's interior. Lord Marcus scanned the situation from the upper floor before returning to stare into the battlefield. A series of loud explosions erupted all over the sky of the cityward, and blast waves carried a cloud of dust with them. The Groan of skyscrapers echoed across the cityward before beginning to topple. Metal I-beams, concrete chunks, and whole sections of walls smashed down across the ward distorted the view of the Tannhauser gate, but he could make out shadowy figures in the dust cloud. The figure in the middle of the melee appeared to be the size and shape of Commander Verdas striding toward the battling enemy leaders smashing into the center of the gate. Shadows of enemies approached in the dust cloud, drawing his attention back to the battle at hand. He motioned to troops in the direction of the incoming attack. A flash of beams cut through the thick dust slamming into the approaching enemies.

***

"So, is it possible to transfer the demon to me?" Lord Whelsey looked to Lord Galen, but the silence was the only response as data poured onto the screens.

Lord Galen watched the scans of Lord Whelsey coming onto the screens set up for display. A holographic matrix constructed a model next to Lord Galen, granting him a look at the working brain in real-time. Contrast scans between Angelica's and Lord Whelsey's first scan showed similarities in certain regions of the brain likely caused by genetic relation in Lord Galen's hypothesis, but the base structure of her brain was so much more advanced. Matthew was the only other member of the original Alcatraz crew with such dense dendrite structures. Perhaps there had been something more to Solomon's absurd notion of a perfect bloodline. Fear rose up in Lord Galen's nerves when he realized Lord Whelsey wouldn't be able to contain Levart, but that wasn't a truth that was going to be told to the tyrannical man of the so-called one true God.

"It should be possible to transfer the consciousness of Levart, which is just living sentient negative energy, but I fear the result could be fatal for your granddaughter." Lord Galen looked to Lord Whelsey for his decision already, knowing the temptation of power would erode any reason.

Terror trembled through Angelica's nerves, but she knew it wasn't her own fear. It was Levart struggling to escape Angelica and the prison of flesh he would be transferred to next. Energy surged through the nerves fueled by fear. Black energy crackled louder between Angelica's wrist and shackle.

With each passing second, the metal heated up from the coursing of power through it. Heat radiating from the hot metal burned her skin, but she bit down hard, grimacing from the pain. Black energy coursed all over her skin, leaping onto the medical bed, and her eyes began to turn black once more, but neither Lord Whelsey nor Lord Galen noticed the situation. Engrossed in the science of energy transfer, he didn't hear the nearby noise while explaining to Lord Whelsey, who hung on every word being spoken.

"I'll have to use a positive energy force of significant power to draw Levart from your granddaughter's body and a negative energy channel to force him into yours. Our only hope is the laws of positive to negative energy exchange, but of course, this is all purely theoretical. No one has ever held scientific proof of demons, let alone tried to channel their negative power from one host to another." Lord Galen prattled on, drawing the attention of Lord Whelsey, standing to look over his shoulder with the machine still hooked up. Steady whirring of the computer drowned out the crackling from behind the two men.

Glancing around the room, Angelica spotted the doorway to escape, but her eyes darted instead towards the energy whips. There was no sign of her power armor, but the feeling of power coursing through her filled her with a feeling of invincibility. Heat radiating from the shackle seared at her skin, but with Levart's help, she didn't feel any pain. Only the feeling of pure ecstasy of power coursed through her mind now from the deepest subconscious. Levart's full power hummed through Angelica's nerves, and his whispering voice fell away to her bubbling inferno of rage, thundering with each beat of her heart. Black energy coursed rapidly across her body with each hammer of the muscles.

"Odds are Lord Whelsey that this procedure will kill Angelica" Lord Galen scanned Lord Whelsey's eyes for any hint of remorse. He could already sense Angelica's death wouldn't stop Lord Whelsey from trying to seize the demon's power.

"That's none of our concern. Just make her death look natural and unavoidable in the autopsy. No need to draw the ire of my daughter into the mix with the plans to deal with Matthew." Lord Whelsey turned to sit back down but saw the sight of Angelica. Pure black eyes glared from the olive countenance twisting with rage before the shackles began to resonate.

Ringing grew louder, drawing Lord Galen's attention to what was happening. Rushing to the intravenous drip, he tried to slam a needle of the most potent sedatives. Crackling electrical energy sparked from Angelica tearing through the laboratory, striking the walls and ceiling. The first squeeze did nothing, and so he dumped the entire needle into the drip before backing away to notice the intravenous tube had been severed. Panic gripped both men tight, holding them still for a second. Lord Galen was first to snap out of it, who sensed the resonance frequency was about to cause an explosion of force between Angelica's arm and shackle.

Darting back to the computer Lord Galen inputted his command override, trigging an emergency system to pop up on the main screen. With the taps of a few buttons, he began dumping the data he'd collected into his safe lab. Glancing back over his shoulder, he felt the pressure of time bearing down upon him. Resonating frequencies vibrated louder, with the chiming metal of the shackles adding to the growing cadence. Data dump continued on the screen with file names cycling in a blur, percentage points increasing at a steady rate, and sweat beading upon his forehead with the ticking of time in tune with the rising tempo of resonance.

Power surged through Angelica's body, causing black energy surging across her body to slam into the growing resonance. A loud banshee screech sent both men covering their ears. Shackles exploded outward, ricocheting off the metal walls. Lord Whelsey stumbled backward, trying to go for the door, but Lord Galen had already exited. The door to lab refused to budge, and the computer showed the lab's emergency seal was active. Containment alarms blared in the chaos of swirling black resonance of Levart's power now under Angelica's control. She walked slowly through the lab, her black eyes fixed on her grandfather, and black bolts of energy surged across her dilating pupils.

"Mother told me how important God and the bible were to you, grandfather, but I never understood until I saw the cathedral that you cared for more than your own blood. Gold and God are all that matters to you. You don't even read the bible, do you?" Angelica's fingers slid across the console towards the handles of her energy whips as she watched her grandfather's eyes dilate in fear. Sweat beading on his head smelled of delicious fear. Reaching out with one hand forced Lord Whelsey to flinch, backing away and retreating until he bumped into the wall.

Lord Whelsey backed against the wall and stared at his granddaughter, speechless. Terror consumed his mind, body and trembled in his eyes. His trembling hand reached for his energy blade but far too slow. Angelica grabbed her energy whip, ignited it, and cleaved her grandfather's hand away with a flashing snap and crack. She smiled, seeing the pain mixed with the fear emanating from her betrayer. Rage burned hot inside her, flicking off in black and crimson sparks, her nostrils flared, smelling the burning blood from the stump, and she licked her lips with a devious smile before reaching for the other whip.

"Religious people never seem to read the bible. It's quite beautiful. Micah 7:6. Do you know it, grandfather? Can you recite it for me if it meant me sparing your life?" Angelica pure black eyes flashed with a deep crimson crackle of energy.

"We're family Angelica! I was just trying to save you and save us all!" Lord Whesley managed to protest, but the words came out with the feeble power he possessed at this moment. Angelica's cackling laughter blurred with Levart's causing Lord Whelsey's terror to spike. He glanced around, trying to find some means to escape, but he was pinned against the door.

"Do not rely on a friend. Put no faith in a companion. Seal your lips from whom lies in your arms, grandfather. For a son dishonors his father, a daughter rises against her mother because enemies are always the members of one's own houses hold." Igniting the second whip, Angelica pulled them back behind her with a grin. She stared into her grandfathers' eyes for just a moment to make sure he realized his hypocrisy. Widening in realizing Lord Whelsey saw the whips slashing in with the revelation of his hypocrisy. "I paraphrased, but it's not like you read the bible."

For a moment, Angelica stood above the decapitated corpse of her grandfather. She'd expected to feel something, but there wasn't any feeling, positive or negative, just the empty void of nothing. She felt only numb, which alleviated a small fraction of the rage bubbling up, pounding in her heart, and coursing through her skin in black and red crackles of energy. An explosion shook through the foundation of the Whelsey compound, bringing her focus of escape back to her. She had to rely on her natural senses without her power armor, but the door only looked reinforced in the center. Flashing the energy whip, she cleaved the entire frame from the metal walls of the lab before moving out of the way. What remained of the doorway fell inward under the weight of the door itself.

Racing up the stairwell, Angelica cleaved her way through the last door leading to the foray to see the commotion of soldiers. Lord Marcus was outside on the patio coordinating defense of the estate, but Lord Galen was nowhere to be seen. Screeches of the chitterers above, sounds of the W'hyish S'yevel attacking force, and the monstrous size of the Arachne warriors drew Angelica to the balcony alongside the defenders surrounding her in power armor. Lord Marcus approached, recognizing Angelica and immediately trying to comfort her, but his hand was quickly grabbed by her, overpowered, and the skeletal manipulation brought him to his knees. Only then did the black crackling energy flared out again with the anger, instinct, and reaction she channeled.

"Who the hell do you think you are touching me?" Angelica glared with pure black eyes.

"Angelica, I'm Lord Marcus, I'm with your sister Nemesis, and we've been worried about you. What the hell happened to you?" Lord Marcus's eyes dilated, watching the black energy coursing across the skin of Angelica. Monitors echoed warnings of heightening neurological anxiety, extreme cardiac stress, and strange neural patterns, but for Marcus, that was the tip of the iceberg of strange as his eyes flashed, reflecting the black energy he was seeing.

"My life is none of your concern. Where is Lord Galen?" Angelica demanded.

"I've been coordinated defense. Commander Verdas has been overrun, and the enemy is beginning to overrun this position. Our forces are being driven back. You need to get out of here before they kill you." Marcus pleaded with Angelica from the position of powerlessness.

"Looks like fun if you ask me. Time to join in!" Angelica released Marcus' hand to push her way to the front of the barricade. Glancing out across the battlefield, Angelica saw the three combatants fighting. In the distance, through the haze of dust. She could make out the massive Arachne fighting Nubrek, Commander Verdas fighting his way toward the enemy leaders, and the swarming armies breaching the Tannhauser gate. Imperials soldiers froze up, staring at the black energy coursing across the woman with crimson flickers sparking off. Most of them froze up, watching her leap over the barricade.

CHAPTER 61

Tides of war were crashing down upon the Imperial forces spread throughout the Empyrean sector. Nemesis stared at the retreating *Sentinel* and *Iliad* on the tactical screen, moving towards the inner defensive ring with *Templar* moving to assist despite the pursuing Serpentine fleet. Her eyes narrowed on the strange movements in the Serpentine armada. Whispers of intuition told her that the Serpentine were holding back, waiting for something. Her eyes darted across the battlefield, trying to figure out what the Serpentine were waiting for. Neural networks buzzed with the raging battles, but the *Empyrean station* battles kept her attention preoccupied.

With a flash of epiphany, Nemesis saw the Serpentine's plans. Fighter craft battles between the Serpentine and battleforges appeared to merely be a smoke screen diversion. Inside the Serpentine armada, the biggest battleships were targeting the A.S.A. interior platform defense systematically, and that's why they advanced so slowly. Green blasts of massive energy sparked in quick flashes. The long recharge time threw her off, but her eyes were wide with the realization. Tapping the communication on the captain's chair, she narrowed the transmission down to the *Sentinel, Iliad, Templar,* and *Victory*.

"Joshua, target those battleships disrupting those A.S.A. platform defenses. It seems that's why the Serpentine are holding their advancement speed and allowing Lord Cornelius and Hector to slip away. Lord Oswald, you must get moving to engage those enemies at point-blank range!" Nemesis adjusted the tasking orders while giving orders to her own crew. Alarms blared, and interior scans showed advancing W'hyish S'yevel forces across most decks and the struggling crew trying to stop the advancing enemy. A quick glance towards the *Dawnbreaker*, *Olympus*, and *Brisingamen* reminded her that she could deal with those Arachne crawling on the ship's hulls.

"If we halt, those Serpentine ships will overwhelm us," Lord Hector warned.

"Not if you link shield in a phalanx the way the *Dawnbreaker*, *Olympus*, and *Brisingamen* are doing. Hold your ground or the *Empyrean station* is lost. They can't afford to deal with a third army attacking the station. We must stop the Serpentine from landing an attack force." Nemesis directed fire at the W'hyish S'yevel worldship watching the approaching Pandoran armada led by the *Death's Reaper*.

"Those serpentine weapons hit harder than you think, Lady Nemesis, but fuck it. Today's as good of a day as any to die." Lord Cornelius's ship began to turn on the battle scans before Nemesis. Communications fell silent between her and the subnet for a moment.

"Don't worry, Lord Cornelius, you're not alone, and I'll be honored to die by your side." Joshua's ship accelerated speed approaching the side of the *Sentinel*. Two ships opened a full barrage of weapons fire, with the *Iliad* began to turn, joining the fray. Explosions erupted across the front line of the serpentine armada halting their advance. Battleships green blasts adjusted aiming at the two ships, but the collective shields dissipated the focused neutron beam. Reports across the subnet showed the damage to the combined shields were minor.

Shrapnel splintering through space slammed against the *Divine Retribution* hull and more of the W'hyish S'yevel troop pods. Hundreds of the pods dotted the hull of the ship like splinters. Nemesis kept the ship moving parallel to the enemy fleet, trying to force them wide, but the armada was now moving directly towards her, firing past. Inner ring defenses couldn't keep pace with the incoming attacks even with Celeris' assistance. Lord Oswald's Victory was still holding position as well on the edge of the inner defense ring, firing only half of its weapons at the W'hyish S'yevel transport pods while his fighter craft assisted against the Serpentine.

"Lord Oswald, move to assist against the Serpentine now!" Nemesis' anger ripped across the subnet, provoking the first movement of the *Victory*.

"There's no way I'll be able to help cover against the transport pods, but I'm on my way. Not sure I'll make it in time to even help." Lord

Oswald's soft voice was ignored by Nemesis, who switched her attention to the *Icarus*. With a quick series of thoughts, she sent the plan to her sister Celeris through the subnetwork to charge the W'hyish S'yevel ships.

"Are you mad, sister?" Celeris' ship remained unmoved, still firing at the incoming transport rounds being shot by the W'hyish S'yevel armada at the *Empyrean station*. Data showed that despite the fury of Celeris and her skills, most of the transport rounds were still reaching the station.

"You're not stopping enough of the pods even with the A.S.A. help. We need to destroy the ships. Get your ass up here and help. Pandora's armada is almost here. Perhaps all of us together might be able to destroy these enemy worldships fast enough to stop the rain of enemy forces pouring at *Empyrean station*. My ship is being overwhelmed as we speak. I'm not sure how much longer I'll be able to keep the *Divine Retribution* combat operational. My troops are in steady retreat, trying to bide time for the defenses of the critical ship systems to maintain combat operations, but it's looking grim over here." Explosions erupted across the hull of the Divine Retribution, causing Nemesis transmission to cut out for a second. Static echoed into Nemesis's mind, but she stayed focused on the battle watching the feeds.

Icarus began to move following Nemesis' order, but the W'hyish S'yevel armada was fast approaching the *Divine Retribution*. Enemy fighter crafts were achieving space supremacy around the ship now targeting the weapon systems. Darting fighter craft weaved through point defense turret fire targeting those defenses first. All along the hull of the *Divine Retribution* point defenses, systems were blinking off faster than nanomachines could repair them. She was focused on restoring communications when they came screaming back to life in her mind's eye.

"Stop targeting the transport pods. My people have figured out which ones are most likely to be destroyed. They've been sparing our dead by ensuring that most of the pods you intercepted were unloaded. We've got bigger problems if you don't deal with my people now. You don't need to destroy the worldships if Pandora and her people launch full invasions. Those worldships are almost entirely empty of troops. Target the bridges like throats Pandora and cut your way into the ships. Uploading targeting data now to the network." A'zyren information poured across the subnetwork and gave Nemesis a moment of pause to check over it.

At first, Nemesis wondered why A'zyren had taken so long to reveal this information and assumed this must be some sort of enemy trick. Confirmation and verification of signal source placed it on the *Sesh'yna*. Realizing the Arachne gravitational webs and weapons must have interfered with communications until A'zyren got far enough away, but that led only to the next question haunting Nemesis. Sesh'yna appeared to be moving away from the Arachne towards the interior defense ring that wasn't being threatened.

"We sure could use your help in this battle, A'z," Nemesis stated.

"Follow my plan and trust me. Did I abandon any of you on the outpost?" A'zyren words betrayed pure focus on something she deemed life or death important. What little Nemesis knew of A'zyren did show that the warrior code meant something to her. Whatever A'zyren was doing, there was the intention behind it, and at the moment, there wasn't much Nemesis could do, even if this were a betrayal. All she could do was hope that A'zyren's plan worked.

Fire erupted from the Pandora fleet, now fully in range, and the *Death's Reaper* led the charge. Tasking orders to the *Death's Reaper*, Nemesis charged her father with ensuring the Pandora fleet could lead the invasion of the worldships. Data showed the lead ship was the *Orphan's Call*. The scan showed it was the strongest, largest, and centrally located ship of the W'hyish S'yevel armada, and so Nemesis tasked her sister with ensuring Pandora's force could land.

"You think this plan is something your people can pull off, Pandora?" Nemesis's question echoed across the network for a moment. She could feel all the minds turning attention to the silent response.

"We're pirates! This is what we live for. All Pandoran forces engage. Rape and pillage to your little heart's content but remember to bring back something pretty for me. Remember, I prefer things on spikes with lots of blood." Pandora laughed with maniacal glee across the communication as the *Queen's Gambit* adjusted course on the sensors.

Smoke wafted across the bridge ceiling with another series of cascading explosions rocking the bridge of the *Divine Retribution*. Inertia compensators failed, but none of Nemesis's crew were bothered by the tumult of battle. She walked across the bridge inspecting her forces and the growing tide of internal reports. All her soldiers followed her mental commands, but she needed to help the internal defenses, which meant giving commands to her first officer. Pulling her back from the work at the weapon systems, Nemesis locked eyes with her first officer.

"Inquisitor, I'm doing my best to keep the weapon systems firing."

"You're in command of the bridge first, officer Krima, and you must keep the battle lines while I deal with these invaders. This is in your D.N.A., you've served beyond your duty, and I'm proud to serve alongside you. Now keep this ship in one piece while I slaughter our enemies." Nemesis stared into Krima's eyes, and she nodded in understanding. The two women separated, marching towards their different objectives.

Reaching the bridge gateway, Nemesis pointed to the guards to hold this position and prepare to fuse it. She glanced back to see First Officer Krima taking the captains' chair before the neural network flooded with her commands. Nemesis watched the Pandoran fleet moving towards the worldship armada through the viewscreen, and with a deep gulp, she marched through the opening bridge gates. Drawing both machine pistols, she checked their clips as her elite guards formed on her side, heading towards the central lift. Already in her mind, she knew where to start the counter-offensive against the invaders of her ship.

Enemy forces were pressing toward the central reactor core of the *Divine Retribution*. With a thought, Nemesis set the elevator lurching down. Sounds of clips locking into guns, tugs on power armor to check for weaknesses, and then silence fell over the elevator. Interior scans and video showed Nemesis and her assault team the situation on the core level. Before the elevator doors could whisk open, she and her troop were already moving. In the distance, the sound of battle echoed down the corridor. Soldiers and defense turrets lined the corridor checkpoints where bulkheads were sealed in case of emergency. Steady magnetic boot thuds were drowned up by the screams of warriors, gunfire, and explosions growing closer with each step.

Rounding the corner into the main corridor of the core level, Nemesis saw the damage in the distance surrounding the melee of combatants. Corpses of W'hyish S'yevel lined the floor with dotted imperial power armor, black blood splattered across the walls and decks, and apexinels, chitterers, and the warriors of the tribes slammed against the steadily retreating Imperial forces. Without a word, Nemesis opened fire, driving back the flailing apexinels and slamming into the front lines.

Allied troops retreating back joined the elite troops marching behind their Inquisitor. Cheers erupted as the Martyr's head exploded under the burst of the machine pistols, and W'hyish S'yevel warriors charged at Nemesis. Short, controlled bursts dropped the incoming soldiers, and the rest of the elite guards opened fire alongside their commander. When the machine pistols ran dry, Nemesis holstered them with a fluid movement, drew her energy blades, and charged with a bestial scream that bellowed down the hallway sending terror through the enemy forces.

Apexinels charged down the corridor at Nemesis, causing the other W'hyish S'yevel troops to stop retreating for a moment. Two bellowing warriors charged at each other, but Nemesis pulled back a blade and threw it with all her might, catching the apexinels completely off guard in mid-attack sweeping multiple arms at her. An energy blade whizzed through the air slamming through the apexinels skull. Death spasms send arms flailing wide, smashing into allies around the apexinels as it toppled forward. Leaping through the air, Nemesis ripped the blade from the skull, somersaulting onto the back of the collapsing enemy. She'd already leaped to the next apexinels smashing both energy blades through the creatures' eyes, sending blackened blood sizzling in spurts in every direction. The impact of Nemesis' weight combined with the strike toppled the creature backward.

Subnet linked all the warriors' minds together on the *Divine Retribution*, and at this moment, Nemesis could feel the tide of moral shifting in the conscious connections. Imperial forces weren't retreating slowly into the core anymore. Nemesis stood upon the face of the apexinels, collapsing as it slammed to the ground before stepping off. Silently she glared across the retreating army of W'hyish S'yevel before unleashing another bestial scream the moment her troops arrived alongside. She charged once more into the breech with her troops at her side. They slashed through the enemy like they were air. Not even the Martyr's stood a chance against the fury of Nemesis' blitzkrieg.

"Status report Death's Reaper," Nemesis commanded.

"Everything is fine up here. Leave this to me, and you focus on the battle ahead. You always did struggle with focus in battel relying way to much on your instincts." Gabriel felt his daughters mind break connection from him bringing a smile to his face. Now he could focus on the battle.

Missile lock blared in the cockpit of the *Death's Reaper,* but Gabriel ignored it for the moment. Inertial dampeners were running hot from the evasive maneuver he was pulling. Diversion drones splintered the warheads off his tail while they open fired with everything the ship had on the wave of fighters sweeping before him towards the *Queen's Gambit.* Pandoran fleet was already diverting and picking targets like it was feeding time for a group of starving animals. From the throne room of the *Queen's Gambit,* Pandora watched her armada feast as ships slammed into worldships.

"I'm beginning my attack run on the *Orphan's Call,*" Pandora reported through the coms.

"There are still too many enemy ships in that area. Give me time to peel some of them away." Gabriel darted the Death's Reaper along a worldship destroying the turrets with precision shots.

"Come now, Gabriel, tell me this isn't the most fun you've had in a while and that this battlefield isn't the true home you've always longed for." The silence was enough of a response for Pandora. Taking a sip of her wine, she pointed to a ship on the screen and stared at her gunner while doing so. With a single nod, the soldier activated a few buttons, causing a steady hum to build inside the ship resonating loud enough that it could be heard and felt.

On the viewscreen was a bright, massive flash before a yellow beam of pure quantum beam of energies exploding from the spinal mount Pandora Cannon. Screeches of delight erupted from Pandora, and wine splashed from the glass all over her hand and floor. Fractured pieces of the worldship drifted away from the wreckage of the hole the quantum beam punched through the worldship. Metal and organics stretched and bent, trying to hold the two ship halves together. A chirping message beeped in the throne room and Pandora motioned to a soldier to put it on screen.

"Who dares interrupt this glorious battle?" Pandora glared into the gloom of the viewscreen.

"Pandora, what a surprise you've ventured beyond your little box. I'd not guessed you'd be brave enough to lead this attack yourself. I was expecting to parlay with one of your incompetents, but I guess it's more fitting we leaders discuss this matter civilly to ourselves. It's been a long time since we last saw each other, Pandora, and it seems you're still not pleased with the visage of M'hat." Shadows cloaked the visage of M'hat, but that wasn't something Pandora was shocked by.

"Still hiding that scarred face of yours?" Pandora giggled, taking a sip.

"These scars were the only damage you could inflict, and your pirates preying on my tribe have done little damage. You should know this from the pitiful hauls they've returned. Tell me, how many of them have you killed for failing to kill me, Pandora?" M'hat leaned into the viewscreen to reveal the jagged scars across his face from knife and claw. The only response of Pandora was to chuckle while tapping her long nails against the wine glass.

"Seems I'm about to do a lot more damage. My armada is about to take your worldships for our own." Pandora finished the wine with a smile before holding the cup out to be refilled.

"What if you were to come to meet me for a parlay? We both know you don't forgive or forget, but I'm certain the treasure on the *Empyrean station* far outweighs what you can take from my tribe or the W'hyish S'yevel. Our ships are inferior to the glittering prize behind you. Take this last offer of friendship, for I still hold and bear no grudge to your people. I could even get you a meeting with the Em'Pharis and his soothsayer." M'hat stared into Pandora's eyes across the viewscreens.

Glugging the wine, amphora gurgled next to Pandora, considering the offer for a moment while watching her soldier refill the crystal glass. A slim sliver of starlight from the almost finished *Divius Oculus* glinting off the angular crystal surface caught her eye. She leaned forwards with all the jovial expression fleeing her countenance leaving only two grim eyes staring at M'hat. In that silent moment, she considered the pirate's code, the situation on the scans before her, and the gravity of the situation. Leaning back, she shook her head no.

"There's no way I can trust you to honor any arrangement."

"Come to my ship and parlay as the code demands. I promise it'll be me, you, and only our honor guards at our side. I give you my word as a man of honor." M'hat's eyes sparkled on the screen for just a second. Long enough to tell Pandora he was serious bout his offer. There was only one last assurance she needed to secure, and standing up, she approached the screen slow, ponderously, and with a grim expression. Taking a large gulp to down the entire wine glass, she gazed into M'hat's eyes glaring right back.

"Swear on your ancestors that you will honor these terms and any future ones you'll offer."

"I swear upon my ancestors that I speak the truth," M'hat declared without hesitation.

"Prepare the hanger bay for my arrival but be warned, I've no tolerance for treachery." Pandora motioned to cut the viewscreen link, stood up, and marched across the bridge, walking towards the gate from the *Queen's Gambit* throne room bridge. A Snap of her fingers sent the elite guard to march behind her through the gates. The sounds of the battle dissipated behind the shutting gate doors leaving only the echoes of marching soldiers in unison onto the elevator pad.

Lift sped down the tunnel with the steady whooshing of the passing decks whizzing by in steady whomps. Tapping a foot, Pandora waited impatiently, and the second the lift stopped, she was already moving forward before the gate could even open. Commotion from the hangar bay came to a grinding halt when the troops saw their Queen appear. Work resumed moments later when Pandora ignored everyone to march towards her transport. Several of the troops broke away to take command of the best fighter craft on the *Queen's Gambit*.

Marching up the ramp, Pandora pointed to the escape pods along the transport's walls, directing her best soldiers to occupy them without any further words. None of the soldiers questioned her but marched towards the pods with resolute silence. Once the pods were full, she marched back to the ramp to scan for more troops. With a loud whistle, she drew a huge crowd of Pandoran troops who wanted to impress their queen racing towards the transport craft. She studied each warrior coming up the ramp rejecting any of the soldiers who didn't seem strong enough by throwing them off. Thuds of the inferior soldiers provoked laughter from all but Pandora.

"Alright, you pirate scum aren't my first choice, and those soldiers are already loaded into the escape pods, so they'll be no retreating. We're about to head to a parley on the *Orphan's Call*. You know me by reputation, so pay attention and fall to my commands. When I order you to shoot, you shoot, and when I order you to die, you say thank you. Death is your only escape from my sovereignty, and my blessing is your only chance to live. Do you understand?" Pandora marched towards the front of the transport making eye contact with each of the various troops on the ship.

Doors whisked away, allowing Pandora entry into the cockpit. She sat down, wasting no time to fire up the engines and systems. The flicker of the scanners revealed the data sync between the Empyrean defense networks and the Pandoran craft. Engines powered up with a dull hum that echoed through the transport and vibrated through the hull. Fighter craft linked to the tactical system before the first craft accelerated towards the raging battle beyond the hanger bay. With the press of a button, she released the locking clamps allowing the engines to propel the transport forward.

"This is your Queen speaking. We'll be flying today through a field of overlapping fire that will likely get you all killed, but don't worry, I'll be fine my vassals. Instead, please say whatever prayers to whatever gods you believe in, load your weapons, and fasten those seat belts because this will be a bumpy ride. For you few true warriors, this is where the fun starts." Pandora pulled the craft into a steep decline from the hanger bay, evading the first bursts of enemy fire coming towards the transport. Fighter craft formed a tight screen around the transport darting towards the *Orphan's Call*.

Deft finger movements activated the transports point defense turrets on the bow of the ship beyond the viewscreen in front of Pandora. Bright beams of red energy struck soaring missiles headed towards the craft, sending smoke and debris rocketing past the transport. The continued firing of the beam weapons cleared the way for the transport while she directed the transport through the path being cleared ahead by the fighter craft escort. Darting in a spiral evasion gave her a clear view of the rest of the battlefield around her through the viewscreen. Pandoran vessels surged through the ranks of the W'hyish S'yevel worldships, absorbing the kinetic rounds while firing tractor beams to lock down the enemy's ability to maneuver.

Jets flared upon the backs of the Pandoran shock troops launched from the maneuvering craft onto the hulls of the worldships. Fighter craft weaved between the flow of bodies launching through the void, beams blasts vaporized people in bright flashes, and explosions erupted, blasting holes across the hulls into the worldships. Pressure vented into space, but W'hyish S'yevel forces adapted, opening fire from their damaged vessels at the approaching invaders. Reaching the emergency escape pod system, Pandora typed in her personal override codes and pulled the manual ejection release system. Escape pods lit up on the battle scanner around her vessel as she activated chaff and distraction decoys.

Drone shot from the spiraling transport weaving towards the *Orphan's Call*, and the escape pods began to head in the same direction with each thrust flash Pandora saw in the spiraling chaos of battle. Pulling back on the flight stick, she aligned the transport on a perfect approach to the hanger bay. Escort broke away at the last second when the transport crossed the forcefield. With a smirk, she glanced at the massive M'hat standing in the almost vacant hanger bay. Only the personal guard stood behind their Niab, waiting for the transport to land. With a jerk on the flight stick, Pandora spun the transport around before reducing the throttle to begin her descent toward the landing pad. Flicking on the autopilot, she pushed out of the spinning chair towards the door. Striding in towards her new temporary retinue, she took a moment to drink in the confusion at what was happening, but the reverence of not questioning asked. Slow footsteps carried her through the ranks of troops of various races looking upon her.

"When I give the signal, unleash hell, you'll know the signal." Pandora's fist smashed the button to lower the ramp. Grinding and clicking of weapons echoed in steady thumps. Lines of troops formed up behind her. She glanced back with a smirk as the ramp slammed across the deck before locking eyes with M'hat waiting for her arrival.

Marching down the ramp, Pandora motioned with both hands for her troops to spread out as she stepped onto the deck plate. Walking towards the Niab, she saw in her peripheral vision the troops reaching the same point as the enemy force backing M'hat. He stood there, draped in the black armor of the fallen, a large series of four claw-like scars on his mutated deformed face. There was a moment of silence between the two leaders staring into each other's eyes when they reached a meeting point in the middle. Looking down at the diminutive, Pandora gave M'hat a smirk that told her he was already too overconfident. She crossed her arms and waited for her host to break words first.

"I must say it's good to see you again, Pandora, but I didn't suspect to see you under these circumstances. War's not agreeable with your mercurial disposition, so I find it strange that you're here helping these humans.

Even stranger that you've come to parlay. I don't remember you being this reasonable, ever." M'hat narrowed his gaze upon Pandora pacing around in front of her.

"Scars I gave you last time suit you. Make you just a tad bit prettier, I think."

"Insolent and provocative as ever. Not that sounds more like you." M'hat glared.

"Yea, being reasonable doesn't exactly sound like me, does it? Sounds wrong, doesn't it? Like me saying, those scars make you look prettier." Pandora smirked without any further flinch in her body language. Her eyes stayed locked with M'hat's during his pacing.

"There's no time for your games, Pandora. I suspect you've come prepared to listen to my reasonable offer. If you join forces with the W'hyish S'yevel to help us conquer this station, we'll share all the spoils with you. Perhaps even introduce you to our patron." M'hat studied Pandora's unflinching countenance. The leader's eyes locked firm on each other's pupils, searching for the slightest micro expression.

"Well, I must admit you're as honorable as you've always been. I suspected you might set some sort of trap for me here in this massive hanger bay, but it seems honor is still your driving motivation." Pandora smiled up at the M'hat. Compliment sent him taking a backstep, and he glanced around at the Pandoran honor guard surrounding their Queen. Silence lingered between the two for a moment while the war raged in explosions in the void beyond the hangar bay doors behind them. Closing hanger bay doors blocked the sounds radiating from the nearby battle.

"Honor is life, and death demands life. It's the way of my tribe if you'd had listened when I tried to teach you. The power we could still have together. Join me and help my tribe plunder this technological wonder of the ancients." M'hat saw the dazzle in Pandora's eyes.

"How could a girl refuse an offer like that?"

Pandora drew the energy blade from behind her back with a flick of her wrist, sending it spiraling through the air up into M'hat's throat, and her other hand drew her energy revolver to unload a single round aimed at the heart. Every troop member behind her opened fire before she could even move the corpse out of her way. Standing there, she chuckled, blowing the smoke away from her barrel. She looked around, seeing the dead

W'hyish S'yevel. Motioning with her hand, she sent the troops forward to check the hallways. Flipping open the wrist combat computer Pandora established communication with her elite team with the press of a few buttons. Escape pods had managed to evade fire by remaining undetectable through intermittent thruster firing. So far, her plan was still intact, and there wasn't any sound of alarms. She looked down at M'hat's corpse to spit in his face.

"Gabriel, come in. I'm on the *Orphan's Call* now. You're free and clear." Pandora sent the secret message using her pirate code before marching to join her troops. With revolver drawn, she surveyed the corner seeing that most of the W'hyish S'yevel troop's numbers were depleted by the sacred housing of the revered dead. She glanced back with a smile at M'hat's corpse just to let his spirit know the truth. Every little secret he'd let slip had been absorbed for a moment like this.

"Alright, be careful, Pandora, but stop that armada at any cost. Both of our futures depend on it." Gabriel's words reverberated in Pandora's mind with each echoing footstep into the empty, quiet corridors of the *Orphan's Call*. She couldn't imagine how many troops the humans were fighting on the *Empyrean station* with the ship this deserted. Reports from the elite unit showed they'd almost prepared to breach into the bridge from outside the hull.

Watching the combat computer, Pandora pressed the button to activate the attack on the bridge. Explosions couldn't even be heard from this distance, but the alarms blared to life and told the team the breach had begun. Scanning back and forth, she expected some kind of enemy attack by now, but the halls remained far too lifeless for her liking. She'd never experienced this unease before but pressed her troops forward towards the bridge, watching the status of the elite team on her combat computer.

CHAPTER 62

Razor claws flailed behind Commander Verdas, striding towards the enemy leaders. Screeches from the dying Arachne were silenced with a single shot from his hand cannon, but the death knell drew the leader's ire. Eight blackened eyes divided between Nubrek and Commander Verdas to maintain defense while the leader shifted attack. A series of claw swipes, smashing leg stomps, and a burst of gravimetric webbing tied up Nubrek, leaving all the Arachne leader's attention to fall upon Commander Verdas, taking slow steps back to clear space to fight.

All eight blackened eyes fell upon Commander Verdas, and he noticed the surging Arachne forces weren't bothering with him. Instead, the screeching leaders seemed to be directing the attacking force toward the defense lines. W'hyish S'yevel forces were skirmishing with the Arachne being driven further back to the walls on the outer ward edges, and raging battle from beyond the Tannhauser gate echoed the ensuing chaos between the two belligerent forces. Locking eyes on the eight blackened orbs, Commander Verdas gripped his energy blade and opened fire with the hand cannon. Round after round exploded across the hardened chitin of the charging Arachne leader, raising four claws high and rearing up on approach.

Slamming front arms cleaved into the deck plate, forcing Commander Verdas to dodge backward, but that moved him into the pinching side attacks from the other two arms. Piercing claws sheared the power armor enough to set off damage alarms along his abdomen. Alerts showed that the damage compromised the power armors defenses, leaving his torso vulnerable, but he side stepped backwards, cleaving one of the arms and channeling the back peddling motion through the sword stroke. He tried to dodge the center limb strikes of the last two limbs. Metal crushed under the force of the strike tearing the claws through the weakened power armor. Blood and claw pierced through the back, lifting him into the air, his eyes still locked on the eight black orbs.

"Strong for a human, almost admirable, and one of the few of your kind to die well, so fear not, my noble brood shall feast upon your flesh, noble warrior, as your body gives them succour to grow strong. Your blood shall make the Areop'Enap broodings strong indeed." Mandibles clacked with the words spoken by Areop'Enap, staring into Commander Verdas' cybernetic silver eyes. Not a single sound of pain erupted from the grim clenching teeth. He held the energy blade behind his back for a moment of pause while being lifted in the air.

"One day, you monsters' of the Great Maw will learn the truth."

"Oh, do tell this truth, so I can teach it my brood you shall give birth to." Areop'Enap brought his prey in face to face. The smell of decay filled Commander Verdas' nostrils with repugnance, but he focused his will on this singular moment.

"Humanity is the real monster that you should all fear!" Slashing the energy blade in a wide cleave forced Areop'Enap to snap backward to dodge, but Commander Verdas expected that. Severing the left arm brought him down, tore the right wound wide, and caused a moment of hesitation allowing him to cleave that arm away. He hit the ground with both feet, ripped his remaining limb free, and retreated back to pull out his energy shield in a snap-hiss. Steady drips of blood pooled beneath him. Alarms blared in his mind of the blood loss he couldn't compensate for.

Enemies circled around Commander Verdas, but none of them made a move. He glared beyond the energy that crackled along the shield, and suit reports showed clamps deploying on his arm to stop the bleeding. The energy edge of the shield wobbled uncomfortably close to his eye with each step backward, but he had to keep his focus on Areop'Enap. Disorientation was already fading fast, being replaced with fury. It was a cycle of violence all too familiar to Commander Verdas. Warnings echoed in the back of his mind that he needed to finish this fight fast. Nubrek approached with a malicious laugh drawing Areop'Enap furious attention.

"At least we agree on the real prey. Allow me the honor of watching you finish this wretch." Nubrek glared up with a malicious grin on his face.

"Tell me, human, why should we monsters fear this frail feeble flesh?" Areop'Enap advanced slowly towards Commander Verdas, staring him down and to the chitter of the Arachne watching.

"Allow me to instruct you in pain!" Angelica screamed, charging towards the battle. Black energy crackled off her skin, leaping into the fray. Whips of energy lanced out, shearing through Areop'Enap limbs, but black tendrils slashed out, slicing through chitin, forcing him backward away from Commander Verdas, still maintaining his defensive stance. Striking the ground in between him and their enemy, the unarmoured woman crackled with black energy seething from her spine. Seven long ethereal tendrils lanced out from each side, slashing through the enemies.

Cracking energy whips were pulled into flailing, whirling death beams dancing around the blackened tendrils tearing through the Arachne. All eight black eyes of Areop'Enap were focused now on this strange woman continuing her offensive. One whip line lashed out, forcing the Arachne to dodge, and Angelica sidestepped, sensing the attack of Nubrek, who found the second whip cleaving his head from his shoulders before being redirected to slash through Areop'Enap leg. Losing balance, he had no time to react before both whips were slashing toward his face.

All fourteen of the ethereal tendrils redirected, sensing the final moment. A furious frenzy of blackened ethereal energy tore Areop'Enap to pieces moments after the whips cleaved through his skull. Not a single drop of flesh, bone, or blood was left when the frenzy ended. Only the screeching lament of the retreating enemy receded away from Commander Verdas, still retreating. Crackling black energy receded around Angelica, who glanced around to ensure there were no more challengers before turning towards Commander Verdas.

"Lady Angelica, you must be a guardian..." Commander Verdas coughed up blood.

"Not an angel! You'll die if you don't get back to the defense lines quickly." Inspecting the wounds, there wasn't anything Angelica could think to do to help. At best, she could ensure the enemy forces were dealt.

"Lord Marcus, if it's convenient, I need an immediate rescue team sent to my locations, and if it's inconvenient, do it all the same under the Imperial authority of Lady Angelica." Commander Verdas drops his energy blade to apply pressure to his wounds. Stepping forward, Angelica's hand sparked with blackened energy she used to sear the wound shut. Pain brought Commander Verdas to his knees, grunting in jaw clenching grimace. Heavy, labored breathing rose lasted for a moment before Angelica sealed another wound. Abyss of pain overtook Commander Verdas's perception, time lost meaning, and when sense returned, all he felt was pain seeing Angelica walking towards the Tannhauser gates. Crackling ethereal tendrils lanced in every direction tearing through any living creature they could reach. She continued charging forward with reckless abandon. Lying on the ground Commander Verdas watched to the sound of medical alarms of the power armor blaring, but he didn't feel the smile that crept onto his face watching the carnage.

Monsters fled in fear from the approaching Angelica. Dancing across the battlefield, her movements mesmerized Commander Verdas. Not even the sight of approaching allied gunfire broke his stare, fixated upon the darting Angelica, leaving a wake of corpses behind her. Allied troops took up a defensive position from the Fleshweaver to assess the damage forcing him to struggle to try to see through their legs. Not even Lord Marcus' pleas to calm down stopped Commander Verdas' clawing to haul his body forward, but Fleshweavers pulled out their nanite syringes.

"Commander, be still; the wounds are severe. All you're doing is making it worse." Lord Marcus motioned to the troops surging forward through Angelica's path of destruction to reinforce the reclaimed front line. Troops rained fire on the divided enemy forces from the central position. Rumbling stomps of warforged resonated up the buildings causing intermittent shard falls from the creaking buildings above. An explosion echoed from either side, but Commander Verdas focused on only Angelica in the distance.

Fleshweavers pulled Commander Verdas back onto his feet, watching the nanites' progress on their medical feeds. He looked away from the angel of death in the distance for the first moment, but it was to find his instrument of death. Snapping to life, the energy blade hissed at his side. Enemy forces were scattering in every direction. Internal battlefields showed the W'hyish S'yevel transport pods were slowing, and the Arachne would soon arrive only to see the angel of death slaughtering her way forward.

"Have our forces begin pushing forward. Catch the enemy in between our pincer movement." Commander Verdas stared off at Angelica, knowing that nothing would stop her.

"Shouldn't we assist Lady Angelica?" Lord Marcus stood next to Commander Verdas, watching the massacre ahead. Arachne, W'hyish S'yevel apexinels, and soldiers died in flashes of black. "It's almost like watching fire. Mesmerizing…"

"Death commands us, Lord Marcus, and we mortals merely obey.

"I'm glad you're still with us, Commander. Your mere presence inspires the troops." Lord Marcus pointed to the surging troops launching counterattacks from their position. Gunfire erupted in steady bursts all around Commander Verdas, bringing a smile to his lips. Limping forward, he pushed towards the front line to keep his eyes on Angelica. Her charge carried her further beyond Tannhauser gate beyond the line of sight.

Commander Verdas motioned for troops to move towards the Tannhauser gate. Once the gate was resecured, the Imperial forces would decimate the remaining enemy forces inside. Empyrean defense network buzzed with his orders to all the relevant troops. Not even the buzzing alarms from the crippled power armor slowed his mind. Missiles soared in a volley to clear the corridors of enemies trying o retreat to ensure the gate wasn't cut off. Waves of flames crashed from the incendiary missiles cascading explosions erupting in steady bursts down the narrow corridors. Flames raced in both directions in whooshes devouring even the largest monstrous apexinels in bright flashing screams.

"We're never going to be able to hold the Tannhauser gate Commander even if we can retake it." Lord Marcus urged the warning but didn't dare supersede the orders. He knew the Commanders combat expertise far outweighed his own.

"You've not seen what Lady Angelica can do, but our goal is to support her, not hold the gate. During that time, we'll do what we can to finish off the enemies inside the cityward. Fresh troops are pressing forward, new defensive emplacements are being prepared, and the wounded are being evacuated toward the Infinity Nexus, where it's safest. This is our duty Lord Marcus and your best off to shut up, observe, and learn from me how warriors win wars." Commander Verdas marched towards the Tannhauser gate with an energy blade crackling at his side.

473

Troops collapsed around the Tannhauser gate, with Commander Verdas marching urgently toward the center of the gate. Inside he saw the path of destruction left in Angelica's wake. Pieces of enemies lay strewn across the battlefield with signs of retreat evident from smears of blackened blood, trampled corpses, and strewn sinew of Arachne splattered across the area. A frenzied blur of blackened energy darted in the distance, still charging forward and driving the fleeing enemies back. Gunfire opened from the troops, with Commander Verdas directing the lines of fire. Focusing fire on the extremities freed Angelica to focus her attack on driving forward. There was a brief flash of black when she came to a halt to glance back, nod at Commander Verdas, and smile before returning to her wanton slaughter of the enemies.

Warforged marched through the gates to bring forth their salvos of missile fire to rain down upon the retreating force. Empyrean defense network showed Commander Verdas the flood of retreating enemies had erupted into a massive melee in the outer ring. He took a moment to scan through the battle reports surging across the space battle returning his grimace. Directing the troops again, he began fortifying the Tannhauser gate, to Lord Marcus's shock.

"What's wrong, Commander Verdas?"

"If any of the Imperial forces in space fall right now, there'll be another surging wave that Lady Angelica won't be able to stop despite the grievous damage she'll inflict. We need to shore up the defenses here and at the other gates. Reports show the enemy is considering other options to gain entrance into the wards. We've got no choice but to divide up our forces now, or the enemy could break through to have a clear path to the Infinity Nexus." Commander Verdas stormed across the Tannhauser gate to assist with the defensive emplacements.

Lord Marcus stared out at the havoc being wrecked by Lady Angelica before glancing back at the troops rushing towards the Tannhauser gate. Gunfire exploded in all directions, missiles whooshes in steady trumpets from warforged, and screams echoed all around. He watched Commander Verdas set up the defensive walls for troops to control the gate. Arachne, chitterers, and W'hyish S'yevel forces could be heard in the distance of the city ward, but the thunder of guns drowned out the noise in regular symphonies of destruction.

CHAPTER 63

Flashes of light erupted across the stellar battlefield on the *Titus Andronicus* viewscreen. Arachne vessels in the armada divided in the distance to continue delivering troops to the *Empyrean station* and the front vessels latched gravity webs to aid in transport. Thousand of tiny Arachne jutted across the gravity webs through A.S.A. defense platform fire towards the station where acid left gaping scars on the otherwise pristine hull. Viewscreen focused on the Mirror of Solace at the center of the panoramic view of the battle for the sector.

"Lord Genji's vessel has been captured, Captain." Lady Marimba turned to nod at the soldier, taking a moment to read Lt. Uhura's name tag.

"Have him brought to the bridge immediately, Lt. Uhura. I must speak to him immediately and should Lord De'Vayne be involved in any treachery; we'll unleash hell upon *Mirror of Solace* before he can mobilize any treachery against us." Leaning back into the comfortable captain's chair, Lady Marimba smiled at the viewscreen. The status of the weapon systems showed her the readying armament, but she was enjoying the moment where she was the unsuspecting predator preparing to pounce. Her fingers rapped off the armrest with a steady growing impatience of excitement beaming from her grin.

Inputting manual targeting perimeters, it was hard for Lady Marimba to calm the glee she felt. The idea of witnessing the destruction of this traitor firsthand played in her mind. Each beep of button press caused her grin to widen ever so slightly. She was just about finished when the bridge door whisked open, drawing her attention toward Lord Genji being led in by her soldiers. With a wave of a hand, she shooed the troops away before returning to the task. Stepping forward, Lord Genji bowed before speaking out softly, drawing Lady Marimba's attention away from her task with its elegance.

"Please don't seek vengeance this way, milady, for we shall all be doomed. You'll rouse the entire fleet of De'Vayne amassing beyond the minefield, and it's still currently offline. We must be careful that whatever we do, Lord De'Vayne does not realize until we are prepared fully to make a move. May I show you what we're dealing with, milady?" Both eyes looked up into Lady Marimbas from the bowed position Lord Genji maintained with ease until she waved him to act with one hand.

Marching towards the scanners, Lord Genji politely moved the officer out of the way before setting to work. Deft movement of his fingers adjusted the scanner's field to show the gravity waves being emitted by the masses in space. Gravity waves radiated out from the star and all the objects in the sector. Even the smallest objects radiated some gravimetric waves. He drew Lady Marimba's attention to the gathering De'Vayne ships cloaked just beyond the edge of the minefield nearby. Armada amassed steadily with new ships moving from out of the system towards the rally point.

"Well, I assume you have a plan for dealing with this new threat you've just revealed?" Lady Marimba gazed sternly at Lord Genji except for a glint of emotions in her eyes. It was an emotion Genji knew too well from dealing with Lord De'Vayne. Lady Marimba concealed she was impressed by the technological display but didn't want her people to see that. It almost made Lord Genji chuckle if it wasn't such a pale reflection of the Great De'Vayne's madness that brought them all to this point.

"Best bet would be to prepare for their eventual attack while trying to free up our allies before Lord De'Vayne realizes we're onto his plans. His instinct would be screaming to launch his ambush now if he was truly a cunning warrior, but he hasn't. We need to maximize this mistake. Imperator Kain, Lady Freya, and Lord Hephaestus are tied up on the verge of complete collapse, and the ambush of De'Vayne forces could ensure that before anyone else had a chance to respond. Lord Cornelius and Lord Hector are tied up with Consul Joshua's forces dealing with the Serpentine, conserving their strength for the same reason as Lord De'Vayne. Both sides refused to truly commit to battle until victory appears assured." Lord Genji looked at the W'hyish S'yevel, Pandoran, and Imperial forces cluster with narrowing eyes.

Divine Retribution was bogged down, almost dead in space. Only a fraction of the turrets and weapons systems were functional from the scans' readings. Fighter craft pulled back, trying to defend their hive ship, but enemy fighter craft made it impossible to land on the *Divine Retribution* for rearmament or repairs. Defense subnets echoed the mental exhaustion of the pilots struggling against the tidal waves of W'hyish S'yevel fighter craft still swarming in the sector. It was clear to Lord Genji that Lady Marimba didn't care what happened to Nemesis or Celeris on the other battlefront, but only how that battle impacted their attempts. Her interests glazed in and out in the way she looked at Lord Genji explaining the situation.

"W'hyish S'yevel forces might be the weakest of the belligerents in this battle, but they've managed to tie up two ships and splintered three more into the Arachne trap. Right now, would be the precise best moment for Lord De'Vayne to launch his ambush, but his desire for perfection has rendered him the inferior leader in all of this. At least the Serpentine are fighting, but the De'Vayne and their need to be superior in all things demand waiting until victory is certain. We'll use that to defeat both Lord De'Vayne and his gathering armada by waiting until they make a move." Lord Genji began accessing the minefield locking in a prepared series of detonations. "Minefield can be recoded into small clusters we can rearm slowly to evade cognitor detection."

Dividing the mines into small clusters seemed a brilliant idea to Lady Marimba, but she remained quiet while observing Lord Genji, dedicated to learning his tactical thinking. Each cluster of mines was set up to their own detonation series to be easily triggered for precision detonation. Fingers keyed in rapid series of mathematical calculations that considered De'Vayne armada disposition, all possible variable reactions to the mine detonations and set contingent series of mine clusters for detonation against any stragglers or retreaters. Every possible plan was quickly countered with mathematical equations, his mind inputted with rapid keystrokes.

"This process would be much faster if your people didn't prefer such primitive interfaces."

"Well, your time is just about up, Lord Genji." Pointing to the movement within the De'Vayne armada beyond the minefield, Lady Marimba revealed the truth of her words with a slender finger and sweat beaded upon Lord Genji's forehead. With a grimace, he bore down, typing mathematical equations into the defense network system with all the speed he could muster. Blips on the scanner moved closer toward the minefield with his fingers dancing across the keystrokes to input his equations to the Empyrean defense grid. With a sigh of relief, he inputted the last command before the first De'Vayne ship entered the minefield.

"Plenty of time to spare, milady, and now we just wait for the right moment."

Lady Marimba finished the manual coordinates to target the *Mirror of Solace* but didn't submit the command yet. She knew that the sudden movement of the turrets would be enough to reveal the plan to Lord De'Vayne. One finger hovered over the input command, her eyes narrowed on the moving armada approaching the minefield, and she grinned with anticipation of the impending moment. Each second brought the blips closer to the minefield.

One after another, the De'Vayne armada slipped between the mines floating in the void beyond the raging stellar battle flashing around the *Empyrean station*. In the center of the viewscreen, the *Mirror of Solace* remained stationary. Sweat dripped down Lord Genji's face feeling the pressure of the moment. Thousands of his brothers and sisters would be wiped out in the cleansing flames of the mines. Gulping hard, he pressed the button and glanced back with a nod to Lady Marimba. She pressed the command to set the kinetic cannons into motion, and the bridge filled with the roar of the cannons unleashing a torrential salvo of fire.

Blasts erupted in the distance on the viewscreen spreading with Lord Genji's directions to ensure none of the De'Vayne armada pressing forward would survive. Kinetic rounds rained upon the *Mirror of Solace* at the center of the viewscreen, but the engines flared, sending the craft darting towards the exploding minefield. Before anyone else could react, Lady Marimba had already taken over manual control of the pilot, projecting Lord De'Vayne's path. She glanced at Lord Genji with a look that told him what to do. He darted towards the weapons control taking over control with a polite shove from the officer.

Cascading explosions ripped across the outer rim from Genji's mathematical algorithm predicting the De'Vayne ship movements before they reacted to the mines. Scans showed the real-time destruction of the De'Vayne ships trying to outmaneuver the trap, but only the ships that turned to retreat had any chance of surviving Lord Genji's plan. Turrets poured fire at the fleeing *Mirror of Solace,* retreating towards the minefield. Communications beeped across the bridge for a second before Lady Marimba threw the holographic displays on to allow Lord De'Vayne to appear.

"You're treacherous scum, Lord Genji, betraying your own people. I swear you'll suffer in ways you can't even comprehend yet for this." Venom spewed in words and the gaze from Lord De'Vayne's holographic image until it turned in reaction to Lady Marimba's laughter.

"Words of a fleeing coward being driven are a sweet lamentation I'll savor for some time. Flee, great Lord, from the thunder of my rage and lightning of my furious cannonade." Lady Marimba leaned forward, staring into the holographic eyes of Lord De'Vayne, commanding silence in return.

Thundering kinetic cannons echoed through the bridge with Lord Genji's smiling. *Mirror of Solace* was moving fast away from the *Titus Andronicus,* yet steady flashes of shields revealed the difficulty of dodging the razor storm of shells pouring from the turrets. Caught between the wall of fire decimating the De'Vayne armada and the fury of the *Titus Andronicus* left, Lord De'Vayne forced to begin blasting a way through the minefield. A.S.A. defense platforms opened fire at the approaching De'Vayne force stuck in the minefield. Scans showed that most of the De'Vayne armada were aborting any attempt to enter the minefield with blips diverging away from the system.

"Don't let that ship escape, Lord Genji!"

Blue energy blasts leapt from the *Mirror of Solace,* igniting mines before the ship reached the minefield. Darting around the ship took extreme evasive maneuvers, but Lord Genji gritted his teeth, realizing what his master was doing. Kinetic cannons tracking tried to lock target, but rounds soared from cannons setting off mines and smashing into the field. Burning debris from the De'Vayne armada drifted outwards, setting off mines, forcing the *Mirror of Solace* to take erratic, unpredictable last-minute choices to avoid sudden shifts in the minefield. Kinetic rounds poured through the debris and mines, setting chain explosions erupting in arcs through the minefield.

Damaged De'Vayne ships trying to retreat opened fire at the looming *Titus Andronicus* moving slowly towards the edge of the minefield. Lady

Marimba glared back at Lord Genji, sensing that Lord De'Vayne was about to slip away, but the joy of the thrill of victory caused her to slip a true smile despite her best attempts. With a smug eye roll, she returned to watch the viewscreen.

"Fire at will, rain, death, and destruction Lord Genji to make sure our enemies never forget the cost of betraying the Empire." Relaxing into the chair, Lady Marimba's eyes fell on the fleeing enemies on the viewscreen amidst the fading explosions and thundering torrent of kinetic shells raining across the battlefield sparking new explosions. In her mind, she memorized every detail of this moment she planned to recapture one day for the glorious Emperor.

A nod was Lord Genji's only response adapting the algorithms to tighten cannon accuracy. Each target was carefully selected from his list of enemies, with the De'Vayne society easily discernable by each ship's unique design. Another one of the Great De'Vayne's superior vanities that only proved now to be a weakness to Lord Genji unable to prevent the disgust he felt. A question echoed in his mind about how he'd admired Lord De'Vayne for so long. Disgust twisted inside Lord Genji, mixing with the sorrow he felt for the death of his children. He was unable to prevent the smile of delight creeping across his countenance with each destroyed De'Vayne ship. Every ship destroyed thinned the herd of the Great De'Vayne's glorious vision of the future.

Death of Genji's children had made him believe for a moment that the future he was building towards was lost, but this battle, moment, and each destroyed ship proved his will to power very much alive. Each destroyed ally of his former master weakened his influence, and that would ripple across the power dynamics of De'Vayne society. For this moment, he was as powerful as Lord De'Vayne, but with a different view of the future. Accuracy across turrets rose rapidly with the narrowing focus of Lord Genji's desire to change his people's society. For his power to be felt and for the chance for his ideas to flourish, he needed to kill as many as possible right now. It was just an added benefit that Lady Marimba seemed to revel in the art of destruction being showered upon the De'Vayne armada.

CHAPTER 64

F ield emitters exploded across the *Dawnbreaker* on the engineering
screen, but Imperator Kain was too busy trying to direct internal
defenses. He couldn't attend to the next gravimetric web attack that
the enemy was amassing. There wasn't anything he could do to prevent what
he could see the spindled ship's arms weaving together on the viewscreen.
Reports poured through the *Dawnbreaker* defense network showing the
status of the repairs on the *Olympus*. Despite the cover provided by the
Brisingamen with Kain, the status of his brother's ship still wasn't good.
Reactor readings still weren't stabilizing yet. Arachne continued to race
across gravimetric webs onto the *Dawnbreaker* and *Brisingamen,* pouring
through gaping wounds in the hulls.

Thanks to Kain's instructions, interior defenses were holding so far,
but enemy forces were moving across the hull, heading towards the bridge
on the hull. Fighter craft whizzed across the space beyond the bridge with
engine traces fading lights whipping in their wake. Bright flashes erupted
across the hull of the *Dawnbreaker* before Kain precipitated the impact
of the explosive waves. Battle scans showed the Pandoran fleet slamming
into the W'hyish S'yevel worldships, Joshua and the Lord's counterattack
halting the advance of the serpentine, and the *Titus Andronicus* moving
towards the Mirror of Solace. Gravimetric readings still showed the buildup
of enemy forces beyond the minefield, but the mass effect combined with
the gravity webs made communications interference impossible to cut
through with the power available.

Mass effect compounding with the web's gravity waves ensured
neither the *Dawnbreaker* nor *Brisingamen* were moving. Both ships rocked
with the surge of gravimetric webs smashing against their hull, but they

blocked the majority from hitting the *Olympus* behind the defending ships. Instinct burned across Kain's nerves, his eyes fixated on the dwindling mass of enemy ships falling to the thundering kinetic cannons, and he coordinated fire with Lady Freya felled ships in a rain of razor-sharp metal storm pouring from the two ships. This was the moment to strike the victory, but the gravity effect prevented any attempt to charge the enemy line. Arachne ships were clustering to protect their biggest vessels, but the strategy forced the armada to reunite to deal with the two Imperial battleforges. Battle scans showed the approaching *Death's Reaper*, but the vessel was still well outside of weapons range to be any help to Kain. It was just a sliver of future hope.

Internal defenses were holding the invading Arachne at bay for the moment, but the real problem facing all three of the captains was the gravimetric damage being done to the ship's fusion reactors. What data Kain could get through the Empyrean defense network on the *Olympus* showed that Hephaestus had gone to the core to stabilize it personally. Repair teams from the *Dawnbreaker* reports couldn't confirm this, but none had been able to find a safe route to the core. Scans showed the *Brisingamen's* core suffered the least damage from the attacks. Arachne armada unleashed another series of attacks while absorbing the incoming salvos of joint fire coordinated by the two Imperial battleforges.

Several small eruptions flashed in the enemy formation on the viewscreen, but Kain was busy directing internal defenses, and repairs, and praying the *Dawnbreaker* would hold together. Damage reports poured through the ship's defense network into Kain's mind's eye, telling him exactly how bad the situation was. Buckling hull crumbled along with the bulkheads vented entire segments of the ship into the Great Maw, Arachne invaders pressed the critical corridors towards the core, and the core was slowly destabilizing until it exploded unless it was shut down. Arachne sensed what Kain knew that two of the three Imperial vessels were on the verge of destruction.

Detonations across the minefield on the battles could do more than just draw Kain's attention. A brief reprieve in enemy attacks that gave Kain's troops precious seconds to effect repairs. Joy was pushed down to welcome fury, Kain unloaded everything he could muster on the enemy armada, and the combined fire of Lady Freya forced the enemy to scatter for a moment in panic. Arachne vessels dropped mass to dart away quickly, but instinct was on the Imperator's side. Unleashing divergent salvos, he programmed the attacks sensing the enemy breaking. Arachne vessels erupted in exploding infernos of antimatter. Sensors blurred a warning to Kain in time to see the singularity missile fired by the *Death's Reaper* detonate in the center of the enemy's former formation. Communications crackled with the approach of the *Death's Reaper*.

"Always have been good at taking a beating, Kain, but you're giving as good as you get this time. I can sit this out and let you finish this off or give you a hand. Your call, Imperator." Gabriel's voice came clear through the network into Kain's head. There was only one response; it wasn't yes or no, and not even spoken out loud. It was the list of tasking orders designating targets for the *Death's Reaper*. "Roger that. I'm on it, so just try to hold in a little bit longer."

Field emitters surged with Kain's attention, trying to isolate the right gravimetric frequencies to cancel the webs out to free the *Dawnbreaker*. Rows of turrets tracked enemy targets on the viewscreen, thundering salvos of kinetic weapons at the scattering enemies. Lowering mass to the maximum movement made the Arachne ship vulnerable at higher speeds, and Kain had that time out in his algorithm freeing him to deal with the field emitters personally. Isolating the right gravimetric waves, he directed all his power to free the ship. Accessing the Empyrean Defense network, he sent direct transmissions to Lady Freya and Lord Hephaestus.

Mechanarium of Gyros adapted to the gravimetric frequencies programmed by Kain to direct a counterfeit to the gravity webs. Three ships maneuvered together free of the gravity mass effect fields trying to coordinate fields of fire to fend off the collapsing enemy forces. Sensors showed Kain the Arachne forces on the hull of the *Dawnbreaker* were approaching the bridge level arriving in only a few moments. Troops are ordered to the bridge window to plant explosives while Kain focuses on destroying the enemy forces. Decreasing mass effect fields helps to stabilize the ship's cores but dissipates the interference blocking the communications.

"Imperator, Kain, this is A'zyren of the *Sesh'yn*a. Please respond." Transmission repeated.

"We're in a bit of a shitstorm here, A'z. If you don't mind, either join in or shut up."

Arachne vessels charged at latched onto and dove past the *Dawnbreaker* in a surge away from the *Death's Reapers* swarm missiles, seeker drones beam lances, and the antimatter cannons unleashing a fury of destruction on any target within reach. Explosions rippled along the bow with swarm missiles slamming in waves into Arachne, skittering onto the *Dawnbreaker*'s hull. Turret thundered in succession, locking fleeing enemy ships. Kinetic rounds tore through space smashing through the Arachne hull, rupturing antimatter sacs, and causing a massive explosion in a bright flash. Sweat dripped down Kain's brow to race down his cheek, breaths were regulated with disciplined thoughts, and his nostrils flared to draw in the extra oxygen, but Kain was searching for the optimal targets in the enemy swarms to drop the numbers to a point where victory seemed impossible.

Arachne forces darted around the *Dawnbreaker* and *Brisingamen*, charging at the most vulnerable ship. Cannons swiveled, trying to keep locks on targets selected by Kain as thundering rounds fired into the void. Enemy ships racing between the two Imperial battleforges tried to cause chaotic friendly fire, but neither Lady Freya nor Imperator Kain fell for the ruse. They both directed their minds to the ships darting wide around their ships. Words weren't necessary between the two warriors' whose thoughts and intentions blurred together in the Empyrean defense network uniting in the mutual offense. Antimatter explosions slammed against the hulls of the ships peeling back metal with a screech that joined the chaos of surging kinetic rounds. Fighter craft veered away from the two ships' defensive formations to strike at the darting enemy ships.

Explosions rippled along the torn and shredded hull of the *Olympus*, sending debris splintering into the Great Maw. Reports from the ship echoed across the defense network of the failing, beleaguered ship. Firing slowed with the failing of the *Olympus* Power grid just as a massive explosion rippled through the center of the battleforge. Alarms blurred to Lady Freya and Imperator Kain, but both stayed fixated upon the surging enemy ships darting towards the *Olympus*.

"Hephaestus, you've got to flee the ship. We won't be able to stop the enemy before they launch another salvo on your ship." Kain's thoughts flowed through the network, were received, and the lack of a reply told him that his brother wasn't abandoning his ship.

"Kain, we've got to get your brother off that ship," Lady Freya urged.

"Arachne forward attack line is about to reach the bridge, Freya. What the fuck do you want me to do?" Kain motioned for his troops to take a defensive position. Officers began retreating from the bridge to the secondary bridge under the escort of Kain's elite troops. Clicking the bolt, he pushed up from the captain's chair, sensing what Lady Freya was doing. The last command he input into the defense system was the priority algorithm to clear a path for Lady Freya to reach the *Olympus*. Battle scans showed the surging Arachne forces splintering around the *Dawnbreaker* and *Brisingamen*. Only a few of the enemy forces had broken off to pursue the *Death's Reaper*, darting away from the battlelines while the *Sesh'yna* held position.

There wasn't any time in Kain's mind to deal with A'zyren or his other allies with the clacking sound of skittering limbs outside on the hull. Demolitions were planted along the bridge viewscreen, now turned off to see through the window to the raging battle beyond. Flashes of lights erupted in the distance around the *Divine Retribution* caught in the swarm of worldships, but kinetic cannon rounds exploded through the hulls of the enemy ships. Reports told Kain his sister was in the heat of combat, and the neural connection allowed him to feel the hammering beat of her heart, the rush of adrenaline flooding her blood, and the thrill of bloodlust her mind focused on. In the distance, Pandoran and W'hyish S'yevel ships crashed into each other.

Consult Joshua led the Lords Cornelius, Hector, and Oswald in a charge against the scattering serpentine ships on the battle scans. Charge took the Serpentine by surprise from what Kain could surmise based on battle scan showing ship movements, but he focused on the demolitions his team was doing the final check upon. Glancing back, he saw the bridge had been evacuated of all key personnel leaving only him and his soldiers. Defensive positions were being taken around the bridge, with mobile shield generators being hidden behind consoles. Hum of the forcefields joined the combat chorus echoing around Kain while he directed his troops to take position. Detonators linked to his neural implant, scanners showed the approaching enemies outside, and rifles clicked with firing bolts locking into position around him.

Clacking sounds echoed beyond the viewscreen glass, shaking with the fury of the approaching enemy. Alarms warned Kain that enemy forces were breaching the hull several decks below the bridge, but he smiled, knowing full command was already transferred to the secondary bridge where his crew would continue the fight. He reached down to pull his energy blade free from his belt to grip it tight in his hand. Eyes narrowed on the glass, seeing the first sign of the enemy's arrival. Arachne claws came crashing down and splintered the glass viewscreen, with webbing cracks expanding with each crash of the spindle arms. With one last look around the bridge, Kain drank in his troop's preparation for this moment, and with a single thought.

The detonation blasted the glass of the viewscreen into the enemy, causing the sharpened, hardened shards to tear through their reinforced chitin. With the triggering explosion Kain and his troops opened fire on the enemy forces with their energy beams and kinetic rounds. With a hand firing a rifle, Kain stormed towards the largest of the enemy igniting his energy blade. Massive claws darted into the bridge, slashing at the defenders, but Kain unloaded on the massive leader, drawing the energy blade behind him. Ready to strike, he had the enemy's undivided attention. Metal screeched, being bent under the terrible force of the Arachne leader, forcing a way onto the bridge.

A massive explosion tore from the *Olympus,* shaking the *Dawnbreaker* and *Brisingamen* with the power being released. There wasn't any time for Kain to focus on either his brother with the massive monster ripping through his bridge. Razor-sharp teeth trembled in the Arachne leader's howling maw, screeching at Kain clawing through the bridge. Gunfire poured from all angles at the creature clawing through the broken viewscreen. With powerful slashes, he severed each limb that attempted to strike him down on his stroll through the chaos. Other enemies skittered around their leader, trying assist the attack against the Imperator, but precision gun shots ripped through their darting blackened masses of eyes without Kain so much as looking. His mind gave into the flow of battle from all points directing the defenses with pure subconscious ease. With a singular cleave, he slashed through the leader's snapping mandibles trying to grasp him, spinning he slashed down the collapsing spindle arms and spun around to drive the blade into the center of the leader's eight blackened eyes, all staring at the crackling blade as he heaved the monstrosity from the bridge.

Kinetic rounds exploded from Kain's gun, but he stayed fixated on the corpse of the Arachne leader drifting away into the Great Maw. Battle scans showed the De'Vayne forces had retreated, the *Titus Andronicus* was on approach, firing at the Arachne ships, and the serpentine forces fled back towards the minefield, trying to escape the sector. Reaching out with a thought, he scanned the *Olympus* for any sign of his brother. Sweat beading down his face, there wasn't any sign of Hephaestus's mind in the defense network, but the explosion splintered the ship's subnets. He stood at the edge of the viewscreen he unleashed fire on the enemy while scouring for his brother with all his mental focus. He could sense Lady Freya's efforts to find Lord Hephaestus in the network when their thoughts slammed against each other.

"Do you think he's still alive?" Worry echoed in Lady Freya's thoughts.

"Hephaestus would have been near the reactor, given the situation, and it's still in one piece. We just gotta give him time and get rescue and repair teams over there. You know, A'zyren, this is a perfect time to help." Kain looked out at the ship floating beyond the fleeing Arachne ships being pursued now by the *Death's Reaper*. Communications crackled on the captain's chair, forcing him to march back to activate the connection with A'zyren aboard the *Sesh'yna*.

"I'll make sure if your brother's alive, Kain, but Pandoran forces have begun seizing the W'hyish S'yevel worldships. Shouldn't the spoils of war be brought before Emperor Solomon before being divided?" The words drew Kain's attention towards the situation that now lingered in victory he'd never considered. Arachne forces were attempting to flee, De'Vayne forces had managed to escape, and most of the Serpentine were going to escape being driven back by Consul Joshua's forces. Several disabled ships were being captured by Lord Oswald's forces, pulling up the rear of the advancing triumvirate of ships still pursuing the fleeing enemy.

Falling into the captain's chair, Kain stared out across the Great Maw and drank in the remaining flashing of battle echoing in the victory he still wasn't sure how they've achieved. Battle scans showed the remaining Arachne forces were fleeing the sector. Transports for search and rescue launched from the *Brisingamen* towards the broken *Olympus* with the help of the approaching *Titus Andronicus*. Reports from the *Empyrean station* echoed the victory of Commander Verdas, Lord Marcus, and the A.S.A.

forces working together, but strange reports of Angelica troubled Kain's mind forcing his gaze to fall upon the station. He wondered how much of the battle Matthew had seen beforehand and which pieces of information had been selectively withheld. There was an understanding in Kain's mind of this behavior, but it troubled him in a way he hadn't expected. Rather than feeling proud of his brother's growth, only fear echoed.

"This is Imperator Kain. All allied forces will answer directly to me. All Niabs of the defeated W'hyish S'yevel forces are to be secured and brought to the *Empyrean station,* where Emperor Solomon will determine the fate of the tribes. All wounded should be prepared for transport to the *Empyrean station* medical facilities for those with the most severe injuries. Empyrean medical network is prepared to receive any reports to prepare for incoming wounded. All damage to allied ships is to be reported to the Empyrean Defense Network to begin prioritized repairs. Docking permissions for the station are being sent out while we deal with the last remaining enemy forces. Anyone with any problems with my orders can feel free to take it with me." Kain cut the transmission to lean back into his captain's chair, already feeling the buzz of the communication requests.

There was only relief washing across Kain's mind at that moment. He didn't even answer the incoming message from Emperor Solomon, knowing his brother knew exactly how he felt at this moment. Search and rescue were underway on the *Olympus,* and he had no intention of leaving until he ascertained Hephaestus's fate. For a moment, he just wanted to drink in the victory, consider the cost, and prepare for the future. Staring into the void of the Great Maw, one repeating truth echoed in the back of Kain's mind. This was just the second battle of his war for survival that kept everyone alive, and the sight of new allies, fallen enemies, and the torment of uncertainty about his brother's fate compounded the realities of the new universal order.

Only one power in the universe mattered now, and it wasn't the concealed star hidden by the *Divius Oculus.* Emperor was the shining center of power in this universe now, and whether Kain liked it or not, his entire family's survival now weighed on his shoulders. His eyes narrowed on the *Death's Reaper* chasing down fleeing Arachne ships. His father seemed to have all the fun while he always got all the responsibility. With a deep sigh, he turned to the scans of the *Olympus,* trying to focus his thoughts on what he could do to help. Communications crackled in the defense network between the three ships.

"Don't worry, brother, I'm still alive. A little controlled chaos to keep the ship in mostly one piece seems to have paid off, but I hope I never have to blow up part of my ship ever again. Glad I could count on you and Lady Freya to have my back." Lord Hephaestus's voice echoed across the network with a jolt of occasional interference crackling it.

"You reckless son of a bitch." Lady Freya cursed over the coms.

"Be careful. Just because we won this battle, Lady Freya, doesn't mean you want to start another war. Our mother would be far harder to defeat than what we just faced and more ruthless." Kain warned, glancing at the *Empyrean station*. Tractor beams launched from the *Dawnbreaker* and *Brisingamen* stabilized the damaged *Olympus* before towing the ship to the shipyards. He weighed the situation they were all in for a moment, wondering how Angelica would respond.

Battle reports spoke of the strange situation with Kain's youngest sister, and scans showed the *Death's Reaper* on return vector. What was about to happen would bring these two forces back into contact, and Kain could only wonder how his brother didn't see this coming. Worse was the realization that maybe he had seen this coming and was working towards his own objective. There wasn't any way for Kain to ascertain the truth, no time for a private moment with Emperor Solomon, and all things coming to a head on the *Empyrean station* with the arrival of the triumphant victors preparing their procession of celebration. Glancing at the *Divine Retribution* left Kain wondering how Nemesis would react to all this once she realized, but there would be no time to bring her up to speed. For the moment, they were all in the singularity of the moment, being sucked in by the chaos of victory and about to unleash the power of the uncertain future.

CHAPTER 65

Ramp hissed, lowering towards the deck plate, allowing Imperator Kain to march down with his honor guard. Power armor still covered in the blood and filth of the battle stormed behind him, marching toward the Infinity Nexus. Damage to the station could be seen glaring from every structure still standing. Deep scrapes in the deck forced him to be careful of where he stepped. Some of the gouges were over a foot deep. He glanced around, drinking in the triumphal scene.

Chained W'hyish S'yevel were prodded by sparking energy lances forcing them towards the Infinity Nexus, soldiers shared war stories, and several showed off impressive trophies collected from the dead. Several captured Arachne were being bartered and sold by troopers to Pandoran slavers who were haggling with their own spoils of war. Some of the captured were being sold to the Pandoran using the Alcatraz slavery system, from what Kain could see, but he averted his gaze to focus on the task at hand. Whatever the Emperor had planned needed to be explained to Kain so that he could help or at least figure out what he had to tolerate or avoid.

"You hear about Angelica?" Nemesis's voice drew Kain from his somber introspection.

"Apparently, she's still leading a one-woman attack on the remaining enemy forces. Commander Verdas is apparently backing her up, but I'm guessing from the look on your face you got that information from Lord Marcus firsthand?" Kain looked his sister up and down to see she was still covered in the gore of combat, so at least she hadn't given in to baser desires.

"If she finds out fathers here were all pretty fucked. From how Marcus tells the story, she's got some crazy powers like Matthew and Lord Void. Why are you so calm?" Nemesis brought her brother to a standstill with one arm before she stepped in front. The siblings' eyes locked upon each other for a moment before Kain tried to move his sister, but she broke his hold with a defiant glare.

Two siblings stood there for a moment, just glaring into each other's eyes in silence. Without a connection to the network defenses, at least both of their thoughts were their own this moment, but neither sibling could conceive the other actions. Nemesis knew her brother was well aware of the vengeance brewing in Angelica's soul, and given firsthand experience, it was shocking Kain hadn't made a move against their father himself. None of this was simple for him, and he couldn't comprehend why Nemesis tried to boil this complex family situation down to simple terms of battle. Especially given the reports of Angelica's new powers, Kain focused all his attention on the truth that Matthew was operating in the dark, which terrified him.

"When has losing our shit ever helped us survive, Nemesis?"

Question brought Nemesis' mind to a grinding halt with the sheer brutality of it. Her finger had already darted up, her tongue already summoning the counterargument, and one question brought that force to a sudden stop. She tried to catch herself to adjust to the question, but Kain's hand grasped her firmly by the shoulder, leading her forward on a slow, quiet walk. Their eyes met again, but she saw empathy of concern glimmering in her brothers' eyes.

"Listen carefully to what I'm saying Nemesis, because I'm not repeating it. Our brother, Emperor Solomon, is playing at something he's keeping from me and, I suspect, from you as well. He told me he couldn't see past this battle, but I find it strange that Angelica is off dealing with the remnants while our father and Pandora are welcomed like heroes. Perhaps this is just some clever politics on Matthew's part to avoid direct conflict, but my instincts tell me there is something bigger and much darker at play. Matthew would have seen the De'Vayne treachery, the Serpentine feint, and yet didn't tell either of us or anyone that could make a difference in the battle?" Kain's question provoked anger from his sister, but he smiled because at least anger meant she was thinking.

"Wow! Kain, that's some serious disloyalty right there, and I doubt Father let you think that way about him when he was in command." Nemesis kept her voice down, glanced around, and ensured no one else was paying too much attention to her or her brother.

"Shows how little you knew about the operation of the *Alcatraz*. This is the exact reason Father chose me as his first officer. I know when to follow orders and when to challenge them and don't rush ahead just yet, acting like I'm betraying Matthew because I'm not. Some things concern me, and it's our job to keep our brothers and sisters safe. If we had done a better job of this on the *Alcatraz* maybe our sister would still be here…" Nemesis glared at Kain.

"Never ever bring even the idea of your treachery up again, or so help me, God, brother, I will rip your tongue out of your mouth with my bare hands." Bones cracked in Nemesis's trembling hand, forming a fist. She tried to contain her burning rage flickering in her eyes, but her entire body convulsed with fury. Only the sound of approaching magnetic books grasped the sibling's attention.

Idea echoed in Nemesis's mind of her brother's intentions forcing her to take deep breaths, trying to calm her rising heart rate and trembling rage echoing in her nerves. Everything he said rang with truth, her instincts whispered, but whether it was the lust of battle, fury of memories, or just her natural reaction didn't make a difference to how she felt right now. It took all her willpower to force the fake smile for her approaching sibling seeing Joshua, Celeris, and Hephaestus with arms locked with Lady Freya approaching. The joy of the moment would have to be the emotion Nemesis relied upon to sell her little charade to hide her true feelings.

"Well, at least when I see my ugly brother, I get to see your beauty, Lady Freya. Kain was regaling me with the fact this gearhead would be dead if it wasn't for you." Nemesis hugged Lady Freya with heartfelt thanks squeezing her tight enough that their power armors groaned.

"How about next time we're in battle, you pick the fight with the toughest enemy first, Kain?" Hephaestus wrapped his arm around his brother with a jovial laugh bellowing forth. Kain just smiled and nodded in agreement, waiting for the laughter to subside.

"I'll keep that in mind for you, brother." Kain mirrored the emotions trying to be part of this moment, but his eyes darted around at the gathering alien forces. In the distance, he spotted his mother marching with an entourage of guards towards the Infinity Nexus, sending his mind whirling again. Without a thought, he tried to connect with Emperor Solomon via the neural link, but the request was rejected immediately. His eyes followed the movement, and he noticed Nemesis making the same observation with Kain as their eyes met with their mother's disappearance behind the gate.

Warforged guards moved in front of the Infinity Nexus gates preventing anyone else from even approaching. A.S.A. forces were clumped entirely around the Infinity Nexus, scanning anyone approaching the closed gates. Empyrean network failed to reach the Infinity Nexus elevating Kain's suspicions which fell in a mutual glance with Nemesis. The others failed to notice. Station scans showed the area where Angelica and the remaining enemy forces were locked down, but all outside access was severed. No footage, feed, or information leaked the perimeter, but Kain's agent fed the data through the network to show the situation to him. He glanced at his sister with a wary eye knowing she'd already have her own agents investigating.

"Those Serpentine ships sure can take a pounding. We're just lucky that the didn't show up with a thirst for battle like the others. Though what happened with the Mirror of Solace and a *Titus Andronicus* still seems strange. Anyone ever seen Lady Marimba since the ship docked?" Joshua looked around at the others to see them shrugging.

"We'll raise a mug to her next time she comes to the Original Sins." Lord Cornelius nodded to Lady Nemesis with a smile she merely mirrored back. Her mind was in tune with her brother Joshua and the silent Celeris standing next to him, looking through the crowd. Intrigue written in the black expression of her features told Nemesis that all the siblings seemed to be aware of the strange occurrence near the end of the battle. Silence fell across the group, with all eyes turning when Lady Marimba's troops appeared in the distance.

Leading the procession was Lord Genji holding the hilt of his sheathed blade. Honorable position at the front told Kain all he needed to know, and a quick glance at Nemesis revealed she agreed with his estimation. Whatever happened on the *Mirror of Solace* it was clear Lord Genji had betrayed Lord De'Vayne to ensure the ambush failed. Guilt bubbled up deep in Kain, but he swallowed hard, thinking maybe Matthew had seen this coming. Each thought sent a shiver down his spine, setting his hair on end underneath his power armor.

Empyrean network buzzed in the Solomon siblings' minds. Silence fell across the group, leaving Lady Freya to glance around at the others, momentarily confused. Each of them turned marching towards the Infinity Nexus without saying a word. Warforged moved back, allowing the siblings to enter the Infinity Nexus, where they saw Helena standing in front of Mathew speaking softly. Kain and Nemesis led the sibling procession, trying to get close enough to hear what was being discussed before the two stopped talking, but Helena turned with a smile towards her children, with Mathew standing behind her to the right side.

"Welcome, my victorious brothers and sisters. This victory marks the beginning moments of our birth as a true Empire and one that will grow to create a new verse. Your sacrifice, valor, and tenacity will echo for as long as our new empire lasts. We must begin laying the foundation for this empire while our enemies lick their wounds. Mother wishes to organize a triumph procession. It's only fitting that Imperator Kain, Lady Nemesis, and Lord Hephaestus, with Lady Freya, lead this triumph. Your courage brought us to victory after all." Matthew's smile beamed down on his family.

A cane tapped the deck softly, but even that noise drew the Soloman's attention to Lady Clotho making her way toward the Infinity Nexus. Silence fell over the group watching the old lady approach with each tap of the cane. Helena's eyes widened, fixating upon the soothsayer whose prophecies had all come true to her, and she tried to hide the fear from her children. Lord Hephaestus offered his hand to help Lady Clotho make her way up the stairs. She just smiled at the massive man, took the offered hand, and approached the Infinity Nexus.

"Emperor, it seems you've fulfilled your purpose well. We're all safe for the moment because of you, but I'm here to warn you that in this moment of victory comes a moment of danger. Enemies are already here aboard the *Empyrean station*, within this chamber as I speak, and you can never be free of them. You must use wisdom to separate poison from power." Lady Clotho took a deep, rasping breath, struggling for a moment before bowing.

"You've no need to bow, Lady Clotho. As always, we value your advice, but perhaps you could tell me who these enemies are that not even I see?" Eyes locked between Matthew and Clotho.

"We're all biased by our own perceptions, Emperor. It is our greatest weakness," Clotho warned.

Mordekai stood nearby, watching the situation. He wasn't sure how Clotho had managed to bypass his warforged security at the gates, and scanning the Empyrean network revealed no recorded instance of her entering through the gates. All his processing power was dedicated to unraveling this intrigue that made no logical sense, but the glint in Emperor Solomon's eye told him he already knew how it happened. That didn't stop Mordekai from searching for the answers through the system. Matthew turned to deal with the situation before him.

"Well, I will rely upon you to continue to expand my perspectives, Lady Clotho, but for now, we must focus on dealing with new allies. A'zyren, Lord Genji, and Pandora have risked a great deal to help us secure this victory, each of them has their own needs for their help, and we should take care of our new friends. Consul Joshua, your job will be to keep these factions under control while we move toward the next major event. Don't take the task lightly, brother, for Pandora's nature is to keep everything she can grasp, which will put her at the throats of the W'hyish S'yevel trying to follow A'zyren now. Pirate forces will need to be watched Celeris. Nemesis, you'll need to find ways to keep these people entertained. Our stellar forge will be busy at work, keeping Hephaestus more than content for the next little while. Already the Cacophony of Discordance has heard of their failure and moved to rally against us. We must press forward united." Matthew took the moment to look into his sibling's eyes, his mother's, and Lady Clotho's. Each showed their commitment in the returned gaze at their Emperor.

There was no telling which of the many futures Matthew could see, unraveling from this moment, that would become the truth. For this moment, all was safe for his glowing star hidden behind the *Divius Oculus* powering the stellar forge already repairing his fleet and forging the new ships. His eyes locked with Nemesis, Kain, and his mother, Helena. Each had their own agenda and beliefs, and each wanted a different future, forcing Matthew to gulp hard. He couldn't see a future where they all stood together, but he refused to accept that. Anxiety spiked with the echo of Clotho's warning to heed wisdom. His mind narrowed on what he wanted, focusing on Angelica's fury decimating the enemies. Her blackened eyes locked with his in astral space beyond the Infinity Nexus, where the rest of their sibling stood discussing Helena's intended triumphal procession.

CHAPTER 66

Insidious Seduction warped into the system of Pandora's Box, appearing close to the damaged and disabled *Jinnestan* floating in the wreckage. Caught in the nearby black holes pull, the *Jinnestan* was being slowly pulled toward the event horizon. There wasn't any distress call from the ship or any sign the crew needed help which made Lilith smile. Pointing with a finger, she directed her minion to send a hail to Tenno Asmodeus, waiting patiently for him to answer.

Scans showed that the Pandoran detonated their reactors to generate a strong enough light flash to damage the *Jinnestan*. Residual energy traces showed Lilith the intensity of the blast. All she could think was Asmodeus was lucky to be alive. There was no response to the hails, so Lilith motioned for scanners to be brought online. Steady scans showed that the crew was still alive by the reading of negative energy readings inside the ship. She focused on the ship scanners seeing the two massive power sources. One was located on the bridge, but the other was deep in the bowels of the *Jinnestan*, where prisoners would be held, forcing her to push out of the captain's chair.

With steady clicks, Lilith marched off the bridge down through her ship to the sounds of screams of torture and ecstasy. Several of her eldest children followed behind her, heading towards the hangar bay. Energy crackled off her with snaps and hisses fading into oblivion behind her like the thoughts receding into the void of her mind's eye. Why had the Cacophony of Discordance not been notified of Magnus Void's capture, and worse, why did Arachne's intelligence lead Lilith to this system where Pandoran pirates had neutralized the Jinnestan? Pandoran weren't interested in capturing a Reverie vessel only highlighted the strangeness of this situation. Only one thought echoed in her mind: Tenno Asmodeus had best have some good answers.

Doors whisked back, revealing the hangar bay to Lilith, where she could see her transport awaiting. Several demons worked on the vessel until they saw their Tenno approaching. Crackling blackened energy fell silent amongst the demonic crew around the transport. Marching up the ramp, Lilith headed straight for the controls, only stopping long enough to seal the ramp once her children were on board. Lilim filled the back of the transport with a cacophony of their revelry, but they fell silent when they felt their mother's gaze fall upon them. Engines hummed, carrying the transport out of the hangar bay towards the *Jinnestan,* being pulled towards the accretion disk of the black hole in the former Pandora's Box sector with only the floating debris as a sign.

Scans showed the *Jinnestan* weapons were offline once the transport got close enough to cut through the singularity's gravimetric interference. Hails were still going unanswered despite Lilith not detecting any damage to the communication arrays. A negative energy build-up in the hangar bay warned that Tenno Asmodeus was perhaps preparing an ambush, but that thought made Lilith smile before setting the automatic landing sequence. Standing in the doorway, she smiled at her children's strength, beauty, and devotion.

"Well, my Lilim, perhaps we shall arrive to find a feast of battle or a revelry of flesh, but as always, we'll enjoy life to the fullest." Lilith smiled at the infernal beauty of her children's claws, fangs, and wings. Silver eyes gleamed up at her willing to follow their mother into the abyss if that was where she wanted to go. One after another, the Lilim stood to march behind their mother towards the descending ramp into the *Jinnestan.* From the ramp, she could see the armies of Jinn spread throughout the dock, but there was no sign of Tenno Asmodeus, just the fiery glare of Ifrit.

Marching down the ramp, Lilith held her hand up to keep her children at bay for a moment. She glanced around, sensing the power in this room from the reverie assembled. Her eyes locked up the flickering visage of Ifrit, who was the only reverie who could do any harm, and that wasn't even close to being a threat to Lilith. With her one handheld up, she told her children to wait by the transport as she approached Ifrit with a smile and black crackling energy leaping around.

"Tenno Lilith, we've experienced a bit of damage dealing with the capture of the rogue Lord Void, but we weren't expecting your sudden arrival. Unfortunately, due to the damage, we could not return your communications, but it seems you've invited yourself to the *Jinnestan* I've been sent to receive you." Ifrit bowed with respect but kept his eyes locked on Lilith.

"I was following a lead on the Minister of Injustice and was told he'd be here in this sector only to arrive to find this situation." Lilith hoped her ruse would fool Ifrit. He motioned for his guest to follow, heading towards the bridge of the *Jinnestan*.

"We can promise you there was no detection of the Minister of Injustice, his vessel, the *Infernal Pact*, and Pandora fled with her little pirate brigade thanks to the deception of Lord Void. Don't worry. The damage is minimal. It just caught us by surprise. Tenno Asmodeus tried to warn us to sweep the Pandoran base when he captured the rouge but matters involving that criminal kept our Tenno diverted." A chuckle broke free from Lilith's lips drawing Ifrit's attention.

"Oh, it happens to the best of us eventually, Ifrit, but I'm sure Tenno Asmodeus will look past this one monumental failure that has made him look ridiculous in the eyes of the Cacophony of Discordance. His forgiveness is infamous amongst our Infernal kingdom, but I care less about your troubles than you care to conceive believable lies. Shut up, lead me to Tenno Asmodeus, and perhaps I'll spare you any further indigitations in front of your Tenno." Silence fell across the corridor leaving only the clacking of Lilith's feet echoing her footsteps.

Following the orders, Ifrit fell quiet except for the flickering crackle of his flames. Warning spoken by his Tenno echoed in his mind to not lower his guard around Lilith. Now he understood why sensing the coiling power beneath the crackling visage of Lilith. There was a much greater power than any of the reverie in the Cacophony of Discordance ever knew was almost palpable to Ifrit at the moment. Power emanated in the quiet demeanor, the clacking footsteps, and the focused gaze of Lilith carrying her down the hallway. The gate to the bridge whisked open, with all the demons on the bridge careening to see the visage of Lilith entering, only averted by Ifrit's fiery glare.

"Tenno Asmodeus is waiting for you in his private quarters, and I have a ship to attend to." Ifrit pointed towards the quarters off of the bridge on the far side. Walking towards the door, Lilith didn't even look back at Ifrit or the others, and when she arrived, she didn't even bother knocking. Nothing happened for a moment, but then the doors began to retract slowly. The darkness of the quarters welcomed her, but she hesitated to scan the room first to ensure there wasn't a trap. Everything seemed quiet inside the quarters. Only one energy signature echoed from inside.

Sitting behind a fine desk made of ancient marble that stood in contrast to the blackened walls of the Jinnestan captain's quarter. Artifacts from across the span of the cosmos time decorated the walls. A wooden cup stained with blood sat next to a blood-encrusted spearhead from ancient Earth, unleashing a coppery smell that Lilith took a moment to savor. Ancient, plumed helmets rolled papyrus scrolls locked inside glass cases, and models of ships across time decorated the room. Artifacts that lacked any worth to anyone but Asmodeus, but the beauty of these keepsakes inspired Lilith, who marched into the quarters to take a seat across from Tenno Asmodeus.

"So, you've not come to make some kind of move against me." Asmodeus sat cleaning a shining revolver that caught Lilith's attention. She narrowed her eyes on it, recognizing the weapon.

"I was sent here by my agents who detected the presence of the Minister of Injustice in this sector, but had I known you had it under control, I'd save myself the time and trouble. Is that a new toy to add to your childish collection?" With a chuckle, Lilith pointed a long-curved nail to the revolver Tenno Asmodeus polished in his hands and leaned back in her chair, relishing the moment. "Boys and their toys, I suppose."

"This was just something the rogue had on him. Strange that such an upstart like Magnus Void could get his hands on one of only two singularity pistols in creation. As a collector of things of unique historical quality, I can promise you this Lilith, items like this are not easy to acquire and even harder to keep your hands on. They tend to find their way to new owner's hands." Asmodeus took his time attending to the weapon carefully before placing it on the shelf.

At that moment, Lilith's eyes fixed upon the Ancients 'singularity revolver, trying to scour eons of memories to place where she last saw this particular gun. She couldn't quite grasp the stands of memory slipping through the sight of her scouring mind's eyes. Shadows of memories blurred together in the eternity of her mind. Only when Tenno Asmodeus turned did Lilith control herself to avoid any slip of information that could be spun against her. She intended to stay in control of the power exchange with Tenno Asmodeus as he turned to face her. The two stared into the abyss of each other blackened eyes in silence, trying to ascertain the nature of the game.

"Well, unless I can find the Minister of Injustice, I fear that locating Lord Void won't do much good for the Cacophony. Perhaps you'd be willing to allow me to interrogate the prisoner?" Lilith leaned back into the chair, relaxing with a smile at Tenno Asmodeus.

Taking an inventory of the damages to the *Jinnestan* only showed Asmodeus he'd have to spend several hours before he could get underway to *Pandemonium* to bring in the prisoner. Instincts whispered to him that something much larger was going on with Tenno Lilith. It seemed she was doing everything in her power to act natural, keep her eyes from the Ancient's revolver, and now the request to interrogate the prisoner all spoke to something Asmodeus could profit from. All he needed to do was be patient, give Lilith a bit of rope, and pay close attention to what she did. It was almost too easy of a power play, but Asmodeus convinced himself there would be time later to add his artful flourish to how this scheme played out to truly ensure his brilliance was written upon it.

"Do you believe Magnus Void might be involved in the Minister of Injustice's disappearance?"

"Anything is possible, and that's why I need to see this, Lord Void." Lilith glared at Asmodeus.

Delight at the power to deny, Lilith tugged at Asmodeus's thoughts that were delicious to just imagine. The flavor of emotions tempted Asmodeus, almost bringing him from reason, but he motioned with one hand towards the door before any further thoughts unhinged his mind. He focused on the fact he'd be watching the interaction of the tormentors from the hell cells. Fixating upon the possible revelations that this so-called Lord Magnus Void could reveal filled Asmodeus with delicious thrills. He watched the seductive sway of Lilith, leaving the captain's quarters silently to only the sound of clacking footsteps on the volcanic floor.

Staring at Tenno Lilith walking across the bridge, Asmodeus wondered what revelations she'd learn from this Magnus Void, and that would be power he could use against the Cacophony of Discordance. Captain quarters door shut behind, leaving Asmodeus alone in his darkened room to contemplate the situation while staring out the port window at the accretion disk of the black hole event horizon, slowly pulling him and his ship in. He couldn't help by wondering how his ship, the singularity revolver, and Magnus Void all fit together at this moment. Asmodeus brought up the torment cell holding his prisoner by accessing the prison levels video feed.

From the data feed, Asmodeus knew he should be hearing a lot more screaming, yet all there was almost silence in the room. Only a soft whistling tune could be heard emanating from the torment cell. The tune seemed vaguely familiar to Asmodeus, as if it was a piece of a half-remembered dream, but the feeling was ominous, echoing through him with each note. Locking eyes with Magnus Void, they both spent a moment staring at each other through cameras, but Asmodeus could feel the reach of this upstart power even through the cameras. Picking up the pistol, he aimed it straight at the screen at Magnus Void's head to watch him grin, revealing his razor teeth at the camera.